Religion's Hidden Dark Secret

Religion's Hidden Dark Secret

Journey of the Twin Flame

R.R. BARNARD

First published in the United Kingdom in 2022

© R.R. Barnard 2022

AUTHOR'S INTRODUCTION

Hello, my name's Richard Barnard. Please allow me to share with you a magical multi-dimensional adventure stored deep within this soul. The epic novel you're about to read has been a long time in the making – because, although I only recently realised this, I believe I began collecting material for it at the age of just 12. It was then as a confused child full of negative emotion, sitting crying on a park bench, the universe kindly presented me with Rosella – a young Romany woman who came and sat next to me that day. We began chatting and Rosella helped me self-hypnotise, taking me into my first ever past life regression experience. We both, Rosella and I, actually became conscious as members of our ancient African soul tribe; the joint reading showed we both lived physical lives in the same tropical coastal village. Until recently I kept this experience a secret, but I never forgot it throughout my teenage years and as a young adult, and around ten years after my meeting with Rosella that spiritual vibration was repeated. In 1987 when I was 23, the universe guided a select few, myself included, to the actual birth of the British acid house music scene. I was invited to a liberated nightclub gathering on Charing Cross Road, London called "The Future", a venue where secretly the guests attended to "get on one" – to take ecstasy. The quality of the high at the beginning of the ecstasy scene could only be described as a mind-opening heavenly experience. I made friends at The Future and was invited to another Saturday night venue, The Fitness Centre Southwark Bridge, a club called "The Shoom" run by acid house DJ Danny Rampling and his beautiful wife Jenni – two of many beautiful, loving souls that have entered my life. The atmosphere at Shoom created an even more intense heavenly feeling. I knew it then and still know it now: something was there among the guests, a familiar positive spiritual presence. One night dancing at the club, tripping on a mixture of ecstasy and LSD, I began to feel exactly how I felt during my past life regression experience as a 12-year-old; I was present at this ancient African village again, but thought I could still hear the musical beat of the modern-day Shoom Club. The thing was, the beat of the music played in that previous life was identical to the original acid house music. Villagers on that African coastline were doing the same dance moves, jacking their bodies to the same beat; and I knew some of those Black Africans had been reincarnated among the people of different races dancing under the strobe lights of Shoom – spirit had brought us together again. Yes, we were buzzing, high on ecstasy, but it was more than a blissful high; every week we attended there was always actually something there. Spirit pulled us to the divine blessed energy connected to the beat of the music – a feeling that we'd come home. The revelation would later play a huge part in the creation of this novel. By the following year, 1988, the acid house scene had become commercial. There were huge cool party venues such as Sunrise, Energy, Biology, Rain Dance, Rat Pack and many others in and around the UK's inner cities, and although these had an amazing vibration, for me, nothing could recreate the blissful energy of the previous year, 1987. I never again found that blissful vibration, and incidentally I never saw Rosella again. Maybe she'll one day read this story and get in contact with me. That would be special because now, like her, I'm spiritually awakened, at one with the ascended masters – with God – and we'd have lots to talk about.

PREFACE

Spirit recently revealed I'm Twin Flame and the Twin Flames' union manifests the most powerful spiritual connection an individual can experience during this and every lifetime. Each Earth-based Twin Flame soul has a divine life purpose, our missions each contributing to working together as a whole for the good of humanity. The universe devised a plan for Twin Flames in this and every other lifetime to meet together in union, evolving, spiritually enhancing the love energy of the planet – another revelation revealed to me that has influenced this novel in a major way.

The universe's magic shared within the adventure reminds us what humanity was, who we were before being forced into separate races and before invented religions and Satanic instilled racial hatred ultimately threw the human race into the negative utter chaos you've become used to today. This madness has to stop, and while there's a breath left in this body, I for one can no longer allow humanity to suffer this way. Therefore, this story aims to help reconnect every other Twin Flame couple around the globe, bringing love again to planet earth. We're here to make a stand for our planet, created by God for the en-"joy"-ment not just for some but each and everyone; God is everyone. The content of my novel and my screenwriting is my soul mission, contributing to end colonialisation of the African continent, joining with other activists around the world in the struggle to end global poverty and hunger. Nature created the origin of the Twin Flame for a purpose. We Earth-based angels will now come together and collectively fulfil our life purpose. So, Twin Flame couples on Earth, it's time to become actively involved in Mother Earth's preordained reawakening. If you are not already in union or actively seeking union, when you're through the challenging runner-chaser phase, reconnect with your Twin Flame to fulfil the life purpose we were sent here for.

During creation, creating me – the soul I embody – God instilled within a spiritual gift to carry out my soul purpose, part of which is creating this story to share with you what's been hidden from humanity throughout the ages. Spirit's initial plan for this book is so that I can have a voice to play a part in helping change the world into a better place for humanity, that beautiful loving place God designed it to be. My soul purpose and contribution toward the reawakening is to join with others as an activist to help Africa in particular out of what the colonialists purposely created, the so-called third world poverty. I have a moral duty to get back what they stole and, to this day, are still stealing from Africa.

Slavery played a crucial role in the development of the modern world economy. Sadistically kidnapped generations of Black African men, women and children were forced to provide the labour necessary to settle and develop the new world as you know it today. In order for the world to regain harmony, it's imperative the Motherland and her descendants are repaid in line with the laws of compensation applied in English, European and U.S. law courts, which will amount to a long and hefty package of reparations. It is only fair the rest of the world should stop feeling good about having someone to look down on and should ultimately bring equality to Africa. We are to seek reparations for the Motherland's indigenous people and stop the continuous unjust oppression and racism against the Black race.

Humanity needs to wake up to the fact this on-going oppression, vicious separatism and racism is the Devil's work. This story portrays a powerful anti-racist undercurrent based on the concept the cycle of life, the soul reincarnation, meaning we – each and every soul – reincarnate continuously to different races and genders. This is in part a pro-Black novel, which doesn't mean it is anti any other race but basically promotes the equality that's lacking within the Black community after centuries of slavery, and in some countries, continued slavery and oppression through colonialisation. Part of my soul mission is to increase the love and wealth campaigning for reparations and equality for those that are born Black Africans in Africa and around the world. Through my work, I've been granted the power to bring together divinely blessed souls such as the music artist Akon, activist Dr Arikana Chihombori and all others who are here to help humanity, beginning with the most violently oppressed, helping Africa eradicate its third-world poverty.

The truth needs to be told. No more pussyfooting around – a little human rights speaking here, a little one knee and Black lives matter there, and it all goes quiet again. No, no, fuck all that; European, Hispanic and Asian nations need to admit their wrongdoing and pay back Africa. Empty their royal vaults and return Mother Africa's stolen wealth. The Black race has been taken into a complex maze, our spiritual culture lost now after being forcibly taken through many turns, and the deceptions of religion etc. Our psyche has been stripped of humanity's original spirituality, stripped of knowing our glorious ancient civilisation, oneness with God and now many feel as though our history only goes as far back as the colonial slavery. If truth be told, Black Africa was once Earth's only race and when Mother Africa gave birth to other nations the Black race was the only civilised race, building pyramids and palaces, creating huge glorious statues, practising mathematics and astrology, when all others were roaming their lands in a savage state and living in caves. The Black race was satanically stripped of the knowledge and in a few thousand years went from being the teacher of the rest of the world to the seventh-class citizens of the Earth. Black people are held in a complex maze still. Today, still following the Arab Asian, European Christian and Hispanic Catholic religions of those that enslaved us is mental oppression that will only help keep the Black race at the bottom of the barrel. The only way out of the maze is to understand how Black Africa was tricked into entering and getting lost in it, making all those wrong turns. We need to backtrack, reverse the process, free the mind to get the fuck out – this story explains how.

When the missionaries arrived, the Africans had the land and the missionaries had the Bible. They taught us how to pray with our eyes closed. When we opened them, they had the land and we had the Bible.

Jomo Kenyatta

Religion was back then, and still is today, the tool used to fuck us over. Invented religions removed our true spirituality, forced us into false beliefs, and the Black races still have their eyes closed if they continue to worship the different Gods of invented religions who apparently had no problem with the inventors of those religions enslaving the Black race. The time has more than come to stop following the religions of those that enslave and oppress us today. The Koolah tribe's not playing this game any longer; it's time to ask direct questions. Whichever religion you follow, prove to us when you pray and worship you're praying to God and not being tricked into a delusion that simply empowers the negative spirit, prove it and I for one, Richard Barnard, will join you. We of the Koolah tribe want to ask the modern-day people of religion how do they know, how do you know? All this daily praying and the world gets worse. God provides enough food to feed the world, but there's no end to innocent babies starving to death, wars, violence etc. The greedy nations such as the Belgian and French Catholics raping Africa, profiting from stealing, drinking the blood of the starving of babies. I'm sorry to sound so harsh, but I'm here to raise awareness, and this has been the situation since the documented "Scramble for Africa", the conquest and partition of Mother Africa. It's God's universe, for sure, but at present the Devil rules Earth not allowing Mother Africa to come together. All negative-influenced nations of the Earth need to set Africa free and stop raping and starving the mother that gave birth to them.

We were raised to think heaven's angels are blonde with blue eyes: White females flying around with their wings. What if I was to tell you when the invisible intangible angel souls descended on the Earth the human bodies of our entire Earth population were

Black African? I say our, because you – whether Asian, White, Hispanic or whatever – you originated from Black Africa. Maybe it's easy to dismiss inhumane cruelty and suffering on the highest level if it's happening in other countries, but as you're reading this text, your descendants, people you've shared lives with as mothers, brothers, sisters, are still slaves and starving in Africa. You have lived the lives of oppressed Africans, and if you were one of those kidnapped or starving men, women or children, wouldn't you like to know someone's coming to rescue you from that misery? In the words of Barack Obama, "We are the ones we've been waiting for." Before I pass onto my next incarnation, I have chosen to do the world some good, to help right the wrongs. Evil has had its time. We keep speaking about changing the world, but nothing gets done; so, who's with me? Are you scared of people thinking you've lost the plot and gone nuts? Well, that's what they want us to think about anything not in line with their guidelines, any "thinking outside the box". I'm calling on as many wealthy people as possible to "invest" in African infrastructure, economy, education and growth and show Africa how to create their own export companies etc. Begin by building just one desirable "African" built coastal town tourist attraction on par with the best on the planet, the first of many.

A story dedicated to my mirror soul, the other half of me. The universe has presented us to one another to fulfil our divine purpose as it does in each incarnation, my Twin Flame.

CHAPTER 1

Santa Eulalia, Ibiza, Balearic Islands, Spain
Summer 1992

On a perfect, typically warm and breezy, early summer morning in Europe's party capital island, twenty-nine-year-old Black Londoner Yanson Bailey lies head rested on his luxury villa's balcony sunbed. He's an adorably handsome man, slightly resembling the famous boxer Muhammad Ali but with darker skin. A Black man with brown slightly oriental-looking eyes and full lips, six-foot-one tall and as athletically muscular as Ali was in his prime. Although his eyes are closed, he's awake, still buzzing from the ecstasy he's taken a couple of hours earlier, and his mind is semi-consciously amid a familiar ancient African dream. A dream that always gives him the same sensation, an unparalleled, immense feeling, a joy not of this planet. His attractive brown eyes gradually open to his surroundings. Wearing just designer jean shorts, white training shoes and an expensive gold Rolex watch, he sits up, nodding his fresh barber-trimmed skin fade head to the house music while sharing a smile with his latest casual girlfriend, Linh. Linh's a uniquely pretty female, a mixed-race Vietnamese-Black disc jockey who's playing music on the decks at one of his regular, cool, cosmopolitan villa gatherings – the regular crowd invited in from all around the globe that Yanson calls his Ibiza family. His mind's still partially in the dream. During the dream he'd opened his eyes to find himself looking around at a large space with the entire ground a gleaming, engraved, glossy-black-coloured rock covered by an off-white, pink mist. He dreamed he was situated in a densely misty dip of the rock surrounded by a large circle of indigenous African people, men, women and children sitting in a meditation position

15

facing him, all with eyes closed. He recalls being conscious in that other dimension with a childlike, carefree, but uniquely spiritual mindset, looking up to the full moon, around the coastal area and downward to his feet. Although in the dream he has the tiny feet of a toddler child, he's dancing impressively to the same beat of the house music being played at his plush party gathering. Still partly amid the recurring ancient African dream, he always somehow knows that the music has the same beat as the modern-day house rave scene but with the purest sounding instruments and vocal. Whilst conscious in the dream, Yanson knows he's present in ancient Africa but his psyche can see into the future, including what's happening during the current modern-day life he's living. Now, he fully regains consciousness at his villa party, looking up at the Balearic full moon surrounded by stars. He recalls that whilst in that ancient dimension, eyes closed, he could clearly see and feel his Ibiza villa party gathering. See what he was actually doing, speaking to his friends before lying down earlier and drifting into dream-filled sleep in his intoxicated state on his sunbed. Fully conscious now in the modern-day dimension, he looks around to see he's sat on the large villa sunbed surrounded by the group of a dozen male and female friends, the exact scene he'd just dreamed whilst conscious in ancient Africa. Four of the males are an Albanian, a Romanian, a short stocky Paris France–based Black man and an Italian called Riccardo and also known as 'Rome'. These gentlemen currently make up one of Europe's most prolific, highest-earning jewellery heist gangs. Although still not identified by them, they're Interpol's most wanted. All members of the gang are attractive men, but Rome is uniquely the pretty boy, a calm-natured, witty, joking character, forty-five years of age with strikingly gorgeous olive skin – a silver fox with a full head of grey flowing hair and a little designer stubble. In many ways he resembles the Hollywood actor George Clooney, and he's the closest out of his gang to the Londoner Yanson by far. The highly intoxicated Yanson rises from his sunbed and falls into a brotherly, manly hug with the Italian and tries to explain the emotion of his deeply spiritual ancient African dream:

'Wow, Brother, some of these ecstasy dreams, had them since I was a kid...' Yanson pauses as he looks again towards his girlfriend. She's the product of a US military Black GI impregnating an indigenous Vietnamese female during the '60s war. The young lady's blessed with the Black womanly shapely backside and legs and elegant feminine upper body. Yanson and Linh share a smile and he wonders why his heavily intoxicated state now has him reminiscing, thinking deep into a joyful childhood memory he and one of his lifelong White London friends, Benjamin Jarvis, share. It's an event, which happened eighteen years ago.

Walthamstow Market, East London, England, 1974

Ten-year-old Yanson Bailey and his friend Benjamin Jarvis, a White, blond, part-gypsy kid of the same age, are waiting in the crowded market across the road from North's Amusement Arcade. Julie Marney, another member of their juvenile criminal gang, leaves the arcade and walks over the road to join them. She's the same age as they are, White with dark hair and huge blue eyes, slight of physique but confident and assertive. She gives them the rundown:

'Yeah, get ready, he's bagging up the 50p's, then he's got one more run after that.' She opens her beautiful, large eyes wide. They look towards the exit door. 'We do it now, fucking get ready.'

As she speaks, the adrenalin has both boys' hearts start racing due to the sight of the coin collectors, a short balding man and his younger colleague, exiting the arcade struggling with two large, hefty leather shoulder bags filled with cash in coins. The boys wait until the men are on their way back to the arcade and make their way to the parked car in a relatively quiet side street where the men have put the money. As planned, Benjamin and Yanson shatter the window of the car with an iron bar, pushing the glass through before making off with two of the bags. They hide the money in a secluded front garden under some bushes a short distance away and leave the area.

Later the same afternoon, the boys have already recovered the money from its hiding place and given it to the local fence, a man named Charlie Baker also known as 'Uncle' who was to change the stolen coins into bank notes for them. All safe and well, they're joyfully chatting, sitting eating their burgers and fries, and drinking milkshakes in the Wimpy Bar.

Yanson has a habit of suddenly being quiet, adopting a vacant expression as though his mind's in another world before sharing his deepest spiritual revelations with others. During that moment the Black child's sitting in deep thought of the girl who's always vividly on his mind. He's picturing the most beautiful girl. He's dreamed of her for years, a continuous on-going dream where she's always been his own age. She's dark-skinned European, fair-haired, and has one blue eye whilst the other is half dark brown and blue. Yanson drinks some more of his milkshake. His mind wanders on; he recalls a futuristic adult dream, sitting down on a plush beachfront villa balcony and the same angelically faced, unique-eye-coloured girl is now a woman stood speaking to him with an amazing sun rising behind her. Yanson explains the dream, the dream he keeps having while awake, to his young criminal accomplice:

'Ben, when I'm a big man, I'm going to live in a palace with my beautiful Princess.'

His friend Benjamin's intrigued by Yanson's smile. It's a smile that's due to the feeling, the vibration, Yanson shares with the beautiful girl in those dreams. He nods reassuringly to his friend and continues, 'I dream about it quite a lot, Ben, and know that I'm going to marry her one day...'

Santa Eulalia, Ibiza

Suddenly a deeper sensation comes over the adult Yanson, causing him to stop thinking about the childhood memory. He takes out his mobile phone to make a call. A groggy-sounding voice answers, and Yanson says, 'Hello ... hello, yole Jarrod, fucking hell, listen sorry if I woke you, had to call you about something on my mind...'

18

Essex, England, 1961

Three years before the boys Yanson and Benjamin were actually born, wealthy, young East London gangland boss Eric Nevin, aka 'The Little Feller', is nervously pacing the first-floor landing of his posh Essex mansion. He's nicknamed Little Feller because, although a naturally muscular stocky man, he had never grown more than five-foot-two-inches tall. Despite his stature, he speaks with the deep intimidating voice of a giant and has a loud hearty laugh. He's dark haired with cute boyish looks but notoriously cold-blooded. He has a nasty cold-hearted streak, finding amusing anything sadistically evil inflicted on enemies and people he feels he has to intimidate. That and his height, build and, at times, comical characteristics cause him to resemble an English version of Joe Pesci playing Tommy De Vito in *Goodfellas* or Nicky Santoro in *Casino*.

His trophy wife, Cindy Nevin, on the other hand, resembles a more tanned version of the actress Catherine Zeta-Jones – albeit with fuller lips, a more voluptuous figure and, as with her husband, a strong Cockney accent.

As Eric lights another cigarette, only moments after he's put the last one out, he hears his wife's loud scream from behind the bedroom door – making him look more nervous still. Inside the master bedroom, Cindy's in labour and the midwife, a chubby, buxom young woman in her late twenties of Caribbean descent, is giving her words of encouragement in a sweet and calming voice:

'Come on dear, here's the head coming through, not long now... push lady, push... worst is over...'

After what seems like an eternity to Cindy, and to her great relief, her baby girl is finally out. The midwife gives her a little smack and shake to successfully set her off breathing. She waits for Cindy to stop being sick in a nearby bowl before handing the baby to her. Now drained and perspiring, but with a huge smile, the young mother takes the newly born, then looks towards the midwife and the younger, white, timid-looking, tall, slim assisting nurse who is also present. Cindy smiles as she repeatedly whiffs the pure scent of the baby's head. She again sniffs the baby's head and its scent now from her own hands, shakes her head with a confused expression, but smiles.

'Fuck me, nah,' she says, 'this feels strange. I've somehow seen this and smelled my beautiful baby before.'

'Seen what, Mrs Nevin?' the tall young assisting nurse's gentle voice enquires.

Cindy continuously smiles at her baby taking another whiff of her head and confidently looking at both women. 'Me 'aving this baby, her actual scent and you lot in 'ere.' Cindy continues to sniff at the baby's head and smile.

The young assisting nurse smiles too. 'Like déjà vu, Mrs Nevin?'

Cindy's squinting of her eyes shows how puzzled she is by what the nurse has said. It was the first time in that life she'd consciously heard the words déjà vu. The young girl turns her back to the young mother and begins tidying up. Cindy's loud and at times demanding voice of authority, as on this occasion, shocks her. 'You fucking what? Fucking déjà vu?

Cindy's voice makes the young assistant midwife nurse jump and startled she turns to Cindy whilst catching her breath, smiling as she explains, 'Yes, Mrs Nevin, déjà vu, a knowing; having already experienced the present situation...'

The young nurse is still breathless through being startled, and Cindy's voice is suddenly calm as she speaks. 'Déjà vu, must remember that fucking word.' The way Cindy pauses in silence looking at the two nurses makes them nervous, feeling as though what had been explained offended her, but then she begins to explain, 'Strange, suddenly you lot and my baby have reminded me of the clearest dream, a weird but beautiful dream I once had. How fucking strange. I woke from the dream the very morning I fell pregnant with little Nicole here. I'd forgotten all about it and haven't dreamed anything the entire nine months since and now suddenly it's as clear in my mind as it was when I woke from it. Mind was so clear in the dream; I know I was somehow living another life as a Black woman in the future, could see flying cars. I woke up from the dream knowing we had successfully made the entire continent of Africa one powerful country and I was the Queen of Africa. Our success was due to the western and Arab and other countries morally embarrassed into paying back what they'd taken from us by way of reparations. Also help from an evolved alien planet showing us many things to make us more advanced as a country, including environmentally friendly ways to fuel the Earth technology which we will introduce to the world. In the future we are aware the destruction and sorrow on Earth today are purposely constructed by Satan. As it was designed in the beginning Africa will lead and will bring world peace, putting an end to world hunger. A futuristic alien planet shows us the way.' She pauses, looking around the room. 'But in that future life my mind fucking knew of this life I'm living now; even remember being White and having this White baby.'

The midwife and her assistant's fascination at what this London Cockney White woman was speaking of is suddenly disturbed due to the bedroom door opening. Eric Nevin enters, happily smiling at the White assistant young nurse but frowning in distinct racist disapproval of the Black midwife.

The midwife nevertheless responds by giving the usual welcoming Caribbean sunshine smile. 'You got a beautiful baby girl, sir,' she says.

Ibiza, Spring 1993

Over thirty years later and several months after the break-up with the Vietnamese woman Linh, Yanson and his latest girlfriend are alone at his Ibiza villa. It's an opulent five-bedroom property that he purchased from a high-profile Hollywood actress. The rooms at the front have a perfect ocean view and the interior is fitted with every luxury imaginable. He had debated which villa out of the three he had shortlisted to buy, but during the viewing of this one, certain dream déjà vu memories had played vividly in his mind: visions showing the girl from his dreams present in this one villa. He knew then it was the right choice. Its luxurious features include a huge top-of-the-line ipool deluxe designed pool, and a ten-person Canadian spa hot tub situated in front of the villa's outside cinema screen. His carport boasts a fabulous fleet of luxury and sports cars, Japanese and Italian superbikes, a powerboat and Jet Skis. The villa interior's equipped with an indoor/outdoor balcony kitchen able to comfortably entertain over a hundred guests, and an emperor-size bed appearing tiny in the huge master bedroom. The react-to-light windowed area and terrace houses a state-of-the-art spa-gymnasium with beach and ocean view. Yanson's favourite spot to unwind with friends or a girlfriend is his indoor cinema, where he likes to watch sports with local friends or movies with a girlfriend.

Just as he's always dreamed her from childhood, his new, Romanian Gypsy girlfriend, Princess, embodies a mix of Hispanic olive skin complexion and Nordic blonde hair and blue eyes. She has ice-blue eyes but her right eye is half-blue half-brown. Her eyes are especially designed the way they are by nature for her Twin Flame to physically recognise his divine counterpart, the other half of his soul in this incarnation. Her blonde hair has a natural dark streak growing from a birthmark just inward from the temple. She's in her early twenties, stunningly pretty with her facial features perhaps resembling those of the actress Penélope Cruz. Her body is golden tanned and athletic. Purposely she's provocatively stood in heeled sandals, wearing a lightweight white silk mini-negligee that sits high on the impressive hip and protruding bottom. Apart from the unbuttoned sexy negligee she's naked, and in her hands she holds two coffee cups. The way her tiny waist, nipples and enlarged silicone breasts shape her silk garment and the way her trimmed bushy vagina's outer lips slightly twist to one side as she crosses her legs while smiling turn Yanson on, giving him a full erection almost instantly. Noticing his erection, Princess looks into his eyes with a facial expression that displays her feeling of contentment. She smiles as she looks out across the ocean. The two of them share the continuous thought in their minds that from the moment they'd met, just days before, they'd felt an awesome powerful connection between themselves from their very first touch. It had instilled them with a vibration of becoming whole for the first time in their lives. Princess looks away from the sunrise back to Yanson laying on the sunbed, and kneels next to him as she attempts to explain her feelings, speaking softly in her Romanian accent:

'My first night back in Ibiza and making love with you on this sunbed, under the moon and stars last night was by far the best night of my life…'

She looks away from him again, towards the ocean sunrise.

'What made it better was I fell asleep and woke for a moment thinking I was still held captive and only dreamed you'd rescued and brought me here. Yanson, just now I woke opening my eyes to the beginning of the sunrise, saw your face asleep and knew it was real…'

As she speaks of her love for the soul of Yanson Bailey, his thoughts recall the precise moment of their meeting from a childhood dream where the beautiful woman's smile matched the vibrant sunrise. The sentiment was the same now, in adulthood, as then. He too is besotted and has the same feelings towards her as she has to him. The unique love vibration has him listening but at the same time not taking all her literal words in; their souls subconsciously communicate on another frequency.

'…Darling, a more meaningful love story movie couldn't be made. I'm now living the sweetest dream. I've fallen deeply in love with you, you bastard. You've got to me. Don't you dare ever fucking break my heart…'

Still half asleep, Yanson explains the thoughts on his mind: 'Weird, I told you when we were in Moscow, I dreamed this as a kid, exactly as we're here right now, you, this balcony, the sunrise and most of all this feeling I always felt dreaming. It's so fucking powerful and unique.'

She answers: 'It's what they call déjà vu. I get it a lot also. I saw you many times before we met.'

Princess looks out to the sunlit ocean in silence and turns to see Yanson has fallen back to sleep.

Ancient North East Africa
10,000 years ago

At the foot of a small mountain, amid the pitch-blackness of the night, a gathering of a hundred people create a perfect silhouette against the backdrop of an ultra-bright vibrant full moon. A few metres from the waterline, there's a large circular rock floor, around fifty metres in diameter and partially covered with seaweed growth. Most of the people are congregated in the central sunken area, which is around ten metres in diameter and lit by fire torches. They're taking part in their village's African magic ritual. A small band of musicians produce a distinct, sweet, ancient instrumental rhythm that's accompanied by female vocalists whose singing creates a harmonic energy at the full moon ceremony. Although the rhythms are ancient, they somehow prefigure modern-day techno beats. This is original tribal-Afro-House. The sublime beat of the bongo drum, the other early instruments and the angelic female voices are complimented and enhanced by the sounds of large waves rolling in and froth suds licking at the white sands. Some dance to the music while others pay rapt attention to the young, slim-bodied, female psychic medium called Chikelu who's sitting facing the moon in meditation. Despite the reverence in which she's held, she's still only a teenager. The moonlight glistens in her light brown horizontal-teardrop shaped eyes and illuminates her dark skin and high Afro hair.

Up in the sky, out across the ocean, the energetic full moon shines among many distant bright twinkling stars. They illuminate the beach gathering, also the mountain hills, the lush jungle vegetation and the picturesque tranquil waterfalls that surround it. A potent ray of moonlight beams through a gap between mountain rock and cascading water. It shines through the falling water gleaming off the dripping smooth rocky mountain wall and reflects directly onto an attractive young couple, both open-mouthed and engrossed in erotic joyful sex. The Afro-haired girl has full lips, huge round eyes, and large breasts complementing her powerfully fit and sexy body. Her lover is taller, muscular and handsome with natural shoulder-length matted dreadlocks. On their secluded ledge, hidden behind the tranquil falling water, the lovers are tucked away in privacy. To them, the music from the beach gathering, that would be complimented by the therapeutic sound of the waterfall, is muffled almost to a silence.

On the beach, Chikelu begins to receive a vision from another world – a vision of the technologically evolved alien planet Delica.

Planet Delica, in line with Earth dimension, 1616

In contrast to the primitive world of the African tribe with their fire lights burning and mainly naked natives, Delica is an evolved hi-tech planet. Delican beings appear human apart from a specific feature: their eyes are between two and three times the size of human eyes and have no whites to them. Their world is filled with self-driving passenger vehicles, skyscraper buildings and space stations. Space travel to and from their planet is an everyday matter, and their buildings have many varied and fantastic shapes, some with the exact same design as the African pyramids.

In a futuristic-looking room of metals and white surfaces, an elderly Black Delican male called Benser lies wearing short pants on a raised bed. He's surrounded by twelve other Delicans of different races and nationalities. In contrast to the otherwise gleaming sleekness of the surroundings, a tatty wooden hoop, about a metre in diameter and fashioned from pieces of bamboo that have been soaked in water to shape, hovers vertically, without any apparent means of support, in the middle of the room. From within it, sights and sounds from ancient Africa can be seen and heard: the psychic medium Chikelu, her coastal tribe, Earth's vibrant full moon and the small band of indigenous musicians.

The situation is mirrored in Chikelu's mind. She can visualise the elderly Benser's smiling face and hear him speaking to her: 'Chikelu, open your eyes.'

On Earth, she does as she is bid and opens her eyes slightly to see a knee-high, dazzlingly bright, off-white, slightly pink mist coming in from across the ocean. The others present at the gathering look around in wonderment at the sight. They not only see but feel the energy of the mist: the positive spiritual vibration it carries.

Chikelu closes her eyes to see the elderly alien Benser's face as his body says its final words:

'I'm coming; I've one request and that is to be delivered from my next resting in peace in heaven, inside the womb. Myself, and its next body is to be delivered onto the psychic blessed stone, heaven on Earth amongst God's other Twin Flame angels, my soul tribe again. Please be there on my return…'

The other alien Delican angels watch through the hoop as Chikelu smiles, nodding in agreement before fully opening her eyes to the mist. Looking upward to the sky, she answers:

'We feel it and see it; spirit is beginning to prepare for your return connecting with us, your soul tribe angels. We're here waiting.'

Her gentle smile is exchanged for a look of excitement and intrigue; her face now lit up due to the vibrant energy the mist has carried in. Again, she addresses her soul tribe member Benser, recalling the times she has often used her psychic powers to become conscious in future incarnations on Earth including lives she's spent in the company of the soul of Benser:

'Ah yes, I feel and see you again, Koolah spirit. You've suddenly reminded me of the later indigenous African lives we've shared. Welcome back… it's time now.'

Ancient North East Africa

An elderly tribesman, feeble and frail with age, respectfully approaches the young clairvoyant witch and sits next to her. She smiles, and he speaks:

'Chikelu, you receive visions while awake. I've been watching you since sunset. What do you see that brings a mixture of joy and sorrow?'

She giggles, then turns to him with a proud smile. 'What do I see that brings my emotions…? It's not just what I see; it's more what I feel.'

Realising that the whole crowd huddled around her, not just the old man, are hanging on her every word, she raises her voice and explains the vision and the vibration she feels:

'The alien body, it's near death; the chosen one comes…

'The Messiah has lived out that futuristic alien incarnation; the Delican-being Benser body is near death and ready to release the soul of the chosen one back to Earth.

'You know the Messiah reincarnating and coming to the Earth from a futuristic planet is what we will record, but they,' – she shakes her head as she says this – 'will change it to the soul of the Messiah as a man called Jesus who came down from heaven. We will record the process revealing itself now: the fact we are born from heaven, the womb, also us angels are alien soul; but later on, into the future, man will invent religions and translate the location of heaven and describe us, God's true angels, so wrongly.

'Goodness, the universe's never-ending manifestation soul cycle, birth in one dimension being death in another continuing eternally. God's chosen one comes now…'

She looks up to see a flock of birds flying silhouetted against the moon, and her smile turns to laughter.

'The chosen one is on its way back to this heavenly spot and us. The Messiah's soul will live and die reincarnating five lives on Earth. At each point of death another female within our tribe will conceive, accommodating the soul and giving birth in a continuous rebirth cycle. When physically reborn a leopard cub will also be reborn and the soul within the animal will reincarnate many times during each life of the Messiah as a cub and growing into adulthood.'

The eyes and faces of the indigenous tribe gathered around pay rapt attention to the young psychic medium. Among them are many other spiritual clairvoyant witches, their minds capable of sharing her future life progression readings.

Chikelu falls silent and again closes her eyes, her consciousness slipping away from the present and returning to her vision. After a few moments she speaks again:

'The Messiah has sent a vision, again showing us as souls passed on, again reincarnated, this time reborn alien to the futuristic planet Delica. I'm being shown just one of the amazing future dimensions.'

Planet Delica

On Delica, Benser's wife is by his side. She's an elderly grey-haired Black Delican of around his own age, and although grey, she still has her high bouncing Afro hair. She holds her husband's hand, knowing her partner, the body of the Messiah, is dying and utters the words, 'You're going back to ancient Africa, the very spot where we angels began on Earth?'

He nods, struggling to speak. 'Yes, I'm going back...' He pauses and repeats himself, looking directly at his wife. 'I'm going back, back to where it began. I will live as Koolah again. You my twin soul, you still have work to do here. You'll reincarnate to our ancient African tribe, born not so many years behind me. As always in this and every other life, the universe will bring us together in Twin Flame union...'

He smiles, and all those present observe his weakening chest movements. Each breath appears shallower than the one before it, and there are long pauses between each breath he takes. His chest eventually stops still, and a faint, almost invisible, multi-coloured intangible shape leaves the body and slowly begins to move away. Benser's wife takes a small, tatty, brown suede purse from the now- loosened clutches of his palm. She pushes her head into his chest and says goodbye.

The others present watch as the soul disappears.

Ancient North East Africa

In that very moment the psyche of the clairvoyant medium Chikelu at the beach picks up on the soul, having been divinely transported to them across the vast universe. Moments later, the same silhouetted flock of birds she saw earlier have reached the centre of the moon. And as the birds pass, Chikelu opens her eyes to witness the multi-coloured soul of the Messiah against the face of the moon. She raises a finger in concentration, closes her eyes again and her clairvoyant mind is switched to a visual of the young couple making love behind the waterfall.

Rested on her back, the young indigenous female now has the backs of her knees squeezing her lover's shoulders, a specific sexual position for maximum penetration, and they eventually, vocally climax, reaching sexual orgasm together.

The sex visual leaves the mind of the young clairvoyant witch, and she opens her eyes smiling as the alien soul glows in the darkness, hovering above the gathering, gradually moving to the waterfall location where the couple are making love. Chikelu looks around at the slightly off-white, pinkish mist that's covered the entire stone floor of the beach area. Then, eyes closed looking towards the moon, her mind picks up a visual of the female's ovary. Benser's miniaturised, now microscopic-sized soul attaches to the fertilising sperm within the young female's body.

Chikelu ecstatically exclaims in explanation to her tribe:

'Heaven, a female womb, within our village has assisted the Messiah back to Earth; the soul has begun human form again.'

During the alien Benser's final heartbeat, on behalf of her ancient African tribe, the young woman behind the waterfall conceives during intercourse, welcoming the Delican soul Benser back to heaven. In a moment, the evolved, futuristic soul is reincarnated back to ancient Earth ten thousand years before today's timeline.

Chikelu opens her eyes to the mist and with her face now lit up with a vibrant energy, she speaks:

'It's back, the divine creative spiritual energy of the universe. Creative energy has no form; the mist has been attached to it to show its potency. Its strength is always abundant when the Messiah is present. The anointed one has come… it's done, the soul, the universe's Messiah has returned to this blessed location, physical heaven on Earth, back to be re-born among our tribe. It's begun. We are safe and all is well.'

The young witch says no more. Instead, she rises to her feet and loses herself in the moment, happily dancing around with other tribe members to the sweet musical rhythm.

Planet Delica

Even when it was just the year 1616 on Earth, life on the far-away planet Delica had evolved, technologically, spiritually and otherwise, beyond the point where we are today on 21st century Earth. Delica's rapid evolutionary process began when their people became victorious in a non-physical but spiritual holy war, against our evil adversary, the Devil. Satan had previously deprived Delica and many other planets of their crucial subconscious-reality psyche. The universe presented a unique soul, a spiritual warrior who came in the name of love and led them to reap the essential benefit of the universal subconscious mind. The benefits of the victory included receiving nature's love vibration to create the infinite spiritual conscious mindset to eradicate Delica's third world and all other negativity from their existence. The Delicans came to understand what humanity have yet to learn, that amid our subconscious reality we naturally know the solution to bring world peace and they understood facts such as time being non-existent. Delica discovered it's a spiritual multi-dimensional universe where time has no place. The soul is the energy of God, which created the universe as souls reincarnating eternally. Spiritual Delicans evolved from conversing primitively with the voice, making sound with vocal cords, to communication by telepathy. One of the positives of communicating telepathically is you don't vocally speak or even hear a sound in your head. Instead, you use the oneness of universal language; you, as in the soul, silently communicate. You feel a vibration, an awareness, to understand what others are saying. Everyone, even random strangers are able to tap into one another's thoughts; you allow others to know your every intention. This created total honesty, therefore stopping all forms of secret hatred, evil acts and deception. Delica had returned to how it was before they and other planets fell under satanic control; speech could no longer be used as a form of trickery, a way to deceive. Having defeated the negative side in the spiritual holy war, the Delicans discovered each soul, Delican, human and that of every other alien, is jointly the universal spirit of God, and this revelation abolished all forms of self-righteous favoured religious beliefs that took them away from God. The Delicans rediscovered we are God, the entire universe, the galaxy and everything in it. God created the physical universe as ingenious waves of energy manipulating matter, forming the galaxy. All beings are part of a universe, a universe that consists of uncountable divinely intricate frame-by-frame spirals of dimension phases, therefore creating a time and ageing process illusion that primitive human souls perceive as lifetimes.

CHAPTER 2

Ancient North East Africa
10,000 years ago

It is later and the beach ceremony is coming to an end. Chikelu rests, sitting back in her meditation position facing the full moon and closing her eyes. She no longer feels the vibration of her tribe or hears the music; in her mind there is just darkness and a sudden distinct feeling of fear and inadequacy. Her clairvoyance, a vibration of her soul, has transported her mind ten thousand years into the future, to modern Earth in the year 1962. She feels the vicious racial prejudice shown to Black people around the globe at that time: the hostility Martin Luther King Jr faced in the USA to his peaceful civil rights movement for human equality, the endemic racism of the day in Britain, apartheid in South Africa...

She feels the pain of millions before the general vibration of her psychic FLP, her future life progression, focuses itself down to a single location: her home in her future incarnation, an English suburban-Essex thatched cottage.

Epping Forest, Essex, England, 1962

The small television that rests on the deep bay window ledge is turned off, but the radio is on, and she listens to it with the large handsome black cat she's named Jojo sleeping by her side. Conscious in her future incarnation, Chikelu listens to the radio news bulletin reporting the latest sickening activities of the Klu Klux Klan in America, legal terrorists murdering Black families, innocent men, women and children. Suddenly, she's disturbed by a knock at the door, and she feels herself rising to answer it and sees her hand – her hand is now that of a White woman – sliding the bolt across to open the door. The visitor is another White woman, the stunningly pretty Cindy Nevin, wife of the gangster Eric Nevin, whom she happily greets.

Back in ancient Africa, as Cindy Nevin's face enters the psyche of Chikelu in her deep trance, the tribal elder sitting next to Chikelu notices her momentarily giggling, hand over mouth. Conscious in her future incarnation, Chikelu maintains her clairvoyant ability, the characteristic of her soul. She's reborn as the English-speaking Romany woman Rosella, who is now sitting in the living room of her cottage speaking to her visitor Cindy. It is a year after Cindy gave birth to her daughter Nicole. Cindy and Rosella sit in opposite armchairs directly facing one another. Rosella is guiding her fellow soul tribe angel Cindy through an ancient future life progression waking-dream therapy. Both psychic clairvoyant women are totally relaxed in a deep self-hypnotic state, their minds able to explore future life dimensions. Unlike PLR, past life regression, a practice that concentrates on the personal history of your past lives, FLP shows events in your future life. It reveals possibilities that your past and current life actions are creating from paths we choose to examine. The women sit with eyes closed, and a joint reading opens up in their minds. Instead of experiencing one of their usual future life progression readings, spirit has them experiencing astral projection out-of-body. Their astral-body souls have separated from their physical bodies, capable of travelling the dimensions throughout the universe and viewing others' lives. They find themselves present in astral-body form in a future setting, thirty years later in the year 1993.

Bucharest, Romania, 1993

Their out-of-body experience, their astral projection, takes them to a plush five-star hotel room. A young lady in her early to mid-twenties, around Cindy's own age, sleeps in the huge king-size bed alone. Suddenly, Cindy and Rosella are joined in the hotel suite by another astral-travelling body, that of Rosella's mother, Dinah, a no-nonsense Romany woman in her mid-forties. Rosella and Dinah speak with each other but Cindy can't understand what they're saying as they converse in their native Romanian. However, they soon fall silent, interrupted by the sight of the girl waking in her bed. She's simply gorgeous, the Ibiza-based Black London gangster Yanson Bailey's Romany girlfriend, Princess. Princess is the niece of Rosella and granddaughter of the elder woman Dinah. She yawns, opening her uniquely different-coloured eyes that light up her pretty face. Princess is actually the only physical body within the room, but she's aware the room has presence. Both Dinah and Rosella follow Princess's eyeline and notice that Cindy's astral body keeps changing on and off to that of a beautiful Black woman in her mid-forties. Princess, a young White woman, speaks to Cindy in Earth's first civilised language, ancient African Koolah. She says a single word, a word which means 'Mother'.

Ancient North East Africa

What begins to unravel has Chikelu respectfully nodding. With eyes closed, conscious in her future life, she smiles a huge smile as the futuristic vision she's receiving presents her with its surprising revelation in regard to Cindy Nevin.

Ten of Earth's authentic months and full moon rituals, nine westernised months, since the arrival of the soul of the Messiah, the scene at midnight at the stone circle is an incredible one. The sky above the stone floor is full of clusters of visible multi-coloured souls: thousands of intangible souls continuously leaving and returning to the location. If you could see them, you'd be reminded of the rainbow-coloured bubbles that children make with bubble blowers, blowing liquid through the small hoop; but with the shapes having less form and the colours a greater other-worldly vibrancy. Others of the souls are clear with a glowing white dot in them. The music of the early Koolah tribe plays tonight as it has done for many nights leading up to this moment, raising the vibration. At the sight of the incoming souls, the clairvoyant medium Chikelu dances along with other tribe members till sunrise.

As the sun rises it illuminates the ever-present pink mist that covers the stone floor, now knee-high and densely covering the entire ten-metre diameter of the sunken area and, with less intensity, spread out over the remainder of the stone. The now heavily pregnant waterfall lover, soon to be mother, is in the centre of the stone circle dip with Chikelu and other women of the tribe.

Suddenly, her new-born baby can be heard crying and the soul of the futuristic alien Benser is born reincarnated a gorgeous Black girl, who will be called Abiona. The clairvoyant angel Chikelu picks her up and holds her above the mist, up against the now faint full moon. The new-born stops crying as she looks up at the spiritual activity above her, the clusters of visible souls in the sky. Chikelu speaks as much in explanation to the rest of the tribe as to the infant, saying:

'Welcome back to heaven on Earth, God's chosen one. I promised you before your death on Delica, that I'd be here in the circle when you arrived from heaven…'

The unique alien soul, the authentic Messiah, had been reincarnated back to a dimension ten thousand years back in time, the alien soul of Benser reincarnated attached to a wriggling microscopic fertilising human sperm, subsequently reborn a pretty Black African baby girl to the tribe.

Three years later

By the tender human age of just three, the authentic Messiah Abiona had already enlightened her coastal soul tribe, revealing to them the universe's most complex magical realms of spirituality. She had not achieved this by use of the spoken word but by means of a deeper, more complex type of self-hypnosis that unearthed her future and past lives to herself in lucid dreams that she was able to share with other psychic minds within the tribe. Through something akin to past life regression and future life progression, after a bright-light flickering sensation she would become conscious in past and future life dimension phases, and her subconscious soul could share her visions with those on her psychic frequency.

In one particular vision, she's conscious in a future dimension, a future incarnation around three hundred years later where she's born male and named Koolah. He, as she, is the Messiah – as with each body her soul reincarnates to. Through Abiona's future-life-progression vision, the psychics of Abiona's village could see their village transformed. They looked around them to see what was once a small village now a densely populated city with a grand palace built on the hill, half as high as a pretty waterfall situated behind it. As far as their eyes could see, there were clay-built buildings for miles around – a thriving city, Planet Earth's first civilised society. On the beach, the stone floor was still present and recognisable but its surface was now clean and a gleaming glossy Black and had it not been for the familiar off-white, pink mist covering its centre they would have been able to have seen the beautiful engravings there. On the stone floor, a hundred or so men, women and children were sitting, surrounding the future incarnation of Abiona, who was talking to a young boy covered in a swarm of friendly bumblebees. Next to them stood a fine-looking beast, a fully grown male black panther.

Following these future revelations, Abiona asked all the villagers to remove the jungle trees from around the off-white, pink mist–covered jungle coastline floor. As every individual began the work, a divine energy force surged through each and every soul, making the work lighter and instilling a strange knowledge in everyone that they'd actually performed the task there before. The Messiah Abiona then explained that they were also to remove any sand from the rock floor and scrape away the hardened film of seaweed growth that covered the huge flat surface. After many days of intense scrubbing a beautiful carved symbolic black stone floor began to reveal itself, and then what seemed an endless North East African monsoon rainfall came and washed down the rock surface leaving it clean and gleaming. The clearing to be known throughout the ages as the magic circle, Earth's spirit world or even heaven on Earth, had again been revealed.

Presently, Abiona sits eyes closed in her meditation position on a slightly raised rock in the dip of the magical circle. It is midnight and the moon is full. Around fifty villagers, Chikelu and other deeply spiritual angel souls, sit with eyes closed in a circle surrounding the child Messiah, their minds receiving her multi-shared past and future dimension visions of many past and future lives. Eyes still closed, Abiona smiles brightly as she begins to share a particular vision, one that reveals Earth's most unique dimension. She speaks as she shares the vision of Black Africa at the universe's introduction of the human race dimension phase with the minds of the other angels: 'This area is the magic circle; we angels arrived here on Earth a dimension long ago.'

The child Messiah stands, looking towards the full moon, and shares with the other angels the images of her and seventy-two thousand other angels arriving on the Earth – intangible colourful teardrop-shaped angel souls approaching in the distant skies, arriving at Planet Earth in waves like huge flocks of glistening tiny aluminous raindrops, hovering around the pristine magic circle stone on the East African coast.

'When we came, Black Africa was the only inhabited land of the Earth. We witnessed Earth's original man: Black humans, men women and children.'

Abiona looks to the impressive stone floor area, then closes her eyes again.

'We have always used the energy this spot holds; the stone marks the spiritual passageway to connect us with other angels, to astral travel and cross dimensions throughout the universe. Travel back to the beginning of creation and forward to the future far-reaching heights of humanity and alien planets.'

The image Abiona is now feeding into the rest of the angels' psyches shows the development of Planet Earth in reverse, a much-speeded-up, light-year speed Earth coming back together as Pangaea – the world as one land supercontinent before it divided as we know it today. As the continents can be seen joining back together, the vision shows the symbolic stone-floor rock magic circle to be the centre of Earth's land.

'God created this spot as the exact centre of Earth's original one land – Pangaea, when all the land of the Earth was joined – vibrating at the highest frequency, producing the source's purest love energy. The magic circle is where I will share with you future dimensions, future lives you will later reincarnate to.

'I will reincarnate to our village here many more times before remaining in the world of spirits, but during my final incarnation I will perform a powerful spell ensuring we meet in every life we reincarnate to, in all those future incarnations receiving vivid dreams to keep us in tune and connected.'

Abiona's shared vision now shows that as Earth's first primitive female humans across the land conceived, the angels' alien souls split in two, becoming twin souls, each possessing the ovary- fertilising sperm and growing with the foetus one soul split within in separate wombs of those early Black primitive human female bodies, each divided soul having now become Twin Flame.

'The land we inhabit today will one day be known to Western civilisation as Africa.'

Abiona's shared vision now shows Africa in the relatively less distant past, the indigenous people leaving the motherland to take up residency across the world – Black Africans leaving the land by mankind's first ships and venturing around the globe.

'A hundred thousand years before Earth's 21st century we will begin to migrate and when we evolve White and Asian appearances the Devil will exploit the fact and inject racism and separatism into the human psyche.'

Abiona's shared vision now shows angels of the Earth having settled on lands all around the planet, indigenous peoples in what's known today as Australia, in Colombia, in China, in European countries such as Romania, and the Native Americans in the lands known as Canada and the U.S.A. today.

'Some of us Earth-based angels left here to venture to other lands and now we are twin soul, Twin Flame angels all across the globe.'

Abiona's shared vision changes again, showing the angels of the circle future modern-day countries of the world and how their inhabitancies have evolved.

'We Twin Flame angel souls are now scattered all around the globe living human lives, but the Black African bodies are naturally evolving to adapt to whichever climate they've had to deal with. The motherland has given birth to all other nations, Asians, Europeans and others. But whatever happens, no matter how far apart we are in the physical world, how scattered around the globe we are, there will never be distance between God's angels; we will stay together through our one soul divine spiritual connection.'

Abiona's shared vision now shows a future world that is different to our own: a world in which Africa was not invaded by Asian Arabs nor colonised by the European invaders who claimed huge chunks of the land for themselves and divided Africa into countries as we see it today. The entire land of Black Africa is flourishing, thriving as one country with a president, one currency and one bank – one-nation Africa, the leading economy of the world.

'But that is but one Earth dimension, one of many parallel existences of Earth. Humanity will be reduced to one-dimensional consciousness, but in reality the universe is multi-dimensional. I have just shared such a vision...'

Suddenly, Abiona's vision changes and with it her previously joyful expression turns to a sorrowful frown and tears repeatedly run down her cheeks. This is the first time she's received the negative images she's seeing now. She and the others all now get to see visions of the world which is our own: the world where Africa was invaded by foreign nations, imperialist and colonialist. The visions show the bloodshed caused while invading nations stole Africa's riches: gold, diamonds and other precious minerals. But stealing and looting wouldn't be enough for the invaders; as they accumulated their wealth, they went a step further, stealing the African people themselves to build their world, beginning the satanic transatlantic slave trade. Again, the visions show all those assembled the true brutal horror of this reality.

'During this dimension the entire African population will have invented religions forced upon them, when our prayer should be the entire indigenous inhabitancy joined together in deep meditation as God. Many different nations will divert us from our oneness with God, instead instilling religion, reaping havoc here and around the world.'

Her psyche shows the inside of a future modern-day church; behind the altar there's a huge depiction of a pearly-white-gated heaven in the sky above puffy white clouds with a long-bearded White God and blond-haired and blue-eyed White angels playing floating harps.

'They'll invent different religions all around the world and this is the image they'll portray to disempower Black Africa. As you've just seen, when we angels came to the Earth possessing bodies, there were only Black humans on Earth; therefore, God's only angels were Black. We left the motherland giving birth to other nations, White, Asian, Oriental and others. Those angels you see in that picture will mislead the entire planet, for periods even mislead Black people also. We are God's true angels observing the deeds of man and leading up to the awakening; the love we create coming back into union will keep a balance against the evil. Each of us angels arrived with a life purpose; we split into two bodies becoming twin souls.'

The child smiles brightly again.

'We will come into union, join with our twin in almost every life we reincarnate to, creating an unparalleled feeling of love, a coming home. It's essential for us to begin our purpose even before physical union and what we've begun will flourish when we find our divine union. Our Twin Flame union is crucially important, because when we reunite, it's not just to bring our own soul back into alignment as divine love, it's also for the greater good to fulfil a mission beyond our personal development and aid the spiritual awakening of the planet. When we Twin Flames come together, we don't just do so to heal our union, and ourselves, but to heal the world at large and help others do the same. Healing is done in so many different ways, dependent on the Twin Flame soul's shared purpose, but it will be done naturally and lovingly.'

A frown crosses the child's face as her shared vision changes again and now shows modern-day Western archaeologists raiding African tombs and finding thirty-thousand-year-old ancient African hieroglyphics, paintings of large boats used for the migration, painted pictures not of later invading Arab-looking men but men of Black African skin colour.

'Look! The fools are troubled by what they have discovered. It does not fit in with their view of the world. A negative force will be made aware of our future, the prosperity of Africa, and they'll fearfully intervene. The reason we angels came here is because many dimensions into the future we will consciously reawaken. During the reawakening Africa will get back what's rightfully hers'

Abiona's final vision shows Africa in the end getting reparations to bring it to the stage it would have been at if European countries had never robbed its land, kidnapped and abducted its people and most importantly forced them away from their spirituality. 'Our African descendants once taken away by force will reincarnate returning back to the motherland and reap the rewards.'

As it finishes, Abiona opens her eyes and looks around at the magical circle.

CHAPTER 3

Five years later

Abiona is now eight years old. Like her, the village has grown too in the past five years, and now might be more properly called a town. There's been a vast carving into the jungle, with many trees removed and the Earth's first clay-built sheltered homes newly built all along the coastline and inland jungle. The population too has grown, now into the thousands as people came to learn of Abiona and the village.

Eight-year-old Abiona sits with legs crossed in the lotus position in the dip section of the off-white, pink misty magic circle. Outside the circle many musicians and vocalists combine creating the authentic beat, recognised today as blissful modern-day house music. Some tribal villagers surround her, dancing, and others sit on the stone floor; the floor now showing its beautiful engravings seen in Abiona's earlier shared astral-travel sightings before the floor was cleaned.

Presently, around fifty men, women and children take their places sitting in a circle surrounding the child Messiah, all facing inward with their feet touching one another or some holding hands to create the circle.

Among them is the clairvoyant witch Chikelu, now in her late twenties, who addresses the child Abiona:

'Abiona, we feel your soul, its joy.'

The child Abiona rises to her feet, smiles and speaks:

'This stone floor and its unique energy was designed during creation. I'm always at joyful peace here, where I was born. Spiritual energy itself has no form; the cloud rests here with the positive spiritual energy to show its presence.

'This very spot is the physical heaven on Earth, but intruders will later come and steal our vast knowledge and translate our teachings wrongly.'

The little girl Messiah laughs dismissively.

'They will later have the human race fooled that God is a White man who lives in a place called heaven above the clouds in the sky...'

Chikelu nods her head in understanding as Abiona continues speaking:

'Here, this rock circle, from where my soul travels the universe, is physical heaven on Mother Earth, and that's why you are able to receive my future visions here. This is Earth's physical heaven. Many generations of our ancestors, my future incarnation Koolah included, have layered our spirit within to create this unique vibration...'

Abiona turns her head to face the ocean as she continues:

'I will repeatedly be re-born to our tribe, to the circle's positive energy, another five times, remaining here more than three hundred years. Each incarnation, each time I return, I'll further develop my astral travel and share my sightings with the psyche of many specific angel souls among us. My mind will convey my astral-travel visual to each soul present within the magical stone circle.'

Abiona now lowers herself to the rock floor until she is lying flat on her back, palms to the floor, with eyes closed. As though it were a signal for it to do so, all the joyful dancing stops at this moment, the music dies down until only a single sweet bongo drumbeat remains, and everyone sits. Abiona opens her eyes wide but then they, like her body, are lifeless and the members of the circle know that Abiona's soul has left on astral travel. Their minds are filled with the vision she shares with them of a future dimension...

The magic circle tribal angels are being shown violent bloody scenes of the Asian Arab invasion of the African continent in 700 BC. They vividly witness the brutality; they see the mass bloodshed, the killing of indigenous men women and children, women being raped and taken by the men as the Muslims' sex slaves, indigenous men separated from their wives and children and viciously enslaved... all the acts of pure evil associated with the enslavement of Africa. In the name of Islam, sword in one hand and holy book in the other, the vision shows them forcing their religion onto the indigenous people of Africa.

Abiona's voice is heard throughout the collective psyche of the magic circle:

'As you can see, I've crossed into a future dimension. This is what awaits us and the motherland God gifted us. These viciously cruel people you see in this vision will cross from Asia; the first of many intruders will come in the name of Islam, instilling their invention, religion. The plan will be to forever oppress the people of our home, to divide and rule, and under no circumstances again allow a reunited Mother of the Earth, a united Africa. They will force us into a religious belief, a God that favours them and allows them to viciously enslave us...'

The visions she shares leave members of the circle disturbed, and once Abiona's soul has returned to the present she sits up and addresses the circle, at first with her attention directed towards three tribal elders, two women and a man:

'There are no coincidences in God's universe, no exceptions. God created each soul of the universe putting us into soul groups.'

She looks around the magic circle before continuing:

'We here are a unique soul tribe: six hundred of us; our original coastal tribe are alien angel souls now each split into two bodies having become mirror souls, Twin Flame. We will reincarnate together as a spiritual warrior group throughout the future dimensions, meeting in each life we live, finding our twin physical and spiritual perfect match, our divine counterpart, to become whole again. Before the first of the invaders arrive, our unique spiritual energy will have assisted us, creating a divine magical spell out into the universe.' Abiona smiles reassuringly.

'Empowered by the oneness spirit, the universe, I've begun the process to combat their plan. The process has begun and will be initiated fully when I cross to the spirit world. Future incarnations have been created and installed into the universe's multi-dimensional phases. Our soul tribe will be born into lives to oppose Satan. We will reincarnate in future dimensions. We may be Black, White, European, from any nation around the globe... We will be put in strategic positions. As we move through future dimensions, I will guide our soul tribe from the spirit world, keeping us connected by feeding your minds continuous intense vivid regression and progression existences, helping you become conscious in other dimensions, future and past lives – lifelike dreams that will subconsciously show you your other lives, how you connect with members of our soul group in those lives. This will keep our energy high and make you aware that there's more to the universe outside the control system they'll have instilled into the human psyche. So, fear not; we have a plan also.'

280 years after the death of Abiona

Throughout her life on Earth, Abiona astral travelled the entire universe, moving back and forward in time and to near or far places, including the future planet Delica, from where her soul had arrived. Eventually the Messiah's human body in the form of Abiona died of natural causes in old age, but over the next centuries the soul of the Messiah was reincarnated back to Abiona's coastal tribe four times. Each time the body died, the soul returned to a conceived womb. And each time the reborn Messiah was able to perform breath-taking, heart-pounding feats of God's magic, and to astral travel whilst communicating telepathically and multi-sharing images of future dimensions as visions with the tribal angels, spiritually enlightening the tribe – the divine magic being characteristic of the unique Messiah soul.

Then, two hundred and eighty years after the death of Abiona, the Messiah soul reincarnates to the coastal tribe for a fifth and final time. Onto the mist-covered magic circle rock floor a baby boy is delivered from heaven, from the female womb, to be given the name Koolah.

23 years later

It is the morning of the customary full moon ceremony, and by now the psychic circle of angels has grown in number. Now, more than a hundred alien angel souls gather to form the circle. They are men, women and children, and they take their places, holding each other's hands, sitting with feet touching one another to form an unbroken circle around Koolah and four others. The entire circle is now so large it no longer fits within the central sunken area of the rock floor and therefore occupies the area around it. The off-white, glowing pink mist still lingers all around the circle rock floor, but as always it is at its densest in the ten-metre-diameter dip, where Koolah and other ascended angels now congregate, showing the potent spiritual energy of God's presence.

Koolah has grown from being a cute baby boy to a tall, handsome man. He has very dark skin and an athletic, muscular body. In some ways he bears a slight resemblance to a young modern-day American rapper 50 Cent, but Koolah wears his hair in long, flowing Bob Marley–type matted dreadlocks, and his face carries a continuously smiling expression.

Like the spiritual ring, like Koolah himself, the village has grown in size over the past years, and now might be properly called a city, with a population of twenty thousand. The crowd surrounding the spiritual ring is larger – many along the beach and around the city practise nature's yoga and deep mind meditation. The band too is made up of many more musicians, who create the city's sweet powerful musical heartbeat, playing sounds that foreshadow those of a modern-day house music festival. In the magic circle, condensed raindrop-shaped souls rise and fall, appear and disappear. Some are clusters of intangible, wonderful colours; others transparent with a bright white dot. The moment bodies on Earth and around the universe die, some of the souls appear and disappear again before reincarnating and beginning new lives.

Koolah takes his place sitting in the lotus position in his usual spot at the centre of the magic circle, and quickly falls into a trance. He is accompanied by his constant animal companion, the handsome black panther named Jojo, who lies down at his side and too falls into a trance state, and by three deeply spiritual ascended angels of the tribal soul group: the child Imani, and adults Ode and Akachi.

Koolah begins his astral travel, opening up his angels' minds of the magic circle. The sights he sees travelling the multiverse are placed into the surrounding angels' psyches daily, a continuous stream of psychic visions. Presently, they are witnessing another vision showing the future history of Africa. The Messiah's multi-shared visions reveal how Satan would show nations the way to weaken and conquer Black Africa and other indigenous lands around the globe.

The spirit Messiah narrates the images he's sharing. Koolah's voice can be heard clearly in the heads of the hundred within the circle.

'The intruders will be taught to remove the divine knowing from the indigenous psyche, remove Africa's spirituality, remove our knowing from Black Africa, the knowing we are God. The invaders of Africa, Asian Arabs and Europeans, will use psychology against us, to weaken us. They will seek to turn Africa against human nature. The Asians will preach that the universe's authentic spirituality, original Black magic, is non-Muslim 'Kafir'. The word Kafir in Arabic refers to a person who disbelieves and denies the authority God in the Islamic tradition; the term is often translated as 'infidel', denier, nonbeliever and so forth. We are not infidels! Later, the European invaders will seek to instil into the psyche of indigenous Africa that anything that does not fit in with their so-called Christianity is pagan.

'Indigenous Africa will be divided and conquered; our great land will be divided because our psyche will be tricked into following the intruders' religions; we'll even take pride in fighting their violent wars. They'll twist the minds of the indigenous African into believing humanity's oneness-God spirituality is an evil witchcraft, the work of Satan, making us believe that we the

African people are not Earth's original humans, and that our true universal magic from God is a black magic Devil cult. Europeans will persecute those they call pagans in our and in their own lands. Both Islam and Christianity will come here attacking our Black African psyche; our gifted divine spirituality will suddenly be portrayed as evil black magic. They'll forcibly manipulate our souls, instilling religion into the land of Africa to make us subservient, trick us into thinking they're our saviour and the way to their fake God. They will trick us into believing their modern-day bible is the word of God. Look! Read! See what their modern-day bible says: "Exodus 21:20-21 – Anyone who beats their male or female slave with a rod must be punished if the slave dies as a direct result, but they are not to be punished if the slave recovers after a day or two, since the slave is their property." Black people of our land and descendants of Black slaves around the world will actually believe their book is the word of God. Without our spiritual connection, we will become gullible and fall for their books of lies. Religion will make it easy for them to make our homeland theirs, steal the wealth of the land, sorrowfully loot the people, steal and enslave us, carry out the work of Satan...'

The psychic visions continue to show events from Africa's future history: the thousand years of brutal slavery oppression by the Asian Arabs that would become a major contribution to the beginning of the global slave trade by them trading indigenous Black human beings to the White Europeans; the atrocities committed by the Belgium King Leopold II in the late 1800s and early 1900s in the part of Africa known as The Congo, seen through his own eyes – millions murdered and the hands of men, women and children's limbs, hands and feet amputated if rubber collection quotas were not met. Within the circle some gasp at the visions of horrific mass genocide, the savage murder of God's beautiful people of central Africa's rainforest; others record what they see in the visions, writing down the name Leopold II, a Satan-commanded terrorist, one of the human souls who'd made a deal with Satan many incarnations previously.

'This soul we see through the eyes of is another scourge to

humanity who's made a deal with Satan, continuously reincarnating, awarded privileged positions and terrorising the souls of those of God during each incarnation. Whilst in this body form, this future European King will be responsible for the horrific murder of more than twenty million and the savage torture and mutilation of another twenty million innocent indigenous men, women and children – murdering almost three times the total murdered during the Nazi holocaust that my astral-travel sightings have already shown you and that we've studied. The massacre of the Congolese will be the unknown and hidden holocaust, an indication of how Black people will be valued and regarded in future society. The people of Africa will never colonise, enslave or commit acts of genocide upon any nation, but it will be the Black people deemed the scourge of every society.'

Koolah's voice falls silent and disappears from the joint psyche of the magic circle. One of Koolah's four spiritual companions speaks. It is the child witch Imani, who has thousands of bumblebees on the front of his neck and shoulders. He's a cute-looking boy, slight of build. His facial expression currently carries a look of bewilderment.

'Kill millions why, for what purpose? Children, babies?'

The visions Koolah shares with the magic circle now change, switching away from Central Africa to East Africa, a decade or so later into the 20th century at the beginning of World War I. A party of British and American archaeologists are seen in the process of excavating some of the ten-thousand-year-old Koolah Palace ruins.

Again, the spirit Messiah narrates the images he's sharing, and Koolah's voice can be heard clearly in the heads of those in the magic circle.

'The fools have unearthed mystical artefacts they did not expect to find. In the 16th century Turkish intruders had previously taken over the City of Koolah claiming they'd built it as their own. Evidence of their civilisation is what these archaeologists expected to find; instead, they have unearthed evidence the Turks thought they had destroyed all trace of, evidence of the more sacred ancient Koolah tribe coastal buildings, evidence of Earth's authentic Messiah and God's true angels of the Earth. They have discovered intact some of the basement dwellings and hieroglyphics on the walls – not just sacred carvings showing Earth's entire solar system but also alien planets and their solar systems. But that alone is not the peak of their discovery; they have discovered methods of exactly how we have direct communication with evolved intelligent alien life, and how we become the first civilised humans learning from shared astral-travel visions, placing future modern Earth and evolved alien activity into the psyche of the magic circle.'

In the vision, the party of archaeologists can be seen and heard discussing their find. The party is now large with scientists, military and members of a powerful Masonic fraternity within its ranks, and even includes a member of the British royal family. It is night and the archaeologists stand on the seashore holding their discussions. One of them, a handsome, young, blond Englishman wearing a Moda Fedora hat and gold-rimmed spectacles, announces in his posh voice, 'But students around the Western world are being taught Christopher Columbus discovered the Earth was round four hundred years ago!' He laughs, before continuing. 'Seems those students are being lied to, because by all accounts, on the evidence that we keep finding, someone on Earth knew this ten thousand years ago!'

One of his more senior colleagues, a high-ranking priest of the Vatican Catholic Church, intervenes, saying, 'For now, we must continue to hide this and all else we've discovered in Africa over the centuries. We cannot allow Black people to know of their glorious history, the great wonders, the true Messiah, their gifted magical power... We and others took that from them and we now use their magical powers for our benefit to actually keep them oppressed. If they knew the truth, that they're the true angels from heaven, we would lose our authority over them, they would unite and there would be a war on African soil that we couldn't possibly win. Converting them from nature's spirituality to religion has played a major part; now half of them look to Islam to show them the way to God and the rest of them look to us Europeans to show them the way to heaven. Control the psyche and you oppress the entire race! At some stage, when we have secured our worldly financial position, we'll have to publicly concede that the Black man is the original human and subsequently pay something back for the atrocities we've carried out. I fear it will be unavoidable; our clairvoyants have explained it's to happen in the future, but I hope it's for the next generation to worry about.'

The shared vision shifts to show some of the archaeological team in the process of unearthing an artefact inside the basement of an excavated indigenous home. It's a large wooden box presently covered in dusty sand. Inside that box they discover, covered in an appropriate preserving grease gel, a tatty old ring made from entwined bamboo – an object familiar to the members of the magic circle as being a ring similar to the one the early clairvoyant Chikelu used to communicate with Koolah's earlier Delican incarnation, the dying body Benser; a magical communication portal ring deliberately preserved and hidden to keep it from the invading Turks and others. The 20th century archaeologists also discover written papers in the box, operating instructions written in a language – man's first ever language – that they do not understand. However, the party are suddenly shocked and astounded to find some of the writing is in English and French typed text. As the members of the magic circle know, the Koolah tribe were able to read modern-day European and Arabic languages eight thousand years before the then-savage Europeans and Arabs knew how to even converse in any language, let alone read and write. The vision now shows one of the archaeologists showing the written papers to a young Black female, who it appears the group hold captive. Moreover, it seems she can understand or at least read aloud the ancient language contained in the scrolls. They force her to read aloud from the scrolls, and it becomes clear that these words are those for operating the age-old African magical spiritual portal which enables a two-way connection with evolved alien planets or even with future Earth dimensions. She reads continuously from the scrolls and her words create the vibration activating the portal. The astonishment of the 20th century archaeologists is palpable as the ring elevates and hovers vertically, connecting itself with a similar portal also rising and hovering vertically. Inside the perimeter of the hoop the Earth-based party now see Delican alien beings living their daily life on board their huge highly evolved futuristic spacecraft bound for Earth. Some are amazed at this sight, and in particular astounded by the strange appearance that the Delicans' eyes possess. However, it seems at least one of the archaeologists, who appears to be their leader, understands exactly what is happening, not just who the Delicans are but what they will do. He begins to explain the alien mission:

'Their estimated time of arrival here on Planet Earth is around our year 1940 and we'll be there to greet them. Their mission and the message they bring is to show the way to instil peace, love and equality to Planet Earth, to enlighten humanity about us illegally obtaining what God awarded to the African natives and reveal the truth in regard to the Earth-based Twin Flame angels – that they arrived here to raise the consciousness and love vibration on Earth and in the future will demand reparations on behalf of Africa, but their message must be delayed as long as possible.'

One of his colleagues asks of him, 'How do you know all this, sir?'

Another of the archaeologists appears to interpret this as rudeness and answers on behalf of his leader, 'Goodness, Lucifer has shown visions to our wizards for centuries, talking of which I've seen futuristic visions showing the Blacks ruling the world, aided by their superior futuristic knowledge and their connection with the evolved alien species; their own powerful Black magic, and resourceful lands putting them top of the food chain in regard to the world economy. They were to be the gifted rulers, but Satan continuously shows us how to make it ours, take the wealth for ourselves to rule over them and others.'

Koolah's shared vision changes again to now show the same

group back in London months later, where they've taken the portal to a secret location. The magical bamboo ring is again out of its box hovering vertically, and they're using it to spy on Delica. One of them points to another of those present and says, 'Our own spiritual mediums have stated that we are on a collision course with the souls of awakened ancient Koolah tribe Twin Flame alien souls and when they demand reparations, we'll ultimately have to give back the bulk of what we have literally bled from Africa. If not, we run the risk of humanity turning against us, the establishment. By the year 2050 whilst they're in the process of making the entire African land a single country, the combined-African elected leader is to receive the first major instalments in reparations. The European colonialists will be ordered to compensate and will only be welcomed in Africa if they use their business interests to invest in the welfare of Africa, bringing employment to Africa and handing back a portion of their business.'

One of his colleagues, an American, replies, 'Yeah, that's right but at least we'll have accumulated untold wealth and have built our society.' As he speaks, his scientist colleagues present are making notes while looking through the hoop.

All present at the magical circle hear the voice of Koolah narrating the vision he shares with them:

'These men are members of a Masonic fraternity. Their leader, the Master Mason is the Duke of Sussex. Their scientists study the Delican technology, which they will copy. They will study the alien prototype of what will become Earth's future aircraft, the Stealth F-117 Nighthawk jet. They will copy what will become known as the microwave oven from the aliens. But there is a more sinister motive to their work; they are working on ways to further develop their superiority to oppress Africa, including keeping third world poverty maintained for as long as they can.

'As my futuristic vision has shown you, they will find evidence of us connecting spiritually to the evolved alien life form. The vicious intruders themselves will use our methods to begin spying on other planets of the universe, Delica and others. Under the guidance of Satan, they'll continue to use the findings to further develop Earth's technology for negativity.'

Koolah's vision continues to show the American-European Masonic group watching the Delican aliens though the portal hoop, but the collective psyche of the magical circle can also feel the emotional pain of the child angel Imani still visualising the Belgium King's horrific atrocities in the Congo rainforests, and hear him asking telepathically:

'But why the mass murder of God's humans, Koolah?'

Again Koolah's voice is heard in the minds of all in attendance and Earth's Messiah answers:

'So that the Devil can live out its pleasures and reward those who assist with slavery, colonisation, splitting the motherland and continuing to disconnect us with the harmonious oneness as God; they will receive the wealth and dominance of the Earth; all part of the evil plan. By the 20th century around fifty thousand metric tons of gold will be discovered to have been stolen by the colonialists, most of that from this land, Africa. They'll have used over a hundred million of God's kidnapped Black humans to forcibly build their society – a society to oppress us further, but in the end they will be made to compensate, to give it back and free the psyche of the oppressed. Human shame from the masses of the countries involved will play a major role. The compensation will be judged fairly on the guidelines of their modern-day European and American courts, but the debt is great: five hundred years of unpaid work from over a hundred million people and the suffering inflicted onto their extended generations who will be born into slavery, and also the oppression of Black people that will endure to their present modern day. Africa's to receive compensation for the crimes against our people – the intimidated victims of trauma, rape, fraud, sodomy, paedophilia, murder and forcibly removing our spirituality. They exchanged our spiritual truth for unfounded religious beliefs, instilled for humans to control humanity. Asians and Whites will eventually be shown how they were manipulated by the Devil to feel justified enslaving other humans, souls of God. The masses will put pressure on their governments for reparations, and in fear of a worldwide rebellion they will concede. Huh, evil bastards, they will do everything to hide the truth and, in the process of keeping it hidden, wrongly denounce their father who has created them, God.'

Imani protests further, 'But that is the future, Koolah. God created you to be continuously present in every inch of every dimension of the universe and become conscious anywhere you choose, past and future. You are ever present within the psyche of every soul of the universe, the entirety of God's spiritual energy. You show us sights through the eyes of anyone, human or alien, while they're performing their wrongful deeds. We can change the future.'

Koolah answers vocally, 'Yes, we could, but no, we have to let it play out. The Devil is, after all, God's creation and certain human souls will be tested, exposed by Satan. In the future dimensions when Africa receives its reparations and naturally becomes the world leader, these evil acts will never again be repeated in future dimensions. A lesson to the human race that evil is the work of Satan. Trust me, we did this during our Delican incarnations.'

The angels of the magic circle are shown the darkness before creation and the manifestation of the tangible universe whilst the Messiah narrates:

'On my astral travel, I often share the visual showing God beginning creation. You angels embraced the sights of the intangible oneness energy source, of God manifesting the physical universe and saw when creating everything living that God embedded parts of itself, the one energy source, the intangible spirit of God, within all physical beings, all people, animals and insects, becoming our universal soul to experience physical pleasures of love, loving and everything joyful through us, everything living. The Devil will later influence some races to feel they are different and superior to others because of the colour of their skin, but as a world-famous angel musical prophet Koolah angel in the future will explain in his own written lyrics judging a man by the colour of his skin is the same as judging a man by the colour of his eyes. Satan experiences its pleasures – manipulation, hatred greed, inflicting sorrow, pain, fear and oppression, actions that stem from human weakness, from greed, jealousy, anger and other negative emotions. Many thousands of years from now future generations of our soul tribe will be tricked by the Devil, deceived into inviting the enemy into our home, our city and to share our magic. Satan will manipulate the minds of our soul tribe to allow them to steal our gift with their intention of oppressing the Black race forever. The universe is God, but during creation God planned to allow the Devil to reign on Earth through some dimensions.'

Koolah's shared vision now shows scenes of the 21st century modern-day Iraq and Afghan wars and the faces of the British Prime Minister and the American President who started those wars.

'The world leaders will reject the options that could achieve their aims with minimal casualties to either side. Their armies know exactly where the accused is hiding and with their superior military expertise could arrest the accused without bloodshed. Instead, the US and British governments will continuously lie, the media lying to the human race, saying that he has weapons of mass destruction, and the Western world will feel justified when the American and British leaders send in around a quarter of a million troops to go to war, even at the cost of four thousand five hundred of their own troops being killed and many innocent lives on the other side lost. They could easily make the accused stand trial, but for one, there'd be no charges, and two, it will benefit them financially if they, the culprit perpetrator British and American leaders, allow the fathers and husbands of many, the people they've sworn to protect, to die for their financial gain. Another case of human families losing loved ones, poor men unnecessarily dying in rich men's wars. The viable alternative of peace will be rejected because they can profit majorly from war;

the Devil will play on their greed and Satan will reap its joy from the bloodshed and sorrow of the war.'

The vision focuses specifically on the British prime minister in London, the day after giving the British Army the order to attack Iraq. He's sitting at his family breakfast table with his wife and children watching the live coverage. It is all smiles and laughter; there's no remorse, knowing he gave the order for his own greedy future financial security.

'He's started the war on the pretence that Iraq has hidden weapons of mass destruction. The problem for Tony Blair will be that Saddam Hussein's regime won't have them, and the highly educated scientists and weapon inspectors they will send will return from Iraq without evidence of any such weapons. The problem for one inspector will be that he won't be prepared to go along with the government and media by lying, and his dead body will be found in the English countryside, in woodland a few miles from his home.'

Koolah's vision shows the face of Dr David Kelly to the magic circle.

'So, we've seen, I've shown you the future leaders who will have the option of sending in an elite squadron of US and British special forces to arrest the man they will tell the world has weapons of mass destruction, Saddam Hussein. But instead, innocent children like the British leader's own you saw at that breakfast table will die for his decision fuelled by personal greed. The European countries that rape our lands they will remain corrupt, and the Western-world leaders, including those of Britain and America, will form the secret society illuminati orchestrating wars, wars that their companies will supply material arms to. Specific privately owned companies will supply many wars, but the Iraq War alone will be supplied with material weapons, transportation, men and women soldiers, and vehicles at a cost of three trillion dollars of taxpayers' money, all going to the bank accounts of the government-selected privatised supply companies, nominated before the decision to go to war was even announced.

Questions will be raised of how the British Prime Minister accumulated such wealth, but at first because of his connections with the secret society he will not face trial. In time, the British Prime Minister's integrity will come under serious scrutiny, forcing the public to want to know the answer to a simple question, how his relatively modest salary led him to quickly accumulate an eighty-million-pound fortune. The British Prime Minister and US President will eventually face trial.'

Koolah's visions continue to show the magic circle horrific events in Earth's future history.

'The evil spirit will take pleasure in genocide, human enslavement, wars, racism, and many other vile acts of evil. Some human souls will make a pact with the Devil in exchange for being reincarnated in each life into influential wealthy positions of power. Such people in the media, in government, in high society, wealthy bankers, religious leaders, film makers, music producers, will have control over the minds of humans, but their wealth and power will be at a cost of having traded their souls.'

Koolah now shares a vision of London in the year 2021, modern-day London – images of gangs, Black inner-city youths fighting with knives and shooting one another with guns.

'The Devil will take the minds of these Black children and take its sadistic pleasure in inflicting on them all of those negative emotions, and physical pain, and emotional pain to the families involved – both the spiritually manipulated killer who goes to jail and the murdered child bringing sorrow to both sets of parents and loved ones. It will be a win-win situation for Satan in its bid to inflict sorrow, oppressing the Black race and empowering the world governments. Each Black youth in prison gives society someone else to point the finger at.'

The modern-day images flow as Koolah speaks.

'As one spirit, our soul group will oppose the souls who have made the pact with Satan.'

Koolah's mind now unveils an image of the French astrologer Michel de Nostredame, known to the world as Nostradamus. He is in a dark room accompanied by others, who wear hooded brown cloaks.

'See the powerful illuminati European clairvoyant psychic mediums, Nostradamus among them. Male and female, they are revealing their prophecies and past-life Koolah magic circle visions to their cloaked group. They know members of our magic circle soul tribe will be born in later lives such as Nostradamus and the other Europeans you see in the vision. Satan will reveal our identities and keep our tribe apart in certain dimensions. Magic circle souls will be tricked into empowering satanic secret societies with our knowledge, and by revealing future dimensions will keep them technologically advanced and able to invent powerful sophisticated weaponry to enslave and oppress. The Devil will create what will be known as the illuminati and grant them our magical powers and vision by manipulating our minds.'

The magic circle are now shown visions of the bitter conflict of World War II.

'Nostradamus and others will reveal the optional negative dimensions available, world wars and so forth. Our visions will reveal that dividing and enslaving the Black race will grant them power over us and all humanity.'

Koolah's visions switch back and forth throughout future human history showing the magic circle the dawning of civilisation in European and Asian societies.

'Owing to our knowledge, they'll no longer live as savages but in stone homes and become civilised like us.'

Koolah sighs.

'Our own magic will give them the ability to rule and conquer us, inflicting on us the future colonisation and enslavement of Africa. The evil they'll carry out is part of the deal they've made with Satan. The Devil will orchestrate and thrive on what the evil Asians and Europeans will force on the Black people – making us believe God's original African spirituality is dark, satanic and blasphemous, and that their control-based religion's our saviour. Satan will thrive on the wars that religion will cause, and religious leaders will secretly allow the Devil to conduct its vile behaviour within their establishments. They will wipe God's spirituality from the psyche of Africa, claim our land, and our indigenous nation will be physically valued as livestock cargo on board the slave ships around the world – weakening the Black race by degrading men, by raping our women, trading our new-born babies, and for generations, leaving our men feeling inadequate, spiritually broken.'

Imani protests, 'Surely with our intelligence and divine spirituality we can do something to stop them. For five generations the astral-travel future visions you've shared with us have even taught us to speak all future European, Arabic and Greek languages, languages that aren't spoken by the people of the lands yet. Your visions showed eight thousand years from today the Greek philosophers would be highly regarded. But Aristotle will have spent twenty-five years in our African lands learning from our African philosophers. We will educate him and the European nations with the knowledge we know today. We are and always will be the educational capital of the ancient world. They will only become the Ancient Greek civilisation after they put Aristotle's name on as many African written books and manuscripts as they can lay their hands on. Aristotle will take the glory from the African written mysteries. The Greeks and other European nations haven't invented or begun speaking their languages yet or forming their secret societies. Our spiritual minds are at present superior to scientists of the future modern Western society and European civilisation. We know more about civilised planets than they'll ever discover…'

Koolah places a palm onto the shoulder of the child. 'Satan will need to white out our great history in order for others to appear superior and keep the Black race as wandering lost sheep to be led and controlled by their religions. Let them carry out their vile wicked acts, but always remember, Imani, as it was in the beginning so shall it be in the end.'

Koolah's vision places an image of the iconic Jamaican reggae star Bob Marley in the minds of all in the magic circle.

'The universe will present many spiritual prophets and the magic circle angel I show now will be born to convey our message of peace. Reincarnated, born of mixed Black and White nations as a sign we are one people, one blood, one God. The oppressors' glory will be short lived; the world will one day know of God's spirituality and the fact they stole their great knowledge from us. Some groups will assist Satan oppressing Earth's subconscious reality, keeping humans in a prison of a one-dimensional consciousness. In Earth's future dimensions our soul tribe will reincarnate occupying bodies of all nationalities.'

Koolah's shared visions show images of John Lennon, Martin Luther King and others to the collective psyche of the magic circle.

'Reincarnate, born musicians, DJs, politicians, sports personalities, freedom fighters – human and also alien beings on other planets opposing Satan. The spell I cast in the days of Abiona will include a reawakening thousands of years from now, beginning amid a bloody and sorrowful world war, their year 1940. The year 1994 will also be of great importance, the start of our spiritual exodus.

'Imani, do you remember the vision I once shared where we visualised the USA, their calendar year 2021?'

The angel child nods his head with certainty. 'Of course, yes Koolah, and a virus will cause a state of confusion, spiritually disrupting a racist Western government. Amid the pandemic their police will kill a Black man called George Floyd, but his death will spark worldwide protests that will split the world population, uniting non-racists, opposing racism.'

Imani pauses in thought while thinking back to the future vision Koolah shared, before continuing:

'White people reincarnated from Africa who have lived previous lives of slavery and oppression or White people that have empathy will understand, and White people that have not and don't have empathy won't understand a phrase "Black Lives Matter." The event will awaken enslaved African souls now conscious in White bodies and bodies of other nations…'

Koolah smiles. 'You always observe the visions and listen well, Imani. Now, young wise one, we need you to become conscious in a future dimension and reconnect our Queen Lulu to our Koolah tribe vibration.'

The ten-year-old smiles, nods, closes his eyes and begins breathing deeply and slowly to balance the psyche. The magic circle still surrounds him, all its members in a trance, feet facing inward towards Koolah, Imani and the others. After a short while, the child angel becomes conscious in a future life —a female incarnation, Claudette Fontaine.

CHAPTER 4

Pétion-Ville, Port-au-Prince, Haiti, 1993

Claudette Fontaine is a wealthy landowner. In her grand Haitian suburban mansion home, she kneels at her Voodoo shrine and falls into a deep trance. As she opens her eyes the Koolah circle angels see through her eyes, the eyes of one of Imani's future incarnations, this Voodoo high priestess, the Haitian witch, Claudette.

She lives a reclusive life in Haiti despite being one of the wealthiest citizens throughout the entire Caribbean and a beautiful woman. She is in her mid-forties, a dainty, brown-eyed, mixed-race, quarter-Black, brunette who wears her long hair up in an almost 18th century style with a lock of long hair twirling to the side of her exquisite feminine neck. Her body is as beautiful and sexy as her face and over all she closely resembles the British soap star actress Jan Anderson.

Among the elite ascended masters of the spiritual universe, she's known as an important ancient Koolah tribe angel, close to the Messiah in each incarnation, dating back to the days of the Koolah city, and respected for her remarkable powers.

Now, she rises and goes to look out the master bedroom window of her Haiti mansion, out over the vast estate, its land stretching further than the eye can see. As ever, she's accompanied by her handsome black cat Jojo, who if he is not by her side will be found on her lap or, at the very least, nearby. Jojo's a healthy, strong-looking cat with a glossy black coat, who wears a brown, platted leather collar with a hollow gold jingling bell attached. As Claudette walks across the short cantilever balcony, Jojo jumps up onto the wall brushing his body against her. She leans her elbows on the small wall and smiles, looking out over the grounds and down towards the modern vehicles on the spacious circular forecourt and the staff washing the cars, tending the lawns and otherwise looking after the general maintenance of the estate. As she and Jojo hold their gaze, the ancient Koolah circle see through her eyes the same view she sees, but slowly the scene changes. The view is from the same window but now the lawn isn't as well attended, the four huge oak trees by the lake, against which the sun is setting, are only half their former height and their branches overhanging the out-house buildings appear shorter. Claudette and Jojo hear the sound of a stagecoach and see a large number of horseback Black Haitian revolutionary soldiers surround it as it approaches. The road is no longer concrete and the horses' hooves and carriage wheels sound as they near, trampling the dirt road. As the carriage reaches the cobbled pavement round the circular forecourt, the hooves make their loud clopping sound before the carriage is bought to a stop at the grand four-pillared entrance. Amid what seems like the tightest security, with riflemen taking positions all around protecting them, three men and a woman exit the stagecoach: a ruggedly handsome White man in his fifties with matted dreadlocks and scar through his eyelid, and who walks with a slight hobbling limp; a younger handsome Black man dressed extravagantly; a Black woman dressed in the finest 18th century ladies' garments; and an equally well-dressed young White man with a pretty face and thick curly dark hair. They're accompanied by a lively white, black-eye-patched English Bulldog, who jumps down from the stagecoach and stretches his body.

Claudette calls out to the dog by its name, 'Patch!' She knows she's now conscious within a different dimension, a life two centuries earlier at the height of the Haitian revolution, the slave uprising against the French slaving nation and ultimately Napoleon Bonaparte.

Patch quickly looks up, and responds to Claudette's call by running on ahead of his human companions and entering the foyer.

The arrival of the men, woman and dog cause Claudette to be

filled with an intense sensation, to be caught in the atmosphere during that dimension, to feel the sense of liberation, freedom from imprisonment, slavery and oppression in the air. She looks on with nothing but admiration for the Black soldiers despite the mixture of different raggedy uniforms they wear.

The young White gentleman, Jarrod, looks up to the balcony. He sees not the lighter skinned brunette Claudette but another equally beautiful and voluptuous woman, physically how the soul of Imani appeared during the height of the 18th century Haitian slave uprising. Jarrod and the lady share a smile, and the young Black woman also looks up to the balcony. Speaking in her French accent, she calls out to the woman, 'Hello Lana.' Noticing the cat, she adds, 'Ah 'ello Jojo, how are you?'

The older White man displays his trademark twitch as Jarrod comments, 'No matter where your sister Lana goes, the cat Jojo is always close by.'

The young Black woman replies, 'The cat is the reincarnated soul of the ancient black panther Jojo. Jojo reincarnates as a domestic cat in later dimensions. Always remember when you encounter Jojo, the spirit of the Messiah is always close by…'

Jarrod nods respectfully.

Then the 18th century vibration, Jarrod and his companions, the revolutionary soldiers, the stagecoach and horses fade and disappear. Claudette is conscious again in her modern-day world; she again sees the modern-day cars and staff working around the grand estate.

The Koolah magic circle has been tuned in to two of Imani's future female incarnations, his 18th century life living as Voodoo witch Lana, during the Haitian slave uprising, and modern-day Voodoo high priestess witch Claudette in the dimension of 1993. The magic circle angels still watch as Claudette re-enters her master bedroom suite and then walks downstairs into a vast high-ceilinged reception room. Visitors have told Claudette how the room always gives them a spiritual sensation, a vibration taking them back into the 18th century during the Haitian revolution. A Black man dressed in the trends of the day sits eerily alone in the spacious reception room, seated at a huge antique desk typing on a desktop computer. Behind the desk, in between two floor-to-ceiling windows is a huge, magnificent antique rectangular mirror showing the reflection of the entire room. Claudette pauses, closes her eyes, and stands still, reminiscing over the memories the room holds, feeling the warm upbeat vibration, the sense of liberation, the echoed voices of the slave uprising generals and their leader Toussaint Louverture deep in discussion. Aside from the computer, every object and every item of furniture in the room is as it would have been two centuries earlier when the estate was occupied and used as the rebel base – fountain pens, bamboo sticks, enemy maps: all perfectly preserved. The tinkling of Jojo's bell as he moves across the room to her brings Claudette's mind back to the present, and they share a smile as Jojo brushes himself purringly against her. She doesn't acknowledge the male typist, and he doesn't acknowledge her, instead concentrating on his work. Beside him are huge piles of ancient papers that have been taken from an ancient book that was bound in suede-like animal hide and tied with lace. Among the pages of text there are artistically drawn sketches. One drawing in particular depicts a man's features combined with the body and feet of a big cat. The face is that of the original human, of a Black man with large lips, full nose and long hair in dreadlocks. The writing on the papers is in ancient Koolah and it's the typist's job to convert it into modern French and English.

Claudette and Jojo make their way to her impressive Voodoo shrine in the corner of the room. The main feature of the shrine is a pair of reindeer horns, accompanied by olden-day hung scrolled parchment paper, lit candles, Voodoo dolls, tarot cards, a crystal ball and many other collected objects. Its mass of candles provide a significant glow, creating a warm and welcoming feel. Claudette takes one of the two beautifully designed male French officer's blazers that hang by the shrine and puts it on. It's a few sizes too big for her dainty body. She kneels and begins chanting in a mixture of ancient African and broken French Creole. As Claudette and Jojo settle down in a comfortable spot among the objects of the shrine, the typist has a brief look over but otherwise takes no notice. Claudette and the cat are seated with their eyes closed.

For the members of the ancient magic circle the 18th and 20th century visions fade, and their minds are filled with only darkness and silence until as though in the distance they hear the sound of a baby crying, which grows increasingly louder.

The Nevins's Essex Mansion
Spring 1962

In the master bedroom the beautiful one-year-old baby Nicole cries in her cot as her mother Cindy Nevin tries putting a bottle of milk to her mouth. As the baby quiets, Cindy turns her attention to giving instructions to her babysitter and getting dressed ready to go out. She puts on over her sexy underwear, a short-sleeved thin blouse, a cardigan, and fitted chess-board-patterned trousers, before slipping on her stiletto sandals to complete the outfit. She gives her baby Nicole a kiss and is ready to leave.

As she walks out the house, she's surprised to see a black cat sitting on the bonnet of her plush Mercedes sports car. She shoos the animal away and the golden bell on his collar tinkles as he jumps down from the car, but rather than scurry off the cat stands by the car moving his tail side to side, staring and loudly meowing. Cindy feels a quiver of emotion at this, perhaps very slightly intimidated by the cat's behaviour, before the cat's apparent owner, a beautiful woman who's stood nearby, calls to him.

'Jojo, come now,' Claudette Fontaine calls out in her French accent. 'Jojo come on.'

Although she'd not yet tapped into her clairvoyant gift, knowing they're her soulmates, Cindy feels strangely drawn to them, but equally is puzzled by the presence of this foreign lady and her cat so near to her home. 'Hello, have you just moved into the neighbourhood?' she asks.

'No, not exactly, just on my travels, and, by the way, enjoy today; you're going to have so much fun. Prepare yourself to physically meet your Twin Flame...' Claudette does a kissing-mouth-smiling-face expression and walks away followed by Jojo.

Although Cindy feels this altogether strange and doesn't have a clue what the woman's speaking of, she feels from somewhere she has an odd sense of familiarity with this beautiful lady and her cat.

Darkness again enters the collective psyche of the Koolah soul tribe angels, before they suddenly begin to hear all the sounds of a busy early 1960s London street. Crowds can be heard, and modern-day traffic before suddenly the images begin to appear to them.

Oxford Street, London, England

The bustling crowds that fill Oxford Street are oblivious to the presence of Claudette and her cat Jojo, but the members of the ancient magic circle see the busy street through her eyes. As she and Jojo walk, Claudette starts to linger behind, her attention drawn to a strikingly handsome Black man across the street, who resembles the boxer Cassius Clay but with darker skin and with hazel-blue eyes.

Cindy Nevin too is on Oxford Street and is startled to suddenly see the same cat she saw on the bonnet of her car that morning. A chill runs down her spine. She knows the cat is the same one because of, not just the unusual brown, platted leather collar with a gold bell it wears, but a vibration she feels. The cat stops and stares at Cindy and Cindy looks up, drawn to the smiling face of Claudette who is walking towards her. Claudette stops her in her path, lightly placing her hands on Cindy's shoulders. When they are face-to-face Cindy splutters, 'That cat and the bell ringing..., and you...?'

'Yes my Queen, I put the bell around the neck of my companion Jojo as a reminder. The evil bastard slavers locked metal collars with large pronged bells attached to the necks of men and women to stop us trying to gain our freedom by running away. Every time I hear Jojo's bell ringing, it's a reminder that our soul tribe still have important work to do.'

CHAPTER 5

Koolah Palace, Ancient Africa

What was once a village community is now a thriving city with Koolah Palace, situated halfway down a hilly tropical palm-tree-filled mountain, a jewel in its crown. The original beach huts and wooden homes of four generations earlier are no longer, but the development of the city has not spoilt the beauty of its natural surroundings. The palace is set among many low pastel-tan-and-beige-colour, rocky, stepped, cascading waterfalls, one of which is where behind its falling water Abiona's mother conceived the Messiah, accommodating the alien soul back to Earth. Its water runs out to a stream flowing through two hundred metres of lush vegetation, secluded by overhanging tree branches from either side that meet creating a lush vegetation tunnel cool spot with sporadic, scattered, isolated sun rays beaming through, that might be called paradise on Earth.

King Imarmu wakes and walks naked from his bed to gaze out the window. From the bed his Queen, Lulu, looks on admiringly at the physically strong body that has served him well for his forty-five years, at his huge chest and muscular backside. She, as naked as he, is equally fine-looking with her elegant Black voluptuous womanly body, her seductive eyes, cute feminine nose, high Afro, and her ruby-red full kissing lips that compliment her other features perfectly. He is wise and cultured, and she his inspirational eternal Twin Flame, highly sexed lover and vital clairvoyant soul. Her clairvoyant spirituality and inner strength are naturally crucial to their kingdom in the same way that the insect beehive has its divine selected queen bee for its vital spiritual and functional purpose. From his window, Imarmu looks out on the magnificent buildings and clay-tiled-roof homes that make up their glorious city, Earth's first civilised society – thriving amongst the lush, vibrant tropical jungle.

On the beach, still in a trance, the magic circle is tuned into Koolah's astral-travel sightings. Koolah moves through the universe putting different time period dimensions into the minds of the angels. For a short while they see a powerful bright light flickering and then their collective psyche is shown the future in the shape of a prosperous Africa as Koolah's telepathically narrates them through what they are seeing:

'By the Earth year 2222 the soul of every looted, kidnapped, enslaved indigenous African will be reincarnated back to enjoy a prosperous Africa. Here you see the African continent in 2140.'

The angels of the magic circle are shown a vision of future Planet Earth seen as though from a satellite. They see the outline shape of the African continent before the vision takes them in to see the new developments that are being built or have been built: state-of-the-art hotels, government buildings and royal palaces; enormous skyscrapers; huge airports with African airlines; and even spacecraft. Everywhere there is evidence of a booming economy and thriving export trade – Africa, the world's fastest growing economy.

Then, the vision of the now liberated Earth focuses in on one particular building, the Wax Museum, in the Land of Koolah, Capital City of Africa in 2140. Koolah takes the collective psyche of the angels of the magic circle inside the museum for a guided tour.

The tour begins in a section that displays characters from the Earth where Satan had reigned in the future dimensions. The angels are shown hundreds of Earth's leaders, Adolf Hitler, King Leopold of Belgium and Donald Trump among them. All the wax images have written documentation detailing the parts they played throughout the history of the Satan-led one-dimension spiritual confinement.

Then the images they are seeing suddenly change. They see the inside of a modern department store with Chinese women clamouring to buy handbags and other accessories. Some buying as many as a dozen handbags, some spending up to a quarter of a million pounds. Koolah narrates telepathically:

'This is the Gucci Store Selfridges in Oxford Street, London, England in one-dimension Earth in the year 2022.'

Suddenly the vision changes completely again and the angels of the magic circle are shown Black women watching their children starve to death in Africa while the Chinese mining companies are taking out all the gold, taking the wealth back to their own lands.

'This is what they'd always wanted for us; the Chinese are just another nation who will take from our lands. By right, before anyone else should be, Black African women should be enjoying reaping the benefits of the wealth nature bestowed on the indigenous people.

'The evil spirit will mask the reality that Earth and the universe is multi-dimensional, hiding the fact there are countless parallel dimensions where Africa flourishes abundantly. Humans will be tricked into believing the relatively dismal existence humanity will call life in the Devil's one-dimensional conscious Earth is all there is. Humans of all nations in that satanic dimension will not know that in other dimensions there wasn't a colonisation of the native Indians nor Africa, and neither slavery nor the takeover of any indigenous peoples; instead, humanity flourishes as nature planned. Satan will control only the conscious Earth dimension putting in place its world governments, religions and so forth to control the psyche of the human race. Humans will be made to feel it's part of life to have greed-fuelled bloody wars, racism, the enslavement and oppression of an entire race, mass genocide and so forth.'

The vision the angels see switches back to the museum and they are taken through a section of it rightly and gloriously displaying once-hidden, unsung, powerful, clever Black heroes. At one of the displays, which shows a gallant Black man, Koolah reads aloud what is written about him:

'Born in AD 145 in the prominent Roman Libyan city of Leptis Magna in Africa, Severus came from a wealthy and prominent local family. In AD 162, Severus travelled to Rome and was granted entry into the senatorial ranks, after his cousin Gaius Septimius Severus had recommended him to Emperor Marcus Aurelius. In AD 193, Lucius Septimius Severus was named ruler of the Roman Empire and in doing so became Rome's first Black African Emperor. After emerging victorious from a period of civil war, Severus expanded the border of the empire to new heights, ushered in a period of imperial transformation and founded a dynasty.'

Koolah moves further along through the future African museum, looking at other Black men and women throughout history: those who opposed the Devil's manipulated Earth dimension; those who campaigned for peace and equality; those who displayed acts of heroism.

There is the beautiful Black woman known as Queen Nanny, Granny or Nanny of the Maroons, the leader of the community of former slaves on the island of Jamaica. She led pitch battles against the British army, who finally gave in to her demands. Having failed to defeat her on the battlefield the British sued for peace signing a treaty with her. Moving through the wax museum, next in line is the 18th century Haitian Voodoo witch Lana Cartier, then Toussaint Loverture, Martin Luther King Jr., Malcolm X, Nelson Mandela... also there are White heroes and campaigners for peace, pirate captain Jim Morgan, John Lennon and others. The vision zooms in on another character and Koolah reads his description:

'Chenu Bechola Barca, also called Hannibal translated "he who has the favour of Baal (God)" born in 247 BC. As a child, he accompanied his father Hamilcar to battles, by the time he was twenty-five, he took up his family's legacy after his brother-in-law died, Hasdrubal the Fair...'

The vision continues through this section, which also shows Shaka Zulu, founder of Southern Africa's Zulu Empire, along with other indigenous heroes trying to defend and keep their homeland. The vision then turns a corner to arrive at a section of the future museum with Black and White alien Twin Flame heroes on Planet Delica: Blee and others who campaigned for peace and equality on a planet where the Devil reversed the arrangement, where the Whites were the ones enslaved and oppressed. Then, again, the vision moves onwards, into another section of the museum that has the models of the ancient Twin Flame tribe angels of Koolah: Koolah himself, Imani, the King and Queen of Koolah and others. Koolah's voice in the heads of the magic circle angels explains:

'Part of our ancient spell cast will ensure that in the year 2140 the soul of Queen Lulu will again be born indigenous female crowned Queen of Africa by us, the true angels of the Earth. After living the life of Cindy Nevin, Queen Lulu will reincarnate Black African, married as always, eternally to the soul of her Twin Flame King Imarmu. She'll disband all the countries, banish corrupt politicians, Chinese and other exploiting nations and abolish borders. A single central bank will be created. Finally the Devil will not be able to corrupt the weak minds of greedy leaders; we'll only appoint and empower those who will put the land and people's welfare first. No more corruption in politics. Asia and the West will also be embarrassed into financially compensating for their ill-treatment of our people, raping Mother Africa for almost two thousand years. They claim to be the civilised race but will allow children and babies to starve to death when nature provides enough to feed the entire world. Wealthy Black individuals and powerful business people of other nations will come together and one day the entire land will become a non-exploited united Africa, the leading world economy. Our spirituality will command our parliament to be built around the spiritual magic circle and the ruins of the ancient City of Koolah.'

Koolah's vision shows this future development, and although there are modern structures, trains running round the coast of Africa and wide motorways, much of the lush vegetation jungle, as the government has ordered it must, remains intact.

'Our Koolah City will be the trusted capital city of Africa, the most prosperous on Earth.'

Koolah smiles proudly, then turns to address Imani.

'What is meant for you in this universe shall not pass you by.

You see, we too have a plan, Imani. Negative forces will delay our success, but they'll only delay the inevitable. As it was designed in the beginning, so shall it manifest in the end.'

Some within the circle sit designing and drawing futuristic year 2100 steel buildings as Koolah narrates the vision. Due to Koolah's ability to astral travel and share his visions with them, their technical ability is second to none. The constant stream of clear and precise future revelations has also taught the ancient spiritually evolved tribe how to both write and speak English, as well as other European languages, Arabic and Greek. The Koolah tribe were fluent in Earth's modern-day languages thousands of years before they were developed. They could speak Greek thousands of years before the Ancient Greeks underwent the process of becoming civilised, practising their twelve-god Greek mythology. The Koolah tribe's knowledge was not limited to Earth either; it included in-depth outer space and future space-age technology as Koolah's astral travel connected them with evolved alien activity, conversing with aliens including the Delicans.

Planet Delica

Whilst Delicans might, apart from their eyes, resemble humans and share similar ethnic diversity, there being Black Delicans and White Delicans and so on, their rapid spiritual evolution caused their planet to develop in many ways. They'd won the authentic holy war, a non-physical but spiritual conflict defeating Satan. The victory prize was regaining their subconscious reality, uplifting the burden the Devil imposed. Nature was now allowed to flow, and this included accepting the love- vibrational musical sounds from space and carrying them back to their planet. Thus, they could hear subtle bursts, light beats of the ancient bongo drum and echoed heavenly female vocals – music from ancient Africa, instruments played in the early days of the coastal tribe when surrounded by burning torches the young, slim female psychic medium sat in the dip of the magic circle in meditation posture facing the full moon.

As if in answer to this call, the Delicans planned a space mission that would have as its goal freeing the minds of those on another planet. Seventy Twin Flame couples were selected from all the different countries of their planet to take part. Theirs was to be a sacrifice for which other Delicans would cheer and congratulate them on, as the mission required in their present body form none of them would ever return home or set foot on any other planet. Instead, they're to travel a distance that would take many lifetimes and are to die of old age on board the spacecraft, allowing their future generations to complete the journey. The journey would last the equivalent on Earth of four lifetime generations. The Delicans on board who'd exit the spacecraft and converse with far-away Earth aliens were not yet born. When born, they'd be taught by the previous generation the purpose of their journey. The plan was for the eighth generation on board the craft to eventually arrive back on Delica.

On the night the mission was to leave, millions of Delicans gathered under the light of their full moons to pay tribute to the travellers. The sending off party was an international celebration enjoyed and televised throughout the entire planet. Amid the joyful atmosphere, when the spacecraft was about to leave none were aware of the intangible spirit, the invisible astral bodies of Koolah and his faithful companion Jojo. Having been called on for spiritual assistance, the spirit of the ancient African Messiah Koolah and his black panther companion had arrived in spirit form by way of astral travel from the magic circle.

As it left Delica, the space-based solar power craft would soon be turned to invisible silent mode, rapidly moving in total silence, with just the sounds of it cutting through the air.

Ancient City of Koolah

Surrounded by deeply spiritual members of the tribe at the magical circle, Koolah sits in the lotus meditation posture in a trance, with, as always, his companion black panther Jojo by his side – the animal also in the same state of trance. Around him, at this divinely blessed location, millions of intangible colourful raindrop-shaped, returning souls rapidly appear and disappear, setting off to begin life again; whilst the bright, glowing, off-white, pink mist covers the rock floor of the magic circle. The huge swarm of bees usually rested on the child Imani are attached to the bottom of a rock as it meets the rock ground.

Once again, Koolah shares his astral-travelling visions by way of telepathy with the tribes' clairvoyant souls who are gathered sitting in a circle of one hundred around him. Koolah shares visions of the alien planet Delica with them as he explains telepathically:

'Time does not exist; instead, the universe consists of dimension phases, thus creating the illusion of time. Freeing and exploring the subconscious mind allows spiritual knowledge to flow. Souls reincarnate to next lives, but in reality all lives past, present and future are all in the paralleled moment. A subconscious dream, no matter how bizarre, is just you, the soul, existing in another body, one of the infinite number of paralleled lives you're also living. Through the visions I have shown you, you are well aware of the vastness of the universe multiplied an infinite number of times.

Through my teachings, you will learn how to use the full capacity of the universe. The human soul and the alien soul are part of the spirit of God experiencing physical lives within each of us. Humans on Earth and alien beings are God existing as part of a beautifully complicated multi-dimensional universe. The conscious universe is vast, but in fact God created an infinitely boundless subconscious universe. You can become conscious in any of the so-called subconscious dimensions your soul is living in, any dimension in history – past, present or future. I say "so-called subconscious" because your subconscious dreams are in fact some of your other conscious realities. When your mind's at rest sleeping, your third eye naturally sees and feels you actually cross over, becoming conscious in another life dimension that you, the soul, are actually living. In the future, the majority of humans will just label this phenomenon as having unexplainable dreams. If you wake from a dream of being fearfully attacked or running from a frightening situation, there is a reason why you awake relieved, your heart beating furiously. Or if you awake from a wet dream, for instance, a dream you're disappointed you woke from, you felt the emotion and pleasures of intercourse that you were actually experiencing in the moment of now. We have knowledge of nature's reincarnation and subconscious that will be taken from us when our lands are invaded and our people are forced into Muslim, Catholic and Christian religious beliefs.'

The images the clairvoyant angels of the magic circle begin to receive are of the joyful crowd on Delica as their mission is about to set off. At first Koolah's vision shows the backs of the heads of the futuristic Delican crowd, families looking up at the stage. Suddenly Koolah's view turns to face the crowd and some newcomers to the magic circle gasp as they're shown the unexpected, extraordinary but beautiful, large eyes of the alien faces. Others gasp and begin smiling excitedly as Koolah's view rises to show the many futuristic buildings and also many built the shape of the Egyptian pyramids. All the while, although there are no physical instruments being played and neither is there any type of hi-fi equipment, just a sound energy passing through, they hear music: four sweet bursts of an ancient trumpet repeatedly sound after long pauses; a lone bongo drum then flute joined by maracas and the chime of another instrument follow the trumpet sound. The instruments can be heard sounding separately as though it were running through an electronic musical recording studio echo chamber. It's an unearthly sweet repetitive musical beat that carries the purest vibration. The Koolah clairvoyants smile and joyfully sigh as they see in their minds Koolah's telepathic images of the Delican crowd dancing around the huge alien craft that has just completed its invisible test modes. It's the size of two football pitches, the rear of the craft up to ten storeys high. Koolah joins the passengers boarding the gigantic spaceship to be greeted by more distinct, subtle, soothing, echoed, sweet sounds from the universe, man's earliest music. The greater the celebration, the sweeter and more whole the energetic music becomes, till it finally encompasses all the sounds of the complete orchestra and vocals. The telepathic mind of the planet could be described as having its own DJ. Delicans don't just listen to and enjoy music; their souls actually get into it, entering the vibrational sound wave within the air.

Eyes closed and in a trance Koolah smiles, knowing he's showed the alien planet Delica how to receive nature's love sound and vibration of the free multi-dimensional universe whilst leading the alien Delican spiritual holy war conflict. The joyful vibration of the planet Delica's occasion, the echoed music, is linked to indigenous tribes throughout the universe, combined to produce what can only be described as an authentic chilled house music set. Koolah continuously smiles as he sees on board the craft some of the adults practising the multiverse's ancient Delican/African magic. They're asking their early spiritual ancestors and ancient Messiah for protection and a safe and successful voyage. The Delicans sit huddled in groups on the craft, and one young petite mixed-race blonde female who is in a trance can in particular feel the unique and intense love vibration of Koolah's presence. She reaches out telepathically to him:

'Spirit of Koolah, we are your evolved tribal City of Koolah angels. We're familiar with your astral- travelling spirit now present on board this craft, watching over us from Earth's magic circle, heaven. We know you're often present on our planet with us. Spiritual warrior Prince, you've achieved much greatness, helping Delica find world peace, but please carry on the fight in preventing Satan suppressing our subconscious reality ever again. Assist us in helping humans locate the love we've found. Please accompany us on our voyage back to Earth, estimated time of arrival late 20th century, the year 1940. On arrival, assist us helping Earth in reaching the promised love vibration we have here on Delica.'

Koolah and the angels of the magic circle pick up on her vibration, and they are gradually able to see through her eyes as well as hear her. She looks around and her Earth-based ancient Koolah soul tribal angels see what she sees: a mixture of nationalities, huge Delican eyes peering back. As she looks among the huddled party on board, Koolah obliges by revealing his most recent Delican image, a young fit and healthy smiling Benser, gradually changing to the faint ancient African intangible physical image of Koolah, showing them all his spirit is present. Earth's magic circle angels smile as Koolah takes over, showing the image of the alien party; Earth's magic circle angels are now looking through the eyes of the astral-travelling Koolah. The young mixed-race girl points her finger at him, becoming tearful and excited, but he smiles reassuringly. Her heart begins to pound, excitedly. Tearfully she gasps, 'My god, the soul of my sixth great grandfather Benser is here among us. The soul of the now Earth alien Koolah is present, he showed us how he appears reincarnated on ancient Earth…'

CHAPTER 6

Delicans possess the ability to communicate telepathically from an early age, and on board their spacecraft children play virtual reality games telepathically connected to their psyche, with no controller or computer being used, instead using the power of the mind to bring through the virtual reality images. The children will live out their lives on board the spacecraft; their grandchildren who will be born on the last leg of the journey will be the ones who will arrive on Earth assisting Earth-based Twin Flames to show the primitive aliens there how to instil world peace into the human race. Their grandchildren will be the ones to fulfil the voyage's mission of exposing the satanic enemy among the Earthly alien beings, freeing their subconscious psyche, fighting the true spiritual holy war and defeating Satan.

In the ancient City of Koolah on Planet Earth, some of the magic circle angels, having awoken from their trance and regained consciousness, are writing of the visions they have seen of sights on board the alien craft. Others still hear the voice of Koolah explaining his astral-travel visions:

'What you see is part of our soul tribe reincarnated to a future dimension on Delica. Some of us evolved Koolah souls are leaving the alien planet to come to Earth and will arrive here at a point in the 20th century. Our music is on Delica. No matter how deep the future dimension phase we reincarnate to, we always pick up our ancient sound wave and vibration; our energy will always be our guide.'

On board the huge craft, some of the children have their eyes closed and are communicating telepathically so that some within the Earth-based magic circle can be conscious in the future and be shown what their future Delican minds see. This will later be masked by the invaders of Africa; in fact, all nations of modern-day Earth will later have the angels of Koolah's discoveries to thank for their proud and relatively primitive civilised histories.

When not practising his soul's spiritual gifted magic, there is nothing the Messiah Koolah likes better than to use his mind drawing and designing grand stone buildings or occasionally working with his hands on his carpentry, skilfully using tools.

At sunrise in ancient Africa, ten thousand years ago the people of the entire continent's way of prayer began with a joining with others around the universe chanting the vibrational Aum or Om to begin full moon soul-healing meditation. As God prayed, the City of Koolah's dark moonlit ocean and night sky begin their magical sunrise transformation. The striking mixture of carbon-black trees, buildings and mountains silhouetted against dark and light shades of blue sky with a gleaming white full moon, bright glistening stars and calm dark ocean is all swiftly transformed. Suddenly a sparkling glint, the pastel golden yellow tip of the sun, alters the night scenery. The tiny but potent brightly glowing golden dot appears on the horizon directly under the moon. It radiates a powerful energy, glowing in the blackness, gradually expanding, changing all moonlit white to its vibrant golden yellow. The rapidly expanding circular glowing ball suddenly appears in the sky as large now as the faded moon. Sunlight beams across the deep blue sea, taking away the chill of the night, steadily rising, bringing daylight to the colourful rich and lush tropical beach. Its light unveils along the coast a rich variety of magnificent golden stone buildings until then hidden by the night. A tribal elder reads from the pages of a large textbook six-inches thick. He smiles as he closes it. The morning meditation is complete and greeted by a customary silence.

After a few moments, a lone baby is heard crying among the massive crowd, followed by the distant morning roar of a lion, then squawking birds and the sounds of a waking alpha-male gorilla. The second section of prayer is about to begin, God's joyful partying. A band of around three hundred musicians joyfully congregate outside the circle. With eyes closed, Koolah stands above the mist facing them, his body gently swaying side to side, head nodding, his fingers making piano-playing movement. The sound of his voice is in the head of each band member and vocalist, acting as the musical orchestra's conductor. He nods towards the tribal elder Akachi within the magic circle. Akachi begins shaking the maracas attached to his six-foot long walking stick and chanting. His chanting spreads quickly outside the circle as many others join in tune. With a brisk waving of his hand Koolah orders them to stop and then raises his palms upward, signalling a group of female vocalists to take over the vocal. Beginning with a drummer to provide a beat, he then in turn turns to face sections of vocalists and musicians – bass drummers, guitar, bongos and so on – signalling to them to contribute with their vocal or instrument creating a sweet music. The ceremonial full moon party begins. Everywhere there are vibrant smiles, and around the city and along the coastline women sing with pure divine energy and angelic melody, their voices blending with the sweet-sounding rhythm of the orchestra. Expert instrumentalists play their trombones, bone flutes, bongos, mankind's earliest guitars, mouth organs, and a host of other instruments. Strong men pound in tune four-foot diameter bass drums, creating that heavy but sweet bassline "BOOM BOOM" sound. Others shake maracas or simply dance. Thousands dance under the surrounding, still-burning firelight torches, adults and children. Large sections of the crowd's natural reaction to the musical vibration is to raise their hands in the air whilst dancing, joyfully cheering in appreciation of the way the music makes them feel. The entire beach and jungle becoming one vibrant festival.

For miles along the coast many bands and orchestras make their music as adjoining villages join in the full moon celebration – the entire coastal tribal city and neighbouring tribes enjoying the ceremonial party. Handsome, athletically built men dance, jacking their bodies to the drumbeat. Pretty, shapely, seductive, laughing and smiling women naturally and provocatively twerk, shaking their bottoms and gyrating their hips to that thumping bassline. Then there is silence just for a moment and a lone tribal drummer hits that sweet hypnotic break beat rhythm. In appreciation, a man places fingers inside his lips and blows a few prolonged, loud, high-pitched mouth whistles.

Our inner souls remembered and repeated all of this ten thousand years later during the 1987 early underground British and American acid-house parties. The smoke machine and strobe light were important, reproducing the Koolah City off-white mist and flickering visual as Koolah crossed dimensions, transferring his visions. There was a cultural sophistication to those indigenous events in ancient Africa, never yet revealed in a modern-day Hollywood movie. The music they played was that of modern-day house music, ranging from acid house through to the bona-fide deep tech, Afro-tribal, and all other house music including the drum and bass beat. The vibration and hypnotic beat the coastal tribe created was the exact beat enjoyed by millions of reincarnated African souls on the modern-day house music party scene in clubs and house parties in London, Ibiza, through the US and around the globe to Thailand and Australia. The City of Koolah was simply good times and quality loud music. Ten thousand years after the ancient ceremonial parties, during the modern 1980s, the vibration had repeated from our ancient souls. Millions of reincarnated modern-day 1980s revellers partying, jacking their bodies to house music in fields and warehouse venues all round the world recently was no coincidence; it didn't just happen. It felt right, Black and White ravers, humans of all nations; our reincarnated inner spirit remembered when it enjoyed partying on the African continent ten thousand years ago. The old African vibration is what influenced the minds of reincarnated music makers to replicate the beat and pure bassline so that we all could reconnect to the ancient love vibration once again. The '80s acid house scene changed the vibes of a generation on a global scale; from tormented serious-attitude Black youngsters to purpose-made racist separatist Whites, they came to the Koolah love vibration and partied as one, no colour. The modern-day 80s/90s atmosphere took our souls through an awakening process to feel a taste of what we did in Africa before intruders transformed the continent and the world, staging their religious wars in Africa. Before religion was forced on the African continent, we did God's will, relaxing the mind by way of meditation and joyfully partying in peace. The universe's one soul God created the human, alien beings and animals to experience life, regardless of colour, and although some choose to allow themselves to be manipulated by Satan, every human and alien soul in this life is part of the oneness spirit, God. Bowing or kneeling and praying, eyes closed, for God's help is something man invented a relatively short while ago, and invented for the purpose of control. Man's religion has brought nothing but greed, assisted slavery, oppression of fellow humans, separation, war and bloodshed, a fear-based method of control. Constant daily prayer and the world gets worse by the day; nothing changes, we're still having to deal with oppression, paedophilia, violence and other vile acts carried out by the human race, much of it within religion. Prior to man's invented religion, for millions of years God's joyful soul peacefully partied to the musical heartbeat, the drumbeat.

Koolah awakens from his latest trance having again shared with his angels visions of the futuristic Delica-Earth-mission vision. As one of the female angels also regains consciousness from the shared Delica dimension, she nods her head happily and vibrantly, her fingertips touching her chest as she speaks of the shared astral travel Koolah has placed within her psyche and that of the other angels:

'Those aliens are us, future Koolah soul tribe angels, reincarnated to Delica…'

From her window in the palace, Queen Lulu, looks out at the sunrise. Her clairvoyant mind receives psychic medium images of her daughter Gabi running from her Twin Flame, totally ignoring him and their connection. Lulu too feels the frustration of her daughter's divine counterpart, Koolah, and his yearning to form union with Gabi. As the images fade Queen Lulu smiles with a shake of her head.

Just down the hill in the dip of the magic circle, a very low-on-energy-looking Koolah lies next to Jojo on a slightly raised rock part of the dip. Gabi, Princess of Koolah, enters the magic circle vibrantly smiling and running towards Koolah full of emotion. The Ancient African Princess is twenty years of age and stunningly beautiful, like a darker-skinned Halle Berry with fuller lips and a wider nose. Her eyes have a similar unique colouring to those of Yanson Bailey's future White Romanian Gypsy girlfriend Princess, although Princess Gabi's eyes are brown with one of them half-blue. Her soft Afro hair hangs loose owing to a recent shower. Although otherwise jet-black in colour, it has a blonde streak that grows from the temple. Gabi kneels next to Koolah, resting her head upon his chest. She looks up into his eyes and she and Koolah share the long-awaited loving smile that tells him she has surrendered to their union, and as the two kiss they feel the unparalleled intense passion that comes with the first Twin Flame kiss during every incarnation.

Gabi squints her eyes, protecting them from the bright sun, as she smiles and says, 'Koolah, the morning meditation was beautiful; my mind is so relaxed. I'm going to the palace to rest, take a little time and enjoy this entire sensation. You should rest too. I feel your sharing your astral travel with the other angels has taken your energy again.'

Koolah smiles sharing twenty-year-old Gabi's mirrored Twin Flame emotion, the sensation of having finally joined in union, becoming one angel soul again. Gabi emotionally kisses Koolah's lips again, tongue slightly inside his mouth. Twirling tongues, they French kiss.

Ibiza, Balearic Islands, Spain, 1993

In Ibiza in 1993, twenty three year old Princess kneels in a similar position to that of Princess Gabi and French kisses her lover Yanson Bailey, who lies on his luxury villa's outdoor sunbed. Although he is asleep, subconsciously his mouth and body respond to their Twin Flame kiss. As they pause from kissing, Princess smiles brightly and Yanson Bailey speaks the Koolah language in his sleep explaining his feelings for his Twin Flame:

'My intuition told me you had stopped running from our divine union, thank God.'

Looking out to a beautiful Ibiza sunrise, Princess feels there's something familiar in the language Yanson has just spoken, having heard those exact words before during her ancient African dreams.

At the magic circle, Koolah looks into Gabi's two-toned eye and quickly falls to sleep.

Yanson regains his consciousness, waking from his magic circle dream with the image of Princess Gabi's beautiful face on his mind. His thoughts linger over the dream he's just woken from: of Princess Gabi kissing him while in the magic circle and him falling asleep into the lucid dream of the present modern-day Princess. Had the dreamer become aware that he was dreaming and taken control over the dream? Was he wide-awake in a dream? He looks into the same two-toned eye – now present within the face of his Romany girlfriend – and gently pulls her towards him. Their lips touch and as they're emotionally French kissing it ignites that divine heavenly Twin Flame vibe. As it intensifies the sensation causes a pleasurable dizziness. Princess staggers to her feet and looks back out over the ocean towards the Ibizan sun. She walks a little way along the balcony and begins making Yanson another coffee at the machine.

CHAPTER 7

The familiar ten-thousand-year-old African Twin Flame sensation Yanson and his Romany girlfriend, Princess, feel increases their desire to be physically close to one another, knowing subconsciously that their soul is now whole. They find that their kisses now carry even yet more intensity than their first kiss a few days earlier. It is better each time their lips touch. Nature designed the effect of the Twin Flame kiss this way, enabling the Earth-based alien angel to raise the positive vibes of the planet and all beings around them. Ecstatically happy, Princess looks towards the waking Yanson Bailey as he stretches his body on the luxury sunbed, yawning with his cute and contagious smile. Pleasurably overcome with the tenderness of an unearthly love vibration, she looks away, up to the sky, smiling as she explains her thoughts:

'Yanson, what is this beautiful feeling, this love that we've found? I have to tell you I never felt I could ever be this happy, as though I want to burst open and let the world know what we got. It's because of our coming together; we're making each other feel this way. Darling, last night's full moon felt so fucking surreal and so familiar at the same time.'

She turns away from the ocean, back to face him, looking deep into his eyes, and the subconscious soul telepathic vibration tells her it's a mirrored energy; he shares the emotion simply because they're one soul. Princess finds her mind thinking back to some of the beautiful Koolah Palace dreams she has, dreams she's had this entire incarnation, which have become more meaningful the past months while living in Russia. She feels a subconscious knowing that those dreams were preordained, sent in preparation to ready her, assure her of their coming together in divine Twin Flame union. Princess and other Koolah Tribe Twin Flame angels are unique sensitive souls who dream whilst consciously awake.

They're evolved alien-beings, the Messiah having highly tuned them to the deepest regions of their subconscious. Princess suddenly begins thinking of the vivid dream she's had just then while watching Yanson sleep and as he woke. The dream revealed that, after a long separation from Koolah, she'd entered the magic circle and passionately kissed him while he lay on the rock. She also feels a guilty confusion in regard to the realistic dream, worried that she feels an equal love for Koolah as she does Yanson. At this stage, she's not consciously aware it's a parallel incarnation and Yanson's the reincarnated soul of Koolah. Not wanting to speak of it now and change the mood, Princess pushes the thoughts to the back of her mind and says, 'There's your coffee, baby,' as she passes Yanson the cup.

He looks deeply into her eyes, and she smiles as she tries to put some of her thoughts into words:

'When you woke earlier you began speaking that foreign language in your sleep. It sounded African and seriously familiar; I've heard it before. You spoke the same language in your sleep when I left your guest quarters in the Moscow palace. That was a beautiful moment. I didn't know if I'd ever see you again, so I kissed you. We kissed twirling our tongues forever as you slept, and I never wanted the heavenly kiss to end. The feeling's always incredible. We felt it again just then. I kissed you the same way as you slept...'

Her words cause him to think about the dream he's just woken from. He again feels the vibration of the ancient African Princess Gabi kissing him while lying on the magic circle rock. Twin Flame is a mirrored energy between both halves of the soul, and both Yanson and Princess subconsciously know somehow part of them, the soul, is still out there in that ancient African dimension and their other lives are playing out. Yanson cannot separate in his mind the uniquely divine way Princess just kissed him from the way it feels Gabi passionately kissing him as he closed his eyes to sleep in the magic circle. He tries to think of it in terms of an amazing coincidence, but nothing can explain away the feeling he has that somehow it all continuously connects on a higher frequency subconscious level within another dimension. He doesn't want to upset the mood, but knows he cannot lie or keep anything from her.

Princess smiles at him and asks the question, 'Why are you staring?'

He sips his coffee and looks out at some noisy seagulls whilst thinking how to answer that in a tactful way. Eventually he says, 'This is going to sound like fucking "out there", but your eyes, I know them, what you've just explained, the kiss…' He points to her half blue-half brown eye and explains his observation:

'The two colours of that eye, I see your eyes in someone else all the fucking time, just now when my eyes were closed but I was in another place, like a reality dream, another place I've always gone to in my dreams since I was a kid. The person I see in that world, her eyes are brown with a touch of blue. Sometimes I feel like I'm someone else, conscious in a place that's much better than here…'

'And this other person,' Princess interrupts, feeling suddenly annoyed, 'is it someone better than me?'

Yanson shakes his head gently and smiles. 'That's the thing, we met less than a week ago, but already I feel no one could ever be better than you or take your place.'

Princess relaxes and smiles. 'You know, Yanson, you say the most beautiful things'

'Saying it the way I'm feeling it, Princess. In that dream I don't recognise your beautiful eyes just because of how they look. This is going to sound fucking weird but the feeling your eyes give me make me know the other person is somehow you… I feel as though I've known you forever.'

Princess feels Yanson's sincerity and understands somehow, but neither yet have the knowledge that they are divinely created Twin Flame counterparts, created perfectly in each and every way, physically and spiritually; unaware they meet in each life they reincarnate to, unaware that what they have experienced is themselves actually coming to union in the days of the Koolah tribe. Neither of them are consciously aware the opened eyes are the mirrors to the human soul and their truth cannot be hidden.

As he sips his coffee, Yanson notices that the swimsuit Princess wore partying last night in the nightclub is now rested on the chair, reminding him how great she looked, taking his mind back to the nightclub Pacha, where they were the night before, and her choice of party clothing.

'You looked proper stunning in that Gucci swimsuit and thigh-high stiletto boots in Pacha last night...' He looks at the side view of her angelic bottom and slightly protruding vagina mound, the sight causing him to smile. Holding his hands up and slowly shaking his head, displaying a submissive gesture, he adds, 'But seriously, I'll settle for the way you look right now; I'm seriously not fucking complaining.'

Princess smiles with pride as she puts her boots back on and shakes out her swimsuit. She goes to sit with Yanson on the sunbed and they look at each other face to face.

'Yanson, your moving around and speaking that foreign language in your sleep woke me and I began kissing you while you were asleep...'

'Princess, God, the dreams I keep having where the black panther is by my side. I'm never scared of him; he always feels like he's my friend.'

She kisses his lips. He goes to speak, but she holds her index fingertip to his lips and says, 'That's crazy, we were out here sleeping and you woke me with your talking in your sleep... waking me from an on-going fantasy I've had since I was a little girl. My dreams helped my sanity when I was held prisoner in Russia.'

She pauses for a moment, thinking back to her recurring dream; the clear-as-life picture memory comes into her mind bringing a smile to her face.

'You mentioning the black panther Jojo has reminded me. I've dreamed so many times I lived in a magical palace on a small mountain. You have to understand, Yanson, these dreams are so fucking real...'

Yanson is speechless at Princess knowing the black panther's name Jojo, and she herself stays silent as a thousand thoughts race through his mind. Princess closes her eyes, reminiscing over the dream. She is looking out of her window upward to a tranquil cascading waterfall that flows down limestone rocks, weaving through a lush, tropical African jungle. A monkey's shriek causes her to turn her head higher upward, and she sees a baboon on a higher window ledge with her baby attached to her back. There are men diving from great height into an amazingly picturesque tropical deep lagoon. The sweet vibration, the BOOM BOOM bassline, of music causes her to look down to the jungle floor to see people all around really getting up and down to the beat rhythm of the music, a party rocking the utopia community.

Princess smiles, nodding her head, as Yanson's voice interrupts her reminiscence:

'Princess, the music is always the same as our house music, the instruments we used made it sound sweeter, more ital, like pure...'

His words instantly instil Princess with a pleasantly eerie feeling. With a smiling look of surprise on her face, she says, 'How did you know I was thinking about the music being the same as our house music in the clubs?'

Yanson looks equally surprised and chuckles. 'You were thinking it as well? It gets better, babe, I always dream my mind can tell each musician and vocalist when to sing or play his or her part. The black panther's named Jojo; you just mentioned it.'

The look on her face shows that what he's just said just clicked together in her mind. Her expression causes Yanson to pause for a tender moment before he says reverently, 'Babe, we have some sort of deep spiritual connection.'

'Yeah, fucking scary,' she agrees.

She smiles and gets up from the sunbed. Yanson reading the sexual desire in her eyes puts down his coffee cup. Without hesitation, she drops her dressing gown to the floor revealing the entirety of her angelic naked body. The expression on his face shows he's mesmerised, thinking from the day that he was born he's never experienced these magical sparks, these feelings, a love anything close to the intensity of the Twin Flame vibe he feels with his new Romany girlfriend, Princess, before.

Princess, naked apart from her thigh-high white stiletto boots, pulls at Yanson's boxer shorts, removing them to reveal his full erection. Looking deeply into her different-coloured eyes, he pulls her to him on the sunbed. She excitedly pulls off his t-shirt, revealing his perfect ripped body, boxer- physique. They begin making love, extremely creatively, erotically, spiritually in the uniquely structured Twin Flame dimensions. He initiating sweet oral sex, swivelling her into position on the edge of the sunbed, gripping her buttocks shifting her closer to his energised tongue, the tip of which strongly begins masturbating her clitoris leading her to pout energetically open-mouthed while she fondles her own enlarged silicone breasts and nipples.

Ancient City of Koolah

In the Palace of Koolah, Princess Gabi lies resting on her bed, in the afterglow of her morning Twin Flame union kiss with Koolah at the magic circle. She drifts into sleep and whilst sleeping begins to feel sexually turned on. Outside her window, the tranquil sound of a cascading waterfall can be heard, coupled with the sounds of a resident tribe of friendly baboon monkeys outside noisily squabbling and shrieking among themselves.

The cries and moans of an animated, prolonged, elated female orgasm sounds from within Princess Gabi's palace quarters. Gabi sleeps in a subconscious dream, conscious in another life dimension experiencing sexual orgasm. Eventually the shrieking of the noisy palace baboons begins to bring her back to consciousness. Waking, she still feels Yanson Bailey's masculine hands tightly gripping her buttocks; his tongue having initiated oral sex, massaging her clitoris, has Gabi's mind in ecstasy. Opening her eyes, she's shocked to find herself at home in the palace because within the same moment before opening her eyes the dream making love to Yanson Bailey on that Ibiza sunbed was so real. There wasn't a doubt in her mind it was actually happening. Wide-awake from the wet dream, Gabi, slightly perspiring, breathing heavily, still feels sexually turned on. Her clitoris still experiences the distinct sensation of pleasure, her mouth pouts as she fondles her own oddly larger breasts, and in her mind her unique eyes look out to the Ibiza sunrise. Now in deep thought, Gabi knows somehow she's actually the tanned, White Romanian Gypsy girl squinting her eyes at the magnificent Ibiza sunrise making love to Yanson Bailey, firmly caressing his muscular, ripped body, and unavoidably ripping her nails into his back while he's giving her energetic oral sex and she climaxes on the Ibiza villa sunbed. She remembers her hand excitedly fondling her own nipple, breast and then her middle finger joining his tongue at her clitoris. She lies there looking at her hands and body, the puzzled state of her mind showing in her facial expression. She stands, goes to the window, and stares out of it, thinking deeply into the futuristic dream from which she's just woken, questioning why she's not her own colour but instead a young White woman. She sighs, sits back on the bed, and says to herself, 'Now then, let me make some sense of this. Why am I that colour and always dream of him?'

The sensation of the dream is so real that she actually feels guilty in regard to her new conscious lover within the tribe, the Messiah Koolah. Part of her feels relieved because up until the last two mornings she'd had a string of negative nightmares in regard to Yanson Bailey: pregnant with his child and not knowing why but scared to face him, nervously always avoiding him as though worried about her inner secrets being exposed, her not being enough for him and him falling out of love with her because of that and many other complex complications. She lies back on her bed smiling at the fact she was no longer running from him and felt secure with him now. 'The love I have for that man and the beautiful love we make in my dream is always so real. Who is that sexy man I'm always very much in love with?'

CHAPTER 8

Later that morning, taking a prolonged shower beneath the paradise setting of a lush falling waterfall accompanied by the sound of the hypnotic musical drumbeat, Gabi smiles, feeling she's finally over an insecurity that had been plaguing her mind continuously for many moons over the recurring negative futuristic dream. The dream nightmare consisted of a negative, distraught feeling, not being able to face a man she'd strangely fallen in love with and been intimate with in the deepest realms of her subconscious dreams – a terrifying fear that when the love of her life in that other dimension, Yanson Bailey, finds out her secrets, mistakes she's made in that life, he'd take his love away. Nodding to the beat, she smiles as she washes her hair, happy because her psyche's now visiting the events of recent contrasting positive dreams. For the past few mornings she's woken with dreams of dancing with the same romantic lover, Yanson Bailey, in a futuristic nightclub and making passionate love with him on the Ibiza villa balcony under the stars. Waking at sunrise, dreaming Yanson's tongue bringing her to sexual orgasm causes her to recall a dream that followed later that morning showing she becomes pregnant in that futuristic dimension and later all is well in the relationship where she's not running and hiding from him. A sudden pleasurable energy rush sends a tingling sensation throughout her body as she then recalls consciously, romantically, kissing Koolah for the first time at early sunrise that morning within the magic circle, and the equally positive vibration keeps her energetically smiling. Although ecstatically happy, she's still slightly confused, feeling guilty in regard to Koolah for the love she also feels for the man in her futuristic dreams.

Some of her family members arrive and Gabi begins larking

around in the lagoon as they join her taking a shower under the waterfall. Her smiling mother, the clairvoyant Queen of Koolah, Lulu, also approaches. Gabi waves to her and shortly joins her. Shortly, the pair sit together on a nearby rock as Lulu begins to explain to her daughter:

'Gabi, your father and I took five years to come into permanent physical union in this life, longer and shorter in other lives. My darling, this entire incarnation subconsciously you've been fully aware that the Messiah is your twin soul...'

Gabi's look is one of wide-eyed innocence, causing her mother to smile, before continuing:

'Twin Flame Gabi, forever deep inside yourself you've known your Twin Flame is Koolah. In some cases, it's perfectly normal for us to consciously deny our feeling towards the connection. Fact is you and Koolah share one soul, you came here to Earth one soul, now always born in two bodies.'

Lulu's words begin to make sense of the things that have been troubling Gabi, what the spirit was in some way telling her.

'I thought it for a long time, but you knew, Mother.'

Queen Lulu laughs. 'Yes, it's my duty to know; you're my daughter. In each incarnation spirit guides us to signs letting us know we're Twin Flame, bringing us together, as it did in your case. The revelations of your soul that the energy rush carry can be daunting at first, and one half of you running from the other is also quite common. Although we're totally in an unparalleled love with our divine counterpart, they often trigger subconscious fears from our past or future history and unearth embarrassing things about us we'd rather not face. I've had this conversation with many Twin Flame angels of the magic circle, not just you. Things happen in other lives, and the subconscious insecurities uncovered from those lives made you run and reject coming into union with your Twin Flame. You ran because of your inner fear. You were full of insecurity, past and future life hurts, feelings of not being enough, or the other half of your soul reminding you of embarrassment that you are afraid to face.

'The fear you feel in that future dimension could have come

from any given life you've lived or will live, Gabi. Our future and past lives are all in the moment of now, such is the complexity of God, the multi-dimensional universe.'

As she sits beside her with her hair drying naturally, Gabi is absorbed by her mother's words, but she is not surprised her mother knew exactly what's been on her mind, The Queen of Koolah would often surprise family members with her magical clairvoyant revelations and spiritual knowledge.

'The other angels and I are continuously doing work on you, concentrating on your connection releasing you from those fears... Have you felt better just recently? Had better dreams?'

Gabi smiles delightedly in reply, and her mother returns her smile.

Lulu allows her thoughts to momentarily drift off into the recollection of a future incarnation of her own: the uniquely pretty, White, tanned-skin Brunette young mother, Cindy Nevin. The year's 1962 and Lulu's inside the Epping Forest cottage with the soul of the early coastal tribe psychic medium Chikelu reincarnated as the clairvoyant Romanian Gypsy named Rosella. Rosella's black cat is the soul of Koolah's big cat companion reincarnated, in both lives named Jojo. Both Cindy and Rosella are aware that during Rosella's ancient African incarnation she initially made contact with Benser on Planet Delica spiritually assisting the alien soul back to Earth to be reborn as Abiona and subsequently, four incarnations later, reborn Koolah. Cindy and Rosella are in the state of joint future astral travel, having crossed thirty-one years into the future to Rosella's homeland, modern-day 1993 Bucharest, Romania. There they are joined in that future dimension by Rosella's Romanian-based biological mother Dinah, who has also astral travelled from an earlier incarnation to Yanson's girlfriend Princess's Romania Bucharest hotel room. Whilst in that 1993 dimension the psychic soul African Queen Lulu uses her powerful creative energy to repeatedly change her astral body from Cindy Nevin back to Queen Lulu.

Sitting looking into the waterfall, Lulu remembers doing this to remind the future incarnation soul of Gabi who she is, so she'd take the advice to join in union with her Twin Flame Yanson for the purpose of raising the vibration of the planet. The clairvoyant Queen nods in excitement at remembering that future incarnation and the future astral travel adventure, and turns to her daughter to explain:

'Gabi, both you and I in future incarnation are born White, living in European lands. You're pregnant, accommodating another Twin Flame angel soul to rest in your womb, in heaven.' Lulu smiles as she pictures the twenty-nine-year-old Yanson Bailey she'd seen during astral travel. 'When you miss your period and run from your Twin Flame partner – your partner always the soul of Koolah, of course – you've allowed that subconscious negative fear vibration you'd kept from your Twin Flame in your future incarnation to also surface in this life, in part the cause of your half of the twin soul to run. You were also running from yourself through fear your Twin Flame would take the love back due to your low self-esteem and lack of self-love. There's many other reasons: terrible mistakes you've made in past and future lives, fear of repeating them. The insecure layers stored within your subconscious made you hesitant and fearful in this life.'

Lulu looks deeply into the eyes of her daughter, who's now surrounded by a beautiful faint rainbow that's appeared in the misty spray of the falling water. She sees Gabi's eyes gradually change from her natural both brown and one half-blue eyes to both eyes being blue and one half-brown as spirit shows Queen Lulu the face of Gabi's future incarnation, the Romanian girl, Princess.

'Gabi, in that future incarnation myself and another angel reincarnated, Rosella, see in the crystal ball and by way of other psychic methods you running from your Twin Flame; you leave your new home and run away to your homelands, lands in Eastern Europe that will be named Romania.'

Lulu pictures the future progression, seeing images of the beautiful Romany girl revealed in the waterfall: of Princess, a little older than Gabi, in her early twenties, sitting upon the hotel bed in a modern-day futuristic setting.

Gabi meanwhile recalls looking through the eyes of her future incarnation, the Romanian Gypsy Princess, seeing from her hotel bed Cindy changing to and from her beautiful Black African mother Queen Lulu. She recalls her Romany grandmother Dinah excitedly smiling, exclaiming as Cindy's astral body keeps swapping revealing her mother Lulu, 'My God, our other angels are showing us Cindy's the soul of the ancient clairvoyant Queen Lulu of the Koolah angel tribe.'

Epping Forest, Essex, 1962

In Rosella's Epping Forest cottage, she and Cindy regain consciousness from the future life astral travel, and Rosella speaks most excitedly:

'We were present in that future dimension; that was my Romanian niece named Princess sitting up in bed; she won't be born for around eleven years. Also, that was my very spiritual mother Dinah who joined us by way of astral travel.'

Rosella pauses for a moment, staring at Cindy with an energetic smile. 'Cindy, don't you see? The reawakening is near and is to happen in this incarnation. There's no more waiting; we are the ones we've been waiting for.'

It usually takes a lot to get Rosella excited about anything, but she is excited now having felt the presence of the angel soul African Queen Lulu.

Cindy too, who in this life has only in recent months been reintroduced to the spiritual realms of the multi-dimensional universe, shares Rosella's excitement and splutters out, 'I know we were there in your country with that pretty girl who's connected, but fuck knows how we did it!'

Rosella stands, her hands gently caressing her own face, looking down at Cindy. 'Cindy, you revealed you are Lulu, and the purpose of the reading was for you to tell Princess to surrender to her Twin Flame in this life thirty years from now, to go home to the island of Ibiza and join in union with him. Never before has a reading felt so heavenly. You are the soul of the ancient angel

Queen Lulu, Queen of the Koolah tribe. My God, the mother-in-law of Jesus... well, his name was never Jesus, Koolah I should say.'

Ancient City of Koolah

Sitting by the waterfall, Lulu continues to explain as her psyche reveals Gabi's future incarnation's new Ibiza home:

'Gabi, you've been running from Koolah in this dimension due to future mistakes. Koolah has always known this, but wanted to let you go through your running phase.

'There's no reason to feel the guilt of being in love with the man in your dreams, Yanson. He is the reincarnated soul of your Twin Flame, Koolah. You form joyful union in that and every life.'

As Lulu turns away from looking into the waterfall and back to her daughter, she finds she's looking at the image of the Romanian Gypsy rather than her daughter Gabi; then the image changes again, the eyes lingering – Princess's blue eyes rather than Gabi's brown – before she is once again looking just at her daughter.

Recalling speaking to Gabi in her future incarnation at the hotel room, Lulu continues:

'The other angels and I went to your future to guide and encourage you. The fact you've stopped worrying in that future incarnation has helped you reconnect with your Twin Flame in this life. I've been shown by spirit that you've stopped running; you're now ready to join in union with your Twin Flame in this present life incarnation. You surrendered yourself to him this morning.'

Gabi interrupts her mother. 'All you say is so true; I knew of the connection. I'm now able to face him and have joined in permanent union. Mother, thank you.'

Gabi smiles at Queen Lulu as the water falls behind her, an image that would remain in the psyche of the African Queen forever.

'Mother, your gifted psychic powers are astonishing, for you to know the reason why I couldn't face it... It wasn't even clear to me why I was running from my Twin Flame.'

Queen Lulu gives her daughter a motherly stare. 'What are mums for? Don't thank me angel, thank God.'

With her mother's blessing, Princess Gabi leaves the palace to join in the full moon ceremonial celebration party.

CHAPTER 9

After leaving the palace, the stunningly beautiful Princess Gabi's sexy legs carry her through joyful partying crowds, the pounding bassline drums becoming louder as she approaches the beach area. She wears just tan suede, slightly heeled, clog-style type shoes and G-string type animal-skin panties. Gabi stops and queues behind three others scooping and drinking the Koolah tribe's mind-expanding love juice from one of two magical large elevated floating steel pots. Both pots hover four feet high, slightly tilting side to side in rhythm with the beat of the music.

The natural hallucinogenic party juice is a concoction that's a more potent form of the plant-based Ayahuasca still commonly used today in South America, with select psychedelic boiled mushrooms and herbs added. Its high is like an LSD-ecstasy mix but from the clearest mind-opening, purest drug. It gives the Koolah tribe heightened awareness and endless energy. The natural high and their freethinking magical vibration allows the tribal souls to witness other real dimension phases that most one-dimensional human minds do not. The real life of the universe comes alive for them. The oneness spirit of God connected, injecting its awesome sensation to trigger the souls of the Koolah tribe, setting the mind free from Satan's grasp. Colours became authentic, animals of the jungle sounded and appeared significant, birds flew with elegance, and the now-glowing sun danced along with the music, the sweet hypnotic rhythm, the real life. A magical vibration takes their minds literally into the music.

The party juice helps the tribe connect and tune into other indigenous Twin Flame angels on Planet Earth and also other dimensions of the universe, receiving flashbacks and flash-forwards of the universal psyche – even becoming conscious partying in future reincarnated lives. Some in attendance display a variety of bleached insignia, actually including the odd smiley face logo and even CND symbol on their animal-skin suede clothing.

The young Princess drinks a cup, fills a second and then goes to look for Koolah, who she finds sitting at a table with the long-bearded tribal elder Akachi. Akachi is tall, strong, with very dark skin tones – shades almost the actual colour black – long and flowing grey dreadlocks, and a serious-looking face, which is actually mismatched to his jokey character. He is an important angel of the magic circle. The two men sit across the huge table opposite one another, playing the ancient African dice game backgammon, watched by another man the shorter and stockier Ode. The wooden playing board's rested on the table amongst a number of large sketches.

On seeing the three men, Princess Gabi initially keeps her distance, standing back to admire Koolah's endless joyful expression, ripped physique, and beautiful matted and well-oiled Bob Marley–style dreadlocks. She peers into the magic circle intrigued by a man whose soul has moved his body so that it lets off a unique mesmerising vibration to the rhythm, the exact way only the modern-day Michael Jackson could, not dancing to the music but actually becoming part of the music. Gabi turns her attention back to the table as the black panther with the piercing green eyes, Jojo, arrives to take his place by Koolah's side, who now continuously strokes the glossy fur of the muscular animal. After a little while Koolah wins the game and Gabi smiles. Koolah then looks as though he's just remembered something; he stands and reaches into his man-bag type pouch and tosses four solid gold coins onto the table. There's a large coin, over an inch in diameter, and the rest are gradually smaller, the smallest being less than half an inch in diameter. Koolah speaks to his friend with an air of confidence, saying, 'Ode, I recall these belong to you…'

As Ode picks up the coins, Koolah closes his eyes facing the sun.

There's a serious expression on Ode's handsome face as he examines the largest coin. It's perfect apart from a light dent on its edge. He pushes his thumbnail into the dent and thinks for a moment, realising he's continuously visualised the coins at the magic circle thanks to Koolah's multi-shared astral-travel visions. Ode then uses all his fingers to expertly set all four coins spinning on the table simultaneously. The coins weave in and out of one another's way, as though the coins were actually dancing to the music. Then Ode snatches up the dented coin while it is spinning, to show it to Akachi and Koolah. 'I remember these coins from an astral-travel vision you shared at our magic circle. Other angel souls and I had reincarnated to a life on board a futuristic ship.' Ode smiles as he pictures the 18th century French slave ship in his mind.

With the other coins still spinning on the table, Ode complains to his friend Akachi, 'Get up Akachi, let me play. Come on, it's my turn to play against Koolah.' He gently pushes at the older man's shoulder and hands him his walking stick. 'It's winner stays on, you lost, let me sit, winner stays on…'

Koolah doesn't get involved in the argument, but instead sits back down, his eyes closed and his mind in tune with what was now taking place at the palace.

CHAPTER 10

The Koolah City Palace functions in line with nature, like a lion pride. It houses the King's five chosen female concubine wives and a dozen other children, but the King and Queen Lulu have three children who are theirs together: first-born daughter Princess Monifa, a Prince and youngest daughter, Princess Gabi. Shortly after Gabi had left to party at the full moon celebrations, the King and Queen of Koolah are joined by one of the King's lower ranking concubine wives, the latest and youngest, Awitti. She wears a cornrow hairstyle, is young – around twenty-five – pretty, short in height, with huge breasts and a shapely backside. The three are quickly engaged in an erotic threesome orgy – all three completely naked apart from Queen Lulu wearing her glossy black pearl and glistening diamond necklace, an item which on the instruction of the Messiah she is never to remove, and the King's wearing a platted elephant-leather neck strap he too is to always wear. The trio experience a unique sexual sensation, an unparalleled blissful vibration, when in one another's company. Queen Lulu and Awitti break from their lesbian sex to jointly perform oral sex on the King; then, after a short while, the women kneel on the edge of the bed, welcoming, accommodating arses in the air, sides of their butt cheeks touching one another, as the hugely well-endowed King Imarmu switches back and forth penetrating both women. He always uses his hand to give pleasure to one whilst making love to the other, a sexual habit characteristic of the soul.

After the highly charged sexual threesome and a short, delightful nap, King Imarmu wakes and lies contentedly looking at his Queen, Lulu; she sits looking out of a window, still naked apart from her black pearl and diamond necklace. She's nodding her head to the sweet sound of the ceremonial music, and turns her head back to face him with a vibrant smile.

'You've awoken, my King …' The excited beating of her heart causes her to pause in thought for a moment before delivering her next words:

'The magic of this full moon ceremony, the souls of our original tribe from our days of Abiona will be made to realise we'll reincarnate and meet in every physical life for an eternity.'

As she explains, Queen Lulu keeps taking lingering whiffs of her fingers.

'…My King, the dream of a woman giving birth is one of the most beautiful, assuring spiritual visions you can receive. On waking, I was just shown myself giving birth in a future dimension, a life I'm to reincarnate to.'

Lulu pictures a beautiful, pleasant-natured future 1960s Caribbean midwife.

'There was a woman helping with the delivery, she actually handed me my baby…'

The King smiles with pride as his Queen falls into deep psychic thought, as he has seen her do many times, on this occasion thinking about her own Cindy Nevin incarnation. Queen Lulu smiles vibrantly as she smells her hands, still thinking back of being conscious as the young White smiling mother repeatedly whiffing the pure scent of her baby's head and her own hands. Lulu shakes her head in a state of confusion, but smiling at her King, she says:

'I still have the scent of my baby, even remember giving her the name Nicole.'

The African Queen shakes her head in wonderment as she speaks.

'My God, the magic of our subconscious universe, my King please listen...'

The King stares silent in admiration and listens as requested. 'The woman helping with the delivery was Black. She actually set my baby off breathing and handed my little girl to me. I had a White body and my baby was White...'

She pauses in deep thought before delivering her next words:

'Imarmu, the magic of this full moon ceremony, the Messiah has put us the souls of our original coastal tribe together, creating a unique Twin Flame angel soul tribe. Koolah has asked the universe to ensure we will reincarnate and meet in every physical life for eternity. We're to be guided through dimensions in a deeply spiritual way by a more advanced type of lucid dream but far more beneficial because not only are we aware we're dreaming, we are – the soul is – actually able to physically become as conscious in other dimensions.'

She smiles at her King, and as she fixes her gaze towards the waterfall images, the physical memories of her dream experience reappear.

'I was just then conscious in one of those lives I shall live. The vision was so real; I still have the spiritual scent of my baby from ten thousand years into the future. Goodness, this spiritual universe...'

She suddenly looks sad.

'I have a White body, White husband and baby, but I knew my White husband's soul wasn't yours but another soul, my King. I'll have to investigate. Koolah and other angels within the circle assured me you and I are eternal Twin Flame, our soul joining in union each life forever for an eternity.'

A loud alpha-male baboon's shriek suddenly causes their ménage à trois partner Awitti, who is still present and was asleep in the bed, to wake. She finds herself still part-conscious in a dreadful detailed nightmare in her own future incarnation in a 1964 London maternity ward, conscious as a mixed race Jamaican-Chinese young mother. She recalls being about to get hit by a lorry and waking lying on that maternity ward bed. She rises from the bed and goes to share her thoughts with Queen Lulu:

'Queen Lulu, I've just experienced a dream of myself in another life. I was in a marriage with a White Englishman... just been left heartbroken... there was a love affair with a strikingly handsome Jamaican. I'd just given birth to the Jamaican man's baby... feeling depressed, harbouring a strong emotion of guilt towards my White husband while speaking to my Black friend Elsie, a madam prostitute they called Tricks. I clearly remember my Black Jamaican friend by the bedside suggesting the baby's name, "Yanson … yes of course, Yanson, we have to call this boy Yanson.'"

Awitti looks out into the amazing African waterfall, continuing to visualise the future incarnation dream: her mixed-race toddler boy and the new-born Black baby in the dream were her children, but there's a strange knowing that the Black baby she'd just given birth to was to cause a lot of hurt to herself and her partner...

The clairvoyant mind of Queen Lulu picks up on Awitti's psyche and the disturbing dimensions she's becoming conscious within, and gives the young concubine wife a reassuring smile. She comforts Awitti and her gestures of comforting soon turn to caresses, and before long the trio of Imarmu, Lulu and Awitti are once again intimate, engaged in joyful, erotic sex.

Outside, the chants of some of the female vocalists along the beach complement the sweet ancient party music, while one of the monkeys, a mother, sits on her regular window-ledge perch with her baby on her back. The scene is exactly that Romanian Gypsy Princess saw in her vision.

Oxford Street, 1962

Cindy's puzzled by the presence of Claudette and her black cat in Oxford Street, and unaware none of the hordes of people about her can actually see them. Cindy stands face to face with the vibrantly smiling Claudette unable to speak or move. Gradually she can no longer hear the crowds, passing cars and buses; they're replaced by the sounds of the full moon ceremonial music and the playful shrieks of monkeys, as she begins to feel she's no longer there in that bustling busy street. She becomes aware of the sensation of someone gripping onto her shoulder and a pleasurable feeling in her vagina as though she's actually having intercourse. Without knowing how or when it happened, she finds herself nose-to-nose next to a smiling Awitti with her cornrow hairstyle, kneeling alongside her doggie style on the bed. She can actually, physically feel the warmth and sexual energy of the sides of their bum cheeks touching and the unique blissful vibration of the threesome encounter ten thousand years earlier. She watches Awitti pleasurably gritting her teeth as King Imarmu's large hand squeezes one of her buttocks before his fingers find and massage her clitoris. At the same time the King is having intercourse with Queen Lulu, and Cindy Nevin's now conscious in that early incarnation, feeling Imarmu holding onto, gripping his Queen's shoulder – gripping *her* shoulder – for extra leverage, and she, Cindy, is moaning with pleasure.

Ancient City of Koolah

The ancient African Koolah Queen smiles at the faces of her King and the young concubine, giggling speaking her mind in London Cockney:

'What a wonderful feeling. I'm really here; it was your hand I could feel pulling on me shoulder. I know this fucking atmosphere and you people, sexiest feeling ever, fuck me...'

She turns to face the King of Koolah. 'You're my Twin Flame, my King and husband.'

The King, Awitti and others in the palace are used to hearing Queen Lulu speak different futuristic languages while asleep, awake and even during sex. Lulu begins thinking about that morning's magic circle experience, remembering word for word the multi-shared telepathic spiritual teachings of Koolah and what he'd explained about becoming conscious in other dimension phases, in future or past lives. Koolah's soothing voice is still on her mind, in the head of Queen Lulu:

'Every being of the universe, human and alien, is able to do this because our soul is part of the intricate spirit of God; collectively we are God the oneness soul, the Holy Spirit. We are the creator of our multi-dimensional universe. Our supreme individual subconscious mind has the infinite number of our past and future lives stored, and we're able to become conscious in any of those dimensions.'

Lulu is still part conscious in one of the soul's stored subconscious incarnations, on this occasion conscious as Cindy Nevin. Cindy still feels the magic of the palace orgy as the sight of Claudette and the sights and sounds of the busy 1960s Oxford Street reappear. Looking into Claudette's eyes, in appreciation of the familiarity of Koolah's voice and his explanation in regard to becoming conscious in other dimensions, other incarnations, Cindy Nevin reverently utters the words, 'That voice.'

Whilst sitting at the backgammon table, Koolah tunes the angels into combined visions of the palace bedroom's threesome orgy and Claudette's view of the modern-day early '60s Oxford Street, staring up the iconic street to see Selfridges store up ahead towards Marble Arch. In the London vision Koolah concentrates on two reincarnated Koolah souls, White brunette Cindy Nevin and a smartly dressed Black man on the opposite side of the street. In the palace vision Koolah's psyche connects to the vibration of King Imarmu, Queen Lulu and the young concubine Awitti engrossed in their erotic threesome orgy.

Oxford Street, 1962

On Oxford Street, Cindy looks into the smiling eyes of Claudette and as Koolah's psychic vision switches between the palace threesome and the modern-day 1962 street in London's West End, Cindy still feels the energy of the sexual orgy.

Claudette speaks, her words in the language of ancient Koolah: 'Queen Lulu, the reawakening has begun.'

Open-mouthed, Cindy looks at the Haitian witch with a look of bewilderment. She now finds herself gripped by the sexual energy. Leaning her back on a shop window, Cindy puts one hand to her crotch and with the other she fondles one of her breasts, her facial expression a sexual mouth pout. Some of the surrounding shoppers stop and stare in astonishment at her actions.

Claudette points with her eyes to the other side of the busy street, indicating to Cindy, as at the same moment Cindy physically hears and understands the unique unmistakable sound of Koolah's voice speaking to her in their ancient indigenous language: 'Lulu, across the street, Imarmu...'

With a puzzled expression, Cindy looks across to the other side of the road to a smartly dressed tall and strikingly handsome Black man, Mr Nathaniel 'Cutty' Robinson, walking. Cindy's eyes fix on the handsome man but also somehow she's still faintly in tune with the palace bedroom. The sights and sounds of the palace have disappeared but subconsciously she knows the man across the street embodies the vibration of the ancient palace threesome. He's across the street walking past, walking with a purposeful stride, as she mutters under her breath, 'Fuck me ... talk about the man of my fucking dreams,' and smiles in the direction of the Jamaican.

CHAPTER 11

Ancient City of Koolah

As Koolah, seated at the backgammon table, is about to begin another game, Princess Gabi sneaks up behind him, watched intently by the big cat Jojo. She places one hand over Koolah's eyes, and he does his usual when thinking, twisting his lips to one side whilst squinting an eye. He speaks before turning to her:

'My eternal and forever Twin Flame, Princess Gabi.' He looks up to her, they share a loving smile and Koolah explains how he knew it was she:

'Our unique energy gave it away, has done forever.'

She looks deep into her soul within his eyes, feeling guilty about previously running from the connection. 'I'm sorry,' she says simply.

He doesn't answer verbally but she feels him saying, 'There's no need to apologise, we are one and there's no need to say sorry, to apologise, to your own self.'

They kiss and both feel it's actually more magical than that first kiss that morning. She passes him the cup and he drinks it down in one go, a huge smile appearing across his face.

'Did you have a good rest and enjoy waking from your future incarnation, Princess?'

She immediately realises Koolah's speaking of her making love in their future incarnation. Reassured by her mother having told her that her previously mysterious future dream lover is the soul of Koolah, Princess reacts with a smile and slight nod of the head.

'Gabi, I'd been chasing you to join in union for more than twelve moons and you finally surrendered to the connection and stopped running today, this morning.'

His words cause her to remember those Twin Flame sparks as they kissed that morning. She smiles as she listens to his further words:

'I've been waiting to explain our purpose: how when in union, we're one of the original seventy-two thousand angels sent here to the Earth. We and other indigenous soul tribe angels were sent here a dimension long ago as guides or healers to remain performing a divine mission assisting humanity. Gabi, on arrival as an intangible angel we, the one angel soul, split as two females conceived, each half of us attaching to one sperm-foetus becoming Twin Soul. Born from separate heavens, separate female wombs, reincarnating each life into two separate bodies; creating the divine counterpart and from birth guided by the hand of the divine to join in a blissful union. In each life we repeatedly come together in union, back as a complete angel, therefore oneness with the source, God.'

She looks continuously and deeply into his eyes, subconsciously feeling and recognising her own soul, herself, within him as he speaks:

'...In each incarnation, firstly from the infant stages, we're linked to one another by way of connecting subconscious dreams. We've seen the future modern-day world's computers and mobile telephones with their digital clocks. In future dimensions we'll be known as the one hundred and forty-four thousand Twin Flame souls and during their 20th century we will send messages to one another through sequences of number digits. The number digit sequences you will randomly see throughout your daily routine will hold a message and guide you on your next steps towards Twin Flame union. The universe then presents us to one another into physical union for the purpose of carrying out our soul mission, our life purpose, healing the planet. When we become whole again, our love vibration naturally aligns the planet to more unity and divinity, just out of choosing unity and loving each other.'

Feeling and seeing her soul within him causes what he's explaining to resonate with her soul – with *their* soul. They passionately kiss again and in doing so experience that twin soul shock.

Akachi meanwhile studies the Messiah's drafted drawings on the table. He looks up from the sketches and smiles as he sees Koolah's manly body holding his pretty girl in a loving embrace, before passionately kissing her.

Akachi remarks to Ode, 'Oh, the Twin Flame runner has come into union, finally.'

As Koolah and Gabi kiss, they grip one another tightly and begin dancing, rocking to the party music.

Akachi explains further to Ode, 'Twin Flames individually but when combined back whole as one of heaven's angels; the love we create in union vibrates at the highest frequency. We again create the universe's unique divine love energy vibrating on not just the Earth but throughout the entire multiverse.'

Hearing this, Gabi stops still from dancing and says to Akachi, 'I know, I felt its vibration this morning when we kissed for the first time in this life. It felt like I'd come home...'

Her mind drifts into pleasurable deep thought about what her mother had said in relation to Koolah and Yanson being the same soul. Suddenly she laughs for actually feeling guilty for also experiencing that same coming-home Twin Flame sensation when kissing and making love to Yanson Bailey in her dream, that morning and in many other dreams.

Akachi's continued explanation interrupts her thoughts:

'...Our purpose will, in the future, be a threat to the evil spirit's dominance of the human race, and they will try to eradicate us, breaking the spiritual links around the world.'

Then Koolah himself takes over the explanation, saying:

'In future dimensions, for a period of thousands of years we will lose our homelands, lose our spiritual way of life due to losing our bible. We will be viciously, systematically enslaved, and in modern dimensions systematically racially abused and oppressed as lower-class citizens due to being of Black skin. We will, I repeat *will*, relocate it and steer Black Africa back to nature's plan, again regaining our spiritual knowing, our oneness as source; we angels opening our minds realising we are the twin soul, Twin Flame, angels on our divine mission, each playing a part to fulfil our combined life purpose.

'The natural potion we take frees the mind allowing us to connect to the psyche of future dimensions, alien planets anywhere, spiritually interacting with other Twin Flame tribes globally and in the far reaches of the universe; this is the real life.

'Our concoction consumed all around the universe helps keep ourselves free of negative energy that could build up stressful emotions. It helps raise us to the vibration needed to spiritually connect with various future and past dimensions' human and alien beings. Future dimension indigenous tribes in South America will take it in less potent form and call it Ayahuasca, as will other Twin Flame tribes who'll keep it turned on. On my astral travels I've witnessed future dimensions' humans using our concoction, experiencing deep mind transformation contributing to the most amazing positive life changes. It gives us an energy to dance and party non-stop for days. False religion will come to try and hide the truth that partying is the human soul's natural way of praying, heightening the global vibration; to hide the truth that naturally anything to do with prayer was designed to be joyful, like for instance the action "fucking" is a beautiful joyful experience, the blissful feeling designed so because the action gives life, but an experience religions will make a taboo subject in the eyes of their Gods and within religious buildings. God will never build buildings for us to stand in, head bowed praying.

'Our work will be complete at the point of modern-day Earth's divine awakening, the beginning of healing the world, the reinstatement of Africa and other indigenous lands. Mother Earth, her lands will never be happy unless the indigenous again create the natural vibration of its original spirituality. The Earth will get sick without the missing original spiritual vibration, the indigenous people's spirituality's there for a purpose, as are the trees, the bees and everything else. The African lands will never belong to the evil spirit of the colonisers, but the spirit within the indigenous people and animals belong to the land; God made it so.'

Koolah passionately kisses Gabi and speaks directly to her:

'Princess, a King cannot rule his kingdom without the strength from the love of his Queen. You've acquired your mother's spiritual strength, a soul now designed for me.'

She smiles into his eyes as she answers, 'You are the chosen spiritual King and I will forever love and adore you, my Koolah.'

Her eyes are drawn to the four gold coins the indigenous tribesman Ode's again spinning on the table. She asks, 'Ode, where did you get those?'

Ode pauses before responding, his mind visualising his hands are those of a White man expertly spinning the same coins on a ship captain's table. He points at Koolah with an inquisitive smile, and says, 'Yes Koolah, where did you get them?'

Koolah smiles back. 'I took them from your cabin.'

The angel Ode smiles nodding because Koolah's words have caused his mind to flashback clearly to a memory of a magic circle astral-travel sighting, a memory from his own recurring futuristic dreams. In one dream of a future incarnation in particular, the sun's shining through an 18th century ship porthole window on stacks of gold coins and jewellery that are scattered all across a huge ship-captain's table. Ode recalls sitting spinning the exact four coins but his hands are deep-tanned White; he's a White man in the dream and future incarnation. He also recalls that his hair is styled in long dreadlocks and he has a thin scar through an eyelid.

Ode explains his thoughts: 'I often dream of my future ship and you physically crossing to us reincarnated angels into that dimension. Now I always wake from dreams living that life.' He picks up two of the coins. 'Koolah, these are some of the exact coins you took from the ship. I recall you taking them. You crossed into that dimension and came to me.'

The Messiah smiles with a light nod of the head, and, the effect of the party juice having kicked in, begins dancing again with Gabi.

As Ode sets all four coins spinning again, his mind takes him into a waking subconscious regression dream of another different future life he'll live – in this life he's a Black child, around five.

But in this life there is pain, pain that Ode now begins to feel, an aching chest sensation that spreads to his arms, jaw and back, followed by nausea, fatigue and dizziness. Ode manages to break the train of thought by focusing on the coins, expertly flicking them to send them spinning in coordinated circles, weaving in and out of one another as though they're dancing to the music. It feels natural to Ode and easy to do, and he knows it's something he does in at least one other life.

Meanwhile, the spiritual elder Akachi is studying the detailed artistic drawings that Koolah has drafted. The Messiah had sat doodling the crayon drawings without any specific intention. Out of love for his black panther companion Jojo, many of the drawings were of combinations of himself and the beast as a symbol of eternal togetherness. One sketch shows Koolah's own face, with his long dreadlocks and handsome Black African features, combined with the body and feet of his beloved faithful friend, his black panther, Jojo.

Whilst nodding to the music, Akachi's clairvoyant mind has a flash of a future African statue they'll create with the face in Koolah's likeness. His psyche recalls the magnificent statue from Koolah's shared future visions in all its glory sitting with the pyramids and other amazing African buildings and statues from that future dimension era. He joyfully smiles as he realises that sketch in particular would turn out to be an early draft design drawing of what would be known later to the world as the Egyptian Sphinx. But then a pang of sorrow suddenly grips his soul as he remembers others of Koolah's multi-shared future visions: visions showing Greek armies invading, and also 7th century Asian armies, followed by European nations enslaving the indigenous inhabitants, taking the land, stealing its wealth also ridding it of nature's spirituality. The wise elder sadly shakes his head thinking sorrowfully of the visions showing those invaders disfiguring African statues: ordering their armies to remove the Black African noses and lips from Koolah's Sphinx and all other statues commemorating the Koolah tribe and all early Black civilisations to rid the world of any evidence of them. Koolah's visions showed the invaders foolishly removing all larger Black people's noses and lips from the statues in a bid to cover up Black Africa as the cradle of civilisation, Earth's first civilised race, and hide the fact from others that would come to Africa that every nation became civilised thanks to the true Egyptians who in fact were naturally Black.

A saddened Akachi places the drawing into a large book folder with an animal-skin brown suede binding tied with lace.

The exact same book is the one that finds its way to the year 1993 and sits on the huge antique desk in the reception room of Claudette's Haitian mansion. The job of the Black man who sits at the computer at the desk is to translate the sacred ancient magic to modern English and French. The content of what he's translating is what they'd recorded from Koolah's shared visions, including of Delica and other futuristic planets thousands and thousands of years into the future of today's Earth alignment. The Book of Koolah has all the secrets of the universe, spiritual enlightenment to be at one with God, all the ingredients for peace on Earth; it is nature's authentic bible.

Koolah pauses from dancing with Gabi as he notices the upset look on Akachi's face and senses the thoughts his soul mate's having about the future enslavement and colonisation of Mother Africa, the purpose of which is to oppress the Black race. Koolah smiles causing Akachi to return his smile. In turn Akachi tunes into Koolah's thoughts and suddenly both are nodding, then laughing, as they think about the present potent full moon ceremony linked with the preordained future 20th century reincarnation reawakening.

CHAPTER 12

Koolah looks deeply into Gabi's eyes. The effects of the Koolah tribe's Ayahuasca-like potion have truly kicked in and the natural high is bringing the real life of the universe alive. In Gabi's eyes he sees now directly through them to her soul. Her face also smiles as she does what will become the modern-day common shuffle dance, dancing around to the music. She hugs him up close, goes to whisper in his ear but instead twirls her tongue inside it, giving his whole body a beautiful tingling, fluttering sensation. He smiles as he explains the reaction, 'Gabi, each time, in each incarnation you surprise me with your tongue, it gives the same blissful feelings.'

She smiles. 'Koolah, join me, you know my soul exists to dance with you.'

Of all the women dancing, Gabi's soul moves her body to the beat the sweetest, creating an angelic movement. She and Koolah, gripped in a romantic embrace, dance the morning sunrise away.

After spending hours dancing in Koolah's arms, Princess Gabi releases her grip from him and dances off on her own, although staying close by, rotating around him. Her dancing is feminine and elegant but rhythmic and the moves she makes will be ones repeated by today's modern-day youngsters' souls. As she's moving to the beat of the sweet bongo drum rhythm, a burst of lightning and thunder causes her to open her eyes and she suddenly finds herself looking on a mixed-race female Delican alien being directly in front of her. The female alien is stunningly beautiful, Black and White mixed race, with curly ringlet hair to her shoulders, and an amazing physique that resembles Gabi's own. The alien is dressed in futuristic clothing, a sexy outfit with a skin-tight navy t-shirt, mini skirt and brown, shiny, heeled thigh-high boots, and actually looks like a perfect lifelike and life-size doll. She smiles ecstatically at Gabi and Koolah as she dances to the music. The strangest magical feeling comes over Gabi that she definitely knows the extra-terrestrial being very well but can't work out how, why or where from. More extraordinarily Gabi has the feeling that the alien somehow knows more about Gabi's own self than she does herself. Gabi also, of course, finds herself drawn in fascination to the alien's eyes, which like all Delican's, are almost three times the size of human eyes and the whites are the same colour of the iris, in this case a glossy dark brown.

Akachi too stares at the stunningly pretty Delican alien, but it seems that he, Gabi, Koolah and Ode are the only people in the crowd that can see her. The alien female gazes up to the sun above the treetops, as she dances, mouth pouting, feet shoulder-width apart, gyrating her hips, rocking her head side to side and twirling her index finger at eye level while shaking her backside to the beat. Princess Gabi feels the extra-terrestrial is inviting her to copy the moves and she does so beautifully. The alien responds by physically kissing the Black Princess. During that moment as they hug Gabi has the strangest feeling, like it was a reunion with a long-lost adult sister she'd been separated from since birth but a sensation a hundred times more intense.

The alien looks to Koolah and speaks to him by way of telepathy: 'Hello again, Benser.'

Koolah smiles. 'Hello to you again, Blee.'

He nods smiling at both females and Blee smiles vibrantly at Gabi for a considerable amount of time before nodding reassuringly and finally walking away.

Gabi looks to Koolah, her face expressing a look of puzzlement, as if to say, 'Did that just happen?'

Although Gabi didn't hear their voices by way of sound, her soul felt the vibration and she understood perfectly the telepathically communicated words between Koolah and Blee, and she can't escape the strange familiarity she has with the alien girl's name, Blee, or the name she's just called Koolah, Benser.

'Koolah, tell me you saw that strange-looking woman showing me how to dance like her. She was dancing, she just then looked right at you, and had some connection with you. Tell me I wasn't just imagining things due to the love juice.'

Koolah laughs as he watches the Delican mingle in the crowd, but Gabi begins to look genuinely anxious.

'Koolah, you both shared a moment.'

Suddenly he too begins to look nervous and instinct makes her hug him.

'Koolah, you're trembling what's wrong?'

His face slightly cringes as his mind scans a life he lived as the White blond blue-eyed slave boy on the alien girl's planet, Delica. He looks deep into Gabi's eyes with a brighter smile and she holds him tight, listening as he explains:

'Gabi, a planet we reincarnate to, the White beings are the enslaved and as in every reincarnation the soul of the female you just saw, Blee, and I are deeply in love.'

Immediately she's confused. 'Slavery, you've only told me of future slavery coming to the land where we live and now you say you lived as a White slave…'

'Yes Gabi, the Devil did the opposite on planet Delica; instead, the Whites were colonised, enslaved, oppressed in society and later compensated by way of reparations.'

Koolah notices that Gabi too has seen the Delican alien still present in the crowd. 'No,' he says, 'you're not imagining things, my darling. I too can see the Delican alien enjoying the vibration of the party with us.'

Gabi moves her head side to side watching the alien girl dance away through the crowds out towards the beach. 'What was she like as a lover, Koolah?' she asks, now visibly confused.

Koolah smiles proudly. 'As a lover…? Divinely structured as a lover, my Princess, perfectly designed for me. One that continuously instils the knowing it's actually impossible for anyone else to complete me, to complete this soul,' he laughs.

Gabi reacts angrily. 'What do you find so funny? You told me I was your other spiritual half of you.'

Koolah points with his eyes and finger towards everyone around having fun dancing and explains:

'My astral travels have revealed to the angels of the magic circle that we, our soul tribe, reincarnate to live lives on futuristic Planet Delica and more of the universe's evolved planets.'

Gabi faces Koolah and holds her palms firmly to his cheeks. The pair stand still as the drum beat bassline has the party rocking about them.

'Koolah, you're not answering my question,' she says. 'I felt a deep familiar love connection between the two of you... and I too feel a close connection to her...'

'Gabi, the alien girl just here *is* you,' Koolah interrupts her, rendering the Princess speechless. 'In another parallel dimension phase that's your soul reincarnated living on a futuristic alien planet, and named Blee. She wasn't just showing you how to dance, she was telling you she is you. Gabi, could you not feel it? You came back from Planet Delica, a future incarnation, and came through by way of crossing a dimension to make contact with you. Look, the alien Blee is us both; she is the other half of me in that incarnation as well as every life we live forever...'

With a vibrantly ecstatic smile, Gabi manages to get a single word out: 'How?'

'In the future the intruders of Africa will ransack our cities looking for what our writers are recording now, the magical Book of Koolah, which will contain our entire history and explain our Twin Flame existence using energy to become conscious in our other dimensions. They'll make a feeble attempt to rewrite my teachings in creating their religious books, calling me by the name Jesus. In future dimension phases Asian and Western religions, scientists, philosophers and others will feel they understand the vastness of our universe looking at it from a one-dimensional aspect. But due to their greed, hatred and fear–based God strategy, they will never discover the complexity of the multi-dimensional universe and true intricate mind of God, therefore never understanding we, the soul, have already lived all past and future lives. Every life and dimension phase is in the moment of now. It's written in our bible, our bible they will one day have in their possession. If their scholars were to study it from a high frequency love vibration, they too would later know how to cross dimensions as we have. God is love and the only way to find the key to access the magic and miracles of our great universe is to truly centre yourself, your soul, talk to your inner being, the soul, and tell yourself what you desire. God's spirit, the soul within each of us has no limit; we're talking God here. The secret is to truly know that the positive energy within is your vibrational state to manifest fates just as your future incarnation Blee has just shown you. Always maintain the positive vibration of love and the law of attraction will bring what you desire, including how to travel the multi-dimensional universe. Love will conquer all, Gabi. It's as simple as crossing from one dimension phase to the other, knowing is the key and you, the soul, can only know while in God's pure state of bliss...'

The shocked but much-relieved Gabi holds her palms to her chest. 'Koolah, that was I. I felt a strange familiarity within her. Goodness, that was I, my soul reincarnated myself in another body, crossed from another dimension. That makes so much sense and answers my inner feelings towards her. I thought you were speaking of someone else earlier, but you were speaking of me...'

She nods smiling and he returns her smile.

'Princess, this full moon ceremony will reveal even more amazing cross dimensions and cast the spell to keep our soul tribe together in future dimensions, not allowing the evil one to break the universal angel Twin Flame cycle...'

Relieved and relaxed, Gabi's eyes are mesmerised looking back into his. 'Tell me more, my influential spiritual being. Koolah, tell me how... make me understand why.'

Koolah leads Gabi away from the high volume of the party towards the quieter beach area where they walk as they talk. Jojo the black panther follows on behind them.

'Gabi, you and I are twin souls, one soul split in two; we, us one soul, live within two bodies. As you've suddenly realised, there's not a deeper love to be found in the universe than the Twin Flame union. My Princess, our soul tribe consists of just the divinely chosen original five hundred mystic members of our coastal village. You and I returned from Delica joining the village making it a population of five hundred. When I, the soul, returned from Delica and was re-born Abiona...'

He thinks of Gabi's particular Delican incarnation, the Black, grey-haired high-Afro woman next to the bed when his Benser body dies.

'You soon followed from Delica and have repeatedly, continuously reincarnated reborn within our now vastly populated city as have the rest of our soul tribe. We as a soul group of five hundred will remain together forever. When each of us reincarnates, they will re-join us in some capacity, continuously in another body in every life we live for an eternity.'

Gabi excitedly gasps, 'That makes so much sense, Koolah, and the name Abiona ties it all together. Your words have got me thinking about your early incarnation, the female Abiona. I remember dreaming you when you were the early incarnation of the female Messiah. Yes, I dreamed the early magic circle; the more I think about it, I was confused thinking how I was a young man in love with a female, Abiona. I remember calling you the name Abiona. It all makes sense; I just know it happened.'

She begins to think about something he'd said earlier. 'Twin soul, Koolah? Twin Flame like a soul mate, Koolah?'

They embrace on the beach, slowly rocking to the now distant music, and smiling he explains:

'A Twin Flame is something entirely different; twin souls are true power couples, my Princess Gabi. A soul mate is a soul identity created near you at the same time, in a similar geography, while a Twin Flame is a rare soul. There are only seventy-two thousand angels on Earth that have split into identical twins, not physical twins, spiritual twin souls. You and I are one soul. The five hundred of us, our soul tribe, make up two hundred and fifty of God's Earth angels. Twin souls will be known as Twin Flames; in the future one soul in two bodies, but in the spiritual we are one soul. When Twin Flames reunite in each life, it's not just to bring our own soul back into alignment as divine love; equally important, we are also here to help others do the same. We are here for the greater good to fulfil a mission beyond our personal development, to also aid the spiritual awakening of the planet.'

The twin souls Koolah and Gabi continue to hug and gently rock to the distant beat of the music as Koolah visualises the future intruders' bible, the modern-day King James and New Testament bibles:

'Many intruders of Africa will ransack our land and civilised cities over thousands of years. Their armies will return to their homelands and their scholars will translate what we've recorded thousands of years before into their religious books. But they'll distort everything because they won't want others to understand the twin soul are the true angels of the universe, but from our twin soul love stories they'll create the story of Adam and Eve. They will write several passages in their bibles, in particular in Genesis. However, their future powerful, controlling Bible will unintentionally fully acknowledge the spiritual union that two individuals can have. In Proverbs 18:24 it will teach, "but there is a friend who sticks closer than a brother". God made Twin Flames and the bible will inadvertently show proof of this. I showed the magic circle a future Christian bible during astral travel and we read Genesis 1:27 and it reads, "in the image of God He created him; male and female He created them." It says "him" and then "them". When speaking of God they speak of the spirit, the split soul in separate bodies male and female. Gabi, that's us; you and I are one soul in two bodies but in the spiritual one soul. The universe, God, planned it so around two hundred and forty-eight Twin Flame couples were present during our arrival from Delica…'

As he speaks, he shares a vision with her, visualising when his alien body Benser was dying with Gabi's future incarnation by his bedside when he passed on and the soul reincarnated to the ancient indigenous African tribe. In acknowledgement of her realising it was one of their Twin Flame unions, she smiles with a look of relief. Koolah continues his explanation:

'Part of the reason behind the vile future Asian and European slavery that will be inflicted on our land, and oppression of the Native Americans, indigenous Australians and others, will be because they will find who are the true angels of God. They will attempt to eradicate nature's spirituality, ridding all evidence from the minds of Black Africa, but in the later dimension the 20th century, twin angels will surface again.'

CHAPTER 13

'Gabi, our identical twin souls contain polarities, like a yin-yang, black-white, male-female, reflector- reflected, and when we come together in each lifetime and reconcile one of those polarities, we release one of the greatest creative powers in the universe, zero-point energy, because we are a recursion of the original act of creation. Angel, we are twin souls incarnated on Earth during this and every time to help the planet transition onto a new level of awareness and into a new reality. My Princess, God created you, I and other unique souls to make the constructive difference in the physical world.'

Koolah shares the visions in his mind with Gabi, showing Earth's future in 2023.

'A shift will take place; humanity will change; humans will truly question the religions they follow, those people and their preaching as to who the creator is. We're here to show them everything that comprises the entire universe is God. We select few souls are God's angels, created to change future Earth's way of living in order for this planet to survive.'

Koolah looks out at the ocean and glances back at his Twin Flame to see Gabi's physical smile is as radiant as he's ever seen it. She walks on past him, and he turns his head to see Gabi and Blee fall into one another's arms and the pair begin dancing on the white sandy beach.

Gabi looks deep into the huge eyes of the female alien, and says simply, 'I know.'

Blee smiles at Gabi's words, and replies, 'Good, now you know it's possible, you shall do it.'

Blee releases her grip and walks away along the beach, and Gabi holds the Messiah tightly. He begins to speak softly into her ear as he, the Princess and Jojo begin walking back along the beach towards the magic circle. As they walk, they hear the music getting louder and they sense the love they feel from the divinely blessed Twin Flame connection growing ever stronger, in turn causing Koolah to smile ever more brightly as he speaks of their deep inner emotion:

'There is no deeper love than finding the other half of your soul, no stronger attraction than being attracted to your own lost and found soul in a divinely designed body, our beautiful love story each incarnation. "Love at first feel" the energy vibration created is part of the shift process. It combines with our purpose, which is focusing on improving ourselves and being the best people and souls we can be, taking active and intentional steps to shift our own energy and the energy of those we come into contact with. We're angels roaming the Earth as humans, raising the vibration of the self and others, my Princess Gabi. We each, the soul within us, are a unique part of God's spirit and the responsibility of creating heaven on Earth will always lie with us. The future controlling religious leaders will have us wait for some greater force to come and change it knowing it will never happen. We will show how to rise up and step forth with our power, increase the glow and collectively create heaven on Earth by each being their highest possible vibration...'

Jojo brushes up against Koolah's leg and he and Gabi both pat and pet him. Koolah playfully wrestles Jojo to the sand of the beach. There are families on the beach, bathing and enjoying the festival, men, women and children, but none are fearful at the sight of the muscular, black, glossy-coated handsome big cat.

'...You and I forever, our soul will come together in union in each life for an eternity. We are one soul in two bodies, my Princess.

'When we're apart, even many miles away, our Twin Flame telepathy makes us able to see what one another's eyes see because our eyes share one soul, my Princess. The powerful unique energy we create makes us able to share with everyone what my eyesight and third eye sees. Twin souls are divinely orchestrated, brought together in union in each life to become whole to heal one another. The high vibrational love energy all Twin Flames create is important to our universe. I love the way God plans the way our pleasurable actions help others. We twin soul angels come together not just to heal our union, and ourselves but also to heal the world at large. The love we create fights against the negative forces that threaten to hijack our beautiful planets.

'Our love will grow and grow deeper each reincarnation; we are one soul, Gabi. Before sunset, I'll show you how to become conscious in our subconscious reality, the real life.'

They stop walking and Gabi lies down next to Koolah in the dip of the magic circle, closing her eyes to the glare of the sun.

'That's so beautiful,' Gabi says. 'How Koolah? Please explain how.'

'To dream of being somebody else is just another dimension phase your soul exists in. So, when dreaming you have to allow your psyche to know your desire to become conscious within the body of that dimension... To become conscious in that subconscious reality or any body from any dream...'

As Koolah speaks, the sensitive soul of Gabi begins subconsciously dreaming while awake, a recurring dream being conscious as the pretty European Romanian Gypsy girl called Princess – of being in Ibiza, aged in her early-twenties, and in love with the Black Londoner, Yanson Bailey. Gabi continues to hear the voice of the Messiah as she visualises her future incarnation:

'Gabi, in future dimensions when our souls astral travel, our images will only be seen by our original soul group unless we choose otherwise.'

The Ibiza dream fades from Gabi's mind and the African beach, Koolah and Jojo come back into focus.

'It's also up to us who we allow to see us in cross dimensions, as you did earlier crossing and appearing as your future dimension alien Blee body.

'Your reincarnated soul living in another dimension phase as a Delican alien just purposely crossed with us in this dimension and you revealed yourself to us. Our tribe are able to experience other dimensions of the universe. Other planets including Delica learned this from us…'

Gabi, fascinated by his words, asks, 'How Koolah?'

'The magic circle is the most spiritual spot, heaven on Earth and we are heaven's angels. I was born to the magical energy of the stone magic circle for the first time when we arrived here in a dimension long ago, and many more times before, but this is my most recent cycle. We within the magic circle learned how to free our minds from the conscious one-dimensional restraints the evil one has on the rest of the human race. We're here to show again in these later Earth dimensions and stage the reawakening. Delicans will also one day physically travel to Earth and reclaim the subconscious psyche. Think of all I've just explained and I'll pull you through…'

'Why do you not just do it now, Koolah, and save the Delican aliens the trouble?'

'No, we need to build our soul resistance by doing it for ourselves. Princess Gabi, your spirituality will also evolve to an even greater level.'

Gabi nods to show that she understands what the Messiah has explained. High on the mushroom concoction, she happily continues partying to the sweet music bongo beat and thumping bassline. The off-white, pink mist in the dip in the magic circle has risen to such a height that she and Koolah can at times barely see one another. As the mist falls to chest height, Gabi begins being silly as they dance. She crosses her eyes, repeatedly rolling her shoulders, moving her torso back and forth, wobbling her head, wiggling her gorgeous bottom. As she dances, she notices a powerful, divine, pleasantly bright light flickering all around. She dances up against Koolah, her nose almost touching his nose. Koolah holds her in his arms and looks through her dark brown and one half-blue eyes, deep into their soul. After a short while, his view comes from deep within her and Gabi's eyes have changed from her dark brown with one half-blue to ice blue with one eye half-brown, and her physical face and body have changed to the White Romany Princess.

Amnesia Nightclub, Ibiza, 1993

The smoke machine and strobe lights at Amnesia are in full effect and Gabi's conscious in her future incarnation, her body continuously doing its silly dance. In ancient Africa the Messiah smiles, realising their souls are actively conscious in other bodies, future incarnations, a dimension where the beat of the music is exactly how they'd left it at the Koolah ceremonial party. Gabi's mind is suddenly trying to work out when she'd fallen into the future-life progression recurring dream with Yanson Bailey again. Yanson begins speaking to her in English as they dance, and she understands the language he's speaking in, but what he's saying comes across as a continuation of Koolah's words of explanation:

'Princess, all humans continuously experience this crossover and call it dreaming. But we angel souls are evolved to a level able to consciously, physically explore the experience in-depth and be in control of our subconscious reality during this consciousness. Gabi, your spirituality will evolve to an even greater level. Earlier you were shown yourself living in another dimension phase conscious as Delican alien, Blee. You purposely crossed into the magic circle dimension and revealed yourself to us. Our tribe are also able to experience all other dimensions of the universe. I taught this on planet Delica where we reinstated our subconscious reality; it was a major factor in achieving world peace, eliminating third-world poverty and all other negative aspects of the planet. Our purpose on Earth is to do the same...'

A highly intoxicated Princess interrupts Yanson. Princess Gabi's soul's now fully conscious as the Romany Princess. Dancing to the music she looks puzzled and says, 'Yanson, I just had the craziest surreal vision that we were someone else, somewhere else...'

'That's because we are, Princess...' Yanson replies seriously.

'Yanson, why are you looking at me that way?'

'You know why, I explained I'd pull you through earlier, and have, Princess Gabi...'

She shakes her head, feeling as though she's hallucinating the divine revelation, and interrupts him saying, 'Darling, I'm buzzing off of my face, or as you would say in London… off my fucking trolley.'

He smiles at the Romanian's attempt at the London accent. 'Gabi, allow your mind to feel your Koolah Princess consciousness.'

The soul of Koolah is fully aware he's looking through the eyes of a future incarnation, that he and his Princess are conscious together in the future in the year 1993, but it takes Gabi time to grasp the situation, to realise that in the familiar subconscious dream state she can heed Koolah's advice and for the first time take control of herself in that physical dream, to determine what happens and be in control of her every word and move.

Her soul moves her modern-day White body to the rhythm. The beat of the music's the same as back in ancient Africa and she makes the same sweet body movements dancing. As she moves her body, clad in a sexy, stylish, cream-coloured modern-day classic Gucci designer swimsuit, with stiletto-heeled boots zipped up tight and slightly squeezing her gorgeous athletically toned thighs, Yanson notes that most of the nightclub, male and female, are mesmerised by his stunningly beautiful blonde's body and way of dancing.

She smiles as she dances, knowing in this life she's partying with the man who's rescued her from her kidnappers, high and happy on her favourite island, so happy she can't help continuously laughing; but also understanding so much more.

She calls out to Yanson, 'I've got it now, know I've fallen into a subconscious dream state, conscious in another incarnation, but for the first time I have total control; I dictate what I do. You helped me into this strange phenomenon.' Addressing him by a different name, she adds, 'I thank you, Koolah.'

She and Koolah's reincarnated bodies hold one another, and she looks over to the DJ stand, taking in the futuristic surroundings of the 1990s house music nightclub. Then Gabi's soul looks out of the eyes of her reincarnated body into the face of her Twin Flame: the Black Londoner, Yanson Bailey. They close their eyes and during a prolonged kiss he hears the sweetest words:

'Koolah, I want us to have our first child.'

Ancient City of Koolah

He opens his eyes to see his Black Princess, Gabi. She grips him tightly as they dance around, now back in the coastal jungle City of Koolah. The reincarnation love vibration he's just witnessed, combined with the hallucinogenic party tea, has only enhanced his natural love for her, and for the utopian lifestyle the people of the City of Koolah enjoy.

A bird's-eye daytime view of the City of Koolah would show amid the vibrant, lush jungle, the glorious sun shining on a magnificent stone city, golden stone buildings surrounding a tranquil rocky waterfall. The fresh clear water weaving through the huge rocks, cascading down onto indigenous families showering, bathing and swimming in an aqua-blue lagoon, and a stream running through the city and out to the nearby ocean. The adult members of the population spending their days swimming in the sea, getting high, acting silly partying, dancing to a sweet rhythm, then sunbathing, making love and cooling off by bathing under nearby lukewarm falling waterfalls, before sleeping and waking to glorious sunrises to enjoy the daily tranquillity of their deeply magical spiritual existence once again — a lifestyle of only good vibes and peace.

The central feature of the city is the large opening they called the magic circle, Earth's spirit world or simply heaven on Earth. Day and night huge clusters of clear-then-colourful raindrop-shaped particles, unable to be touched and not having any physical presence, dart around it like the children's bubbles blown from a tiny hoop, souls having left their dead bodies, appearing in the circle, then selecting which life they wish to live and disappearing off to their appropriate conceiving womb. They could too be seen all around the city and out at sea but were always clustered more densely around the magic circle with its sacred engraved stone floor. It and many other authentic divine spots around the African continent were used to stay connected with the multi-dimensional universe before intruders came and forced man's invention religion on the African continent.

Invaders wouldn't begin to impose their separatist religions and borderlines on the people of the Kingdom of Kush, the land of the Black people in North East Africa later renamed Egypt, and the African continent as a whole until nine or ten thousand years later. Back then, the pristine land was of the spiritual oneness, one blood, one people, one love in God and the knowing of nature's soul reincarnation, the divine cycle of life. Much later, many thousands of years later, the more-than-curious Asian scholars would travel by land and or across the Red Sea into Kush. They'd be welcomed on the seashore with open arms and smiles, taken into the city. They were shown the same spiritual mind-blowing Black magic by the much later descendants of the Koolah tribe. Subsequently, the enlightened Arabs continuously returned to their Asian continent and their leaders, explaining the Black Koolah soul tribe's many magnificent, great spiritual wonders.

CHAPTER 14

In the ancient City of Koolah near sunrise, joyful party music plays as the usual knee-high, still and calm, off-white, pink mist blankets the magic circle stone area on the beach. The mist gives off a welcoming vibration, a safe feeling that would pull you in towards it. One tribal angel chants as he uses a bamboo stick to push artistically painted pebbles together. Koolah and another angel look into one another's eyes and the woman gives a reassuring smile and vigorous nod of the head. Koolah then speaks to two male soul tribe angels:

'Akachi, Imani, open your eyes. Claudette has reopened the passageway; she awaits you on the other side. Go through and intensify our awakening; you're to join another of our lost souls with others.'

The cute boy Imani who is lying on his belly slowly rises to his feet, accommodating thousands of bumble bees attached to the entirety of the back of his body, head and legs. With the aid of the boy's hand and a six-foot-long walking stick, the towering tribal male elder Akachi too stands. Once on his feet, he loosens his grip from the boy and gently strokes the black panther Jojo on the neck. Attached to his stick are hollowed containers filled with dried beans, exactly how old Rafiki in Disney's *Lion King* movie has them. In fact, Akachi resembles Rafiki but in human form, being wide-eyed, bald on top of the head, with a greying beard. He's responsible for helping perform ceremonies, but always has a youthful attitude and is fond of joking around. Jojo stands against the vibrant full moon creating an immaculate big cat silhouette as heaven's angels look out towards the ocean and moonlit African night sky. Akachi looks downward to see the pink mist covering their shins has become unsettled. Part of the misty cloud begins twirling, swirling and twisting, small puffs becoming entwined, and the continuous movement creates a tightly formed two-metre high ten-metre-long tunnel passage. Suddenly a pitch-dark opening appears at the end of the tunnel. The man and boy walk through the passage and stop at the pitch-dark opening. As they focus deeper into the blackness a different shade of black, a tall large upright rectangular shape comes into focus. The child is the first to confidently walk through, followed by the more cautious older, tall, grey-bearded Akachi.

Instantly amid the darkness of the room they've entered, the whispering French accent of Claudette greets them. As the indigenous tribesmen walk forward, they suddenly see her mesmerising brown glistening eyes faintly in the darkness – beautiful eyes which once seen, you'd never forget. Then her petite brunette form becomes clear to them and they see the Haitian witch before them. She speaks native Koolah to the man and boy: 'Come come, follow me, he's in here, shush…'

Claudette, Imani and Akachi congregate in the middle of the room and the boy turns his head looking back to see he has entered the room through a gigantic beautifully crafted antique floor-to-ceiling mirror. Within the mirror the pink cloud tunnel, Koolah magic circle and ancient African moonlit coastline can be seen in the distance.

Elsewhere in the world, moments after resting his head on the pillow and switching off the bedside lamp and TV, twenty-nine-year-old Black Londoner Daniel Cottle feels at first an eerie, then pleasurable rush throughout his entire head and body, causing his heart to beat hard; then the silence is broken by Claudette's softly spoken feminine French-accented voice:

'Breathe in deeply, mon chéri. Breathe in positive energy, Jarrod, and out the negative…'

Later Imani and Akachi return through the tunnel onto the magic circle and the angels of the Koolah tribe stand to look through the mist cloud opening to see Daniel Cottle looking through the Voodoo mirror to them from the other direction. They can see the darkness of the room and Daniel can see the brightness of the vibrant ancient city. Outside the stone circle, the party's in full flight, with a joyful sweet sounding rhythm and dancing all around the city, in the jungle, along the clear water beach and even into the sea – humans enjoying the purest heavenly vibration.

Leyton, East London, England
December 1974

The peace of the afternoon is shattered by the high-pitched screeching of car tyres followed by a prolonged sound of a car horn.

The commotion wakes Detective Sergeant Jan Harris who's recently fallen asleep alone in her warm, parked Ford Escort. For a moment her mind's still present in the serene dream she'd been having, a dream of being present in the ancient tribal City of Koolah. She feels the vibration of the bright off-white, pink mist carrying the unique creative energy and thinks fondly of the spiritual elder Akachi, the bee-friendly boy Imani and the others, and of Koolah and the black panther at his side. She knows all present share Koolah's telepathic astral-travel visions and the sound of his voice narrating the visions. But the dream of the vibrant lush jungle city with its blissful spiritual vibration fades and she looks out her car's windows at the contrasting, grotty, bleak 1970s London council estate that surrounds her. She's an attractive, cute-featured, spectacle-wearing, pleasant brunette who now yawns and stretches her neck, slowly moving her head left to right as she manually raises her reclined driver's seat.

A huge dog starts barking loudly from a high-rise's first floor balcony in response to the car horn, and an enraged Black man is out of his car hurling Jamaican-style abuse at the Pakistani lady who's pulled out in front of him, causing him to swerve to avoid a serious accident to himself and his family. After a short while the cars from both parties go on their way, memories of the near miss taken with them.

Jan stays in her car. It's a bright sunny but bitterly cold winter afternoon and she had left her engine running and heater blaring whilst parked outside one of the three high-rise tower blocks of the estate and drifted off to sleep. She looks at her watch and huffs, 'Useless blooming watch.' It had stopped, so Jan turns up the radio and catches the national radio news bulletin being read:

'...Police have confirmed the foreman of the jury from the Lewin-gang armed-robbery trial accused of perverting the course of justice has been released on bail, having surrendered his passport and a curfew order having been imposed. The juror, who cannot yet be named for legal reasons, stands accused of having manipulated fellow jury members in order to attain a not guilty verdict in the trial. The case had attracted widespread media attention because the men accused are allegedly the nation's most prolific and wealthiest armed robbery gang who appear to have a number of celebrity friends, among them the British Hollywood based film star China Marie and her now estranged husband Ronnie Day.

'On to sport now and Derby County remain top after destroying Chelsea in the midweek clash last night at Stamford Bridge...'

Jan knew the case; it was all some of her colleagues talked about. Ricky Lewin, more commonly known as Flash Ricky his brother Geoff and six other members of their gang had been arrested months ago but the attempt to bring them to trial and conviction had been troubled from the outset. Of course, it didn't help that Flash Ricky had connections. The actress China Marie might be a Hollywood name but she was born in West London and her husband Ronnie Day was an East End gangster if ever there was one. Then there was Lewin's childhood friend, the now notorious Eric Nevin and, of course, another close friend Nevin's love rival and bitter underworld adversary the flamboyant wealthy Jamaican property magnate, Nathaniel 'Cutty' Robinson. The Robinson gang were still heavily implicated in the disappearance and possible murder of East London pub landlord and once convicted murderer himself, Gus "Piggy" Andrews.

Initially the Lewin robbery jury at the trial failed to reach a verdict and when continuously asked by the judge to keep deliberating they came in with not guilty verdicts on all defendants. Police officers who'd attended court were seen seething at the fact Ricky and company had been acquitted of all charges. Since the acquittal the foreman of the jury, who in Jan's view was obviously guilty, had been indiscreet, having seen to have been on a flamboyant spending spree, including a holiday to Spain, a new car and jewellery...

Still yawning but having paid rapt attention to the newsreader's words, Jan turns the radio down. Placing her hands in front of the heating vent and rubbing them together, her mind wanders back to her dream.

In her head she can still hear the tribal music, and she shivers pleasurably, laughs and says out loud to herself while shaking her head: 'That has got to be the most beautiful and real dream I'd ever had. That waterfall, jungle and what was that pinkish cloud and black panther all about...?'

She looks at herself in the interior mirror and thinks back on her life that has led her to be outside the high-rise tower blocks of the Oliver Close council estate waiting for a child and two social worker colleagues to emerge from one of their graffiti-covered, rubbish-littered exits. She had never set out to be a police officer; neither would she ever like or get used to the idea. It all began with her being an abused and battered but rescued young mother. Before that Jan had been a passionate teenage follower of the '60s flower power hippie movement and had enjoyed every high available those days. Her unintentional police career began when she decided to help other battered wives, putting a little back. Before she knew it, she'd developed a passion for her job and her paid profession became assisting the police, liaising with victims of any sensitive nature. One thing led to another, and a female detective suggested Jan would make a great contribution by joining the police. On the understanding that she was only doing so to make a positive difference to any victim, she fell into becoming a police officer and subsequently made sergeant. Her active sergeant role in the force included normal detective duties in the local area. For these she didn't much care, but she did care for her specific occupation within the Metropolitan Police of being a Family Liaison Officer, of which she was now a highly experienced and effective one having done the job for many years. She was drafted in on delicate issues such as those surrounding tragic child abductions and murder investigations. Her work took her anywhere in Britain helping families come to terms and cope with their grief. Police had also called upon her expert advice flying her across the world to places including Australia, Europe, Japan, the United States and what were becoming the hotspot kidnap zones of Latin and South America.

Call it fate or coincidence, but Sergeant Jan Harris was first on the crime scene at both the horrific Cottle family tragedies. Over the years, she'd learned not to take her work personally, but there was something about these cases that preoccupied her in and out of work, and this had contributed to her marital separation. What Jan couldn't have understood was the spiritual connection she had to Daniel Cottle and his mother, the fact of her Koolah angel soul sharing an ancient bond with the child and in fact also his deceased mother. It just felt to Jan as though she had developed more than a soft spot for the child victim, feeling a strange love for him as though he were her own.

She looks up suddenly to see the two women from the children's social services emerge from the exit to the flats accompanied by Daniel Cottle – two White women escorting a ten-year-old Black kid – and her heart begins to have palpitations. She hadn't seen the boy since assisting with both separate family tragedies over the past year. The social workers are struggling with two heavy bags each, some of his personal items, and the sight of him only causes her to feel worse. She's shocked how Daniel Cottle has deteriorated from the last time she'd seen him. Only months previously, he'd been full of himself; a once spirited, immaculately presented, healthy boy, now withdrawn and bowing his head in the presence of others, his hair untidy – and most shocking of all to Jan was his weight loss, which was now more evident as he got closer to her and she could see the scrawny look of his face. She searches his hazel/blue eyes for a hint of some of their former sparkle. Once they reach the car, one of the care workers opens the rear door behind Jan and seats the boy in the car, whilst her colleague loads the bags into the boot before going back to retrieve two more bags from outside the tower-block lift.

The sight of the child now up close in her car causes Jan to re-live the horrific memories of both gory scenes, and although she knows she has to try emotionally to keep it together, the feelings come flooding back, recollections, the aftermath. She holds back from crying and forces a smile but finds herself unable to maintain eye contact.

'Hello again Daniel,' she manages to say. 'How's things been with you, young man?'

He doesn't answer and as soon as the other social worker returns with the bags and has loaded them in the car, Jan begins to drive the car slowly away.

Up on the seventeenth floor of the high-rise, Daniel's chubby Jamaican aunt Joy, who's been looking after him is stood tearful on the balcony with a framed photo in hand. Watching as the car drives away, she says quietly, 'I'm so sorry Daniel, I didn't know what else to do.'

Inside the car both care workers know Jan's feelings towards Daniel and feel at any moment she'll break down. Jan sniffles and her voice is almost breaking as she tries again to engage the boy in conversation:

'It's me Jan, you remember me, I stayed with you at your home in Pretoria Avenue, Walthamstow with you, your brother and sister the odd night.'

She thinks back and a smile comes across her face at the memory.

'Came and got you from school with my daughter, Sally. Remember you two playing over the park opposite your home?'

The mention of the park, making him think back to happy times he and his Jamaican mother shared there, saddens the child deeper. At the sight of his expression, which she glances in the rear-view mirror, a tear rolls down Jan's cheek.

She perseveres, but it's apparent to both welfare officers that her words and happy act are ever more strained. 'So tell me, what've you been up to?'

Again there's no reply from the boy.

'Remember I was helping when your mum…'

Suddenly Jan stalls the engine as the car is moving along the busy street in slow traffic and it lurches to a halt. The welfare officers can't understand why the police officer's gone and mentioned the child's mother; it feels like a terrible blunder, and Jan herself feels the same. As Jan restarts the car, the three women are surprised to see a bright smile on the pretty, hazel-bluish eyed Black boy's face.

He excitedly looks into their eyes and politely speaks: 'Please… can you take me to my mother? I want to tell her sorry for what happened to Dad…'

He takes in the appalled looks on the welfare officer's faces and his demeanour changes rapidly. 'Where is she…? Could you please take me to her?' Raising his hand to his mouth, he shakes his head and begins to quietly cry, 'Please… I want my mum… mum. I want my mum…'

The policewoman looks at the tearful child's image in her rear-view mirror and has a flashback of him dressed in his blood-soaked Paddington Bear pyjamas that were once white. All three women are completely lost for words and their silence causes the sobbing, pleading boy to again look downward.

Back at the Oliver Close council estate, looking out from her seventeenth storey balcony, Daniel's aunt Joy is still distraught. She sobs hysterically, now carrying the feeling she's let her best friend down. She's allowed her deceased friend's youngest child to be taken by social services. Looking up to the sky, she cries and cries, repeating, 'Lord Jesus… God forgive me. Me sorry, Pearl. On top of my anxiety, depression an' high blood pressure, I just couldn't deal with it.'

Eventually Joy comes in from the balcony and sits on the sofa holding a framed happy photo of the Cottle family. Looking at the smiling image of Daniel in the picture, she sobs, 'Son, so sorry, son, me never know what else I can do…'

In the back of the car, ten-year-old Daniel has fallen back into silence. The words he has just spoken are the first he has said to anyone in a year. The only time he spoke was asking when his beloved mother was coming to get him. His mind is in a distant, cold place, and his depression is so deep he takes little notice of the outside world. He doesn't recognise Jan Harris as the person that helped the children of the family, him especially, through the shocking trauma; and she can see in his vacant eyes that her familiarity is having no effect. His soul is numb with the pain of suddenly being alone.

Church Hill Children's Care Home, Walthamstow

After the drive of three or four miles to Walthamstow, Jan parks her car outside Church Hill Children's Care Home. As Daniel and one of the social workers get out of the vehicle, a local pretty Black Jamaican mother Shirley Bailey and her children approach in the distance. As they get closer and slow down, it's apparent that the Bailey family are shocked at the appearance of the now scrawny and depressed-looking child Daniel Cottle. Neither her nor her children have seen him in the neighbourhood or at the school since it all happened within the past year.

Jan Harris can't hold back her tears as she addresses the other social worker. She wipes away her tears as she speaks, but the sorrow in her voice is obvious:

'Why hasn't anyone mentioned anything? The child can't know the details but needs some kind of closure. He hasn't got to be told of her death until he's old enough but needs to get used to the fact she's not coming to get him. It'll be a shock to his system, but the uncertainty is torturing his young mind. The longer it goes on the more it will affect his adulthood...'

The welfare officer shares Jan's sorrowful emotion, but just reacts with a shake of the head. She gets out of the car and Jan follows.

The other social worker, standing with Daniel outside his new place of residence, points upward to the first-floor window and says, 'That will be your new bedroom, Daniel. Isn't it a lovely house?'

Shirley Bailey's children are all mixed race except the second eldest, the darkest of the five, her ten-year-old boy, Yanson Bailey. Yanson slows looking sad to see Daniel Cottle being escorted into the notorious children's home. He's not seen him since the horrific Cottle family tragedies first became the much-talked about and on-going international news story. The fascination of the moment causes Yanson to lose concentration and walk directly clattering into the front wing of Jan Harris's stationary vehicle. Jan turns to look, the boy's and the policewoman's eyes meet and her immediate thoughts are, firstly, how much Yanson and Daniel Cottle look alike and, secondly, she recognises Yanson as someone who'd been in trouble with the police before. However, she nevertheless feels herself drawn towards him. Shirley curses her son for being clumsy, but the choked-up police officer smiles with a shake of the head, and raises and waves a hand in a manner to say 'It's ok.' As Jan and Yanson exchange looks, their eyes lock and she feels a strange connection that causes her to smile through her tears.

Later, having said her goodbyes, Jan drops off the social workers and, now officially off duty, begins her drive home. Nevertheless, she switches on her police radio. Immediately she hears of a local incident: a young White couple, husband and wife, are victims of a horrific car crash. A WPC's voice sounds over the airwaves:

'...hit and run driver, fatal collision, caused vehicle to turn upside down spinning into a lamppost both passengers crushed, driver fatal... on the lookout for a white Ford Escort M registration. Fire crew cutting out pregnant passenger in urgent need of assistance, ambulance on route, over...'

Jan snatches up her police radio's microphone and says, 'Sergeant Harris here. How's the mother doing, over?'

'Jan, doesn't look good; she was due to give birth, actually driving to the labour ward, Whipps Cross Hospital. WPC at the scene trying to keep her talking but doesn't look hopeful, over...'

Meanwhile, Daniel Cottle sits in his new bedroom alone with his painful thoughts, feeling responsible and riddled with a guilt that's been eating him from the inside out for months. His depressive state has brought him to an unimaginable crossroad in his young life. He doesn't want to wake another morning, at times wishing he were dead. He sits on the edge of the bed, too distraught to cry. He eventually looks up to take in his new surroundings. In contrast to the cosiness of the warm pastel-coloured bedroom he once had in his clean, loving family home, dirty scuff marked white walls in much need of redecoration now surround him. The new unfamiliar environment carries a distinct cold and industrial feel and creates a longing in him for that snug pillow, motherly cuddles and nightly bedtime story. Instead, one of the night staff is arguing loudly with an aggressive older teenage male youth in the room next door. Their raised voices cause Daniel to look up at the partitioning wall. He sits thinking how he detested seeing his mother going through the brutal suffering and wishing he could somehow turn back the clock with the exclusion of his father relentlessly brutalising her.

Jan Harris's home, Chingford, Essex

Now back at her Chingford home, Jan Harris listens on the phone to what a male colleague speaking from Chingford police station is saying:

'...lost the mother, she didn't make it, Jan, but managed to save the baby, mother had already named her Melissa. The baby's aunt and uncle have taken her in overnight and the older children are under expert supervision of care workers. Doctors managed to deliver the baby successfully... hello Jan, are you still there...?'

Jan doesn't reply; instead she just hangs up the receiver and slumps down on her sofa.

Church Hill Children's Care Home, Walthamstow

The next evening outside the Church Hill Children's Care Home a blond-haired White man, the typical flash East London wide boy gangster type, looking not unlike a young Ray Winstone, sits in his car smoking a marijuana cigarette and looking up at Daniel Cottle's bedroom window. The man is Charlie Baker. He's only twenty-two years old but is already a seasoned arm robber. His waking dream of that morning had been at the front of his mind all day, dictating he had to drive round to the children's care home. He still pictures the dream clearly in his mind, a dream he often has of being an 18th century pirate in the company of a cute White dark-haired hazel-bluish eyed boy who shared Daniel Cottle's nickname, Jarrod. During the dream and often thinking while he's awake Charlie always finds himself drawn to a young Black woman, a Haitian Voodoo witch called Lana. She's always practising African Black magic in each and every dream he has of that time period. In his most recent dream, the white boy pirate Jarrod had woken from a nightmare explaining to him and Lana that he'd dreamed being a black boy called Daniel Cottle and killing his father. The White boy Jarrod is actually adamant he is the Black kid Daniel Cottle. Both the boys, Jarrod in the dream and the Cottle kid Charlie's seen in person have the same eyes, not just in colour and physically but subconsciously Charlie knows both boys' eyes mirror the same soul. The vibration of what young Jarrod explained in the dream causes Charlie's mind to connect both kids as one. He finishes his marijuana cigarette and drives away, now consciously feeling sorry for the child Daniel Cottle having to carry the heavy burden, the guilt of killing his parents. The young villain deeply feels he needs to do something for the lonely Cottle child but doesn't yet know what.

CHAPTER 15

The next evening Charlie Baker is moved to actually ring the doorbell of the children's home. The door is answered by Kim Davis, the senior care worker in charge there for the evening. She's mixed race, Black and White, originally from Liverpool, young, attractive but slightly on the large side. She'd been watching the early evening news on TV and certainly wasn't expecting any visitors, so she'd peered through the pane of glass to study the face of the ruggedly handsome Charlie Baker before opening the door. She knows for a fact she's met him before, just can't be precise as to where.

The first thing she says as she looks into his eyes is, 'I've seen you before…'

Charlie assumes she must have seen him hanging about in the market, but the reality is she had seen him at his father's High Street betting shop, the local hangout for the local villains. Her psyche also relates to subconsciously knowing him, the soul he embodies, in a previous life where he physically appeared identical.

Charlie smiles as he speaks: 'Yeah, me name's Charlie Baker; me family have always owned the betting office in the market.'

She smiles nodding. 'That must be it. Anyway, what can I do for ya?'

He looks sincerely into her eyes. 'The boy Jarrod.'

A puzzled look appears on Kim's face. 'Jarrod, that name sounds very familiar, but we don't have a Jarrod child resident at present.'

Charlie chuckles slightly. 'Oh sorry love, I mean Daniel. Jarrod's a nickname we've given him locally.'

She smiles a relieved smile. 'Oh, I've only been down from

Liverpool a short while, not that familiar just yet. Daniel Cottle, yeah he's here, but what's the connection?'

'I was close to the parents and he's practically a son to me. Called me uncle since he was a toddler.'

Kim looks deeply into the young man's eyes with a sudden smile. 'My God, I got it now, you and the rest of the Lewin gang have recently been released from prison. I've watched the news headlines on the telly.'

Something tells Kim it will be ok to show Charlie up to the Cottle boy's room, and she does so. They enter to find Daniel just sitting on the edge of his bed with a vacant expression. Other than slightly rocking his body back and forth, he is motionless. Charlie sits himself down on the empty bed next to Daniel's so that he's sitting opposite the boy.

Charlie's visibly saddened by the physical and mental state of the boy now that he sees him so close up. He tries to make eye contact with Daniel and shuffles himself a little way towards him.

'Hello son, it's me, your Uncle Charlie.'

Daniel doesn't acknowledge him at first, but as Charlie takes out a fifty pence coin and sets it spinning on the bedside table between the beds, the boy briefly returns his smile before looking away again. Kim sees this and gasps joyfully, but the smile is gone as quickly as it appeared, and as Charlie reaches into his pocket for another fifty pence piece and flicks the two of them spinning simultaneously rotating in tandem, there's no further response from the boy. As the coins begin to slow and their spinning subside, Charlie repeats the action but there's still no reaction from Daniel. Nothing gets a response from the child.

Eventually Charlie decides it's time to go and a smiling Kim says as she holds the front door open for him to let him out, 'Didn't think he had a smile left in him, at least you got a reaction, that's more than anyone else… The only words he's said to me is he don't want to take his coat off because he wants to be ready when his mum comes. Breaks me bloody heart to hear him say that… his little face…'

After letting Charlie out, Kim makes her way to a shared boys' room that's literally next door to Daniel's. Daniel hears her speaking to the two occupants, the Stephens brothers who are two and three years older than Daniel and strapping Black boys for their ages:

'Albert and you Alex Stephens, I've noticed a lot of unfamiliar items in your room lately. I hope you haven't been out there bullying and taxing again…'

The younger of the two, Alex, replies, 'No Kim, I promise… relatives gave them to us.'

Alone in his room, Daniel cries.

CHAPTER 16

Pirate Vessel, *The Haitian Witch*, Jamaica, Caribbean, 1756

On board *The Haitian Witch* the child pirate Jarrod and others of the crew have just finished eating their breakfast. The ship's a huge ex-slave cargo ship taken from its original French owners and renamed *The Haitian Witch* by its pirate captain Jim Morgan, and commonly known within the criminal underworld and even among Royal Navy officers as simply *The Witch*. Captain Jim Morgan, male Haitian pirate Raphael, and petite female Oriental pirate Yu Yan, sit around the huge circular table in the captain's cabin. Morgan looks the image of Charlie Baker, the only differences being that Morgan has matted dreadlocks hair and beard, is deeply tanned, has a thin scar through his left eye and hobbles with a slight limp. The captain's nephew Jarrod is also at the table, but the infant sits on the table with his feet rested on the chair. He has the look and skulduggery character of a boy who's jumped from the pages of the Charles Dickens novel *Oliver Twist*.

Also present are Haitian Black Voodoo witches Lana Deframe and her younger sister Natasha, but they sit on the floor in front of a Voodoo shrine practising old African magic. Lana's twenty-six years of age, attractive with a pleasant smile, huge lips and eyes that look as though she's purposely always got them opened wide. She could be said to be weighty on the legs but carries it wonderfully well. The pirate ship is actually named after her, due to the magical protection spells she casts for the vessel and crew. Eyes closed, Lana speaks to the boy, and the pirate crew respectfully quieten down: 'Jarrod, tell me more of your on-going dream you was explaining to your uncle this morning, the same scene you've dreamed for years. You say you killed your father and still don't know where your mother is…'

The boy pirate's mind flashes through the terrible bloody scenes, from the death of Clinton Cottle to his waking dream of being in the 1970s children's home, Charlie on the opposite bed with Kim present. Jarrod looks towards his uncle Jim Morgan and breaks out into a huge smile as he explains the most recent of the recurring and on-going dreams.

'Uncle Jim came to me in my dream again last night. I was in a room, a room I hadn't dreamed before.'

Natasha looks on as her big sister Lana's smile becomes brighter. Eyes still closed, Lana says to the child, 'Yes. I see it too, Jarrod.'

Jarrod explains more as the Haitian witch sits smiling nodding her head: 'Uncle Jim always looks different, short hair, no beard or scar on his face and his skin's lighter. But it is Uncle Jim…'

The cuteness of the child's voice causes Lana to break out in a smile, as does Yu Yan at the table.

Jarrod stops thinking about the dream and looks across at the cabin mirror to see himself reflected in it: a White child with thick curly long dark hair, a mass of freckles and blue-hazel eyes – eyes that are identical in every way to the child he dreams of being, the future Black child Daniel Cottle's. He looks deeper into the huge eight-by-twelve foot uniquely engraved Voodoo mirror and sees the reflection of modern-day Haitian witch Claudette smiling back. In the mirror's reflection she's seated at the table, but when Jarrod quickly looks back to the room she's not actually present, and then neither when he quickly looks back to the mirror.

The crew notice a sincere look of sadness on the boy's face as he speaks confidently with a strong London Cockney accent:

'I feel terrible, Lana, a strange feeling. I'm the Black kid Daniel. I dream about my father beating my mother, dream I wake to her screaming as he punches and kicks her, and I wake to her screaming out in another part of the house…'

Jarrod points to his own face as he's explaining:

'I, me Jarrod, I killed my father. I was dreaming. It was as though I was angry, inside the Black boy's body, and decided to kill him. I still feel the guilt every time I dream it because he's feeling so terrible. I really miss my mother.'

It's hard for Jarrod to explain how he's actually conscious experiencing the emotion of being heartbroken over his mother. Lana opens her eyes and, with a reassuring smile, looks directly into the eyes of the child. 'How do you know he misses his mother?' she asks.

Confused, Jarrod raises, then lowers his shoulders in a slight huff. 'I miss her because I'm him, Lana. I feel all that he feels. When I'm him I haven't the heart for killing. Lana, when I dream of being the Black boy, my mother calls me Daniel, but most people still call me Jarrod.'

Captain Morgan suddenly looks intrigued, and Lana's easy smile encourages the boy to say more and Lana laughs and turns to the mirror speaking to the child's reflection. 'How do you feel about his mother, Jarrod?'

The child begins to cry as he explains. 'Honestly, as though she is my mother and really love her as much as my real mother in Australia. That's why I killed him, he was hurting her.'

Lana gets up and walks to the table. She stands behind Jarrod and puts a palm on each of his shoulders, comforting him and he turns falling into an emotional hug with the Haitian witch. 'I'll call on spirit and see what they reveal, Jarrod'

Church Hill Children's Care Home, Walthamstow

In the Church Hill Children's Care Home at midnight Daniel is woken from his sleep by the sound of his room door opening. He wakes in panic but relaxes at the sound of a soft female voice saying, 'Well hello.' He looks up to see a smiling, chubby, friendly-faced, young teenage White girl.

'Your light was on,' she says, 'and you're still dressed. You should get your pyjamas on and get into bed; it's well past half eleven. I'll tell you what, would you like a hot chocolate, Daniel? Kim's asleep in her chair; I'll sneak into the kitchen, make us one and get some biscuits. I'm having one, really delicious, yummy...'

Daniel nods and as she goes off he gets up and walks to the window to see it's raining and he can just about make out two figures sitting in a prestigious navy-blue E-type Jaguar parked directly outside.

Although Daniel couldn't know it at the time, the men were two well-known Black London gangsters, Nathaniel Robinson and Flash who were sat having a conversation actually about Daniel. Men didn't come tougher or with a colder streak than Mr Nathaniel 'Cutty' Robinson. He was among the nation's elite wealthiest gangsters and had personally killed men in cold blood on more than one occasion. Cold-blooded killer that he was, he still sat in that car riddled with guilt believing there was no one but himself to blame for creating the hardship and sorrowful situation the Cottle boy found himself in. Day and night, Mr Robinson knew he alone was responsible for the deaths of the boy's parents and that the child would one day carry the burden being responsible for the death of his beloved mother. What made it worse was the London-based Jamaican gangster was very close to the boy's parents when they were alive.

His fellow gangster Flash points up at the window and the sight of the boy's silhouette there causes Nathaniel's heart to beat faster and his body to break out in a cold sweat.

'Flash, man seriously need fe take the boy out of there, him muss be suffering.'

Flash replies earnestly, 'An' fockin' take him where, Cutty? I understand how you feel, the boy is family but think about what that would create, how it would look. It would get people talking and create a huge problem for you. It soun' sad, the child is suffering but we can't do nothing about it right about now.'

Daniel sits back down on the bed as he waits for the girl to return, and the memory of Mum always making him a chocolate before bed comes flooding back to him. His thoughts flit between memories of his present life and memories from his dreams. He thinks of the 18th century ship's cabin, the large Voodoo mirror and his face as the White pirate boy Jarrod reflected in it – a face with eyes that he knows are his own eyes.

Sitting on his bed the Black child Daniel Cottle holds his hands up in front of his face and turns them backwards towards him. He says to himself in his mind, 'I was White, I know it was me but how...?'

Then his thoughts drift to a time just before the horrific incidents the previous Christmas – thinking what could have caused his father to become a violent, abusive drunk constantly relentlessly battering his mother? He hears the boys' voices from the room next door, but tries to block them out by focusing on the scuff-marked wall. He recalls his father, Clinton Cottle a powerhouse of a man, just getting increasingly more drunk and violent as time went on, but even so Daniel's mother Pearl, still gave her husband, and all three children, love and affection throughout. Daniel always felt she was the gentlest soul in the world and few who knew her would actually disagree. His mind keeps coming back to the question: Where is she? He misses her desperately. He knows his father is dead, but no one has told him where is mother is. What's more, he hasn't seen his brother and sister for months. He doesn't understand why he's been separated from them or know where they are either.

He tries to clear his mind, at least for a moment, of the negative thoughts that have been circulating in his head for the past year, having taken him to the point where each morning he wakes up thinking that if things can't go back to how they were he'd rather not wake up at all. However, his thoughts just take him back to a time just before the first of the two horrific incidents.

CHAPTER 17

Things were so different for Daniel just a year ago. One afternoon in December 1973 Daniel had been sitting in the large private back office at the Jamaican gangster Nathaniel 'Cutty' Robinson's barbershop on the Tottenham High Road, North London. With him in that back office were a group of North East London's criminal elite, Black and White, men and women, among them the stunningly pretty Jamaican madam-prostitute Elsie, aka 'Tricks'. Daniel clearly remembers her words to him that day: 'Daniel, you're too soft … you a mummy's boy.' He also remembers Cutty Robinson's prescient warning of this sorrowful time approaching, and he recalls how much the Jamaican gangster reminds him of the great heavyweight boxer Muhammad Ali. In Daniel's mind both Tricks and Cutty have what he thinks of as a cool vibration, and thinking of them picks him up a little.

That afternoon his drunkard farther Clinton embarrassingly burst into the office and began beating Daniel, slapping him about the face, shaking him and eventually almost choking him to death. It was Nathaniel 'Cutty' Robinson that had ordered Clinton Cottle to stop. The memory of the strikingly handsome, hazel-eyed Mr Robinson coming to his aid causes Daniel to smile – properly smile for the first time in over eleven months.

The teenage White girl arrives with his hot chocolate, but sensing Daniel to be deep in thought and not wanting to disturb him, she puts his drink on the bedside table for him with some biscuits and goes to leave the room. Daniel smiles again at the memory of Cutty and picks up the mug of hot chocolate and begins sipping at it. Noticing this, the girl turns back and bids him 'Goodnight,' and as she does so both she and Daniel hear the car engine start up outside.

Inside the car, Flash gives his boss some reassuring words,

before they drive away: 'My friend, in this case time will be the healer, trust me.'

CHAPTER 18

As Daniel continues to sip at the hot chocolate, which the girl was right about being delicious, his mind takes him to the memory of the next day following the barbershop-choking incident. It was a cold, dreary December day and already getting dark when Daniel heard a continuous tap, tap, tapping sound outside. He looked down from his second-floor bedroom to the lower addition roof to a smiling but scary-looking middle-aged White workman and his two companions. The rugged, bearded man was using a roof slater's hammer to knock away concrete with the hammer end – the other side of the hammer being a six-inch long sharp metal spike that's used for piercing through slate without effort. He looked up to see Daniel at the window, and the sight of him caused the frightened child to jump backwards, falling back onto his bed, breathing heavily in a panic.

Captain's cabin, *The Haitian Witch*

Jarrod lies asleep on his bed in a dream state, conscious in the dimension of his future incarnation Daniel Cottle. The sight of the scary-looking man causes the 18th century child pirate's body to jump and him to loudly hit the side of his head off the bed's wooden headboard, waking him.

In his mind, Jarrod can picture the scary workman and specifically the spike end of his hammer vividly. He, himself, probably wouldn't have been afraid of the man in that situation but he feels the fear transferred to him from his future incarnation, Daniel who obviously was scared.

Through the partition that divides his bed from the captain's own sleeping quarters, Jarrod hears his uncle drunkenly shout: 'What the hell was that bang? Woke me from me sleep'

Jarrod doesn't answer and after a few minutes the pirate captain's lightly snoring again. Jarrod snuggles his face into the pillow again and, knowing he has no one to fear, quickly falls back to sleep.

Cottle family home, December 1973

After a short while Daniel composes himself. It's only some workmen, he tells himself. He gets up and creeps toward the window. He looks again through the tiny gap between the curtain and windowpane to see the three men working away. Downstairs in the living room a Tom and Jerry cartoon's just beginning. Daniel hears the theme music blasting from the TV and goes down. He stops by the kitchen seeing his mother speaking to one of the workmen but then hears his sister calling him and goes and sits on the sofa with his brother and sister. He shifts himself nearer to his sister because a branch of the Christmas tree slightly blocks his view. As usual the cartoon cat, Tom, is being bad, provoking the mouse Jerry into striking him on the head with a hammer and a huge lump appears on Tom's head. The children laugh hysterically and the sound of their laughter fills their mother Pearl's soul with joy as she enters the room carrying a tray bearing mugs of hot chocolate and a plate of cookies.

Nine-year-old Daniel happily shouts out, 'Bad Tom, bad Tom,' pointing to the cartoon cat on the screen, then noticing his mother exclaims, 'Yeah! Hot chocolate, thanks Mum.'

Pearl continues to smile at her children's happiness as she hands out the mugs of hot chocolate. 'Small cup's yours, Daniel, not too hot, I cooled it...' she says, and the three children each take a cookie from the tray as she goes to them in turn. Before leaving them to go back to cleaning the kitchen, she takes a lingering stare at the three children's beautiful, happy faces and quietly utters the words: 'My world, the three of you are my world.'

As the cartoon is finishing, the children hear the heavy vibrating rumbling sound of their father Clinton Cottle's V8

Rover parking in the garage, and Daniel's face suddenly loses its smile.

Church Hill Children's Care Home, Walthamstow
December 1974

Daniel's thoughts drift back to the present and he sits looking up at those lonely industrial care home walls. Still fully clothed but now very tired, he lies back down on top of the bed, closes his eyes and quietly falls asleep. At the moment Daniel falls asleep, Jarrod wakes and Daniel drifts into a dream, consciously awake in his previous incarnation Jarrod on board *The Haitian Witch* pirate vessel.

Two weeks later

Charlie Baker's visit to see Daniel became the first of many, and he quickly fell into the routine of visiting the boy each morning before he opened his uncle's High Street betting office.

As Charlie gets up to leave now, Kim smiles warmly at the young London gangster, impressed by the loving care he's shown young Daniel Cottle over the past fortnight.

'Jarrod, I'm here for you and never gonna give up on you or leave you, alright?' Charlie says, addressing Daniel as he always did as Jarrod.

Despite Charlie's visits, Daniel was still very much in his depressed state. There had been glimmers of hope, faint smiles, but no real sign that the youngster was coming out of the depression.

For his part, Daniel desperately wanted to ask Charlie where his mother was, and somehow Charlie instinctively knew this. There was a deep-rooted soul-to-soul love between the two and Charlie hadn't got over the death of others close to his soul, Daniel's parents Mr and Mrs Cottle.

Charlie turns to address Kim and says, 'His parents were among my closest friends and I've always felt close to this one.

They made my dad godfather at his christening. He's got no one; what else am I supposed to do?'

He looks sadly one last time towards Daniel sitting at the breakfast table before leaving the room. Also present at the table are the older children of the fatal hit and run victims, now also resident at the home.

Kim walks with Charlie to the front door to show him out, but Charlie finds his mind occupied by the events of an afternoon in December 1973, the same thing Daniel thought about when he'd arrived at the care home.

Twelve men and women, a mix of Black and White, including among their number some notorious gangsters and even members of the IRA, were met in the backroom of Nathaniel 'Cutty' Robinson's barbershop. The meeting was good natured and civilised and the room cosy and warm. No one had any particular concerns about nine-year-old Daniel being present. Suddenly a loud clattering and the sounds of breaking glass and shouting came from the adjoining barbershop to disturb them. Charlie remembers the noise actually waking him because he'd just nodded off at the time, the warmth of the room or something having had a soporific effect on him. Clinton Cottle burst in and began brutalising his son Daniel. Cutty in particular stepped in and ordered him to stop. After Clinton and Cutty had had words, the drunkard Clinton broke down crying. Just then Cutty and Charlie exchanged glances. Charlie remembers continuously looking back and forth between Daniel and Cutty, realising that they shared the same shape head, eyes and other facial features.

The madam Elsie had nudged him then, saying, 'You must have been frightened out of your wits being woken like that. Are you alright, Charlie?'

'Yeah Tricks,' he'd replied. 'I was in a deep sleep just then, dreaming I was lying on a bed. A Black woman, Lana, was talking to me and a Black geezer sewing up a deep gash, flesh wound to me back. Crazy fucking dream.'

'Sounds like you've been smoking too much weed and hash,' Elsie had mumbled.

The sound of Kim's voice brings Charlie's thoughts back to the present: 'Are you alright, Charlie?'

He nods, and once outside the building he looks up and points in the direction of Daniel's room. 'It wasn't the boy's fault, you know,' he says.

Kim gives him a disbelieving look. 'Wasn't his fault, Charlie? Yeah ok, they found the murder weapon, him covered in his father's blood and he admits doing it! His father brutalised his mum that was the reason, end of.'

Charlie pauses to light a cigarette. 'Oh, Daniel killed Clinton alright, but there's more to why Clinton began laying into Pearl.'

Kim still looks puzzled, but the love she knows she's starting to feel for Charlie also shows on her face.

45 Teckwort Park Road, Walthamstow, East London

It's now almost Christmas and ten-year-old Yanson Bailey wakes at the family's modest three-bedroom mid-terrace home to find himself disappointed by the dream he's just had. He and his friend Benjamin Jarvis had been walking through the early evening packed market in Walthamstow High Street. Darkness had just fallen and the rain had left them cold and wet. They'd met an older lady with her brown hair worn up with a huge curly lock of it hanging down over her beautiful face. She'd spoken with a French-accent and had a cat with her that she called Jojo. She'd led them to a Jaguar car parked near to the Chequers Pub, situated near the halfway point of the lengthy Walthamstow market. She'd said to Yanson: 'Open the door, Koolah. Inside that jacket, there's what you've been looking for, what you want.' And he'd opened the car door to be met by the sight of a glowing off-white pink mist that appeared to be coming out from the jacket rested on the driver's seat. He'd searched the jacket only to find a single penny coin, which then somehow disappeared, miraculously dissolving into his hand. Both he and Benjamin had looked disappointedly towards the woman.

Although disappointed at the lack of finding anything more

promising in the jacket in the dream, Yanson feels there's something familiar about the off-white pink mist he saw and something joyful about it too. He smiles at the memory. He has similar pretty facial features and smile to Daniel Cottle – same shaped head, mouth, nose and ears – but his skin is lighter, and due to his oriental grandfather, his brown eyes have a slight Asian look to them.

As he continues to wake up, Yanson thinks back, as he often finds himself doing lately, to the day he saw Daniel Cottle being taken into the children's home. The uncharacteristically sad, depressed look he saw on Daniel's face that day is still vivid in his mind. And he somehow senses Daniel is still in distress. The strange thing is, though, he and Daniel didn't really know each other. The Cottle children were the local well-to-do rich kids and up to this point he and Yanson had never exchanged a word.

Suddenly he hears the ding-dong sound of the doorbell. Downstairs, his Black Jamaican mother Shirley goes to answer it as her White English husband Brian carries on reading his morning newspaper. Upstairs Yanson experiences a feeling of panic, thinking perhaps it's the police come to arrest him again.

In fact, the person Shirley finds standing on the doorstep is Yanson's friend Benjamin Jarvis, looking cute in his school uniform and giving her a slightly buck-toothed smile.

He speaks with a confident tone in his 1970s Romany accent: 'Morning Mrs Bailey, is Yance ready ta go ta school?'

Shirley looks into his eyes, reminded of the Artful Dodger character from the Oliver Twist movie she and the family had watched the previous Christmas, and thinking how his family and their crowd are always getting into trouble and barred for stealing from shops in the local market. Nevertheless, she can't help feeling a liking and being drawn towards him.

'Yep, hole on,' she says, and shouts up the stairs, 'Yanson... Yanson...'

As she calls repeatedly, Benjamin sits himself down on the doorstep, squinting looking towards the bright winter morning sun in the clear blue sky. It reminds him of a recurring dream he has of the North East African sunrise and the associated pink mist that covers a circular symbolic engraved black stone clearing.

'Yanson… somebody at the door for you.' Shirley continues to call her son, and eventually he gets himself out of bed. Wearing nothing but a pair of Y-front underpants he takes a look out the bedroom window and is relieved to see there isn't a police car there.

'Yanson, it time fe school. Your friends are always ready before you.'

Yanson begins to breathe normally again. He puts his hand into his pillowcase to take out the money that he's keeping hidden in there. It's twenty-three pounds, a lot of money for a 1970s ten-year-old to have. He puts a five-pound note and five one-pound notes in his pocket, hides the rest back in his pillowcase and smiles. He then kisses his old lucky gold coin, a secret sentimental and valuable gift from his Aunt Elsie. It always reminds him of the day she gave it to him. As always, he can't help rubbing his finger over the distinctive dent in the coin's edge. In his mind he sees other hands doing the same thing, and also setting the coin spinning on a table along with three others. The hands he sees are in one case Black, in another grubby White hands with dirty fingernails. He thinks back to that day six years ago when his Aunt Elsie gave it to him.

He'd only been four then, but he could remember it vividly. Aunt Elsie, his mother's best friend, Black Jamaican, pretty, always well-dressed and perfumed like a movie star, had hugged him emotionally. Then she'd delved into her handbag, taken out her purse and the gold coin from it and handed it to him.

He remembers feeling an instant familiarity with the coin and asking curiously, 'Where did you get this, Auntie? I see it and other gold coins in dreams.'

'It's a lucky coin,' Elsie had replied. 'It came to me on a day I'll never forget, because it was the actual night you were born…'

Cutty Robinson's brothel/gambling house, North London
December 1964

It's around midnight and Elsie in her early twenties is the classy young madam of the brothel. She zips up her shoulder bag containing the entire day's takings and places it on her desk. She then walks, heels clicking, to check in on one of the escort girls in another room, and has to explain to her paying customer that his time's up. When she returns, she's annoyed to find her handbag and purse open and ruffled. Her immediate thought, of course, being that she has been robbed of the entire night's takings, she rushes to the desk to investigate; but she's relieved to find all the banknotes present. But then when she looks to the bottom of the purse, she's surprised to find, although slightly dented, a gleaming gold coin in with the wad of money.

At that moment her psyche revisits a reoccurring bizarre dream she usually has of a drunken pirate captain looking almost identical to Charlie Baker. He's full of hearty laughter and on this occasion sitting spinning the very same dented coin and other gold coins on his huge captain's cabin table. In the dream one of the gold coins falls from the table and she picks it up. It's the same coin with the same dent in its edge, but in her dream again bizarrely her hands are those of a White woman.

45 Teckwort Park Road, Walthamstow, East London
December 1974

Yanson's sure he can recall almost word-for-word what his Aunt Elsie said to him that day as a four-year-old:

'It must have come from someone, one of the girls at work or I don't know who. I just found it there in my purse. Later, I came and sat by your mother's maternity ward bedside. I told your mum Shirley to give you the name Yanson, the name of my forbidden first and only ever love and up till this point, love of my life. I broke his heart when my parents and family in Jamaica separated us because he was poor… couldn't even afford a pair of shoes. I loved him because he was loving and smart. He's now a married US medical school lecturing doctor in America and I've just come from prison! A day doesn't pass when I don't dream or think about him, Yanson. Always follow your own mind, little man, and don't let anyone or any situation dictate your destiny. You're a lucky soul, Yanson Bailey; I can feel a lot of happiness, love and luck coming your way. The coin's brought me nothing but better luck the minute I got it, but something tells me it's connected to you – that you need to have it to make you whole and that it was only passed to me to give to you...'

CHAPTER 19

From the day Elsie had given him the coin, Yanson had begun having ever more vivid dreams of ancient Africa, of the magic circle, the soul tribe, even of himself in adult form handing the exact same lucky coin with the dent to a man who was called Ode. The secret dreams and visions helped him cope with life. He'd often visualise ancient and modern-day soul mates, Claudette and others.

'Yanson, come on!' Yanson's mother is still shouting for him to get ready and come downstairs. He washes and dresses quickly but lingers on the staircase coming down when he realises he can hear his parents talking about the Cottle family tragedy. He sneakily listens in to what's being said:

'...Yes Brian, that must be why they were taking him into Church Hill, his aunt Joy could no longer cope and the rest of the family will only take the other two.'

'They're blaming the little one for everything. I don't feel it's fair they hold the child responsible...'

That's all he hears before his parents move out of his earshot as they go into the living room. He comes down and follows them into the room.

When they see him, they stop talking, but Yanson asks, 'What's that about Jarrod Cottle? Who's blaming him, blaming him for what?'

His mother snaps slightly as she answers him, 'Mind you own dyam rarted business, Yanson.'

His father, adopting a calmer approach, adds, 'Yanson, son, it is none of our business. Please don't repeat anything you've heard us say about the Cottle family outside or at school.'

Yanson goes to join his friend outside.

As they walk along the street together, Yanson hands Benjamin

165

five folded pound-notes. 'There you go Ben, there's the rest of your cut from Charlie.'

Ben smiles and pockets the money. 'The arcade fifty pence swindle Yance, nice one.'

Suddenly, Yanson again recalls the dream of the penny coin he'd found in the blazer pocket inside the Jaguar car.

Church Hill Children's Care Home

At the same moment Yanson is thinking of his dream, Daniel Cottle, lying on his bed in the care home, is startled by the brothers Albert and Alex Stephens and two other older boys bursting into his room. They start going through his drawers and the older brother, Albert, takes out a beautifully knitted jumper, which he squeezes into despite it obviously being at least a size too small for him.

Daniel tries to protest. He hadn't even worn the jumper yet because it was slightly too big for him. 'Hey, my mother gave me that. My grandma in Jamaica knitted it and sent it for me, put it back.'

Forest Road, Walthamstow

Yanson and Benjamin have now reached the main road on their walk to school.

At the same time as Daniel Cottle is being bullied by the Stephens brothers, from nowhere Yanson feels a sudden sense of sadness for Daniel, and having thought of Daniel, he turns to his friend and says, 'I keep forgetting to tell you, Ben, I saw Danny Cottle a few weeks ago. He was really sad getting taken into Church Hill.'

Ben just laughs. 'Who? Rich boy Jarrod Cottle? Fuck that, them Stephens brothers and the rest of the Selbourne Park boys will have him for breakfast.'

'I know, Ben, they're all expelled from their schools for bullying and stealing stuff.'

Ben takes the five pound-notes from his pocket, looks at them, puts them back and smiles. 'Thanks for the dough, Yance. Oh yeah, me mum said the Cottles were in the local papers and on the news again. Kids on me estate are calling Jarrod Cottle the exorcist.'

Yanson squints his eyes with a puzzled expression. 'I know his mum recently died and his dad had been killed as well, but what actually happened, Ben?'

Ben pauses in thought but doesn't answer, instead changing the subject and speaking about his own family's latest escapade: 'Me mum and sister Zoe, they got chored by gathers Friday night. They been in all weekend. Probably got sent to jail again this morning.'

Yanson's about to press Ben about the Cottle family tragedy, when he notices his friend's smiling face is preoccupied, looking far up the main road, through the rush hour traffic, into the distance. Yanson follows his friend's eyeline to see Ben's mother Jasmine and her eldest daughter, Ben's seventeen-year-old sister Zoe, up ahead. Both share Ben's blond hair and blue eyes.

'Mum… Mum...!' Ben shouts hysterically as he rushes towards her, dodging in and out of slow-moving traffic to get to his mother. When he reaches her, she excitedly hugs and kisses him, lovingly ruffling his hair.

'Mum,' Ben exclaims, 'the magistrate let you out! Thought he said you come before him again and he'd send you back to jail.'

She holds his head as she explains: 'No, got to go to court a few weeks into the new year. We got bail and let out from the police station. We're home for Christmas, thank God. Fucking starving, son. Got any money?'

Ben's hand delves into his trouser pocket secretly separating a pound note from the rest. He slips it out and, smiling proudly, hands it to her. Her instant reaction is to start excitedly kissing and cuddling him all over again.

Forest Road Bakery, Walthamstow

Yanson notices there's only one other customer in the shop as he, Jasmine Jarvis, Zoe and Ben enter the local bakery. The customer is in her mid-forties, petite, stunningly pretty with long dark hair and immaculately dressed in old-fashioned clothing that looks a little out of place in 1970s Walthamstow. Yanson stares at her, knowing he recognises her from his dream that morning, and the more he thinks about her he realises she appears in other of his dreams too. Both she and the black cat lurking at the entrance to the bakery are strangely very familiar to him.

Yanson joins the others at the bakery glass counter looking through at the freshly baked cakes and deciding what to have. One of the shop's three sales assistants, a woman of Jasmine's age called Samantha, approaches.

'Hello Sam,' Jasmine says, 'just got let out the police station, fucking starving. Nothing like the smell of freshly baked pastry when you're hungry... Thought we'd had it getting nicked on Friday the 13th.'

One of the two older assistants chips in: 'Thirteen, lucky for some, unlucky for others.'

'Yeah, I'll remember that,' Jasmine says, 'unlucky for some'

Samantha looks to see if the other customer wanted serving because she was there just before Jasmine's lot. But she judges the earlier arrival hasn't decided what she wants yet, so she turns her attention back to Jasmine and the children.

'Arrested again, Jasmine? You'll never learn... and what can we do for you today?' A thought crosses Samantha's mind and her attitude suddenly changes. 'Oh fuck, I almost forgot, we can't do any tick, Jas. You nearly got me sacked the other day. Manager wanted to know why the till was short. You promised you'd come back and pay before closing Friday...'

Jasmine smiles with a silly shake of the head as she shows Samantha the pound note. 'Sorry we got chored, and nah, not asking for tick, Sam. Got money, look. I'll pay what I owe as well. Didn't do it on purpose, got nicked...'

As Jasmine and Sam carry on talking, Yanson tunes into the conversation the two older assistants have started having:

'Flo, did you see a few nights ago, they were on the news again?'

'Oh yeah Doris, still don't seem real. It was only this time last year Pearl came in for the last time with her children. What a sad turn out, for God sakes.'

'I know Flo, everyone thought the Cottles had it all, that huge house opposite the park, nice car, beautiful-looking couple and three adorable kids. Something must have been horribly wrong, that's fucking obvious. You never know what happens behind closed doors; no truer words have ever been said.'

The woman called Flo notices Yanson's listening. She smiles, turns her back and lowers her voice before continuing; but Yanson can still just about hear every word she says:

'Clinton Cottle's death was shocking, but they found his wife Pearl, her body cut clean in half at the waist. She was literally found in two, both halves of her body thirty feet apart, blood everywhere.'

'Awl, I know,' Doris replies too adopting the whispering act, 'but the bit that gets me, Flo, is all the relations blamed it all on the poor little one, Daniel. They took in the other two, but he's been left with a lady he calls his aunt in Leyton, and I've been told she's been suffering deep heartbreak depression. What must he be going through in his head, adored his mother, must be well lost…'

'That's right Doris, dad killed at Christmas, mum dies the way she did in April just months after, and they're blaming him for everything, the death of both parents…'

Flo breaks off as she spots Yanson still trying to listen to their conversation. Seeing how much interest he's taking in the details of the Cottle tragedy, Flo decides to save the rest of her conversation with Doris until the boy and the others he's with have left the shop.

Having nothing further to listen in to, Yanson turns to Benjamin and, pointing surreptitiously at Claudette, whispers, 'I've dreamed about her loads of times. Had a dream of her last night.

She was showing us where some money was hidden but when we looked there was nothing there, just a penny.'

Samantha overhears him and with a smile says quietly to him, 'Dreams are often the opposite, son.'

The expression on Yanson's face makes it clear that what Samantha has just said makes no sense to him.

Samantha laughs and speaks to Jasmine: 'Seems it was only the other day we were sitting next to each other in the classroom round the corner.'

Jasmine agrees with a smile. 'Yeah, hard to believe. Where does the time go?'

Samantha looks around the bakery to see that Claudette and her cat that was waiting at the door have suddenly disappeared. She looks toward Jasmine and the children. 'Jasmine, where did that woman go?'

Doris looks puzzled and says, 'What woman… where?'

'The woman who was just in here,' Samantha replies. 'See her sometimes, always being followed by her cat. It was just at the door waiting for her now.'

Both Doris and Flo look confused and Flo remarks, 'I didn't see a cat.'

Later, as other children are still walking to school, Jasmine, Zoe, Ben and Yanson sit on someone's garden wall across the road from the bakery, eating the food they've bought and larking about. Jasmine's eyes show both Benjamin and Yanson pure love and affection. It's in moments like these that Yanson knows what perfect love between a mother and son should feel like. Yanson loved his mother more than any child loved theirs and Shirley loved him deeper than any mother could love a son, but for more surface reasons she lacked emotion for him. Benjamin hands his mother, Jasmine, another three of the one-pound notes he has and she excitedly kisses him again.

'Fuck did you get all of that?' she says. 'You lot make more than me… I'll go get something for your supper and Sunday dinner later. Come on you two, when you finished eating, off you go to school.'

Benjamin looks sincerely at his mother. 'Mum, don't go to the pub…'

45 Teckwort Park Road, Walthamstow

Sitting at the table with her husband, Shirley Bailey's in the middle of expressing what's on her mind:
'…Yes Brian, the boy who just knocked for Yanson was the little thieving boy whose family are always in trouble with the police. They live on that rough Priory Court Estate.'

Forest Road Bakery, Walthamstow

Back in the bakery, Samantha looks over the road to see Jasmine and the children speaking, smiling and eating. Her older colleagues are still talking about the Cottle family tragedy, Daniel in particular, and Samantha interrupts:
'Talking about young Daniel, Yanson over there don't half look like him. Hasn't got his blue eyes but fuck me, don't they look alike?'

171

CHAPTER 20

Charlie Baker's betting shop, Walthamstow Market 1993

Again accompanied by her black cat Jojo, the woman who'd disappeared from the bakery twenty years previously still appears the same age, around mid-forties, as she slowly journeys upward a long single flight of stairs and reaches the top. Claudette stands outside Charlie Baker's office door at the top of the flight of stairs accompanied by her cat. If anyone could see her, they would think her clothes out of place: an 18th century outfit with a tight white upper corset, a dress with puffed-out style layered skirts and a matching hat. And if they'd have seen her in 1974 and 1993, they'd be surprised to see her apparently still in her mid-forties nearly twenty years later. She stops, turns to the left facing Charlie Baker's office door, focused on the sounds from the other side of it.

Listening at the door she can hear the bassline of Bob Marley's 1970s hit 'Stir It Up' and amid the delightful sounding reggae music, the sexual rhythmic bumping and pleasurable moaning sounds of a couple thoroughly enjoying sexual activity. A mobile phone begins to ring inside the office, but Claudette hears it gradually fade as she goes downstairs and out through the door that leads out to the market street.

It's very early in the morning, and outside, stallholders and street vendors are setting out for the hustle and bustle of the day's market trading, but none of them seem to take any notice of Claudette or her odd, old-fashioned appearance. She crosses the street and stands opposite the betting shop, smiling looking up at Charlie Baker's first floor office as she says to herself, 'Huh, still ze adorable, womanising bastard. Forever ze characteristic of your soul, Jim Morgan.'

It seems something changes her mind about leaving him be, and Claudette goes back into the premises, upstairs to the same office door. Again she hears the mobile phone still ringing, the bassline of the music and the muffled ecstatic moaning of a female sounding as though she's at the early stages of orgasm. There's first the delicate soft vocal stutter, then the sounds of the voice gradually become intense and animated. Claudette raises her eyebrows as her smirking face looks towards Charlie's office door. Once she's inside the sounds are now louder and clearer: ecstatic moaning coupled with a now louder knocking sound, Bob Marley's *Exodus* album playing, the mobile phone still ringing and vibrating. Claudette stands in the lobby area where there's a stylish low-level fridge, which has on top of it a small mountain of cocaine powder, many made lines on a small mirror and a rolled snorting fifty-pound note resting next to it. She hears the heavy panting and joyful moaning getting louder as the woman reaches the sweet ecstasy of sexual orgasm.

King Louis XVIII Hotel, Amsterdam, Holland

Meanwhile in Holland, twenty-nine-year-old Daniel Cottle and his Swedish-Moroccan mistress Emy are in bed in their luxury, antique-themed, five-star penthouse suite in the King Louis XVIII Hotel. The plush hotel suite boasts fine, opulent antique furniture, including bed, mirrors, pictures and a four-poster king-size bed complete with luxurious bedding. Resting on the bedside table are an expensive half-full bottle of VSOP Cognac, napkins and two glasses, all placed on a silver room service tray. Also in the room, there are plenty of recent expensive purchases: clothing, jewellery and the like. Louis Vuitton and Gucci baggage lie strewn around the large hotel suite. The room's lit by the television, on the screen of which there's a female presenter speaking Dutch.

As a twenty-nine-year-old adult, Daniel's a fine figure of a man: six-foot-two and athletically muscular with the physique of a champion boxer. He lies propped up in the bed speaking on his mobile phone with Emy's face resting on his manly chest. He ends the call and places the mobile on the bed next to the TV remote, which he picks up and uses it to turn the TV off, plunging the room into darkness. He closes his eyes.

Church Hill Children's Care Home
December 1974

The Stephens brothers and two other boys have entered the ten-year-old Daniel Cottle's bedroom. One of the gang is Sammy, a tall and slim, tough, Black thirteen-year-old whose frustrated facial expression carries an especially negative vibration. All the boys have taken at least one item belonging to him but Albert Stephens wearing a beautifully knitted jumper causes Daniel to speak up. 'Hey, my mother gave me that, my grandma in Jamaica knitted it for me and sent it, put it back …'

Sammy's reply is accompanied by the menacing sound of his flick knife opening: 'Shut up, likle poom poom crying for his mum. Now give me some fucking money before I stab you up in here …' Sammy holds his knife to the face of Daniel and the boy nervously protests.

'I haven't got any money, I promise…' Daniel stutters.

Mercifully the flick knife doesn't get used, but mercilessly all four members of the gang turn on Daniel and give him a beating.

'Stop it please…' cries Daniel, 'alright… I've had enough…'

King Louis XVIII Hotel, Amsterdam, Holland, 1993

It's daytime but the 'do not disturb' sign is on the outer door handle. Inside the thick curtains are drawn, leaving the plush and swanky five-star olden day Dutch theme, classy hotel room in darkness.

Daniel Cottle tosses and turns in his sleep, speaking unclearly whilst his head's moving side to side on the pillow. The ringing of his mobile phone wakes him as he cries out, 'Stop it please… alright… I've had enough…'

His cries, sudden waking and the sound of the phone are

enough to wake Emy in shock too, so much so she has to breathe a few times to catch her breath.

Daniel gasps and screams out, 'Mummy, where are you?' before sitting up, open-mouthed trying to catch his own breath as he comes out from his nightmare.

Emy feels his body trembling with fear. She grips him, hugging him tight, and gradually he relaxes. Both of their breathing settles and she rests her head on her pillow.

Daniel's mind still reels from the dream he's had of himself being bullied as a child, of the Stephens brothers and Sammy taxing his clothing and personal items. It happened nearly twenty years ago, but the memory still haunts him in vivid dreams, made worse by that deep feeling of guilt he's now carried through into adulthood.

He pats around the bed, trying to locate the phone that's still ringing. He leans over to turn on the bedside light, exposing the huge, expertly created, artistically detailed Chinese dragon tattoo that covers his entire back. Eventually he finds the phone but only after it has stopped ringing and he takes a look at the caller ID as he picks it up. Emy, awake now, pulls him to her and kisses his lips.

'Daniel, you had a bad night dreaming. You sat up earlier. I could feel how distressed you were.'

He looks into her glistening hazel eyes and nods. 'Yeah, I had a nightmare I was in the care home getting hassled by them lot before I got tight with Yance.'

All of a sudden, Daniel feels a strange, beautiful sensation all around him, a feeling he's not felt since childhood. He associates it with a time when at his lowest point as a child there was a major turning point in his life. Yanson had visited him in the care home and life was never to be quite the same afterwards. He still doesn't understand how he experienced it, but he recalls Yanson Bailey sitting on the bed opposite him changing into the authentic Messiah Koolah as he spoke of the magic circle and activities in the ancient City of Koolah. The modern-day Haitian witch Claudette was also present. There was a moment he recalls where it was like the visions of the ancient City of Koolah had been paused like a movie on TV and Koolah as a child and Claudette were the only ones moving and speaking to him. He specifically remembers the words of the child Koolah: 'Release your fears…'

'Again?' says Emy interrupting his thoughts and bringing him back to the present. 'You certainly have no reason to be fearing those guys today, darling.'

'No, you know I fear no one today, but the dream always gives me that fucked up feeling I had to deal with, being responsible for my parents dying. Still an 'orrible feeling now I'm a grown man; it gets me every time.' He closes his eyes, gently shaking his head. 'I've really got a lot to thank Yance for when he came. He really helped me.'

Emy smiles. 'Yes Daniel, he's certainly a cool friend, no doubt about it.'

Daniel looks at his phone again and uses it to make a call.

Charlie Baker's betting shop, Walthamstow Market

Charlie Baker's ringing mobile goes unanswered as he and his latest pretty young mistress help themselves to a couple of fat lines of cocaine each. Claudette hides in the shadows and sees first the lady's then the gentleman's hand pick up the rolled-up fifty-pound note to snort the drugs through.

Charlie's lover's mini-skirt's still hitched up over her tiny waist and he gives her impressively soft, delicate peachy bottom a gentle squeeze. 'I'll be honest, you've got the best little ass I've ever seen. Come on treacle, let's have you back on that fucking desk, eh babe?'

Instinctively clasping her hand to her mouth Claudette suppresses a laugh and with a smirk on her face leaves the office as she'd entered it, her astral body moving through the unopened door.

Moments later forty-one-year-old Charlie Baker and twenty-eight-year-old Stacey Holley are again enjoying cocaine-fuelled sex. Stacey's a slim, petite, hazel-eyed blonde with a remarkably sexy body, especially after baring two children. Her face has a youthful innocent look that belies the down-to-earth reality of her personality. He's chosen again to take her from behind and he pants heavily with each thrust, his blond hair and black shirt soaked in sweat, actually thinking to himself the occasion could give him a heart attack, but he carries on regardless. His trousers and boxer shorts lie on the floor, whereas Stacey's still fully clothed, her tight-fitting leather mini-skirt inside out and half folded up, hitched up around her waist. Apart from that, she's dressed in a skin-tight blouse and white thigh-high stiletto-heeled boots. One of Charlie's hands holds her skimpy knickers to one side allowing clearance for his large and during that moment pleasurably throbbing penis, as his other hand reaches in, his finger masturbating her clitoris. She's positioned with her knees, palms, forearms, breast and one side of her face resting on his office desk. Knees situated close to the edge of the desk, peachy little ass in air as he's penetrating her. Charlie stands rigorously pounding the delicate-looking blonde with a continuous rhythmic motion, using the power of his pelvis and thighs to slowly but firmly thrust his penis in and out. As his pelvis hits against her bottom there's a continuous rhythmic beating sound due to the force he's using rocking her body back and forth. Their motion's also causing his desk to repeatedly hit against the wooden doorframe. He uses a hand to hold on to her shoulder for extra leverage whilst ejaculating his sperm inside her. Although now seriously struggling to breathe, he can't help in that moment but aggressively tear her knickers completely off, snapping a suspender in the process.

Charlie pulls himself away but Stacey's face and breasts still rest on the desk. She's panting hard, her upper body and backside pleasurably juddering; her vaginal area's feeling pleasurably numbed and she has a contented smile on her face. She slowly, gently rocks her body back and forth and her soaked vagina makes that contented after-sex squelching sound.

Stacey attempts to speak but instead what she first comes out with is uncontrollable vocal gibberish. She joyfully giggles, stumbling as she climbs down from the desk, and smiling as she watches Charlie's large semi-erect penis swaying from side to side as he walks across the room.

'Oh, my cunt loves that feeling when your cock keeps throbbing like that,' she says, 'you squeezing me arse as ya spunk comes shooting up inside me… Your powerful body gripping me, ripping me knickers off…'

She sits cross-legged on Charlie's legendary throne-like office chair, her blouse unbuttoned and her shapely, outward-pointing, firm breasts on display.

Charlie focuses in on them with his trademark twitch. 'You look a treat sat there with your little thrupneys out.'

Stacey looks puzzled. 'Thrupneys, Charlie?'

'Thrupney fucking bits, your tits, babe. Thrupney's the old three pence coin, thrupney bit, just old East End Cockney rhyming slang, a word granddad and the ole boys used ta secretly talk about a bird's knockers.'

She laughs. 'Well I fucking never, Charlie, and I feel like the Queen of England sat up here on this comfy chair. Tell ya what, you're the oldest man I've fucked, but easily by far the best I've had. It's your strength and the size a ya cock, I'm certainly not complaining and I bet Tracey wasn't neither. No wonder you couldn't get rid of her…'

Charlie smiles proudly as he picks up her shredded laced knickers from the floor, tosses them on the desk, and snorts another line off the top of the mini fridge.

'Oldest feller maybe,' he says, 'but a well-worn and used saxophone always reaches that sweeter note, princess… What was that you were thinking about earlier?'

'Oh, nothing, I just get the feeling we're being watched here sometimes. Not by the police but like a ghost from the past here with us.' She shakes her head and smiles. 'That's the coke comedown talking. Don't know why the fuck I just said all that.'

They both laugh. He stands in front of her and rests his hands on the desk as she picks up her knickers and begins to examine them.

'Oh Charlie, I loved these knickers. They were special 'cos of the look on your face and the feeling it gave me when you chose 'em. You've fucking ruined 'em now, look.' Still smiling, she holds up the torn panties for Charlie to see. 'Got a thing about ripping me drawers off. And what is it with you always wanting me on ya desk lately? Used to be the recliner – that's far more comfortable, by the way. Me knees are wearing out.'

Charlie returns her smile. 'To be honest, on the desk I love looking down at your little ass, angel. Then enjoy it sat here all day thinking about it when I'm working.'

Stacey laughs again. 'How dare you! You are a naughty man. D'ya know what, it would be nice to be fucked in a bed just once in a while.'

'Funny you should say that, treacle. I thought we could do with a little luxury holiday, bit of sunshine...'

Stacey holds one of her nostrils closed and sniffs to draw the cocaine powder that had lingered inside her other nostril. She excitedly interrupts, saying, 'Me sister's just come back from honeymoon, Caribbean cruise, loved it.'

As Stacey mentions the Caribbean, a sudden rush of excitement causes Charlie to smile proudly because she's reminded him of something supernatural that occurred connecting him with his recurring dreams. She's brought to the surface a strange but wonderful sensation he gets every time he visits Jamaica. It began the first time he travelled there with his friend and fellow gangster Nathaniel Robinson, and for many reasons he'd never forget the mind-blowing experience: twenty years earlier, high on marijuana, laying out on a beach looking out at the ocean, his subconscious revealing to him he'd been there in various lives many times before. With genuine sincerity, he tries to explain to Stacey: 'We'd just been acquitted by the jury for that high profile robbery conspiracy but during my time in prison I started having the clearest déjà vu dreams showing I'd been to Jamaica in lives I'd lived before.'

But Stacey begins excitedly sniggering. 'Déjà vu, Charlie, not a word I'd usually associate with you, I mean...' Charlie interrupts her and continues seriously, 'We got acquitted for that big armed robbery conspiracy and I went to Jamaica, came back and after Christmas 1974 got rearrested on another armed robbery conspiracy and kept on remand for another two years. I thought about my Jamaican experience every day in prison and again had the deepest fucking dreams. I wrote me mum explaining me dreams and coincidently Cindy Nevin was up visiting her cousin on the next table. Mum called her over and she was the one who explained about déjà vu past lives and all that. She said her and me are always quite close in every life we live, even once been lovers and, that's right, she said there are no such things as coincidences, it was fate she was on the visit.'

Charlie pauses for a moment, lingering over what he's just said, then adds, 'Good mate a mine Cutty Robinson's got a lovely gaff out Jamaica, right on Negril Beach.'

'Yeah, Cutty Robinson,' Stacey says recalling the handsome, flamboyant Jamaican. 'I remember once seeing him come out of this place when we were kids, but he's your mate...?'

Charlie's mind drifts back momentarily to the day he first saw Cutty.

Eleven-year-old Charlie and the other kids were playing football in the street when the sharply presented Jamaican skidded up in a flash, convertible, gleaming off-black/navy Jaguar E-type V-12, got out the car dressed in a waistcoat and cravat, and began fighting with three men: Charlie's next-door neighbour, who himself was a tough Jamaican gangster, and his two equally tough brothers, over a money dispute. Mr Robinson beat them senseless, leaving two of them knocked out cold, whilst the other one ran away. His white shirt covered in the men's blood, Cutty Robinson winked at Charlie, putting a shush finger to his lips. They shared a smile before the Jamaican gangster got back into the Jaguar and drove away.

'Yeah Stacey, he's had that house in Jamaica since 1974. Fuck me, that visit to Jamaica was twenty years ago...'

Stacey interrupts him. '1974? I was just nine, Charlie, don't time fly...?'

'Yeah, he's had most of it demolished and re-built, modernised. The whole of the beachfront side's glass, every room. Fucking amazing gaff, pucker morning view of the ocean waves rolling in.' Charlie proudly smiles as he thinks back to the vibration of the island's sun setting. 'Fantastic feeling sat watching the sunset. I love the music, food...'

Stacey still excited at the idea of Charlie being mates with the handsome and notorious Cutty Robinson, interrupts Charlie mid-sentence:

'The Jamaican gangster Cutty Robinson's ya mate? Wow, you're one serious heavy bod. Fucking hell Charlie, Mum says Cutty's mob kill loads a people. Heard he was once arrested in America for killing two policemen in Jamaica...'

As she's speaking Charlie's mind revisits an unforgettable moment he and Cutty shared on that Jamaican visit. He clearly remembers it and the recollection causes him to shake his head and laugh as Stacey speaks of the much talked about Nathaniel Robinson-Cindy Nevin love affair that took place many years ago.

'...Charlie, I remember being at school and it all came out about the Black Jamaican gangster, he'd been fucking Nicole Nevin's mum, Cindy. Fucking hell, everyone knows what a racist bastard her husband Eric Nevin is...'

Charlie doesn't pay much attention to what Stacey's saying; instead his mind's fixed on the pivotal month of his life, a time he and Nathaniel Robinson shared in Jamaica.

At first Stacey thinks he's thinking about what she's speaking about, but as she goes on about the high-profile love affair that took place between the man people thought of as the Jamaican Godfather and the wife of the equally successful but racist White gangster Eric Nevin, she eventually realises by his silence and vacant stare that Charlie's mind is now elsewhere.

In fact, Charlie's mind is firmly in Negril, Jamaica in 1974 and the deeply spiritual memories of that time. He was staying at Nathaniel Robinson's Negril Beach villa, and Charlie recalls the conversations they were having in regard to modernising the property. Nathaniel's business associate and close friend the extremely wealthy Jew called Jach Marco had introduced him to a Scandinavian futuristic property designer for the part rebuild and refurbishment of his beach villa. As they were stood speaking and Nathaniel was excitedly sharing his ideas for the property, a group of seven Hispanic Colombians walked past, their ages ranging from a boy called Raul who was around ten to a senior who was aged around seventy. There were many unforgettable things about Raul: his appearance and the fact he spoke fluent local Jamaican patois. As the group walked past Nathaniel and Charlie on the beachfront, the boy Raul translated for another of the group, seventeen-year-old Diego Juan Carlo, explaining to Charlie that he repeatedly sees him in his dreams. Just days later into Charlie's stay a revelation occurred that put him and Nathaniel into a state of shock. Neither could say a word; they just sat next to each other on the sofa completely freaked out, staring at a family photo of two children, a pair of young Black Jamaican boys dressed in classy suits both around the same age, the boy with the lighter eyes being a four-year-old Nathaniel Robinson.

The moment brought Charlie and Nathaniel closer than any pair in their entire criminal organisation, bringing about an unearthly beautiful familiar vibration and unbreakable bond. Charlie recalls Cutty Robinson's serious expression coupled with a familiar vibration that commands respect. He could never forget the moment and the words Cutty said that day:

'Charlie, I want you to take what I'm about to tell you very seriously, like your life depended on it. Don't repeat what we've discovered here today to anyone, understand?'

Charlie felt so tense he couldn't find the words to reply but nodded his assent.

Cutty then smiled and said, 'Good, that's good then, alright my friend,' and Charlie felt reassured.

Although it was a magical moment they shared, for Cutty's own spiritual reasons he'd made it clear he didn't want to discuss the subject and it hadn't been spoken about by either Charlie or Cutty the entire twenty years since.

On the final day of the same lengthy visit to the island, Charlie sat outside looking out to the beautiful ocean wishing he could stay longer but knowing his flight was booked for the following morning and that he had business obligations back in London. At first he took no notice of a middle-aged woman who came walking up the path from the beach end. She was a lighter-skinned Jamaican woman in her late fifties with a friendly face with slightly droopy eyes, who was called Charmaine. She'd been talking to the gardener asking him to pick certain herbs for her to make specific oils, and as Charlie heard her voice his subconscious picked up on her more than familiar vibration. He recalls saying to her, 'Lana said I'd see you here and you'd have a message.'

She'd smiled and replied, 'My goodness you've met Lana already. Message, yes, of course…'

His mind jumps on to later the same day, to him having fallen asleep on the living room armchair and waking to see Charmaine sat opposite him holding what looked like the neck strap his friend Nathaniel always wore. They shared an unforgettable deeply spiritual conversation in which she'd explained the platted strap she held belonged to her son Gerry who'd sadly passed on.

The following morning would turn out to be an unforgettable sunrise. Charlie remembers standing barefoot in shorts, water up to his knees, gazing out at the beautiful Caribbean ocean, then joining Charmaine, her daughter Andrea and her daughter's children at the breakfast table on the veranda. Andrea had been in her mid-thirties with three beautiful children, a toddler girl and two older boys. He remembers the entire experience and the conversation that morning had such an emotional impact on him that he, already a tough London gangster then, broke down in tears of happiness. There had first been the photo of the boys on Nathaniel Robinson's wall, then the moment when he met Charmaine, then their conversation that morning – experiences that would change the entire way he'd ever again perceive the universe.

The recollection of it all and the upbeat spiritual vibration, soon has Charlie picking up and spinning his coins, an action that relaxed the soul.

CHAPTER 21

Stacey begins getting ready to leave and watches Charlie's expressions change as he reminisces; at one point he's smiling pleasurably and even trembling with excitement. Then he starts spinning his coins.

'I remember the first time I ever see you do that with them coins. I was only a little girl,' Stacey says, and her mind thinks back to the occasion. It was one Christmas and she, her friend and her aunts were in a local pub and at a nearby table there was Charlie sat with the Lewin gang spinning his coins.

They share a smile, but Stacey's still excited about what Charlie has told her, and says, 'Can't believe you went out on holiday with Cutty Robinson. Seriously, he's a mate of yours, Charlie? You that close?'

Charlie nods. 'More than a holiday, spent a month there. If I didn't have to get back to go on the bit of work, I'd have stayed another month and probably another. Wish I did now,' he jokes, 'I wouldn't have got nicked with the Lewin mob for conspiracy to rob the city bank, Bank of America.'

Charlie pictures the face of Charmaine at the breakfast table and recalls the words she spoke to him just before he flew back from Jamaica:

'The ocean view will stay in your mind an' help you through some more difficult jail time. All will be well in your life after some turmoil, alright son. We are at work for you and they won't be able to hold you for long.'

Charlie laughs heartily as he thinks of those words and says almost to himself, 'Mum knew, she fucking knew we were nicked.'

Stacey looks at him. 'Mums always do, Charlie.'

He nods assuredly and says, 'Cutty's a lot closer than a mate.'

After pausing in thought for a moment he asks, 'You believe in spirituality, treacle?'

As she gets dressed, she squints her eyes as she answers: 'Oh all that hippy type a stuff, dunno. Charlie, you?'

'Yeah, I have to say I do.'

'Why, who's taught you about all that?'

'My mother,' Charlie says with a smug smile, which Stacey doesn't see.

Then Charlie decides it best to change the subject and finally responds to her talk of Cutty Robinson's affair with Cindy Nevin:

'Fuck me Stacey, how could anyone forget that fucking nightmare? The little fella was never the same after he found Cutty knobbing his ole woman; he ended up in Claybury nut house. Cutty's Yance's dad as well, by the way.'

Stacey looks shocked at what Charlie had just told her, and he equally disappointed that he's drunkenly blurted it out.

'What...' she says, 'your Yanson Bailey? Use' to have the long dreadlocks, still call him The Dread. Cutty Robinson is Dread's dad. Really? It makes sense 'cos Yanson's a good earner as well.'

She excitedly smiles but he looks at her straight-faced.

'Cutty couldn't resist Yance's mum, tidy sort in her day, our Shirley, still looking well today in fact. Listen, you got to keep all that to yourself, understand?'

She nods, maintaining her feeling and look of surprise. 'I remember being a little girl and me ole man and mum talking about Cutty Robinson's gang getting arrested and questioned for the disappearance of an East End pub landlord, a gangster nicknamed Piggy. Piggy went down for murder and got it dropped to manslaughter at the appeal court. God, him disappearing seemed like gossip around the fucking neighbourhood for years, still is.'

Charlie raises his eyebrows; Stacey has reminded him of a situation he and many villains around the East End are glad to have seen the back of. Secretly he's fully aware of the details of Piggy's disappearance and her speaking of him has refreshed some old eerie memories.

'Charlie, I heard Piggy was well racist against Black people…'

Charlie laughs, relieving his nervousness in regard to the lingering Piggy affair. 'That cunt, racist against anyone that wasn't White, sweetheart, cunt was even racist against northerners…'

Stacey smiles nervously. 'I use' to hear Mum and Dad speaking, saying that's why the police feel the Robinson gang killed him. He'd been disrespectful, racist towards them.'

Charlie doesn't answer, instead thinking back to long ago when all the local villains got picked up and taken into the police station for questioning about Piggy's disappearance.

Stoke Newington Police Station, North London
1964

Charlie's just eleven years old and sitting with his mother in a gloomy 1960s police interview room once painted white but now a cigarette-stained dingy yellow. The questioning officer's White, fortyish, of stocky build with a wide face and thick military moustache. He aggressively questions young Charlie, voice raised in a military tone of authority:

'Have you heard anything about Gus "Piggy" Andrews's crashed vehicle left outside Nathaniel Robinson's premises? He's since disappeared without trace. Come on, you've heard something, boy, tell me?'

Charlie adopts an innocent expression, looks into the eyes of the questioning officer and replies, 'No comment.'

'Son, I see you've been trained well by your father,' the officer says with a defeated smile, but presses on regardless. 'Mr Andrews was seen entering the premises shortly after crashing his car outside. What have you heard boy?'

The child Charlie Baker's solicitor interrupts. 'Constable Morland, my client's a child and has repeatedly explained he's heard nothing. He was safely tucked up in bed at the time of the alleged incident. I really must insist you let him go without any further questioning…'

Charlie Baker's betting shop, Walthamstow Market, 1993

The ringing of his mobile phone disturbs Charlie from his not so pleasant childhood memories. The phone's away on a shelf and it stops ringing again just before Charlie finally retrieves it. He throws himself onto his luxury comfy recliner, puffs his cheeks, and breathes a sigh of relief that the Piggy situation is well and truly behind him. He scrolls through the list of nineteen missed calls on his phone. He stops scrolling as he notices one of the callers' IDs, the seventh, and says in annoyance, 'Jarrod, fuck, fuck, fuck, fucking forgot to call him back. He must have the right hump.'

Having made herself look respectable, Stacey stares lovingly at Charlie as he pours himself another glass of vintage Dom Perignon Champagne whilst scrolling through the other missed-call numbers.

He points to the bottle, and says with a raised eyebrow, 'Fancy one for the road before I call your cab?'

'Nah Charlie, I think I'd better go, and oh yeah, I keep meaning to ask. Why do you lot always do that... you call Danny Cottle, Jarrod? Mum asks everyone who gave him that nickname?'

Her question prompts Charlie to think of his on-going 18th century Jamaican pirate dream and the cute, White, dark-haired hazel-blue-eyed, freckled-faced boy called Jarrod who appears in it. Charlie smiles, shakes his head and says:

'Can't remember, the boys and me suddenly began calling Daniel by that name, and I suppose it just stuck. It's even got me calling someone else Jarrod when I'm dreaming sometimes. Just seems normal now, I guess. Funny you've asked, I often wonder why suddenly everyone started calling Ben Jarvis, Jaden.'

'That reminds me, Charlie, Ben's sister Zoe, fucking strange one her... round at hers for a sniff last night. Bit like your reason, she said she's remembered calling Ben the name Jaden in a dream. Something about it wasn't Ben in the dream but was and he wasn't her brother, she was his mum instead. I get on with them alright, but always been a bit weird that lot...'

Charlie ponders on what she's just said because the name Jaden relates to a sorrowful event stored within his psyche, a family, mother and siblings crying for their son and brother. Nevertheless, he listens with half a mind to what Stacey's saying:

'…Charlie, I feel sorry for Jarrod's wife June; everywhere he goes women are throwing themselves at him. It's them beautiful blue eyes, look lovely on a Black man and his deep cool voice, the way he speaks… He don't half look like Yanson Bailey, just different eyes…'

Charlie calls the local mini-cab firm on the phone, and ends the call by saying, 'Five minutes, sweet, mate… tell him to bib when he's outside.' He then reclines his chair, the headrest almost leaning against the open window, through which can be heard the loud clattering and voices outside of the stall holders pulling out stalls and setting up pitches. He eyes his freshly dry-cleaned suit, tie and Crombie overcoat hanging on his office door, then looks towards the television. 'Stick it on the news channel and turn it up a bit, babe,' he says to Stacey.

She does as he's asked, and comments, 'Fuck me, don't time fly?'

'Sorry about them little Alan Whicker's, treacle,' Charlie says.

Stacey looks puzzled. 'Little who… who's Alan Whickers? Ain't he that geezer off the telly Mum use' to watch back when I was a kid?'

Charlie laughs, looking lovingly at her and shaking his head. 'No, I mean, yeah, he was, but when us lot say Alan Whicker's, we mean knickers, my sweet little princess.'

She's amused by the explanation and laughs.

Charlie joins in, laughing uncontrollably before he recovers sufficiently to say, 'You think that's funny, the Jamaican's, sometimes even Jarrod and Yance call a bird's knickers the "Baggy", fucking baggy, for fuck sakes!'

Then another thought comes into his head: 'Fuck me, that was it, the TV programme, *Whicker's World*. Fucking lucky ponce Alan Whicker, it was his job to fly around the world making documentaries. Had to think then for a minute.'

Charlie looks at the knickers on the desk, then to Stacey's beautiful eyes. She smiles back and both share a moment that would last in their Twin Flame soul forever.

'What's the matter, Charlie? Why you looking at me like that?'

'Your eyes, feel as though I've known 'em forever.'

'What a beautiful thing to say.' She holds her head to one side with a vibrant smile; his words have triggered deep feelings within her.

'Look Stacey, get Ann Summers to drop some more samples and I'll help choose again, babe. I'm going to chill here for a bit before I get washed up. Don't fancy going home to her indoors just yet. After a night of that type of pleasure with you, that's the last fucking face I wanna see and voice I need to hear. I'll pop indoors after the prison visit tonight.'

She giggles, then stares proudly. 'I listen to Mum and Tracey – after all this time, she's still heartbroken over you. Auntie's best mate's ex or not, I ain't gonna let you go now. Want you all to me self my "Champagne Charlie". Remember the first time we fucked, that beautiful feeling, it felt like we'd been together all our lives. Still get that feeling now. It's like you told me that night, you said it's fate and told me I was the one. You fucking knew, Charlie. We'll find a way, I promise, so stop ya worrying.'

'Why d'ya say stop worrying?' he asks a little nervously.

'Come on, I can see it in your eyes, Charlie Baker. I get scared as well sometimes, Mum finding out. I want you to listen, when Mum and Dad moved us out to Essex to get me away from it, I just left school, I started dreaming about you. Hadn't seen you all them years since I was a kid and when I come back here to live in my twenties, I still kept dreaming about you.'

'You remember our first fuck, Stacey?' he asks.

'I just said so, didn't I? Come on Charlie, how could we ever forget? It was like playing a real-life part in one of them romantic far-fetched TV adverts or something. I'd thought of you, even dreamed of you, so deeply in love every day for years, and all the sudden I was shocked to see you at that party. It gave me that incredible feeling like I didn't know what had come over me.'

Charlie smiles brightly. 'Me too, babe. I felt it all as well.'

'You were putting out a line, you just naturally put some out for me and pointed to it. See, I never forget. It was like it was orchestrated, that song came on and everyone darted into the living room to have a dance, and we were all alone. We didn't even talk, you didn't even know it was me when you sat me up on the worktop and we just fucked there and then...'

Stacey begins to laugh as another part of the memory comes back to her. 'The girl whose party it was, Linda, came back in after a few minutes and caught us. Normally I'd have been right embarrassed but didn't give a fuck...'

She then notices Charlie's in deep thought, and says, 'Charlie, what's wrong?'

'Never forget all them years, twenty years ago, Mum had always got Cindy to give me psychic readings, insisted on visits to give me psychic readings to see how things were going to turn out during trial and put some protection around me. Suddenly every night in the boob I dreamed about this stunningly beautiful woman. I kept dreaming about her and twenty years later I'm in Linda's kitchen minding me own business and who walks in, literally the girl of my dreams, you Stacey.'

Stacey's starry eyed. 'Love it when you explain it, Charlie. Proper fucking love story. There's me growing up and when I first left school I use' to see you in the market, had a mad crush on you. Even dreamed of being with you.' A more recent memory then pops into her head. 'Oh, and Cindy was round at me mum's the other day, fucking weird her, just kept smiling at me. Always done it in a way that makes me feel as though she knows something about me. Her eyes stare, not in a horrible way but always make me think she knows something about me. She's always done it to me since we were kids. Still fucking beautiful her, no wonder she was with Cutty Robinson.'

Charlie begins to laugh. 'Hey, fucking hell why does he get all the women lusting after him? What's he got that I ain't got?'

She laughs with him, but then says, 'Charlie, all fun and jokes aside, I'd be devastated if we had to break up...'

He pulls her to the recliner for a hug, a kiss and a soft delicate squeeze of her moist vagina, causing her to pleasurably pout.

'Stacey, I actually saw you before I started dreaming of you in prison in the 70s. Listen to this, listen how, it will properly blow your fucking mind. When I dreamed of being that pirate I'm with this right familiar Black woman and she helps me see the future and shows me you just as you're stood here with me now.'

'Charlie, stop it you're giving me goosebumps.' She shivers and smiles as she speaks. 'We been on the coke all night, me two nights straight. Better be off, got a busy morning today. I'll need a couple of hours sleep and a hot shower to get me started. You better get some sleep, you're up to visit Kieran with Danny, Countess Nicole and little Jess.'

Charlie picks up on the sarcastic way Stacey has just referred to Nicole: 'Stacey, I know she speaks posh, but come on, leave it out; it's Kieran's wife for fuck sakes…'

'Well, I know she was raised in posh Chigwell, but it doesn't mean she has to speak as though she's looking down her nose at the rest of us over 'ere. Her mum and dad usually speak like us, although I've heard mum Cindy can be a bit of a wannabe toff because they had a nice few quid.'

Charlie gives that puzzled expression of his. 'Dunno why Cindy does it, but you can excuse Nicole, born in that Chigwell mansion, posh school and neighbours all her life; but I couldn't tell you why her mum Cindy talks that way at times. She was born and raised over here in East London like the rest of us.'

Charlie watches Stacey's beautiful bottom as she leaves the office. Then he hears the adjacent door open and close, the patter of a dog's paws, and Stacey making a fuss of his English Bulldog. There was always something familiar in the way Stacey kissed her lips for Patch. Subconsciously it stirred a loving vibration within the psyche of the gangster Charlie Baker. She continues to kiss her own mouth and says to the dog, 'Morning Patch.'

As she re-enters the room, she says to Charlie, 'Oh yeah, you had an English Bulldog when we were younger.'

'Yeah Stace, that's right. Granddad and uncles over Canning

Town have always bred them for a living. When the other one died of old age I went over and picked out this Patch as a pup.

'Funny, both times choosing one I just sat and waited. One out of the litter will always come to me. Tested him four times, put him back among the pups and he came walking back again and again; he was the one. Love 'em so much, got them in the olden-day dreams too.'

As Charlie's talking, the dog firstly runs around his office, then jumps straight up onto the recliner to his chest and begins licking his face. As Patch jumps off, still full of energy and running around, Charlie expertly and powerfully flicks a coin from the chair. It bounces on the side table and begins spinning. He uses different fingers to make two coins do different movements, repeating it twice and suddenly there's four coins spinning at once. Both Stacey and Patch move their heads watching the coins rotating around one another.

'Charlie, why have you always done that with the coins? I remember you doing that when I was a kid in the market pub.'

'Everyone asks why I like doing it, done it since I was a kid for as long as I can remember. Sort of relaxes me.'

As Charlie pauses to think, Stacey asks the question, 'What ever happened to that Black woman Bernice?'

The mention of her name makes Charlie smile as he recalls the sight of the Haitian lady, then in her mid-thirties, sitting at the Christmas-decorated pub table twenty years ago – a memory he'd never forget.

'Bernice took the kids back to the Caribbean, Haiti. From what I've been told she's either still there, in Miami or Jamaica now.'

As his mind drifts off into thoughts of his recurring 18th century pirate dreams, Charlie sets another two coins spinning, so that there are now six of them weaving in and out of each other as they spin.

'Charlie, I must say, the way you do that with the coins is fucking mesmerising.' She giggles as Patch studies one of the coins rotating. 'Poor Patch is getting fucking dizzy, look.'

In Charlie's mind he suddenly pictures his 18th century grubby tanned hand spinning gold coins. 'I dream of being an olden-day pirate spinning them sometimes.'

'I know you told me that already, always a sign when you're tired and had too much to drink.'

He gives Stacey a look of curiosity. 'Just had déjà vu again then; someone had said that to me before. Here, listen I always dream of being a pirate; a clairvoyant witch once told me the dream is of an actual life I've lived.'

'Who told ya, Charlie?' Stacey asks adopting a serious expression now.

'De sweetest lickle Obeah ooman. Mummy did tell me so.'

Hearing Charlie talk in perfect Jamaica patois and the mention of Obeah gives Stacey shivers.

'You said that just then like a real Black Jamaican man, like Bob Marley or someone. Heard load of White geezers try to speak like that but they sound nothing like a Black man. Lived with a Black man once. Anyway, don't know about all that Voodoo stuff, I'm told all that's to do with the Devil.'

'Don't believe all you hear, my little princess,' Charlie replies knowingly.

His mind is filled with thoughts of two events: one from his on-going 18th century dreams when the Haitian witch called Lana was doing future life regression reading; the other from his stay in Jamaica and what the woman Charmaine had told him. Lana's reading had showed him a vision of his twin soul, and it wasn't until he met his mistress that he realised the woman he and Lana had visualised was her, Stacey Holley. And Charmaine in Jamaica had said these words to him:

'Oh my God before I forget. Your Twin Flame is obviously an angel within our soul tribe. You've already met in this life but for many reasons she isn't ready. There's a ten-year age gap but in twenty years, you both will be ready to join in union again.'

He then thinks of the visions he has when he sees his hands as those of a Black man spinning the coins. He also recalls a black panther and other visions of the ancient Koolah tribe.

'It's a bit like what Cindy Nevin goes on about,' he says, 'Déjà vu, like I've done it in many lives before or something, babe. Like with spinning the coins, I even dream of being a Black man doing it.'

Stacey laughs. 'Black man, fuck me Charlie, what goes on inside your head? Crazy dreams and always coming out with stuff like that.'

He smiles. 'If only you knew, treacle; you don't know the half of it.'

Suddenly they hear the sound of a car horn outside. Stacey stuffs a plastic Ann Summers bag into her leather shoulder bag and goes to leave.

'Babe,' Charlie says, a nervous thought striking him, 'I know you'll keep it quiet about Cutty Robinson being Yanson's dad, won't ya? Not many know it.'

She nods reassuringly and gives Charlie a final quick kiss before she goes. Charlie stays on the recliner, and with Stacey gone, still high on coke he mutters a few incoherent words to Patch, before picking up his phone to call back Daniel Cottle, better known to him as Jarrod. As he listens to the prolonged, monotone abroad ring tone, he reaches for a screwdriver and pops a small section of skirting board off, revealing a prepared hole in the wall. Inside there's a black tea cloth, which Charlie takes out. Patch watches him as he opens a small box that's sitting on his desk and takes out from it a brand-new, gleaming automatic .38 calibre pistol. He cleans his fingerprints off it, wraps it in the cloth, and places it in the hole, before clipping back the skirting board. The ringtone's still continuously sounding as Charlie rests back on the recliner.

'Answer the phone, Jarrod, for fuck sakes,' he mutters, as Patch hops up onto his lap and makes himself comfortable, resting his head back on Charlie's stomach.

CHAPTER 22

Priory Court Estate, Walthamstow
1974

It's a week after ten-year-olds Yanson Bailey and Benjamin Jarvis stole the amusement arcade takings from the parked car. Yanson is sitting on the sofa in the Jarvis family home whilst Ben's in the kitchen speaking with his mother, Jasmine. Yanson's always intrigued by the modern-day Oliver-Twist-style Fagan's den vibe that the home of the Jarvises has. Owing to the antics of their constant skulduggery, their home is filled with many modern luxuries, including in the living room, a three-piece leather sofa and a state-of-the-art modern colour TV. Ben's twelve-year-old sister Nancy Jarvis sits in an armchair opposite Yanson. They're not saying anything to each other, but the looks the pair sometimes exchange suggest there's something like puppy love between them. Nancy looks like a prettier female version of Benjamin, sharing his blond hair and bright blue eyes.

In the kitchen, Benjamin looks disgustedly at the two empty vodka bottles stuffed in the bin and opens the fridge door. He sighs, rolling his blue eyes. 'What, no milk for cereal, Mum?'

Jasmine, nursing a hangover, lights a hand-rolled cigarette she's just made from dog ends and is too embarrassed to face her son. Instead, she stares out the window.

Ben, frustrated by his mother's behaviour, runs to his bedroom crying.

As Nancy leaves the living room to go to the toilet, Yanson decides to see what's happening elsewhere. The door to the kitchen isn't fully closed and peeping through the gap he sees and hears Jasmine on her knees politely praying:

'Please Jesus, I only ever call on you when I got a big problem.

Please can you help me and the kids have a decent Christmas. Jesus, please help.'

Yanson comes away from the doorframe as he hears Benjamin coming down the passageway. As she gets to her feet, Jasmine hears the front door slam.

Yanson and Benjamin have gone out and are in the lift travelling down from the fourth floor. Ben's most upset and begins crying in frustration.

'That four quid from the arcade swindle I gave her on the way to school the other day, she's spent it all on booze.'

'You're joking,' Yanson exclaims.

'No, am I fuck. We're skint again. She gets carried away in the pub and buys her whole family and their friends drinks all night, then brings the whole pub back to ours and they eat the food. Christmas soon and I woke up to nothing in me fridge.' Ben bangs the side of the lift with his palm. 'Yance, there was no milk in me fridge this morning.' Calming down a little he adds, 'Not Mum's fault; she's just kind-hearted. And she can't go out on the thieve at the moment, as she don't want to be locked up this Christmas. Me big sister Zoe always tells people in our house it's either feast or famine, no in-between, and she's fucking right.'

Yanson shrugs his shoulders sympathetically and tries to find some encouraging words to say to his friend. 'Yeah but at least yer mum's not in prison, Ben. Remember this time last year? Come on, let's go into the High Street, see if we can find Iftica, Liam and them lot; they may have something we can get involved with.'

Benjamin wipes his tears and with a look of sincerity says, 'I swear when I'm big my kids will have a normal life.'

Walthamstow Market

The mile long street market is packed with Christmas shoppers on a dark winter's evening. For well over a decade Britain had seen a huge influx of migrant Caribbean workers and recently the beginning of the Pakistani and Greek migration, all changing the culture of East London and other parts of Britain. Benjamin walks through the market feeling envious towards the normal families of all nations he sees around him buying their Christmas treats from stallholders and stores.

After a short while, Ben and Yanson are happy to see Julie Marney, the look-out girl on their recent amusement arcade escapade. She's stood on the corner of a slip road outside the butchers next door to the Chequers Pub, with little nine-year-old Stacey Holley alongside her, watching the hordes of people of all nations go by; both girls fascinated by the ethnic languages and accents. Julie and Yanson have been close friends since the age of five, but Stacey's especially pleased to spot Yanson, as she's recently become his secret admirer – a childhood crush brought on by his handsome face, strapping physique and stylish clothing he always wears.

Suddenly a commotion erupts, as the middle-aged Black Caribbean woman Bernice starts shouting at passers-by. She's a large lady with a larger-than-life personality, now magnified by having had a bit too much to drink, and a part of the market comes to a standstill as onlookers stop to observe the fuss surrounding this Afro-haired, light-skinned, loud-mouthed Black lady.

A Cockney stallholder shouts, 'Oh her again, someone should lock up that nutcase and throw away the key.'

Julie feels sad at this lack of compassion towards Bernice. As Ben and Yanson approach, she says, 'Hello you two, just waiting for Mum in there. What you's up to…?'

Inside the butchers, Julie's dolly bird mother, Stella, her friend Tracey and the butcher's female assistant are having a conversation. Stella and her daughter Julie look alike, sharing the same beautiful dark hair, loving face and remarkable huge blue eyes. Her friend Tracey's glamour relies more on hairstyling and make-up, without which she might be called plain. Tracey's looking after nine-year-old Stacey for the day, while Stacey's mum and aunt visit Stacey's aunt's boyfriend in Pentonville Prison.

All three women look outside at Julie speaking to Yanson and Benjamin.

Tracey turns to Stella and says, 'You'd better watch little Julie with them two out there; that's one of them Jarvis pikey lot she's speaking to, and as for them vicious, dirty thieving wogs…'

A pretty young mother in the queue with her three mixed-race Black infant children sighs, all too used to hearing this sort of racism, then commonplace in the 1970s. She promises herself that if her children have heard it, she'll say something, but they're happily playing amongst themselves and clearly aren't listening to anybody else.

Tracey points to Bernice outside being detained by the young bobby on the beat as more of his colleagues move through the packed crowds to join him.

'Well,' she says, 'as you can see out there, you know their kind are always nothing but trouble as well …'

Stella Marney objects: 'Tracey, that's unfair; there's good and bad in every kind.'

The young mother smiles at this as she hears it.

'That coloured boy there Yanson,' Stella continues, 'my Julie reckons he's her best mate.'

Tracey looks disgusted. 'Yeah, well if I were you, I'd keep me eye on your Julie. She's always been well clever and had her own mind…'

Stella laughs. 'Oh now you've just said it, she hasn't half got some imagination. Our Julie's got an imaginary little sister; her sister and her are both Black princesses. Julie's ever so specific about her Black sister having a half-blue-and-brown eye and a strand of blonde hair growing.'

Both Tracey and the butcher's assistant start to snigger, but Stella continues, 'She's sort of growing out of the imaginary friend bit now, but when she was younger…'

Tracey interrupts with an abrupt shake of her head and delivers her words with venom:

'Black Princess, how can a wog be a princess? Who'd ever heard of such a stupid fucking thing? Fucking gollywog Princess, indeed, you're right she must have some fucking imagination. Whatever next, a wog married to our royal prince Charles, a White prince? A coon and coon kid in our Buckingham Palace, don't make me laugh.'

Both Tracey and the butcher's assistant are laughing, but the young mother in the queue and Stella show obvious signs of disgust at Tracey's vile racism. The young mother looks to her oldest son who's five years old, thinking by the distraught look on his face he must now have heard, but Stella speaks, determined to explain more, and the young mother with the children's too intrigued to want to interrupt her.

'Well,' Stella says with a look of concentration on her face, 'her Black Princess little sister, Julie always calls her Gabi. Gabi has a male best friend who's got a black leopard as a best mate and they live in a sort of like jungle town with a palace and many beautiful waterfalls, music playing and people dancing beautifully. She said it's heaven and they are the angels.'

Tracey angrily butts in. 'Are you for fucking real? How silly, we've seen how them coons all dance around in the films like wild fucking animals.'

Stella presses on with her explanation:

'I showed her White angels and Jesus in some religious books, but she won't have it, actually gets angry… I asked her if any of her family are there and she looks at me strange and says, "No, well sort of. Just Black people, the countries always hot like Spain." She says they speak another language. I asked her what, Spanish? And she says, "No, you are there but you're not White, Mum. Yanson's there but looks different with his long hair and the black leopard friend." When I put her to bed at night, she's talking a strange fucking language in her sleep. She even does it sometimes when she's playing on her own, or with her imaginary sister and other friends… Oh yeah that's it, she says her name's not Julie, it's Monifa.'

Having finished, Stella laughs and gives a proud nod of her head, bringing a smile from the young mother in the queue.

Tracey frowns at her friend and says, 'Stella, if I didn't know better, I'd think you're a secret wog lover.'

Her words get a laugh out of the butcher's assistant. Stella doesn't respond and instead addresses the butcher's assistant in a business-like manner: 'Right, please don't forget to deliver the turkey on time. We fly out to Spain on Christmas Eve and it won't be Christmas out there without it.'

The assistant nods as she remarks, 'I couldn't do Christmas out there, wouldn't seem real, got to be here in the cold, Father Christmas's reindeer and sleigh for the kids and all that.'

CHAPTER 23

Outside the four children are larking around, but Yanson's expression changes as he notices the Jaguar being driven down the street. The crowds part for it before it comes to a rest parking halfway up the street at the turning of the Chequers Pub.

Julie notices Yanson's concerned expression, and says, 'What's wrong, Yance?'

All three kids watch as Yanson crosses the street to get a better view. He sees a huge, dark-haired, heavy-set man get out. The man takes off his blazer, throws it on the driver's seat, exchanging it for a warm Crombie-type beige mac. He opens the passenger door for a tall, classy, brunette woman to get out, and helps her on with her coat, before engaging the central locking with his key.

As Stella and Tracey walk out of the butchers, the lady and gentleman respectfully exchange hellos with them. Tracey gives the boys a cautious warning look, a piercing stare that unsettles them, then turns her head back as the woman from the Jaguar addresses her excitedly:

'Hello Tracey, I hear you're going out with Charlie Baker. Lucky bitch, you pulled one of the Lewin blaggers.'

Tracey smiles reminding the lady, 'Yeah, you ain't doing too bad either...'

Not wanting to listen to what might become a long conversation here, the man from the Jaguar says to her, 'See you inside,' and walks on into the pub.

The lady grabs both Stella and Tracey's arms, saying, 'Come on, won't take no for an answer. I want both of you to pop in for one drink with us. Come on, it's Christmas for fuck sakes.'

Just then the young mother from the butcher's shop queue emerges from the shop laden with her Christmas turkey. She decides she must say something and approaches Tracey.

'I was raised to date my own colour but now date only the Black man. I've found they're far cleaner, more compassionate and grown up than any of the White men I used to go out with.' Looking Tracey directly in the eyes, she adds, 'And you talk down about Black people, but the Black Jamaican Cutty Robinson's got the look of a Prince, and I'd bet you'd give him one.'

As the woman walks away, pushing her pram up the market, Stella laughs, 'She's got a point, girls. Cindy Nevin couldn't resist him and I wouldn't say no, that's for fucking sure. Besides, your new boyfriend Charlie's quite fond of the Jamaican. In fact, the Lewin mob and other heavy villains all over the East End got respect for Cutty Robinson.'

The lady in the fur says her piece, 'Tracey, you don't want to let his mob hear you talking all that wog talk... We all remember what happened to Piggy when we were kids...'

Tracey stops smiling, thinking about what the woman has just said, before noticing the changed look on Stella's face and then the fact that the whole of the market, stallholders, customers, the police officers who were handling the Bernice situation, everyone, has suddenly stopped what they were doing to stare at what's happening behind her. Headed by Ricky Lewin, a large group of White men, all well-respected, elite East End gangsters had begun appearing from around the corner. Due to the silence, the sounds of car doors could be heard shutting as others were getting out of their parked cars to join them on their way towards the pub. It seemed their vibration had caused the whole of Walthamstow market to stop and stare.

Stella quietly exclaims, 'Well, if that wasn't a fucking coincidence; there's the Lewin mob coming along now.'

As they get nearer, Stella acknowledges Ricky Lewin and his shorter, less good-looking brother Geoff. Also present are Ludwig Epstein AKA 'Bigwig' or 'Brains', Patsy Fagan, their youngest active member twenty-two-year-old Charlie Baker, and the members of four other London-based armed robbery gangs. Nineteen seventy-four was a period where there wasn't a lot of money in the mainstream East London working class community.

It wasn't till the following year Margaret Thatcher would lead the Conservative Party and begin to transform working class Britain, giving the poor the opportunity to buy brand new cars, become entrepreneurs and self-made millionaires. The contrasting bleak poverty of 1974 East End London enhances the way these high-earning, flamboyant celebrity villains present themselves and the vibration they create. Some of them, including twenty-nine-year-old Ricky Lewin have just arrived back from Spain with suntans, but all are dressed to the nines, to perfection, the very highest order. Some dress formal, in Crombie coats, three-piece suits, shirts and ties; others appear very smart and casual; all dripping with expensive gold jewellery and watches, and many trendy 70s haircuts on display.

Even so, Mr Ricky Lewin always stands out from the rest. He's six-feet-three-inches tall with a muscular body. The sun from his recent trip to Spain has turned his natural tanned skin a glowing golden brown enhancing his renowned pretty-boy looks. He wears a black cashmere V-neck jumper, 70s fashionable unbuttoned collared light blue shirt with the collars out, navy fitted slacks, a trendy pair of Italian imported shoes, gold watch and a huge carat pinkie diamond ring – the kind of get-up that has earned him the nickname Flash Ricky, along with his flamboyant lifestyle and extremely lavish habits. He wears his brown hair in a 70s-pop-star style, cropped up top but long at the back, coming down way past his shoulders. His eyes are a seductive hazel and his teeth display a perfect natural Hollywood whiteness. Nevertheless, despite all the flash, he's known for his kindness and generosity, and speaks in an old-fashioned manner.

Tracey has a slight panic, wondering whether her new boyfriend's there, and can't turn to face them just yet. She begins fixing her hair and whispers, 'Is my Charlie with 'em, Stel? Don't want him to see me unless me make-up's alright?'

Stella looks up to see Charlie Baker larking about with some of the older crooks. She smiles and looks back at her friend. 'Yeah Trace, Charlie's with 'em.'

The rest of the colourful group of villains walk into the pub, but Charlie Baker and Ricky Lewin stay behind outside. Ricky's intrigued by the commotion concerning Bernice and at first doesn't see the face of the policeman in charge amongst the crowds, a tough-looking, no-nonsense Irishman, Sergeant Ted Riley, whose cauliflower ear and crooked nose are souvenirs from his ABA boxing champion days. Charlie stops to talk with the boys, Yanson and Benjamin. 'Fuck me,' he says to Yanson suddenly, 'I nearly forgot, that gold coin that Elsie gave ya...'

Yanson takes the gold coin out of his pocket and hands it to Charlie, who begins rubbing his finger over the distinctive chip to its edge. He knows it's the same coin he's seen in his recurring dreams, the same coin he took out of his leather pouch in the 18th century in another life. Charlie's face turns serious as he looks into the eyes of Yanson Bailey and his mind takes him back to a memory buried deep in his psyche, the Black Haitian witch Lana dressing his wounds and her lover a Black Haitian pirate Raphael sewing up a nasty opened gash wound on his back.

Caribbean Sea, 1754

It had been early morning on board the pirate vessel when with more than a hundred cheering pirates surrounding him, twenty-five-year-old James Morgan had fought the drunkard pirate Captain Grimes, a ginger-haired, long-bearded man twice his size. Towards the end of the fight, the powerful pirate captain had picked up the badly beaten and bloodied Morgan and slammed him onto a deck table with ease, and then he'd delivered what he was sure would be the coup de grâce by means of an axe blow to the younger man's chest. But then Morgan had stuck his dagger through the windpipe of the pirate captain, causing blood to spurt from his mouth, killing him instantly.

Later the victorious young James Morgan lies on his side as Haitian witch Lana tends to his cuts and wounds. She removes his leather pouch from his breast pocket, revealing a distinct bruise covering the entire right side of his chest. The brutal pirate captain's axe had penetrated his jacket and the thick leather wallet, the pressure of which caused the bruising. He opens his pouch revealing part of his share of gold coins he's accumulated, and specifically the one that had saved his life. As Lana's dressing his wounds, Morgan takes the coin out which took the brunt of Grimes's axe and it gleams as a sunray from the porthole shines against it. Grime's axe had left a distinctive chip into the edge. Although in excruciating pain, the young pirate smiles excitedly and with a croaky voice says to Lana, 'This coin will always be me lucky one.'

'It has to be,' she answers. 'Where many before you failed, you've killed that evil monster Grimes. Look, this means it's your time to lead the men now, they hated him…'

Morgan interrupts her, 'But how did you already know? You told me I would one day captain the crew?'

She doesn't specifically answer his question but shakes her head and simply says, 'It's your time to lead the men; they hated him. New name for a new life, your name's no longer James Morgan, it's pirate Captain Jim Morgan from now on.'

Black pirate Raphael enters the cabin and helps Morgan onto his belly. He yelps in protest, pressing his face into the pillow, as Raphael pours neat alcohol on the rear shoulder wound and begins cleaning it up.

Lana kneels on the floor, closing her eyes as the same porthole sunray shines directly into her face. 'Relax, Jim Morgan,' she says. 'I want you to breathe, take a deep breath in and breathe out all your negative energy. Relax your mind. Slowly fill your lungs with air; breathe in the positive, completely emptying out the negative contaminated air.

'When you're ready, close your eyes and concentrate on the sound of my voice. Your mind is about to enter the deepest levels of relaxation you've ever experienced in this life…'

After a few minutes of Lana's guidance, Morgan's view of the cabin appears blurry. He closes his eyes, but still hears the voice of Lana:

'As your breathing slows, notice the gentle relaxed expansion and retraction of your chest. You are completely relaxed now you are safe and all is well… Soon you'll see it.'

Morgan feels his sense of time slip away; he couldn't say how long he's had his eyes closed for, just feels he's been lost in that blissful trance state for a long period.

He hears Lana's voice say, 'Your soul has become conscious in a future life progression…' and feels a warm, calm atmosphere, before he begins to hear voices of laughter and becomes conscious in that future dimension, his future incarnation.

Cutty Robinson's barber's, North London, December 1973

In the backroom gangsters' meeting, Charlie Baker wakes abruptly from dozing in his chair as the Jamaican Clinton Cottle bursts into the room and starts slapping his son, nine-year-old Daniel Cottle, about, screaming at him in Jamaican patois: 'Me did tell unu wait pon de chair out dessar when the barber finish unu rarted skiffle. Me no want you out back here and hear certain tings.'

After Cutty Robinson has stepped in and ordered him to stop, Clinton Cottle breaks down crying. He's a large man running to fat and his body shakes as he sobs and says, 'Cutty, I wake everyday confused, man…'

Cutty and Charlie exchange glances. Charlie continuously looks back and forth between Daniel and Cutty, realising that they share the same shape head, eyes and other facial features.

Then the madam Elsie nudges him, saying, 'You must have been frightened out of your wits being woken like that. Are you alright, Charlie?'

'Yeah Tricks,' he replies. 'I was in a deep sleep just then, dreaming I was lying on a bed. A Black woman, Lana, was talking to me and a Black geezer sewing up a deep gash, flesh wound to me back. Crazy fucking dream.'

'Sounds like you've been smoking too much weed and hash,' Elsie mumbles, as she then turns her attention towards young Daniel. 'So Daniel,' she says to the boy, 'when you get bigger you going to be a builder like daddy?'

Clinton Cottle listening expects the boy to say yes and make him proud, but instead Daniel says, 'No, not gonna be a drunk like me dad,' and turning with a proud smile in the direction of Mr Robinson adds, 'I'm going to be a gangster like Cutty Robinson.'

Most of the room including Cutty himself can't help but laugh at this, but Clinton Cottle immediately flies off the handle, lunging again at Daniel, now tightly twisting his school cardigan choking him as he applies powerful back and forehand smacks to the face. He grips and screws up the school jumper so tightly against the boy's windpipe that he's actually cutting off Daniel's air supply.

Cutty Robinson stands and shouts at Clinton, 'Let the boy go now, before you kill him.'

One of Cutty's henchmen, a huge powerhouse of a man nicknamed Bull, prizes Clinton's grip from the boy, and Daniel runs and huddles up to Cutty Robinson.

Again, Charlie keeps looking back and forth to the exact same colour eyes and certain facial features of Daniel Cottle and Nathaniel Robinson, and now firmly wonders if his beloved friend, the ladies' man gangster, had somehow fathered Daniel Cottle. Charlie looks to the boss of his gang, Ricky Lewin, and wonders if the puzzled look on Ricky's face is due to the same thought. Then Charlie finds his mind lingering, concentrating on Daniel's eyes realising he knows them from a character in his recurring 18th century pirate dreams. The one he's just woken from is still vivid in his mind. The unique vibration of the White pirate kid suddenly becomes clearer, a conscious knowing he has a deep love for the child. He sits picturing the White child pirate Jarrod, his freckled face and long curly black hair, at the same time looking into the eyes of Daniel Cottle, realising the young White kid's eyes are just the same. He doesn't consciously realise that it's not just that they look exactly the same but that they mirror the same soul. He wonders if the affection he feels towards the boy Daniel is because of the affection he feels towards the boy Jarrod in his dreams.

Walthamstow Market
December 1974

The returning hum of the market brings Charlie Baker's mind back to the present. Momentarily he's surprised to be where he finds himself. 'Fucking hell, wondered where I was just then,' he says.

He takes another deep look at the gold coin in his hand before handing it back to Yanson. 'There ya go, Yance. I must have thought about that coin before I went to sleep the other day and had an olden-day dream about having the exact one with exactly the same dent and scratch on it.'

Ricky Lewin gives his younger friend an enquiring look. 'What's up, Charlie? You look concerned about something, stood there in deep thought for a few minutes... What were you thinking about?'

Charlie shakes his head as he answers: 'What am I thinking about, Rick? How things were so much different last Christmas, Clinton and Pearl alive, and little Jarrod Cottle was a happy kid.'

Ricky Lewin asks, 'You love the kid little Jarrod Cottle, Charlie?'

'Yeah, just something about him, felt close to him since he was a baby, have done ever since.' Charlie beams with happiness as he thinks back to an earlier thought. 'Strange one, Rick, listen to this. I dreamed I was someone else in the olden days and in that life I dreamed being me today. Difficult to even say...'

Ricky doesn't answer and instead jokingly gives Charlie a look as if to say he's lost his mind. In truth, Ricky's a bit distracted by taking an interest in the commotion outside the pub, trying to see who the police officers have surrounded.

Charlie turns to Yanson. 'I've been to see Jarrod Cottle,' he says to the boy.

Yanson nods sadly as he replies, 'Yeah, I saw him getting taken into Church Hill.'

'I been there to see him a few times, Yance. He'd feel better for a visit from you, as well.'

Yanson looks puzzled. 'But I hardly know him, Charlie...' he says.

CHAPTER 24

Ricky's no longer taking any notice of what Charlie and Yanson are saying; instead being more interested with what's happening with the nearby disturbance. When he sees it's Bernice getting carted away to the police van, he shouts out, 'For fuck sakes, no!'

'Afraid so, Mr Lewin,' a familiar voice says to him.

He turns to see Sergeant Ted Riley, and the Irish man continues, 'Someone called in, made a complaint about her causing a disturbance, been arrested for threatening behaviour, resisting arrest...'

It's the first time the pair have seen each other since Ricky's release from prison along with the rest of the Lewin gang, for a major armed robbery conspiracy, and Ricky greets the police Sergeant respectfully: 'Evening Officer Riley, didn't know it was you on duty.'

Riley shakes his head. 'You trod one of your brand-new boots in something special as a kid, Lewin. The feck did you lot get out of all those armed robbery charges? Thought that was the last we'd seen of you.'

'I really have no idea what you're going on about, Officer,' Ricky replies with a straight face. 'We were all innocent and had been stitched up. Thank God the jury realised'

'Oh come now Lewin,' says Riley abruptly, 'feck off, we go way back, you may be able to buy or fool those gullible women jurors, but you'll not kid me with that feckin' look. That was a shocking not guilty verdict.' With a smug smirk he adds, 'Always remember, we've only to get lucky the once, Lewin, understand?'

Once inside the police van Bernice looks to the seated bench opposite to see a pair of brown eyes looking back at her and a smaller pair of glistening cat's eyes lower down. As her eyes adjust to the darkness she sees her fellow Haitian Claudette's unmistakable pretty face and mystic eyes looking back at her. Claudette shakes her head at Bernice and gives her a disgusted look.

'Oh, it's you again,' says Bernice addressing Claudette in their native Creole Haitian. 'You're always there to lecture me, telling me what to do...'

Some of the onlookers laugh at Bernice's outburst inside the van. Among them are the Stephens brothers and the rest of the gang of Black youths called the Selbourne Park boys. Albert Stephens shouts loudly, 'Watch Bernice, mad woman, always a chat to she self.'

Meanwhile Ricky Lewin pleads to Sergeant Riley:

'Come on copper, it's Christmas and you're gonna lock up poor Bernice, away from her kids. She just likes a drink, she can be a bit loud, but never physically harms anyone, has she?

'You know she's never got over her husband leaving her for that young bird. Tell ya what, my driver will take her home. Come on, bit of mutual understanding, season of good will and all that. You ain't gotta be that tough bastard copper all your life. We're on the opposite side, but come on, show everyone here you lot can be alright. Use your authority, Copper...'

Sergeant Riley holds his chin and nods his head slightly, pondering over what Ricky has said and on the edge of being persuaded, helped by the younger man's charming smile.

Tracey, watching what's going on, turns to Stella and whispers, 'Why's Flash Ricky speaking up for the spade?'

Inside the police van, Claudette says to Bernice, 'The man there speaking to the police is one of us. Most of that group of men he arrived with, you just saw walk into the pub, are angels of our soul tribe.' Indicating Charlie Baker, she adds, 'Him and the blond man there as well, Morgan.'

'His name's not Morgan,' Bernice objects. 'You mean Charlie Baker. I knew his father, knew Charlie when he was at school. He's been around this market since we first came to England.'

Claudette smiles brightly. 'That is correct, Bernice, but both the soul of myself and Charlie Baker's shared an amazing experience two centuries ago and I renamed him Jim Morgan. Nature designed Charlie physically the same so that we, his fellow angels, would recognise him from our regression dreams.'

She looks out at Ricky Lewin and the Irish police sergeant, who are still face to face in conversation, and continues, 'Koolah has surrounded the police officer with spirit and they are conversing with him, the soul. They will help the Koolah angel Ricky Lewin into letting you go.'

Bernice snaps drunkenly, 'He won't let me go. I'm off to the police cell to sleep it off, stupid.'

'You've got to start listening,' Claudette replies patiently, 'Drinking every day will not remedy your feeling of being left heartbroken by your husband. You need to come back home to Haiti and your soul cleansed, unblocked. An island bloodbath will once again open your soul to our spirituality...'

Claudette pauses allowing Bernice to sob and after a short while adds, 'Tell you what, let's make a deal. If the police let you go, when you see Charlie next call him Jim Morgan. If he asks who said, tell him I did and explain my name's Lana.'

Bernice stops sobbing as Sergeant Riley and another colleague walk in their direction towards the police van.

Riley stands resting a hand on the top of the opened door. 'Come on Bernice, out you get... Up ya get before I change my mind.'

As Bernice emerges from the van, Riley points to Ricky Lewin and says, 'I'm letting you go on this occasion and you've got that man there to thank.'

Ricky smiles and calls her over. 'Come in Bernice,' he says. 'I'll arrange to have ya driven home. I'll have the pub call a taxi in a while.'

She walks to him, and he gives her his arm and walks her into the pub.

Watching them, young Julie Marney proudly smiles as the loud-mouthed stall holder, who had been the one shouting for Bernice to be locked up, now moves respectfully out of the way to allow Mr Lewin and Bernice to pass.

Inside the pub, it's a joyful Christmas family atmosphere. Food on the tables and Christmas music playing greets Bernice. Ricky takes the place that's been saved for him at a table with his brother and other leading members of the Lewin gang. Geoff Lewin calls the barmaid over, to order drinks for all the new arrivals, including Bernice, Tracey, Stella and the young girls, but leaves out Charlie Baker.

'No need to tell me what yours is …a glass of champagne, Charlie. Got it coming up, handsome,' says the attractive barmaid as she walks away to get the drinks.

Once she's gone, the talk at the Lewin table takes on a more serious tone. Addressing the other men, Ricky says angrily, 'I told them when they brought the poxy juror in on the swindle not to pay him till much later. It was fucking obvious he'd start spending like that, fucking idiot. What did I say? Not to let him have the dough till it had all properly died down. Fucking works on a production line in the local toy factory and gone from being in debt with no car to recently paying everything off and owning a BMW. What is he, a cunt?'

Outside in the market, as the final police car drives off, Yanson leads Benjamin round to where they saw the Jaguar park. As they're walking round, the sight of Ricky Lewin's gleaming white Rolls Royce Corniche Convertible brings a huge smile to the face of Yanson. He says quietly to Benjamin, 'I'll have a car like that someday.'

Benjamin smiles and nods. When they get to the Jaguar, Yanson peers through the back window and, exactly as his dream showed, sees the blazer on the driver's seat. It gives him a mixture of a feeling of eeriness and an overjoyed rush of excitement. He kneels and his hand scrambles around on the ground. Having picked up a suitable pebble, he stands and his smile is exchanged for a look of concentration.

'Right, you keep watch, Ben,' he says, then throws the pebble, at the second attempt shattering the quarter-light window of the driver's side. After taking a quick look around him, he pushes the shattered glass in with his elbow, and reaches in to open the door.

He grabs the gentleman's jacket and rolls it up as Ben has a quick look inside the empty glove box. Then after closing the car door behind them, they run off heading towards a nearby regular spot where their friend Liam Donahue's father was a caretaker at a local youth centre.

Once there, they sit in the darkness of the tool shed, lit only by a fuel lantern. Yanson pushes his hand inside the inner jacket pocket and retrieves the bulky, neatly banded wads of money, two thousand pounds in twenty notes. The sight of the money in the child's tiny hand sets both boys hearts racing, bringing smiles to their faces and they begin joyfully jumping up and down.

'Fucking hell, we're rich, Yance. How did you know it was there? How did you know it was in the jacket and not search the glove box?

Yanson, counting one of the two bundles as he speaks, replies, 'Put it this way, if Julie wasn't there we'd have walked straight past it. We'll give her a small cut.'

'That's true, yeah Julie deserves something, but how did you know?'

Yanson concentrates on his counting and ignores the question for the moment. He finally counts out the fifty twenty-pound notes from one of the bundles and double checks it's the same size as the one he's already counted, then says, 'I told you last week, that woman in the bakery, Claudette, showed us it in a dream. Fucking hell, Ben, there's two fucking grand here.'

Yanson thinks back to the off-white, pink light he saw in the dream of Claudette. It triggers his mind to show him a glimpse of the pink light hovering over the ground of the ancient Koolah spiritual circle. For a second, the black panther Jojo's present in the shed stood looking directly at him.

Ben laughs and says, 'Yance, we got a grand each. I never ever thought I'd ever have a grand.'

Both boys again begin jumping up and down, hugging one another, but Yanson's smile leaves his face momentarily. 'No Ben,' he says, 'we're giving some to your mum, five hundred and we split what's left, seven fifty each. We'll give it to Uncle Charlie to look after. But listen not a word to no one else.'

The boys resume their happy laughing and hugging, before Yanson says, 'Come on Ben, let's go. We'll leave our share here and take it to Charlie tomorrow.'

Meanwhile in the pub, Tracey and her friend Stella Marney sit with the children Julie and Stacey, a table away from the Lewin gang. The kids are drinking a coke and eating a packet of crisps each as the adult women both drink spirits. Some of the Lewin gang table and the children from the next table are sat mesmerised, watching as Charlie Baker continuously has his coins spinning. No one takes much notice of Bernice stood next to the table. Everyone's used to seeing her talking to herself, and she presently appears to be having an in-depth conversation in broken-French with an apparently empty wall:

'I hope you haven't come in to keep lecturing me... Yes, I will call Charlie, Morgan... Yes, now go and leave me in peace.'

Bernice then goes to sit down at the same table as Tracey, Stella and the girls. The racist Tracey looks uncomfortable, but Bernice laughs, smiles at Tracey, nods in the direction of the Lewin table, and asks, 'Charlie Baker your new boyfriend?'

'Yeah, what's it got to do with you? And how did you know his name?'

Bernice laughs. 'My husband worked for his father before he ran away and left me when our children were babies. Listen, spirit is here with me and tells me you and Charlie will have one or more children together, but you have to be careful not to push him away, understand?'

Tracey's expression softens a little. At the least, she's intrigued by this.

'Your whole extended family despise Black people,' Bernice continues 'and have made you this way. Like most racist White English, you were born into being racist and the hatred bred into you. Similar to religion, racism's embedded in the breeding. You don't feel comfortable being racist, just do it because now you feel it's to be expected...'

'How do you know?' Tracey asks.

'How? Spirit is here with us… Soul tribe spirit is here with us. Our soul mate tells me her soul was very close to Charlie two centuries ago. Her name was Lana during that life.'

Tracey moves her head in closer and looks serious. 'Spirit… two centuries ago, what do you mean… what you on about?'

'She tells me your soul's not that of a racist; you've helped us many times, in many lives. Listen, if Charlie's soul felt you didn't like Black people he could not stay with you.'

Tracey's feelings are a mix of confusion, upset and intrigue, but she feels herself warming to this larger-than-life Black woman who seems to know something of her past and future.

'Bernice, a mate of mine told me about you people with the gift you've got and I didn't believe her up until I've just spoke to you. Who's this person that's telling you this?'

'Gift, young lady? You haven't seen anything yet; you have no idea.' Bernice smiles. 'Tracey, listen carefully…'

Bernice's mind pictures a beautiful secluded Caribbean beach with a few huts, and she explains:

'Today my young cousin Claudette's in her twenties, physically living in a Voodoo beach hut back home on our native Haiti with her sister and infant nephew, Hercule. Claudette astral travels from a future life, a dimension twenty years from now, 1993 where she lives as our wealthy spiritual Voodoo Queen between Haiti and Jamaica. In the future 1993 dimension Claudette's reached spiritual realm high priestess, ascended master, and is able to travel through to any dimension in history or into the future in just a moment. That's how she's with us now. She specialises in many forms of spiritual time travelling, including astral projection, a powerful out of body experience as well as physical crossing of dimensions. She even travels back in history to visit her own self and assists herself two centuries ago during our slave uprising.'

A faint vision of Claudette wearing mid-90s clothing appears before Tracey who stares in disbelief.

'Yes,' says Bernice, 'she's showing herself to you. She appears in this form throughout history; her astral body image appears the same age regardless of which period because she's forty-five when her soul astral travels.' Bernice laughs a long laugh. 'Thought I was just the local drunk crazy woman speaking to myself, didn't you?'

CHAPTER 25

Later, Charlie eventually leaves the Lewin table and comes over to Tracey and Stella. By this time, he's got himself quite drunk and takes a huge wad of bank notes from his pocket, shouting so that the whole premises can hear, 'I'm buying for everyone who knows me in this pub...'

'Charlie,' his girlfriend Tracey instinctively protests, 'everyone in here knows you'

He smiles drunkenly. 'Tracey, my ole man always says and it's true, you got to enjoy it because you can't take it with ya.'

Charlie leans down and kisses the seated Tracey. Their lingering kiss causes the children, Julie and Stacey, to giggle with embarrassment.

Tracey, now quite drunk herself, places a palm on Bernice's neck, and says, 'Charlie, I tell ya what, I been speaking to this woman all night and she's changed the way I feel about the world, especially Black people. She knew things about my family and myself I never knew...'

Charlie sits and spins two coins on the table as Tracey kisses Bernice's cheek and the Haitian gives Charlie that motherly stare and speaks lovingly, saying, 'Hello Jim Morgan...'

The name she's called him in her French accent sends a shudder through the soul stirring a memorable familiarity. The subconscious soul hears its 18th century name and Charlie immediately responds by stopping larking around and looks into the eyes of Bernice. He stands up, palms gripping the back of Tracey's chair, and his face appears strained as the coins fall flat. Tracy gives Bernice a friendly, light slap across her shoulder as Charlie tightly grips the back of Tracey's chair. His mind tells him the name she's called him is somehow connected to his recurring olden-day Jamaica dreams, but his drunken state doesn't allow him to concentrate fully.

Tracy gives Bernice another friendly, light slap across her shoulder and says, 'His name's not Jim, you know it's Charlie, can see Bernice's fucking drunk…'

Charlie's mind begins to question the situation, wondering if Bernice could have overheard when he was talking to Yanson and Benjamin outside the pub. But then no, she couldn't have because she was in the police van when he spoke of his dream to Ricky Lewin and neither did he mention the content, especially not names connected to his on-going pirate dreams. Not wanting to look like he's losing his mind, he puts on what he hopes looks like a light smile as he asks, 'Who mentioned that silly name Morgan, Bernice?'

Bernice is about to say Claudette but remembers the deal she made with Claudette to say her name was Lana. 'Silly you say, Charlie? Oh, it was mentioned by someone I was in the police van with earlier, someone you may know as Lana.'

Bernice smiles brightly because she can see from the expression on Charlie's face that something has connected for him. His mind drifts deeper into specific 18th century recurring dream memories, of himself as Morgan and of the attractive Black Haitian Voodoo witch called Lana.

Caribbean Sea, 1756

It's a sunny day out on the ocean and the youthful Jim Morgan, drunk and wearing just short pants, stands spinning gold coins on his captain's cabin table. He calls his dog Patch by way of continuously kissing his lips, but suddenly hears Lana's voice behind him: 'The scar on your back has healed well, Jim Morgan.'

Her voice surprises him, as he'd not realised she was there, seated silently on the floor at the ship's Voodoo shrine. Morgan glances at his reflection in the mirror then downward to the floor. He picks up a small handled mirror and turns his back to the huge cabin mirror.

'Yes Lana,' he says, 'I used both these mirrors to have a look earlier. Thanks to your Raphael, he did a good job on it getting the two sides of flesh to hold together. Lost a lot of blood, even he said it was by the grace of God I made it.'

Morgan's English Bulldog comes running in from deck and begins sniffing the cat Jojo at the shrine. The dog then jumps onto a chair, puts his paws on the table and stretches as Morgan feels the dog's underbelly while making a fuss of him. The scar on Patch's belly brings back a bittersweet family memory. Still with his back to the Haitian witch, Morgan says to Lana:

'Do you know what, Lana? Both me and my wife Haley kissed our lips and called the name Patch when choosing him as a pup from the litter. I remember me mother doing the same thing with our dog when I was a kid. She'd kiss her lips making that sound. Haley my wife did the sound and I called the name Patch and this one came walking to me. I put him back among the others three or four times, called the name and the same one always came.'

Lana smiles. 'Funny you should say that. Every time in past and future lives I, the soul, also choose the kitten that comes to me. Some coincidence, hey Morgan?'

He doesn't pick upon the intended sarcasm, and replies, 'Yeah coincidence, Lana, for sure.'

Suddenly Jim Morgan feels a sharp pain in the back of his head. Startled, and rubbing at the pain, he turns to see the angry face of Lana and realises she's thrown one of her clogs at him.

She snaps at him, 'Have you not listened to anything I've taught you? There's no such thing as a coincidence within God's universe.'

He squints his eyes. 'God Lana, that bloody hurt, why did you have to...?'

Her frown quickly turns to a smile, but she still says, 'It was supposed to hurt... The spirituality I've shown you may just save the lives of the men and us one day. Listen to me, the reincarnated soul Patch comes to your vibration each time because he's our soul mate and spent countless past and future lives together with us. You are spiritually guided back to one another; Koolah angels are always around guiding Patch to your vibration and sound.'

This said, she returns to kneeling facing her shrine. 'The blessed coin,' she calls back to Morgan, 'let me bless it on my shrine. As the Koolah spirit angels pass, they'll strengthen its protective powers.'

He lifts a hanky, which lies on the table, revealing the coin with the chipped edge, the very coin that saved his life. The pirate captain expertly flicks it to set it spinning on the huge table. Lana smiles looking up at the coin spinning in the reflection of the huge cabin Voodoo mirror, then closes her eyes.

Morgan snatches up the coin as it spins, and looking back at Lana in the mirror reflection, he flicks it upwards towards her. She catches it with her eyes closed and without turning to him.

'Good catch,' he says.

'No, I don't take credit for anything. When you're one of God's angels and submit your self, the soul, eternally back to God's spiritual guidance, you cannot miss. I consciously wasn't aware you were to throw the coin to me; I subconsciously knew. Why do you think I spend most of my days dedicating my services to the other angels of our universe? Including you, Morgan.'

Although Morgan trusts in the magic of Lana, he's still not able to fully consciously understand. With an animated nod of the head, he changes the subject to another of concern to him: 'Lana, my special mirror soul love you speak of... tell me more about this future life and her, please...'

Lana sighs. 'How many more times do you want to hear it? I'm tired of explaining this future incarnation.'

Jim Morgan sets many of his other gold coins spinning and says, 'I know it gets on your nerves, Lana. I'm sorry but I just like when you talk about her, that's all.'

She opens her eyes to see he's looking at her with a pleading smile, and acquiesces. 'Alright Morgan, as you know, she's the soul of your murdered wife Haley. You've already met her in this life and obviously won't again...'

Lana notices Morgan looking impatient and says, 'Alright,

alright Morgan, I know what you really want to ask me, I'm not stupid.'

They both share a loving smile, and she says, 'We're to do something different today. I'm not going to accompany you in future life progression; instead, I will transfer to your mind my future life progression. Get a feeling this one will fascinate you…'

He and Lana sit huddled together comfortably at the shrine as Lana begins speaking mixed Ancient African and Creole and in time the pair fall into a trance.

CHAPTER 26

Claudette's home, Haiti 1993

Morgan sees through the eyes of Lana's future incarnation, the beautiful dainty recluse Haitian Voodoo priestess Claudette, one of the wealthiest people in the Caribbean Islands.

Claudette looks out from the master bedroom balcony of her huge elaborate European-style ex-plantation mansion house across the estate with its hundreds of acres and its own lake. The property was once owned by a French trading company, trading in slave cargo from West Africa to the rest of the world. Petrified with fear the horrified humans were terrorised in to working the kidnappers' lands producing sugar and coffee. After taking in the view, Claudette goes back inside and makes her way down the elegant wide staircase followed by her cat Jojo. They enter the reception room where the young man at the typewriter sits at his desk surrounded by loose pages of handwritten ancient text. Claudette and Jojo then make their way to the large hanging mirror and the Voodoo shrine.

At first there is only darkness seen through the mirror. Then the sounds of the Bob Marley song 'Stir It Up' and a couple making love can be heard. Jim Morgan's mind accompanies Claudette as she's present in Charlie Baker's office, and the 18th century pirate's actually witnessing his own self in that future life progression incarnation: he and his twin flame Stacey Holley enjoying intense, erotic cocaine-fuelled sex.

Caribbean Sea, 1756

In the captain's cabin, deeply in a trance Lana smiles excitedly as the vision of Charlie and Stacey's sexual activity comes through.

Morgan's face smiles too as his psyche shows his identical-looking reincarnated self making love to Stacey Holley on his office desk.

Later when the vision is over and they've both come out of the trance, Jim Morgan and Lana sit on the floor innocently holding one another and talking softly. Both still have their eyes closed as Lana says, 'Morgan, as you saw, you will appear as you do now in a future life, exact face and body shape.'

The pirate captain is more interested in talking about his lover. 'Lana, I could see her clearly, she's fair...'

'Naughty, naughty man Jim Morgan, she will match your every passion and very creative sexual nature. Your passion for making love is your soul characteristic, even way before you lived as Ode within the Koolah tribe. From creation each soul has its unique nature.'

Lana opens her eyes and as she turns to look at Morgan he opens his too. Looking into his eyes, she continues, 'You never gave your mirror soul Haley the chance, too busy giving your love to others with that big penis of yours. Spirit is showing in that future incarnation she will be younger than you and when you're both ready to come into union you will fall deeply in love. My God...' Lana holds out a hand revealing she's still holding the chipped edge gold coin. 'Morgan, this coin will forever be in the possession of an angel of heaven, moving around to whichever Koolah angel needs it at times when their soul's vibration is low in certain incarnations.'

Jim Morgan closes his eyes again and faintly hears the Christmas music and other sounds of the joyful market pub...

Chequers Pub, Walthamstow Market, December 1974

Charlie Baker sits with the sobering thoughts of the intense spiritual dream of Lana. Bernice's mention of the Voodoo witch's name had brought Charlie's hidden, subconscious, parallel past-life dimension to the surface, leading him to consciously concede he'd actually somehow lived his on-going recurring dreams in another life.

He looks up to see Bernice tapping her own shoulder and speaking in agreement with apparently no one but in fact speaking to Claudette. She turns to Charlie with a smile and says, 'Lana tells me you're thinking about a time on board your ship *The Witch*. You were enquiring of your future eternal twin flame, am I right?'

Her words render the young gangster speechless. He knew for sure he'd never quite look at Bernice the same way again.

'Morgan,' she says, addressing him by that name, 'Lana took you, the soul, on astral travel to her future home in Haiti where a man was sitting at a huge desk translating ancient Koolah teachings. Our bible was being prepared in book form so that Claudette was able to physically cross dimension back to ancient Koolah with it...'

Charlie looks perplexed, but Bernice continues:

'Yes, I mean why do you think all those Asians, Arabs and Europeans travelled many thousands of miles through scorching deserts and treacherous poisonous snake- and spider-infested jungles. They came for the knowledge we shared with the aliens back ten thousand years ago. They all came for the hidden magical spells, the teachings of the universe's true Messiah, Koolah. We here on Earth, and our soul tribe angels on certain alien planets knew of the love, how to re-instil world peace, a loving world without disease, misery or hunger.

'They stole the wealth and also horrifically kidnapped and looted, taking the African families as their own possessions, satanically stealing humans, oppressing souls. Degrading us to the lowest depths was just a part of the Devil's plan. The Devil created an elite group and showed them the knowledge for their civilisation is in our Koolah bible, including reversing the love spells to turn them for hatred and greed, creating advanced weaponry to use to enslave and oppress us. This is why they came. The cheek of the Devil!

'Well Satan... We have back our bible now and will soon reactivate the more powerful intricate secret spells none of your intruding nations were able to, the fools!

'Silly Morgan not to believe, did you not recognise our lucky gold coin Destin showed you outside the pub before you came in?'

As Bernice was speaking Charlie's mind was filled with various visions, of the man at the desk of the huge reception room typing on his keyboard, of intruders raping the African continent, of the gold coin under the hanky on the table on board the 18th century pirate ship.

Hearing the name 'Destin' causes another different vision to fill his psyche. He repeats the name out loud as he hears it, and in his mind he sees the reception room of Claudette's mansion house not as it would be in 1993 but as it was two centuries earlier when it was the rebel base where the historic leader Toussaint Louverture and his Black generals discussed battle strategies in their anti-slavery war against Napoleon Bonaparte and the French. He sees himself, a much older and tanned version of himself with long past-shoulder length dreadlocks, there as one of only two White men present. The French-speaking Black leader Toussaint is telling off his younger brother, shouting his name Destin; and it somehow feels fitting to Charlie that Bernice uses this name to refer to Yanson.

'Bernice, how do you know all this?' he asks.

Bernice smiles and says, 'Morgan, who do you think you're speaking to?' I'm Lana, a soul attached to and able to influence Bernice or any other angel of our soul tribe.'

As she speaks, Charlie sees Bernice's eyes change before him to those of Lana. He nods and replies, 'I know, Lana. I see your eyes and feel your presence. It didn't feel as though I was talking to Bernice.'

'Alright Jim Morgan, you will soon travel to Jamaica where our Koolah angel Charmaine has a message for you. You will find some of what she has to say disappointing, but it's part of your journey, you are – the soul you embody is still – in much need of rest'

The name Charmaine too sounds so familiar to Charlie and there's a beautiful loving energy attached to it. What's more intriguing is after recently being released from prison he'd planned to visit the island of Jamaica in the coming weeks. 'Who is Charmaine?' he asks, but there is no reply. Bernice has moved away from him and is now talking to the children, Stacey and Julie.

'Stacey, young lady,' she says, 'you are a Koolah tribe angel and when you're much older you will be made to realise it, ok?'

The girl doesn't answer and just looks back at Bernice in a strange way. She then looks to Tracey, who gives a shrug of the shoulders and an expression as though to say she doesn't know either.

Bernice turns her attention to the other girl, Julie Marney. 'Julie, or should I say Monifa, you regularly become conscious in our Koolah tribe dimensions – in your dreams – so you know what I'm speaking about.'

The name that Bernice has mentioned 'Monifa' gets the attention of both the adult women, Tracey and Stella. Bernice's psyche visualises a future 1990s café on the Spanish island of Ibiza and the beautiful face of the Romany gypsy Princess. She's sitting with a group of friends and a now grown-up Julie Marney.

Bernice looks directly into Julie's eyes and speaks to her in ancient Koolah, saying, 'Julie when you're around thirty you will meet your sister Gabi, also the soul of your Koolah era brother again in this life and Koolah will be present. The promised mid-90s spiritual awakening will almost be upon us.'

Julie feels a deep spiritual familiarity with the language having remembered speaking it in her dreams and it being buried in her subconscious soul memory. The vibration takes Julie's psyche to the days of the Koolah tribe, her childhood subconscious dreams of Koolah, Jojo, the magic circle angels and the full moon ceremonial music. She totally understands what the spirit of Lana within Bernice is saying to her. In the language of ancient Koolah, she replies addressing Lana by her Koolah tribal name: 'I know of this, Imani.'

Stella remarks to Tracey, 'There she goes, Julie's off again, told ya earlier, she use' to speak like it all the time as a kid.'

After talking more with Julie in ancient Koolah, Bernice gets up to leave, and now speaking English with a French accent, says to Stella, 'Take care of Monifa.'

Why do you call my Julie, Monifa?' Stella asks.

The older lady laughs and says, 'You too, Stella, are a member of my tribe.'

Then as Bernice necks her shot of rum, Tracey enquires, 'You off?'

She nods and on her way out stops to kiss Ricky Lewin on the cheek. 'Thank you for rescuing me earlier and Merry Christmas, Mr Lewin.'

'No problem Bernice, this is what mates are for.'

Bernice shakes her head. 'Oh, you're more than just a friend, Mr Lewin, I assure you.'

Ricky looks surprised at this out-of-character comment, and Charlie decides to try asking his question again, 'Who is Charmaine?'

'Charmaine has special revelation messages for you, Jim Morgan,' she replies, but says no more and Charlie no longer feels the spirit of Lana present, instead seeing Bernice as purely herself. Charlie straightens himself up as though to snap out of it, not wanting to continue sharing his on-going pirate dream revelations with Bernice.

Farewells are said as the apparent mad woman of Walthamstow market leaves the pub, winking at Ricky Lewin as she goes.

Both Stella and Tracey are left astounded at their spiritual encounter. Tracey feels a spine tingling feeling as she says, 'Can you believe she's just called her by the name she gave herself when playing with her imaginary friend?'

Tracey nods. 'Fucking weird night with that one Bernice, but there's something in it...'

Ricky Lewin and his brother Geoff are back to talking business.

'Rick, there's an opening at Spitalfield's and we can have a major part...'

Ricky interrupts his brother, 'You mentioned this the other day, sounds like work, Geoff. Remember what the ole man use' to say: only fools and horses work. Just take the money, have a demand up.'

An older member of the gang at the table comments, 'Your ole dad was the last of the bandits. Did you know his hero was Dick Turpin? Anyway, Rick, hear our Geoff out. He's proposing something from a Moroccan firm. Easy money.'

Geoff shows his brother a huge quarter kilo chunk of hashish. 'This is getting more and more popular, Rick. The robbery game's too risky now it's on top. I can sell as much of this as we can get in. The Moroccans can get it across to Spain and from there if we got our own lorries bringing fruit over. Well, do I need to say any more?'

CHAPTER 27

Priory Court Estate

Ben's mother and his older sisters stand silently looking at the £500, a fortune in 1970s cash, that Yanson Bailey has just put down on the kitchen work surface. Having been penniless and literally hungry for a few days up until this point, they are intensely excited at the sight of all this money.

After a minute, Jasmine's slightly trembling hand picks up the wad of notes and begins continuously flicking through it. Smiling, she breaks the silence, speaking in regard to Yanson:

'Boy's got his ole man's money luck. From the day our Benjamin brought him to us, I've noticed he's been able to pick up the scent for money.'

She hugs her eldest daughters and warns them, 'Zoe, Sharon, not a word of this to anybody. It had to belong to one of the local villains…'

Mississippi, Deep South, USA, 1751

In an upper-class Christian church, the reverend preacher delivers his Sunday morning sermon to hundreds of well-dressed, wealthy slave plantation owner families, men women and children. The backdrop of the stage boasts a huge portrait covering the entire wall that depicts a White God in the clouds, a White Jesus and White blond angels up in the clouds with them. The preacher speaks about the contents within their bible and tells the congregation to pray to Jesus.

After the Sunday service is over, the in attendance owners of the huge four-pillared estate mansion and huge cotton-picking plantation entertain their English Royal guests, the Duke and

Duchess of Kent. For entertainment a young autistic boy slave Jaden is paraded upon a raised scaffold, in front of an audience of around three hundred: plantation family and guests, many from the church, White men, women and children, the sermon preacher included. A redneck hangman holds the child Jaden's arm, and the child's wrists are bound tightly by rope.

Two wealthy redneck male guests sit at a nearby table engaged in conversation:

'The charge-hand boys over at my place stopped using the whip. Yeah, cuts into the skin but niggers always got some kine of ointment to treat it with and that pain is soon forgotten. Firm strike across the head with a three-foot length of four-by-two's far more effective. Coon never forget the shock pain of that...'

'Yeah,' his companion says nodding, 'myself and the wife were saying the same thing as we came out of church.'

His wife smiles, nods in agreement and comments, 'Beautiful service...'

They and the other churchgoers, the church minister included, sit eagerly awaiting the hanging as sorrowful and scared Black slaves nervously serve them food at their tables. Nearby there's alternative children's entertainment. A huge sign on a fairground stall reads 'Hit the Nigger Baby'. Little White boys are throwing objects to hit the real-life Black baby on display to win a fairground prize.

Not too far from the scaffold, a mother and her three young Black kids are stood surrounded by confederate soldiers. The family look on crying hysterically for their son and brother as the hangman places the rope around the autistic boy's neck. His siblings suffering is apparently just another part of the diners' entertainment.

Nearby, where the more distinguished upper-class guests and English royalty are situated, a scuffle suddenly breaks out. Young James Morgan dressed in his glamorous Royal Naval officer's uniform heroically comes to the aid of the Black family. He succeeds in knocking five burly confederate soldiers senseless, but then, just as he is about to free the boy, the young naval officer is overpowered as more soldiers, and even some of the guests, pile in to stop him. As he's being pulled away, with the stage now impregnably guarded, he breaks away and rushes towards the boy's family. Whilst shouting in protest, Morgan takes the Black mother and children away so they don't have to watch their son and brother being hanged.

CHAPTER 28

Priory Court Estate
December 1974

Early in the morning, Jasmine Jarvis wakes and reaches under her pillow for the wad of money that she put there the night before. She's excitedly flicking through the banknotes, when a horrific feeling hits her: a knowing she was the sister of the autistic boy getting hanged.

'Fuck me what a nightmare. Poor boy. Fuck me that still feels real, he was me brother...'

She hears her son Benjamin yelp out from the bedroom he has to share with his sister Nancy, she on the top bunk, he on the bottom bunk. Ben's frantic body movements shake the whole bed; he's freaked out, feeling for the rope still around his neck, scrambling to free the noose rope that isn't there.

'You alright, Ben?' his sister asks, awoken by the disturbance. 'Bad dreams again?'

Ben lies looking at the underside of Nancy's mattress and thinking into the contents of his nightmare: the local gangster Charlie Baker oddly dressed in British Royal Navy uniform and beating up on the American confederate soldiers at the 'pic-nic' garden party and later the noose tightening around his own neck.

He massages his throat, telling himself it was just a terrible nightmare, before getting up to go to the toilet.

Church Hill Children's Care Home

Daniel Cottle is living the nightmare of sharing a house with the local market kids he's feared and before now felt protected from all his young life. The Stephens brothers are again terrorising

233

young Daniel Cottle in his room, this time with three other boys in tow. Albert starts it off by punching him hard directly on the nose and then the rest of the gang of five join in relentlessly, mercilessly beat him up. When they're done Albert holds Daniel by the scruff of his collar, lets him go and picks up another item of his clothing.

'What else you got for us, man?' Albert says. 'I'm taxing this for a Christmas present.'

As he speaks, the boy called Sammy is looking curiously at Daniel's face.

After a moment, Sammy laughs and announces, 'Oh yeah, I remember the face now. This is the rich boy, the one they call Jarrod Cottle. Fucking hell, what you doing out here with us?'

Albert Stephens joins his laughter. 'What he's that rich boy who lives the other end of the High Street in that big posh yard?'

'That's why he's here,' another of the boys says, realisation dawning on him. 'He's the one that killed his mum and dad.'

Albert looks surprised and he gives the order, 'Let's give him more licks.'

The five beat him senseless again and take anything that's left that they think worth having from his belongings, leaving young Daniel not only depressed, lonely and beaten to a pulp but now more anxious than ever – deeply concerned at what the kid said about his mother being dead and worst of all him killing her.

Stadbroke Grove, Chigwell, Essex

Cindy Nevin in her mid-thirties is still stunningly beautiful, if anything perhaps even more attractive than she was twelve years ago when she experienced the extraordinary meeting with Cutty Robinson on Oxford Street. She sits at her dressing table in the plush master bedroom thinking about the nightmare she has just awoken from: the Deep South pick a nigger 'pic-nic' garden party with her English Royal husband, there seeing the unfortunate child stood on the scaffold with the noose dangling in front of his face. Then the chaos breaking loose as Navy officer James

234

Morgan began beating the confederate soldiers and subsequently him taking the boy's mother and siblings away from seeing their brother being hanged. Her psychic medium capabilities make her fully aware Morgan subsequently reincarnates to Charlie Baker, but she makes a joke of it all the same.

'Wow, fucking Charlie Baker, what's he doing in me dreams and what a fucking fighter,' Cindy says to herself, as her daughter Nicole bursts in the room.

The now-teenage Nicole is dressed in her school tie and blazer, with her hair neatly brushed and ready. 'I beg your pardon, Mother?' she says in disgust, delivering her words abruptly in the posh accent she's acquired from the expensive school she goes to.

'Mother, it's almost eight. Will you please hurry? You know I don't like being the last in. Honestly, I wish you'd make more of an effort in the mornings driving me to school. Yesterday you actually wore your dressing gown.'

'I'm in a car, who's gonna see?'

Priory Court Estate

Over in East London, worlds away in terms of the type of neighbourhood, on the rough Priory Court council estate, Benjamin Jarvis gets up and goes to the kitchen to get himself some cereal for breakfast, still reeling from his Deep South nightmare.

From her bed, where she's still enjoying flicking through the wad of banknotes and even giving them an occasional sniff, his mother Jasmine calls out, 'Is everything alright, Jaden?'

'Yeah Mum,' Benjamin calls back, feeling a strange familiarity with the name she's just called him.

Jasmine shakes her head and mumbles to herself, 'Fucking calling you Jaden now,' before realisation dawns that not only did she just call her son by that name but he answered to it too; she's hit by a feeling of eerie surprise.

In the kitchen, Ben's pleased, at least, to see some Christmas treats now stored in the fridge and cupboards, which his sister

Zoe had already been out that morning to buy from the local corner shop.

Leabridge Road, Leyton

A couple of miles away from the home of the Jarvis's, thirteen-year-old Terry Lewin, son of armed robber Geoff and nephew of Ricky Lewin, wakes from a nightmare in his upstairs bedroom of their family pub. He's filled with a sorrowful feeling for his Black brother in the dream who was being hanged for the Christian family entertainment. He feels he loved that brother dearly and vividly remembers sorrowfully crying out for him in the dream.

Now awake, he repeats the words he cried out in the dream, 'Jaden... fuck, what was that for, why were they doing that? Jaden...'

Church Hill Children's Care Home

Later that same day, Yanson Bailey sits in Daniel Cottle's room at the care home looking at a very depressed boy on the bed opposite him. Not only is Daniel distressed, his face shows the signs of the recent beating he's taken from the Stephens brothers and their little gang of bullies – a fat split lip and a swollen eye.

Daniel looks away from Yanson in embarrassment. He doesn't express it outwardly but feels Yanson has no idea how much emotionally he needed to see his friendly face there and then.

Yanson unexpectedly stands and places both hands on the top of Daniel's head. The Messiah Koolah had become fully conscious; at this moment his full spiritual presence is within his future Yanson Bailey incarnation. A divine magical healing runs through the soul causing Daniel to close his eyes and gradually a relaxed smile comes to his now suddenly unswollen face. Yanson begins speaking ancient Koolah:

'Jarrod, you are an angel from my soul tribe and I'm here to reconnect you. Come, I'll take you home...'

Immediately Daniel responds. For the first time in months, his face carries the self-assured expression it used to do, and his wide open eyes look directly into Yanson's. As Daniel falls into a deep trance, he begins to feel the familiarity of their ancient magic circle and finds himself filled with a totally relaxed and stress-free feeling.

He and Yanson feel a subconscious familiarity with one another's souls, causing both to smile brightly – the life that had come back to Daniel's psyche apparent in his face. They speak to one another in ancient Koolah.

'This feels too nice to be real... I'm dreaming,' Daniel says as he finds himself in a lucid dream – dreaming but aware that he's dreaming. He's no longer in the care home but instead within the more densely clouded dip of the magic circle – heaven, with the entire angel tribe and some of their alien angel souls, their spiritual ancestors, present. Yanson now appears as a boy Daniel's own age, ten-year-old Koolah, with his spotted leopard friend, an earlier incarnation of Jojo by his side. In the North East African night sky there's vibrant soul movement, millions of souls in transition. The soul Daniel embodies is now fully energised, conscious now in his magic circle dimension, his physical form now that of a Black female child – a child whose face shows elation at Koolah's rescuing of the soul she embodies from its former depressed state. Over sixty other angels sit holding hands forming a circle around the centre of the dip where the Messiah's located.

As Albert Stephenson bursts into Daniel's room, the sight that greets him is of Daniel sitting smiling with his eyes closed. He recognises Daniel's visitor Yanson Bailey, but is amazed when the ten-year-old Black boy gets to his feet and begins shouting at him in Jamaican-English street slang:

'Hey, fock orf bwoy, fock orf nah, run from round here, pussie...'

The older boy feels the opposing powerful, overwhelming spiritual vibration of the Koolah magic circle. He would normally not feel threatened by Yanson, but now he sheepishly backs away out the room. Yanson uses his foot to push the door closed and sits back on the bed smiling.

Daniel's lucid dream continues undisturbed. Strangely he is in a trance with the rest of the magic circle receiving the ten-year-old Koolah's multi-shared vision of his own care home bedroom. The entirety of the magic circle angels' psyche is being shown exactly what the future Koolah incarnation, the child Yanson Bailey's eyes see.

In the bedroom Yanson begins to explain to Daniel Cottle and every angel hears what's being said:

'Relax your mind. Stop trying to think. I'll explain. The reason for this relaxed, beautiful feeling is you're now conscious with us in a parallel dimension phase – an early life your soul also exists in. You're experiencing a more complex combination: part past life regression and part lucid dream state.

'We've just awakened you from a sorrowful future dimension, where you are now unconscious in a trance.

'In this future dimension, our soul tribe, we are about God's business opposing Satan and setting Mother Earth back to its divine nature. Africa and the people of our land will thrive, defeating Satan and bringing peace and love back to our planet.'

Daniel Cottle feels himself to be conscious in his magic circle angel incarnation as the child Messiah Koolah opens his amazing glossy dark brown eyes and turns to address him directly via his own early Koolah tribe incarnation:

'We here in the heavenly circle, your ancestors, watch over you every day in your future incarnation and will protect you from harm. When you again become conscious in that dimension do not be sorrowful. When you emerge from your trance you will gradually begin to realise your mother Pearl's body died through no fault of your own. Her soul came and rested here with God's angels while choosing her heaven, the womb transition to the next life. She's reborn an Earth human again, very near to you and will be back with you quicker than you would ever have thought possible. She's one of our soul tribe. Therefore, she subconsciously knows of your sorrow and chose to be close to you in that future dimension with you again. Our soul tribe, the soul of your mother Pearl are forever connected, so be positive from now on. We have important work to do; be brave. It was not your fault, Jarrod.

'Now to talk of our spiritual purpose. There are no coincidences within this glorious universe; everything is divinely guided. The Devil has become a threat to humanity. God is the multiverse, every dimension of the universe, but the Devil rules God's Earth with wars, slavery, oppression, purposely creating and maintaining the so-called third world. Mother Africa gave birth to all nations, White, Mediterranean, Asian; they are all the descendants of the motherland, Africa. Mother Earth has lost her children to the Devil. Now they're Earth's lost children under the Devil's rule, tricked into turning on and oppressing other nations along the way, but in reality in need of their mother's love and divine guidance. The elite rulers of the world within each controlling nation know this, but because of their treacherous greedy deal that they made with Lucifer they can't go back on it, even if it means instilling sorrowful oppression upon others. It's imperative Mamma Africa smiles again; if Mamma's not happy, the world family isn't happy. A shift is upon us; the preordained reawakening to fight the evil spirit has begun, and step by step Mother's children will come home. During adulthood you will be witness to the reawakening, but in the meantime you will receive the protection of the magic circle, and we will come through at the appropriate time and reawaken your soul. All of our soul tribe will be guided to meet one another in each life we reincarnate to.

'Now Jarrod, when you come out of spiritual regression and become conscious again in your future life, you will only consciously remember parts of this experience vaguely, but you will be fearless and a master of your emotions.'

Tesco Supermarket, Walthamstow High Street

On the final shopping day before Christmas, Jasmine and her children push two large shopping trolleys through their local supermarket store, filling them with everything they need for an extravagant Christmas, to go with the handsome Christmas tree they've already bought from the market.

Ben's eldest sister, seventeen-year-old Zoe, places some Christmas puddings in an already packed trolley and says to her mother, 'Mum, that Yance is a lucky kid...'

Jasmine, who's currently eating from a pack of chocolate biscuits resting on the trolley, nods and clears her mouth and swallows before replying, 'Sorry I'm fucking starving. Told you, he'll be a clever top villain. Gets it from his father.'

'His mum still ain't told him Brian isn't his real dad, has she...?'

Jasmine looks at her daughter in annoyance. 'No, and you gotta keep it quiet, Zo. Tricks told me that in confidence.'

Priory Court Estate

Benjamin looks down from the fourth-floor window at the activity on the estate while Yanson, who's watching the world-famous boxer Muhammad Ali on the TV, dips a chocolate biscuit into his tea.

As he turns around to notice the TV screen, Benjamin can't help thinking to himself how much the boxer reminds him of a man who'd been to his home on occasion, Nathaniel Robinson. He doesn't mention his thoughts out loud, though, instead saying jokingly, 'At least Mum won't spend that lot as fast.'

Both boys laugh, but Ben's face suddenly takes on a worried look as his mind drifts back again to his nightmare, this time visualising the actual face of the redneck hangman.

Yanson notices the look on his friend's face, and asks, 'What's the matter, Ben?'

Benjamin pauses before replying, 'Woke from a scary dream this morning, getting hung. I remember feeling a hand putting a noose round me neck and the man's voice saying, "Don't be making a fuss, just happens to be your time, boy. You is this week's picked nigger. I'm goin' ta place this round your neck..."'

Yanson recognising the self-same dream his friend is talking about reacts excitedly. 'That's weird, Ben...' he begins to say, then sits in silence, thinking deeply.

'Why d'ya say weird? What you tinkin', Yance?'

'We've both dreamed about someone being hung. I dreamed someone, a Black kid, was getting hung. This is the really strange bit, Ben: I knew you were there. I can always feel us all there... all the people we know. I feel that in all my dreams.'

'Yeah, fucking coincidence, Yance. In the dream I wasn't scared, but when I woke up, fucking hell, it was so fucking real.'

There's a lot Benjamin doesn't yet understand, not even realising that he was a Black autistic slave child in the dream; it felt to him that White Benjamin Jarvis was being hanged.

Tesco Supermarket, Walthamstow High Street

Zoe stands looking at one of her fellow shoppers, a pretty woman who in some ways reminds her of the nightmare she woke from that morning. Zoe recalls the wealthy redneck crowd watching the autistic child Jaden being hanged. Her mind vividly recalls the entire smiling, happy crowd but she remembers the royal guest Charlotte Ortice, Duchess of Kent in particular because, other than the brave naval officer, the young Duchess was the only White person who showed any sadness at the satanic treatment of the autistic child being hanged in front of his siblings. Though she can't remember hearing them in the dream, the boy's mother's words spoken in a Black Deep South accent now come clearly to her mind: 'Why yole hurting my boy? Done yole nothing, little simple at times is all. Gi' him back now y'hear.'

As with her brother Ben, there's a lot Zoe doesn't yet understand. She certainly doesn't realise that within that dimension she actually was the Black mother to the boy, Jaden, mother to the soul of her brother Benjamin – and that that was her most recent incarnation in the soul reincarnation cycle of life, accounting for the otherwise inexplicable way she herself talks with a slight Deep South drawl.

The shopper who Zoe finds herself staring at says with a nervous smile, 'You're staring at me. Can I help you? Is there something wrong?'

'No,' Zoe replies, 'you just remind me of a girl from a sad dream I woke from this morning, is all.'

Priory Court Estate

It took the Jarvises two taxis to get them and their shopping home.

Later that evening, Yanson sits in the Jarvises' living room with Benjamin's two youngest sisters, Sharon and Nancy. He's engrossed in the TV, concentrating on the repeated Christmas movie, *Oliver*. Since watching it at home with his mother and family the previous Christmas, it had become his favourite, and ever since he first came to Benjamin's home after watching it the first time he's felt the Jarvis home reminded him of Fagan's den. Sharon smiles looking at Yanson and Nancy sitting next to each other on the sofa eating mince pies. She doesn't look much like her little sister, and in fact, Sharon's the only Jarvis sibling with the darker complexion, brunette with dark eyes. 'Yance,' she says, 'I remember you came round last year and said you watched this.'

'Yeah, love the film, Shal, my favourite,' he says, barely taking his eyes from the screen.

'Hey, just a thought, imagine that, Yance and Nance, rhymes dunnit?' Sharon giggles as she says it then gets up to leave the room.

Nancy runs to the door to make sure her sister's gone off, then comes back to the sofa to give Yanson Bailey the magic of his first proper kiss, a wet one that lasts a few seconds. He'd never ever forget the surprise, Nancy introducing him to the natural high, her amazing smiling eyes and the texture and sweet taste of mince pie particles still in her mouth. Afterwards they smile sitting next to one another, spellbound, both lost in the puppy love magic.

Her eyes look into his. 'Yance, thanks for the best Christmas ever.'

He blurts out in reply, 'Nancy, thanks for the best kiss ever,' then appears embarrassed at having said it.

At that same moment, at 45 Teckwort Park Road, Yanson's mother Shirley Bailey looks up at her living room clock and says to her husband, Brian, 'It's Christmas Eve tomorrow, where is that dyam bwoy Yanson? Him always out ina de street.'

There's a sudden knock on the Jarvises' front door and Zoe runs to answer it. She opens it to find a pretty smiling Black Jamaican woman, thirty-one-year-old Elsie, aka 'Tricks' facing her. Tricks is dressed smartly in a classy dress, heels and a jacket.

Zoe's smile beams. 'Hello Aunt Elsie, what a nice surprise, thought yole was still in jail...'

The pair hug, and Jasmine having overheard from the kitchen speaks quietly to herself saying, 'Fucking hell, my mate Tricks. That's a lovely surprise.'

CHAPTER 29

Elsie enters the living room, and both Yanson and Nancy smile. Elsie has a habit of lighting up any room or situation; she's every connected local kid's auntie.

Nancy's the first to greet her. 'Hello Aunt Elsie.'

At the mention of her name, Yanson looks away from the TV and saying nothing goes to Elsie and gives her a prolonged hug. He then reaches into his pocket and produces his shiny antique gold coin with the tiny chunk missing from the edge.

'Don't ever lose it, Yanson; it's your luck and protection,' Elsie says sternly.

'I know, Auntie,' he replies as she places her palms on his shoulders.

'How's mum?'

'She's fine, Aunty,' he says smiling.

Later, Elsie joins Jasmine in the kitchen and noticing all the freshly purchased food and alcohol about says, 'Someone's having a nice Christmas. We spent the last one in Holloway.'

'You only got out this morning,' Jasmine says. 'I wasn't expecting you for a few days. Vodka?'

Elsie nods and Jasmine makes them both a large vodka and tonic. They touch glasses and the conversation turns to the subject of Yanson.

'Hadn't seen him in eighteen months before tonight, but him look like him father now,' Elsie says.

'Do you know what, Tricks? I was just thinking that and said to our Zoe, the boy's got his dad's money luck.'

Jasmine takes £100 out from one of her hiding places in the kitchen and shows it to Elsie, who's surprised and even more surprised when her friend says, 'Tricks, you couldn't have timed it better, take that. Was sitting here starving skint the other night,

244

but Yanson and Ben had an earner, put five hundred quid on the table!'

'He's got a lucky coin I gave him. Don't know where that coin came from. The night Yanson was born I was doing a shift at Cutty's and all the sudden it was in me purse and whoever put it there could have nicked the night's takings. Strange because it was as though someone had crept in and put it in there. The whole thing made me know the coin's lucky and we were meant to have it...'

But then Elsie lets her words trail off as she notices the time, and instead says, 'Look, I better drive Yanson home. It's getting late and Shirley must be worried sick.'

Chequers Pub, Walthamstow Market

'Charlie, your go, can you lay your card or do you have to pick up?'

Charlie Baker's thoughts aren't on the game of cards he's supposed to be playing; instead, his thoughts are occupied by the dream he's had: the dream of him knocking 18th century confederate military men out cold in a fistfight, of him helping the Black family...

But the voice of the fellow villain at the card table brings him back to the present, and the six other men he's playing cards with. He hears one of them saying, '...left two grand in the motor last night and some fucker's got lucky...'

Charlie smiles remembering that morning Yanson had explained to him how he'd robbed money from a car and asked Charlie to look after some of it. He laughs and makes the comment, 'Someone's having a good fucking Christmas.'

Churchill Children's Care Home

The following morning, Christmas Day, Kim Davis answers the door to Charlie Baker and her face is beaming with happiness.

'Hello again Charlie,' she says, in her enthusiasm physically pulling him inside the main entrance while explaining, 'You won't believe the change in Daniel. He's had a lovely day with a visitor, school friend I think, what a transformation.'

She shows Charlie up to Daniel's room, and Charlie enters to see the child smiling like he used to before the family tragedies. As his instinct tells him to do, Charlie sits on the bed opposite Daniel and starts spinning his coins on the bedside table.

Daniel smiles vibrantly and says, 'Side to side, Uncle, circle Uncle...' urging Charlie to do a specific motion with the coins.

For Charlie, it's a magical déjà vu moment. He recalls the White child pirate Jarrod saying those exact same words to him in an 18th century dream he's had.

Speaking with the same confidence that Charlie remembers him having long ago, Daniel says, 'Uncle, Yanson Bailey visited me and spoke in a foreign language that I could understand.'

Porto Banus, Spain

'Julie! Breakfast getting cold, darling, lovely fry-up on the table sweetheart,' Stella Marney shouts upstairs to her daughter Julie as the rest of the Marney family gather around the Christmas breakfast table.

The sound of Stella's voice wakes Julie, who gets up yawning and goes to her bedroom window to look out on the villa's impressive swimming pool in the warm bright Spanish morning light. She smiles as she stretches, before her dream comes back to her. She remembers crying hysterically over her beloved Black brother Jaden and recalls the uniformed naval officer who came to their aid and tried to rescue him. She can see his face clearly in her mind, and it's a face she recognises – the face of the man she'd seen a couple of days ago in the Chequers pub when she and Stacey Holley ate crisps and drank soft drinks. The man who was speaking to Tracey and Bernice at their table: Charlie Baker.

Downstairs in the kitchen, with the sounds of her beloved Sam Cook Christmas album playing, Stella feels the Christmas turkey with her hand and says, 'Thawed out nicely, ready for the oven.'

Kim and the rest of the staff have made an extra effort to make all the children feel special this Christmas and there's a happy feeling at the dining table as the children eat a delicious Christmas morning fry-up breakfast – Daniel Cottle included. His mood has seemed to improve by the minute since Yanson visited him.

Kim leads an attractive mixed-race couple and their three children into the room. They're the aunt and uncle of the children whose parents were killed in the car crash and they've brought with them baby Melissa who survived. Their nephew who's five and their niece who's seven, both resident at the care home, rush to greet them and to see their new baby sister again, who responds to the situation by crying.

Daniel recognises the couple. He knows they've been visitors to his family home in the past, and the sight of them makes him feel a little uneasy; it reminds him of his mother.

Kim detects there's a slight awkwardness and says, 'Well, get your coats off and join us for breakfast.'

Daniel and the children's uncle, a handsome Black man in his thirties, exchange looks. The man says nervously, 'Jarrod, want to hold her?' Daniel nods with a smile and the moment he touches the baby a memory of the Koolah circle comes to him. He looks into the baby's eyes and gently rocks her side to side; she stops crying immediately. He feels the aunt and uncle who have come to visit have somehow given him a feeling of protection, a vibration familiar from long ago, and he doesn't want them to leave.

As the uncle begins talking with Kim, the aunt can't help herself but look at Daniel. The boy's smiling face and beautiful eyes remind her strangely of Cutty Robinson. She thinks back to a christening party at a house she'd attended ten years ago and it all begins to come together in her mind. A man was killed for disrespecting one of Cutty Robinson's gang member's wives, and during all the excitement with hordes of police coming to the house, Daniel's mother Pearl had driven off with Cutty Robinson in his Jaguar at a time when her husband was away in Jamaica.

Albert and Alex Stephens arrive down from their room and can't help but adopt their usual rude boy attitude, giving all the kids including Daniel attitude stares. Albert says abruptly to Daniel, 'Hey you bwoy, how long you known dat Yanson?'

Daniel doesn't answer, being too wrapped up in the vibration of Melissa and another waking thought, the face of a beautiful woman playing on his mind, to even listen to Albert properly.

Taking Daniel's silence as disrespect, Albert says threateningly, 'Oh tink you bad man now you got Yanson? Liam and Iftica dem boys deh, we'll see about that?'

Daniel doesn't stir, still deep in his thoughts about a beautiful face from a vivid dream he's had, not understanding it's a vision from twenty years into the future and the stunningly pretty face is that of his future Swedish-Moroccan mistress who was raised in Holland, Emy.

King Louis XVIII Hotel, Amsterdam, Holland, 1993

In their plush hotel suite, Emy kisses Daniel, places her head back on his chest, closes her eyes and falls asleep. He raises his wrist to look at the time on his expensive Rolex. He takes the watch off, places it aside then massages his wrist. His mobile phone rings and he answers it, blinking his glistening bluish hazel eyes and gently massaging his designer goatee beard.

'For fuck sakes Uncle,' he says to the caller, 'd'ya know what the time is? I've been trying to call you for ages.'

On the other end of the line Charlie Baker is not feeling in great shape. Drunk and coming down from the cocaine high, he sits in his office recliner with Patch asleep on his belly and replies, 'Sorry Jarrod, I was busy with my young lady…'

'Uncle,' Daniel replies in protest, 'I called you hours ago before football started. I must have fell asleep watching the Porto Champions League game. What was the final score?'

'Porto won it,' Charlie replies before breaking into secret slang – a mix of street and East London underworld – and saying, 'Listen, Dreadie said you'd sussed cloggy Coover bod up there ain't moving right, may be at the fuck game,' words which meant: 'Yanson said you were concerned about the Dutchman cocaine supplier there in Holland, thinking he might be out to rip you off.'

'Yeah, I'm sure of it, the pussy hole,' Daniel says angrily. 'Fucking liberty, I'm fuming, Uncle.'

Charlie picks up a pen and writing pad. 'Jarrod, what time's ya flight in?'

'East Midlands, 11:40, look when you pick us up I'll explain it on the way ta check Lickle Kieran in shovel.'

'Alright Jarrod, we'll be at the airport waiting.'

In London, Charlie hangs up, and leans back in his recliner chair, thinking over the memory of the cocaine-fuelled sex with Stacey but then beginning to worry about what he told Stacey – about Cutty Robinson being Yanson Bailey's biological father. He thinks of phoning her but remembers her saying she had a busy day ahead and needed a couple of hours sleep. He dismisses the idea with the thought that when he sees her next he'll tell her again to be sure to keep it quiet.

In the King Louis XVIII Hotel, Daniel places his mobile down on the bed and looks towards Emy, naked and beautiful beside him, who's had her angelic hazel eyes open for a little while listening to Daniel on the phone. He's wound himself up over the matter of the Dutch conman, and as he always does when in need of calming, he pictures an angelic female face, a person he's practically grown up with by way of subconscious dreams, even though the last dream was ten years ago. Sofia's Hispanic and beautiful, with long silky brown hair, the darkest brown large Spanish eyes, a cute small nose but the largest lips more associated with a Black person and a smile that lit up your world. Resting his head on the pillow, Daniel feels an eerie but pleasurable familiar rush and his heart begins to beat harder. He hears a softly spoken French-accented female voice saying, 'Breathe in deeply, mon chéri.'

At first he thinks it's Emy speaking, but knows she doesn't have a French accent and besides which he's sure the voice is coming from another part of the room.

A welcoming familiar vibration enters the psyche of the Black Londoner and the voice continues:

'Fill your lungs with God's pure oxygen, breathe in the positive energy within this room, and each time you breathe out we want you to let go of all that negative energy, bad feeling and guilt. Slowly breathe in the positivity and out the negativity, letting it go.'

With a knowing of being guided he rests his head on the pillow looking upwards, and with every breath he feels his whole body and facial expression totally relax. All the negative issues weighing on his mind appear visually to him and then disappear. He sees Herr the blond smarmy-looking Dutch conman, the deaths of his parents, and the face of his heroin addict child's mother, Victoria, as though he were looking at her face to face. Then after a few moments' darkness, the Koolah circle's glowing off-white, pink light appears before him, a swirling pink cloud the size of a pumpkin that sends two thin cloud beams of light directly through his eyes, entering his being. At first its beautiful blinding light causes Daniel to squint, but he doesn't shut his eyes, pleasurably allowing the light through.

Beside him Emy's fallen back asleep, oblivious to the sudden spiritual presence. In his relaxed state Daniel can now hear a blissful sweet bongo music and the prominent repeated sound of maracas. He's back to the pitch-black darkness, the pink cloud having entered his being, and the sound of Claudette's voice coming as if from inside him only enhances the pleasurable feeling:

'Relax Jarrod. I've joined you, the soul you embody.'

Daniel smiles and answers, 'Your voice, this music, bright light and energy rush I now feel throughout my body. For some reason I remember it. For the first time since I was nine years old, I feel pure and free again. How did you do this? I'm so relaxed and feel as light as a feather...'

Lying there in this blissful state of mind, he begins to hear a faint, recognisable, quality house music song. He welcomes its rising volume, the subtle echoed African bongo drum sounds and angelic female vocal seem to complete the experience and he exclaims, 'What a fucking tune, never has a song made me feel this way inside.' The music apparently even causes Emy to stir under the sheets.

Suddenly he feels it's like his body is being submerged in lukewarm water. He raises his head up from his pillow but instead of a darkened hotel room he sees a vibrant sunny tropical day. His body up to his neck is submerged in water, and he feels the sounds, sights and vibration of a dimension where his soul's now become conscious, the ancient civilised City of Koolah.

He's bathing in a shaded area, looking up to sunrays and rainbow combined in the distance above the beautiful Koolah City cascading waterfall. Suddenly he looks down at his refection in the calmness of the pool and is surprised to see his face is that of a young pretty indigenous female. He looks across the water to see his identical twin sister swimming towards him to join him. He consciously knows he's female and it's his twin; everything about the city feels like he's lived there his whole life.

But then he's conscious back in the hotel, no longer in bed but finding himself standing in the centre of the room. So overcome by what he feels is a beautiful strange dream, he pleasurably whispers, 'Fucking hell, that felt so real, the city is so familiar.'

As he says the words, he finds the dark room becoming illuminated by a brightness coming from the huge mirror in front of him. There's an image in it that is not his own: the silhouette of a woman with a cat, its tail swishing from side to side. Gradually the image of the black Haitian Voodoo witch Lana becomes clearer and moves towards him. She wears 18th century clothes – a corset dress and hat – and addresses Daniel in her strong but soft Creole-French accent with a tone of authority:

'Jarrod, your soul was actually just conscious in that Koolah City dimension, one of your early incarnations living as one of the twins. You were both born from the same heaven, the same womb, physical twins, but you each of you are in your own Twin Flame connection. Whilst sleeping you become conscious in a parallel subconscious dimension you, the soul, exist in; humans

251

call it dreaming. Our other magic circle Twin Flame angels enhanced the vibration so you knew it was real…'

He interrupts her. 'Strange, I know I'm dreaming right now. I've always had strange clear dreams'

'Yes Jarrod, you are dreaming; you're actually in trance with myself and all our soul tribe in the City of Koolah's magic stone circle. You've crossed over here and become conscious in just one of an infinite amount of lives your soul also exists in. This is what dreams are, just other played-out parallel dimensions. Listen, we've come from the sacred heavenly stone to reawaken you, Jarrod.'

Lana disappears behind Daniel and he can't see behind him that she exchanges her image to become her soul's modern-day incarnation, Claudette. Claudette's now wearing the enemy leader Napoleon Bonaparte's impressive French military leader's uniform, white-fronted dark navy jacket with gold buttons and epaulettes, white leggings and knee-high black boots.

As Daniel sees her, he can't help thinking how sexy she looks wearing the French officer's uniform and white leggings.

She displays her amazing smile and says, 'I'd appeared as my 18th century image Lana to remind you, Jarrod. Two centuries ago I lived as the Haitian witch Lana and during that life we knew you as Jarrod, the nephew of our pirate captain Jim Morgan. We are reincarnating Twin Flame angels, meeting in each physical life we're born to.'

Claudette disappears behind Daniel; Lana appears in front of him again but still wearing the same military outfit. Daniel looks confused, still trying to make sense of who she is as she switches back to Claudette. He stutters as he says, 'Nah, this is just a dream and I'm going to wake.'

Claudette shakes her head in a slight huff. 'Dream or whatever else you choose to call it, mon chéri. Regardless, I'm here to remind you of lives we've shared. Were you not consciously awoken in a Koolah City dimension where you lived as a twin female? That lagoon you swam in, I defy you. Tell me, that waterfall cascading, the fresh-smelling water falling onto many others and us. Tell me, was it not real? Me just now showing my body image the 18th century revolutionary Black Haitian witch Lana was appropriate in regard to beginning your reawakening process. You lived as the legendary pirate Jarrod and I, Lana, the two of us fighting side by side during that dimension phase.'

Daniel still looks just as confused. 'I'm sure I know you. Have we met...? How did you get in here?'

Claudette smiles. 'Have we met... Ok, ok this is the thing, Jarrod. We've physically and spiritually met in every dimension, each life we've lived from the creation of the universe. We're God's Twin Flame angels, also belonging to the same soul tribe. Have we met...' She tuts at the Black Londoner. 'Qui, qui, yes, we've physically met because each dimension is in the moment of now; we've experienced every past and future dimension. This is why you recognise my face on the Earth one-dimensional plane. We will meet physically very soon. You will come and find me and other angels of the magic circle.' Claudette moves closer to him. 'Jarrod our dear soul, how did I get in here?' She points to the large glowing floor-to-ceiling mirror situated within the plush hotel suite. 'Crossing dimensions by way of spiritual tunnels. We'd not have freed ourselves from the vile slavery inflicted by the French on the 18th century island of Haiti without them. Spiritual mirror doorways, entrances and exits to underground passages, most effective during the 18th century Haitian revolution and other conflicts, Jarrod.'

'Eighteenth century, did you say? Mirrors...?'

'Yes, for instance the mirror in this room is an ancient Voodoo mirror connected to every other mirror in the universe. We, God's angels, bless the mirror with magical spells from ancient Africa and it becomes a much more complex psychic crystal ball, Jarrod. The blessed mirror's a crystal ball with intricate spiritual travel dimensions. Your psychic mind's been reopened by Koolah and other angels of the heavenly circle, my darling.'

Claudette looks down at Emy who looks unnaturally still, and says, 'Emy, she's called in this life. It's alright, she's under self-hypnosis; we call it past life regression today. The soul Emy embodies is conscious occupying her ancient Koolah body and will remain in that state while I'm here with you.'

'Koolah?' Daniel asks.

She looks him directly in the eyes. 'The city with the divinely blessed stone circle was named after the Messiah's fifth incarnation, reborn within the tribe, Koolah. Emy's present at the Koolah magic circle, Earth's physical spirit world – an amazing soul and one of us. Emy's been contacted by her Twin Flame but partly because of you she hasn't invested in the connection, running instead. You will soon physically have your Twin Flame. You know her; she's called Sofia in this life.'

As Claudette mentions her name, the image of Sofia in all her flawless Hispanic beauty enters Daniel's mind and causes him to smile, stirring within the soul memories of the deepest beautiful dreams they used to meet in. In particular, he thinks of her astral image coming to his aid at one of the lowest points of his life when as a twenty-year-old in 1984 he was held in the segregation unit, the block, within Brixton Jail.

The sound of Claudette's voice brings him round from thinking back to that sorrowful period:

'…Koolah is Earth's authentic Messiah, the true soul that recent religions have rewritten as a person called Jesus. Earth's authentic Messiah repeatedly reincarnated, reborn to our tribe five times, and when born male for the second time his mother named him Koolah. The fifth and final time he reincarnated to our tribe he decided to stop joining us physically attaching and becoming somebody, instead residing in the spirit world watching over us in our fight against evil. We named our city, our tribe and our language after the name of the Messiah's last Earth incarnation, Koolah.'

'You mentioned Sofia?' Daniel says, wanting to know more of the one Claudette has called his Twin Flame.

'Jarrod, your Koolah tribe eternal Twin Flame love Sofia was born and raised in Bogotá, Colombia in this dimension, but subsequently she and her mother had migrated to the US to find work and a more prosperous life.'

This makes perfect sense to Daniel. In his dreams Sofia always had a Spanish accent and he remembers seeing the climate and terrain of South America in those dreams years ago.

'The universe, God, made it so you continuously meet and are together in all other dimensions, or, if you like, dreams.'

As Claudette then says some words in ancient Koolah, first they notice a bright light flickering sensation and then magic circle mist begins swirling around the room, filling it with its off-white pink light. Daniel can hear the city's ceremonial party music and feel its energy. Still speaking in ancient Koolah, Claudette says, 'Want to see her, our Sofia?'

Daniel nods understanding her words.

'Ok Jarrod, I'll remind you of the power of the Koolah magic. We'll go back ten years.'

All this is so much for Daniel to take in that he finds himself leaning against the doorframe for support and shaking his head. 'You're from the 18th century, did you say...?'

Claudette doesn't answer, and as a gap in the mist clears he begins to see not the hotel bedroom but a different room in a different time and place – a plush bedroom in an apartment on Madison Avenue in New York in 1984. Sofia is asleep in the bed. She's the age he dreamed her last, twenty, but she's with someone else now.

He hears Claudette's voice saying, 'That's her Italian-Jewish, New York mafia boyfriend, Justin Gambini, twelve years her senior,' and he feels a sharp pang of jealousy seeing them asleep in bed together.

He looks away from the bed and out the apartment's window to see the spectacular Manhattan night skyline with all its illuminated skyscrapers, as Claudette speaks reassuringly: 'You'll soon have your Sofia...'

Then he's back in the King Louis XVIII Hotel in his 1993 present, but Claudette is no longer with him. Instead, as he turns round to look for her, he's faced with the sight of two male members of the ancient Koolah tribe entering the room through a tunnel of the off-white pink mist: the elderly Akachi and the child

Imani. Akachi expertly shakes his walking-stick maracas to the beat of the Koolah tribal party music that fills the room. The bumblebee-friendly boy Imani meanwhile walks towards Daniel. As he reaches him, his body evaporates through Daniel; for that moment their souls connect as one and the familiarity of the recoupling of souls causes Daniel to be filled with joy. His eyes shine with happiness and he smiles so brightly that his face breaks out in laughter.

He turns back round to find the Black 18th century Haitian witch Lana's reflection staring back at him in the mirror. She's still wearing Napoleon's uniform. Gradually right in front of Daniel's very eyes he watches as she transforms into Claudette and comes out from the mirror, entering the hotel room to stand before him.

Daniel shakes his head with an impressed smile. 'How do you keep doing that? You were a different woman in the mirror and changed when you came into the room. I saw it'

'Yes, you saw my earlier incarnation when I occupy the body of Lana. The idea was to awaken your mind, show you who you were during the Haitian slave uprising, Jarrod. That's where I've just come through from, the 18th century where we're at war with the French on the island of Haiti. We're going to awaken you in that dimension, your earlier incarnation, to become conscious during our slave rebellion, part of our reawakening.' Looking him up and down and smiling, she adds, 'Jarrod, our Jarrod, it's been a while. Don't worry I'll show you how to do it for yourself shortly.'

Claudette stands directly in front of the large, uniquely engraved, antique hotel mirror and lights the candles situated on the purpose-made shelves halfway up on either side of the mirror. Then, turning to face the Black London gangster, she says, 'I'm here to assist and reveal to you who you are. This mirror is a magically blessed Voodoo tunnel. Now, stand in front of our mirror, Jarrod.'

Daniel does as he's requested, and addressing Claudette's reflection in the mirror, says, 'That jacket you wear...?'

Claudette laughs. 'Oh yes the jacket. We borrow it. I cross into later dimensions and physically cross back with this and many other items of enemy leaders' clothing. It's actually occasionally worn by Napoleon. He has four identical ones. Each time he exchanges one to be cleaned our people, his servants, bring it to us and we send back the one we've worn and blessed at the shrine.'

'Why do I get the feeling you are still at war with Napoleon?' Daniel asks.

'Because subconsciously you know all the universe's events are parallel. In this moment we are at war with Napoleon, Hitler's Nazi Germany and the Confederates in the American Civil War. I've come through from spying on our French enemy and reporting their plans to the slave rebellion rebel base. You are there present with God's other angels, myself, Toussaint and others. You're there with your uncle, Jim Morgan.

'The spirits of our indigenous African ancestors, Koolah and others, are present whilst we're casting Voodoo spells at our shrine where the blazer is hung. Koolah and other angels assist by empowering us with the positive energy and attach our opposing vibration to the garment. Our positive energy is the opposite for them. At this moment Napoleon's wearing an identical blazer which will unbalance his negative-energy mind.'

'His negative-energy mind?'

'Yes Jarrod, a soul that wants to enslave humans. *Chaque humain a le droit de sourire*. Every human has the right to smile. Oppressing God's loving people, God's innocent loving families; that level of cruelty can only be the negative work of Satan. God never created just some races; but created the human race. If you have a problem with a race of people, you have a problem with God, and they're soon to find there couldn't be a worst problem to have. Anyway, not to worry about Napoleon, we're waiting for a more personal item of his, and at the point we receive it, it will be over for that bastard.'

Claudette smiles reassuringly at the thought and points to the mirror. 'Relax and allow your vision to become a little hazy. Slightly cross your eyes, allow yourself to drift deep within... This is a magical mirror. You're about to re-live, again become conscious in a life you lived. It was a special dimension phase for our soul tribe, an incarnation when the vibration was high and it will show your relationship to us all during our slave uprising.'

She moves forward, leaving the hotel room passing through into the mirror. Daniel's eyes follow her and gradually a scene from another time and place appears before him in the mirror. The mirror no longer shows the hotel room's reflection; instead, he sees a grand reception room occupied by around fifty Black men dressed in decorated military uniform stood discussing matters among themselves. He walks closer to the mirror and gradually hears the voices of the French-speaking Black men, but then subtle bongo, bass drum and horn instruments playing. Looking deeper into the mirror, he begins to see his own hazel-blue eyes looking back at him. A face begins to appear around them, but it is not his own but a face with White European features and a tanned, freckled skin.

In an instant Daniel's no longer in the plush, modern 1993 hotel suite looking through the mirror; he's actually in the huge occupied reception room, now conscious as the psyche of the pirate Jarrod and looking back at Daniel's reflection in the mirror.

Reception room, occupied slave sugar plantation, Haiti, 1781

As a thirty-two-year-old, pirate Jarrod has become a handsome man, today dressed in the most elegant gentlemanly garments, sky blue lapelled jacket, white collared shirt, and cravat. He stands at the mirror looking as though he's frustrated by something. He hears the words: 'Turn and face me when I'm speaking to you, Jarrod,' and turns to face the speaker, his uncle pirate captain Jim Morgan, the only other White man in the room.

Morgan's annoyance with his nephew fades a little as he looks into the younger man's hazel-blue eyes and explains, 'Jarrod, you and Destin were caught by our troops. We've been through this, you're not supposed to be listening in on these meetings. Our strategic attack methods are top secret, only the generals and I'm to be present...'

King Louis XVIII Hotel, Amsterdam, Holland, 1993

Daniel rubs at his eyes and shakes his head. He's back in the King Louis XVIII Hotel bedroom and all would be back to normal but for the presence of Claudette.

'The man there,' he splutters, speaking of the White pirate Jarrod. 'I've seen him, dreamed being him all my life. I was somehow him just then, fucking weird. Now I come to think of it I've been in that room, this very scene...'

'You were just conscious in a dimension phase living a previous incarnation. You're the legendary White pirate who lived two centuries ago, Jarrod,' Claudette explains.

'And there was the tanned, scarred, dreadlocked version of Charlie Baker I've always seen in dreams...'

'Yes,' Claudette encourages him to go on as Daniel looks at one of the generals looking back in his direction.

'And the general looking back at me...?'

'A member of our soul tribe you shared heaven with in the magic circle dimension. You are to merge with him in this dimension, Jarrod.'

French Military Headquarters, Haiti, 1801

Surrounded by his military generals in the officers' mess, the leader of the French military, Napoleon Bonaparte, is getting a haircut and a wet shave. A kidnapped Black slave woman assists the barber by bringing him hot water and handing him the tools of his trade.

When it's all over and the officers' mess is empty, the slave woman sweeps up the clumps of the French leader's hair that lie on the floor. She picks up one lock of Napoleon's hair and places it into a small black leather pouch. She then drops the pouch out the window for a teenage White girl who's waiting for it to catch. The teenager then travels through the night making her way to the edge of the woods to where a group are holding a Voodoo ceremony around a blazing fire. Claudette stands naked by the fire awaiting the girl's arrival. She takes the leather pouch from her, and all present watch as the naked modern-day Haitian witch Claudette walks toward the dark forest and gradually disappears into thin air, finally becoming invisible.

Twenty years earlier

Claudette reappears walking in exactly the same spot in the woods at an earlier Voodoo ceremony. She tosses the small black leather pouch to the foot of the shrine and takes her place among the group, who greet her with vibrant smiles, all knowing that she's crossed dimensions from twenty years into the future, a dimension nearing the ending of the Haitian Revolution.

Reception room, Occupied slave sugar plantation, Haiti 1781

As the pirate captain Jim Morgan's telling off his nephew for listening in on the meeting, the French- speaking revolutionary leader Toussaint Louverture is also telling his younger brother off, Jarrod's closest friend, Destin:

'…Destin, I keep telling you not to listen in on our top-secret meetings. Our ancestors, now Dutty Boukman and others, risk their lives for us to have reached this far. If the enemy catches and tortures you for our methods and who's working our African magic, then all this will all have been for nothing'

Toussaint points to the shrine where Lana, her younger sister Natasha and their assistant, a young and a pretty Colombian witch called Esperanza, sit. Lana and Natasha both wear decorated blazers confiscated from the enemy, and other similarly confiscated items form part of the myriad collection of objects surrounding the shrine's central feature, the huge pair of deer horns.

'Lana, Esperanza and Natasha's ancient magical powers give us insight into the future, spying on future leaders, Lana's future incarnation Claudette unveiling the knowing of our victory. The enemy cannot know of our magic, our true spiritual identity. We revealed it once before and that's what got us in this slavery oppressed system mess in the first place.

'Destin, they don't and cannot know the identity of Lana, Natasha and others moving through blessed mirror spiritual tunnels spying on them. The French have magicians and sorcerers able to break our spell. If we're not careful they'll have us back in chains, raping our women and children again. You know European men slavers have a love for raping us men to.'

Eventually both Toussaint Louverture and Jim Morgan return their attentions to the military meeting with the generals, respectively leaving Destin and Jarrod alone.

Jarrod glances at the mirror and sees in it the reflection of a laughing, smiling Claudette standing among the men, but when he looks back at the room itself she's not present. Looking a little sorry for himself, Jarrod rubs his fingers around the frame of the mirror.

Lana smiles towards Jarrod and beckons him over with a movement of her head. He goes to her, joining her in sitting on the floor, next to three young musicians who are also present near the shrine.

'Jarrod, you must listen to your uncle,' she whispers. 'He knows best.'

As Jarrod frowns with embarrassment, Lana lights more of the candles that sit on purpose-made shelves around the mirror and says to him, still whispering her words so as not to disturb the military meeting that Toussaint is currently addressing, 'Jarrod, remember as a kid you used to tell us about dreaming of being the Black boy Daniel and I'd tell you he is you.'

Jarrod nods, and Lana gently tugs at his arm coaxing him to stand before the mirror, which now has many candles burning on either side of it.

'Look into the mirror, Jarrod. Concentrate, allow your focus to go...'

As Jarrod stares into the mirror, he sees his reflection change before his eyes. His eyes in the reflection remain the same but the face and body surrounding them changes – his tanned White skin replaced by Black skin, his baby-blue lapelled fitted coat exchanged for the bare-chested Daniel Cottle.

'Just like in the dreams,' Jarrod excitedly gasps, 'he always has my eyes…'

Jarrod's thoughts and the conversations of all in the room are interrupted at first by the low-hum vibration and then by the louder rumbling sound of many horses approaching, trampling the approach mud-dirt road. Then there's the sound of hooves clickety-clicking on the cobbled stones immediately outside accompanied by the sounds of some horses neighing. Some of the generals present rush to the window to see what's happening. The guards outside have halted a group of around twenty-five on horseback. They recognise the riders and as one of them, a young masked Black horsewoman, dismounts they admit her entry into the reception room. As the door opens, those in the room see the young woman enter, remove her mask and approach the shrine to place the small black leather pouch she carries there.

Lana smiles delightedly as she thinks back to an early incarnation as the bumblebee boy, angel Imani in the presence of the Messiah Koolah. Reminiscing about the magical circle helps her explain the item the rider has brought and how Lana's future incarnation Claudette had travelled across dimensions into the future to retrieve it.

She looks towards Destin and smiles at him before she makes her speech to all assembled in the room:

'Civilised ancient Africa, the indigenous vibrated within the fifth dimension, we heaven's angels within the tenth dimension and even connected to the highest eleventh dimension. Thanks to the invaders of Africa, the world today exists with a what-you-see-is-what-is mentality, thinking in just three physical dimensions, thinking reality is only what can be physically touched. The human mind no longer has the desire to reach the spiritual realms, instead looking for heights in the material world, holding onto a religion-based God. This will have a catastrophic effect on the future of humanity. The masses will not seek the truth, accepting everything from the mainstream media, the invention television and its news, from corrupt governments and blinkered education. Humanity will fear appearing foolish by speaking of the spiritual universe even when God within them questions the wrong teachings of the world's rulers and religious leaders.

'Creating the energy in oneself to be able to physically cross dimension only works from the state of the purest unconditional love consciousness. The intruders came to our lands seeking the divine knowledge, including the universe's eleventh dimension spiritual realms. The Book of Koolah, the authentic bible, has more than a thousand pages of futuristic modern-day typed text. Two thirds consist of powerful magic spells including exploring and practising the magic of the higher dimensions. None of the intruding Asian or European nations were able to access this intricate magic from our bible because they arrived motivated by greed and hatred in search of the power the bible possesses. They had the option to share the love so that the planet would continually progress in peace but chose to keep it to themselves for their own agenda, destroying all evidence of it and our existence. Instead, they use the magic to oppress and keep humanity away from the knowing of God and dependent on them. They were able to remove the spirituality from the mind of the indigenous and therefore since diverted the consciousness of the Earth into a negative wilderness of the three-dimensional physical world alone. With their leadership and beautiful religions, this is where we are today. We've ended up in situations such as this war, us fighting against those who've chosen to enslave humans.

'Well my comrades, Koolah is present with us in this room and wants us to continue fighting and win this bloody war – part of the process to bring future equality, joy and peace to the world.'

All in the room look on in rapt attention as the powerful Haitian witch turns and picks up the leather pouch containing a lock of Napoleon's hair.

'Conscious in my future incarnation Claudette, in the mindset of unconditional love consciousness, I'm able to vibrate at higher frequencies. I was able to cross dimensions two decades into our future to retrieve the future French Emperor Napoleon's biological DNA, which as we know carries his spiritual energy DNA.'

Lana holds the pouch open for her sister Natasha to remove the lock of hair from it. Natasha takes the hair and binds it to a prepared potently cursed, white cloth Voodoo doll representing Napoleon and his army. She then soaks the doll in prepared prayer oils before placing it among a cluster of blessed lit candles.

All three of the witches, Lana, Natasha and Esperanza, now lead a chant calling on the angels of the Koolah circle and other positive love vibration alien souls around the universe. During the chant Natasha begins to place prepared Black Voodoo dolls representing resistance fighters around and on top of the doll representing the French.

Lana closes her eyes and speaking in French, says forcibly:

'We, the angels of the universe have bonded as one to weaken the might of the Satanic-influenced French. God has assured we're to be confident in the victory.'

She turns to look into the mirror, which now shows a vague image of the future French military leader.

'Ayibobo,' Lana smiles. 'Monsieur Napoleon Bonaparte, it's time we met. Allow me to introduce myself.'

With that, she places another doll next to the one representing Napoleon, and the three women smile at one another, before resuming their ancient Koolah and Voodoo chant as music fills the room.

Napoleon Bonaparte's quarters, French military base, Haiti.
1801

As the sun rises on a beautiful Caribbean morning, Napoleon wakes in what was for so long a French-dominated stronghold but now had been taken by the Black resistance fighters. They had finally captured Napoleon, his officers and some remaining men, and begun beheading them, placing their heads on spiked spears.

The seashore runs red with the blood of French soldiers. A bloodied and beaten Napoleon Bonaparte looks up and down the blood-red seashore awaiting his own beheading.

Gasping for breath, Napoleon tries to shake off the nightmare – a glimpse of the tail end of bloodied defeat on a coastal beach where he was about to be beheaded by the once oppressed slaves, now freedom fighters. Although relieved to have woken from the shocking nightmare, he feels the Voodoo presence, a surreal experience causing his body to lie stiff, pressed to the bed and unable to move. It has him in a nervous sweat. With difficulty, he raises his head to see a smiling Claudette sitting on the end of his bed.

He converses with her in French, stuttering his words as he tries to get up but his body won't respond:

'Who are you? I must be still dreaming. Why are you wearing my military blazer? Only I've the right to wear it. What are you, some kind of evil witch that has entered my nightmare?'

Claudette laughs and begins nodding. 'Witch? Yes. Evil? No. I've just crossed from a dimension twenty years ago where you're not yet the French military leader. I'm here to issue a warning on behalf of myself and other Koolah angels. No, you're no longer dreaming, although your living nightmare is about to begin if you carry on trying to enslave poor Black men, women and children, of that I can assure you, you will not enjoy your destiny...'

He angrily attempts to alert his officers, but his body uncomfortably tightens no longer allowing him to speak. His discomfort makes her smile as she thinks of her own 18th century incarnation Lana, her sister Natasha and Esperanza using his hair and Voodoo dolls, carrying out the spell which has the French leader and his army in the weakened state.

'Your mind is strong, but the flesh is weak. Can't move, can you? And now you can't speak properly...? Want to know why? I'll tell you. Within this moment but in a dimension phase you'd regard as twenty years ago myself and other angels around the galaxy are using the positive unique energies from around the universe against you.

'Oh, what's on your mind, brave little gallant military hero? The bloody dream, showing a possible future dimension, frightening you? It was alright when you were beheading, hanging and enslaving the Black man, wasn't it?'

The sudden vibration of an astral travel soul memory causes Claudette to frown with despair. The specific memory takes her below deck on board a French trading company slave ship crossing from West Africa to the Caribbean, where a frozen crying toddler bearing the cold sits next to her neck- and ankle-shackled, coughing, sick, dying mother. Claudette gathers herself in spite of the heart-wrenching sadness.

'Napoleon, you cannot and will not win this war. Spiritually what you stand for is wrong, your wanting to oppress and violently force other humans to serve you against their will. You cannot tell me it's God's way; you know you are assisting Satan. For the sorrowful trauma, pain and suffering you've inflicted on beautiful souls of our world you will feel the wrath of God.'

Napoleon is mesmerised as the Voodoo witch looks into his eyes.

'Our gifted spirituality enabled us to accompany those kidnapped humans amid the unbearable stench and depravation of those vile slave ships from Mother Africa. You see, in exchange for power over other humans, you traded your soul, and for this will join your ruler in hell.'

Claudette confidently struts around the bedroom.

'It may shock you to learn one day Africa will again be the ruling continent as nature intended. I often travel to the future to see it and it thrills me.'

She stops to look directly into Napoleon's now fearful eyes and says, 'Look, enough of that. I will give you one opportunity to take your army back to France; if not, the angels here on Earth will unleash a fury like no other. You've been shown the outcome if you proceed.'

Daniel Cottle lies still, eyes open, wondering about the amazing dream he's had: Lana, Claudette, the leader of the Haitian slave uprising and the enemy Napoleon Bonarparte, the amazing vibration of the magic circle, Koolah tribal angels entering his hotel room. The Koolah full moon ceremonial music is still in his head as he looks towards the gap in the middle of the curtains. He looks at his watch on the side table; it's five o clock in the morning. As he turns his head back, he realises the hotel suite's mirror is the exact huge uniquely engraved framed mirror from his Haitian revolution Voodoo dream. The memory of his dream gives him an incredible, pleasurable, continuously pumping headrush. He swivels his body out of the bed, walks to the mirror, and begins running his Black fingers over the unique frame as he did his White Jarrod fingers during the dream of two centuries ago. Breathless with excitement, he sits back down on the bed. Emy's still fast asleep.

When he looks back to the mirror, he sees Lana standing in front of it smiling.

'Hello again Jarrod,' she says in her Creole-French accent. 'Are you getting the picture now?' Her eyes scan the room. 'No coincidence you are in this room here and now, Jarrod. No such a thing as a coincidence within the entire universe...'

Daniel gets to his feet and joins Lana by the mirror. As he looks again at the mirror's antique form, Lana says, 'No coincidence that the very mother Voodoo mirror we used in the Haitian rebel base during our spiritual slave uprising is here now helping create the vibration for all of this magic to work – you becoming conscious in your 18th century incarnation, my crossover from that same dimension phase... Yes, the earlier owners of this hotel were influenced by myself and others to acquire our mirror from the Kingston Jamaica museum, and yes, for her own personal reasons Emy booked this room but hers, yours and all Koolah angels actions are always influenced by our unique magic within.'

Although she's only standing a foot or so away from him, Daniel doesn't notice when Lana physically changes to her modern-day incarnation Claudette. Claudette smiles at his reflection, walks away, then stands still next to the bedroom fireplace. She looks to the mirror and she shakes her head as her expression changes to a sorrowful stare. Daniel looks round at her then back at the mirror to see a reflection of the room not as it is now as a hotel room but as it was when it was part of a family home. In the room reflection sits a tall, greying blond man wearing spectacles.

'As you can see, Jarrod,' Claudette explains, 'this room still has its original features and furniture as when it was a glamorous family home – home to a White Afrikaans-speaking Dutch family before it was subsequently converted to this five-star antique-theme hotel. The disturbed-looking man in the mirror is the grandfather of the family that lived here.'

The vision in the mirror changes to show the tall blond homeowner and other White Afrikaners brutalising indigenous Black people on their own South African land.

'The father, a successful businessman and landowner, and his father before him brutalised, even killed, many indigenous Africans of South Africa and were very influential within the apartheid regime.'

Claudette looks towards Emy asleep on the bed. 'Emy will explain the Dutch history of the wealthy trading company landowner you see before you in the mirror. It's still a mystery to most people why he went crazy, flipped out one night and committed suicide.'

As Claudette speaks the mirror shows African angels from another soul group, South African Twin Flame soul tribe angels, having entered the family home through the Voodoo mirror. Daniel doesn't notice the ghost of the racist homeowner leave the mirror and make its way through the hotel suite wall. Instead, his mind's still occupied with thoughts of wonder at the amazing dreams he's had.

'That dream about Napoleon was real?' he asks.

'Of course, it was real. What do you think dreams are? You, the soul you embody, became conscious in a parallel dimension when you lived as the pirate Jarrod. You were just awoken during our war with Napoleon and the French in Haiti in the late 18th and early 19th centuries. Koolah sent us through to here, the year 1993, to awaken your soul. All Koolah soul mates are at present in the process of a potent spiritual awakening.'

Daniel looks perplexed. 'Parallel dimension?'

'Yes Jarrod, you see time doesn't exist, only the moment of now. Every past and future date is in the moment of now. That's how come you're able to cross over to the 18th century Haitian revolution, the future planet Delica or ten thousand years back to the ancient Koolah circle in an instant'

In the bed, Emy begins to stir, moving under the sheets and talking in her sleep, words in the ancient language of Koolah.

Claudette smiles vibrantly. 'I've seen this mirror during the 18th century on board *The Witch*, but I've also seen it, on dry land in the 1940s on one of my astral travel visits. It was part of the confiscated 18th century pirate ship exhibits in a Jamaican government museum. One of our angels was there conscious then as a Jamaican man called Fitzroy, a strapping Black man who was cleaner and night watchman at the museum. I explained the mirror's history to him.'

'Come Jarrod,' she adds looking directly at Daniel now. 'Look into the mirror...'

He stands before the mirror and images appear to him through it.

Magic circle, City of Koolah, Ancient Africa

All the Koolah tribal angels sit, eyes closed in trance, feet facing the middle, many holding hands. In the centre of them, in the denser mist in the lower dip, Koolah in his early twenties sits in the lotus position, his big cat companion Jojo by his side. He speaks of the evil future atrocities and purposeful lingering oppression soon to be inflicted on the Black race of the Earth:

'…They will steal the knowledge from the magic God has guided us around the universe to retrieve, and when in their possession, they will translate or use it wrongly. We, the indigenous people will be forced into deluded man's invented religions.'

Koolah opens his eyes and looks around the stone circle at the off-white pink mist covering his body from the waist downwards. He shares a vision with the tribal angels of a modern-day Christian church and its picture of a White God in the sky surrounded by winged White angels. He slowly shakes his head.

'They will translate our knowing wrongly, invent religions which will teach people to believe our divine mist that's always here at Earth's heavenly location is a cloud in the sky…'

Koolah points his eyes to the sky.

'… And that heaven is just above the clouds up there. The intruders will have the Black people of our lands believe God is a man who is White, his angels are White and the Black people of the Earth have no soul or a place in heaven. Black people will actually subconsciously later feel we won't fit in with the God, angels and pearly heaven gates above the clouds because we're not White. They'll do this to keep the true glorious history of the Black race hidden from the subconscious of especially the Black people. It will be for us to disclose we are God's true angels and the purpose of our Twin Flame existence.'

The true Messiah looks at all angels within the circle with a vibrant smile.

'My angels, we are to go on a journey reincarnating throughout many lives and you must remember on our travels the Black gene is the original and therefore strongest, healthiest physical form.

'A sign when the awakening is near will be a dimension where White and other non-Black people, women especially women naturally want back their Black facial features and body attributes. All young men of the world will adapt the latest Black attitudes…'

The vision Daniel Cottle sees in the mirror of Koolah addressing the tribal angels fades to be replaced by the image of Koolah conversing in the tribe's ancient language with one of the tribal angels in particular, a young woman. Daniel suddenly finds himself looking back and forth from Emy talking in her sleep to the mirror and the Koolah circle female angel who's speaking. They speak word for word in tandem. He looks towards Claudette with a questioning look on his face.

'Yes,' she replies, her voice soft and soothing, 'that is Emy's Koolah tribe incarnation we're being shown; that's her speaking with our Koolah.'

Daniel says nothing and Claudette continues her explaining.

'Jarrod, when you become conscious from dreaming, as per usual you will only remember vague parts of what's been revealed. You and the rest of our soul tribe are currently on a spiritual mission conscious in your 1993 dimension where shortly we're to relocate God's one true bible, the Book of Koolah. We're about to complete the spell begun in our tribal city dimension, which means life on Earth is about to become magical for humanity. We are to lift the Devil's curse, allowing us once again to choose whatever subconscious reality we feel we want to experience and remember everything when we wake – the real life. The process has begun...'

Claudette stands near to the mirror, kisses the tips of her fingers, smiles, and blows a prolonged kiss at Daniel. The Koolah tribe's ancient ceremonial music can be heard in the room growing louder. The vision in the mirror shows Koolah's ancient city, its palace and waterfalls up on a distant low level hilly mountain. The angels of the Koolah circle rise to their feet and join in partying. As Daniel looks deeply into the mirror some of the Earth-located angels come closer to greet him. The smiling and dancing Imani and Akachi come towards him, and then, as though they evaporate when passing through the mirror's surface, they are in the room with him. Daniel looks amazed, not least because the boy Imani's back is covered with the thousands of bees he hasn't seen him with before. He slumps down to sit in a comfy chair in the hotel room, open-mouthed. As he breathes out a glowing off-white pink mist clouds from his mouth, taking with it all the stress of the situation from him, leaving him in a state of blissful wonder. Then the mist gathers and seems to collect the two Koolah tribe members with it as it passes back into and through the mirror. Then there are no visions, no Koolah tribe members, not even Claudette or Lana, just the King Louis XVIII Hotel room as he has known it before, and a huge part of Daniel Cottle feels alone.

Charlie Baker's betting shop, Walthamstow Market 1993

Still wearing Napoleon Bonaparte's uniform, Claudette reappears standing over Charlie Baker as he and Patch sleep on the comfy recliner. The TV is on switched to Sky News, Charlie's set of clothing ready for the prison visit he's planning to make hangs on the door, and the note he's made of the time of Daniel's flight's arrival sits on his desk.

King Louis XVIII Hotel, Amsterdam, Holland, 1993

Daniel lies down on the bed. Next to him, Emy wakes feeling horny and begins caressing him. The vibration as they begin to make love reminds him of her presence in the Koolah City magic circle.

Every slight touch feels even more loving and welcome than before as she hugs, kisses and strokes his body. His body responds giving him an immediate full-blooded erection. The spiritual experience has only enhanced for him her beauty– her tanned complexion, hazel eyes, freckles, jet-black hair, daring 1990s-style designer blonde streak highlights, all appear flawless to him. She climbs on top of him, sets her vagina into position and grips hold of his penis, pushing and pleasurably inserting it. They

French kiss open mouthed as she begins fucking him. Daniel firmly grips her defined buttocks and repeatedly pushes himself upward, and after making passionate love for a few minutes, Emy climaxes early, not used to the higher-level intensity. They kiss lovingly and he swivels her to the side of the bed and on his knees gives her a beautiful combination of oral sex followed by penetration with his firm penis, repeating and varying the mix at length, fondling her breasts and bottom, before he climaxes.

They lie nose to nose looking into one another's eyes whilst gripping each other in a romantic embrace. She lovingly repeatedly kisses his lips in between her words: 'My God, your heart honey, when you woke earlier this morning I could actually feel it beating so fucking hard.'

After pausing to choose his words very carefully, he says, 'When's the last time I told you how truly fucking beautiful you are?'

She feels his vibration as he delivers this sentiment and her hands begin stroking his head, face and body. 'Wow-wee Daniel, you're trembling again.'

As Emy closes her eyes, feeling physically and spiritually connected to the love they've just made, Daniel gathers himself emotionally and gets to his feet.

'Emy, you got to listen, this room has a presence, haunted by ghosts...'

He pauses to light a cigarette and his words set her thinking about the death of the father of a wealthy White family that once owned the premises as their magnificent home.

However, Daniel says, puffing out a plume of smoke, 'It was that exact same people I dreamed and the same beautiful feeling I got one day the first time Yance came to visit me at that care home when we were kids. There were two women, both spoke with a French accent, an old man, and a boy who had loads of bees on his body. Both the man and boy spoke an African language I didn't understand but as they spoke something inside me knew what they were speaking about... Come to think of it, I think it was one woman, with two different appearances. Anyway listen, it was like they were assisting me through a meaningful dream but took me to another time, or other times...'

As he's speaking, Emy's conscious thoughts are still about the family that once owned the hotel. She recalls the receptionist telling her of the ghost sightings, and her wealthy friend Fenna who was a childhood friend of Tess, the granddaughter of those that owned the property when it was her family house. However, her subconscious hears every word and when she looks into Daniel's eyes, she finds herself again tuned back into the Koolah tribal vibration. Past life regression images begin coming to the surface caused by the corresponding descriptions her subconscious mind had been gathering, and they bring an excited smile to her face.

Daniel ends by saying, 'Strange fucking dreams. Deep but really nice spiritual dreams, Emy.'

To his surprise, Emy replies, 'Same here, things have been getting a little crazy for months now. My dreams are so real and clear.'

He looks into her eyes as her psyche scans her many recurring dreams, her other parallel life experiences, associated with the ancient magical circle. Suddenly a memory of the magic circle appears in her mind too, and Emy begins to explain:

'Up until recently they'd never made sense, but lately it's as though I'm being told a story. I just then woke from an amazing coastal dream, a bright mist always settled on our large rock clearing...'

Magic circle, City of Koolah, Ancient Africa

Imani, Akachi and Jojo rise to stand against the full moon creating an immaculate adult male, boy child and big cat silhouette against the vibrantly bright moon as they look out towards the moonlit ocean and tropical night sky. The off-white pink mist slowly gathers itself into a form, creating a two-meter-high, ten-meter-long tunnel passage with a pitch-dark rectangular opening appearing at the end of the cloud tunnel. The elderly tribal angel

Akachi and angel soul bumblebee boy Imani pass through the passage, stop at the pitch-dark opening, then go through.

King Louis XVIII Hotel, Amsterdam, Holland, 1993

'… Daniel, the dream's as clear in my head as though I was there. They travelled through the light pink cloud tunnel to begin the reawakening of one of our soul tribe.'

Emy's description reminds Daniel of part of his own waking dream, looking from the opposite angle through the hotel mirror at the bright mist tunnel leading to the cloud covered magic circle.

'The misty tunnel on the moonlit beach?' he asks, and she somehow knows he's been shown the exact same spot as she.

Suddenly the mood is broken by Daniel's mobile ringing. He looks at the caller ID, and with a concerned look says, 'Weird, Yance calling at this time… Let me quickly get that; it's got to be important.'

He answers the phone and hears Yanson Bailey saying excitedly, 'Hello… hello, yole Jarrod. Fucking hell, listen sorry if I woke you, had to call you about something on my mind…'

He's talking loudly against the house music and party sounds in the background, but Daniel can sense the exuberance in his voice, and even before Yanson finishes his sentence, as always, the vibration between the two souls reminds them both of the deep inner-soul familiar love energy bond the pair create in every dimension they share from the days of the ancient city to the modern day. On this occasion in particular their minds share their 18th century dimension during the Haitian revolution that Lana/Claudette had taken Daniel to earlier that morning. Subconsciously, deep down, the soul Daniel embodies knows the soul of Yanson's earlier reincarnation is the young man caught with him spying on the top-secret meeting: Destin the younger brother of Toussaint. For a short while, Daniel's mind drifts, tuning into his own thoughts about the connection and only subconsciously hearing what Yanson is explaining. As he tunes back into Yanson's words, he hears his friend say: 'In the dream

I've got this French-speaking older brother, kept calling me the name Destin…'

Daniel interjects excitedly, 'Fucking hell, Dread, I was taken there… Listen, you ain't gonna believe what I've fucking seen this morning. I was taken where you're talking about and was with Destin…'

As Daniel continues speaking, Yanson suddenly thinks of his friend's eyes, and knows his 18th century friend Jarrod is Daniel's earlier incarnation.

In bed beside Daniel, Emy begins to stir as her mind becomes semi-conscious at the ancient circle during the full moon ceremony as Akachi and Imani pass through the cloud tunnel.

Suddenly Daniel's concentration is interrupted by her voice: 'It was you, Daniel. We came through to awaken you…'

Not understanding what she's talking about or immediately noticing her trancelike state, Daniel gently places an index finger to her lips and says softly, 'Shoosh, quiet baby. I need to hear what Yance is saying; this is fucking deep, babe.'

Having now missed a few of Yanson's words, he says into the phone, 'Dread, yeah, what was you saying now?'

'Speaking to you has made me remember that in some of my dreams I'm in the psyche of every living human, know their every intention. Seriously deep Jarrod, fucking deep, my brother. Gonna have to get a meeting with Cindy Nevin and her mate, the psychic medium who Uncle's been to visit and always going on about lately, the woman who lives up in Epping Forest…'

CHAPTER 30

As Daniel and Yanson continue talking, Emy's mind is present at the magic circle dimension telepathically receiving the teachings of Koolah. The Messiah enlightens her and other angels, specifically speaking of future religions' misleading teachings, of their White God and angels above the clouds in the sky. Daniel feels the vibration, the spine-tingling sensation travelling through the soul and physical body of Emy, a sensation caused by Koolah.

In Ibiza, Yanson stands looking out across the ocean to the amazing Balearic sunrise, at the same time thinking of his 18th century dream and picturing the face of the legendary pirate, Jarrod.

'Jarrod, I dreamed you, blood, but in the olden days and you were White. We called you Jarrod there as well. I already knew it was you because of your same eyes, not just the colour...'

Daniel doesn't quite hear what Yanson has just said, the music in the background getting in the way of the words and making him want to actually be there with his friend at the party. 'I couldn't hear what you said just then, Dread...'

Yanson doesn't reply immediately, his mind having drifted into deep thought about the 18th century dimension. He recalls being present in the reception room of the rebel-occupied slave plantation's grand mansion. He's stood in front of the Voodoo mirror talking to his elder brother Toussainte who's calm now after telling him off about sneakily listening in on meetings. Yanson recalls explaining himself to his elder brother saying, 'Jarrod and I only want to help in the fight against the French,' and his brother replying, 'I know both you and Jarrod are very brave, but there's nothing the French would like more than to kidnap either of you to weaken myself, Morgan and others. The less you know the better, Destin.'

277

He tells Daniel about this and Daniel reacts saying, 'Destin… fucking hell… Listen, me and Emy just here speaking about the same thing and you ain't gonna believe this Uncle Charlie was in the dream. Funny thing I knew you were somehow present. I could feel you there; I can always feel you're there.'

Yanson explains further, 'Jarrod, this is the real crazy part. You know I didn't listen to a word our French teacher said at school. Didn't learn a word, but, blood, I was speaking and understood French in the fucking dream…'

Daniel interrupts with laughter at first. 'French, Dread, are you fucking serious?' Then it starts to make sense in his mind; yes, his dream was the same.

An intense feeling of euphoria rushes through Daniel, a happiness he had never felt in this life, caused by the knowing their dreams are all linked.

'Must fucking mean something,' he gasps. 'Me and Emy's dreams are linking as well.'

'Jarrod,' Yanson says, 'ask one of the elders, Cindy Nevin, about it. She's properly into all that clairvoyant psychic stuff. Uncle can ask her. She'll break the spiritual meanings down.'

Daniel hears Yanson getting distracted by the party going on around him, especially as one of Yanson's female friends passes him the cocaine snorting tray.

Eventually Yanson gives up trying to hold the phone conversation as well as the party and says, 'Jarrod, I'll call you back.'

In a way, Daniel's relieved by the call having ended. He's having difficulty adjusting to all the recent startling revelations.

'Sounds like Yanson's having quite a party at home,' Emy's says having overheard the party sounds on the other end of the line.

Emy grips Daniel and attempts to wrestle playfully with him, but she quickly realises how tense he is and that he's not in a playful mood.

'My God, your heart, honey,' she says, 'it's still beating so hard, and wow, you're trembling again.'

Daniel gathers himself emotionally and smiles. 'No, it's

nothing, really. Yance just fucking freaked me out, that's all. Hey Emy, listen, as I was saying earlier, this room has a presence; just seen fucking ghosts.'

Emy comforts him and the pair come to lie together, nose to nose, holding each other in a romantic embrace. Emy closes her eyes and, unbeknownst to Daniel, her mind is filled with visions of the Koolah tribal angels, the bumblebee boy Imani and Akachi in particular, leaving and returning through the cloud tunnel onto the magic circle.

Daniel too closes his eyes, and begins to fall asleep in her arms.

CHAPTER 31

Daniel loudly calls out a name in his sleep: 'Sofia!' And both he and Emy are startled back to consciousness.

Emy raises her head and sits up resting on an elbow. 'Goodness Daniel, you must have had a nightmare. It was probably the end of a bad dream. You shouted the name Sofia.'

Instantly at the mention of the name, a slightly nervous expression comes across his face.

'Did I?' he says and feels a pang of guilt.

Emy's words have reminded him of a specific part of Claudette/Lana's guided dream, of being present in Sofia's apartment in a parallel dimension ten years ago. He feels an awkward sense of disloyalty towards his loyal mistress Emy. Daniel doesn't yet understand the Twin Flame connection, the constant emotional attachment he feels towards a woman he's never physically met – a Twin Flame connection that is more real than any relationship he's had. Sofia is designed in every way, physically and spiritually, as his perfectly balanced divine counterpart – a love that overrides any other previous lovers he's ever had or would ever encounter through his illustrious string of amazingly beautiful women, a love so deep he could never describe it to himself.

Feeling emotionally insecure, Emy holds her index finger mid-air and says, 'Oh yes, that's it, that's where I've heard the name Sofia. When we first met and got high you told me of her ghost always visiting you in times of need and constantly meeting in dreams. She came to you when you had the nightmare in jail, dreamed seeing your father you killed and just the bloodied torso of your severed-in-half mother. Sofia came to tell you it wasn't your fault and to stop feeling guilty about their deaths. Daniel, you called out for her. Why did you feel you needed her help just then? Did your dream re-visit that London prison cell…?'

Her words have an effect on Daniel, and seeing how uncharacteristically vulnerable he now looks, she hugs him tightly yet gently. 'Daniel I'm so sorry, how could I have been so insensitive?'

He shrugs it off and smiles. 'It's funny you should say that. Claudette did mention Sofia…'

The name Claudette means something to Emy; she recalls the Messiah speaking of her.

Meanwhile the image comes to Daniel's mind, which he tries to dismiss, of Sofia in bed with her lover in their New York bedroom.

'…There was two of 'em, different ones. I've never dreamed of this boy or woman before, but their presence and faces were so familiar. By the way, that was no dream, Emy.'

A spine-tingling inner feeling grips Emy and seems to move around her entire body. Her psyche is again filled with visions of the ancient Koolah tribe, of Jojo, Akachi and Imani silhouetted against the vibrant moon, of the hump shape on the child's back caused by the bees attached to him, of the pink mist tunnel: visions she now consciously connects with Daniel's descriptions, realising that the pair of tribal angels had left the magic circle to awaken him, the Koolah angel, Black Londoner, Daniel Cottle.

Her mind partly lingering in the magic circle dimension, she says softly to him, 'Tried to tell you earlier when you were speaking to Yance…'

Daniel looks confused at her words, his mind still not making the connection.

'Don't be afraid, darling,' she continues.

Daniel speaks excitedly: 'Wasn't fear babe, the reverse. The woman actually told me not to be afraid. Emy, she called me Jarrod, gave a deeper meaning to me nickname, Jarrod, like reminding me I'd had the name before. They all gave me a feeling they were on my side, like I knew them. I feel like a different person and a life I'm familiar with when she calls me it…'

Like all subconscious human dreams, Daniel could only remember patches as he explains it.

'To be honest it was more the shock of it all. Their presence took me off guard, that's all. The beautiful music was so fucking familiar and I'm trying to think where I've seen their faces. Fucking bugging me now.'

Emy leans across him, the warm skin of her gorgeous body feeling heavenly to him as she picks up his gold Rolex to see the time.

'You've got another hour, Daniel,' she says to him soothingly. 'Get some more rest.'

But instead he stands, wanting to jolt himself out of the disturbing vision that's just filled his mind: Claudette's 18th century vision of the freezing baby crying on the slave ship sat next to her sick, shackled dying mother.

'Babe,' he asks, 'you ever thought of how many millions of Black people there are in the Caribbean, America, South America, Europe, the UK and other countries?'

Emy looks at him slightly confused.

'The reason I ask is Black people don't come from those countries but were taken there as slaves from warm lush tropical climates. Fucking lot of slave ships over four hundred years. You got any idea how many million were tossed overboard because the ships ran out of food to feed them? How many got sick, died because of heat, disease or froze to death down below deck. We're talking people here, beautiful human beings bolted to a wooden plank, packed in shoulder to shoulder, literally on top of one another like sardines in a tin down in that rat-infested shit-hole sewer?'

The hardened London gangster suddenly appears emotional; he gulps and fights against becoming tearful.

'When we arrived on plantations us Black men of a so-called strong breed were forced to mate with our mothers, and sisters with their fathers. Proud Black people forced to mate with our parents, even sisters with brothers. I never knew any of this before. As the pink light entered my head, it felt as though it began to open my thoughts, like reminding me. The moment she blew the kiss, something clicked; it was as though our souls connected and she began turning the wheels inside me. They keep sending visions…'

The mention of the pink light causes Emy to sit up on her bed, and before she even speaks her silence commands his attention like never before.

'Daniel, I've been having a mixture of beautiful and horrific dreams lately: enslaved Blacks in America's Deep South, White rednecks taking new-born babies and toddler children from their screaming Black mothers and forcing the male Black slaves to place the babies on riverbanks for bait to catch crocodiles…'

Daniel feels a different but familiar vibration within her voice. Looking into Emy's eyes, he pictures a certain middle-aged female from the magic circle, his soul recognising it to be Emy's incarnation from the days of the Koolah Tribe.

Now looking increasingly sorrowful Emy continues:

'I once saw one of the other babies get taken under the water by a huge crocodile, eaten alive in one go, and the White catchers weren't bothered about saving the child. They laughed and joked "plenty more where that one came from". Thing is, I researched the history and this is something they did; they used Black babies as alligator bait for God sakes. How evil, and they have the cheek to call Black people savage.'

She rises from the bed as Daniel shakes his head and places his face into his palms.

'Funny you mentioned that presence earlier,' she says as she gets to her feet. 'You've reminded me of a trippy familiarity a few friends and I constantly get after going out partying, getting high and waking having experienced the same – well, it's not like a dream, but wow, it's as though we were actually there, a deeply spiritual ancient stone city, all dancing to a sweet African bongo that's like house music. Baby, the music is exactly what we listen to today. The city is in a lush jungle, on the coastline. A bright, blinding light pink mist often covers a particular sacred stone area clearing with billions of tiny multi-coloured dots appearing and disappearing, Earth's spirit world, souls returning through the spirit world before they head off to the womb, heaven...'

He interrupts her, 'Emy, I've seen heaven, the pink mist; I was shown it last night and this morning.'

His words come as no surprise to Emy; somehow she already knew. She smiles, nods and carries on speaking calmly:

'We knew a lot back then in Africa. Baby, we could see the futuristic slave colony from the circle, the Messiah shared his astral travelling vision. At first it was frightening but turned out to be a beautiful dream in the end. In around thirty years from today, events around the world will raise a consciousness that will begin a preordained long-awaited transition, a dimension phase putting us back on track where we're to be no longer dependent on the West. The Messiah astral travels the universe and even shows us living on futuristic planets...'

Daniel hasn't heard her speak like this before, hasn't consciously in this life experienced this part of her soul. He senses she's now the one freaked and feels her shivering as she's thinking about being present at the magic circle communicating with others on an alien beach at night: around a hundred or so of them gathered listening to music, watching as the huge spacecraft approaches in between the planet's two moons.

'Daniel, we at the magic circle were taken aboard the alien craft. The beings were almost human except they have much larger eyes with no whites to them. Their crafts, all their vehicles are guided by the power of the mind.

'I used to think Africa was just lions, natives and zebras... but now I know it as the beginning, the cradle of civilisation. We were aware of alien activity thousands of years ago on Earth. We meditated for the survival of the universe's honey bumblebees. Those strange alien bees, they came through with it...'

'Came through with what, Emy?' Daniel enquires, but immediately something in his subconscious somehow picks up that she's talking about a black pearl diamond necklace.

Emy doesn't answer his question, but carries on: 'And people with those eyes, it was as though the bees had carried it through...'

Still in a trance-like state, she pauses then places her hands to her throat and chest, and says, 'Well you think the light's going to be blinding, but actually it feels pleasant and healing when it enters your being.'

Daniel wants to ask her more questions and wants to tell her how much he relates to what she's saying, but seeing her eyes in a vacant trance-like state, he knows she's currently too deep in a vision to respond to him.

Magic circle, City of Koolah, Ancient Africa

It is the time around a year before Koolah and Gabi finally came into Twin Flame union. The sun is setting and lit fire torches surround the sacred circle as twenty-two-year-old Koolah shares his astral travel sightings with the tribal angels who form a huge circle around him holding hands. Also within the circle is the child Imani, but his form is unrecognisable, his complete upper body and face covered by thousands of honeybees.

The necessary ceremonial music plays throughout the city as Koolah's powerful mind also directs the souls of hundreds of musicians and vocalists, who feel and obey his psyche creating the sweet sounds that ring out into the jungle and out along the coastline. Near the circle, two slim neat flames come out from thin air, each heating an elevated floating steel pot, both pots hovering around four feet off the ground.

In a trance, the elderly male witch Akachi gets to his feet and begins walking around shaking the maracas attached to his walking stick to the hypnotic rhythmic beat, his shins and feet covered by the off-white pink cloud blanketing the entire stone floor. His magic raises the Koolah circle vibration ever higher and Koolah's astral sightings become yet more vivid within the angels' collective psyche: visions showing an alien sky, two moons and the shape of a nearby planet.

Futuristic beach homes lie along the Delican shoreline, all with fabulous designs in materials that look like steel and glass. Music plays at a beach party full moons gathering, but no electronic gadgets produce the sounds; instead the sweet, clear music comes from what look like many entwined wooden bamboo hoola hoops bound together hovering vertically in mid-air. The music is precisely in tune with the exact sound wave and energy of the African Koolah tribal ceremonial music being played on Earth in a dimension phase more than ten thousand years earlier. A small Delican crowd watch as a gigantic spacecraft that hovers above them moves off out to sea, for a moment silhouetted against one of two visible moons before it disappears off into the darkness of the sky.

A loud buzzing sound can be heard emanating from a thick branch of a tree where there's a huge colony of bees in a hive. Nearby the extremely pretty, mixed-race Delican Blee stands looking up at the moons. In her hand she holds the small tatty brown suede pouch she'd actually took from Benser's grasp as his elderly body died in an earlier incarnation, another dimension phase. From it, she takes out a glossy black pearl and glistening diamond necklace, which she holds up above the beehive. Then she replaces the necklace in the pouch and holds the pouch containing the necklace above the beehive, and communicates with the universe, telepathically saying, 'God, please ask the queen bee of their kingdom for her assistance.'

Immediately the queen bee takes instruction from spirit and she orders the congregated bees to create an opening. A burst of activity breaks out among the Delican bees. They're similar to bees on Earth but with larger eyes, longer legs and antennae, and more vibrant in colour. Blee lets go of the pouch, and it hovers and gently rests itself on the hive. The bees become more agitated, some flying around her but none are aggressive or sting. The Delicans around Blee watch as the bees' movements cause the pouch to nestle into the hive until it has buried itself within and is no longer visible. Then the hive is quiet and settled once more.

The wooden ring from which the music on Delica emanates tilts and within it images of the Koolah tribe in Earth's ancient Africa appear. As Akachi shakes his maracas, the bee colony attached to the child Imani becomes noisy and unsettled as some of its number mutate from being Earth bees into Delican bees. The magnificent black panther Jojo stands and the part of the swarm that have become Delican bees begin to leave Imani. Imani smiles as he watches the Delican bees settle themselves in clusters around Jojo's neck until they have formed a complete ring around the beast's muscular neck. Then as Jojo begins walking around the circle, the alien bees leave him to re-join the Earth colony, and in their place the black panther now proudly wears a glossy black pearl and glistening diamond necklace.

On Delica, Blee excitedly jumps up and down, clapping her hands and telepathically speaking, communicating with the others around her:

'The magical wonders of our amazing universe, they took it through… the bees took it through.'

Blee remains looking into the hoop, watching as Koolah who was lying on the stone circle floor rises, with his long flowing dreadlocks and immaculate physique becoming visible above the mist. Blee speaks telepathically to Koolah as the two share a romantic smile: 'I see you, my darling.'

Magic circle, City of Koolah, Ancient Africa

A louder buzzing can be heard from the bees. Then, having intermingled with the Earth bees, the Delican bees seem no longer to be present among them, having either disappeared or mutated back into Earth bees.

The visions Koolah shares with the tribal angels now show Blee and her crowd at the Delican beach party beneath the low-sitting moons. He narrates telepathically for the angels:

'The vision is showing us, our soul group; what you're seeing is another future life, a dimension we angels are to reincarnate to.

287

We, our original tribal village are to evolve from human to Delican beings…'

CHAPTER 32

The King and Queen of the ancient African Koolah tribe walk onto the circle with their three adult children, nineteen-year-old Princess Gabi, her handsome older brother, and her older sister Princess Monifa.

Koolah slips the necklace off the slightly growling Jojo and with a smile and reassuring nod holds it out in his hands to present it to Lulu, the Queen of Koolah.

'It's ready, our Queen; the blessings and love vibrations it carries are from the farthest reaches of the universe, including having already been of service on our planet Delica. The angels attached will only react to your soul, Queen of Koolah; as always they're responsive only to your spiritual DNA.'

'Spiritual DNA...?' she asks, giving Koolah a puzzled look.

'The spiritual DNA,' he explains, 'is essentially responsible for the multiplication of our biological DNA, mind and body, our enlightenment and our wisdom. Studying and knowing it will be vital for the future of the whole human race as spiritual beings and for Earth's freedom. The necklace will leave you in certain lives you'll reincarnate to, my Queen, but it will always come back to you; it's part of you.'

She smiles. 'Thank you, our spiritual warrior Prince.'

Koolah respectfully returns her smile. 'The vibration of this necklace will take you to an unparalleled level of spirituality. Positive and negative demon spirits attach themselves to objects and people. Be careful of people and or items that are given to you; the giver's soul may be under the spell of evil, an assistant of Satan and mean harm...'

He reaches out to put the necklace around Lulu's neck and clip it in place, saying, 'The spiritual energy within this necklace is pure. It has the spirit of the most beautiful angels attached. Now and in each incarnation, each lifetime, it will take a little time for you to settle and get used to the universe's powerful force, the magical vibration, the necklace holds; it has to be this way.'

As soon as the necklace is in place around her neck, Queen Lulu feels the divine force of the entire universe empowering her body's inner soul, instantly taking all negative fears away, creating an immense joyful childlike feeling and bringing an effortlessly vibrant smile to her face. She begins twirling her index finger around the pearls and the powerful energy from the necklace continues to fill her with an unparalleled euphoria, pleasurably breathlessly causing her to collapse to the stone floor as though she's experiencing a spiritual orgasm. A combination of Koolah's presence and the powerful force of the heavenly stone have begun to transfer clear visions to her psyche: visions of joyful liberated uprisings. She feels as though she's actually there, hearing the sounds of gunfire and seeing the wars of the positive revolutionaries against aggressive unjust oppressors of the Earth and alien planets. Her mind takes her on a blissful journey through the victories and she feels the elation resulting from good triumphing over evil. Her visions culminate with one of the oppressed kidnapped Africans' bloodiest battles, the slave uprising of the Haitian revolution.

Then suddenly in an instant her mind is calm and the visions have switched. She realises she's still conscious in the time of the Haitian revolution but now finds herself across the Atlantic inside an 18th century Essex cottage living room in England. Her psyche visualises her reflection in the mirror; she's reincarnated again stunningly pretty, this time White, blonde-haired and speaking to a man who's stood behind her. She can see his reflection clearly, his face also facing the mirror, hand on her shoulder, having buckled to her neck the exact same black pearl and diamond necklace. He's a well-built, heavily tanned, ruggedly handsome, well-dressed White man with a thin scar through an eye. He has matted-style dreadlocks, his hair poking out from a beautifully embroidered Royal Navy Captain's bicorn uniform hat. Having had the necklace put around her neck, the same powerful sensation has her future incarnation now twirling her now White fingers around the glossy black pearls as she did when it was put on her there in her earlier Queen Lulu incarnation ten thousand years earlier in her Koolah tribe dimension.

Now almost fully conscious in the 18th century dimension, Lulu knows she lives in a huge castle on the Kent coast and knows everything else she's experienced in that future life, feeling a familiarity with her husband, her children, her undercover lovers and all others in that life. The White man who had just clipped the black pearl and diamond necklace to her neck is the legendary pirate captain Jim Morgan. Also present in the room are a Black woman, a White woman, a Black child and an English Bulldog. The Black woman is Natasha, the Haitian witch Lana's clairvoyant sister, the White woman is Charlotte Ortice's royal maid Alice, and the Black child is a girl called Anci. She knows too that the dog is called Patch, and that she herself is the sexy and promiscuous Charlotte Ortice, Royal Duchess of Kent.

Jim Morgan stands beside her at the mirror and the pair smile at their reflections. Charlotte, Royal Duchess of Kent somehow knows that Koolah placed the same necklace around her neck ten thousand years earlier.

'Goodness, I remember, that was I and the true Messiah, Koolah.' Through the mirror Charlotte sees a vision of the Koolah tribe communicating with the larger-eyed alien beings from the faraway planet Delica by means of a wooden hoop. Gradually Charlotte Ortice is becoming aware of her spiritual angel ancestral roots.

Jim Morgan sees only his own and Charlotte's reflection in the glass. Eventually he goes to sit on a comfy rocking chair by the fire from where he spins his gold coins on a low-level table.

As Charlotte looks towards Morgan, she doesn't notice Claudette's image appear in the mirror, or hear her sigh and say, '*enfin*,' – the word that means 'finally' in French – in relief at Lulu being back in possession of her divinely blessed, magical necklace.

The music at the magic circle has risen to a higher vibration and people on the magic stone floor are getting down to some

291

serious partying. After a short while, looking downward something distracts Akachi. He stops dancing and picks up the tatty suede cloth he's spotted on the ground. It's the pouch the Delican Blee had inserted into the bees' nest. He sniffs it hard with his nostrils, smiling whilst looking to the full moon.

Planet Delica

Blee and the Delican adults and children that surround her watch the visions of the Koolah tribe through the tatty wooden hoop that hovers in the air before them. Their huge eyes gaze at Monifa, Gabi, her brother and other Koolah angels helping their mother, Queen Lulu, to her feet. Blee and some of the others notice Koolah and Gabi exchange looks but Gabi purposely doesn't hold eye contact.

Koolah communicates telepathically with Blee, saying, 'You're called Princess Gabi here.'

Blee laughs and explains to the Delican beings around her, 'I know... Oh my God, that's me before coming into union with my Twin Flame Koolah in that life, our eternal twin soul love.'

Blee looks deeper within the diameter of the hoop, and as Koolah returns the smile she's sending out to him, she urges him on:

'Koolah take me; you know the half of our soul also exists within the body of Princess Gabi.'

CHAPTER 33

Koolah smiles, then turns his attention to and addresses all the angels of Earth's heaven circle.

'In a few short years the time will come for my fasting and my body will only last five nights without water, at which time I shall leave, cross into spirit world and remain in transit. Write the instructions to reactivate my soul for our reawakening. I'll physically appear, my brief second coming, and sixth reappearance in this dimension for one lifetime in the 18th century dimension.'

The tribal angels are shown a vision of Destin at the Haitian revolution slave rebellion base.

'My full second coming two hundred years later will be the year they will record 1964, my birthday, born in heaven, my seventh reappearance as a human body.'

The tribal angels now see the face of the Messiah's future incarnation. At first they see Black Londoner Yanson Bailey as a child in the 1970s walking to school with his White friend and fellow Koolah angel, Benjamin Jarvis; then his face as a teenager; then as an adult.

'Thirty years on, the year 1994... Well, they'll register it 1994 AD, but the correct date will be 10,707 AD, more than ten thousand years after my death as the man, the body you know me as today, Koolah.'

Turning to address the bee-covered boy Imani, he adds, 'In that year you, the then reincarnation of the soul you embody, will be responsible for releasing my mind from my voluntary physical exile. You will perform the ceremony to reactivate my mind to realise I'm the one chosen who came to the Earth in the name of love...'

All the while Koolah speaks a writer with a set of scrolls sets down Koolah's words, and a young female angel oils and tightly plats the three thin strands of blessed elephant leather separate travelling witch doctors had brought to the ceremony.

One of the tribal angels, an elderly woman, speaks up, saying, 'Koolah your spell woke and invited many of us here today to receive certain warnings. Put more of your astral travel sightings into our minds, show us what you see, the distant future of our soul tribe…'

Koolah takes up the lotus position and projects his clairvoyant voice into the minds of the tribal angels, not actually speaking vocally but communicating telepathically:

'Thousands of years from now the Asians will come across the Red Sea from their continent into Kush, the land of the Black people, Africa, and learn much from our knowledge. They'll negatively use the teachings from the Book of Koolah to perform powerful, deep magic. Aided by our magic, they'll cross into early dimensions and change humanity's conscious history. The African continent is naturally created for Black people to be the future leading economy, but sadly they will change all that.'

The visions Koolah shares show 7th century, Asian Islamic army generals and their leader in the process of establishing their religion, Islam, talking, making plans in regard to invading and enslaving the Black people of Africa – an intentional invasion specifically against the descendants of Koolah's and other African Twin Flame angel tribes. The Asians recover material, which shows the early indigenous African tribes were in fact more advanced in the knowledge of the invaders' own Arabic than they were. The visions show the intruders stealing and hiding ancient written material, crucial knowledge, and ridding all other evidence in a frantic callous act of mass genocide.

The circle are shown an image of King James who wrote his version of the bible.

'The later European intruders will hide our bible and hide the fact they'll find and will keep hidden my present ten thousand year old preserved body. Also in the year 1604 replace our bible with a Scottish, English King authorising a book full of lies.'

'This will happen because they are to be angry at the revelation of our tribe, Earth's first civilisation, God's authentic angels occupying Black bodies. The greed and hatred within the Asian leader and the Islamic armies will initially begin global slavery, enslaving the indigenous people of our peace-loving spiritual African land. They'll not want the world to know of what we discovered and achieved, because our spirituality will contradict their newly formulated invention, religion. For this reason they will continuously massacre any descendants of our uniquely chosen coastal city tribe in a bid to wipe us out. Yes, I'm sorry to say in around ten thousand years from now invading Asian Arabs will travel here to Africa seeking indigenous Koolah to destroy our spirituality and exchange what we know for what will be known as religion.

'Our tribe help uphold the divine force that keeps the world balanced, in tune to nature's justice and truth. We are as one, doing God's will by joyfully allowing the oneness, our inner spirit of God, to experience life. Human and alien races were created each with a soul; the magical soul within us is a part of the one Holy Spirit, the source. Individually and collectively all beings and animals of the universe house the oneness spirit God. Our joint meditation is our spiritual way of being whole again. Acts of kindness, our soul's joy in our dancing, singing, making love, achieving our dreams are some of God's ways of experiencing life through human and alien beings.

'Negative acts are in reality allowing Satan to experience its earthly desires: bad deeds, the future enslavement of humans by fellow humans, aggressive behaviour, hanging, molestation of children, rape, racism, murder, slavery, war and all deeds hurtful...'

The vision shows religious leaders and people with positions of power in the film and entertainment world, in prestigious public schools, and in religious institutions, allowing children to be molested, assisting Satan throughout history.

'A relatively small group will literally trade their souls so that they can repeatedly reincarnate as wealthy leaders having dominion over other humans, but their oppression assisting the evil one will come at a hefty price.

'We will explain to the intruders of our oneness and spirituality, but they will force their religion on Mother Africa. In our own home, the motherland. Believing Islamic conversion will create mutual respect, our people will convert to avoid being oppressed or sold into slavery. But Black slavery will be justified under Islam, stating the message of God says it is legal to have slaves.

'In our home Kush, they will enslave us and claim it an act of God, what wickedness! The Muslim Arab armies and their leader will begin global slavery, enslaving millions of Black African people.

'The Islamic slavers will begin trading us, the indigenous Africans, and then we'll continue to suffer at the hands of another race and their invented religion, which will be called Catholic and Christianity and will be formed by the European Whites. Tens of millions more will be kidnapped, taken in slave ships across the ocean, abducted and enslaved. God's universe, for sure, but the Devil will rule Earth for thousands of years and it will be the job of us, heaven's angels, to put it right.'

The visions that have corresponded to Koolah's words now change abruptly to show the globe nearer the beginning of creation, accompanied by warm laughter from the Messiah that causes the tribal angels to smile.

'The human race was created one colour. Africa was the only populated land and we travelled around the globe giving birth to other lands and their races.'

The visions focus on England in the time of the Koolah tribe's present day. The assembled tribal angels see images of descendants of British tribespeople with beautiful Black skin and loosening hair, some with blue eyes.

'The remains of one of the people of that land today, the land that will one day be known as England, will be discovered thousands of years from now, and they will call him Cheddar Man – a man Black like us but with straighter hair and light eyes, similar to part of Princess Gabi's right eye.'

The tribal angels are shown visions of the colourful African terrain, its glorious tropical weather, native humans, tropical birds, magnificent vibrantly coloured marine life, beautiful monkeys, black panthers, and spotted leopards; followed by different telepathic images of evolved European White people, domestic cats, less colourful birds, and bleak ocean and river life.

'Over time humans, and of course animals, have naturally evolved to their climates.'

The visions now show the indigenous people of the Arctic in their igloo homes.

'In colder lands us Black humans have evolved and developed lighter skin and different-shaped eyes to deal with the snow and constantly reflected bright sunlight. We had the same on Delica.'

Images of the Aboriginal Australians come through to the collective psyche of the circle.

'As you can see we've maintained the dark skin colour but evolved wider nostrils to take in more oxygen in the drier heat of that part of the globe.

'The force of evil will exploit the fact we later evolve with different colour, different facial features, on separate lands. The evil one will manipulate the human mind creating a divide, class structure, oppressing the darkest of our people of the hotter climates, the humans like us that have remained Black. The separation will create nations. Nations will seek our knowledge in order to have empowerment over one another.'

Koolah's visions now show his spiritual angels the formation of the continents from one supercontinent, splitting as though in time-lapse photography to leave the African continent remaining in the centre of the world.

'The world was one supercontinent, what will come to be called Pangaea, before it split into continents, yet the African continent was always at its centre, and even in their future atlases thousands of years from now they will show Africa at the centre of the world.'

Again Koolah shows the tribal angels telepathic images of Asian and European invaders, now crossing the deserts of Kemet heading towards what would later be renamed Egypt.

'We'll name our lands Kush and Kemet, but they will change it because they'll learn Kemet means land of the Blacks. They'll not want the rest of the world to know they travelled here to steal what Africa was gifted. Our future visions will be responsible for nations becoming civilised. They'll use the technology and magical powers to become victorious in major world wars. It's all so ridiculous because everyone on the globe was once Black, and the White people of this world, the souls they embody, will reincarnate to be Black again. The evillest trick the Devil will pull on the human race will be to manipulate and use minds to create racism. Examine what I'm revealing to your minds. Many nations will travel across treacherous deserts seeking the unrivalled power from our gifted magic. Their own futuristic visions will reveal to them the dominion it will award them. World wars will be won and masses of material wealth awarded.'

Koolah's multi-shared vision shows Queen Elizabeth II walking through the royal vault proudly showing off more than four hundred tons of stolen African gold, part of the monarchy's stash.

'This female wearing all the diamonds in her crown is the Queen of England. Just to clarify, there are no gold or diamond mines in their country. Future Europeans will in Earth's future dimension be guided by the evil spirit to steal the wealth meant for our Africa, part of the Devil's masterplan. This is the reason they will come, man's greed, their unnatural Kings and Queens wanting to rule over other nations. They'll come and take, take, take, leaving the people of Africa with nothing but disease that they'll bring from Europe, causing war, famine and starvation. A vile act, the cheek of the Devil reversing the psychology, having the rest of the world convinced we are the evil burden of the planet out to harm them. We'll be the Black bastard, animal apes, the scourge of Asian and European society. The evil Satan will manipulate these nations to inflict and carry out cruelty on the soul of humans, the spirit of God...

'Our tribe have been able to build our advanced city and learn their languages thousands of years before their countries and their languages will exist. My telepathic spiritual astral travel visions have revealed knowledge of Earth's and other planets' future dimension phases to you. These visions have revealed how to build the Egyptian pyramids and attain other fabulous achievements. Later in the wrong hands, the knowledge and magic will be used for negative technology including the invention of guns and other weapons of destruction to be used for oppressive, vile and evil global slavery.

'Saying Black African magic is evil, as they will do, is similar to saying that because a soul is reincarnated born Black the person is evil. The universe's Black African magic truly exists, for sure, but whether positive or negative, well that depends on the intention of the one casting the spell.

'A small minority of souls will be selected from certain nations and will make a pact with Satan opposing Earth's Twin Flame angels. Satan will send some to us and we'll let the Devil into our home to steal the love magic. The Satan-empowered visitors will secretly learn everything from what the future visions have revealed to Kemet and the rest of Black Africa. The unscrupulous guests will take the human race through the Satan-desired dimensions, always choosing greed, staging bloody wars and having dominion over the oppressed when global peace was an alternative. They will help the Devil supress the Koolah spirit and other angels, and in return their souls will continuously reincarnate in positions to have dominion over humanity. Unwitting, assisting souls, this small selected group will have entire nations helping the Devil carry out its plan. Satan will live out its personal pleasures through soldiers of war, slavers, rapists, paedophiles and oppressive nations throughout history. The clause within the deal for those who entered the agreement with Satan: well, they'll belong to the Devil for eternity, residing in hell.'

Koolah's civilised pre-Egyptian community are shown, through more of his shared telepathic visions, their city's tribal ancestors thousands of years into future dimensions. It's revealed to them that in the pre-Ottoman era Turks and people from the neighbouring Asian continent are to be invited into the magic circle to learn Koolah Twin Flame angel knowledge. In the beginning the invited scholars will live in peace with the extremely gifted indigenous tribespeople. The visions show the Turks and Asians meditating in peace, receiving visions at the sacred circle, being taught spiritual enlightenment, as well as bathing, hygiene and massaging techniques in premises that would later be known around the world as 'Turkish baths'. The guests would also play games such as backgammon with the Koolah people, full of joy and laughter. But then all that would change.

Koolah's later visions show waves of invading armies, Turkish, Greek and other European intruders seeking knowledge, the Persians, Assyrians, the Greek King Alexandra, Napoleon Bonaparte of France, and yet further into the future, Hitler's Nazi army – all in search of the sacred power, of Koolah's powerful hidden knowledge.

'The leaders of each nation will be shown by Satan the glory the magic can bring them, and part of the deal will be they have to keep the knowledge of the existence of authentic Earth-based Koolah tribe Twin Flame angels secret from the world. On arrival in places like Egypt, the invading armies will find to their horror gigantic sculptures there of the Koolah tribe's indigenous Black appearance. The intruders will feel it necessary to remove the Black-African-shaped noses and lips from the famous historic statues.'

A vision shows Napoleon riding his horse through Egypt and ordering his men to shoot off the Black-African-shaped noses and lips with their powerful cannons. Then the tribal angels see the Messiah Koolah's nose and lips being removed by a Sufi Muslim from the gigantic statue Koolah designed of himself with Jojo's body, the statue that would become known as the Sphinx.

'This Sufi Muslim is a man named Sa'imal-Dahr. A Sufi Muslim is said to be a Muslim who seeks to find the truth of divine love and knowledge through direct personal experience of God.'

Koolah laughs before adding, 'I take it by the Sufi Muslim's actions divine love will not later apply to the Black humans of the land he had been invited into…'

Then reverting to a more serious tone, he continues:

'Look at what I show you. European and Asian Kings will travel across unforgiving deserts to our great African Kemet cities. Look at them breaking the noses and lips off the statue images of myself and other spiritual angels of our tribe. Future humans will be tricked into believing the original people of Egypt were not of the local indigenous Black skin but instead we were the savages and lower classes of the land. Human intelligence will later tell them the lighter-skinned people they'll describe couldn't genetically be the original people of our lands. European leaders will be embarrassed by Africa's thousands of years of advanced civilisation, during which time they themselves lived as primitive savages. They will come and ransack our lands in search of our gifted magic, using its power to negatively stop Africa progressing, making us slaves to the lighter-skinned settlers, awarding them lifetimes of comfort off the back of our suffering. For a long time their religions will make Black Africans be looked upon as the inferior race of God's earth. Our spiritual teachings will be hidden and instead they'll create their controlling religious books.

'Their findings will make them all realise that it will be imperative to their survival, for many reasons, to quickly physically and mentally enslave Black humanity. The Asian and European masses for a long time will not know why they enslave and have hatred for the Black people of Africa. The evil one will take away Earth's subconscious psyche here and on other planets of the universe. The invaders are on their way to manipulate us to stop loving the God, the soul, in one another and instead fear and pray to a God in the sky.'

Koolah shakes his head in disgust.

'We will no longer know our spiritual heaven is the universal female womb. They will take away the knowing that the individual soul of each human and alien being is the one spirit of God, and that bodies are jointly part of the physical God. They will do all they can to keep it this way forever. Religious buildings of prayer will be the diversion.'

Koolah now telepathically shares the image of the future famous painting by Leonardo da Vinci *The Last Supper* with its White Jesus sitting at the centre of the table.

'They will know of my soul and our Black existence, but we will be portrayed in most cases as the man your minds see right now.'

Imani now can't help speaking out. 'But Koolah, what foolishness, how can modern-day people see a blonde, blue-eyed man originating from darkest Africa?'

Some of the circle open their eyes in disgust; others remain in trance as the voice of Koolah laughs, 'They'll preach I wasn't from here. Our descendants kidnapped slaves scattered around the globe, as well as white Europeans, will have such pictures hanging on the walls of their homes. Our spirituality will be hidden; our names Kush and Kemet, Land of the Blacks, will be changed to Egypt. They'll do anything to take away our identity, enslave us to build their Western modern society, then make us the scourge of that same Western society.

'In the beginning there was just the invisible spirit God and the darkness. They will depict God and the angels White in a bright heaven, but in their own books of religion they will say, "God said let there be light." If God said let there be light, God had to be dwelling as the darkness...'

The child Imani again interrupts the Messiah. 'But why, Koolah...? Why would they want to do this?'

The Messiah smiles with a shake of the head. 'Huh... their findings will reveal the Black African continent was to be the natural leading country. The love of the Koolah tribe was to thrive maintaining world peace, just as we made it so on planet Delica. Many nations will become civilised through us, come to the land of Koolah and steal our thunder by reproducing parts of our scripture to appear knowledgeable. After the Greek visitors arrive in the future, they'll become known globally as the elite and us as the poor backward Africans. They will come to call Ancient Greece the cradle of Western civilisation.'

Koolah telepathically shares the image of a beautiful female indigenous African who has many long thin living snakes in place of her hair, and the angels of the magic circle cringe.

'Don't be afraid; this hideous, snake-headed person will never exist in the physical. The mythical character and story of Medusa will be created for Greek society to demonise Black women, specifically those like us involved in nature's African spirituality, the knowing of our Twin Flame angel existence. In their mythology she'll be rumoured to be beautiful, desired by all who lay eyes on her but at the same time so evil and menacing to look at that even one glance can turn you to stone. Her myth will be created by those in fear of us with the aim of discouraging race mixing, their fear being the genetically dominant Black masses will be a threat to their White genetic survival.'

Koolah's vision now shows the African-Greek Queen Cleopatra, a flawlessly pretty Black woman, the epitome of beauty, a majestic presence that commanded power, a natural Queen.

'Just like many of the angels of our soul tribe, male and female, Twin Flame angel soul Queen Cleopatra and many women like her will wear their hair in natural dreadlocks. The visiting nations' armies will discover the indigenous female presence alone will be so powerful that eye contact with her will stop them dead in their tracks. The talk of her beauty stopping a man in his tracks will add exaggerated stories to the myth. Another mythical rumour will spread: looking into the eyes of the indigenous woman would turn you to stone. This is how they'll try to avoid other mixed-race people being in top tier society such as the future African Queen Cleopatra.'

Within the minds of the angels, Koolah shows images of other races, Chinese, Indian, Scandinavian and European. White slave masters of the Deep South's faces are shown. Gradually the faces of these characters change to show the astounding results of what they look like when Black genes are mixed back in.

'Now and for thousands of years more during our civilisation they'll live as barbarians but finally come here to be civilised. Also, all nations of the Earth, including the Greeks will find when they come to our lands and mix with the original Black human it creates a kind of beauty they never knew existed on God's earth. You've seen from my astral travel that the mindset within modern-day Earth society all over the globe will be of Black women being hideous and undesirable. It will stem from European White-crafted propaganda about Black magic, witchery, spookiness and made-up stories like that of Medusa. Our natural hair dreadlocks are instead described as many snakes and will be added to the myth. Another way of disempowering and oppressing the Black race and part of Satan's integral strategy will be to demonise Black women by their myths. This and other myths will contribute in creating a modern society that legally describes us, Earth's original humans who they've originated from, in their future government U.S. constitution as just two-fifths human, most part animal. Our colour, large lips, curvy body and protruding bottom will become undesirable and this will last thousands of years into modern society. Again, this will be in fear of the world mixing and going back to when the entire planet was Black. We'll invite them in and they'll take our riches, our gift from God whilst not even wanting to mix back with our race, wanting to keep their people White, creating the Black people Voodoo spook mindset to discourage mixed-race intercourse for the survival of the White race. The Greek civilisation will be founded from knowledge gained while bowing at the feet of African angels and the future so-called civilised Ancient Greeks will later claim they discovered the knowledge Black tribes of Black Africa gave to them.'

There's a sorrowful sadness within the collective psyche of the angels and then the voice of the Messiah:

'We will have to later expose our history and how we civilised the modern world in order to regain our spirituality.'

As the angels open their eyes following Koolah's sermon, they see, in the dip of the circle, there are two pretty four-year-old angelic twin girls before them, most oddly dressed in shabby

1970s clothing. One girl is Black, the other White, and it were as though they'd been reversed, mixed up, equally divided. Each of them has one ice blue and one dark brown eye. The Black twin sister has black silky soft fine hair, but the White twin sister has a blonde tight Afro. They watch mesmerised whilst looking up at the magically hovering pots of the Koolah tribe's mind-expanding party juice that adults of the tribe are presently taking turns in scooping cupfuls from.

CHAPTER 34

It is five years later, and the now twenty-seven-year-old Messiah Koolah shares a vision with the tribal angels of the modern twelve-month westernised calendar. He sighs and shakes his head.

'Our birthday is the moment the body's heart stops beating and we leave the body...'

Koolah looks to the sky to see the millions of tiny dots, souls arriving and leaving the City of Koolah.

'...leave the body and come directly here, heaven on Earth, before re-entering a chosen womb, reborn to our new body, in heaven. Born again that moment the soul's new body's heart begins beating. My birthday was the thirteenth day of the third month. It's the moment we begin life as a tiny sperm and usually almost ten moons, ten genuine ancient twenty-eight-day months, later our earth-day is the day we exit heaven, the womb, and born to Mother Earth. My earth-day is Friday the thirteenth in the last thirteenth month, fifteen days before the new year cycle.'

The now twelve-year-old Imani interrupts the Messiah. 'Koolah, why are you telling us things we learned long ago?'

Koolah appears slightly annoyed. 'Imani, you need to listen to what I'm about to say. Store this in your mind because you in a later incarnation, you specifically, will be called upon to activate our conscious reawakening at a dimension they will call the year 1994. You are to set the location for the reawakening reunion as well as releasing us from the negative one's prison. You'll know how to reactivate the spell and bring my soul from my voluntary spiritual exile and complete the spell to open back my mind to make me realise my soul is that of Koolah. The angels attached to the item, our magical book of Koolah, will join forces with all angels across the universe responding to your spiritual DNA and help with the spell.'

The Koolah circle is shown a Ku Klux Klan meeting. None of the racist White men are aware the astral travelling Claudette is present with them listening in on the secret meeting. The vision focuses on one of the robed and hooded men in particular and Koolah explains:

'We've discussed the Devil's cowards terrorising, kidnapping and oppressing defenceless Black people in future conscious dimensions. The son of this man will become president of the United States in their recordings of time, 2017 AD.'

The face of the future US president is telepathically shared as Koolah speaks:

'If we don't intervene, he will become the most powerful man in the world within the conscious reality psyche. Both his grandfather and father will be openly racists and he will follow them.'

The visions show the circle of angels the actions of the US president's ancestors.

Imani is again outspoken. 'Koolah, we can't allow this evil racist negative soul to lead the world. His grandfather will sell women to the public and his father will be a member of the Ku Klux Klan, a group who pray to one they call Jesus while they have humans chained and whipped, and rape adults and children. They stole our magic for prosperity and power.'

Koolah wipes away a tear and smiles. 'Fear not, the power they'll take from the people will be returned to the people. Imani, you will also be responsible for one day reciting our gifted love magic. You will know how to cross dimensions, and at the awakening you're to reunite us, bringing us together from other dimensions. When I'm rested in spirit world, we need to perfect the method of crossing. Only you will understand your written coded wording at your later incarnation.'

Imani nods solemnly and quotes Koolah's own words, 'As it was in the beginning, so shall it be in the end.' The child then asks with sincerity, 'Why do you have to go, Koolah?'

'The powers of the evil one are fierce,' Koolah replies. 'The Earth's consciousness is controlled in spirit world and it is from there where I'll battle with them. Imani, listen, the intruding oppressors will take away humanity's knowing of the magic gifted the indigenous of these lands, the physical crossing of dimensions. It is you who will be responsible for secretly keeping it preserved. Code it into our bible so that one day only your mind can reactivate the knowing.'

Imani again nods and says, 'Koolah, my Messiah, as it was in the beginning, so shall it be in the end.'

Koolah nods and hugs the child angel. 'Imani, ten thousand years from today, the day of our awakening reunion, we Twin Flame angels will begin the spiritual revolution. When we reach that period, please remember to allow mine and Gabi's, our, soul to fall in love naturally, without interference.'

The cute child smiles. 'Koolah, I've already promised to not forget.'

Koolah smiles at the child's cheeky manner of speech and carries on narrating his visions:

'As I've shown you, many years from now invaders will come to our lands and do everything they can to mask our existence and hide the fact that they got their knowledge from us. Our darker skin will be portrayed as a stigma, and through many dimensions when re-born Black you'll feel the Devil's negative curse. Leading up to the reawakening, Black people will begin to realise they've been tricked by the ways of religion and realise they are the original and true blessed people of this planet. The introduction of religion and racism will be partly motivated by the fear of humanity going back to Black. The number thirteen connected to my birth and earth-day will be taught to be a bad omen and an unlucky number within their psyche.'

As Koolah narrates, as ever writers are recording his words, creating what would become the Book of Koolah, the authentic bible.

'They will keep our gifted knowledge hidden at all costs, stupidly hide many things, including actually losing the year's thirteenth month from their invented calendar in protest of and to discard my birth. Simple mathematics tells us there are thirteen twenty-eight-day moon cycles to the year. They'll reinvent, re-write nature's yearly thirteen-moon cycle by scattering the twenty-eight days of one of our thirteen months among the remainder, reducing their calendar to only twelve months. Some moon cycles will suddenly have twenty-nine, thirty or thirty-one days. They'll also re-write our bible; their mistranslated books will teach to celebrate my earth-day, calling it Christmas in their newly designed twelve-month calendar, six days before the new year cycle begins.'

Visions of the famous and historically documented Scramble for Africa are shown, the European leaders partitioning of the lands, the British, German, Portuguese, Spanish, Italian, French and Belgian nations simply claiming vast portions of Africa for themselves. The telepathic visions show the German leader Bismarck at the head of a meeting in Berlin, Germany speaking of the land he and Lord Salisbury of Britain have already claimed. Then the evil mass-murdering devil-controlled disciple King Leopold II of Belgium speaks with regard to taking his share of the Black African continent: 'I am determined to get my part of this magnificent cake…'

Koolah's voice can again be heard:

'Their aim will be not to allow the rest of the world to know that the beautiful statues were made in the likeness of us, the indigenous beautiful Black African people. It's so ridiculous, the lengths they will go to to have power over other human souls, the spirit of God within human bodies. Their actions will be the result from their fear of Africa naturally becoming the leading country. They will put physical borders up to divide us by region, but more importantly they will create spiritual barriers to divide and conquer us by way of religion.'

Koolah laughs ironically. 'The intruders will be us, just evolved to appear different to deal with the climate of their colder lands. With the help of chosen humans, Satan will trick us into oppressing our darker fellow humans, manipulating us.'

The image of a magnificent spotted leopard changing to a British domestic cat is shown, followed by the image of a beautiful Black woman, the true likeness of Cleopatra, changing to the White Hollywood misrepresentation by actress Elizabeth Taylor, then the handsome Black man, the true likeness of King Solomon, changing to a painting that depicts him as a White man.

'The true Kings and Queens of Africa will be shown to the world as European White,' Koolah narrates.

'The invaders will force us to pray empty prayers. For all their efforts they will not be victorious because God armed humanity with the spiritual tools to bring back the love. We will have peace in our lands; we will prosper in the end.'

Koolah laughs and proudly smiles. 'Today's ceremony will ensure the spirit of the Koolah tribe angels stay together, our souls reincarnating and our new bodies physically meeting in every life our souls are born to.'

He turns to Princess Gabi, and beckons her to her feet. 'Gabi stand, let me take you on a journey, a trip which will show the awesome spiritual powers God gifted us. As you can see Jojo is dressed in his best harness for the occasion.'

Gabi looks to see the Black Panther has on a beautiful decorative body harness with glistening diamonds hanging from each of its many tassels. She allows her soul to move her body to the delightful drumbeat, the sublime music that always accompanies the tribe's ceremonies.

Koolah looks on approvingly and says, 'Gabi, empty your soul of any doubt. Remember we are counterparts comprising one soul. With our soul combined and the spirit of God within, our soul tribe will do the rest...'

Using the combined power of her and Koolah's divinely gifted evolved soul, Princess Gabi is able to completely rid her mind of any doubt, causing her to realise naturally that anything you ask for within the universe can be made manifest. High on the tribe's party juice, she and Koolah begin dancing amid the circle's pink mist to the sweet musical rhythm. Jojo too is joyfully excited. The huge muscular immaculate beast starts to prance and leap around.

The mist gradually evaporates; the music, soul tribe angels and stone circle are gone with it. The circle's remaining angels look to see the bodies of Koolah, Princess Gabi and Jojo are suddenly no longer there at the ceremony's coastal party. Instead, the Twin Flame couple find themselves on a Jamaican coastline at a fancy high-society barbeque. Looking around at the pristine island's features and the male and female characters present that Princess Gabi's familiar with from many dimensions throughout history, she inquisitively looks at Koolah and says excitedly, 'Strange dream, Koolah.'

The Messiah looks around smiling with a slow, gentle shake of the head.

CHAPTER 35

Negril Beach, Jamaica, 1994

There are people, Black and White, of all nations congregated at the exclusive party on the tropical seashore, characters from modern day, other characters from different time periods. Gabi looks around to see 18th century pirates and her alien incarnation Blee along with others from her planet in attendance. They dance in front of a fabulous glass-fronted beach villa, in fact an exact replica of Blee's Delican beach home. Gabi notices the faces of the guests around her lighting up in joyful surprise as they come to see the Messiah Koolah and the Black Panther Jojo are among them.

'Koolah,'she says in a trembling voice, 'we're no longer at home. This dream's amazing. It always seems so real; I've been here many times before. Thing is, I always dream myself as being White when I come here... But why are there people from different times and places here?'

Koolah calmly explains, 'No my Princess, a dream is us, the soul, becoming conscious in another of the universe's dimensions. We've physically crossed into a future dimension. We're at our preordained reawakening reunion, their year 1994. The people before you are from many dimensions our tribe are to live.'

'How many dimensions are there, Koolah?'

He smiles looking into her eyes, into their soul, and replies:

'Dimensions, oh an infinite number within our countless paralleled multi-universes. There are a countless number of universes, therefore times that countless number of us physical beings. Rather than travel through life you, the soul, moves switching through what are designed as multi-dimensional time and ageing dimension phases of choice, giving the illusion of lifetimes. Your every move, where you travel, who you go to see, whether to be kind or cruel in situations, every option is available. Every action of everybody's already played out in dimension phases, available life choices. Every action is up to us, the soul, the true vastness of God, our never-ending dynamic universe, the true greatness of God. The spirit of God is far greater than their modern-day religions will ever know. Within the multiverse in all other year-1994 dimensions the Devil had never enslaved Black Africa and, as I speak, the country Africa is, as designed, the leading world economy. In fact, we have only been enslaved in Earth's conscious dimension.

'Dreams are simply souls living other dimensions. This intricate dynamic was far too complex for the relatively low vibration intruding nations' scholars to understand. Instead, they taught nonsense such as God sitting in heaven up above the clouds in Earth's sky and that the Earth was the only inhabited planet. Part of their deal with Satan was to keep what we knew from humanity. The small group who made the deal always knew of our interaction with alien races, our Twin Flame angel existence. They were sent to hide our spirituality and do everything to keep it hidden, create tools such as religion, film, media to make us and other alien beings the bad people who mean harm. Instead of following what we'd revealed, they wrote their bibles and other religious books, but ten thousand years before their intrusion we travelled into their future viewing them forming their religions. The intruders discovered we the Koolah tribe have been aware of the universe from the beginning, actually witnessed it being divinely created, but that has been kept secret. The way in which God designed the spiritual and physical universe is truly great. On our Planet Delica we, in the end, found the way to free our minds, enabling us to cross dimensions as we have now. Humanity will have no idea what the Devil will keep from them, but we angels are here to reveal subconscious Earth to the human race.'

As Koolah speaks, he and Gabi look out towards the ocean, seeing the modern-day yachts moored, people riding jet skis, and overhead a jumbo jet flying in. As Gabi looks around she sees that others have joined them to look at the beautiful Jamaican scenery and to listen to Koolah.

'...And they feel they will get away with the wickedness they've carried out, inflicting pain and still daily oppressing the soul of God within Black people.'

Gabi looks around the gathering crowd with a polite smile and says quietly to Koolah, 'Where is this place?'

'No need to feel anxious, Gabi; you're among the angels of our soul tribe. Many of us have physically crossed from parallel dimensions. It took just a moment for our angel soul to travel ten thousand years into Earth's one-dimensional time frame future, which shows all past and future dimensions are parallel, my darling. Where's this place, you ask; this is the future Caribbean island of Jamaica and everyone you see gathered here is a Twin Flame angel soul. Jamaica will be a safe haven for Koolah angel souls during the Haitian revolution in the 18th century as well as the location for Earth's spiritual awakening.

'My Princess Gabi, we are one soul combining as a Twin Flame angel that vibrates creating the higher states of consciousness to the entire planet, consciousness only accessible when we merge as one, able to create the divine magic which includes crossing dimensions by using the universe's highest energy, eleventh dimension frequency and higher. In just six and seven dimensions our thoughts are so powerful all we have to do is think about a location and we can cross to it as we have now. In these higher states of consciousness there are three key differences, perception of time, power of thoughts, and most importantly the feeling and knowing of oneness, unconditional love unity knowing we, all souls, are God. In these higher states we can fly wherever we want and have a powerful understanding of unity. We can travel the Earth dimensions through time, and other star systems also. The soul can also choose to continue moving up to higher levels of consciousness. This is what enables us, God's angels, to choose when to return to our energy: the source without a physical body, to merge back as one with the spirit of God, including being able to return during the creation of the universe, travelling to different galaxies sharing our visual with other angels of our soul tribe. Intruders won't be able to use our bible correctly, cross dimensions, experience seventh-dimension high-vibration reality, because it can only be achieved with the highest vibrations of love, harmony, unity, joy and peace; not achieved when anger, blame, fear motivated by greed, and worry are involved. When separated, like humans we twin souls naturally vibrate up to a fourth-dimension dream plane and even fifth-dimension high-vibration reality, a space in consciousness that resides in higher vibrations of love, harmony, unity, joy and peace.

'Our tribal city accesses the higher states through our joint meditation and when having consumed the love juice. There is no fear in our states of being, and everything is perceived from a place of pure, unconditional love. During our last magic circle ceremony, I multi-shared, took our Twin Flame angels' combined psyche on a journey showing how intruders will gradually reduce our vibration, taking humanity backwards and ultimately taking away our spiritual knowing.

'Globally, through man's inventions, low-vibe religions, race and nationality, humanity will be reduced to a maximum three-dimension level of separation, conditional love consciousness. Here in this dimension, they'll be represented by feelings of fear, limitations, lack of inter-connectedness, suffering, working hard to succeed and being locked in time and space. Negativity does not exist back in our magic circle dimension; jealousy and shame do not exist there, neither anger, blame, fear nor worry.

'The planet's not aligned with love here. The energies here are out of alignment with the fifth dimension. Gabi, we're twin soul angels able to achieve this in this dimension 1994 because we've retrieved the universe's book of spells here, our Bible they'd confiscated and have held for thousands of years.'

Koolah holds Gabi's hand as they walk back towards the villa where there are plenty of other guests mingling. Gabi finds her eyes being drawn to the man standing talking with her future incarnation Blee. He's a mixed-race Rastafarian, the deceased iconic Jamaican reggae star Bob Marley who has crossed from a parallel 1980 dimension where he's alive and well. Koolah places his hand on the shoulder of Bob Marley.

'He, this soul, is a Twin Flame angel from a Central African soul tribe we connect with. He has also crossed dimensions as a physical body to be with us at our reawakening. This Twin Flame angel prophet reincarnated, reborn on this island toward the end of Earth's World War II.'

The Messiah looks around, still gently resting a palm on Bob Marley's shoulder as he speaks.

'Here in this dimension 1994 us Twin Flame angels have already battled to free Earth's subconscious mind. The purpose of our victory was to show many things, one being time is but an illusion, therefore 1980 Bob Marley, your futuristic Delican self and us from back in the 18th century are able to cross dimensions to all be present in this dimension.

'We interlinked with his and all other Twin Flame tribes here on Earth from our magic circle, together exploring. This is a multi-dimensional universe and this is the result of it, Gabi.'

Bob Marley shares a smile with Koolah and says, 'The modern Western scientist did try to figure out teleportation, but it isn't a scientific ting. The universe is created by spirit, therefore it a spiritual ting ...'

Koolah nods in agreement. 'This soul reincarnated as spirit intended, a prophet born mixed-race showing the world we are of one kind. He grew up in that dimension with the help of his soul tribe angels delivering messages of peace through his talks and music, but they, the men who are the Devil's supporters, created violent political wars and bloodshed in the ghettos, wars on God's Earth, the streets of this beautiful Caribbean island. One hundred and fifty miles long and fifty miles wide, tiny in comparison to the much more populated Haiti, Dominican Republic, and Cuba. Yes, smaller but what an impact its vibration has had on the rest of the globe. Jamaica produced reggae music, soul food, the accent all want to copy, great athletes; the list is endless. Through music Bob Marley here and others before him began the desired platform here, the vibration for our reawakening. Twin Flame prayers designed this island specifically so that the creative-attitude souls reincarnate here. We've crossed into the beginning phases of the spiritual awakening, my Princess Gabi.'

Back at the ancient Koolah City circle, Gabi's cross-dimension view and vibration of the island and the face of the iconic reggae singer Bob Marley enter the psyche of Imani and the rest of the angels.

Bob Marley turns to Koolah and says, 'Koolah, thanks, you fought for us in spirit world, you revealed Jah subconscious mind, the real life, you promised and delivered.'

CHAPTER 36

There's just one tiny cloud in the clear blue Jamaican sky above the marquee of the fancy high-society barbeque. Staff serve from a wonderful spread of meat and seafood, catering for wealthy guests, some part of the elite international criminal underworld.

Princess Gabi's drawn to and staring at the relaxed smiling face of an attractive silky-haired brunette, who's around fifty years of age but still possesses an amazingly voluptuous body and tremendous sex appeal. The White woman is accompanied by an equally attractive, athletically built, strikingly handsome, Black Jamaican of around the same age. The reason the woman has attracted Gabi's stare is the necklace she wears: a distinctive glossy black pearl and glistening diamond necklace that Gabi recognises.

There are around two hundred guests in total at the event, and it seems the crowd feel only pleasant surprise, perhaps a supernatural magical feel, at the sight of Koolah and Princess Gabi, and feel no fear at the sight of the full-grown black panther Jojo's presence. But some look confused as Koolah collects items of food from the spread, cooked barbequed meat and fish wrapped in tin foil and cartons of juice, and bundles them up neatly in a large fancy white tablecloth, collecting some ice too to keep the package fresh. He puts out a hand and the Haitian witch Claudette, who's among the guests, comes to him and places a platted elephant leather wrist strap onto his outstretched palm, which he adds to the contents of the bundle.

Claudette turns to see that the black panther Jojo is rubbing heads with her domestic pet cat also called Jojo, his own later incarnation. 'One soul, two cats,' she says in wonderment, 'the sights and wonders, this universe holds…'

Gabi looks through the crowd and focuses her gaze now on two Black men each around thirty years old. They are Yanson

Bailey and his best friend Daniel Cottle. The pair look similar to each other, albeit Yanson doesn't have Daniel's bluish-grey eyes; his are brown and slightly oriental like his mother Shirley's. In particular Gabi can't take her eyes off Yanson Bailey and his partner, the beautiful White Romany girl Princess. The modern-day London gangster Yanson and ancient African Princess find themselves exchanging curious glances. Koolah laughs, knowing instantly he and Gabi are in the presence of their own later incarnations. Gabi feels a distinct familiarity with the Romany girl but it's not until she notices the black streak in her blonde hair that she remembers somehow being her in the futuristic Ibiza nightclub, wearing a cream-coloured designer swimsuit and thigh-high stiletto-heeled boots.

Gabi finds herself addressing Princess in perfect English: 'It's making sense now, your hair and eyes,

the opposite of mine. I always dream of being you and I actually remember being you...'

'And you I,' Princess answers. 'We share the same eyes.'

Gabi smiles. 'And eyes mirror the soul... Koolah has explained it; we are of the same soul, existing in different bodies and have come together from different dimensions within our multiverse.'

One alien angel soul in four bodies, Koolah, Yanson, Princess Gabi and Princess speak.

Princess Gabi addresses Yanson in native ancient Koolah, saying, 'Oh... we meet again, my Koolah. I've recently been to a dimension of the future and seen and felt you.'

Yanson understands her words and nods, as Princess takes her beautiful mixed-race baby girl from an outside baby chair and explains, 'We've had a baby in this dimension and her name's Dinah.'

Koolah responds with a smile. 'I know, the child from your heaven, your womb, is the soul of your Romany gypsy grandmother recently passed through the magic circle; she's of course another angel.'

A bright pink ribbon falls from a young catering woman's hair and the Messiah uses it to tie the four tablecloth corners together, thus binding together the sack. Suddenly an 18th century Black African child, Anci, leaves her grandmother and little baby brother and approaches Koolah. She smiles ecstatically and speaks confidently to Koolah in her West African language:

'We meet again. I last saw you on the cliffside on the African coast. I understand; your powers are incredible. You're taking the food to me in another dimension.'

Koolah nods and greets the little girl's grandmother and baby brother with hugs and smiles. 'I told her you'd be reunited once again,' he says.

'You are the anointed uniquely blessed soul, the authentic Messiah, Koolah,' Anci says.

Koolah smiles and remains silent.

Meanwhile Princess Gabi again spots the White woman who's wearing her mother Queen Lulu's black pearl and diamond necklace. This time, she cannot help herself and approaches the woman, snapping at her in ancient Koolah, 'That's my mother's necklace.'

The woman laughs and herself responds in the ancient language, saying, 'I *am* your mother, Gabi.'

Gabi feels her mother Queen Lulu's spiritual vibration as she's answered. The woman wearing the necklace is the person Queen Lulu dreamed she'd reincarnated to, Mrs Cindy Nevin giving birth at her plush Essex mansion accompanied by the Caribbean midwife during the early 1960s, only now twice the age she was then.

Another White woman, a beautiful thirty-year-old with an angelic loving face and remarkable huge blue eyes, steps forward and says to Gabi, likewise speaking in native Koolah, 'And I the soul of your sister, Monifa.'

Gabi looks shocked then delighted as she and Julie Marney hug and kiss each other.

CHAPTER 37

The African Princess Gabi scans the entire party and speaks excitedly. 'Koolah, we are all in some way connected. I've seen this more than once...'

Koolah gently supports her chin with two fingers. 'I explained why when we arrived; you're in the company of the future incarnation Twin Flame angels, other twin souls we arrived on Earth with and spend each life with.'

She gives him a proud stare. 'Koolah, your gifted powers are truly divine. You've explained, but how, tell me again how we were able to do that, how did we get here?'

'Firstly, Gabi, simplicity is the key... you have to "know" anything in this universe is possible. Anything you think in your mind you can manifest to your reality. If you can think it, it's possible to do. Beings of the universe are one soul, the spirit energy, God. Modern-day scientists will investigate teleportation to no avail, but as Bob Marley just explained, the universe was created spiritually so you will only have the method by using the universe's spirituality.'

Later, Cindy Nevin hands the necklace to Koolah and agrees what has to be done with it.

'Leave it for Imani, Ode and the others,' she says.

Koolah nods respectfully. 'Yes, my Queen Lulu.'

'Well fucking hell...' Cindy replies with a smile.

Magic circle, City of Koolah, Ancient Africa

The Koolah circle are again visualising Earth's one-dimensional sorrowful dimension. Now Koolah takes Gabi with him on his astral travel as the rest of the circle receive visions of what he and Gabi see. Koolah and Gabi are in the future 18th century west coast of Africa, though they cannot be seen or heard by the people there.

Koolah and Gabi are at the scene of an indigenous family hut that has been ransacked by European colonialist slavers. In a pool of blood, a dead baby boy lies on the floor next to his dead grandmother.

Gabi is distraught, recognising the child and grandmother, having just seen them alive and well at the awakening gathering in Jamaica. She looks towards Koolah with a look of anguished confusion on her face.

He explains to her, 'The power of the magic circle made it possible by bringing Anci, her grandmother and baby brother across from another dimension phase of the multiverse, a dimension where they hadn't been murdered kidnapped and enslaved. The horrifically murdered grandmother and grandson are the very people alive and well accompanying the little African girl, Anci, present at the reunion awakening. In this sorrowful dimension, Anci is shortly about to discover her grandmother and brother's murdered bodies here.'

Koolah then addresses the angels of the magic circle:

'We'll invite them into our homeland Africa, share our gifted material wealth, teach them our magic, and this savagery is what becomes of it – just like a venomous snake saved from harm that would return your kindness by biting and killing you. They couldn't just share, take our teachings back to their lands and the world live in harmony. No, Satan showed them another side where they could have dominance over other nations and the evil one could live out its pleasures. Their fuelled greed got the better of them.'

The spirit of Koolah takes Gabi to a hill where nearby British slavers are gathering and shackling other indigenous families. There are groups, native families, made to sit with single long chains connected to groups of neck shackles. Gabi and the minds of the circle find themselves on a hilltop where a group of four psychic medium witchdoctors are sat in front of a small shrine. Koolah converses with one of them and places the Queen of

Koolah's black pearl and diamond necklace on the shrine.

A confused Gabi protests, 'Koolah, that's mother's blessed necklace.'

'I know,' he answers. 'We're leaving it here. Your mother, our Queen Lulu, will have it again'

Suddenly an eerie darkness fills the collective psyche of the magic circle, and time in the astral travel vision moves forward. It is now a few days later and Koolah shares with the circle a vision of a huge white fortress on the west coast of Ghana where the kidnapped indigenous families have been taken.

It is Ghana's notorious Cape Coast Castle with its 'Door of No Return' through which millions of kidnapped Africans would be forced on to slave ships bound for the United States. Through his visions Koolah takes the circle on a tour through the squalid sorrowful surroundings showing them the atrocious conditions of imprisonment. Parents' loud screams echo from the dungeons. Separated children cry for their parents within other squalid dungeons. Koolah's voice is saddened as he speaks:

'Intruding nations will possess the Book of Koolah, containing our gift, magical powers of the universe. They'll reverse the love magic and use it negatively. Kidnap us, remove the universal natural spirituality, subconscious reality, from the soul of the indigenous, and instead make us live with a one-dimensional conscious mind as slaves by their unjust laws and religions.'

Koolah's telepathic images show previous Asian invaders of the African continent staging and beginning their religious wars, also Asians invading all parts of Africa enslaving the indigenous Black people, contributing to the beginning of the global slave trade by trading the men, women and children that they did not wish to keep as slaves on to European and Westerners to take to Europe, the Caribbean, South America and the U.S.

'Evil times are ahead. Their modern man-made laws and man-invented religion will permit the satanic evil treatment of Black people on our homeland and around the world. Entire White nations will feel they're justified owning human property, forcibly making us work with threats of being whipped, inflicting male rape, sodomising, hanging innocent fellow humans by the neck until they are dead. The immense wealth brought about by their stealing of our precious minerals and Black African enslavement will bring them abundant prosperity in theirs and their other stolen countries.'

The visions now show the dreadful journey ahead for the kidnapped, abducted families. After they are forced through the notorious 'Door of No Return' they will be systematically packed, rammed tight into a slave ship like sardines packed in the can. Then the horrific voyage would await them.

It wasn't enough that the people of Africa were kidnapped and chained in squalor in baking hot and below freezing conditions; during the voyage their captors would perform hideous acts of cruelty on them, including acts of paedophilia, and raping the women, and the men. Many proud Black men are to be raped on-board the ship during the journey at sea. Having reached their destination, for even the least fault, the terrified and more-often-than-not divided families were to receive the harshest punishment. They were made examples of by having horrific cruelty inflicted on them, including the commonly known so-called sugar-juice punishment.

Koolah's vision shows this punishment standard throughout all sugar plantations. An innocent Black woman's entire head and body are dunked in a huge pot of boiling sugar, her skin literally falling off as a deterrent for others not to steal and eat the product. Afterwards, as her corpse lies cooking in the boiling sugar water, the White slave owner family go off to church to pray, giving their thanks to God.

The visions also show many other atrocities. Enslaved Black people, males and females, are transported in secret to farms for the wealthy White owners' personal enjoyment. As was often standard practice for dehumanising and breaking the spirit of the male slaves, the biggest and baddest male on the entire plantation is selected, tied down and sodomised in front of every Black person, a method commonly known as buck breaking. Sacks are placed on the heads of slaves and strong males are mated with 'good breed' females, even their own mothers in order to produce that strong hard-working slave. Because of their handsomeness, great physique and strength, huge manhood and stamina, White women force slaves to sleep with them while their masters are away.

'This sorrowful, vicious, violent future will not be forever. Slavery will one day be abolished but the effects of four hundred years of everything under the umbrella of slavery will remain in the human psyche until the perpetrators will publicly admit wrongdoing and compensate the ancestors of the victims in order to re-establish their culture.'

Koolah's vision now changes to show a modern-day English crown court.

'We've travelled through to the 20th century courts of law, studied their punishments for specific inhumane crimes. When someone committing a crime behaves in a way that shows no compassion, their law courts label his or her actions inhuman. In the words of English law: "Murdering another person is an inhuman act; slavery is an inhuman institution. Inhuman acts can also be described as inhumane, inhumane meaning without compassion for misery or suffering, heartless and cruel." The slavers weren't aware these inhumane acts would be those punishable by life sentences just over a hundred years later in their own modern-day crown courts. In the future victims of these crimes will be compensated. For their inhumane acts, Asia, the West, Europe and the U.S., for the parts they played in the criminal conspiracy will compensate by way of reparation in line with inflation. Compensate for Belgium's mass genocide, their and the rest of Europe's murder, kidnap, abduction, human enslavement, mental trauma, theft of belongings in line with the year 2023 inflation. An estimated wealth we would have accumulated with our precious minerals, again in line with modern-day inflation, more importantly purposely taking away our spirituality, therefore not allowing Africa to prosper. All to be settled in line with modern-day courts' treatment of victims of crime. Reparation is an extremely strong and just word, meaning the action of making amends for a wrong one has done, by providing payment or other assistance to those who have been wronged. Souls reincarnated to Black bodies will be reborn amid an oppressed psyche, into Earth's negative consciousness. For four centuries Europeans not allowing us to read, write or be educated. Degraded, in fear of being whipped, hanged, raped, buggered and molested. We'll be taught we're not human and later in the 20th century they'll promote the question why are Black people behind in economy and uncivilised. Make us feel they are superior within their man-invented religions and many versions of God. Black people will be the scourge of their society, lowest seventh class citizens within their psyche. All people will pray to a God that's alright with enslaving and torturing the Black people, the same God for the evil oppressors and sorrowfully oppressed.'

The inquisitive child Imani's voice is telepathically heard saying, 'But, Koolah, will not anyone question their religious belief in future Asian and Christian Gods, a God that allows us to be enslaved and sorrowfully oppressed to forcibly serve them? A God that will make heaven on Earth for Asians and Europeans and hell on Earth for Black people having to serve them. Do they really feel they are praying to God? Why will not modern-day Black people question why they pray to the same God that has them enslave us?'

'Imani, later in the 21st century during the reparation stages they'll concede, they'll realise the Devil tricked them into believing it was right for nations of human beings to treat entire Black races, souls, the spirit of God, that way. Religious belief, you say Imani, in their dictionary the word belief actually means to not know. We've studied enough of the universe's spirituality to know our knowing is the truth. For instance, Gabi, Jojo and myself know we are travelling through the 18th century and displaying the future visions to sixty of you simultaneously, the authentic magic of the universe. None of their religions will ever be able to show them any wonders; they will write their religious books without substance, no proof. They'll say God showed them things and God spoke to their prophets, but ask them what God looked like and they won't really know. We know the spirit of God is the soul of every being, alien and human and the entire physical universe. They will come and steal our timber, ivory from our animals, precious metals, diamonds and colonise our lands and leave us with nothing.'

'Koolah, do you mean they will kill elephants for their tusks?' Imani asks.

'Yes Imani, ivory will sadly become of value in their modern world.'

Through his telepathy, Koolah now shares with the tribal angels future visions from the year 2023. An image of the attractive, spectacle-wearing face of female Black activist and public speaker Dr Arikana Chihombori-Quao fills their minds as Koolah speaks.

'Now for the reason we twin souls are here. We were brought here during a period when Africa was the only populated land on Earth. It was during the early stages of the human race. Twin Flame souls are present now in every nation of the Earth and each of us angels has a life purpose to bring equality and love to the human race, whether it is here in Africa or for the Native Americans or the Aboriginal Australians. We angels have split becoming Twin Flame angels, and no one must get in our way in creating our one Africa and bringing love to the Earth. If Mother's not happy, no one's happy; the nations of the Earth are the children of Mother Africa; she bore them only for them to come back and viciously rape, enslave and oppress her. All who have taken from her, like the Belgian and British monarchies have, will pay compensation and Black people of the world will wake up and invest financially and reinvest spiritually in the authentic holy war. This is where we begin to make the change. Alright, look now…'

Koolah's psyche shows the angels of the circle cities far more advanced into the 21st century: futuristic Singapore, Dubai, Las Vegas and others, African coastlines flourishing again in Earth dimension 2050s and 2060s with high-speed trains, mile-high buildings, man-made islands, futuristic buildings taller than today's skyscrapers, flying drone taxis – all blending with the African jungle.

'Listen, by the year 2140 nature will have each and every stolen soul returned to Africa. Each soul kidnapped, taken away and enslaved will return by way of a spiritual exodus and inherit the Western wealth in what will be called reparations. We are to be financially repaid; each ton of gold taken by the European invaders will be returned to Africa... with inflation, of course.'

'But of course, Koolah,' Imani chips in.

CHAPTER 38

'...The compensation awarded and the return of stolen goods will enable Black African business to flourish rapidly. New Africa with no borders. Foreign business people, Chinese, European and Asian, will flourish there too but not without financially putting something back into the country. One currency, one bank, one just leader, one Africa. The capital city of Africa will be built along the coast and inland of the site of the ancient city of Koolah, and the banquet room and government building above the coastal heaven magic circle. The spiritual strength will ensure evil will never oppress our lands again. No more Satan-manipulated corrupt Black politicians in places of decision-making. We'll bring Black and White celebrities and business people from all over the world to invest in Africa. The ancestors of the early intruders' biggest fear and last thing on Earth they'll ever want is Africa to have unity and be back to our original solidarity, the wealth of Black people coming together. A balanced Koolah soul natural leader, natural like the queen bee of the hive, will ensure, aided by our spirituality, that we'll never again be colonised, but instead naturally flourish in economy as the most developed, civilised leading country.'

'We will have the power to stop the future atrocities, Koolah?' Imani asks.

'The atrocities the rest of the world put us through will be our lesson, a harsh lesson we'll use to make us strong as a race. Let them do as they wish; they will be brought to God's justice, laws of Karma, Imani. Let nature take its course, but as it were in the beginning, so shall it be in the end. They gave into greed, but evil will not prevail. You don't honestly think on God's earth the Devil's oppression will last forever?'

The face of Donald Trump enters the collective psyche of the Koolah soul tribe's angels.

'Whilst in his short reign of power, a White Western leader will inadvertently begin a mass exodus. He and other racist leaders will provoke Blacks to repatriate. These events and the actions of celebrities, film writers and other influences will pressure them into paying our reparations. Kidnapped indigenous souls will reincarnate to all nations in high-up positions to grant the reparations to this continent, or should I say country. They may take away our knowing, force us to follow their invented religions and not allow us to educate ourselves in their Western society for four hundred years, and the Asians before them for a thousand years, but we will still be victorious. Nature also has a plan: God will heal its spiritual wounds, the oppressed soul within the Black race, heal Mother Africa, the Earth and entire universe. The spiritual underground is always at work. The nations who have enslaved us and taken our wealth, Africa will be greater than them all. In the conscious dimension the reparation payback money we'll receive will help; we'll make the most of it and build our economy. As we move up away from their religions and reconnect with the universe's spirituality evolved alien planets will show us how to prosper economically. The soul of every kidnapped slave, tens of millions, will have reincarnated back in Africa to enjoy the beginning of our new prosperity.'

The Koolah circle are shown future 20th century assassinations of reincarnated twin soul angels: Malcolm X in 1965, John Lennon in 1980, Martin Luther King Junior in 1968.

'They'll kill Earth-based angels from our and other soul tribes, but we will ultimately regain nature's spirituality. We are the chosen gifted ones with abundance of everything. What's to be, will be. If they were the chosen, God would have made their lands resourceful and rich. They'll unnaturally take by force what God awarded us, spilling much blood. They'll delay but won't be able to control the laws of nature, or for that matter, handle its backlash. Reparations from the West, they'll owe much more! They'll interfere with nature's plan by taking away God's gift, stealing God's precious jewels, the chosen people. God created humans so the spirit could experience joy, conscious as us in these amazing lands. Satan made it so that when reincarnated Black you continuously experience a feeling of inadequacy. You don't think God would allow the Devil to carry out this wickedness and forsake its own soul? No, God cannot abandon itself. You see we prosper; we are God and win without compromising our spiritual integrity.'

CHAPTER 39

King Louis XVIII Hotel, Amsterdam, Holland, 1993

Emy suddenly sits bolt upright in bed, her eyes open unusually wide. She's woken from more dreams and visions of the magic circle: Koolah sharing images of the 16th century West Africa slave trade, of futuristic prosperous Africa, and of the reawakening party on the island of Jamaica. She also recalls walking through the mist tunnel leading out of the magic circle, walking towards the end of the tunnel with another Koolah angel, and to her astonishment remembers seeing Daniel and Claudette looking through from the other side, and in the background seeing her own self asleep in the hotel bed.

'Daniel,' she almost shouts out in her excitement, 'we came through to awaken you.'

'Funny, that's what Claudette said,' the London gangster replies, not realising that she's speaking of Akachi and Imani travelling, crossing dimensions, to their hotel room.

'Daniel, we ancient indigenous Africans were shown future visions. Many showed you and Yanson present…'

'Jesus and other angel twin souls could physically appear wherever they wanted, any time in history, and Koolah's psyche, the purest and most potent energy of source able to examine the minds good and bad deeds of every soul on earth and in the universe. We took others from outside the circle on occasion, showing the power of the mind is able to achieve anything. Gabi crossed into what must have been today's Caribbean island of Jamaica and we in the magic circle received her visual. God, I saw yourself, Yanson and others there speaking to Koolah and Gabi'

Emy pauses, the sudden sorrowful turn of her thoughts reflected in her face.

'What is it, Emy?' Daniel asks with sincere concern.

'I didn't see myself at the reawakening, at the glass villa barbeque in Jamaica. Can you tell me why you were present with a beautiful Hispanic woman called Sofia...?'

Daniel, lost for words, says nothing but hugs Emy and they share a reassuring kiss before she continues speaking. 'Gabi explained when we die we, our soul reincarnates to another body but the infinite amount of lives we live run parallel. She met herself in other dimension phases in other body forms, past and future lives. Daniel darling, the Princess Gabi told us she crossed dimensions and physically touched, hugged, even spoke to the person her soul reincarnated to.'

Emy sits back and Daniel feels her shaking with excitement.

'Wow,' she says, 'is that not fucking freaky?'

As she was speaking Daniel consciously felt her words chiming with knowledge buried deep within his subconscious.

'Emy, the twenty-nine years I've lived, that's got to be the most powerful fucking story I've heard on this Earth, fucking deep...'

She smiles brightly. 'Everyone, Jesus and all of us, were Black people. I say we because I didn't see our White friends... But when Jesus and the Princess crossed, she beamed her visual and we saw the reawakening: the ancient indigenous King and Queen had reincarnated Cindy Nevin and Cutty Robinson, and both you and Yance were there.'

Emy jumps out the bed in an outburst of excitement. 'Oh my God, Daniel, how could I forget? Koolah was speaking to Bob Marley – I've always loved Bob Marley. He was explaining how the scientist today was trying to work out how to teleport but it's not a science thing but spirituality. Humanity lost Mother Africa's spirituality and instead turned to religion and science. You, I and all the other people we know, Black and White, our souls are present. Our minds were not influenced or separated by today's modern society; we're freethinking loving Black natives.'

CHAPTER 40

Emy picks up the hotel telephone, and ruffling her hair as she speaks, says, 'Hello room service, can we have some coffee and pastry cakes brought in please? ...Yes for two. Thank you.'

She puts the phone down and carries on, 'Where was I...? Oh yes, that's it. Our sisters, brothers and friends, our parents in today's modern life are all spiritually connected... fucking weird.'

She pauses as she recalls seeing a modern-day mobile phone that had somehow found its way to the dip section of the magic circle, the spot from where Koolah and specific tribal angels share their telepathic visions.

Her mind becomes slightly confused. 'Funny, I heard the music as I woke up earlier, sounded loud.'

'Emy, that is fucking weird,' Daniel says excitedly, for the moment losing his ordinarily cool composure. 'Those ghosts made me feel what you've explained, I swear, that bright pink light, the mobile phone and you heard the group of girl voices singing and bongo…'

Emy's shocked. Shaking her head and breathing heavily she points at him and says, 'I never specifically said anything about that mobile telephone, those guys playing the sweet bongo drum or the choir of girls singing that beautiful African melody. But we heard the same music this morning...? Yes, you must have. And you saw the mobile phone at the sacred circle. I felt seeing the mobile phone was a dream within a dream. That's it; it's all making sense now. Koolah is somehow connected to your friend Yanson Bailey. Koolah brought the mobile to the circle from a future dimension. My God Daniel, you're connected as well...'

Daniel's mind is trying to fathom what she's saying as there's a knock at the door and a male Dutch waiter arrives with their coffee.

After the waiter has left, Daniel asks 'Other dimension?'

She places her index finger to his lips and begins to cry tears of happiness, trying to catch her breath as she speaks. 'Daniel... you, you saw the fucking mobile phone.'

She smiles as the image of Koolah becomes vivid in her mind. He's sitting upright, chest and head visible above the shining off-white pink mist covering the engraved floor. She knows the divine energy has no form but that the pink mist is there to signify its constant presence – its potent magical vibration there to tune the tribal angels' minds into Koolah's telepathic visions, cast spells and perform other aspects of the universe's deep spiritual Black magic.

'Emy, why do I get the feeling what you've just explained is connected to those ghosts in this hotel room as I got up earlier?'

She replies with an extraordinary vibration of confidence he'd never felt in her before:

'Darling, a human sighting of a ghost is just someone in their soul tribe existing in another dimension. Stories you hear about people seeing the ghost of a little boy or woman who'd died in the house is a paralleled dimension when they're alive; all dimensions are in the moment of now. Objects being moved around the house are by people who appear invisible and have crossed from other physical dimensions. Seeing a person that died in the house – so-called ghost sightings – feeling people touching you: all that's happened is you've just shifted, both slightly crossed into one another's dimension. Her walking up the stairs or around a room: at times it's possible to pick up on other of the multiverse's dimension phases...'

Emy suddenly appears freaked out. 'Daniel, please don't ask how I knew that. It felt as though I was being guided as I explained it, like it wasn't even me speaking.'

She pauses in thought for a while thinking back to the City of Koolah.

'It's a strange but beautiful, trippy place, in ancient times but I've seen yourself and Yanson there dressed in modern clothing you wear today, also, on many occasions, an unused mobile phone with other objects on the engraved floor of the magic circle. It's the circle where we all lay meditating and spiritually connecting with one another in other dimensions and futuristic aliens of the universe. Fucking blew my mind the other day. Some Dutch friends I hang and party with share the same visions, one of the guys began checking what our visions revealed. Scramble for Africa, facial features purposely removed from magnificent African statues, ruins of the destroyed and lost city of Koolah in that very coastal spot on the North East African coastline – they keep emailing ancient historical stuff that matches our visions, ruins of our homes re-inhabited by the invading nations, Turks and other nations claiming to have built our cities. Daniel, I freaked the fuck out in my apartment the other day.'

Emy's voice becomes even more excited. 'Baby, I woke from dreaming that in the ancient magic circle we'd received visions of Asian and European leaders and kings removing the Black people's facial features from the great statues. A morning later my Dutch friends and I had a telephone conversation having dreamed the same dream. Days later those Dutch guys emailed printed pictures they'd downloaded online, many of the exact statues with the lips and noses missing, the exact chunks removed by cannon fire. I saw the French leader Napoleon giving his cannon operators the order. We felt their vibration. He found the truth during his trip to Mother Africa and didn't want the world to realise Africa was the cradle of civilisation, the Black African the original human, Black Africa where the Europeans learned to be civilised and knowledgeable from. Oh my God, it's documented everywhere on the internet. The European "Scramble for Africa", stuff none of us knew anything about. Baby, none of us knew what King Leopold II of Belgium looked like or had even heard of him before those dreams. Aside from African slavery, this evil fucking devil Belgium King exterminated twice, maybe three times, the Black Africans than Hitler did White Jews during the Nazi holocaust. Thing is, the African holocaust is not even spoke of today, which shows how much Black people have ever been valued by the rest of the world. Our connected dreams showed us receiving the Messiah's vision of world leaders, the bastards who did it; and now we know why they did it. Jesus's visions revealed Britain, France, Germany, Belgium, Spain, Portugal and Italy's leaders discussing how vital the oppression of the African country would be to their modern – in fact today's European – civilisation.'

His mind recalling his own visions, Daniel urges, 'Emy, tell me more about this magic circle.'

'Baby, the magic circle is physical heaven on earth and we, the psychic Koolah soul tribe, are nature's authentic angels. The true angels of the world are Black. Other human nations, Asian, European and so forth, are migrated Black people evolved differently over a long period to adjust to the globe's different climates. Invading nations and their religions changed the script – just one of the many lies told to disempower Mother Africa.'

Emy pauses and smiles as a previous Koolah circle vision comes to mind. She recalls being in the ancient circle receiving a future dimension image of a five-year-old Yanson Bailey and his best friend at infant school, a White girl of the same age, Julie Marney. Emy recalls the details vividly. The year was 1970, the school Blackhorse Infants School in East London and cute but sad-looking little Yanson Bailey was standing in the playground shivering, inappropriately dressed for the winter cold.

'Daniel these visions are crazy. I saw a young child. The vibration we got from Jesus told us the child was your friend Yanson. All of us in the circle are jointly visualising Yanson and a very pretty little White girl in a London school playground.'

Daniel instinctively knows she's speaking of Yanson's lifelong friend Julie Marney, whom Yanson has many times told him about being best friends with at infant school.

'Jointly visualising?' he asks.

'Yes Daniel, the Messiah Koolah telepathically puts his visions into all of our minds and narrates the detail, sometimes a voice in your head or no voice but a strange heavenly telepathic knowing-what's- being-said way of communicating.

'Don't ask me how, Daniel, but we all knew Princess Gabi's

elder sister's soul had reincarnated to the little White girl stood in the playground. Aided by Koolah, the Princess Monifa could command her future mind and body. Monifa became conscious in her future incarnation and befriended her troubled Koolah soul mate Yanson.'

Emy closes her eyes for a moment recalling Princess Monifa lying in a trance in the dip in the circle. Then as she thinks again of the five-year-old Yanson and Julie freezing in the playground, realisation strikes her that the pretty, blue-eyed, dark-haired little girl grew up to be the beautiful blue-eyed thirty-year-old woman at the reawakening party in Jamaica.

Emy's thoughts are interrupted by Daniel's voice saying, 'Hold on Emy, you mentioned some spiritually connected Dutch people. Something about you and a group of friends sharing visions.'

'Yes baby, angels from our soul tribe, a male and two female friends, cool White people and all three raised in mega-wealthy families where their White Afrikaner parents still have those twisted, extreme right wing apartheid racist views. Wealthy school friends – as you know, I'm not from a wealthy background but my grandparents used their life savings to get me through the top Dutch schooling. I'd known two of them from the age of seven and the other girl, Tess, more recently from teenage years. Tess was more their friend, but we've got the closest just recently. She's fucking deep, baby, tells me of her Twin Flame connection with a cool White dude...'

The topic of conversation and mention of Emy's schooling takes her mind back to one of her many heated discussions growing up as a pupil at her posh Amsterdam school, an argument that would often erupt between her cool cosmopolitan crowd and the opposing right-wing White supremacist group. The racist crowd would often air their opinion on Emy and her friends wanting reparations for Africa. Emy and others with empathy would express the notion Africa should rightfully be compensated for the atrocious crimes inflicted on her over thousands of years. But the racist Whites would always argue the Blacks of Africa were stupid enough to allow her wealth and riches to get swindled from her because Black African countries and Black people of the world in general are backward. Having been raised under the influence of his apartheid parents, one of the racist pupils smugly comments, 'Black Africans enslaved their own, so what's the difference if White Europeans did it to them as well?' Therefore concluding Black African countries had no argument on slavery. As Emy's re-living the in-depth conclusion of the discussion, the memory suddenly brings a vibrant smile to her face and Daniel sees she's in deep thought nodding with a proud expression.

The mention of Twin Flame gets Daniel a little nervous, reminding him of Lana/Claudette explaining that Emy isn't his Twin Flame but Sofia is instead.

'...but my other friends, the other White guy and the girl, pissed their racist parents off by having deep meaningful relationships and children with Black partners. They've since been alienated from their families...'

Daniel laughs out loud. 'I bet they're pissed. Can see her evil racist dad's now thinking of his daughter getting sexed with some huge Black dick, bet he's still shouting, "Kaffir lover".'

Emy smiles at Daniel's accurate imitation of the accent. He and his whole gang had become expert larking around mimicking all racist accents from every racist nation.

However, she soon takes on a more serious tone as she talks more about the friend she had recently got close to very quickly.

'The four of us were out recently at an Ibiza café and Tess broke down telling us of her grandfather who had abused her, molested her for as long as she could remember. Other than her parents we were the only people she'd shared it with. She'd told her parents of her grandfather doing strange things, but they never got the picture. Ok, there's a crazy link between us all; the four of us share dreams. Tess's soul tribe angels sent her father visions showing her monster grandfather sneaking into the room when she was just thirteen, corroborating Tess's on-going nightmare she'd tried to tell them of. Her granddad even used to keep trophies, things like knickers belonging to her; filthy bastard even kept her used tampons next to her kid pictures all in his private chest. In light of the visions, her father secretly filmed him and caught his own father, Tess's grandfather, sneaking into her room.'

All of a sudden Daniel's expression is one of bitter sadness and concern. 'Emy, some rich people are rich because of a deal they made with the Devil: material wealth in exchange for their minds and bodies used to be manipulated and or manipulate others for Satan to experience pleasure.'

Emy interrupts, 'Such is the case of Tess's grandfather evil racist apartheid and paedophile, but how did you know about the deal souls have made to be awarded wealth and dominion over other humans?'

'One of the elders on the firm, White guy called Ludwig Epstein – we call him Brains – he talks about this stuff all the fucking time, deep spiritual guy, knows things about Africa most Black men in the neighbourhood don't know.'

Emy looks around the room, then moves closer to cuddle Daniel on the bed. He feels her shiver nervously as she says to him, 'You do realise Tess was raised in the hotel? It was once her family home; this was her bedroom.'

Daniel's heart begins beating faster as he thinks back to the words Claudette said to him: 'As you can see Jarrod, this room still has its original features and furniture.' He thinks back to the disturbed tall greying blond man he saw in the mirror and knows he was looking at Tess's paedophile grandfather.

He hears Emy saying, 'When the parents confronted him and called the police, he killed himself,' and thinks of Claudette explaining to him how both the man and his father brutalised and killed many indigenous Africans of South Africa and were very influential within the apartheid movement.

Emy herself is thinking back to the time she last saw her Dutch friends. Tess was still asleep and while the toddler children were playing, Emy was talking with Fenna and her partner Troy. Fenna had said to her: 'Emy, I stayed there in the hotel room and felt his presence. I knew he was watching me and Troy, watching us having sex. I remember his face as a kid growing up. He creeped me the fuck out then, the way he'd smile at me driving us to school and around the pool after school. Tess can't bear to drive past her old home no longer. Me and Troy secretly made a promise to make a reservation as a sort of stand of solidarity.'

Emy's mind suddenly focuses again on the heated reparation discussion during her younger school days and the closing argument. Her White friend Fenna's White partner Troy saying to the opposing crowd, 'How would you like it if today Black African people came across to Europe having been awarded some futuristic advanced technological weaponry and a satanic plan installed within their psyche to attempt to violently oppress the entire White race forever. Enter your home, kidnap and force enslavement on yourself, your mother, father, brothers and sisters, babies even and all generations to come, with threats of whipping, other sadistic torture or worse, death by hanging if you didn't comply? See, there's being a little tricky in business and then there's complete outright evil where the Devil gave the unfair advantage against peaceful loving people of God's Earth. Still think it was fair? African countries were stupid enough to allow themselves to be swindled, you say? No, not quite. There wasn't such a thing as an African country before the European colonialists arrived and carried out their documented so-called scramble for Africa. With bloodshed, violence, mutilation, mass genocide and murder, the people of the African land were divided into countries, forced away from nature's spirituality, made to forget their own ancient education and civilised culture, and in the process for two thousand years not allowed to be educated in the oppressive Asian and European regime. Africans are stupid, ok yes, what you say is in some ways is correct. The Black race are more than two thousand years behind in a religious, political and education system they didn't choose to be part of but were forced into, and still purposely handicapped with help from the media, strategically kept at the bottom by those oppressive systems today. The land belonging to the Black race has been divided and its people forced to build Western societies, societies that purposely stop the Black race progressing.' Troy looks into the eyes of all

341

the now quiet racist crowd, then directly into the eyes of the young man who spoke of Black Africans enslaving their own so therefore it was ok for the invading Europeans to do the same.

'Africans enslaved their own? You forever bring this into the discussion as a means of some sort of justification. Ok, let's go on the assumption this is true and out of the one-to-two-hundred million humans kidnapped and enslaved the indigenous may have been responsible for a tiny minority...' As one of the racists goes to answer, Troy holds his index finger mid-air as an indication he's not finished speaking and suddenly his voice is raised. 'Before you answer listen to this. Several Jewish families made a combined contribution of 100,000 RM to Hitler in early 1925. Also elite Jewish bankers and business families actually financed Hitler's war machine prior to and during the holocaust, contributing to the introduction and production of the future Nazi death camps. Germany's largest bank, Deutsche Bank, one of its founders and two of its first members of the management board were of Jewish origin. Some Deutsche Bank Jewish managerial staff actually helped to fund the construction of the Auschwitz death camp by way of compiling and divulging lists of Jewish customers' accounts during the war. Let's put that into context. During the Second World War Jewish families were actually being exterminated whilst a Jewish company, Deutsche Bank, and Jewish staff were helping finance the Nazis. Jewish bankers and businesses financed the Nazis with full knowledge of what Auschwitz and other extermination camps had in store for their own Jewish citizens!'

At this point the racist crowd look on utterly astonished and Troy continues to speak, but quieter again now. 'Some go as far as saying the Rothschild Jewish banking family control the world, financing both sides of every conflict since the 1700s Napoleonic wars and therefore for financial gain responsible for the sorrow inflicted on the Jewish people during World War II.

'Point to all this is at least a tiny minority of the Jewish nation's elite knowingly contributed to the Nazi holocaust, but does this excuse Hitler exterminating six million non-political innocent human families? The answer, I feel you'll agree, is no. So why does a tiny fraction of indigenous Africans contributing to global slavery make it ok for what the evil European Whites inflicted on human families, the human race? You wouldn't say oh many Jewish business families helped toward the holocaust so it was ok for the evil the Nazis did – although it's the same argument you always raise against Africa, same principle. When it comes to the Black race, you're always looking for excuses, a way out for the disgraceful horrific crime that our biological forefathers carried out against humanity, God's people. What actually needs to be established is the question: did they carry out all the atrocities and still carry them out up till this very day because it comes down to who's the mightiest on planet Earth, the leading aggressors and therefore can do what they want or should it now come down to morality? Germany began making reparations payments to holocaust survivors back in the 1950s, and continues making payments today simply out of a moral obligation.'

Troy smiles. 'Our point exactly. By the look now on your faces I feel you agree just as the Jews have been Mother Africa should also be compensated by way of reparation.' The racists don't reply and offer no resistance.

Still reminiscing Emy looks toward Daniel smiling brighter because from that day onward she didn't hear any objections from the racist crowd on the subject.

With both absorbed in their thoughts, there's a few moments silence between them before Emy says, 'I had to book this room. That evening you called and said you'd be in Amsterdam at the weekend and to book a hotel for us, even though I was shit scared, I knew I had to book this one. The historic tale throughout Holland is their Black South African victims had got their own back and performed witchcraft on the family, exposing what Tess's grandfather had done, haunting and pressuring him to commit suicide. The truth is we sent the visions to Tess's father and the Black African angels, and the White racist ghosts are still haunting the hotel, its corridors, landings and rooms. I had to come and stay here after she'd shared that with me, make a stand against the nightmare she went through when she lived here. You see, some of these wealthy people you think they are living the fairy tale but in reality living a nightmare.'

She feels the vibration of Daniel's chest as he speaks. 'Grandfather traded his soul for wealth, Emy. Your friend hated him, so fucking relieved happy when he died because she knew the living nightmare was over.'

'How did you know, Daniel?'

'Fucking obvious, not only that I dreamed it, a lady called Claudette explained it and the strange part is she said you'd explain what you just have. Emy, you and everything else that's happened since we've been here has blown me head off.'

CHAPTER 41

Emy wants to tell Daniel more about the bond she shares with her Dutch friends.

'Ok, Daniel, listen, this was how we, myself and my Dutch friends, first found we constantly fucking share the same strange ancient African dreams. It blew my mind speaking with them after a crazy partying day and night in Ibiza a couple of months ago. Waking from a deep sleep at our villa, having slept it off, we were lounging by the pool...'

Finding it hard to explain, she pauses before continuing, 'Uh, ok, that's the thing, they're not exactly dreams. Fenna also knew we have a spiritual bond, having all lived that life as a soul tribe together. That's not it, there's more...'

She laughs a sort of nervous and seriously excited laugh. 'Listen to this strange connection: just as you did, we all saw the fucking mobile phone in an ancient-like city. Strange, deep vision, baby, it's like we all obviously knew the phone wasn't made or used during those times, but no one in the city was fazed by it being there. Up to just recently, we asked each other and wondered how it could have got there until I was shown Koolah crossed back with it. During those times we also understand the technology of modern-day Earth, and we can speak English and other languages. My Dutch friends and myself concluded that everyone we know, our family, friends, lovers are connected in some way to this city. Each dream, I remember seeing a full moon, leading into a sometimes rainy but always sunny tropical coastline. Our souls couldn't be any happier... Wow, I never knew Jesus was a Black man with dreadlocks up until now and...'

Daniel interrupts, 'You keep mentioning Jesus...?'

'Yes, the Sharoo, that's the word for Messiah in the ancient language. A Black man Koolah is the Earth's true Messiah. Man, alien or what fucking ever. I say Jesus but not the one the world knows today as Jesus; he's fucking fake. The Sharoo lived long before the Jesus bible story, but his name was Koolah and he's the real deal.'

Another recollection suddenly strikes Emy. 'Daniel, I saw you there. Thing was you had the modern- day haircut you have now and dressed in modern-day designer clothing like you do now. You were sat facing the Messiah, his girlfriend Princess Gabi, deep spiritual angels and the black fucking leopard.'

What she's saying strikes a chord with something in Daniel's psyche.

'I know where I've felt that energy and seen the city in the jungle a few times before,' he says. 'A naughty coover firm once held me prisoner in Venezuela and I dreamed the place you've explained. To be honest, I don't know whether or not it was a dream. I felt people hugging me, heard the music; the jungle and ocean was so real. I remember being there, Emy – even getting on one drinking a cup of this juice and partying with the people. And oh yeah, Jesus took me from a tough time I was having in jail. He's the tall handsome muscular man you described with the dreadlocks and his girlfriend had a blonde streak and one bluish-brown eye on the same side...'

Emy looks upwards and her surprised expression stops Daniel speaking.

Staring intently at him and wagging a finger, she says, 'Again Daniel, I never mentioned Koolah being tall and muscularly athletic, nor did I describe Princess Gabi's blonde streak or blue and brown eye...'

Her words trail off and an unearthly energy rush causes them to tightly hug each other.

'Daniel,' Emy asks, 'what the fuck is going on here?'

He pulls away to look at her. 'Fuck knows, but you've just described a detailed dream I had. You was there as well.'

A little later that morning Daniel's mobile phone ringing wakes him from a doze, and as he answers the phone, bleary-eyed he looks up at the ceiling to apparently see two Delican bumblebees buzzing around, with their overlong legs and antennae and overlarge eyes.

He hears his friend Yanson on the other end of the line greeting him, 'Jarrod, wah gwan, blood?'

Daniel smiles at the sound of his friend's voice and says, 'Dread, some weird looking bees here in Dam, fam.'

'I dreamed some mad-looking bees last night,' Yanson says in reply, recalling a vision of the child angel Imani.

But before Daniel can ask him to explain, their phone conversation is brought to an abrupt pause by Emy rushing out from the bathroom having noticed the time and shouting, 'Oh my God, look at the time. You best hurry otherwise you'll miss your flight. I'll drive you to the airport.'

'Fam,' Daniel says into the phone. 'I'll give you a call tonight when I'm back in London.'

Yanson isn't keen to let him go. 'Jarrod, hole it down, yeah. Cindy Nevin always says all of our gang are unique, but for some reason I'm a special soul. I think she still fancies the ole man, always paying me compliments, saying how much I look like him. Heard her and Brains, Ludwig Epstein, talking...'

Daniel interrupts, 'Brains knows his stuff. For a White Jew, man knows our Black history for real, fam.'

'Jarrod, listen, tell Emy to mind who she speaks to.'

'Sure, you've always been spiritual, Dread, no problem, but why?'

'Cindy always says it's not for everyone's ears. She's got her own psychic network now and a lot of people go to her for spiritual advice. She's clued up on all this, knows what she's talking about. Jarrod, listen to this, mad ting still, I dreamed being with you. You were White, but I knew it was you because your eyes were exact as they are today and same vibe, mad ting, blood.'

After he and Yanson have finished speaking on the phone, Daniel turns to Emy and says, 'Look, the stuff we've spoke about this morning, Dread said to keep it to ourselves, yeah.'

She nods with a smile.

CHAPTER 42

'Daniel,' Emy says as she's driving him to the airport, 'Yanson's friend, the Italian Rome, looks so sweet and innocent, hard to believe he's on Interpol's most wanted for daring jewellery heists.'

'Yeah, Rome's quite a character, Emy,' he replies, but before they can do much more talking his mobile rings with the first of a number of calls that occupy him most of the journey, all to do with vital personal and business issues in London. But as he's dealing with them, in the back of his mind he can't help thinking about what he and Yanson had talked about earlier on the phone and about the dream where Lana took him into the slave rebellion headquarters and he became conscious as the White pirate Jarrod.

Time seems to fly and before Daniel knows it they've pulled up at the departure lounge, with him and Emy hardly having had a chance to speak. As Emy's dropping him at an undesignated spot, a police car sounds its siren, hurrying them to move on. He quickly gets out, takes his baggage from the back seat, and they share an emotional kiss before he goes off into the lounge.

King Louis XVIII Hotel, Amsterdam

Back at the hotel suite later that day, Emy wakes from a nap thinking about her spiritual conversations with Daniel, asking herself if perhaps it was all a dream. How much did she really speak about? She hears a loud buzzing noise and looks up at the closed window to see three Delican bumblebees buzzing against it, and gets up to open the window and let them out.

East Midlands Airport, Leicestershire, England

Daniel wakes after a quick nap, feeling groggy as his plane touches down. He yawns, wondering if he's dreamed the whole thing, the ghosts in his apartment, the in-depth conversation with Emy, the warning visions revealed to the tranquil tribal city – visions showing the then future the African continent was to go through, a horrific transformation, intruding Islamic Asian armies enslaving Africa, followed by European intruders including the British Empire inviting themselves in.

Gold Coast, Elmina, West Africa, 1756

Along the entire coastline White Europeans are rounding up thousands of natives, restricting their movement with shackles and chains, placing them into chains ready to take them to the awaiting ships at the coast.

On a hilltop a group of around fifty indigenous men, women and adorable children and babies are congregated, most of them absolutely terrified of what approaches and what's happening all around them. Metal chains jangle. Englishmen shout orders. Human beings, men, women and children are being brutalised. There is screaming and hysterical crying to be heard.

Four tribal trance witchdoctors, three male and one female, are huddled together on the ground in the centre of the group, chanting and working magical protection spells.

They're guarded by twelve brave indigenous warriors with spears. One of them, a young man still in his teenage years, shakes the shoulder of one of the seated witch doctors, alerting him of impending danger.

The witchdoctor, a small thin man called Ajani stands, looks towards the intruders and speaking the local West African language, says, 'They're back. They came long ago; we showed our love, sharing the knowledge of our magic. This is the result of what happens when you allow the wrong people inside your home. They've returned to use our powers to manipulate, oppress and enslave us, as the Asians did when we invited them in a thousand years ago. Take our precious gold and gems, this is how you repay our kindness…'

'Please hurry,' says the young man. 'They've seen us, they're coming up the hill… Hurry, the spell…'

As the slave catchers advance, fearful mothers hide themselves and their children behind the warriors. One of the indigenous warriors, a powerful stocky muscular man, shouts warning the abductors off. But the intruders are not fazed; they are armed with guns and the native warriors have only spears.

The stocky indigenous warrior aggressively exhales air from his lungs as powerfully he throws his heavy wooden ten-foot-long steel-headed spear. As soon as the spear is thrown, the man is hit by a shot from a musket that removes part of his shoulder, turning him to the side, before a shot from another angle lodges deep inside his chest. The rounded bullet continues smouldering and smoking, sizzling inside, cooking his skin and flesh, heart and lungs after he's dropped dead to the ground.

Meanwhile the warrior's spear had found its target, entering a well-built middle-aged blond slave catcher's eye and exiting two foot out of the back of his skull, the pointed steel spearhead covered with fragments of his eye, blood and brain tissue. After being struck there had been a delayed response before the slaver dropped the bundle of ankle shackles that jangled in his hand and his lifeless body fell backward, only to be propped up by the spear in a grotesque imitation of life with his open-mouthed expression and remaining eye looking upward – a sight so grotesque that even some of the already captured and shackled natives look on at his death in horror.

Inside a large well-made hut some distance away, the sound of gunfire disturbs the family of three generations who live there: mum breastfeeding her one-year-old boy, dad cooking turning the meat on the fire, children and grandparents looking forward to the meal. As they hear the unfamiliar faint sound of musket gunfire followed by screaming and commotion, all in the hut look at one another in bewilderment.

Magic circle, City of Koolah, Ancient Africa

None of the four spiritual shamans from the 18th century West African hill realise the change, or how or when it happened, but

350

they now find themselves in safety, lying flat on the ancient engraved ground of the magic circle blanketed by the circle's pink mist. The four witchdoctors had been placed in a dimension the other side of the continent, their souls conscious in a life they'd lived in ten thousand years ago.

The air is filled with those clusters of tiny colourful raindrop shapes, some clear with tiny white dots, appearing and disappearing. A ceremony at the magic circle is in progress, with Koolah, Imani, Akachi, Jojo and around forty more angels present. The four witchdoctors' souls are instantly tuned into one of the Messiah's telepathic visions.

The shared vision shows the inside of the captain's cabin on board *The Haitian Witch* with Black Haitian witch Lana, cute White freckled-faced seven-year-old pirate Jarrod and the captain himself Jim Morgan sitting at the captain's table.

Koolah's telepathic voice is directed at the four souls taken from the 18th century West African hill now conscious in their magic circle incarnations, one in particular Ajani.

'Ajani, shortly you'll be conscious again in that atrocious dimension we just brought you here awoken from, during which you will become close to a man and horrified at his death, killed as he lies beside you. His body will die at your side, but the soul will not instantly reincarnate; instead, it will return to reside here in spirit world. You are to fall in love and impregnate a womb and the soul of the dead man will return to heaven and be reborn your son. Care for him, teach him well and do not put a harness on his warrior spirit; he will be of great assistance during a slave uprising of that dimension.'

Ajani smiles. 'Koolah, firstly I wish to thank you for answering our call for help and bringing us to heaven. You say there's to be an uprising in the dimension we were conscious? We fight back against the wicked Europeans enslaving us?'

All within the circle are in tune with the vision as it now shows packed 18th century slave ships moored along the West African coast.

Koolah's voice sounds: 'Help is on its way. The people you've seen on board the pirate ship are us angel souls reincarnated. Imani's reincarnated soul is there and she has your location and will direct us to rescue you.'

Koolah telepathically shares visions of the massive rebel-occupied estate set in hundreds of acres of land overlooking its private lake – the very property the soul of Imani/Lana's modern-day incarnation, the wealthy Haitian Claudette, would later purchase.

Another of the four witchdoctors asks of Koolah, 'I know we asked for it to be so, but how did you bring us here, to the magic circle, heaven?'

'You live in many dimensions simultaneously,' Koolah replies. 'Your conscious reality is here at the Koolah circle at Earth's spirit world, but in the moment of now your subconscious soul also exists in an infinite number of lives. One of your lives includes being in 18th century West Africa and being captured by evil slavers on that hill, and also another dimension twenty-five years later in Haiti in the Caribbean.'

Koolah's visions now take the minds of the Koolah tribal angels inside the rebel-occupied ex-slave- plantation mansion. The Black leader of the Haitian revolution, Toussaint Louverture, presides over a meeting of his generals, organising the war against Napoleon Bonaparte and the French slaving nation. The two odd men out in the elegant room are the now-greying White pirate captain Jim Morgan and his nephew Jarrod. Morgan still has his confident swagger in middle age and his nephew has retained his good looks into adulthood. Morgan sits spinning gold coins on the huge desk whilst listening to the Haitian leader, Toussaint, speak. The vision places extra focus on a man sat next to Morgan, Toussaint's younger brother Destin, focusing deeply into the young man's eyes as Toussaint speaks.

The angels of the circle hear the voice of Koolah narrating the vision:

'The men and women you see are reincarnated Koolah angels. The older White man present is the reincarnated soul of our soul mate angel Ode, present in the circle in trance next to me now.

Help is on its way and the deaths of some bodies will permit us to reincarnate to positions and later help within our spiritual war against the Devil. As you know, we as souls are reborn to any nationality.'

Then the four witchdoctors taken from the hill no longer visualise the future Toussaint Louverture and his Haitian revolution army generals. Instead, the pink mist completely clears and they find themselves back at the Gold Coast in the 18th century, but now with the confidence and knowledge that Koolah has the situation in hand.

Gold Coast, Elmina, West Africa, 1756

The spirit of Koolah and Jojo also occupy the hill. Koolah dips his hand into a pouch that he has strapped over his shoulder and takes out from it Queen Lulu's distinctive black pearl and diamond necklace. He kneels and speaking with a soothing voice of authority says two words: 'It's done.'

The female witchdoctor looks relieved and turns to assure the women and children, 'It is done. Help is on its way. Koolah pulled us through; we became conscious back in the magic circle dimension and he showed us visions of a future slave rebellion.'

'You were taken to spirit world, heaven?' asks one of the women present.

The female witch doctor nods and the woman and most of the rest of the group express their elation at the news, jumping for joy, chanting, even dancing, but the pleasure is abruptly halted by musket fire aimed towards the group. Some of the warriors are killed instantly, and one callous White intruder comes in close to aim and fire a shot at the tummy of a cute four-year-old boy. The powerful musket shot passes straight through, boring a gaping hole the size of a fist. Some of the natives momentarily see daylight out the other side of the boy's stomach, causing the mother to drop to her knees screaming frantically. The next shot from the intruders puts a bullet through the frantic mother's forehead, blowing the top of her scalp clean off. As she falls to the ground, her murderer comments, 'Noisy savages, shoot a few and they soon calm down, works every time.'

Another White man, his senior, raises a hand and shouts, 'Stop killing our livestock. The cargo's worth nothing dead; we've ships to fill. Come, let's get them shackled. We'll be moving out toward the coast first light.'

Even under tragic adversity, the four shamans remain seated around their makeshift shrine, a wide sheet of animal skin on which are tossed animal bones and trinkets. They, and only they, see before them Koolah, Jojo and now Claudette standing proudly. Gradually a distinctive glossy black pearl and glistening diamond necklace becomes visible where Koolah had placed it on the Voodoo animal skin, not just to the witches but to all who could see.

As the intruders quickly set about shackling all the indigenous people congregated on the hill, a slaver's boot kicks away the rest of the items at the makeshift shrine in its owner's haste to get at the black pearl and diamond necklace. The man dressed in British Royal Navy uniform picks up the necklace and places it in a small leather purse and then later into a small treasure chest with other robbed and stolen items.

A little way in the distance, the slavers reach the home of the three-generation family who had only recently become aware of the mass intrusion. The father of the large household quickly makes for the exit to investigate and is greeted by armed White European slave catchers. The intruders begin violently chaining and shackling the adult family members of the home. As the one-year-old baby cries in distress his chained and shackled mother pleads to be allowed to attend to him. The grandmother of the family looks on completely bewildered. It is the first time she or any of them had seen White men before, and she screams out in her native tongue, 'What are you and what's the meaning of your vicious intrusion?'

One of the slavers, an older man with rotted brown-stained teeth, crashes the butt of his musket to her head almost knocking her unconscious and causing her head to bleed. The baby screams out louder than ever and unwittingly, instinctively raises his arms towards another one of the intruders, a young man still in his teens, asking to be picked up. The older slaver points towards the baby and nods at the teenager. And as the older man continues to rain blows on the grandmother, clubbing her to death, his teenage colleague produces a cutthroat razor and slits the baby's throat.

As the baby's father screams out, physically trying to break the chains and get at the murderer, and the mother faints, falling to the ground pulling chains and others with her, the senior kidnapper speaks, saying, 'We're helping you; it's for the best. The old won't sell, even assuming they make the journey, waste of food and space, and new-borns usually haven't the strength for the crossing; the cold weather part of the journey usually kills them. You don't seem to do well in the cold and anyway both would probably die left alone here. Take it as a sympathetic act of kindness.'

He looks toward his men, who are currently wolfing down the delicious food the family were preparing. 'Get the breeding wench to her feet. Captain's orders, we move them out before daybreak.'

The mother of the dead baby stands to her feet, unaided but still crying; and she and the other of the family's survivors join the thousands of neck- and ankle-shackled forced to walk along the coastline.

Later that day, at the family's hut, the door bursts open, as the family's two eldest sons return home accompanied by their little sister, four-year-old Anci. They're hungry and ready to eat, but instead of being greeted by their loving family and a welcome meal, the gory sight that greets them is of their grandmother lying dead on the floor in a pool of their equally dead one-year-old baby brother's blood.

The little girl, Anci, begins crying for her parents and the rest of the family who have been taken. The shock of seeing her grandmother and baby brother's mutilated dead bodies cause her dark bulging eyes to bulge a little more than usual.

Meanwhile the captured slaves are walked, shackled and chained, for four days with little sleep and little food and water.

Although dehydrated, starved and almost dying of thirst, their nightmare had only just begun. On the shoreline, kidnapped families, more than a thousand in convoy, get their first glimpse of what was to exacerbate their living nightmare, Cape Coast Castle with its 'Door of No Return'.

Blue Mountain, Jamaica

In the darkness of a ramshackle but cosy hut tucked away up in the mountain, Captain Jim Morgan and others of his crew listen carefully to what the Haitian witch Lana is saying.

'The Navy ship will soon leave the West African slave fort. Koolah has placed Queen Lulu's necklace; it will act as a spiritual transmitter. This mission is of the utmost importance. Our soul tribe Koolah angels, material wealth and the Book of Koolah will be on board. I'm to sail with you and with help from Koolah my future incarnation Claudette Koolah will place into my psyche the layout aboard the enemy ship making it easier for attack.'

Morgan smiles. 'We'll make for the coast at daybreak. Sooner we leave, the easier to ambush the *George IV* as she's cutting across her trail...'

CHAPTER 43

Cape Coast Castle, Ghana, Gold Coast

Europeans quickly realised their illegally obtained wealth brought them abundant prosperity in their homelands. The west coast of Africa became commonly known as the Gold Coast because of its richness in natural gold which European nations stole. In light of the growing demand for human labour in the Americas and Caribbean, the Europeans moved on from stealing gold, ivory and other wares into also taking something they simply regarded as another commodity: kidnapped people.

The Swedes had built Cape Coast Castle for use in the trade of timber and gold, but the castle and many others became warehouses for Africans to be rounded up, shackled and shipped to the New World. Cape Coast Castle was one of about forty 'slave castles' or large commercial forts on the Gold Coast of West Africa. The majestic fortresses along Ghana's breath-taking picturesque tropical coastline housed dark dungeons, overflowing with misery and despair. By nature African people pride themselves on hygiene, and nothing could prepare the abducted victims for the horrific smell that greeted them. The crammed dungeons had zero sanitation or washing facilities and their floors were covered with faeces, vomit, urine and female period blood. Cape Coast Castle's 'Door of No Return' was so-called because the abducted indigenous people going through it would be packed on to waiting slave ships taking their last glimpse of Africa and never to see their homeland again. Millions of Africans were shipped from places like this whitewashed fort to a life of slavery in Brazil, the Caribbean and America.

Just before sunrise, above the squalor and misery of the slave castle dungeons and in the comfort of a large plush banquet-style room, four well-spoken and well-groomed White men sit holding a secret meeting. All are middle-aged, one blond, three dark-haired, and all four are members of the newly formed Illuminati, wearing dark brown robes and Masonic rings of gold and silver. One of the men's rings has a prominent initial G in its centre.

One of the men stands to light a cigar from an oil lamp and for a split second he thinks he sees in the mirror a smiling face and pair of eyes looking directly at him, but he brushes it off as it being just his imagination playing tricks on him. At the table his three colleagues are engrossed in studying the book that lies open before them: the authentic bible, the Book of Koolah in typewritten text. Only part of their awe is due to the fact that the typewriter would not be invented for more than another one hundred years.

The man who's standing looks out the window to see, across through the darkness, hordes of indigenous families exiting through the Door of No Return and being loaded onto two huge European ships. The sounds of chains jangling, whips cracking, women, children and babies crying can be heard.

He turns back towards his colleagues and says, 'Before coming here we were privileged to share psychic magic by Henrik and the rest of the King's clairvoyant medium group in London. The psychic group revealed a powerful adversary, a Haitian witch, the Koolah angel soul called Lana in this life. Today she sails with Morgan and other angels.'

Outside the door a ship's captain, a feminine, slim type of a gentleman, passing by stops to listen in on the Masons' conversation.

'Psychic medium, you say his name is Henrik...?' one of them says.

'Henrik the Swede,' the man on his feet replies. 'The clairvoyant alerted our British monarchy of the turncoat traitor royal duchess Charlotte Ortice's deceitfulness and true identity. We are now aware of her suspicious activity especially her adulterous behaviour in regard to the Duke of Kent Cuthbert'

He walks back to the table and gently rubs the tips of his

fingers over the page of the Book of Koolah open before him. 'This writing will be known as being "typed". This was typed in the late 20th century and has been taken back cross-dimension to the ancient City of Koolah when Queen Lulu reigned ten thousand years ago.'

'But how?' one of the men asks.

'The alien Koolah had taught the spiritual mastery of physically crossing dimensions in order to retrieve objects and even people. The Messiah spirit has, but we do not yet have, the power.'

'So if they can physically cross dimensions and retrieve objects, why can't we? We have in our possession their magical bible.'

'Yes, we have the knowledge, but the ultimate spell comes from within the power of love to reach the universe's highest dimensions within the source, God. My fellow freemasons, you have to admire the magic within the universe that was gifted them. The alien soul, the true Messiah, came to them offering gifted magic and showed the prosperity of this world was for them. We destroyed nature's plan, but I can't help wondering how much longer we can keep this a secret. The retrieved and hidden five ancient bodies of Koolah...'

Another of his robe-wearing companions interjects, 'Are you forgetting? We have no choice but to keep this a secret; it's part of our pact with Lucifer. Our eternal life of total domination, repeatedly reincarnating to positions of power is our reward for the part we're playing.'

The cigar-smoking man responds, 'But at the cost of the misery of those poor souls in the dungeons below? Those dreaded ships and beings reincarnated to Black bodies to be forever oppressed...'

His less compassionate colleague interrupts him. 'Part of the plan is to break the spirit of the Black race. Take away their independence, wipe away spiritual knowing, enslave them and give them false hope with religion. Tell me, do you want the Blacks to inherit nature's valuable gift, or us?'

'But with their help from the Twin Flame angels, instead of war, famine and segregation they would keep peace on Earth for the love of humanity. We've been shown parallel dimensions where this is in effect…'

'Will you listen to yourself?' his colleague interrupts shouting angrily. 'What's got into you? You're weak just like your father. Either we carry out the Devil's plan or the Blacks will lead the world's economy in the future. Besides, we can't back out now.'

By daybreak the King's ship *George IV* is being made ready to set sail. Its cargo of Black families, along with animal livestock and precious gems are loaded aboard. The slaves are chained together in groups of up to twenty, with shackles around their necks or ankles – some with the four-pronged bell-sounding neck bracelets used for runaway types. As the abducted families are led aboard – among them the mother and father of the murdered baby – a bible-holding White pastor holds his book aloft. He stands in front of a banner displaying a picture of a blond, White Jesus, whilst suspiciously caressing an infant Black boy's neck and back. He then opens his book and touches his index finger to a page.

'Look, the words written by God himself in his very own King James Bible, serve your slave master and you'll be abundantly rewarded in heaven.'

He looks up smiling at the distraught shackled and bloodied, freshly whipped families being loaded aboard to be packed in like sardines in a can, and then back to the religious book's text.

'The meek shall inherit the Earth for theirs is the kingdom of heaven, Mathew verse five… Take comfort in the word of God and don't resist.'

One of the illuminati members makes his way aboard ship accompanied by a kidnapped Black man forced to carry his baggage. He holds a hanky over his mouth and nose because of the vile smell of previous abducted families having had to piss and shit themselves onto one another where they lay chained to the wooden lower decks packed shoulder-to-shoulder.

The feminine-looking Captain who was listening in on the Mason's conversation during the night orders his men, 'Hurry, get the savages below deck. Order our jailer to put the young, small ones in separate dungeons. Make sure they're watered, can't have the young livestock dying, for Christ sakes…'

The crew begin separating the screaming, terrified children from their parents.

All the children are totally distressed, but one chubby-faced boy in particular begins to scream out,

'Mummy, Mummy.'

The same slaver who'd earlier shot the four-year-old child opens the dungeon and begins whipping the petrified children inside, including those as young as toddlers. He shouts in a loud, deep, husky tone, 'I said quiet.'

Anci and her brothers had walked for days following the slave trail and from miles away they saw the huge castles along the coastline. As they got closer, they could see two huge Union-Jack-bearing slave ships docked, one the *George IV* that had her parents already on board,

A distraught Anci stands with her brothers at the cliff edge watching as the *George IV* sails away over the horizon and cries, 'Mummy, Daddy.' Her older brothers try to quiet her, but she carries on crying, and pointing to the disappearing ship says, 'Mummy, Mummy… I know you are there.'

CHAPTER 44

The Atlantic Ocean

As the *George IV* sails the Atlantic, Claudette spies on the ship's officers by way of using their mirror as a spiritual travel tunnel access and exit point, relaying what she sees and hears to Lana on board *The Haitian Witch* now in the Atlantic.

With Jim Morgan and Yu Yan also present in the cabin, Lana kneels at the shrine in front of the huge Voodoo mirror and Claudette appears in the mirror smiling at Lana. Claudette's actually on board the Royal Navy ship listening in on what's being said in the officers' mess. She smiles and nods as she speaks in French telepathically giving Lana an important personal message and the rundown on the King's Royal Navy vessel:

'Lana, listen, they know of your name and the spiritual work you do, so be careful...'

Lana nods in appreciation of the warning and continues to listen.

'Lulu's necklace is on board... Lana, tell Yu Yan our Book of Koolah is in the secret compartment of a grey, gold-studded treasure trunk. Under no circumstances allow our bible to be taken back to their intended destination, London. Those who await it wish to continue the Devil's evil and inhumane plan. You will be handed the magical bible on board *The Witch* during this voyage, bury it in Jamaica until the appropriate time, Earth's Twin Flame reawakening.'

As the witch Lana's conversing telepathically with Claudette, a powerful feeling of nostalgia hits the pirate captain Jim Morgan, who smiles and says out loud, 'I was among the officers first to sail the *George* on her maiden voyage to India.'

Lana doesn't respond; instead she smiles looking into the

mirror, thinking about the importance of the necklace. Then she turns from the mirror and reaches for a spiritual compass, a pendulum with a diamond-shaped engraved stone attached to a piece of string. She holds it and it begins spinning round. Then after a few moments it gradually comes to a rest, then moves slightly again indicating a particular direction. Lana points the way her dial is displaying and looking at the map says, 'There, the King's ship is there and travelling in that direction.'

A crew member looks at his hand-held nautical compass and says, 'North northwest, Captain.'

Morgan smiles excitedly. 'The *George*, she's cutting across to the Caribbean to unload slave cargo. We'll cut her off, mount the attack, keep her trail and sail directly back to Jamaica to unload our treasure, get fresh supplies and head straight to England... Set new course, head directly north unless Lana advises otherwise.'

'Aye aye Captain,' Lana smiles as she speaks. 'Slave cargo indeed. We'll *putain de* see about that. I'm being told by spirit the Book of Koolah is placed back in the secret compartment of the gold studded treasure trunk.'

CHAPTER 45

Snow clouds sporadically mask the bright ineffective wintery sun. Two months at sea, the slave ship crew are dressed appropriately warmly as they supervise trustee Blacks sifting through and throwing the frozen-to-death and diseased native family members overboard. The Black trustees show empathy as they listen to the crying, sobbing, depressed screams coming from freezing cold kidnapped Africans below deck. One tough-looking guilt-ridden Black trustee emotionally sheds a tear as he looks up to the hazy sun. Snow clouds pass for a minute or so but only to reveal the ineffective sun again.

Gold Coast, Elmina, West Africa

At that moment back at their homeland on the warm and sunny West African coast, Anci and her brothers and three other children with them have dangerously returned to the cliff edge from where they can see Cape Coast Castle a few miles away. Looking out at the ocean, sensitive angel soul Anci dreams while awake. The recurring 1960s dream has her looking out from the Buckingham Palace balcony standing three people away from the Queen of England at a royal celebration.

Anci pushes the dream to the back of her mind, looks out to sea and as always cries out loud for her mother, 'Mummy'.

By way of crossing dimension phases Koolah, Princess Gabi and their Black Panther companion Jojo appear at that moment besides Anci, at first startling the chapped-lipped, now feeble child. She and the other children are all drained and exhausted, near to collapse through starvation. Anci hears the voice of Koolah:

'It's not safe here. Go back to your village hut. Other villagers have buried the bodies of your nana and baby brother. It's too dangerous here; if you stay, they will capture and chain you for the rest of this life. Go back to your village. Our soul tribe will come for you.'

'They killed my nana and brother,' Anci cries out to the voice, 'Please help, we're hungry and have no water, we'll not make the journey...'

'You will be guided and find food on your journey,' Koolah assures her. 'Go back and help will come. Trust me, go home and someone will come for you. You'll be safe back at the hut. They'll not return now they've systematically cleared your particular village.'

His words send a tranquil familiar feeling through her body and soul; she feels she can trust his every word.

Koolah continues to explain, 'Both your parents will be brought back to you, little one, in this life. You are a blessed soul, an original Twin Flame angel of my ancient tribe. You will also again meet your mirrored soul, your Twin Flame, also the souls of your little brother and grandmother in this life. They will come back to you. One day you will physically meet them again at the awakening, you have my word, now go...'

He turns to say to his own Twin Flame, 'Gabi, one day Claudette will explain all to you,' before he, Gabi and Jojo walk away and fade to nothing in front of Anci's eyes.

She's aware that none of the other children noticed Koolah and his companions, and she wonders a little to herself whether the Messiah, Gabi and Jojo were actually real.

Later as the children make their way back to the village under the scorching hot African midday sun, one of Anci's brothers drops to the ground too weak from exhaustion and hunger to go on. As she tries to get him back to his feet, Anci looks up to see a bright white sack bound with pink ribbon a few feet from her that she was sure wasn't there before. The children investigate and are delighted to find the delicious food it contains, food that Koolah had packed at the reawakening barbeque party in Jamaica.

Anci finds the platted strap that the bundle also contained and telepathically feels Koolah's soul communicate with hers:

'The Delican elephant leather is empowered with the purest, positive energies of the universe. Tell one of the others to fix it to your wrist, Anci, and never take it off. We'll come for you.'

Anci nods her assent with an exhausted, pretty, little smile.

Royal Navy vessel *King George IV*

On board the *George IV* silenced abducted Africans listen to the sounds of the huge creaking battleship, the cold icy waves hitting against it, and the officers shouting orders to the seamen. Inside one of the dungeons, one of the male captured warriors taken from the hill questions a shaman spiritual man called Ajani, one of the group, an angel who'd become conscious at the Koolah magic circle. Both men are barely alive and chained shoulder to shoulder to the wooden floor, neither can feel their frozen hands and feet, and their teeth are continuously gently clattering as the man questions the shaman:

'Ajani, you say Koolah, the spiritual warrior Prince himself, has arranged our freedom. What's taking so long? Many of us are dying down here.'

The angel soul smiles and manages to let out a laugh that under the circumstances is a hearty one as he thinks back to his crossing of dimensions and his visions.

'We were taken to our conscious lives, living at Earth's spiritual heaven,' he says as his mind recalls the face of the White pirate captain, Morgan as a young man in his twenties in one vision, then older mid-fifties in the second vision. He distinctly remembers the White man's eyes, the matted dreadlocks and specifically the vibration of the future rebel base, Haiti.

'We will escape from here, this ship, my brother,' he continues. 'I will accompany the White pirate captain and a Black leader in a slave revolt war. When we were on the spiritual hill back home, Koolah pulled four of us through, awakened us conscious in the ancient dimension, Earth's sacred circle, heaven. A powerful soul mate angel travels with other freed slaves. She is guiding them to us to take back the treasure they stole and to set us free to join their revolution army.'

The two men hear the sound of hefty boot steps approaching as members of the crew come to check on the abducted Africans below. The same man who shot the four-year-old boy and whipped other children is among them and the African who was talking with the witchdoctor Ajani proudly says, 'We'll be released from here soon and will kill you, coward.'

The slaver doesn't understand the words of the African language being spoken to him but understands enough of the sentiment to react with anger. 'Why you cheeky Black bastard, you're talking about me, bloody animal,' he says before viciously kicking the captive man in the head and beating him with his wooden truncheon, literally smashing his teeth and skull in until he lays dead in his chains. The slaver is about to set about the dead man's companion Ajani too until he thinks about having been previously reprimanded for costing the slave company money due to his brutality, and instead settles for pointing his truncheon threateningly at the spiritual shaman who's still alive.

Pirate vessel, *The Haitian Witch*

The Haitian Witch is now well on its way to intercept the *George IV*, filled with Captain Jim Morgan's ever-growing army. On the crow's nest two pirates are stationed on look-out duty, whilst below deck Lana and Natasha sit at their Voodoo shrine filled with its remnants of ancient African witchcraft, Voodoo dolls, scrolled paper and many lit candles.

'Come Natasha,' Lana says to her younger sister, 'we have time to venture into another joint crossover existing life…'

Both women excitedly put on the now tattered, well-worn military jackets they have, jackets confiscated from the French. Unbeknown to the French, the personal items of their civic and military leaders were often taken to be regularly blessed at Voodoo ceremonies to help the slave rebellion disempower the enemy, muddling their leaders' minds into making wrong decisions.

'Work it with me, Natasha, let your soul relax…'

The sisters sit with their backs resting against each other, arms locked into one another, with eyes closed, and after a short while the psychic future life progression reading reveals Natasha's crossed over, twenty-five years older in her late forties. She's now sitting in a grand, elegant, eight-horse-drawn stagecoach as it approaches the huge mansion situated in the rebel-occupied slave plantation estate.

Rebel base, Haiti, 1781

Lana has also crossed into the dimension twenty-five years into the future and sits in her opulent sleeping quarters in the huge plantation mansion as her sister Natasha's stagecoach approaches. Lana and Jojo hear the sound of Natasha's stagecoach and many other horses approaching. Lana and her cat enter the balcony overlooking the grounds to see that over a hundred horseback Black Haitian revolutionary soldiers surround Natasha's stagecoach. Horses' hooves and carriage wheels clatter as they round the circular cobblestone forecourt and come to a stop at the grand four-pillared entrance. A lively, white, black-eye-patched English Bulldog jumps down from the stagecoach and stretches its body.

Lana smiles and shouts down, 'Patch.'

Amid the tightest security, pirate Captain Morgan now fifty-two, his thirty-two-year-old gentleman nephew Jarrod, the Black Haitian leader Toussaint, and Lana's sister Natasha exit the stagecoach, and all of them, especially Toussaint Louverture are escorted by riflemen on the lookout for enemy snipers. Just before they enter, Captain Morgan looks up to Lana and smiles. The party enter the huge plantation house, and followed by her black cat, Jojo, Lana leaves her quarters to go downstairs to greet the arriving stagecoach party and the other Black revolutionary evening guests already present.

Morgan, Jarrod and Natasha enter the reception room, which is full of joyful smiling Black generals. Toussaint Louverture's younger brother, twenty-two-year-old Destin, is also there. Natasha looks to the corner of the large room to see her sister Lana and cat Jojo joining other Haitian Koolah angel witches to practise their Voodoo magic.

After a short while, the lower-ranking men, Jarrod and Destin included, are asked to leave the room so that Morgan, the generals and their rebellion's leader, Toussaint Louverture, can begin discussing their strategies to defeat the racist French slaving nation. Lana takes the tall, handsome, dark-skinned Toussaint to the blessed candlelit Voodoo mirror explaining the French battle plans.

Pirate vessel, *The Haitian Witch*

Back on board the pirate ship, Lana and Natasha's vision of the future life regression fades and for a moment they see only darkness with their closed eyes.

Then gradually Natasha begins to feel the familiar Koolah City vibration. She sings a heavenly melodic vocal and many other angels of the Koolah Tribe in and out of the circle of heaven join her contributing to the song. Although her closed eyes still only see darkness, Natasha knows she's conscious in her ancient incarnation, a young girl and angel called Abidu, and at the same time Lana knows she's conscious there as the bumblebee boy Imani.

Magic circle, City of Koolah, Ancient Africa

Koolah welcomes the souls of Lana and Natasha, telepathically:

'Hello again, we saw you conscious in the dimension with our soul group on board the pirate ship and twenty-five years later the headquarters of our rebellion 18th century Haiti.'

Natasha opens her eyes to peek and sees the off-white pink mist in the dip in the circle and the other angels beside her forming a circle around Koolah. Imani, Akachi and Jojo are by his side.

She closes her eyes again and out of the darkness comes one of Koolah's multi-shared telepathic visions. The vision focuses in on the Earth dimension 44 BC and the face of Cleopatra. The true appearance of the African-Greek Queen of Egypt is more like a darker-skinned version of the modern- day pop star Rihanna than being anything at all like Elizabeth Taylor as Hollywood's idea of Cleopatra. Those in the circle hear the soothing voice of Koolah:

'There will never be any doubt, this is Earth's motherland, resourcefully rich, uniquely filled with divine spiritual vibration and knowledge – those are the very reasons they will come. They'll come to this very spot, our city and the vast surrounding lands later known as Kush and Kemet and eventually to be renamed Egypt – renamed Egypt two thousand five hundred years before the Greeks and Romans will come to learn our civilised knowledge, knowledge we and other tribes of Africa understood millions of years before Egypt.'

Koolah's vision shows Greek soldiers smitten by the beauty and shapely figure of the indigenous – God's original – female. The voice of the Messiah is clear in the minds of the angels.

'After the birth of Queen Cleopatra, in a bid to stop further mixed-race breeding they'll invent the Black witch Medusa myth to try to prevent any further Europeans mating with the indigenous of our lands. From then on, as with every nation seeking to conquer Africa, they'll all do anything to disguise the fact Black Africa has the most glorious characters, Kings and Queens throughout history.'

More images stream through as Koolah's shared astral travel visions reveal sorrowful upcoming atrocities. One of the magic circle's ancient indigenous writers records Koolah's words as he speaks.

'They will label our gift, evil black magic but secretly steal and constantly use it for means of power. The intruders will use our knowing to design their own books and invent many religions, all designed to oppress us, teaching that Black slavery is God's will.

They will use our love magic, reversing the positive influence to kidnap, physically enslave Blacks and have dominion over the entire human race.'

The visions show later ancestors of Koolah's tribe inviting Turkish and Asian scholars to share the Messiah's telepathic visions. Although Koolah's physical body would die thousands of years before the Turks' and Asians' arrival, his image would still appear and share the visions. The invited leaders are horrified when the indigenous tribe reveal ancient scriptures showing they'd learned both Turkish and Asian languages before the guests' nations were actually formed. Back home on their lands the visitors' leaders are envious of the continuous reports of miraculous visions showing Earth's Messiah as the Black African, Koolah. Also, the tribe's superior intelligence and the Messiah's alien-being incarnations undermine their religious beliefs. The not-so-happy guests are shown Koolah and his descendants designing and building the Egyptian statues in their likeness. The revelation of the Messiah's image appearing as a Black man, the true Jesus, is too much for them to take. Angering them so much so, the Turkish as well as the Asian settlers turn on the peace-loving indigenous people, killing them, burning and destroying their city and all evidence of their existence. After the mass genocide as Koolah's city burns in the distance, a Turkish general on horseback, confident that the evidence has been safely destroyed, addresses the army officers and scholars who'd witnessed the miracles of Koolah, saying 'Bu şehir dışında dünya, burada neyin şahit olduğunu asla bilemez' – outside this city, the world cannot ever know the magical wonders these people witnessed here.

'The vicious intruders will fade our soul tribe's beautiful magical existence into the sacred lost city of the Koolah people, lost forever and forbidden to be spoken of ever again – or so they will think. Or so they will think!'

CHAPTER 46

The angel souls of the magic circle are now shown some of the worst atrocities that were to happen to kidnapped African people during the slavery era on the US Deep South plantations. The visions range from breeding farms where male and female's relatives were matched, forced to have sex and reproduce, to the treatment of Black people being worse than that the plantation owners afforded their animals, to the brutal rape and murder of men, women, and children. Koolah's words fill the heads of the assembled tribal angels:

'They will embed into the psyche of the Black race that our natural ancestral spiritual legacies are Devil worship when it will be they who come to us with the Devil's sadistic oppression. Our bible and nature's spirituality will be lost to the Devil for a period and Black people will accept the oppressors' controlling religions as our saviour. The magic from the Book of Koolah will be used for many atrocities against us and the African continent, but as a tribe working together we will get the Book of Koolah back for Earth's reawakening. The one-dimensional earth will be taken through the available negative dimensions for many hundreds of years. Having already been invited and welcomed to our lands, they will return as intruding oppressors and steal our scriptures. The nearby Asian Arabs will return in the name of Islam with books of religion and enslave much of the African continent. Our spiritual battle against evil will be changed in their language to a Jihad, meaning a struggle against people not conforming to their religion. They will play a major part in human slavery and keep our women as sex slaves. Around a thousand years later they'll begin trading us, the indigenous people, with later European slavers, who will come in the name of another religion,

Christianity. Although in their hands the Book of Koolah will never be used to its full capacity because the powerful angels attached are commanded only by a state of pure love consciousness.'

The visions show a map of the world with the African continent at its centre. The map comes alive showing early invading army nations returning to African soil with their rewritten versions of the original ancient African scriptures. European slavers are shown quoting passages from the more recent distortions of their Christian bibles.

Then the visions, for a time, focus in on the kidnapped families being loaded aboard the *George IV*. The pastor standing in front of the picture of an apparently blond, blue-eyed Jesus nailed to a cross calls out, 'Slaves, when you reach the New World obey your human masters with fear and trembling, in the sincerity of your heart, as you would Christ. Serve your slave master and you shall be rewarded in abundance by being saved and taken up to heaven... the meek shall inherit the Earth.' He points to a passage in the bible he holds in his hands and adds, 'Look, it's written in God's book by the good Lord himself.' As he speaks, chained and shackled humans are led onto the ship and down into the foul smell of the cargo area.

Other scenes show how the European man will always come with bible in one hand and sword in the other. An African medicine man shakes his head as a European invader orders him to remove the spiritual Ankh symbol that hangs from his neck, and the witch doctor is killed for his refusal.

'They will claim to be servants of God but will kill us for not conforming to their recent man-made religions. African spirituality is not a religion, what we practise is God's intended way of life, God's joyful experiences. God made all humans to be born free. God did not say one race should be allowed to hold another race in bondage. The European invaders will be doing the work of the Devil.'

The faces of the Koolah tribal angels show great distress, but then Koolah tunes the circle into a contrasting joyful future life one of the angels will one day reincarnate to. The vision shows Disney's *Maleficent: Mistress of Evil* premiere in 2019 and the Koolah angel living as the Black daughter of Brad and Angelina, her name Zahara Jolie-Pitt – one of their adoptive children, a magic circle angel born African Black female in Ethiopia. Photographers are taking pictures of the movie star Angelina Jolie and her children.

'Like all Twin Flame, she is born in a position to make a difference to a life during adulthood, again meeting her mirror soul divine counterpart and raising the vibration of the planet.'

The image fades as Koolah stands and his body begins to hover five metres off the ground, tilting facing downward, facing and still passing telepathic images to the circle aided by his telepathic narration.

The party revellers of the city share the breath-taking sight of Koolah's elevated body and Jojo on his hind legs looking up at him silhouetted against the full moon. The ceremonial music ceases and the crowd stand in awed silence. Then a lone male drummer walks holding a huge bongo drum strapped over his shoulder playing the sweetest sounding solo rhythm.

For a moment the angels of the circle see only darkness, then they hear an immense joyful crowd cheering and a modern-day scene comes to life in their minds, the ancient African drummer's future incarnation, modern-day world-famous Cuban percussionist Luis Conte performing live on stage at a Phil Collins concert at the Stade de France national stadium in Paris in 2004. Luis Conte is replicating the drumbeat, beating the bongo drum in tune to the exact note of his early Koolah incarnation. Two other world-famous drummers, Chester Thompson and Phil Collins, play alongside him in the 'drums, drums and more drums' section of the live concert.

The musicians in ancient Koolah resume their playing as Koolah's telepathic vision ventures into the modern-day concert crowd to a seated section. Seated in a line are East London crime boss Charlie Baker, his Twin Flame wife of nine years Stacey Holley, Yanson Bailey, Yanson's Twin Flame Romanian wife

Princess, and Daniel Cottle also with his Twin Flame eternal lover, Colombian Sofia.

The voice of Koolah explains telepathically how their tribal city soul mates have secretly reincarnated to certain modern-day humans, performers on stage and East London gang members, seen in the vision enjoying the concert:

'During creation of the physical universe the oneness intangible soul God divided itself, creating individual unique characteristics repeatedly reincarnating, embodying human, alien or animal – in fact everything physically living. And so life began, our spiritual universe's cycle of life. Individual God spirits in soul mate groups from just a few up to a thousand. Each individual soul meets with its group as soul mates in every physical life they reincarnate to as soul mate lovers, friends, family and so on. Although we the Twin Flame angels fall into that soul mate category, we also form a group blended within those soul groups with a deeper purpose and operate uniquely differently. Unique in the way when we individual Twin Flame angels come together with our divine counterpart in each life, we don't only heal one another. It's not just about the love story within the connection. Twin Flames come together not just to fall into the alchemy of divine love and heal our union and us but also to heal the world at large. We share our complimentary gifts to start our purpose, giving our light and love to all who need it. In unison Twin Flames teach together, working naturally in harmony, spreading love and light to the planet. God created all Twin Flames equipped with a shared life purpose. Healing is done in so many different ways, and is dependent on us Twin Flames' shared purpose. This purpose is different for each Twin Flame connection, but it will always have the same outcome, spreading nature's highest dimensional unconditional love.

'When the intruders of many different nations begin to arrive on Earth's motherlands, the vibrational energies of our planet are to get lower by the day, to just three-dimensional consciousness. The love that Twin Flame angels embody is the very "weapon" that will fight against the satanic fear that threatens to hijack the love of our beautiful world. Twin Flame union is integral for the ascension of the Earth and entire universe to help ensure the energy of love continues to grow. The love that Twin Flames share is a beautiful example of true soul love that must be shared with the planet at designated points in time. The year 2020 will be a joint soul awakening for Twin Flames. Ascended masters will wake the subconscious memory within, directing each angel to their mirror soul. Each time Twin Flame souls become one again, we'll naturally align the planet to more unity and divinity, just by loving each other and choosing unity, and a huge beam of love and light will shine onto the Earth and universe. God, the master planner.

'Later in the modern-day Western world when the masses know of our purpose we'll be known as the good vibe tribe.'

The angels of the magic circle begin to feel the vibration of the huge joyful crowd at the Phil Collins live concert and again they see the performers and the crowd audience.

'What you see is just some of the future lives myself and some of our soul tribe will be living. On my return to the Earth in my first incarnation Abiona I showed a vision to the souls of our original village tribe, showing we're a unique Twin Flame soul group and angels of the Earth here to carry out a mission.'

The vision within the angels' minds takes them in close to focus on Luis Conte's drumsticks; the modern-day drumsticks gradually change into long, thin animal bones hitting the ancient animal skin bongo drum strapped over the indigenous Koolah magic circle drummer Luis Conte's early incarnation's shoulder.

CHAPTER 47

Koolah's multi-shared telepathic images switch to a terrorist Ku Klux Klan mob outside a modest Black family home rapidly burning down in flames in Alabama in the U.S. Deep South in 1963.

Three young children watch in tears as nearby on a hill the traditional burning cross lights up the night, making silhouettes of their innocent young Black parents' bodies hanging by the neck in rope nooses from the same tree branch.

Then Koolah's astral travel sighting changes to images showing the future incarnation of one of the Koolah tribe angels themselves, Dr Martin Luther King. It's a pivotal moment with a seemingly under pressure Dr King struggling with his pre-prepared speech at the 1963 March on Washington. His mind specifically focuses on his waking dream that morning. He woke with the knowing, due to his and many others around the world's struggle, the Civil Rights Act of 1964 would ultimately put an end to a four-hundred-year-long segregation across the U.S., even though it would take more years for some lower courts to enforce it. He had dreamed the change.

At Martin Luther King's side is his vocal and loyal supporter, the Queen of Gospel, Mahalia Jackson – herself too a reincarnated Koolah tribe angel soul.

Her Koolah tribe incarnation sits with Martin Luther King's Koolah tribe incarnation in the circle. She speaks some words in modern-day English with an American accent, influencing her own reincarnated modern-day body. In the 1960s March on Washington crowd Mahalia urges, 'Tell them 'bout the dream, Martin…'

Ready to give his speech in Washington, Dr King recalls dreaming future dimensions where racial segregation in the U.S.

had been stopped. He also remembers a specific heaven-sent dream set in London. Koolah's astral travel had showed the angels of the circle a specific future 1970s East London school where Koolah angel souls Julie Marney and Koolah's modern-day incarnation Yanson Bailey were stood together in the school playground. It doesn't stop there; Dr King's conscious state suddenly recalls dreaming of other phenomenal hidden subconscious dimensions. Koolah had multi-shared visions of Earth dimensions where there was no interference from the Devil and slavery and racial prejudice hadn't been introduced, where there hadn't been a so-called Scramble for Africa where European countries raped and stole Africa from the indigenous people, and where countries such as France would go on raping the fuck out of Africa until the present day. Koolah showed in other dimensions the natural balance exists: equality as nature designed, better technology than in modern-day Earth's timeline, Africa thriving as one country and the natural capital city where the City of Koolah stands where they have Egypt's Red Sea coastline today. In the other dimension Koolah shows White European people travel to the leading economy Africa to get their children educated, the main subjects, spirituality and the history of the authentic Messiah Koolah and the Twin Flame angels of the Earth, the true angels. No invented religion exists. People from all over the world come to see African museums and the Koolah bible is the bible of the world. No wars or hatred. No governments creating wars and committing crimes against humanity. Equal opportunity for anyone to progress financially. Modern-day Africa with Black children and migrated White children, and no prejudice, as designed by nature not seeing colour, just like the not so intelligent animals. No form of colonisation around the world. Migrants who came to settle purchased land from the African government or privately owned individuals. European countries not having to begin the 2025 financial reparations for the many injustices inflicted on the indigenous people of the Earth. Humanity operated fairly: Native Americans ruling America, Aboriginal Australians ruling Australia and other nations, including Europeans, coming as guests.

Recalling all this, Dr King feels elated, uplifted, still receiving the tenth, eleventh subconscious dimensions of the Koolah heaven before Earth was taken back to a three-dimension consciousness. The vibration of nature's hidden dimensions, Africa and the peace-loving world in its intended state, indigenous natives ruling their countries, causes Dr King to let his words fly from the soul and he begins addressing the huge March on Washington crowd, and a sound wave carries his faint sounding but entire iconic 'I have a dream' speech blending within the beat of the ancient Koolah city's ceremonial music. Koolah's telepathic vision of Dr King giving that speech is carried into the Earth-based angels' collective psyche, blended into their music with the sound of the mass Washington crowd cheering as he repeats those iconic words, 'I have a dream.'

Koolah's voice continues in their minds:

'My soul will not reincarnate but instead remain in the spirit world assisting our tribal soul mates, helping recreate love vibrations such as you see in these visions. I will begin taking a physical presence two centuries before the awakening. I will be re-born Destin, younger brother of the Haitian slave uprising revolutionary leader, then also reborn my earth-day in my seventh human vessel of this earth phase in the year 1964.'

Koolah looks to the young male angel soul beside him and urges, 'Imani, show us what you see now. Put your telepathic visions into the minds of us all. We also need to record what you see so that later generations can...'

The writer recording Koolah's words interrupts him by beginning to laugh, and Koolah says to him, 'Why do you laugh?'

The writer answers, 'The irony, Koolah. They will enslave us and not allow us to learn to read and write, but we write and speak English thousands of years before it's become a country or language and they are currently in savage state.'

Imani asks, 'But, Koolah, what will they achieve by oppressing us?'

Koolah nods smiling at the cute child. 'A minority group from each major nation will be brought together as one by Satan to rule Earth. In order to achieve this, they will locate the Book of Koolah and use its spiritual powers negatively, reversing the spells for greed and evil. They'll carry out Satan's work in exchange for dominion over the human race. Their reward will come at the ultimate price; they'll have traded their souls with the Devil.'

As Koolah speaks the angels see the visions he shares of invading leaders ordering their men to smash the Koolah tribe Black African noses and lips off the faces of statues, and of invaders breaking into tombs and secretly digging up parts of the lost Koolah cities in search of treasure and, more importantly, the written knowledge being recorded now as Koolah speaks, then later imprisoning indigenous Twin Flame angels to translate what had been written.

'Problem for us is our love vibration and people of the African continent will be oppressed in the deal. Listen, they also have spiritual witch doctors that will tell them of our magic and evidence of our civilised knowledge. They will come to destroy all evidence of us being Earth's civilised race and hide all that we will have learned. The evil intruders will reverse our love energy spells and use it to oppress the African continent and have dominion over the world. Instead, their newly formed books will show me appearing as an evolved fair-haired, blue-eyed European born thousands of years later than our civilised history.'

Koolah again looks to Imani. 'Come on Imani, show us what you see... what you feel.'

Imani lies in a trance receiving no visions but instead filled with a feeling of deep sadness and an unbearable physical pain around his face, wrists and ankles. Although he sees only pitch darkness, he hears and can share with the other angels the sounds of howling wind, waves hitting the ship, the ship creaking and the voice of one of the ship's English-speaking Naval officers, saying, 'Steady as she goes.'

Koolah notices the proud look on Imani's face as the boy realises he's able to share the sounds he hears and the feelings he feels with the other angels.

'I see nothing,' Imani explains telepathically, 'but as you hear I reincarnate to a life where I'm captured on board a ship by an aggressive and violent enemy… I often see my soul lives the life of a witch called Claudette in the future dimensions. She can travel the universe as you do now, Koolah.'

Suddenly the Twin Flame angels' telepathic images are of another Koolah soul mate angel, future German-born philosopher of science Albert Einstein, who luckily escaped the Nazi death camps.

The scene is New Jersey, USA in 1940 and Einstein sits in his living room in conversation with two other gentlemen speaking on his theory of relativity and also explaining other issues. 'There is only the moment of now, no past or present,' he says. 'Time is but an illusion.'

As another different vision fills the tribal angels' minds, they hear Koolah's voice saying, 'We will have the inner strength to explore the subconscious mind and seek the answers.' The vision is one of Nazi-occupied Poland.

Auschwitz concentration camp, Oświęcim, Poland, 1940

World War II is underway and young Jews Adam and Frieda have been at Auschwitz just a month, placed in separate, adjacent dormitories. Dressed in striped pyjamas, Adam fearfully looks out of a window to see a female Jewish prisoner trustee has come to get young Freida from her sleeping area. She and another young lady are taken from the dormitory, neither knowing why they'd been selected. By Adam's side at the window is an older gentleman called David Marco, who too has good reason to be worried, David's brother Colin having earlier been taken from his dormitory.

At this moment, Colin Marco is standing in the middle of the Auschwitz Nazi Colonel's office exchanging his issued striped pyjamas for smart businessman civilian clothing, surrounded by male and female Gestapo officers. The obese, fat-faced, blond Nazi Colonel converses with Colin from behind his desk in a calm but menacing manner, speaking in German, and saying, 'Marco, if there is no truth in what you've told us, my officers will bring you back here and torture you, keeping you alive for as long as humanly possible.'

Colin Marco nods and smiles but says nothing.

One of the Gestapo officers asks the question, 'By the way, do you not feel anything for your brother you will leave here? Why have you not negotiated his freedom also?'

Colin smiles and even chuckles at the question, then answers, 'Half-brother, and no, fuck him. I detest him and his sadistically brutal father. Always knew his day would come. Yes, he was always the daddy's boy who teased me, the bastard. I, the stepson was always beaten when his father was cross. Besides that, I have my five-year-old son, Jach, to think of. With any luck, I'll be reunited with him and my wife in London.'

As this conversation is taking place, elsewhere in the camp Freida and another pretty teenage girl are being violently and brutally raped by two burly young German soldiers. David's still looking out the window as he sees his brother emerge into the courtyard wearing a smart businessman's suit and being accompanied towards that part of the camp's exit by Gestapo officers. David shouts and screams to him, 'Colin... but where are you going? Colin, Colin.'

Colin ignores his brother, leaving him for as good as dead at Auschwitz.

Outside in the cold open air of the concentration camp, the astral-travelling image of Claudette is present, smiling looking on at Colin's brother David Marco screaming out of the death camp window. Inside, the other Jewish prisoners sharing the dormitory pull him back from the window in fear of him upsetting the Nazi guards and bringing punishment on them all. They sit him down and try their best to calm him.

Car doors can be heard opening and closing, and Colin takes his place in the back of the car with a Nazi guard sitting either side of him. The sound of the powerful engine starting and the car driving away can be heard from the dormitories. As the car heads off into the distance the noise of the engine subsides, but the silence is followed by a burst of machine gun fire, and then another three bursts within a few seconds of one another. David looks towards the bed next to him for Adam's reaction, but the young man is no longer there.

Magic circle, City of Koolah, Ancient Africa

As the vision fades, the circle hear Koolah's voice:

'Human minds will soon be made to experience just the one-dimensional existence. Always remember, no matter how bizarre, your dreams are you, the soul, physically existing in other dimensions. That's what a dream is, your subconscious soul is showing your conscious soul how it's existing in other dimensions in the exact moment.'

Koolah smiles a short while before speaking again. 'Let's bring Claudette through,' he says.

Jojo walks around the circle taking in the familiar scent of the angels.

Imani smiles, excited by the prospect of his own physical future incarnation being brought through. 'Koolah, you're going to bring me through?' he asks eagerly.

CHAPTER 48

Trenchtown Rema Bay, Jamaica, 1984

In the darkness of night, on the edge of a coastal ghetto shantytown, the physical Claudette, in this time period in her mid-thirties, enters a Koolah soul tribe friend's modest place of practice. She's greeted by the usual blacked-out windows and candle-lit aura of the so-called Juju hut. She places $50,000 in brand-new crisp hundred-dollar notes onto the owner of the premises', Betty's, table and explains, 'Those Colombians are making millions now, thanks to our services. Diego Juan Carlo's known as Don Carlo in his homelands.'

Claudette's friend Betty has long Rasta dreadlocks, a glowing dark brown skin colour, thin build, and is naturally wide-eyed and pleasantly smiling. She looks at the stack of money, nods, smiles and hugs her tribal soul mate. Also present in the hut are four others: Claudette's teenage nephew Hercule, a Rastafarian man named Jacque, and two young women twins in their twenties. The twins have identical facial features but otherwise couldn't be more mixed. One twin is Black, the other White. Both have a brown and blue eye on opposite sides. The Black twin has dark brown straight European hair, while the other has a blonde Afro. Hercule is a mixed-race young man, dressed in expensive designer garments, and has the strangest eyes, more than twice the average human size, dark brown but with no white in them. Jacque is short in height but muscularly built. He's a light-skinned Rastafarian Haitian migrant and Juju man, a man who practises Obeah magic. Presently he's almost naked and kneeling in the darkness surrounded by a ring of burning candles.

Betty lights yet more candles, those surrounding the Voodoo mirror that's a prominent feature of the hut.

Claudette has flown in from Haiti specially to visit this particular hut to pick up a unique vibration present, re-live a past life regression and make sense of the pain she feels in it. She joins the Rastafarian sitting near the mirror within his ring of blessed lit candles, as Betty says, 'Jacque's been sat there for days calling on spirit for you; hasn't left that spot, not even eaten, just drank little water during the night.'

Claudette smiles at Jacque then joins him in a trance with eyes closed, and for many hours they see nothing.

All night they remain there until Claudette hears Betty's voice saying, 'We're there!'

Keeping her eyes still closed, Claudette asks in a demanding way, 'Where... where are we... where have we crossed to?'

Betty begins guiding her through. 'Claudette, keep your eyes closed and just concentrate on my voice. Your mind is among the most deeply spiritual in the entire universe, my sister.'

Both feel a sadness and sorrowful vibration, and Betty says, 'Ok, we're there. We've crossed over. You are now conscious in the previous incarnation that's always been in question. I'm receiving the vision from the mind of Koolah, and my God, I see you, Lana. It's not clear, but I know I'm in the dungeon and feel your soul is present and can see out of your steel-barred dungeon porthole.'

In her vision Betty can see Lana chained up alone in one of the King of England's Naval ships' dungeons. Lana's older now, hair now partly grey. She's lost a lot of weight and appears thin and haggard. Her face bears the scars of many wounds inflicted upon her and left untreated. Her wrists and ankles are so tightly shackled that her swollen limbs are bleeding, and the chains that hold her are so short she can't even stand. The King's Royal Navy had captured her on the island of Jamaica, bringing a sad end to her and other angels of the Koolah soul tribe's illustrious escapades, and now she's dying in that dungeon, with no choice but to kneel in her own faeces inside the rat- and poisonous-insect-infested dungeon hellhole.

Claudette hears the howling windy rain and the sounds of the waves hitting the side of the ship. The vessel is creaking and she can hear the faint voice of one of the ship's skippers saying, 'Steady as she goes.' Further away another officer acknowledges and repeats the order, 'Steady as she goes, aye aye Captain.' Then a break in the clouds allows the light from the moon to partially illuminate the dungeon cell. Claudette is shocked by the sight that greets her, Lana's once-lovely face now swollen and deformed by infected facial wounds, and the reason why Claudette felt such pain during previous regression readings is clear to her.

Lana herself can see Claudette's astral-travelling form, and for the first time in months something like a smile appears on her face. 'I know you,' she says croakily. 'The wonders of our universe, actually I *am* you. My soul in a later life dimension, you've crossed over and come back for me. I've seen you many times in Natasha's crystal ball and many of our tunnel mirrors. I know of our gifted powers and the fact you're always watching over us.'

The now frail Lana is shivering as she speaks and she scratches at her face as a tiny parasite crawls out from one of her pus-filled wounds. 'Help me,' she cries, breaking down. 'Help me to get away from these people.'

The astral-travelling Claudette approaches Lana and physically uses her hands to wipe away the poisonous infected wounds of Lana's face. Miraculously the captured witch feels a pleasurable numbness instead of the icy cold and severe pain she'd previously felt.

'My God,' Lana says in awe, 'you're able to physically cross. You've become abundant. You've reached the infinite source in the realms of the ascended master. I feel my wounds healing.'

'Yes Lana,' Claudette responds. 'Although you'll remain scarred for life your wounds have almost completely healed and the rest of this voyage to London will be more bearable.'

Back in the hut, Betty opens her eyes to find the physical body of Claudette's no longer present. She smiles brightly, though, as she watches Claudette re-emerge walking through the Voodoo mirror and back into the hut.

After becoming fully conscious back in the 1984 present, Claudette remarks to Betty, 'It's strange; every dimension is stored within the soul, so how come I wasn't able to access visiting my later Lana incarnation when locked in the ship's dungeon before now?'

'Yes Claudette,' her friend replies, 'they'd previously blocked it from your psyche, part of their evil plan. They used our bible to cast spells blocking us experiencing certain subconscious dimensions. Didn't want us to know of your capture in that 18th century dimension because we'd have prevented it. Our gifted powers have returned, the magic circle has relocated the hidden subconscious dimension, and that is the reason why Koolah asked you to be here today. It's also revealed your full potential, which includes physically crossing dimension and other gifts such as being able to physically heal beings of the universe. As Koolah promised, the Devil's grip on our Earth is loosening.'

In the Voodoo mirror images begin to appear of the picturesque tropical coastline and blue skies of the ancient City of Koolah, and the tribal drumbeat and sweet angelic vocals of the city's ceremonial music can be heard. The tranquil atmosphere of the city fills the Juju hut with its unique spiritual vibration.

All those in the hut gaze into the mirror as the image of the Koolah magic circle becomes clear, and Claudette says, 'I saw this during astral travel. We were there at the ceremony, and through my incarnation twelve-year-old Imani I saw myself arriving at the ceremony.'

Magic circle, City of Koolah, Ancient Africa

Imani's psyche returns directly from sharing a subconscious future life progression of the 1984 dimension with Jacque, Hercule, Betty, the twin young ladies and his future incarnation Claudette present. Now conscious as the bumblebee boy angel at the magic circle, he explains to other angels about his future incarnations Lana and Claudette. As he's speaking, Claudette appears in the distance on the ancient African City coastline having crossed over, pulled through from thousands of years into the future and thousands of miles away. She walks from the beach into the circle of angels.

Claudette's intrigued as she looks into the eyes of the body her soul is occupying in the ancient tribal dimension. 'Hello Imani, my darling,' she says in her delicious Creole-French accent, 'you look like you …' – she pauses – 'or should I say I? – could do with a good hug.'

Imani looks embarrassed but he's also excited. 'I'm speaking to myself,' he effuses, 'my own future body and soul, two of me are here at once.'

Claudette leans in and actually hugs the child.

Now is the time of the Messiah's fasting and after days without food or water, Koolah's twenty-seven-year-old earthly body is weak and dehydrated. He says croakily to Imani, 'Wait till you develop the skill of cross dimensions, many or more of your physical bodies will be in one dimension together…'

Later, the dreadlocked-haired Messiah Koolah sits in trance, with the King, Queen and two of their adult children on one side of him, and his big cat companion Jojo and Twin Flame Gabi on the other.

Along the sandy beach, a heavily pregnant teenage girl walks towards the firelight, bright mist and musical vibration of the city's ceremonial party. She had never been to the City of Koolah before, but since falling pregnant she's been called upon by spirit nightly and has walked many miles to get to where she is now. She nears the circle and stands looking across at Koolah, who's telepathically transferring a modern-day pre-World War II vision to Gabi and the other angels, including among them the young woman that was Emy's Koolah tribe incarnation.

Poland, 1938

Europe stands on the brink of the long sorrowful World War II. Oblivious to the up-coming atrocities, a group of grubby poor White Jewish teenagers are hanging out in the street. Among them are seventeen-year-old blue-eyed Adam and sixteen-year-old brown-eyed Frieda, the only female in the gang. The pair are two reincarnated Koolah tribal angel souls, reborn and growing up innocent young Jewish lovers. They continuously kiss and cuddle: he, the perfect young romantic gentleman respectful of his lover, and she intelligent, feisty, tough and daring – and pleased that he had been the one to take her teenage virginity.

Magic circle, City of Koolah, Ancient Africa

Suddenly the vision switches to an African night sky underneath which a huge Nazi convoy of trucks and armoured vehicles carry masses of troops and weapons across the desert to their African lands, later known as Egypt.

Koolah's telepathic voice and lifelike futuristic visions of the Nazi invasion of Egypt fill the minds of all present in the spiritual circle.

The spirit of the evil one will interfere and cause world wars to rage. These European countries will steal our magical power, reverse and use it negatively for their empowerment over Africa.

'Their leaders will have the responsibility of the welfare of millions, but the leading nations of the Earth with all their joint knowledge, their intelligent solution will be "Let's go to war!" The Nazi Germans will travel here to our lands which will be renamed Egypt. They'll come in search of our spiritual powers and their great leader Adolf Hitler and others will know and keep secret our history as that of the authentic chosen people. They'll keep secret their discovery of the five preserved bodies of the Messiah, my Koolah body included.'

As Koolah's voice is explaining the vision, three witch doctors, two male and one female, each sit with a pile of blessed thin-stranded elephant leather next to them. Each one takes one strand from their pile in turn to give to a young girl, the fellow tribal angel who sits near them and who immediately begins tightly platting the three strands together.

Koolah turns to a tall muscular man from the circle and says to him, 'Your twin soul, she's there in the physical, go out and get her.'

The tall man looks up in a nervous, joyful panic to see the travelling heavily pregnant teenager of his dreams stood at the edge of the stone floor. He leaves the stone circle to greet her and they stand face to face under the moonlight. Although they have never physically met before, she knows she knows the man. She finds herself attracted to him in every way and senses a vibration, a feeling of more than familiarity, drawing her to him. Her mind recalls dreaming of the man, and on many occasions, passionately kissing and being intimate with him during wet dreams, sharing emotions she never thought were of this Earth.

He leads her into the dip of the circle, saying, 'Koolah said you were travelling on your way to us. The Messiah's psychic powers are unparalleled.'

She's shocked to also see the dreadlock-haired man and his Black Panther companion that she also knows from her recurring dreams. Although massively dehydrated his handsome facial expressions still represent love and his eyes seem to smile even though they're closed. Jojo startles her a little by roaring as the tall young man sits her down with him and they kiss as he caresses her face.

With eyes still closed, Koolah says in a soothing tone, 'Don't be afraid. Jojo likes you and says hello. He's not angry with you; it's that he can detect negative spirit trying to manipulate you and the souls residing within your heavenly womb. Please lie in the space by my side.'

The pregnant girl does as she's bid, lying herself down in the spot Koolah indicated.

The Messiah, his eyes still closed, gently rests a palm on her belly, as Queen Lulu joins them to kneel beside her holding her hand. The young mother-to-be finds herself being drawn into the smiling eyes of the psychic Queen Lulu and shares the vision Lulu sees of an English cottage in the dimension year 1756, but the pregnant girl sees it not through Charlotte Ortice's eyes but through the eyes of one of her future incarnations also present, the little infant Black girl Anci.

Koolah speaks, saying, 'The female twins inside you are joyfully enjoying their divine heavenly experience, sharing visions with us. In a later dimension one will be in danger, but the magical spell performed during this ceremony will permit the future temporary merging of these chosen souls, keeping the endangered one from harm. The twins you carry have lived many lives as friends and now share your heaven. Just before Earth's 20th century reawakening they're to merge back as one soul for a period, for one to keep the other safe from harm.'

'Twins,' she says, 'I'm to have twins. I thought so because of the heavy morning sickness.'

A frail looking Koolah opens his eyes, takes his hand away from her belly and smiles at the young woman. Then pointing to his own body, he declares, 'The ultimate magical energy needed from my fasting will kill this body which my soul occupies at present.'

The pregnant girl gasps and says, 'You are to die?'

Koolah laughs with under the circumstances a reassuring nod. 'Please allow me to explain. Your body is not who you are; although special and uniquely crafted, it's simply something you have to use. Your hands, your ears are part of your body. The soul is yourself, who you are, forever reincarnating using new bodies and will always and forever be you. You cannot get away from yourself, so be careful how you treat yourself and others.

As he continues speaking, Koolah begins to address not just the young woman but all the tribal angels present, and as he speaks, as ever, one of the tribe is writing, recording on a scroll what the Messiah is saying.

'Then there's spirit world; spirit world is the world or realm inhabited by spirits in transit, both good and evil of various spiritual manifestations. Spirit world is an external environment for spirits. This is God's universe, of that there won't ever be any doubt but over five generations reincarnating to our tribe I've shared with you what I've witnessed on astral travel. I've travelled the dimensions of the universe and shared with my fellow angels, by way of visions, graphic scenes: vile acts of mass genocide and slavery committed by people who at the same time practised their religions. This will happen because the Devil will dominate the spirit world and therefore have dominion over the Earth. I, the soul I embody, will not reincarnate to another physical body but the other half of me Gabi and I will join back as one soul so that we can instead assist from spirit world, fighting a spiritual battle, playing my part in future dimensions. I've shown man's invention religion will white out our history as Earth's original beings, translate our knowledge wrongly, and in doing so refer to me as the Holy Spirit while in spirit world. In later dimensions we'll use crystal balls to see past and future, use mirrors for the same thing but also for soul travel, tunnels to cross to past and present dimensions. When in spirit world I'll continuously send you, my soul tribe angels, plentiful vivid regression visions, dreams to ensure you stay connected as you, the souls you embody, move from one life to the next, reincarnate. Subconsciously you'll know who one another are when you meet in lives. Those dream state revelations will show you who you've lived as in previous and future lives. From now and for the thousands of years up until the reawakening, our soul tribe will receive a continuous stream of subconscious dreams connecting lives, showing dimensions we share.

'Myself, Gabi, many others within our city and on this planet are inseparable, divinely created twin souls combined creating an angel. The oneness spirit God created the physical universe and divided itself, the spirit, into human and alien beings – everything living around the universe, God's plan and way of experiencing life. A part of God, the spirit, lives within everybody in the universe; the body cannot function without soul. Your unique character – thoughts, emotions, multidimensional dreams – comes from your connection to the oneness spirit. The entire multi-universe is God, the soul within each being of the universe is the spirit of God.

'I've shown on my astral travel that nations will come here maiming, torturing and killing us to steal the knowledge we've been gifted. They'll take it back to their lands and translate it wrongly, creating what will one day become a so-called bible trusted by hundreds of millions around the globe. Whilst studying their bible, they will inflict horrific atrocities on the indigenous people on Earth. We've read and listened to passages from many of their future bibles: New International version, New Living translation, English Standard version, New American Standard Bible, New King James and so many other versions. They all give the same description, Genesis 2:7, "Then the LORD God formed a man from the dust of the ground and breathed into his nostrils the breath of life, and the man became a living being," and Genesis 1:27, "So God created man in his own image, in the image of God he created him; male and female he created them."

'During creation God empowered me to astral travel to any dimension and gave me the ability to share my visions with all at each of the magic circles on Earth and alien planets. Thus, you God's angels of our soul tribe have witnessed the creation of the stars, Earth's sun, planets, rain, watched as oceans fill, as hurricane storms rage, seen huge waves, the physical universe forming and the beginning of alien being and humanity. We clearly recorded that man, humans, aliens, animals, insects, being created in God's own likeness speaks of the soul within being the likeness of God, just the inner soul, not the physical likeness. Nothing breathed life into man; God didn't begin as anything physical, least of all a physical man. God began as just the spirit amid the darkness. God gave the universe light and life and everything created living was instilled with God's spiritual mechanism within, part of the energy source, the soul. God created the physical beings with part of its divided spirit instilled into every living thing created, from the largest whale to the tiny flea. The oneness spirit placed part of the soul into anything to be living, one God and so life began.

'Where the idea of breathed life into the nostrils comes from, I'll never know. They'll make it up to fool the people, but they'll find they can't fool all the people all of the time.

'Our future visions have shown both invading Arab and Europeans' cruelty on a grand scale to people of the African land. The entirety of the universe is God, and what goes around comes back around, the laws of karma will always play a major part. Good and bad deeds are rewarded and punished. It may take generations, hundreds of years, but for every negative word, thought or act of force, or alternatively pleasant action, once carried out there is to be an equal reaction. That negative or positive energy will come back to them. They should be prepared for reaping what they've sewn.

'What we write specifically about Twin Flame will filter into their modern-day bible, and I quote, "In the image of God he created him; male and female he created them."

'I've shown in magic circle visions that seventy-two thousand of us angel souls were sent here millions of years ago to remain over many lifetimes performing a divine mission. They'll get what we're writing today of the Twin Flame, true Earth-based angels twisted on so many levels.'

The pregnant girl smiles at the Messiah as she asks, 'Twin Flame, Koolah?'

Koolah smiles. 'You are a twin soul; the man who impregnated you is a soul mate, a perfect physical match, beautiful connection, a soul you've met and fallen in love with in certain lives.'

He looks to the tall young man now with the pregnant woman, and adds, 'He who impregnated you is also a soul mate of this man sitting with you now. Has to be soul mate to both of you because you're Twin Flame; you're one soul; he is you.'

Koolah points his finger back and forth at both their faces in turn. 'You both are one soul in two bodies; therefore your soul mates are both of yours.'

He then looks at Princess Gabi with under the circumstances a vibrant smile and then back towards the couple. 'The coming together, your Twin Flame union, is deeper than any relationship you've experienced before. It is divinely structured and there is nothing more beautiful in the entire universe. You belong here in heaven with each other and us.'

Again, the Messiah begins addressing not just the young couple but all the tribal angels present:

'During creation God designed it so in each life we twin souls physically and spiritually meet our perfect partner; it's designed, literally a match made in heaven. The person in whose eyes we find home, who is a perfect reflection to us, whose strengths are our weaknesses – our counterpart. We may be relatively weak as individuals but a powerful whole love angel together. Twin soul Earth angels, we'll be known as Twin Flame, a soul split into two perfect matching bodies. One half has the male, the other a female energy, but in the spiritual in union we are one soul, one of God's created angels. Twin Flame union is two people coming together by the will of God, divinely orchestrated into a place of love, happiness, harmony and peace.'

Koolah closes his eyes and tunes the collective psyche of the tribal angels into visions of Twin Flame angel tribes in other parts of Mother Earth's land, lands that would come to be known as North America, South America, Australia, Asia and Europe. His voice fills their minds, narrating the images:

'What you see now are Earth's 16th century Christian missionaries from Spain encountering indigenous Amazonian-basin South Americans using Ayahuasca, and they and their Christian religion will label it "the work of the devil"!'

A different vision replaces it, a vision of England, a county called Essex, and a group of people lovingly huddled together for warmth around a large burning fire in a wintery Epping Forest, a Twin Flame soul group, angels incarnated currently to European bodies.

'During the same 16th century dimension, Britain labelled the European-based Twin Flame angels as Pagan for not following the religions they will have invented.'

Then yet another different vision replaces it as Koolah links the magic circle angels to the psyche of another Twin Flame soul tribe circle, Native Americans, indigenous people of the lands that would become known as Canada and the USA. The vision shows them being driven from their homelands, sick and dying families. Then the focus shifts to a high-ranking 18th century British Army officer.

'This man is Jeffery Amherst, a Lord of the realm and from

1758 to 1763 Commander-in-Chief of the British Army in North America. See him discussing his plans with others. Part of his plan is to exterminate the indigenous people by way of driving them from their lands and in the harsh winter deliberately giving them smallpox-infected blankets taken from the corpses of British soldiers – so that such cruel biological warfare resulting in the deaths of men, women, children and even babies would look like an act of kindness.

'As you can see, future satanic government souls will inflict virus to cause disfiguring scars, blindness and death. The Devil will know of our Twin Flame mystical experiences, our spiritual revelations regarding our true purpose on Earth, the true nature of the universe. But they will try to stop us and by means of colonisation and religion temporarily put a pause on us achieving our purpose. It will be imperative for Satan to break the spirit of the indigenous, break the global joint ceremonial meditation. It's all part of the Devil's plan, and an integral part of the plan will be to divide the global indigenous spiritual angels of the Earth. They'll break the spirit by imposing religious beliefs, on our homelands, on South America, on the Native Americans, on Aboriginal Australians. The Devil's masterplan is to break the one soul global contact, dividing the lands by creating nations, religion and borderlines. These things are all part of Satan's plan.'

Koolah continues with his explanation in regard to the Earth-based angels' purpose. At the same time the angels of the circle share with him his visual of sacred sites around the globe including Stonehenge in Wiltshire, England.

'Twin Flame union is spiritual heaven within the soul. It is the biggest, deepest, soul connection a human or alien being could experience. Our union is also important because it is an example of the truth, the unconditional love that this and alien planets are to ascend towards, humanity's true path. We were created angels, sent to Earth by God to raise the awareness, awaken humanity and release the human soul from the clutches of Satan. Twin souls are the only ones spiritually evolved to receive other angels' visions; also only Twin Flames receive the vibrational energy of this and other sacred stone, heaven locations on the Earth.

'The Earth will enter a negative dimension when the first intruders, the Asian Arabs cross into Africa. Angels of the Earth will be blocked, unable to connect by astral travelling the globe. It will be part of each Twin Flame angel divine mission to get subconsciously back to the real life.

'When the universe brings Twin Flame angels together in union, we're spiritually designed to naturally align the planet to more unity and divinity, just by loving each other and choosing unity. Twin Flames love one another on the highest and purest level, which is unconditional love.'

Koolah turns for a moment to specifically address the young pregnant woman again. 'As you're experiencing now, your heart is bursting with unconditional love for your twin, the other part of you, and you will find in each life there will never be anything that you ever want more than to be with them.'

His mind then focuses in on Earth's 20th/21st century timeline.

'Our truth will stay between us, our secret until the turn of the century around 2020. Our Twin Flame journey will have actually become trendy among the young generation. The idea of Twin Flames will become glamorous. The year 2020 will be the enlightenment awakening for the twin soul.

'I will always and forever love my Twin Flame's bodies because, as in the case of all Twin Flame connections, they are the body and soul divinely designed by God for me to be attracted and drawn to. My Twin Flame's soul and mine is one whole and her biological DNA was created specifically for me.'

The Messiah turns back to address the pregnant teenager and asks, 'Now do you understand?'

She nods, smiling in agreement.

'Close your eyes,' he directs and she does so.

Her mind, along with those of the other tribal angels, is filled with a vision now of the 1960s British royal family on the balcony of Buckingham Palace, among them is a young blonde Princess Michelle.

'Angel of heaven,' Koolah says to the young woman, 'I need you to listen. Part of today's ceremony will also ensure one day you're to reincarnate born a Princess within a powerful European, English family. Our soul group will be there to guide you at the critical time. You will be born into that life for a specific purpose.'

Koolah turns from her, closes his eyes and addresses all the angels of Earth's heaven circle.

'I'm nearing the end of my fasting and my body will only last a total of five nights without water, at which time I shall leave, cross into spirit world and remain in transit. Write the instructions to reactivate my soul for our reawakening. I'll physically appear, my brief second coming, sixth body of this human phase, for one lifetime in the 18th century dimension.'

The tribal angels are shown a vision of Destin at the Haitian revolution slave rebellion base.

'My full second coming and seventh body two hundred years later will be the year they will record 1964, my birthday, born in heaven, my reappearance as a human body.'

The tribal angels now see the face of the Messiah's future incarnation. At first they see Black Londoner Yanson Bailey as a child in the 1970s walking to school with his White friend and fellow Koolah angel, Benjamin Jarvis; then his face as a teenager; then as an adult.

'Thirty years on, the year 1994... Well, they'll register it 1994 AD, but the correct date will be 10,707 AD, more than ten thousand years after my death as the man, the fifth body you know me as today, Koolah.'

Turning to address the bee-covered twelve-year-old boy Imani, he adds, 'In that year you, the then reincarnation of the soul you embody, will be responsible for releasing my mind from my voluntary physical exile. You will perform the ceremony to reactivate my mind to realise I'm the one chosen who came to the Earth in the name of love...' He points to the belly of the pregnant teenager. 'During the same ceremony your mind will recollect how to complete the merging of the twin souls presently in her heaven.'

All the while Koolah speaks the writer with the scrolls sets down Koolah's words, and the chubby female angel oils and tightly plats the three thin strands of elephant leather the separate travelling witch doctors had brought to the ceremony.

Sunrays shine through between the buildings of the city and onto the particular part of the circle where Koolah, the pregnant girl, Jojo and Gabi are sitting. Guided by one particular ray of sunlight, swarms of fluorescent, vibrant butterflies come out from the sunset jungle. Hundreds fly through the pink mist of the circle to come to gently rest on and around the young pregnant teenager's belly.

Another young woman, around twenty years of age and in a state of trance, is led into the circle. She kneels before Koolah and hears his voice in her head:

'You are one of us, you too are clairvoyant, show us what your mind sees… a life you will one day reincarnate to.'

She smiles looking into the eyes of the Messiah and suddenly she can't help but visualise a British royal wedding fifty years later than the earlier scene with the pregnant girl's White blonde Princess Michelle future incarnation. And she knows she's actually there in another dimension marrying Prince Harry on 19th May 2018. She's reincarnated Meghan Markle, Duchess of Sussex, stood in her wedding dress with other royals getting their pictures taken.

Koolah smiles. 'You will one day reincarnate a mixed-race Princess marrying into a powerful English royal family. We will all one day be placed in positions to make that difference.'

The Messiah and all in the circle are suddenly distracted as the midwives deliver the first of the screaming young mother's twin girls.

Lulu helps by casting additional positive spells over the twins. There's a huge cheerful commotion before Jojo lets out an almighty roar and all turn to see the black panther pushing its nose against the prone lifeless body of the Messiah Koolah. This was then to be the sacrificial ceremony of the Messiah. Koolah's earthly body had died. Two of the pretty choir singers come near the circle singing their sweet song. Queen Lulu nearby continues helping with the delivery but joins in with the spiritual chant.

Trenchtown Rema Bay, Jamaica, 1984

Claudette finds herself back in the hut with Betty staring into the mirror showing the scene at the magic circle.

'Betty, you were speaking of my full potential...' Claudette says.

'Just the moment of now is all there ever was;' Betty answers excitedly, 'the Messiah's death is in this very moment. Koolah's frequency is at the highest, his deep faith due to fasting has secured the unique divine energy, therefore able to now instil it within you, the soul you embody. You're now high priestess ascended master in spirit world aligned with the highest frequency within the source, God.'

She looks deeply into Claudette's eyes and addresses her by way of her magic circle name:

'Imani, part of the Messiah's sacrifice was to empower specifically you to activate the magic within the Book of Koolah, also many other aspects, including helping other Twin Flame angels here on Earth into union so that we fulfil our mission helping humanity to spiritually ascend. We've had the breakthrough we've been longing, my sister. Satan oppressed the real life; our natural Twin Flame awareness will begin to surface again over the next thirty-five years, the year 2020. Claudette, you're a Koolah angel that now has the ability to "physically" cross dimensions. Koolah himself had requested your presence at the sacrificial ceremony and his sacrifice awarded you the unique energy. We've seen in other future life progression readings you are the one to translate our bible for Earth's awakening.'

Hedrin Castle, Kent coast, England 1755

Charlotte Ortice, Duchess of Kent's servant Alice wakes from her night's sleep somehow knowing she's one of the choir singers who sang a duet at the ancient sacrificial ceremony as Koolah passed on to the spirit world. She sings the very same ancient Koolah ceremony vocal as she dresses herself in her castle quarters. As she gazes at her reflection in the mirror – a young White woman looking not unlike the modern-day global singing sensation Adele – she says to herself out loud, 'What in God's name was that? I was a Black native, singing the beautiful melody...'

As soon as she's dressed, Alice goes to check on the Duchess of Kent's young children, the eldest Gautier who's five, four-year-old Robert, and the little girl Janelle who's just two. Seeing they're still sound asleep, she goes back to singing the vocal again.

CHAPTER 49

Charlie Baker's office, Walthamstow Market,
1993

Charlie Baker's woken from his mid-morning snooze by the sound of an adjacent office door being slammed shut as a couple of his men, unaware of Charlie's presence, make their way downstairs and out the building, laughing and joking as they go. As the footsteps and loud voices subside, Charlie closes his eyes to try and go back to sleep. Outside his window, the regular crowds – shoppers of all nationalities, street kids, older gangsters – fill the busy market and a stallholder shouts out hoping to attract the passing members of the public, 'Rock hard tomatoes. Come get yar fresh strawberries, picked only this morning.'

A return to sleep doesn't come easily and Charlie sits thinking about the dreams he has: of him with a bicorn hat, the dreadlocks, dark tan and scar through an eyelid; of his pirate crew made up of British ex-military, as well as French and Spanish defectors, mainly White men, but there was also a Chinese woman and many runaway African slaves and Black Haitian revolutionaries. A lot of the crew feel familiar to him as though he knows them too in the present day. He's had the dreams throughout his life, sometimes he's at his present age, other times he's older or younger, but always in his dreams he has the same mistrust of rules and the same loathing for those in authority as he does now.

Eventually his eyelids do grow heavy and he falls briefly back into another dream-filled sleep, this time dreaming himself to be the twenty-eight-year-old version of Captain Jim Morgan.

The pirate ship *The Haitian Witch* is alongside the Royal Navy vessel the *George IV* and although sporadic musket and cannon fire still rages, and hand-to-hand combat is still taking place, with men still dying by gun or sword, the battle is nearing its end; the Navy ship's captain stands captured on the deck of his ship. Some of *The Witch's* crew are tying ropes bonding the skull-and-cross-bones-flying *Witch* to the Union-Jack-bearing *George.*

The then young and vibrant Black Haitian witch Lana, ducking as pistol and musket shots ring out around her, bids her lover Raphael, the Chinese woman Yu Yan, and four other pirates to join her in *The Witch's* Captain's cabin. Among the four is a huge, muscular, recently freed ex-slave who took vengeance on his former so-called masters, who had buggered him in front of the entire cotton plantation as their way of dehumanising and breaking the spirit, by killing one of the culprits but only after slicing off and making him eat his own testicles.

Lana's younger sister Natasha and the young Colombian witch called Esperanza are already inside the cabin. As the others enter Lana quickly bids them sit and says, 'Raphael, Yu Yan, listen carefully, this is of the utmost importance to our soul tribe, each member of our crew, in fact the well-being of our spiritual universe. This attack happening today is not just about retrieving our stolen property, Koolah has sent a message from spirit world. One of the trunks on board the enemy ship, the Navy vessel *George IV*, has a secret compartment...'

Lana has to pause for a moment because of her excitable joyful laughter, causing all in the cabin to smile. She closes her eyes and frowns in concentration before continuing, 'Ah, I see it... Thank you Koolah. The Messiah's surrounded just one of the trunks with our magic circle pink mist... Thank you Koolah, we're truly grateful ... It's the armoured trunk, dark grey metal with the King's emblem studded in our pure stolen African gold.'

She opens her eyes and turns to address Yu Yan in particular. 'Yu Yan, the treasure trunk is of the utmost importance. We can't leave without it. We also need the combination for the secret compartment. Inside it is our bible; we wrote it. The powerful magical spells it possesses have been used negatively for greed, slavery and oppression for more than a thousand years, firstly by the Asians and more recently the Europeans. My God, the bastards all chose greed. Our bible must be returned today by whatever means, understand?'

Yu Yan smiles; she nods towards the muscular Black man beside her, and turning back to face Lana says, 'It will be done.'

Natasha turns to look into the mirror sharing a smile with Claudette and speaks to her.

'What is it?' Natasha asks. 'What can you feel that makes you happy?'

'Koolah,' she replies. 'Just the fact the soul of Koolah soon to leave spirit world reincarnated ...'

HM Prison Lowdham Grange, Nottinghamshire, England 1993

Surrounded by his combined team of police and fellow customs officers, all crammed into a small security room, tired and overworked senior customs officer Robert Beasley has dozed off. He's forty-seven years old with greying blond hair, glasses and a narrow face with eyes remarkably close to one another. He sits head back, nose in the air, open-mouthed and snoring. One of his colleagues nudges him awake from his power nap as the prison visitors they're waiting to observe on CCTV arrive. Beasley clearly recalls the dream he's been woken from, of being the 18th century Royal Navy Captain in command of the *George IV* and having his ship attacked and taken over by pirates, of being held captive by the pirate army on the deck of his own ship as cannon- and gun-fire raged and seagulls squawked above his head.

The prison visitors the Her Majesty's Customs and Excise team and police are particularly interested in are those of the inmate Kieran Sears, also known as 'Little'. Now awake, Beasley stares at the CCTV monitor not quite believing his own eyes. One of the visitors looks identical to the pirate captain Jim Morgan he sees in his recurring 18th century dreams; of course, he doesn't have the pirate captain's scar, dreadlocks and tanned skin, but the build, facial features and even his mannerisms are the same.

Inside the hall, all forty prisoners are sat alone at their tables waiting for their visitors to join them, all wearing their standard prison issue dark mauve colour polo shirts. Outside the glass screen doorway, in view of all prisoners and visit prison staff, two particular visitors are attracting a lot of attention, the high-profile gangsters, Daniel Cottle, aka Jarrod, and Charlie 'Champagne' Baker. Visitors nudge their neighbours and discreetly point at the pair of underworld celebrities in their midst and everyone seems to stare at them.

One of the visitors, an elderly White man called Reginald, who's smartly dressed and looks a little like a chubbier less-good-looking version of the late actor Sean Connery, can't take his eyes off Daniel Cottle in particular: the strikingly handsome Black man dressed in an expensive black fitted cashmere vee-neck and wearing a diamond-encrusted Rolex watch. Reginald's sure the man's face is familiar to him, but he can't think how. The eyes, in particular, he's sure he recognises, belonging perhaps to somebody else, perhaps even a White person he knows from somewhere. But the man with the handsome Black man he does recognise, and soon realises that it's Charlie Baker.

He approaches him and says, 'Champagne Charlie, fuck me it is you; it's been a while, a fucking long while...'

Charlie smiles at Reginald and at Reginald's wife, Mavis, who's at his side. 'Mavis,' Charlie says, 'in all them years, you've hardly changed.'

'Flattery will get you everywhere, Charlie Baker,' she replies.

In the meantime, whilst he doesn't recognise the woman in her early thirties who's with the two gangsters at all, or the little girl who's with her, something has clicked in Reginald's mind, and the elderly Cockney gangster realises who the Black man with the hazel-blue eyes must be. 'Well fuck my old boots,' he says. 'Hello sunshine, I'd recognise them pretty blue eyes anywhere, young

Jarrod Cottle. You haven't half made a name for yourself around town, son'

Daniel Cottle stares for a few moments, his mind recalling a dream of himself as Jarrod on board *The Haitian Witch* witnessing his uncle Jim Morgan reprimanding a pirate called Santiago for pocketing the Queen of Koolah's black pearl and diamond necklace. Bringing his thoughts back to the present, he smiles and says, 'Hello Reg.'

Reginald holds out his hand for Daniel to shake and says, 'Last time I see you, you must have been ten sat in school uniform waiting at Cutty Robinson's barbers for your old dad Clinton to...'

He lets the words trail off, realising he has, as he would put it, just dropped a clanger. His heart begins to beat fearfully and he feels hot under the collar.

Charlie looks to the woman he and Daniel are with, Nicole Nevin-Sears, and they exchange nervous glances, secretly praying Daniel doesn't react to Reginald's clanger.

Thinking quickly, Nicole changes the subject. She smiles her pretty hazel eyes, gently pulls her light brown hair from her face and places her palm on Daniel's shoulder. 'Dan, I saw your Missus, June, and your boys in Walthamstow market last week, ain't they grown up...?'

Charlie smiles with relief, as Daniel shows no reaction to Reginald's comment and instead gets happily engrossed in conversation with Nicole. As it happens, Daniel hadn't even fully taken in Reginald's words or heard him say the name 'Clinton', being still too absorbed by thoughts about his 18th century dreams. A relieved looking Reginald continues his conversation with Charlie.

Atlantic Ocean, 1756

The camp Royal Navy Captain sits, stripped to his underwear, bound and tied, along with his fellow officers, on the deck of the ship now captured from his command, the *George IV*.

'Morgan,' he snaps at the pirate captain standing over him,

'you'll pay dearly with your life for your acts of treason. You're helping savages, James Morgan. Sir…'

The pirate captain has heard enough of this. He cuts the Royal Navy Captain short saying, 'You have a wife and children. Imagine being kidnapped and degraded in front of your children. Your wife taken from your bed and shared around by a drunken mob and possibly killed at the end of her ordeal. Children, new-born babies ripped from your wife's arms sold and raped, used as crocodile bait. You yourself sodomised in public. Are those not acts of savagery? Hung by your neck till you're dead if you protest. Forget what your King and governing departments teach you and ask your own heart, who are the real savages here, Captain? These Black men aren't fighting for glory or profit but the right God gave as a human to be free.'

Thinking back to his recent times with the Haitian generals, training and socialising with men he came to love as brothers, Morgan adds, 'Next major battle on the island the French are gonna know they been in a fight, that's for sure. Can't be wrong and strong.' Morgan begins laughing excitedly and walks away, not wanting to even listen to any more of the *George*'s Captain's whining.

After all, the battle had been won. The Royal Navy officers of the *George* were now bound in their own slave shackles and some placed below deck, chained up in the stinking, rat-infested slave-transporting area. Its former cargo of kidnapped Black Africans had been freed: the African families abducted from the hill, Anci's family and others, half-starved men, women and children now given food from the *George*'s stores.

The pirate captain rests for a moment in the *George*'s captain's cabin whilst the masked pirates of his crew cart treasure chests, maps, uniforms and firearms taken from the *George* aboard *The Haitian Witch*. As he sits at the table, Morgan performs his trademark spinning of gold coins, setting them spinning, with different movements, back and forth and circulating around each other. As he spins the coins, his mind begins to wander and the pirate captain's expression takes on a vacant look; in his mind he

407

sees his hands as those of a Black man spinning the coins and he feels a familiar vibration. He can see in his mind and strangely feel the presence of the tall, athletic body of the spiritual Messiah, Koolah. He feels as though he's pleasurably under the influence of some concoction, and for a moment he feels he's actually there in ancient Africa, his Black hands playing backgammon and the Messiah saying to him in a language unknown to him but which he oddly understands, 'I will return them to you, Ode.'

Suddenly Morgan is bought back to the present by the sounds of an angry commotion. In the middle of a crowd of freed Blacks, the vicious slaver that shot the little child, and brutalised and killed many others is begging for his life. Morgan gets up to see what's going on, and one of his Black pirates translates explaining to him what the evil White man they'd captured had previously done. The pirate captain shrugs his shoulders and smiles as if to say, do with him what you will.

One of the freed slaves shouts, 'Chop his head clean off,' but one of Morgan's crew, a Black pirate says, 'No, got a better idea.' He's seen sharks around the ship feeding on some chicken carcases a cook had thrown overboard. He points and says, 'Lower him to our friends over there.'

A noose is placed around the pleading slaver's neck – which ironically the racist had used to hang a kidnapped Black man days earlier – but it is not tightened around his neck but instead secured under his arms and used to slowly lower him overboard after the Black pirate suggesting the idea had sliced a few deep cuts into the slaver's skin.

'Let the blood drip to the water,' he instructs, and in no time the sharks below gather and become frenzied as blood runs from the slaver's fresh wounds. The man is lowered and even the children share a smile as the sharks begin to tear the screaming brute apart, savagely fighting over his limbs, bringing happiness to the faces of the freed tribal families.

Robert Beasley's thoughts are still on his 18th century dreams. He recalls the pirate attack, being stripped and bound, the pirate captain Morgan, others of the pirates too, a female pirate who even though her face was masked he remembered had the most amazing pretty, oriental eyes...

'Sir, are you alright?'

Beasley's brought back to the present by the voice of his young junior customs officer, Jenkins, who had just noticed a distinctly queasy look on his superior's face.

'Must have drifted off earlier,' Beasley says; then removing the glasses that are as usual resting on the tip of his nose, he unwisely adds, 'Christ, an extended repeat of an olden-day daydream. Our ship had been overrun by vicious cutthroat criminal masked pirates and native bloodthirsty savages. Goodness, they'd fed one of our officers to the sharks. Those dreams are always so real, frightening – glad to wake from it just then.'

The entire customs and police team are listening to this peculiar outburst from the senior customs officer. So much so, it almost distracts them from looking at the monitor as the elderly gangster Reginald is being searched.

In the visits hall, Reginald has hands in the air whilst a prison officer searches him and waves the metal detector around his body. His face has a look of concentration, his mind on thoughts of a dream he's had, the exact same dream as the customs officer had except he, Reginald, wasn't the *George IV*'s Captain but a handsome Mediterranean pirate called Santiago serving under Captain Jim Morgan on the pirate vessel *The Haitian Witch*.

Royal Navy vessel, *George IV*, 1756

Yu Yan and the small group of pirates that Lana had called into the captain's cabin on board *The Haitian Witch* are now back on deck on the *George*, engaged in their mission to find the gold-studded trunk.

She's trying to get answers from the captured and bound Royal Navy officers, but they remain silent until the vengeful muscular ex-slave Black pirate in Yu Yan's group shoots a musket blast through the head of one of the captured men.

'Right, now, the gold-studded trunk,' Yu Yan demands, 'One of our people witnessed it being brought aboard. I have to insist you reveal its location.'

The officer she addresses doesn't reply, so the petite Chinese pirate orders, 'Shoot him as well.'

But as the Black pirate raises his reloaded firearm another captured Navy officer is so scared for his own life that he pre-emptively blurts out, 'The Captain's desk... remove it and the hatch in the floor will reveal a secret compartment...'

Another of the officers, a member of the illuminati, shouts at his countryman, 'You coward,' before turning and addressing Yu Yan to ask: 'But how did you know of the trunk's existence?'

Yu Yan laughs as she answers, 'You, a high-ranking freemason having worked with many wizards, of all people you should know.'

The freemason responds by saying with a wry smile, 'Yes, oh but of course, the legendary Voodoo witch, Lana. The French have informed us of her and others' spiritual assistance. Lana and the powers of Koolah angels are legendary. You wear a mask, Yu Yan, but your existence is no secret. You, Morgan, Lana and the rest of your criminal gang, you will hang.'

As the freemason is speaking, the captured Captain of the *George IV* is becoming increasingly intrigued by the member of the illuminati's bullish attitude and what's being said. He thinks back, trying to remember what he heard listening in outside the closed door on the freemasons' conversation back at the Cape Coast Castle.

'Yes, you're right,' the freemason continues, whilst pointing to a long-bearded cloak-wearing wizard man who sits bound in the same way as the Navy officers, 'we too have wizard clairvoyants, you know. We've been shown your future. For you, your last journey will be a walk up to the gallows within a London prison.'

The cloaked wizard comments on Yu Yan's beautiful smiling eyes: 'Personally I'd recognise those eyes anywhere. We meet again. Your Book of Koolah taught us plenty. One's eyes are the reflection of one's soul, the mirrors of thyself…'

Yu Yan nods. 'Yes, quite true.'

She removes her mask in view of the Navy Captain and officers. 'You speak of us being criminals. For centuries you and other European nations have used our bible negatively, under your British Union Jack and other flags travelled the world terrorising humanity. The land you call America is stolen from people and being built by stolen people. You've taken the land from the indigenous Americans, kidnapped the indigenous Africans, enslaved them to build America, again for your greed. You've raped, hanged, subjected men, women and children to vile inhumane acts, and you have the cheek to sit there and accuse me and my soul tribe of being criminals, mocking us with the fact we're to be hanged at London gallows.'

The freemason attempts to speak but just manages a slight muttering stutter.

Yu Yan smiles confidently. 'See, we both know the real reason you enslaved Africa and colonised all indigenous lands and we both know who you represent. Your wealth and prosperity comes at a cost, a cost so severe my walk to a London noose is in comparison a walk along the beach. See, you don't fully understand; you and others have sold your souls. The magic from the Book of Koolah revealed to your grand wizard that the Black African land was designed to be the leading economy and natural trusted mother of this planet. You felt it right to change history, didn't you?'

With the freemason still in an open-mouthed state of shock, Yu Yan gives the *George IV*'s Captain a wry smile and concludes, 'Dangerous to throw stones at others whilst living in a glass house, isn't it? And when pointing one finger at someone look at your hand only to see you're always pointing three more back at yourselves… '

CHAPTER 50

The studded trunk is brought out on deck by two masked pirates and set down next to Morgan.

One of the officers looks horrified, knowing the powerful spells it contains. He whispers to another, 'My goodness, they have back the authentic magical bible; the Book of Koolah's been hidden from them for thousands of years.'

Yu Yan approaches the frightened officer who gave away the location of the trunk and demands, 'Now tell us the combination to the secret compartment.'

Without hesitation, he blurts out, 'Underneath there are two latches. Push the right latch seven clicks and the left latch six to the right. Please spare me…'

'You, open it,' Yu Yan says, and the compliant officer does as he's told.

The secret compartment drawer opens with a satisfying clunk.

The pirate gang are now ready to shoot all the officers, but as they go to shoot the one who revealed the trunk's location and opened its secret compartment for them, Yu Yan holds a hand aloft, and says, 'Hold on, stop, he could be of use to us.'

Captain Jim Morgan looks on watching the proceedings, his beloved pet English Bulldog, Patch, by his side. Patch had been in the Morgan household when he still had his family, a wife and twin children, and he himself was an officer in the Royal Navy, before circumstances forced him to become a pirate, before his wife and children were horrifically murdered. His daughter had chosen the dog as a pup from the litter and his wife had named it Patch.

An old Black pirate sings a snatch of the Bob Marley song that begins with a line about old pirates and Patch happily gently howls along. Another of Morgan's men, the blue-eyed, bearded

Mediterranean Santiago goes by and accidentally drops from his pocket a piece of swag he'd been hoping to keep for himself. It's the very black pearl and diamond necklace Koolah had left at the witchdoctor's hilltop shrine. Santiago tries to pick it up sneakily, but Morgan spots him, and before the Mediterranean pirate can raise his head, Morgan's stern face is next to his, almost nose to nose.

'No need pocketing items, boy,' Morgan says stonily. 'There's more than enough to go around. Now giss that 'ere, come hand it over. Keep telling you men, don't get too attached to the booty so much so that you deceive your own men. It's not as though you can take it with ya.'

Santiago looks embarrassed and passes the black pearl and diamond necklace to Morgan. Then he turns to the George's Captain, who is still bound on deck and not one of the officers that Yu Yan's gang have executed, and removes the Navy Captain's bicorn hat. Morgan senses what Santiago has in mind and removes his own tatty hat to exchange it for the bicorn hat in Santiago's hand. Morgan puts on the bicorn hat and Santiago places Morgan's tatty old hat on the head of the Navy Captain. Many of the freed slaves and other crew find this amusing and there are smiles all around.

Morgan holds the necklace up and its diamonds glisten in the sun. Something in his mind tells him not only would it make a nice gift for his comrade co-conspirator, Charlotte, Duchess of Kent, but that he absolutely must give it to her. Subconsciously he reconnects to his earlier incarnation Ode and can picture the big cat Jojo wearing the necklace as he came walking onto the magic circle and hears Koolah's reassuring voice speaking to him in ancient African language that he somehow understands: 'Ode, we have back Queen Lulu's blessed necklace'

Among the onlookers is one of the witchdoctors from the hill, Ajani who trembles with delight at the sight of Morgan holding the necklace. 'Thank Koolah, the soul of Ode,' he whispers to himself.

As they're waiting to go through, Reginald places his hand on Charlie's shoulder. 'Fuck me Charlie,' he says, 'last time I see you was Brixton, 1976. You, Ludwig and the rest of the Lewin mob were in for that big city bank of America job. You must have been twenty-four or twenty-five. Never forget it. Just our luck, hottest summer on record and we were banged up cooking in them cells.'

'Yeah Reg, how could we forget? Was hot. But, you've just blown me cover. I'm stood here convincing everyone I'm a thirty-year-old straight goer.'

Charlie's comment causes Reg to smile. 'Charlie, you're fooling no one here, mate. You've got to be forty-odd and you straight, ya crooked cunt!'

Some of the visitors begin to laugh at the old gangster's joke, but Charlie replies, 'Hold fire with the swearing; women and kids here, Reginald me ole son.'

Just at that moment the prison officer opens the door and all visitors move forward. Reginald tugs Charlie's arm and says in a serious tone, 'Funny thing is, I see you in me dreams from time to time, the age I remembered you when I see you last. And don't be getting no ideas, not them sort of dreams, I'm no poof, you know that, Charlie. It's definitely always you 'cos in the dream you always say what you always say, your trademark saying, "Spend it cos you can't take it with ya." You'll have to let me buy you a glass a champagne one weekend for old times sakes, Charlie.'

'That would be lovely, Reg, but let's have less of the old timer bit, I'm trying to impress this new young bird I've recently pulled, and I'm told keeping young's largely a state of mind.'

When Charlie's moved forward, Reginald's wife Mavis nudges her husband and says quietly, 'Always wanted to ask, why do they call him Champagne Charlie?' 'Cos when we got the drinks in, Charlie would always have a glass of champagne, drove some landlords crackers having to open a bottle specially for a few glasses.'

CHAPTER 51

As the clock in the prison visits hall shows precisely two o'clock, the little girl Jessica rushes forward to greet her father. Kieran Sears was nicknamed 'Little' when he was young, just like his unwitting father-in-law he too was and still is by far the smallest of the gang. Nevertheless, he's a little powerhouse of a man, twenty-nine years old, mixed-race Black and White with curly hair, muscular and extremely fit. He stands, lifting his daughter up. ''Ello poppet, missed ya dad?'

The quarter-Black, pretty, little girl answers, 'Yes Daddy, when you coming home?'

'Ten weeks, Princess, and just then you looked and sounded just like your mum then when she's demanding an answer.'

Daniel Cottle, Charlie Baker and Kieran's wife Nicole closely follow Jessica in arriving at the visit table.

Kieran kisses his wife. Nicole Nevin, now Nicole Nevin-Sears, has grown up to be a very attractive woman, inheriting her mother's beautiful facial features if not all her mother's curves. Nicole's slim and fit with light brown hair. She's retained the posh accent she acquired from her school days and is known for her lavish spending habits. The three men hug and there's lots of hearty loud laughter, hugs and hefty backslapping. Reginald too, who's at the table next to them, gets up to come over and give Kieran a hug.

'Lovely to see you again, son,' Reginald says and the pair have a quick chat before Reginald goes back to his table.

Kieran's visitors continue to attract a lot of interest from their fellow visitors. Nicole crouches down and says to her six-year-old daughter, 'Jessie darling, what says we get Daddy and uncles a snack or two from the canteen?' They walk over to the queue for the prison canteen, leaving the men to talk amongst themselves.

Daniel smiles at Kieran. 'Ten more weeks and you're home, bro.'

Kieran looks inquisitively at Charlie. 'Uncle, you looked shattered.'

Daniel butts in with a bout of laughter, 'He's got a hot little hot blonde bit, Stacey, lovely ass. She's properly taking it out of him...'

Daniel's description causes loud laughter among the men and Charlie displays a proud smile.

'How's Dread?' Kieran asks. 'Tell him his Irish mate Liam's just arrived here.'

Daniel answers, 'Dread already knows. He's gonna book a visit to come see him.'

Charlie isn't sure which Liam they're referring to. 'Is that the tinker lot, our pikey Paul's cousin, Liam?'

Kieran nods affirmatively and Charlie pulls both men slightly away from the table, speaking loudly enough so as the police microphone picks his voice up: 'Listen, careful, remember they bug the tables in these gaffs, keep it schtum, alright.'

Charlie raises his eyes to the ceiling security cameras. Daniel discreetly covers his mouth and whispers something.

In the security office, Robert Beasley shows his annoyance. 'Baker, no you bastard, bastard, bastard, fuck...' He angrily slaps his palm against the desk as the CCTV shows Danny Cottle, Charlie Baker and Kieran Sears talking in secret away from the table.

Covering his mouth, Daniel whispers to Kieran, 'Yole, Lickle, what's this I hear about you and Jabber's cousin in 'ere? Terry saw him the other day, said unu jook up his close cousin, he had to go from prison to outside hospital on critical, he was well pissed off.'

The tall, leggy, brunette who's the lip-reading expert in the security office sighs and explains to her superior, 'Getting nothing. They're cute this gang, covering up at vital moments.'

A frustrated Beasley orders the deputy governor of the prison, 'Order our jailer to get the Cottle gang seated, nearer the table microphone, for Christ sakes. We need Cottle to say at least something of his last escapade to begin building our case. The Crown Prosecution Service denied our last request. We need something, anything, to tie them in to the French Calais cocaine-trafficking gangs. I get the feeling our latest request for arrest warrants on the lower-ranking members of their gang will also be denied.'

Meanwhile Kieran is explaining to Daniel and Charlie, his hand hiding the movement of his lips, 'Little bastard Jabber's cousin felt strong, bunch of local hood rats, Notts youngers backing him. Had to open him and one of 'em up in the shower the other morning. It's war with Jabber when I get out, no getting away from it. It was beef before I sliced up his mouthy fucking cousin. Nicole parked her motor on the Roman Road, Jabber opened the door, sat in the car, told her he's gonna kill me when I get out. He got out of her car and ripped her Rolex off, shit the life out of her and our Jessica. I'm going to go see him, pay that cunt a little visit.'

Daniel's about to say something when a prison officer, having received his instructions from the security office, walks up to them and says, 'Excuse me lads, would you mind taking a seat please, not me, the rules I'm afraid…?'

Annoyed at being interrupted and thinking back to his days in Brixton Prison when he was twenty years old and after fighting off a dozen prison officers he'd finally been knocked unconscious by truncheon blows to his head and face, Daniel Cottle is about to tell this prison officer to fuck right off and start a fight with him, before Charlie sensibly intervenes, winking at Kieran and Daniel before he looks at the officer and says, 'No problem at all, governor. Come on lads, let's take that seat, eh?'

Nevertheless, as the officer walks away Daniel says in a voice loud enough for him to hear, 'Fucking hate kangers.'

The men sit and Charlie calmly explains, 'We've all got reason for hating the fucking kangers but, long story short, he's a two-bob screw, equivalent to a local fucking supermarket shelf stacker. Nothing wrong with stacking shelves, but this lot have no ambition to be much else in life except locking men away. We can't have a tear up with 'em here, with Jess and Nicole here; get a fucking grip, pair a ya's.'

Charlie gently places his finger on Kieran's chest. 'Kieran, what you need to start worrying about is how you're gonna start earning when you get out. That bit a dough you left us with is gone. Nicole with her Rolexs, exotic holidays, new motors, little Jess's taxi to and from her posh Barbican performing arts school, mortgage payments...'

Kieran interrupts Charlie's listing of his wife's lavish spending habits. 'Yeah, I know, I know, Uncle, tell me about it. Ain't got a pot to piss in or window to throw it out of. I'd be fucked now if not for Danny here. Just got ta go on a decent bit a work when I get out, no choice...'

Charlie snaps at Kieran in frustration, 'You ain't gotta be walking across the pavement. Robbing banks is old hat now. We'll sort something.'

As Kieran's wife and daughter return, in the security room Beasley starts talking about Charlie Baker as he looks at the man's image on the screen. 'Christ almighty, Baker... he's often in my dreams, usually these days as you see him on the screen there, but I also sometimes dream him as the 1970s younger Baker, the age when he was arrested with the Lewin gang for the huge armed robbery conspiracy and later attempted armed robbery on the Bank of America in the City of London. The previous dreams I've had of him all end on a happy note...'

His colleagues stare at him again in puzzlement.

Atlantic Ocean, 1756

Lana looks out from a porthole in the captain's cabin on board *The Haitian Witch* towards the captured *George IV* and locks eyes with the *George*'s Captain, who's bound in chains on deck. She knows he has seen her, and moves away quickly from the window.

'What's wrong?' her lover Raphael asks.

'I'd have preferred the British Captain didn't see my face,' Lana answers, then turning to her sister says, 'Natasha, my face has

418

been seen, unmasked. I can now be identified; therefore I cannot ever risk coming back to Hedrin Castle. At a function the Navy Captain may recognise me as Morgan's assisting Black witch…'

Raphael can't understand what the problem is. 'I'll just go aboard the *George IV* now and kill him,' he says taking out his dagger.

'No,' Lana says in an uncharacteristic panic, 'I'm being told the Navy Captain has a part to play that will benefit us in this and future incarnations. He must stay alive.'

Two of the rescued witchdoctors that were practising their craft on the hill before being kidnapped, a man and the woman, are shown into the cabin. The woman hugs Lana and speaks excitedly.

An ex-slave pirate with her who understands her language translates her words: 'When the White man came, Koolah took us to the magic circle. The Messiah told us of a powerful Koolah angel soul guiding other Koolah tribe angels to rescue us; it's you, thank you.'

Meanwhile on the deck of the *George IV*, the captured camp Navy Captain smirks and says to one of his nearby officers, 'I've seen Morgan's Black Voodoo witch. That traitor Morgan, why would an officer of the King's Navy want to defect, joining a mob of native savages fighting a war against his fellow White Frenchman?'

CHAPTER 52

Shortly, *The Witch* is on course for Jamaica, closely followed now by the captured *George IV*. Morgan, Lana, Natasha, Esperanza, Jarrod and Yu Yan are in the captain's cabin. Morgan drunkenly sits spinning four newly acquired gold coins on the table and admiring the huge grey treasure chest with the King's emblem illustrated in gold studs on it. Leaving the coins still spinning on the table, Morgan stands and gets up to give one of the chest's golden studs a polish with his handkerchief then scratches at it with his dagger. 'Pure gold,' he says to himself. 'Pure gold, the studdings are of pure gold.'

'Yes Morgan,' Lana interjects, 'our pure gold, stolen from us.'

Lana closes her eyes, presses her palms to the confiscated French officer's blazer she's wearing, then puts her fingers to her nose and breathes in deeply.

Watching her curiously, Morgan asks, 'Lana, are you alright?'

She lets out a relieved sigh. 'Yes Morgan, I'm fine, but my God, I'd know zat vibration anywhere; ze spirit Koolah is present aboard *The Witch*.'

Morgan looks out a porthole from where he can see the *George IV* sailing almost parallel to them, then glances back to the table and is amazed to see all four coins no longer moving but all standing balanced upright on their edge, neatly in a row.

'You didn't leave the coins like that before you looked out the porthole,' Lana says noticing the astounded look on Morgan's face. 'Couldn't put them together like that again if you tried, movement of the ship wouldn't allow it.'

As if in tune with her words, the ship rides a large wave and the coins fall, and Lana continues, 'Morgan, the Koolah spirit's letting you know he's present. I could feel him. Koolah's soon to again join us physically reincarnating to this life his sixth body, but just crossed dimension from the Koolah circle multi-sharing what we're doing here in our future incarnation. We within the circle are joyful we have our magical bible back.'

Yu Yan gets up and walks to the chest. She clicks the right latch seven and the left six times, opening the secret compartment specifically designed in size for its contents. As Yu Yan takes the authentic bible from its compartment, the image of Claudette appears in the mirror.

Claudette's face smiles and her eyes fill with tears of joy at the sight of what surrounds the book of Koolah; it has her beaming with happiness.

Natasha mutters to her sister, Lana, in astonishment, 'My goodness I'm counting over a hundred alien Twin Flame angel souls from around the universe surrounding the bible and haven't left its side since written by us a dimension ten thousand years ago, I haven't seen them for all those generations.'

Lana laughs and Natasha looks at her sister quizzically.

'Natasha,' Lana explains, 'Koolah's in agreement; they've been present around our bible since it was stolen from us. He promised we'd have back our magical bible. It doesn't just give the instruction how to conduct the spells but this item has the power of fellow positive angels attached to remind you how to carry the potent spells from the deepest regions. The forceful intruders used the spells but the intricate deep-rooted power to command the angels attached can only be activated from the energy source God within. From the power of love'

Her tears drip onto the bible as she caresses it with her fingertips and speaks to the Koolah spirit present in the ancient Koolah language: 'We thank you and we're truly grateful.'

Lana speaking ancient Koolah causes Esperanza's mind to recall a spiritual regression, a past life magic circle dimension that recently showed up in one of Natasha's clairvoyant readings, of Koolah speaking to Imani. Her mind recalls it well because Koolah had appeared uncharacteristically a little annoyed with Imani after the child angel questioned him. It plays back in

Esperanza's psyche and she reveals her subconscious soul memory to all present:

'I remember from past life regression we shared, Imani interrupting Koolah and saying, "Why are you telling us things we learned long ago?" and Koolah being slightly annoyed and explaining to him that he needed to listen because in a later incarnation he would be the one called upon to activate our conscious reawakening, and that the angels attached to the Book of Koolah would join forces with all angels across the universe responding to the soul of Imani's spiritual DNA and help with the spell.'

Esperanza confidently nods, her face breaks out in a smile. 'Lana is the unique soul to activate the true magic from our book, the soul of Imani. The forceful intruders used our magic negatively and were only able to action a fraction of its potential. A past life regression reading we recently carried out showed I was present in the magic circle heaven era. Back then Koolah explained about us getting our bible back having reached this far, and in two centuries from now, the year 1994, the soul of Imani's to reawaken and activate the soul of the Messiah. Koolah will expose to the Earth other dimensions where Mother Africa is not a European-divided continent but one world-leading country.'

'It's alright, I too remember, Ezperanza,' Lana says. 'I know how to do this.'

Chanting some words in ancient Koolah, Lana lays her hands to rest on the magic bible and feels the positive vibrating colonised souls of the Earth and all around the universe join force with her. The bible comes alive, beaming what appears as though it were a hologram of the Messiah Koolah into the captain's cabin. He sits with his eyes closed and his body in his meditation position. Then his face begins a transformation, morphing into the face of the modern-day Black Londoner Yanson Bailey.

Lana says three words: 'The second coming.'

Slowly the magical hologram expands and ceremonial music can be heard rising in volume as the hologram gradually takes over the cabin that is no longer, but is instead the glorious coastline of the ancient City of Koolah. All the Twin Flame angels that were in the cabin find themselves conscious within their indigenous Koolah tribe incarnations, with Princess Gabi and the King and Queen of Koolah present. Lana is Imani, Morgan is Ode, Jarrod and the rest all knowing who their later incarnations are.

Then, no one's aware how but in the blink of an eye they're all back as they were, sitting around the captain's table but with Yanson Bailey's image still present and still sitting in the meditation position.

Lana is the first to speak. Staring and pointing, she says, 'Good heavens, the hidden depths of our multidimensional universe, this is Koolah's body during the future dimension of the pre-ordained spiritual awakening. He wants me to know how he will appear. No wonder they were able to dominate the world; the powers this book holds are astonishing.'

Yanson speaks to all present within the cabin: 'Alright, we're here, Lana, and the rest of you, this is my body at reawakening two centuries from now.'

Having said these words, the image of Yanson fades to nothing.

Lana speaks with fresh confidence: 'The King's masonic magicians had carried it on voyages to locate our treasure and perform spells…'

'Lana, what's the book all about exactly?' a confused Morgan asks.

'The Asians, a Greek King, the Roman Empire, the British and many others became powerful and conquered the world with the knowledge and magic within this book. That's what it's about exactly, Morgan. Leave it in my cabin for the rest of the voyage, but when we dock bury it with the treasure in the trunk as normal on our hideout island, Jamaica. I promise when we dig it up, your question will be answered, Morgan; all will be revealed.'

For the remainder of their voyage Lana would spend all her time studying the Koolah bible alone in her cabin, practising powerful Voodoo magic and taking notes.

CHAPTER 53

Hedrin Castle, Kent coast, England

As Morgan and other Koolah souls sail back to the warmth of the Caribbean island of Jamaica, the bright hazy winter sun sets on the icy cold setting of the glorious Hedrin Castle on the south east coast of England. Inside the great hall, the Duke and Duchess of Kent occupy the elegant end-of-table carver chairs at either end of the long dining table that could seat twenty others. After bearing three young children at a young age, Charlotte's body is still athletic with huge firm outward pointing breasts. She has curly blonde shoulder-length hair and an extremely attractive face with large blue come-to-bed eyes and a dainty ski-slope nose. In short, she oozes sex appeal and doesn't expect any difficulty in attracting any man she desires. The dining area boasts magnificent paintings, statues and huge candlelit chandeliers, all adding to the opulent and plush surroundings.

A strapping twenty-year-old male house servant stokes the fire of the elegant ten-feet-high marble fireplace. As he works, the hazel-eyed handsome Black man secretly exchanges looks with the pretty young Duchess, at twenty-three just a few years older than him.

He bows to the Duke and Duchess as he leaves, addressing Charlotte as 'Your highness' in his American accent.

The Royal couple sit in silence as the middle-aged Black maid Martha pours wine into their glasses for them. Meanwhile the Duchess makes an entry in her diary. Her body tingles as she writes:

Each time I see my Bento he brings joy, causing my insides to dance, my body yearns each moment of each day for his wide muscular back, narrow hip, strong masculine grip, gentle touch and my vagina's a slave to his huge manly hot blooded throbbing penis, its pulsating veins... I need this man in my bed. No other will do...

She puts down her fountain pen and takes a few gulps of wine, then bites her bottom lip and smiles.

The Duke noisily clears his throat to attract her attention. He's blond like her but twelve years her senior with a face that has the permanent look of one that has just been slapped.

Charlotte looks up, sighs and exhales. With a look of disdain directed towards her husband, she says, 'Yes, what is it, Cuthbert?'

'I mentioned earlier I had something of great importance I needed to get off my chest...' he replies.

'Yes, yes, what is it?' Charlotte says sharply.

He composes himself and speaking slowly says, 'My dear wife, pray tell, may I ask, why do you continuously refuse my manly sexual advances?' Then having delivered his complaint the Duke takes a huge inward relieved breath and slowly breathes it out.

Charlotte's face displays a catalogue of emotions from firstly surprise to scorn and then outright amusement. 'My God,' she laughs. 'I say, am I hearing correctly did you just ask me...?'

Their Black housemaid Martha also finds it amusing, and intriguing as well, but despite her best efforts at carrying out her duties nonchalantly, the Duke dismisses her. 'Martha, leave us,' he stutters.

Charlotte, rolls her eyes, shakes her head. 'Perhaps you could pour me a Cognac before you leave, Martha. And make it a large one, for crying out loud,' she says.

Martha does as requested by the Duchess. She curtseys to both Duke and Duchess and leaves, closing the heavy oak door behind her.

The Duke returns to his line of questioning. 'Why woman, why do you refuse me? I'm the Duke of Kent, for God sakes, and demand an honest explanation.'

'Demand... you demand. Duke of Kent, you say... for God sakes, you say...' Charlotte laughs. 'Cuthbert, listen once and for all, this lady will choose her words carefully and make herself perfectly clear. Your brother Calvin has to manage the financial and business affairs of the castle as you are not capable. You, you are a feeble excuse for a man, a mere coward if I'm to be perfectly honest. I find you repulsive and cringe at your every touch. There, you demanded an explanation. An honest explanation, so there you have it, my dear husband.'

His dignity affronted, the Duke gets to his feet and tries to defend himself, saying, 'I, a coward? Explain woman, give me your evaluation on how you've come to the conclusion I'm what you say. Men will testify to my bravery whilst hunting the runner. I'm often the leader of the pack in the hunt capturing the picked nigger.'

Again, Charlotte laughs scornfully. 'Huh, very well Cuthbert, as you've brought up your picnic topic. Do you not understand, they let you lead for your ego? Forty of you armed with weapons on horseback and one unarmed Black person running for his or her life. Please tell me Cuthbert, where's the bravery in it? Make me understand.'

She shakes her head sarcastically, and after taking a gulp of her Cognac, folds her arms as though she's waiting for an answer. 'Well?'

Cuthbert says nothing.

'Just as I thought, you haven't an answer. Allowing you to lead is your family's way of pretending to make a man of you. Making you feel you're brave, but in actual fact you're not. I maintain, I have a coward for a husband, a fat and over-protected, pampered bullyboy. A spoiled child in an adult body.'

Her words ring in his mind and set him thinking how he secretly hates leading the hunt at the picnic events but how he does so in a bid to appear macho in front of his family and elder brother Calvin and pretends to enjoy it.

HM Prison Lowdham Grange, Nottinghamshire, England, 1993

It's clear to see on the surveillance monitor that Kieran and his visitors are in a happy mood. The lip reader's busily writing notes, and the junior customs officer Jenkins is speaking on his mobile phone. Jenkins punches the air. Suddenly perspiring with excitement, he unbuttons his top button and loosens his tie. The lip reader taps her pencil on her pad and reports the words she can make out being said: 'War with Jabber when I get out... is all we've got so far, the rest is unclear.'

After ending his phone call, Jenkins comes back to the table, places his fists on it, and locks eyes with his commanding officer. Beasley looks puzzled at his junior officer's sudden swagger and confidence.

'Got some great news to cheer you up, sir,' Jenkins says. 'Looks like you're to have that long-awaited high profile media case, convicting Europe's most successful ever international cocaine trafficking organisation.'

Beasley removes his spectacles. 'Well, spit it out, man. Christ, what is it?'

'The government have ruled we can set up visual and audio equipment throughout the Cottle mansion, vehicles and all business premises. Our most recent approach was a success after all, sir.'

All the officers present share elated smiles. Beasley's face alone displays a momentary look of concern as in his mind an image of Claudette smiling and shaking her head appears, and, as a tingling sensation engulfs him, he can hear her saying to him: 'We meet again, Royal Navy Captain. Molesting a male child and you arrest us to be tortured and hung? You're soon to receive your karma, Navy Captain, oh for sure.'

The senior customs officer tries to shake the presence from his mind and simply share in the joy of his colleagues. 'Just as I was losing the will to live,' he says, 'we can actually bug Daniel Cottle, Yanson Bailey and Charlie Baker here. Team, our case has foundation. This means our government feel there's sufficient evidence mounting against the Cottle organisation. Arrest warrants from the CPS are soon to follow.'

Then, souring the moment a little for his colleagues, Beasley can't help but talk again about his dreams, his subconscious revealing none of the previous depicted art form illustrations of the pirate captain Morgan are correct, instead the face of Baker is the actual 18th century pirate captain. 'Almost forgot that happy outcome. Strange but amazingly clear dream, we're a lot older, Baker was the actual historical legendary fugitive pirate and I the olden-day Royal Navy Captain arresting him, his pirate gang.'

In his mind, Beasley pictures the unforgettable and now disfigured face of Lana as she's sat alongside Morgan and others in the dock of the Old Bailey.

He laughs once more. 'Yes, arresting Morgan, bringing him and his accomplices back from overseas to London for trial at the Old Bailey. If that's not an omen for the future, what is?'

By now the police team and Beasley's fellow customs officers are all feeling more than a little uncomfortable at the senior officer's continuous dream revelations.

CHAPTER 54

Marigold Bay Hotel, St Lucia, the Caribbean

Diego Juan Carlo, who Claudette and Betty spoke about being known as Don Carlo, is now firmly established as Colombia's number one cocaine baron. He had come a long way since bumping into Nathaniel Robinson and Charlie Baker on Negril Beach twenty years ago. He's now a handsome, flamboyant thirty-seven-year-old with a thick-set muscular build, olive skin, shoulder-length black slightly kinked hair and a friendly face with seductive light-hazel eyes that show a romantic side to his otherwise no-nonsense nature.

He's watching CNN News in his luxury apartment in the company of his cousin Natrale, his nephew Pedro, and Hercule the cartel's trusted male Haitian witchdoctor. Also with him, sitting on his lap, is his son Juan, a young boy with short-cropped hair but with a long thin ponytail at the lower back of his head, which his mother, Diego Juan Carlo's wife, Angelina, had refused to cut away.

The international satellite news channel shows cocaine drug busts happening in Miami Beach and throughout the U.S.A., Drug Enforcement Agency officers raiding and burning down labs – *his* labs being destroyed and men of *his* cartel getting arrested. The newscaster intones, 'The U.S. government's DEA is waging war on the fugitive outlaw, the so-called Cocaine Don, Diego Juan Carlo and his violent soldiers operating on home soil across the United States, the Caribbean, the streets of Colombia and jungles of Latin America.'

As he watches the events unfolding on screen, Don Carlo is on his mobile phone, nodding as he listens to what his business contact is saying. He looks at his watch, a 22-carat-gold blue-faced

Rolex Submariner, and explains something will be ready in a few hours.

The man Diego Juan Carlo's is conversing with is Fernando, a slim Hispanic man in his early forties who wears his hair long and is fond of fast women, slick clothing and expensive jewellery.

'You got to think, Don Carlo,' Fernando says. 'Someone close is letting out the info. We always contact one another by way of satellite mobile phones and never mention the locations during our conversations. The Gringo knows too, too much. I'm on the case; got some guys in Miami doing some investigating and negotiating for us. Their price for the info is high, but if they have something it could prove priceless, amigo.'

As he's listening, Don Carlo gets up and walks over to the balcony where the strange mystical-looking Hercule is sat meditating on a sunbed. The drug baron takes great comfort in the company of the cartel's witchdoctor.

Speaking slowly and carefully, he says into the phone, 'Hercule has explained his aunt has spied on them with ways of her magic. She also has news for us and will reveal all when we meet her in Jamaica next week. What's done in the darkness will be brought to light. Always remember, as Hercule reassures me, the spirit of Koolah doesn't sleep, Fernando my brother.'

Fernando is puzzled by the name Diego Juan Carlo has just mentioned, Koolah, but knows better than to question him when the Don is speaking of Voodoo magic.

When he has finished the call, Diego Juan Carlo, turns to Hercule and asks, 'What can you tell me?'

'Spirit is showing there are two informants within our organisation working against us,' the witchdoctor replies in his Creole-French accent. 'I'm picking up on their vibration. Both are extremely worried the cartel will find out about them. Two very distinctive souls, both Hispanic, Colombian. Possibly family members, Don Carlo.'

Diego Juan Carlo's own sadness mirrors that he hears in Hercule's voice. He forces a smile and says, 'You and your auntie Claudette have an amazing gift, Hercule. Tell me, who gives you this knowledge? Who, what is in your head telling you these things?'

'We are shown in many different ways,' the witchdoctor replies. 'An easy way to describe how I just received it then is that it's like waking from dreaming after being conscious in another dimension, present in the life with the people in question, in tune with their vibration in their thinking. Sometimes not actually seeing much, or anything at all, but suddenly within your consciousness there's an intuitive gut feeling, a knowing. I just know many things about them and their lives. I, this soul, just knows stuff, always have.'

Hercule pauses to remove the designer shades that are usually a permanent fixture on his face – Diego Juan Carlo is one of the few people who has actually seen his eyes. They are eyes unlike human eyes, being twice the size of the average human eyes with huge dark brown glossy pupils and no whites to them.

'Don Carlo, when you wake you can't remember hardly any of the contents of your subconscious dream. Even if you see nobody, you know certain people were present and the dream location. The reason for this is what you feel is a short dream is in reality a tiny part of another parallel life, another incarnation you, the soul you embody, living a life as clear as this one. You wake and your conscious mind takes you back over remembering just a tiny part, but your subconscious recalls the events of that day, in fact certain events within that entire parallel life. The human mind is much more powerful and complex than many humans could possibly know. You remember feelings more than sights of other dimensions; this is why you sometimes know who was there and where it was but can't remember much more detail like what was happening. You say to people, "You were in my dream last night, we were walking somewhere local, and that's all I can remember." Fact is you were walking, making love, swimming or doing whatever with that person. What actually happened was you consciously experienced how your life plays out in another dimension or having made different life choices in this dimension, taken a different direction. You have – the soul has –

subconsciously lived all other lives you dream and more. You exist in an infinite number of past, current and future dimensions which are parallel. The Devil has the human race tuned into the conscious dimension and dreams are unexplained. A dream, no matter how strange, in whatever era, is you as a soul existing in one of the universe's infinite number of possible parallel dimensions that are playing out. The human and every alien race combined is one conscious and subconscious mind, all linked as one; we are God. We are all clairvoyant, seeing our own past and future dimensions in dream state, but some of us individuals, such as myself, take it further and see the future dimensions of others as I did just then. I learned to master this and many other magical feats long ago when we were Earth's physical angels of the Koolah tribe. To answer your question, the spiritual universe is so complex, Don Carlo. I receive dreams all day while consciously awake. Our soul tribe, you included, enter each other's dreams receiving clues from many different dimensions, answering our questions and showing us which decisions to make etc, etc. Spirit had just then taken me to a future dimension, into the psyche of one of our soul tribe who's shared with me their clairvoyant mind exposing the two shady figures, informants from within our cartel selling us out. So basically if you like, I've been shown the future of when we've found out who they are.'

Diego Juan Carlo feels it's an appropriate time to ask a huge question. 'We'll talk business as always in your time, but, Hercule, who is God and...?'

The witchdoctor interrupts with a smile, 'God is the universe and everything in it, Don Carlo. Once there was the darkness, nothingness and just the one spirit energy, God. Again and again the newly written religious books are mistakenly translated. Part of the modern bible says, "and then the Lord God formed a man from the dust of the ground and breathed into his nostrils the breath of life, and the man became a living being." What rubbish, what actually happened was in creating the living, the spirit God placed part of itself, the soul, within each of us. Collectively the bodies of human and alien races house the oneness spirit of God.

The one spirit is actually experiencing life having divided itself, now existing within each and every being and animal in the universe. Every being, animal, insect, has a purpose. The soul within us is God's soul, a tiny part of the one spirit, the source. Like the prophet angel Bob Marley and the Rasta man say in Jamaica, one people, one blood, one God my brother.'

After sitting for a moment or two in silence, Hercule gravely advises, 'It's time to take your permanent disguise, Don Carlo. They've been close to getting you. Even gone as far as allowing our opposing Mexicans to attempt assassinating you.'

Diego Juan Carlo's cousin Natrale, who's a flashy short, stocky Hispanic with cropped hair, gets up to come over to the balcony to join his uncle, and is in time to catch what the witchdoctor is saying.

'Yes,' Natrale says brashly, 'we have a top-quality plastic surgeon in Dusseldorf, Europe. Cash, no questions and of the strictest confidentiality. Angelina used him and as you can see…'

Hercule laughs interrupting him. 'Not that sort of disguise. What's needed is a spiritual transformation, something much more unique than the usual face and fingerprint alteration. It's time your soul took up residence within another body, Don Carlo.'

Natrale has heard enough. He looks scornfully towards Hercule and waves his hand as though to gesture him away. Turning to his cousin, he asks angrily, 'Don Carlo, why are you listening to this fucking freak?'

Don Carlo and Hercule simply stare back at him, until Natrale thinks better of arguing further and turns to go, looking at his wristwatch as he leaves them. Don Carlo in turn looks at his watch and notes that it's 11.30am. At that precise moment Black Londoner, Daniel Cottle looks at his watch with the same arm movement.

HM Prison Lowdham Grange, Nottinghamshire, England

Daniel's sitting in between Charlie and Nicole, who's got little Jessica sitting on her lap. Noting from his watch that it's 3.30pm, he smiles at Kieran and says, 'Listen Kieran, Nicole, you ain't got long left. Uncle and me will take Jess out, so you can have half hour of the visit to ya selves.'

Kieran nods and beckons to his daughter. 'Come gi' Dad a kiss. You're picking me up, bringing me home with your Uncle Danny in just over two and half months.'

Jessica gets off her mother's lap, walks around the table to her father and kisses him. 'No more prison visits... swear Daddy?'

He proudly smiles as he replies, 'No more visits not ever, poppet.'

As Daniel and Charlie stand, Kieran says to them, 'She was a baby when I came in. Can't believe been in this toilet a five stretch. Dan, Uncle Charlie, thanks for coming, from the heart, I mean that, chaps.'

He stands, kisses and hugs his friends, then kisses Jessica again.

When the three of them have gone, Kieran and Nicole hug romantically and get themselves engrossed in a loving conversation.

Daniel, Charlie and Jessica return to visits waiting room area, a holding room within the prison. As the two men sit and wait, and little Jessica's amusing herself skipping around the room out of earshot, Charlie turns to Daniel and says, 'Fuck me, Jarrod, it's recently hit me. When I was over in Jamaica with Cutty Robinson twenty years ago the woman Charmaine and Cindy were telling me when I was going to meet Stacey, my Twin Flame and they got it bang on. That new little blonde bit I'm shagging, Stacey. Giving her one early this morning and as I shot me load I ripped the old Alan Whicker's off.'

'Lately you got a thing about ripping them off,' Daniel responds dryly. 'Tell you what, you're turning into a right old fucking serial nonce in ya old age, Uncle.'

'Oi, let's have a bit less of the old, alright,' Charlie jokes. 'Must be the ole woman's at home, big ass and old granny drawers she wears, sending me that way. Somehow, her knickers don't have the same appeal. The fucking passion killers I call 'em.'

After the two men share a laugh over that. Charlie leans in

closer and says, 'Jarrod listen, on a serious note, I'm gonna tell her I'm leaving tonight. Feel terrible, but I just can't do it with her no more. Watched that same fat, flat ass get out of bed one too many times of a morning, son.'

Daniel stifles a laugh at Charlie's description, as the older man continues, 'The worst thing that could have happened between the ole woman and me was me having this type a fun with Stacey. I'm 'appy again, first time in donkey's years for fuck sakes. If truth be known, Stacey's made me realise I've never been truly happy with both me kids' mums, Tracey or Vera, in all the years I'd spent with them. No matter how much money I ploughed into the home getting it looking like a palace, cruises, flash cars, holidays, I was never happy.'

Daniel smiles, slaps his palm to Charlie's neck, presses his forehead against Charlie's and explains to him, 'Uncle, happiness isn't the size of the home; happiness is the size of the happiness within the home. You only live this life the once, Charlie.'

Charlie smiles briefly but a serious expression quickly comes over his face again as he drifts into deep thought. 'Jarrod, when me and Stacey first fucked it felt for both of us as though we'd been together our whole lives and we both had actually dreamed of being together before we were. Dreamed her many times. This is the weird bit, dreamed Stacey and woke up still in a dream as the pirate I've always dreamed being. Anyway, listen to this. I hadn't planned to go to this party and in the last minute I thought fuck it why not. I walked in and there she was stood in the kitchen of the lady whose party it was smiling, giving me the strangest feeling like I'd known her forever as though we were already in a relationship. I thought that had to be a sign we were right for one another. Anyway, we began talking and she was disgusted when I asked who she was. It only turns out to be me ex-wife Tracey's best friend's niece.'

A lot of what his friend has been saying has been triggering associations in Daniel's mind. He's heard the term Twin Flame before, Lana/Claudette having explained it during the night and early morning in Amsterdam. And Charlie's description of what he'd found with Stacey chimed with his feelings towards Sofia, the Colombian girl he's grown up with by way of subconscious dreams. And then there was the pirate connection... to Lana, to himself as Jarrod...

His thoughts are interrupted at that moment, by a prison officer opening the door to let everybody out and back through to the prison car park.

As Charlie, Daniel and Nicole are set to leave, Charlie notices Jessica, who's by nature a chatty child, is talking with a lady who's sat alone. As Jessica rushes to join her mother, Charlie calls out to the woman, 'You coming, love?'

The prison officer and other visitors give Charlie a curious look because they can't see anybody sitting there. Charlie gives the woman a look that says 'please yourself' and a shrug of the shoulders as he turns to go. When he sees the prison officer going to lock the door, Charlie looks concerned but Daniel waves a hand and says, 'It's alright leave her; she must be in there waiting for someone.'

Jessica adds, 'Uncle Daniel, that lady I was just talking to knows my Nan Cindy, Granddad Eric and my mum and dad...'

Charlie turns back to the building and sees the woman looking out the window at him: the smiling face of Claudette. 'Yeah, come to think about it,' he says, 'she does look familiar.'

The party reach the final room that leads to the car park, and Daniel is able to retrieve his mobile from the prison locker.

Charlie rests his hand on Daniel's shoulder. 'Jarrod, you seem in deep thought; what you laughing at, son?'

The familiar vibration of Claudette, the unique Koolah energy feeling, had bought a smile to Daniel's face.

'Yeah, just hit me again, Uncle,' he answers. 'For some reason just now sat in that room brought the exact feeling back. Before me flight this morning had the craziest dreams in Amsterdam. Dreams I've dreamed all me life. Fucking hell, saw ghosts in me hotel room. Thing is, I'm not sure what was real and what were dreams. Bits keep coming back to me.'

'What's coming back?' Charlie asks as they walk across the prison visitors' car park.

Daniel doesn't know how to explain Claudette guiding him to the slave uprising rebel base and him becoming conscious as the White child and man Jarrod; or how he somehow saw that morning in Amsterdam the Black Haitian Lana, still wearing the same military jacket, change to Claudette. All he manages to say as they reach the car is: 'I've always seen you in my dreams, Uncle.'

'I dream a lot as well, son,' Charlie replies, for a moment seeing in his mind an image of the pirate Jarrod with the same eyes as Daniel Cottle. 'Does your head in trying to make sense of them sometimes…'

Kingston International Airport, Jamaica

In the warm morning climate of the Caribbean, Claudette and her elder sister place their travel documents on the check-in desk for their flight.

The pretty, dark-skinned, young Jamaican girl checking passengers in smiles in awe at the classy and sassy Haitian ladies. 'Ok, where are you traveling to?'

'Flying into London Gatwick,' Claudette replies, 'then connecting flight onto Spain, Balearic Islands.'

The check-in girl's smile is even brighter. 'Sounds nice, just a holiday?'

Claudette's smile is equally vibrant. 'Yes, and we're going to meet some very old friends.'

Once the check-in procedure is completed, the check-in girl compliments Claudette saying, 'Your French accent is actually beautiful, my favourite European language.'

'Yes,' Claudette responds after a pause, 'gave the French a great battle and defeated them, more than earned the right to use their language. Oh and by the way, it's a girl.'

Suddenly the smiling check-in girl looks astounded. 'Madam, I only did the positive pregnancy test this morning; how did you know?'

Claudette picks up the paperwork and passports, smiles and leaves.

Charlie Baker's home, Essex

It's the following morning and Charlie Baker wakes from another of his 18th century dreams, and although he could not know it Yanson Bailey in his Ibiza villa was at the same time waking from being conscious, interacting in the same dream.

Charlie lies still for a while listening to his wife Vera's loud snoring. Eventually he decides he can't stand listening to any more of it and nudges her awake.

Without wanting to waste time procrastinating, he says to her abruptly, 'Vera, I don't know about you but this ain't working for me. I'm leaving you.'

In response, she sits up and says, 'You fucking what?'

CHAPTER 55

The Bell Pub, Walthamstow, East London

That evening at around six Daniel Cottle is sitting opposite a notorious, local, street gangster called Jabber, having a beer and discussing recent and possible outcomes of future events. Daniel's mobile rings, he takes it from his pocket, looks at it, but doesn't answer it, instead placing it on the table.

Daniel has an ability to switch accents depending on who he's speaking with, and he matches his underworld associate Jabber's manner of speaking. 'Jabber,' he says agitatedly, 'what the fuck's this I hear about you sticking the heavy on Kieran's missus, Nicole, and me goddaughter, Jessica? You know I got a son with Lickle's sister, Victoria, talking fam here, blood. Told me you jumped in her motor on the Roman Road and jacked her Rolex.'

Jabber's quick to try and defend himself. 'Yole fam, ain't gonna lie, man jacked his baby mum's 'lex, yeah jacked that shit, blood, but, Jarrod, listen...'

Daniel abruptly interrupts him by slamming his hand on the table and shouting, 'No, na you listen, yeah blood...'

But as Daniel notices other people in the pub looking at the sound of his raised voice, he composes himself a little and continues in a quieter tone, 'Man have disagreements, that's all in the game, but we won't have women and children harmed on the manor. Call me old fashioned, but as far as I'm concerned that's borderline noncey, ya cunt. You fucking listen, geeze...'

Jabber nods submissively. 'Yole fam, I hear that, big man. You know I got bare love for Lickle's sister, Vicky, and your son, Nathan. Come on, blood, that goes without saying. I would never disrespect and apologise. I was just pissed off, fam.'

'Man mek it slide this time, just the once, alright,' Daniel replies, adding firmly, 'Won't be a next time.'

Jabber nods nervously and Daniel continues, 'Listen, Lickle's out soon, you both got good women and lovely kids. What you're saying, straight to the point, unu man lough the beef ting?'

Jabber's not so sure he's ready to bury the feud he has with Kieran so easily. 'Jarrod, my peeps have the utmost respect for you. You do a lot for the ends, especially the women and young yutes. Everyone and their youngers praising the way you conduct the food on the manor so that everyone eats. Blood, which other firm takes a percentage of their profit and puts it aside for women and kids whose men are in jail? Who could send a bad word in your direction? My cousin Tina told me to thank you for sending her and the kids to Tenerife the other day...'

Daniel interrupts, raises a hand in protest and speaks calmly. 'Tina's feller's a good man, top robber, just a little unlucky. But get to the point, not about me, it's about this beef ting with you an' Lickle.'

Jabber points to his scarred cheek and pulls it back to show his missing teeth, rotted gums and the rest of the shotgun shell damage inside his mouth. 'Can't lie, big man, tings gone deep. I lost my baby mum due to this. Deaf in one ear, rotting stinking gums wreak, bitch cunt baby mum run leff me 'cos of it.'

'Known you from junior school, Jabber,' Daniel interjects, 'longer than Kieran even. You were both disrespectful; leave it there before it gets right out of hand.'

'What you saying, Jarrod?' Jabber explodes. 'You ain't listened to a word I've fucking said...'

The menacingly cold look that's appeared on Daniel's face silences Jabber, who suddenly looks fearful.

'Your mum's here today,' Daniel says, the anger rising in his voice as he continues, 'Don't you feel I know about fucking loss, rude boy, ee man?'

A look of shock spreads across Jabber's face. 'Oh shit, sorry blood, wasn't thinking, Jarrod, sorry man.'

Both sit in silence for a few seconds, and Jabber's mind drifts back to thoughts of his nightmare night: the night Kieran 'Lickle' Sears shot him in the face.

It was late on a cold night in Hackney, East London, and he was running – running for his life – into an alleyway when he hears the sound of the sawn-off shotgun blast and feels a few of the red-hot pellets from the gun hit the backs of his legs and backside, but the adrenalin kept him moving through the alley and still on his feet until as he reaches the end of the alley he'd literally bumped into two street youths dropping him to the floor. The youths had run off at the sight of the balaclava-wearing man wielding the sawn-off pump-action shotgun, who was quickly standing over him about to blast his head off. He'd pleaded, 'Kieran, come man, please,' begged for his life, as Kieran had his foot on his chest. He'd realised Kieran was waiting for the slow-moving traffic to pass and doing his best to hide the gun from sight, and when the shot eventually came he'd moved his head to one side, and although the blast took the side of his face off, he was still alive.

Through the mouth of the balaclava, Kieran's lips had displayed a defeated smile; he'd known he hadn't succeeded in killing him despite the pool of blood that was spreading out from his head. 'Crying like a little bitch now, innit. What happened to the real bad man?' Kieran had sneered at him. Kieran looks up to an elderly White woman screaming from her upstairs window.

The woman has the entire view of the alleyway where the action took place from her back kitchen window. 'I'm going to call the law…' She puts her head back in the window and inside the flat she excitedly speaks to her Black Jamaican husband and comes back to the window. Outside Kieran wastes no time and runs off as she's continuously screaming from the window, then inside the flat, pointing back at the window. 'Fred, a man's been shot, someone call the police. I saw it all, thought it was just a fight and a man was trying to get away but he fired a gun twice. I saw the big bright flash when he fired it again the same loud noise. It was him, he's running back through the alley...' The White woman persistently nudges her frail looking Black Jamaican husband who's sat watching BBC1 Match of the Day British soccer programme with a bottle of beer next to his marijuana stash.

'Don't bother with the police. You want them come find me gunja? Woman, how many times I got to tell you, come from the blasted window and mind you own rarted business, cha …' He shouts louder, 'Come inside … dyarm rarted ooman, what the dyarm backside …'

The sound of a police car with its loud siren speeding past outside the pub brings Jabber back to the present. The memory of the nightmare has, though, only stirred Jabber's emotions and he can't control his anger as he says aggressively, 'Oh yeah, Jarrod, he tried to murk my little fleshie in jail the other day as well. Lickle wet up my little cousin, you know what. Anyting a anyting, whatever like. Fuck it, it's on, no long ting, no lay lay, blood. Man's no dickhead like, innit, fam…'

Daniel's mobile on the table rings again, but he ignores it as he bids Jabber, who had risen to his feet during his outburst, to sit back down. 'Firstly, sit yourself down, get to know yourself, rude boy. Jabber, Jabber come drop the hype ting, you know that don't work here. Have a little think about the reality of it. Everyone knows you two got beef. One a you's gonna get topped, ok, the other possibly lifed off. Not just that, you lot having murders on the manor is bad for business. Lots more plod stopping man for yogars, no one wanting to run their – or should I say my – gear around. You know what happens to people who disrupt my business.'

'I hear you, big man, but...'

Daniel interrupts Jabber mid-sentence, 'Listen, tell you what's gonna happen, you're both gonna sit down at the table, white flag day. After that, if it don't get resolved or aired out, have ya beef off the manor, alright?'

Jabber goes to speak, but Daniel cuts him off saying, 'Don't wanna hear no more about it.'

Nevertheless, Jabber says, 'Too late for all that, Jarrod. I'm telling you straight, I ain't coming to meet that pussy-hole nowhere.'

Again Daniel's mobile rings. He looks into Jabber's eyes and places a hand on his shoulder. 'Suit yourself, Jabbs. I'll give you some time to have a think and give me a call to sort it. I'll come check you one last time, yeah blood? You know I'm a man of me word. Got to go…'

Daniel gets up, necks his drink, and for a moment he could swear a pair of female eyes were looking at him from the pub mirror reminding him of his recent Amsterdam hotel experience. He dismisses the thought and walks out the pub, leaving Jabber sitting at the table.

Moments later, Daniel is sat in his brand-new customised Range Rover 3.9 Vogue SE 5dr parked opposite the pub. From there he has a perfect view through the window of Jabber speaking on his mobile. A look of sincere sadness appears on Daniel's face. He shakes his head, turns the ignition key, and begins speaking to Victoria, the mother of one of his two sons, through the car's Bluetooth system.

'Pop round, Jarrod, need to see ya, babes,' her voice through the speaker says.

'Yeah, yeah Vic,' he replies, 'I'm only down the road, soon come.'

He speeds off with loud house music pumping through the speakers, and muttering to himself, 'Na, seriously got to put a stop to this tonight…'

CHAPTER 56

Hedrin Castle, Kent coast, 1756

Charlotte Ortice, Duchess of Kent, and her husband the Duke are still sitting in the carver chairs at opposite ends of the long dining table. She takes another sip of her French Cognac and decides that there's more that needs to be said to her husband.

'You and other male members of your American family with your macho, bravado so-called picnic, capture, brutalise and hang petrified Negro men, women and children – a teenage girl on the last occasion, hunted by dogs and drunken cheering men on horseback, a scared barefoot child running for her life through the woods, caught and savagely mauled by the dogs as you and others looked on.'

Her husband forces a smile and tries to respond proudly. 'Pick a nigger, or picnic for short, was invented in America long before we enjoyed the fun. You witnessed one such event when we travelled overseas, my dear.'

Charlotte vividly remembers the hanging of the autistic child, Jaden, and the Royal Navy officer James Morgan having to intervene to save the boy's family from the ordeal of having to watch.

'My cousin Marcus crossed the Atlantic with us to reside within our castle,' the Duke continues. 'You have spoken to him whilst dining at this very table in regard to the U.S. Constitution.'

'Constitution pah!' Charlotte sneers. 'Your cousin Marcus is pure evil. He and the American Constitution deserve to be consigned to the bottom of the Atlantic forever.'

'Charlotte dear, the picnic is a simple symbol of our human superiority over just another animal. Oh, and incidentally if my mind serves me correctly, was it not the Royal Navy Captain

James Morgan assigned to escort us back overseas on our return from America to London docks who turned coat becoming a pirate traitor?'

'Turncoat, you say?' Charlotte's startled at the mention of Morgan's name.

'Yes dear, according to reports coming from the French, Morgan's band of criminals and deserters are acting as mercenaries, operating with the savage out-of-control Negros against the French military's efforts to get the Caribbean colony of Haiti back to order. Morgan's actually releasing and helping, strategically organising, the Negro savages. The man's completely taken leave of his senses. Our King is furious at his actions.'

'I imagine,' Charlotte responds in disgust, 'when you say "get the Caribbean colony back to order" you mean viciously re-enslave poor soul humans against their will to build countries around the world stolen from other people.'

By now Charlotte has had enough of even talking with her husband and returns to writing in her diary. At one point she casually glances towards the blazing fire and sees a faint image she's repeatedly seen from childhood, the astral travelling modern-day witch Claudette smiling; then the image fades to nothing.

Saint Ann's Bay, Jamaica

Across the Atlantic Ocean, the crewmember on lookout duty shouts from the crow's nest of *The Haitian Witch*, 'Land ahoy,' as he sees the Jamaican coast in the distance.

A little later, members of the crew are readying to drop anchor and the young pirate captain Morgan appears on deck. He looks out at the distinctive natural floral beauty of St Ann's Bay and breathes in deeply through his nostrils. 'Jamaica, we're home, thank Jesus,' he says and there's a friendly, relaxed expression on his face as he shares a smile with Anci's family and the other rescued West Africans who are also on deck admiring the beautiful sight of the Jamaican coastline.

Lana and her sister Natasha are tidying their cabin after an ancient regression reading. The past life reading had again revealed to them visions of the ancient Koolah tribe and knowledge that they themselves were present in their Koolah tribe incarnations, Lana as the boy Imani and Natasha as one of the two female vocalists who began singing the sweet melody at the ceremonial party when Koolah's earthly body died.

Lana asks her younger sister, 'I know you are one of the two singers at the ancient ceremony, but who is the other reincarnated as today?'

'Alice, of course,' Natasha replies.

'Be sure to mention it; remind her when you meet with Alice again.'

'Yes sister, I surely will.'

It takes quite some time for the ship to be docked and all the crew to disembark and offload the confiscated items from the *George IV*, including a number of treasure chests. As the men leave the ship, Captain Morgan pats each one on the back as they pass. He's the last to leave the ship, only shortly preceded by the Black Haitian sisters.

Many locals go to work camouflaging the huge docked ship, stacking huge leafy tree branches against it, as Morgan watches, his dog Patch by his side. The pirate captain stoops down to pet Patch and as he strokes the dog and rubs its belly, he feels the huge, deep, healed scar on Patch's underbody.

Morgan thinks back to the event, the night of the horrific family tragedy, the night that changed his life forever, in 1754 but the best part of three years ago...

Commander James Morgan's home on the Kent coast
1754

The low-level Morgan family home is a farm within walking distance of the Duke and Duchess of Kent's Hedrin Castle on the Kent coast. It's a bitterly cold stormy night, but with the log fire blazing away the home is a cosy setting for the then clean-cut

Royal Navy Commander James Morgan and his wife and children, nine-year-old boy and girl twins Benedict and Kiera. The family have just finished eating and Morgan amuses his children by spinning four coins on the table, setting them weaving in and out of one another as they spin, as his two English Bulldogs curl up in front of the fire. However, Morgan never considered himself to be off duty and the twitching of Patch's sensitive ears, even though the dog was half-asleep, set him on alert. It was after all part of his regiment's role to protect Hedrin Castle and its residents, the Duke and Duchess.

Keira looks to the window and thinks she sees a tall male shadow lurking in the darkness. None of the family notice her worried expression as she gets up to close the curtains. She looks out to see the branches of a tree blowing in the wind creating shadows, and reckoning that was all she must have seen, she smiles a relieved smile, draws the curtains and goes back to the table. As she sits back down, a concerned James Morgan looks towards the fireplace to see the dogs looking to the front door, then the roof of the single-storey dwelling, before they begin whining and barking. Morgan quickly gets up, walks across the room and after putting his boots on as quickly as he can, arms himself with sword and pistol. His wife and children look on in alarm as he does so.

'What is it, Patch, someone out there? Come boy, let's go,' he says rushing for the door.

As he opens it an icy blast of wind blows rain into the house and his family glimpse not only a strike of lightning from the raging storm but the figure it momentarily illuminates: an intruder jumping down from the roof.

'Father, behind you,' his son Benedict calls out, and Morgan reacts quickly, raising his pistol and shooting the man dead but not before the intruder had fired his own weapon, the bullet only, though, grazing Morgan's thigh. Before the sharp burning sensation of that wound has had a chance to kick in and whilst Morgan is turning to smile proudly back at his son, he's set upon by two masked men armed with swords. They begin fighting it out in the stormy night, and Morgan can quickly tell the men are well-trained fighters.

'Haley, keep the children inside, lock the door,' he shouts to his wife, and the turn of his head in that moment is enough to save his eye. The attacker's sword instead slices only through his eyelid, leaving him the two-inch scar there he will have for the rest of his life.

After more relentless fighting, a tiring Morgan is finally backed up against the wall of his house, sword to his throat.

Breathing heavily after his exertions, the masked swordsman says, 'Drop it, James. I'll be the first to admit, you're quick.'

Morgan recognises the voice from somewhere, but before he can place it, his assailant saves him the trouble by tearing off his own mask, revealing his identity to Morgan.

With rainwater and blood streaming over his eyes, Morgan sees a face he knows well. 'You, of all people they send you...'

'Sorry it has to be me that kills you, Commander,' the young, well-built, blond assassin replies. 'Always admired you, old friend. The irony is you trained me to kill you. You don't have to ask what this is about, James.'

'How... how did they find out?' Morgan asks.

'The Duchess of Kent, you fucked her with that huge cock of yours, you handsome bloody bastard. The sissy Duke, the King's beloved nephew Cuthbert's wife, what were you thinking? I was sure you fucked her aboard our ship when we escorted the royal couple back from America. I heard heavy breathing in your cabin but wasn't sure whom you were fucking, thinking it was a wench on board. Your affair with her really upset the King. It's already clear to see Janelle's your daughter and not Cuthbert's. Always was one for the women, James. Personally, truthfully I don't blame you; I certainly would have risked the consequences given half a chance. I mean it's plain to see her husband isn't up to much in the sleeping quarters. I should know, stood guard outside their palace door many a night when they were in bed together, not a sound.'

Both the blond assassin and his dark-haired accomplice laugh at this, and the blond man adds, recalling a time when he heard the Duchess moaning in the throes of delight alone in her room, 'Quite the contrast when she was in bed alone, seems as though she's pretty good at entertaining her own sexual desires.'

The dark-haired swordsman, satisfied that his accomplice has the situation in hand, walks away to go and stand at the cliff edge watching what the raging storm's doing to the ocean, high waves crashing to the cliff face beneath him.

Suddenly, out of nowhere Patch jumps onto a log, then a firewood storage shelter and comes flying in, whereupon the dog clamps its jaws on the young man's face, teeth piercing deep into the skin of his cheek. As the dog vigorously shakes its head and growls, the young man tries his best to fight the animal off. Then as the dog comes free, tearing a lump out of the young man's cheek as it does so, the man gets to his feet, raises his sword and slices it into the dog's underbelly.

Seeing him chop into the dog, the horrified Morgan screams loudly, 'Patch!' and as the assassin stands back up Morgan had drawn his hidden short dagger sword from his inner cloak and runs him through the solar plexus of the stomach.

There's a gut-wrenching scream and the blond assassin is impaled on Morgan's dagger.

Holding the dying man with the dagger through his stomach in a standing position, Morgan intones,

'Always knew you'd make a good swordsman, but told you over and over you talked too much, idiot. Warned you of that too many times; good listeners make for good bloody learners. Didn't you listen to anything I taught you? I repeated time and time again, no mercy, instant death. The enemy don't pose a problem dead. Standing telling me stories of the sissy Duke, you should have killed me quickly.'

As Morgan extracts his dagger and lets the blond assassin fall to the ground, he sees the man's dark-haired companion charging towards him and has to face another fight.

Two others come running out of the house, one covered in blood. As they exit, a tall elegantly dressed man, the man who had in fact been responsible for the shadow Kiera saw earlier, also emerges. Morgan catches sight of him and screams out, 'Haley, no, please God, no.'

Patch lies wounded, his underside sliced open and covered in blood. The other English Bulldog, a bitch, tears in to one of the approaching assassin's legs, but he swings his sword at her, almost decapitating her and killing her instantly.

On the cliff edge, Morgan is soon tiring, trying to fend off three trained killers. He fatefully stumbles and falls at least one hundred feet downward towards the icy stormy waves, hitting off the cliff face, and finally crashing to the rocky shore, where the current begins to carry his body away.

At first, the bloodied faithful Patch stands whimpering at the cliff edge, but as one of the attackers aggressively moves in to finish him off, the dog makes its mind up to jump off the cliff after its master.

The assassins standing at the cliff edge look down below at the freezing powerful waves relentlessly battering the shore and one of them says, 'Morgan's dead, for sure. If he's not dead from the fall or drowned, no one could survive that ice cold water.'

Calvin, the Duke of Kent's brother, joins them at the cliff edge. He's the elegantly dressed man whose shadow Keira saw at the window and whose face Morgan caught a brief glimpse of. He's a tall, dark-haired and remarkably handsome man in his mid-thirties, and wearing a full-length black cloak.

'The others, the witnesses?' one of the men asks.

'Dead, they are all dead,' Calvin replies, and looking down over the cliff edge adds, 'and I feel we can rest assured the same can be said for the Royal Navy Commander Morgan. Oh, and incidentally, my brother Cuthbert must never learn of his wife's deceit in regard to Morgan, understood? The very mention of tonight to anyone will be punished by death.'

As the assassins throw their dead comrade over the cliff edge, none of the men can see her but the astral travelling image of Claudette is just feet away from them.

Back at the Morgan's farmhouse the front door is wide open,

with wind and rain soaking the floor, on which the dead and bloodied bodies of Mrs Morgan and the twins lie.

CHAPTER 57

Woodford Green, Essex, 1993

Victoria Sears is at the mirror putting the final touches to her makeup as she hears a car pull up outside her home.

Outside, Daniel Cottle gets out of his car engrossed in mobile phone conversation whilst walking the short distance to her home, apologising on the way to a dainty woman that seemed to come from nowhere who he almost bumps into by accident. As he's pressing the doorbell, although he didn't get a good look at her face, he realises where he'd felt the vibration of the woman before and the deep spiritual Amsterdam sensation suddenly comes alive within his psyche. Subconsciously he feels coincidently she was the one speaking to his goddaughter Jessica at the prison.

But his thoughts about that are quickly driven from his mind by the sight that greets him as the door is opened. Victoria Sears is a stunningly beautiful woman, White but a quarter Black with long blonde curly hair and glistening hazel eyes. Her body is equally magnificent with perfect shapely breasts, a generous ass, and strong but elegant legs. She's what might be called peng, a dream girl, a ten out of ten.

Presently she's wearing high-heeled boots with a long classy black cashmere mac with silk lapels – and she's high on coke.

''Ello my fucking 'ansome man,' she says, continuously sniffing and pushing her tongue around her gums whilst speaking in her mix of London cockney and Black street slang. 'Whum to you, don't answer ya phone to Vicky no more, rude boy? Is it really, like?'

She unashamedly opens her coat to reveal she's wearing nothing underneath but her newest Victoria's Secret underwear:

452

stockings, suspenders and crotchless knickers, which reveal her blonde- haired vagina and tan lines. Daniel gasps, instantly captivated, but manages to compose himself and takes her arm to usher her inside her home.

Inside, Victoria drops her mac to the floor, leaving her naked apart from her revealing knickers, stockings and suspender belt, and her stiletto-heeled thigh-high boots. She slips off even the crotchless knickers as she moves seductively across the room to a low table, where she squats pole-dance style in front of chopped lines of cocaine and an opened bottle of expensive champagne.

Daniel stares open-mouthed, and she laughs and says, 'The big man Jarrod Cottle shy and lost for words! You use' to love telling me how sexy I looked in these boots. What was it you use ta call me? "My little Queen Victoria" Ah bless, you gone all fucking shy.'

Despite the temptation to do otherwise, Daniel sits down on the sofa and tells himself he needs to say what needs to be said. 'Alright, look it's time to set it straight...' he begins in an uncharacteristically quiet voice. 'Look Vic, this is it. I was seeing you and June came along with something different than the fast dolly bird I always fucking attract. You both got pregnant a fortnight apart.'

'We know this, Jarrod,' Victoria replies, 'but why wife her off and not me? You were spratting both of us and we did both push out pickney for man.'

Suddenly she becomes extremely emotional and starts to cry. 'You fucking hurt me, Danny, you bastard,' she sobs, 'leaving me and our little Nathan.'

'Come, babe, sit down, stop the crying. You love the glamour, Vic, whereas June is the homely type that brings out that family man side of me. In my world it's a breath of fresh air to wake up that guy sometimes.'

She gathers herself and goes over to him. Placing her palms on his chest, she bends down and kisses him on the lips.

'You used to love me wearing nothing but these boots. What, no longer got the hots for me, babe?'

He pulls away, leaning back into the sofa. 'Vic, I didn't leave ya 'cos I didn't fancy ya.'

She turns away from him and goes back to the coffee table where the lines of coke are laid out. In the mirror, she notices Daniel taking a lingering look at her bottom.

'I see the way you're looking at me, Danny. Still got that twinkle in your eye.'

'Man's not gonna lie, but I had to make a safe choice; I married June,' Daniel says, continuing to admire Victoria from behind: the way the suspenders slightly squeeze her legs, her curly blonde hair falling down her tanned back almost reaching her tiny waist.

She drunkenly stumbles as she bends down to pour them both a drink. 'I get what you see in June but, be fucking honest, yous two have never created that fire, the passion we get. This is why you still have me as that splurt.'

'We got to stop this, Vic,' Daniel snaps, feeling guilty about his cheating on June with his other child's mother.

'You know you don't mean that,' she replies, handing him his drink.

'Anyway, I hear you've been seen with Tyrone; lowering ya standard?'

'I'm not fucking him. Just company, I guess. Sort a feel sorry for him.' She smiles guiltily. 'Alright, I've slept with him a few times, but I'm lonely most nights thinking about you up in the palace with her.'

Daniel can't help but be annoyed by her admission. 'But he's a fucking idiot. Don't ever let my boy Nathan come to mine telling me anything I don't want to hear about that fucking mug, otherwise he's gone, hear me?'

'He's not just yours, he's *our* fucking son,' Victoria screams, tears running down her cheeks again. 'When are you gonna fucking get it? Besides when you're playing happily families with that cunt…'

Daniel points a finger at Victoria and gives her a scornful stare. 'Stop there, no need for the disrespect, wasn't her fault'

Victoria recovers herself and with an attempt at a smile says,

'Hey, remember the good times we had when this was our home? You used to tell me about some Spanish bird you always dream about, Sophie. You'd put coke moves together and share the stories with me. Still in love with you, Danny, bastard. It was all sweet between us. Why did you leave me for that little stuck-up fucking bitch? You know I'm right, you're still feeling it, see it in your eyes, Jarrod Cottle.'

She holds her hand to her face, chokes up with emotion and covers her mouth. Daniel stands, shakes his head and gently places his palms to her cheeks, looking into her eyes as tears wallow up in them.

CHAPTER 58

Saint Ann's Bay, Jamaica, 1756

With *The Haitian Witch* unloaded, Captain Morgan is supervising the members of the crew digging holes in the night to bury their treasure. When it comes to dealing with the trunk with the gold studs, the chest containing Earth's authentic bible, an excited Lana instructs, 'Bury it as normal, Morgan. I will make a promise, when we dig it up all will be revealed.'

Morgan takes a swig of rum and encourages the pirates working by torchlight to dig deep into the ground. By the time the work is finished and all the treasure chests, including the gold-studded one, are buried, the pirate captain has got himself quite drunk. Still swigging from the bottle he breaks into Jamaican patois, as he often does when drunk, saying to his young nephew Jarrod:

'Jamaica, sonny bwoy, certainly no prettier spot 'pon God eart', young Jarrod. You fe practise dem deh sword techniques at daybreak wid William and the ress a de crew. An lickle more, you is no longer lickle bwoy, unu big man an it will soon time you move out of man cabin an share wid nex yute man.'

Jarrod feels sad at being told he will soon have to move out the captain's cabin and into his own quarter's sharing with another young man, but he takes some comfort in being treated so much like an adult and quietly says, 'Yes sir.'

That night, back on board *The Witch*, Jarrod lies awake in his bed that's behind a partition wall in the captain's cabin. He's woken from one of his recurring nightmares, in fear, breathing heavily. He'd dreamed himself again as the Black boy Daniel Cottle and the events immediately before the Cottle family tragedy, the Christmas of 1973. In the dream he'd looked down from his bedroom window to see the rugged, frightening-looking workman staring back at him – and he'd seen his own White hands as Black hands pulling back the curtain; he knew himself to be the soul of the Black child Daniel Cottle, knew of his father Clinton beating and nearly strangling him in Cutty Robinson's office, knew his father was always drunk and violent toward his mother, knew of life in the 1970s and was fascinated by the baffling existence of refrigerators and TVs.

The Cottle family home, Walthamstow, 1973

Young Daniel goes downstairs to get himself some juice from the kitchen. As he's looking in the fridge for the juice, he's startled by the sound of the back door opening. Before he knows it, he's looking up at the scary-looking White man he saw working on the roof.

In a loud voice that Daniel finds intimidating the workman says, 'You must be young Daniel I've heard so much about…' while all Daniel can do is stare at the man's tough-looking and dirty hands, one of which is carrying a tool bag.

Daniel's mother comes into the kitchen and begins speaking to the workman. 'Ah, you guys finished for the day,' she says in her soft Jamaican accent. 'You can leave your tool bag by the door; it will be alright there.'

The workman does as she suggests, and Daniel notices the roof slater's spike hammer falling from the packed, overflowing tool bag onto the tiled kitchen floor. The roofer picks it up and places it back in the tool bag and at that moment Daniel's elder sister shouts from the living room, 'Daniel, *Tom and Jerry* has started.'

The mention of the TV cartoon has Daniel excitingly rushing towards the living room shouting, 'Tom and Jerry, Tom and Jerry,' over and over.

He sits himself on the sofa with his elder brother and sister, fourteen-year-old Mark and twelve-year-old Donna.

Later that night, at midnight, the scene in the Cottle's family living room is a gory one. Pearl Cottle kneels on the floor hugging her blood-soaked dead husband Clinton, who's lying propped up against an armchair with a roof slater's spike hammer deeply embedded in the back of his skull. In a frenzied panic, she pulls it out and tries to stop the gushing blood with her hand. It's no use; the blood spurts through drenching her and Daniel's faces and bodies as the distraught young mother cries out to her son, 'Daniel, what did you do? You killed him...' before her words become just a series of harrowing screams.

The innocent-looking nine-year-old Black kid's white Paddington Bear pyjamas are now a blood-spattered red. He widens his gorgeous hazel-blue eyes and flinches each time his mother wails with her high-pitched screeching voice. The commotion wakes the elder children, Donna and Mark. When they enter the room, they see Daniel on the sofa with his face buried in a cushion, the movement of his shoulders telling them he is crying.

'Mark, I didn't mean to, he was hurting mum, sorry Donna...' he sobs. For the first time in his young life Daniel has the feeling that his mother's love is not there. Mark goes to him and instinctively tries to prize his little brother from the cushion to hug him.

'Daniel, what happened to Dad?'

'I didn't mean to,' Daniel stutters in words directed at his mother, Pearl. 'He was hurting you.'

Pearl stares at Mark and Donna in silence for a moment before the blood-spattered mother goes into another hysterical bout of screaming.

Captain's cabin, The Haitian Witch, 1756

On board the moored pirate vessel, Jarrod wakes to his dream mother's harrowing screams. He gets up from his bed as though sleep-walking and semi-consciously walks out into the dimly lit main room. Lana is still up, sitting alone at the captain's table, her mind occupied with a vision of Koolah's companion the black panther Jojo. Morgan is in bed asleep. Jarrod stumbles towards the Voodoo mirror, the exact same mirror that would later find a new home in the 1993 Amsterdam hotel bedroom. In the huge mirror, Jarrod's relieved to see his own reflection and not that of the blood-soaked Black child.

'It was a dream,' he says to his own reflection. 'But why does it always feel so real?'

The sound of his voice causes Lana to look up; she gives him a loving smile but says nothing. She watches him rubbing his hands on his face and checking them for blood as he looks towards the cabin mirror. Morgan too wakes looking from his bed and through the opened door and laughs a little at the sight of Jarrod staring at himself in the mirror.

Eventually Jarrod returns to bed but only to enter the nightmare again once he falls asleep. Pearl Cottle's screams ring in his head again. His moaning and thrashing in his sleep bring his uncle, Morgan, to his side.

As Morgan tries to gently help him up, he feels the child's body tense.

Jarrod wakes gasping for air and mumbling, 'Mark, I didn't mean to, he was hurting mum, sorry Donna…'

As he's crossing back from dream state to consciousness Jarrod's mind tries to make sense of what he'd just experienced. He dreamed waking in the children's care home, waking from the gory dream of his mother covered in blood after he'd just murdered his father. As consciousness returns to him, Jarrod somehow knows he more than influenced the Cottle boy to murder his father. He knows he made a decision and carried it through. He knew where the hammer was and what he was going to do with it.

Morgan looks into the child's eyes, the same hazel-blue eyes he recognises from his own futuristic recurring dreams as belonging to Daniel Cottle, and caresses the child's head, gently pushing his fingers through the boy's long black curly hair. 'What is it, boy? Sounds like another nightmare.'

Jarrod stares vacantly as he speaks. 'I didn't mean for my father to die, but he kept hurting Mum. I was sad for her and just wanted him to stop. I'm sorry, really, I am…' He looks around the cabin frantically and jumps to his feet. 'Need to go back there, left Mark and Donna… got to go back…'

Morgan sits him back on the bed, gently caresses the boy's cheek and asks, 'Who in God's name are this Mark and Donna you always speak of when you wake? Your father's not dead, Jarrod. It was just a dream, silly. We left your father with your mother on the coast of Australia; he's alive and well. Remember?'

Jarrod looks frustrated. 'No Uncle James, you really don't understand. I did it and he's getting the blame. I'm not tough when I'm him, haven't seen and done what we have here. I was him, feeling the way he does, and saw my father punch my mother to the floor and start kicking her. Suddenly I felt everything in this life that's been taught me, the Haitian's fearless passion, the merciless discipline within our training. For a moment I imagined him a French soldier and I killed him. As soon as I done it and my mother began screaming, I felt how I do in that life, soft and afraid again. Back there I still feel my Black mother's sadness. I don't know how but I am him feeling the guilt and having to deal with it…'

Growing increasingly concerned and confused, Morgan interrupts, 'Yeah, but it's a dream, boy.'

'I wasn't actually sleeping,' Jarrod responds, looking directly into his uncle's eyes. 'You have to trust me.'

Morgan shakes his head. 'You were walking and talking in your sleep boy. I saw you looking into the mirror. It's just another nightmare, you have them all the time.'

'It's not like a dream; it's real. I can't explain it, but I'm in that world, that body, many nights I sleep. Lately I can feel all the pain and the hurt from what I did. I have my eyes, but I'm Black. You Uncle, you're always with us, you're my Black father's friend, and I killed him; I killed my father. I'm Black, Uncle James. I have a Black family in that dream. You and Patch are always there, only they call you Charlie and Patch's black patch is a bigger black and brown patch over the opposite eye.'

Jarrod's words send a shudder through Morgan. He, Morgan,

had seen the people Jarrod was describing in his own dreams. He occasionally dreams himself being the East London gangster Charlie Baker – with the dog Patch exactly as Jarrod described it, and his Black Jamaican friend Clinton Cottle and son Daniel. He knows their dreams are connected – they must be. In his mind, he promises himself he'll talk to his trusted Haitian witch Lana about it.

Jarrod begins crying and his uncle comforts him again, pulling the blanket over the child's body and gently patting his head.

'Stop ya crying,' Morgan says softly. 'Just a bad dream and it's put the ebee jeebes right up yer. Get some sleep, boy. We're going to have to toughen you up for this life. That's for sure.'

Lana, having been listening to the conversation between uncle and nephew, appears just as Morgan and Jarrod are giving each other a heartfelt hug. She's accompanied by the black panther Jojo and Morgan and Jarrod react in astonishment at that, even though Morgan would have said nothing that Lana did these days could surprise him.

'I was sat there with Jojo listening to your conversation,' Lana says emotionally. 'My God, the spiritual realms of our universe...'

CHAPTER 59

A cock crows as the sun rises on the pretty St Ann's Bay, Runaway Bay hilly terrain – a familiar sight known today as the world-famous tourist attraction, the iconic Dunn's River Falls – on the island of Jamaica. As the mist clears the view comes alive with vibrant colours. A picturesque waterfall cascades down large golden smoothed rocks into a small blue water lagoon. A small log drifts from the waterfall and gets carried along to the opening of the beach, where the pirate army are practising fighting techniques. Jarrod is among those practising sword fencing and he's not given any soft treatment by the others. A slick young White pirate called William shouts instructions to Jarrod as he and another pirate fence off against one another.

When the early morning training session is over the pirates bathe under the tranquil waterfall and swim in the lagoon.

Later at breakfast on board *The Haitian Witch*, Jim Morgan, Lana, Natasha, Yu Yan and Jarrod sit around the captain's table as the sun beams through the porthole window. Natasha shuffles a deck of tarot cards and, instead of dealing cards from the top, allows cards to flip out from the deck as she shuffles – so the cards for the reading are selected by spirit rather than her own energy. At first the cards are all positive ones which she arranges in order, but then she tuts in annoyance as the tower card flips out.

Morgan meanwhile puts the finishing touches to a treasure map. He wraps the paper map around a treasure chest key and places it in a small steel strongbox. Then he begins spinning his gold coins on the table and beckons to one of his men, the pirate who's on guard duty at the door, and orders, 'Ready *The Witch* to set sail for London in a few days. Tell the cook to be sure food supplies are fresh and plentiful, more laying hens and cows to produce milk, this time.'

The pirate captain then decides now is the moment he must give his nephew some bad news. He sets his gold coins spinning on the table and looks towards Jarrod.

His nephew can sense what's coming and says questioningly, 'Uncle Jim…?'

Morgan doesn't answer immediately, but instead with his finger and thumb begins nervously twirling one of his matted dreadlocks. Then eventually he says with a tone of authority in his voice, 'Jarrod, you're not to come on this trip. You're to stay here on the island until our return.'

'Oh, please Uncle Jim,' Jarrod pleads, 'I won't get in your way. I promise. You know that I get scary nightmares when alone. Please, I'll hide out the way…'

Eyes closed Lana intervenes at that moment saying, 'Tell me more of the same dreams you keep waking from recent mornings, Jarrod.'

Jarrod answers, careful not to take an eye off his uncle. 'I told you this yesterday morning, lately I always dream of being the same Black boy; I killed my father…'

'Spirit has revealed to me that's because he *is* you,' Lana says. 'You are the boy Daniel in the future dimension; your soul reincarnates to that life. It's you, and the soul of your White mother in Australia today reincarnates to the Black mother you see in the dream, she's your mother again in that future life Jarrod. You've actually been her father and even brother in other past and future lives. All the time, sleeping or awake you, the soul you embody, are conscious in other lives, your later and past incarnations. Only some sensitive souls are aware of these lives when awake and others don't always remember waking from sleep being conscious in other dimensions. The reason some call you Jarrod in your life as the Black boy Daniel is because their subconscious minds remember the vibration of your soul from this life. Including you Morgan, you know your relationship with Jarrod in that future life.' The pirate captain displays a sort of surprised and happy expression as Lana carries on her explanation.

'Your mother has named you Daniel in that dimension, Daniel,' Lana says and both Morgan and Jarrod look intrigued as the names Pearl and Daniel trigger dream memories in each of them. 'You're to explore the very deepest boundaries of your soul, joy and sorrow during that future life, young Jarrod. Fear not, you're a heavenly blessed soul, divinely blessed by Koolah himself at his very own sacrificial full moon ceremony. Koolah has seen to it I have – my soul has – experienced higher spiritual dimensions in order to evolve and watch over you all, assisting Koolah in spirit world.'

Lana looks to the mirror to see Claudette's face in it and the Black witch and her future incarnation share a smile.

'I've watched over you and the rest of our soul tribe during that future life,' Lana continues. 'In fact, I often travel the dimensions to watch over us. My evolved soul is actually watching over us as we speak.'

Faced with Lana's words and Jarrod's sad puppy dog eyes, Morgan smiles and says, 'There's many dangers out there, the King's men and, of course, other deadly pirates who know of my love for you. There's already talk of some wanting to kidnap you for the ransom of our treasure.'

Jarrod smiles the cutest smile causing his uncle to return it.

'Thank you, sir,' the child says joyfully, 'London it is, Uncle Jim, aye, aye Captain.'

Jim Morgan can't contain his smile. 'I haven't agreed to anything,' he protests, but Lana smiles at him with a shake of her head, knowing he's conceded the argument.

Jarrod lifts his breakfast goblet, drinks the contents of milk, spilling most of it around his mouth, and slams the goblet down on the wooden table.

Victoria Sears' home, Woodford Green, Essex, 1993

Victoria grips Daniel's jumper and pulls him towards her,

passionately kissing him as her hand quickly feels its way up his leg towards his manhood.

Daniel suddenly pulls himself away. 'I'm off, Vic, got to go; this ain't right.' He gets to his feet and shakes his head.

Victoria's distraught. 'Jarrod, you fucking what? You know you don't mean that.'

'Vic, you're one of, if not the most beautiful women I've had the pleasure of, but I'm not going there no more, it stops here. Fuck, talk about complicate things, na, no fucking way.'

As he goes to leave, Victoria moves herself in front of the door and cries, 'Stay for one drink, Jarrod, oh go on.'

'Don't do this, Vic. You know I fucking love you deeply and hate to see you sad. We both know where that one line of coover always goes, time we stopped this. It only takes Nathan to suss something between us and that would seriously fucking confuse him.'

Vnukovo International Airport, Moscow, Russia

At the same time as Daniel Cottle is trying to get out of the door at Victoria's Essex home and Claudette and her sister are checking in for their flight, Yanson Bailey arrives at the Moscow arrivals terminal dressed for the harsh Russian winter – with its temperatures known to fall as low as around eighty degrees centigrade below zero – in thermal hat and underwear, gloves, roll-neck jumper, classy full-length cashmere duffle overcoat and Timberland boots. He no longer has the dreadlocks half the way down his back but, like Daniel Cottle, keeps his hairstyle bald sides to fade into short Afro up top. In ways, Yanson resembles Daniel. Yanson's darker skinned and without Daniel's lighter coloured eyes. Yanson's are oriental in shape. Both men have similar muscular physiques, the same shaped heads and some facial features.

As Yanson clears immigration, two stunningly beautiful Russian girls, a blonde and a dark-haired brunette approach him. Both smile and the blonde one says in English but with a strong local accent, 'Hello Mr Bailey, I'll take that,' as she removes his hand and begins pushing his trolley containing light luggage.

'Yance, you can call me Yance,' Yanson says.

'Ok, Yance it is,' the blonde replies and all three smile as they walk to the exit. Outside, they walk through the snow to where a car and driver are waiting for them. Yanson gets into the back, sitting in between the girls. The Londoner is given a drive-by tour of the sights of Moscow before they drive out from the city. Despite the new sights, Yanson finds his mind drifting – drifting to thoughts of a beautiful pair of eyes he always dreams about, either both blue but one half-brown or both brown but one half-blue, sometimes belonging to a White girl, sometimes belonging to a Black girl. The thoughts so occupy him that he mutters out loud to himself, 'Who the fuck are you...? I've dreamed you constantly all my life?'

'What did you say about dreaming, Yance?' the brunette asks.

'Oh no it's nothing really,' Yanson replies, yawning and smiling.

After a ten-minute drive away from Russia's capital the blonde girl points in the distance to a stunning spectacle, a magnificent snow-covered palace, surrounded by a guard-patrolled security wall.

'There,' she says, 'the home of the Mikhailov family. The Godfather has visited his Moscow palace only three times in the past forty years. He refuses to fly; instead he drove more than fifteen hundred miles just to meet you here. For reasons other than your expert sufficient cocaine supply, he thinks very highly of you, Yanson Bailey.'

Mikhailov Palace

Not much later, Yanson is making himself at home in one of the palace's four huge fifth-tier tower guest suites. It's a suite equipped with every comfort imaginable: Scandinavian state-of-the-art Bang & Olufsen audio, a huge television, a five-six-person Jacuzzi bathtub, log-burning fires, marble fireplaces, and expensive decor throughout. The Black Londoner strips naked and eases his athletically muscular body into the Jacuzzi, feeling the effect of the tub's powerful jets. He smiles as he rests his head and lets memories of the hectic week he has just spent in London and the sleepless inbound flight from Gatwick fade away.

He closes his eyes and those recent memories are replaced by visions of distant times. He sees ancient hands – his hands – rolling dice and moving pieces playing the ancient African board game backgammon. He sees the spiritual circle in the ancient City of Koolah where Imani has just experienced his visit from Claudette, who embodies his reincarnated soul. He hears the voice of Koolah saying to Akachi, 'Show us your future, a life you will reincarnate to. It's important we see at these stages,' and he sees the vision Akachi shares of a man he would one day reincarnate to: an elderly, clean-shaven White man with long matted dreadlock grey hair in a huge, elegant reception room.

Yanson wakes from his dream with the bathwater now lukewarm, but with a deep pleasurable feeling of déjà vu, a knowing that somehow he was in tune with the vibration of this palace. He gets out the tub, dries and dresses himself ready for the meeting he is due to have in the palace's reception room.

He and members of his organisation were used to travelling the world, used to seeing the high life, but nothing had prepared Yanson for the opulence he finds at the Mikhailov Palace. The grounds, the size and structure of the palace, its plush interior – all were breath-taking. Yanson almost felt a sense of intimidation walking across the palace's huge reception room, past the many and various priceless objet d'art on display, towards its huge fireplace. And there sitting in one of the armchairs by the fire, was an elderly white man with long grey dreadlocks wearing a silk dressing gown. Yanson is startled to see in reality the same man he had only just dreamed about lying in the tub. He also now realises the room he is standing in is also the very same room the vision showed.

'So glad you could join us, Mr Bailey,' the elderly man says.

And then as though appearing from nowhere there's a woman by the old man's side, a beautiful woman in her mid-forties with a dark complexion wearing her curly hair styled up but with two strands dropping around her neck. She looks familiar to Yanson.

'Thanks to your supply, Mr Bailey,' the old man continues, 'we have been competitive throughout the Balearic Islands and rapidly moving our operation into parts of southern Spain. In return, please enjoy our hospitality, just a token of our appreciation. I usually stay away from the big cities but had to thank you in person.'

CHAPTER 60

A little later when Yanson has left them, the elderly Russian Godfather Mikhailov turns to face the lady Yanson saw present, the astral body of Claudette, with a questioning look on his face.

'That man Yanson,' Claudette explains, 'the body harbours the soul of Koolah. He doesn't yet know it, but I've guided him here to reunite with the soul of his Princess Gabi, his Twin Flame. The Koolah spirit loved her body so much in that life, he created the exact indigenous body during the ceremonial sacrifice, all part of the process.'

Mikhailov is left astounded not simply by Claudette's words but also by the vision that fills his mind of being seated at the backgammon table watching Koolah and Princess Gabi dancing in that loving embrace, then she performs what would become the modern-day shuffle dance to the bongo beat.

'My God,' he says breathlessly, 'I always knew he was one of us, but the soul of the Messiah itself. Goodness, you say Koolah's twin soul Princess Gabi is here; why did you not tell me sooner?'

'I believe she's called Penelope here at the palace. Listen, before Koolah's sacrificial ceremony, we visualised this point: you present in this palace sat in front of this very fire entertaining Yanson Bailey. It was during that full moon ceremony Koolah said this moment would be the time to reveal his soul to you. Also to reunite him with his Princess, and more importantly we're to allow it to happen naturally.'

The elderly Russian is about to interrupt but Claudette silences him, holding an index finger in mid-air and saying, 'Akachi, we both know better than to question any desires of anybody and that includes the Messiah. Besides, you know better than most I enjoy nothing more than watching a deep love story unfold.

My physical body is presently underneath a blanket on board a passenger jumbo jet heading towards Spain. It's there now in a trance from where I'm projecting my astral body to you. We're due to land in Madrid for our connecting flight to Ibiza. As you know, Yanson is resident on the island and we shall meet again there. You also know Twin Flame union is the coming together of two people by the hand of the divine – divinely orchestrated into a place of love, happiness, harmony and peace. Twin Flame union is heaven on Earth, or whatever alien planet you happen to be on. It is the biggest, deepest, soul connection vibration you could experience.'

'Imani,' the Russian Godfather says, calling Claudette by her male ancient Koolah tribal name, 'this means the awakening, the Messiah's second coming is near. When are you to reactivate the Messiah's inner spirit?'

'Koolah has all us souls, our entire soul tribe working as one. Myself and other soul angels have located the Book of Koolah, the authentic bible. The book has instructions to activate the spell. When I have it in this incarnation… so shall it begin.'

CHAPTER 61

As a sweet acid house beat plays on the room's audio system and Yanson relaxes in his suite, he's suddenly disturbed by a knock at the door. A middle-aged woman is the first to enter, followed by one beautiful Black African and four equally beautiful Eastern European women escorts, all in their twenties. They're all smiling but one of the White women begins slightly moving her hips to the beat of the music and her physical familiarity, her shapely Black-female-shaped bottom, catches the imagination of Yanson. He senses she's distraught and he feels an ever-growing sense of déjà vu, a knowing he's somehow connected to her but not sure how or where he'd seen her before. As he's trying to work it out, the Mafia Godfather and his two sons enter. These are the Russian men Yanson deals with in Ibiza and mainland Spain. They come in and joyfully greet their London connection.

Mikhailov, the Russian Godfather himself, simply smiles at Yanson, but the Black Londoner not only sees but actually feels the older man's smile. Out of the five stunningly beautiful women, Yanson makes no secret of the fact he's captivated by the one his soul recognises. Mikhailov can't help but notice this and speaking native Koolah, says under his breath, 'Princess Gabi, you're here, my God.'

Claudette's astral body appears at the elderly Russian's side and he says to her, 'Goodness, Imani, what have we done?'

In that moment, Mikhailov's ancient indigenous African soul moves his body to dance in tune with the house music, and everyone present is surprised and impressed by the elderly man's dance moves.

The girl Yanson is captivated by is known in the palace as Penelope. She's of Romany descent, five- feet-four-inches tall and wearing white stilettos and a tight-fitting black designer dress that compliments her perfect figure. Her stylishly cut long blonde hair has a dark streak in it and her eyes are those Yanson has seen in his dreams and visions: blue eyes but with one half-brown.

The older woman, the madam type, claps her hands and bids all the girls except Penelope to leave with her. Penelope sits on a comfy armchair near the fire and begins preparing what looks like some sort of tea, whilst Yanson chats with one of the Godfather's sons. Eventually the others leave, leaving Yanson and the girl called Penelope alone together.

Looking at her up close to him now Yanson can tell the dark streak in her hair is natural and not dyed and that her eyes are so familiar to him even though he'd never seen them physically before today. For her part, she too feels an unexplained familiarity with him, and both feel an extraordinary attraction to each other – a coming home of the soul; a magical, intense feeling of unconditional love not of the Earth, a heavenly bliss; a telepathy, although they hadn't yet come to the realisation that they're actually one soul.

Although flustered, she tries to remain composed. 'Your accent tells me you're from England, sir. I have an auntie Rosella who lives there in a forest, a place called Essex. Do you know it?'

'Please stop calling me sir, and yeah, Essex is the county I'm from over in the UK,' he replies.

She can't help smiling as she says, 'Why are you staring?'

'Your eyes, I've seen them my whole life. They make me feel as though I've known you forever and tell me I've been guided to meet you here.' Yanson doesn't know where that thought or those words came from but felt good saying them, all the same.

'Thank you for your kind words, sir, I'm not used to those beautiful deeply spiritual compliments.'

'What's that boiling over there?' Yanson asks, pointing to a pot that his visitors had set heating over the fire. 'Is it like a tea?'

'A pot of Ayahuasca, got a feeling you'll like it, try some.'

She pours some out for him and passes him the cup. There are drink and drugs of every variety in the drinks cabinet or set out on a tray in Yanson's suite and Penelope helps herself to a huge line of cocaine before stripping off her dress revealing her stunningly attractive olive-skinned naked physique. She kicks off her shoes and eases her body into the Jacuzzi, dancing provocatively as she does so, turning away, twerking her bottom, hitting it off the water, turning to face him and smiling whilst fondling her vagina and silicone-enhanced breasts.

Yanson sits sipping the bitter oily-textured concoction she's given him as he watches her performance. Soon the concoction causes his mind to drift to ancient subconscious memories of Princess Gabi in the froth of the lagoon at the bottom of the waterfall dancing to the ceremonial music making the exact same movements as Penelope is doing now.

Penelope gets out the Jacuzzi and dries herself as provocatively as she got in, her fingers finding and lingering over her vagina and clitoris. She then gets into the bed, smiling at Yanson as she does so.

To Yanson something here jars with the deeply spiritual feelings he's experiencing, and something makes him throw her a gown and turn away to look out the window.

'Penelope, get out of the bed. I want you to want it the right way, not as doing your job.'

She looks puzzled, shocked but intrigued by what he's said. She smiles, gets up and joins him looking out of the window.

'Your eyes,' he repeats. 'I've seen them my whole life. I dreamed you as a kid. You lived with me at my Ibiza villa, and...'

She interrupts excitedly, 'You have a villa on Ibiza? Other than Jamaica, my favourite part of the world.'

'Me Dad's got an amazing place on Negril Beach, Jamaica as well; that's where my parents are from.'

'My God, you are so lucky, sir'

'Please, call me Yanson. I'm not a customer.'

'Ok Yanson, why did you pick me out of the other women?'

'Your eyes...' he replies smilingly and, to stop himself from talking about vibrations or visions of the ancient City of Koolah, adds 'and beautiful bottom, of course.'

But something makes her say, 'Yanson, they've renamed me

Penelope, not my name. My clairvoyant spiritual medium grandmother Dinah named me Princess because in another life I was a Black African Princess...'

He smiles. 'Princess, the name more than suits you; you have the look and presence of a fairy-tale princess, darling.'

She looks towards the tray with the drugs laid out on it and says, 'Let's do some of the MDMA; it gives the Ayahuasca a real kick. Come let's party.'

As she goes to the tray, she licks her finger and uses it to dab a huge amount and gently puts it near his lips. He touches it with the tip of his tongue before licking it off. His action gets her excited. He laughs as she licks her finger again and whilst looking directly into his eyes does the action as though she's performing oral sex.

As the couple stand getting high and getting to know one another, neither recognise the phantom astral body of Claudette in a distant corner of the room.

Victoria Sears' home, Woodford Green, Essex

In her hallway, Victoria puts back on her black cashmere overcoat covering her remarkable naked body, as Daniel finally opens the front door to leave. He looks back at the classy-looking Victoria as he steps outside. She slams the door shut behind him, and there's a sad look on his face as he walks the short distance to his parked car.

He doesn't see her this time but the woman he almost bumped into when he arrived is across the street moving slowly away from Victoria's house, the petite form of Claudette.

Daniel decides not to drive home but instead to take a drive through the ghetto streets of the East End of London, something he'd often do to reminisce, and for his senses to remain grounded and in touch.

CHAPTER 62

Mikhailov Palace

'Princess, you don't have to have sex with me,' Yanson says, 'although at this moment there's nothing I'd love more.'

She beckons him closer as if to whisper to him, but instead of speaking she kisses him and lovingly twirls her tongue inside his ear, awakening in the far reaches of his soul the memory of a blissful ancient Africa sensation he so loved when she did this during her Princess Gabi incarnation.

'Good,' she says pulling away, 'I don't wish to have sex with you...'

Yanson frowns and, her face serious, she continues, 'No, I don't ever want to have sex with you, the thought of it actually disturbs me, repulses even...'

Then after a few seconds pause, her face breaks into a smile and she adds, 'I don't wish to have sex; my wish is to make passionate love with you forever, Yanson,' and she begins to laugh excitedly. 'Just fucking with you. Fucking had you, admit it. Go on, Yanson, fucking admit it, you gorgeous bastard.'

As far as Yanson was concerned the pause before her comforting finale seemed to last an eternity. But even her laugh is familiar, and although the MDMA high delays his relieved reaction, he's soon laughing joyfully with her.

Then they share their first physical magical kiss in this life. For both, there's a knowing their whole lives were leading to this moment – an electrifying explosiveness, a knowing that they were kissing for the first time but that they'd somehow done so an infinite number of times before.

Outside, one of the guards is walking the inner perimeter wall with his guard dogs, four huge long-haired black Russian terriers.

To Yanson high on a mixture of Ayahuasca and a potent trippy MDMA they appear as lions, and he's sure he sees Koolah's black panther companion Jojo walking with them.

Princess is still laughing at the joke she's just pulled on him, and their soul grows ever more familiar. The character of her soul from the beginning of time and whilst living the life as Gabi was to be the joker, always fucking with people's minds, in the nicest way. She smiles, open-mouthed, eyes crossed, rocking her head to the beat of the music, moving her face too and from his. Again, her action prompts that familiar ancient feeling in him.

'I've met my soul mate,' he says simply.

'Why do you say that, Yanson? I felt the same the moment you arrived at the palace. Before I was told to get dressed and come up to the guest tower, I knew you were here, fucking strange...'

She breaks out into more joyful laughter, and as they touch they experience the Twin Flame sparks, a heaven-meeting-Earth sensation as though they were the only soul in the universe. They begin dancing around to the music in each other's arms, rocking to the beat as they did in their ancient African incarnations in the party celebration days of the magic circle. She jokingly pushes her palms against his chest, knocking him to the bed. He's surprised at the physical strength her body possesses. She lies on top of him, stops laughing and both smile looking into one another's eyes.

Then both speak at the same time saying, 'We've kissed before.'

They laugh together and she adds, 'Fuck, I've felt this incredible feeling before.'

He nods in agreement as they kiss and begin caressing one another, he undoing her dressing gown and she undressing him. And after a time, it seemed they shared a never-ending pleasurable rotation of sex, oral sex and French kissing – he licking her clitoris, she licking, masturbating and sucking his penis, he lovingly sucking her breasts, kissing and fucking one another, each and every way imaginable. The couple had entered that unique love zone, in tune for hours, as one with the interaction.

Panting with pleasure she asks, 'I know you have many women, tell me the one who is special to your heart, Koolah,' and neither of them realise she's just called him by his ancient African name.

Yanson doesn't know what to say. He thinks of but doesn't mention the only love in his life that's caused him no end of heartbreak, an East London blonde White girl, Joanne. He mentions Gemma, the mother of his Colombian child, but knows he's never felt the same vibration before that he feels with Princess.

Princess stands over him, resting a stiletto on the edge of the bed and positioning herself perfectly so that his stiffened twirling tongue can find her clitoris. The sight at that moment of her feminine abdominal muscles and perfect implant breasts is one Yanson would remember forever. The moment, more than ever, connects their souls with the ancient Koolah days, and he strongly feels the unmistakable sexual vibration of the Black Princess, Gabi.

'Yanson, from the moment I saw you the non-use of the condom was never an issue,' she says.

'I swore I'd never go down on a call girl but...'

She pulls herself away and puts a finger against his lip. 'Silence Yanson, shoosh,' she says before they begin French kissing and masturbating one another.

Downstairs in the main hall of the palace, the elderly Russian mafia boss Mikhailov sits in a trance sharing a vision with the astral travelling Claudette. The vision shows Princess's grandmother Dinah on her deathbed in her gypsy caravan in Romania.

'She's one of us,' Claudette says, 'a powerful Twin Flame foundation spirit angel of the Koolah tribe magic circle. Her soul is to pass on and re-enter heaven tonight. Princess Gabi's heaven will accommodate her, she and Koolah will be her parents in her next life...'

Gypsy caravan site, Bucharest, Romania

Princess's elder brother Django is almost the image of his olive-skinned sister but slim and masculine with light hazel eyes and dark hair. He sits alone at his grandmother Dinah's bedside in her traditional gypsy caravan in Romania Eastern Europe, the home of European Voodoo.

Tears roll down her elderly face as Dinah continuously repeats, 'Where's Princess? Django, where is our Princess?'

Django says nothing of his sister's disappearance; he doesn't want to worry his grandmother on her deathbed. He simply leans down to the bed and hugs her, but with their heads nuzzled together, Django suddenly feels his psychic grandmother knows something of Princess's disappearance anyway.

Dinah whispers in his ear, 'I'm going now, Django. Tell Princess she'll deliver me from heaven and I'll remain with her for the rest of her life. Later you'll both know what I mean. I'm going now, grandson... Your sister's soul is that of the Earth's most authentic Princess. During that life, I was also her grandmother, mother of her mother Queen Lulu, Queen of the Koolah tribe. That is why I insisted your mother name her Princess again. Django, don't let him get away with what he did to Princess...'

Django holds his grandmother's hand as he says, 'Nana, nana, lately I keep seeing the village which you spoke about when me and Princess were children...'

'I'll see you soon, Django,' Dinah repeats, her body weakening. 'Don't let him get away with what he did to Princess.'

'Nana?' As he looks into her eyes, Django realises she has gone and that these were to be her dying words. Through his sobs, he whispers, 'Don't let who...? as he wonders who she was talking about and what it was they must not get away with.

CHAPTER 63

Mikhailov Palace

At the same time as Dinah was dying in Django's arms, Yanson's penis was inside Princess, the pair of them about to climax together, her body shuddering.

As the sun rises, after a night of MDMA and sex, Princess recalls seeing the face of her grandmother vividly during the lovemaking, and without knowing exactly when or how she knows during the intercourse her grandmother Dinah had spiritually connected to her. Dinah's words and face, and the love she and Yanson are creating, are the only things clear in her mind.

Yanson looks to see it becoming daylight outside and realises they've spent many hours making love.

'Bet Gemma nu ti-a dat-o a fel bine ca asta, scumpo,' Princess whispers, words meaning I bet Gemma hasn't give it to you as good as this, darling.

'I don't know what you just fucking said,' Yanson replies, 'but keep the Romanian language coming. I could definitely get into that. By the way, there's something very sexy about the way your lips move.'

'Was it good for you, Mr Bailey... you ok?'

'Oh yeah,' he replies with a look of contentment on his face. 'I certainly am now, my Princess.'

Shortly, both relax contentedly in the hot soothing bath, their bodies at either end facing one another, her legs on top of his torso, feet on his shoulders. Her intoxicated mind drifts to recent dreams of Koolah and his companion Jojo, of the man in her company now, Yanson Bailey. The dream memories and the vibration between them now tell her that in a short space of time, for the first time in her life, she's met a man she can share anything with. And, although she decides she will save talk of her ancient tribal memories until she is more straight headed, less high, she knows, deep in the soul, she can trust Yanson Bailey and decides she's going to ask him for his help.

Her insecurities must have shown on her face as Yanson asks, 'What's wrong? Tell me what's wrong, Princess…'

She gets out of the bath in silence, looks out of the window, her stunning naked body dripping wet, soaked pubic hairs now straightened downward. She makes her way to the centre of the room, gets a towel, and leans in to kiss him.

'Please Yanson, take me from here, you have the influence, they respect you…'

A moment of panic, a fear she will put Yanson in an awkward position with his business partners, makes her break off her words and abruptly change the subject. 'The Colombian Gemma, what has she given you, a boy or girl?'

'A girl called Emily,' Yanson replies automatically as Princess dresses hurriedly and is rushing around getting ready to leave.

'Where are you going?' he asks in alarm. 'And what was you saying about me taking you away from here?'

'Yanson, ok I want you to listen,' she replies after a pause during which the face of Koolah appeared in her mind. 'They'll be here to get me in a minute. Don't think I'm crazy, but I often dream of your face as I see you now and also in another form, another body looking over me.' She begins to cry as she speaks. 'Please help me away from these people. I miss my grandmother Dinah, my mother and my brother Django. Haven't seen them for four months.' With a smile she adds, 'My mother is so pretty. She's known as the queen of our gypsy community.'

Yanson's shocked by what he's heard. 'You're not allowed to leave?'

She looks into his eyes and with a shake of the head says, 'No, they have me here held prisoner.'

CHAPTER 64

Princess's expression shows a sadness she feels; sadness due to the younger Russian Mafia family members having explained to her Yanson's a highly valued contact throughout the international underworld, a trustworthy businessman. She begins to feel an inferiority complex in regard to her teenage call-girl hustler antics, having acted as bait getting other Romanian gang members into the homes and business premises of unwitting mega-wealthy criminal victims, high-earning cocaine traffickers and other wealthy criminals. Eastern European gangs used her uniquely youthful angelic pretty looks, body and naturally provocative mannerism to lure their prey to hotels or other establishments to be kidnapped and held for ransom. The MDMA high causes all types of negativity to begin creeping in. She begins thinking of the gangs she'd worked with and her high-level international cocaine trafficker victims Yanson may be associated with. Princess frustratingly explains her current situation.

'No, my cousin tricked me,' she tries to explain. 'Ok, like every young girl, I wanted to be seen in the latest Gucci designer fabrics, Louis Vuitton accessories, Cartier jewellery, and my own German car. Four months ago I was in Ibiza broke and my cousin talked me into doing one weekend's work for good money. I was photo'd naked and in lingerie, a particular wealthy businessman picked me, and before I knew it, I was flown across and kept here in Moscow.'

Suddenly Princess pictures her nana Dinah in her mind again. She can see Dinah in her vardo, her brightly painted Romany wagon home; see her face; see her on her deathbed.

'Yanson, my nana I feel her spirit sort of within me as though she's suddenly close. She's dying, or for all I know she could be already dead. When I was a little girl, I'd visit her caravan and

481

we'd sit speaking for hours. She'd help me self-hypnotise and practise regression reading on me. I saw myself as a little African girl, an ancient Princess from a royal family. Nana said she lived as my grandmother in that life too. I was the younger of two daughters in Africa thousands of years ago. She explained her sickness will kill her, but not to worry, her spirit will come to me and stay with me my whole life.'

A look of anger crosses her face. 'I trusted and always looked up to my elder cousin, more like an uncle, twelve years older. He sold me. My cousin knew I'm Nana's favourite and she'd be heartbroken. He told me never to try and contact my family because there's nothing they could do and the Russian mafia here would have my family in Romania and Ibiza killed if they tried anything. They own the Russian police; the army's generals come to the palace for entertainment. They have my passport, Yanson. I once asked a guest if I could use his mobile and he told on me. I feel I can ask for your help...'

She begins crying, and, her insecurities heightened by the MDMA comedown, sobs, 'Look Yanson, never mind...'

He caresses her neck and cheek. 'You say that you dream about me, Gabi?'

She laughs through her tears. 'My God, you just called me Gabi! And yes, but you, we look different in what seems a different world. We're both Black and you have a friend, a black leopard...'

Her words send shockwaves through him. 'Princess, I've seen the black panther. I've dreamed him often and my girl. Princess Gabi, you're leaving here with me; I'll not leave Moscow without you.'

She smiles and, looking down at his semi-erect penis, giggles, 'You have to take me with you, I could get use' to that.' Then more seriously she adds, 'You called me Gabi. My God, it's all making sense now.'

'What... what's making sense?' Yanson asks, although he's sure he already knows what.

'Yanson, when I was just a little girl, Nana Dinah told me of this fairy-tale evening, tonight. It's you, you've come to rescue me, you're the one, and we will have a child and one day marry. I promise I'll respect your deepest innermost wishes and have our best interests at heart. You can come and go as you please, but all I ask is you allow me to share your pillow forever.'

'Sounds perfect,' he replies, 'and I have to say I've never met a woman that I feel I instantly want to share my life with like I do you. Princess, I don't know why, but from the moment we met I've felt I had to introduce you to someone dear to me, Julie. It's as though I know deep within me the two of you share a spiritual connection.'

She smiles but says, 'Yanson, I've got to leave now to return to my quarters. I've asked you to get me out of Russia, but I promise I won't ask you again and will leave it in the hands of the universe, God.'

Later Yanson rests in bed, his pleasurably sore penis, aching emptied testicles and aching tongue muscles reminding him of the sexual activity he and Princess had shared. There's a knock at the door, and Yanson wonders if she's returned — already he's feeling as though a part of himself is missing; there's a feeling of emptiness throughout the entire room. He pulls the sheet over the bottom half of his naked body in case it's not her, and calls out, 'Yeah, come.'

To his disappointment a well-dressed male servant enters with a tray. 'Your coffee, Mr Bailey. Mr Mikhailov is expecting you at breakfast in forty minutes.'

After the servant has left, Yanson looks for his mobile to begin making calls. He produces a scrap piece of paper from his luggage and, still slightly high on the MDMA, taps the number that's written on it into his phone. As the receiving mobile begins to ring, Princess's words weigh on his mind. He thinks about the sick grandmother she's not able to see, but most of all he thinks deeply about the personal love feelings he has for the Romanian girl with the eyes he'd previously seen in both incarnations, the African Princess Gabi and the Romany Princess.

CHAPTER 65

Victoria Park Road, Hackney, East London

A tired and exhausted Daniel Cottle had fallen asleep in his car parked next to the huge Victoria Park. The ringing of his satellite phone wakes him and he scrambles around the passenger seat to find it. When he looks to see who the caller is he smiles and answers it, still half asleep but excited to hear from his friend, 'Wa gwan, Dread, ah where you deh?'

'Moscow,' Yanson, on the other end of the line, replies.

'Fucking Moscow, you're moving serious, Yancey Dread. Fuck you doing there?'

'Yeah, head of the family wanted to fucking see me, some Russian mafia bullshit, he can't leave Russia just yet, Interpol would like to speak to him in regards to a few matters. Listen to this one, blood…' and Yanson goes on to explain his encounter with Princess.

Daniel's shocked at what he's hearing. 'You fucking what, Dread? People dem trow you a peng ting and you wasn't gonna tek de slam?'

'Jarrod, she was one of us, an let me tell you, she lickle punany sweet. Bro, I fucked her and fucked her and fucked her till her juicy little poom poom couldn't be fucked anymore, then did it again and again, we both loved it, trust man. Jarrod, I'll call you back in a minute, just got to call Julie…'

'Cool Dread, no problem.'

Mikhailov Palace

Yanson makes his next call to Julie Marney and she answers straightaway.

'Yance, how are you?' she says sounding tired but happy to hear from him.

'Yeah, it's all jiggy here, so stop worrying. Did you get your flight sorted?'

'Yeah,' Julie answers excitedly, 'Stacey booked them earlier, last thing yesterday, and we're booked into a lovely hotel on the strip.'

'You should have come stayed with me in my place; I got five bedrooms.'

'Stacey didn't want to; you know what she's like, likes her privacy and gets all shy and starstruck around you lot. Little bit weird like that is our Stacey.' Julie looks at her bedroom clock and adds, 'Fucking seven, is that the time, Yance?'

'Sorry, I know you're not an early riser, forgot the time difference.'

A little while later Yanson is walking towards the palace's dining room for his breakfast appointment. In all the excitement of the encounter with Princess, he'd forgotten about the revelation concerning Mikhailov himself, arising from the vision he received in his bathtub the previous evening. The sight of the elderly Russian with the grey dreadlocks sitting alone at the breakfast table brings it back to his mind.

'Your hair,' he stutters.

'My hair, yes people often remark on it. I like it this way. Take a seat, my friend.'

Yanson does as he's bid, sitting down in the chair Mikailov indicated. 'I meant to mention it yesterday, I recognise your hair, Mr Mikhailov, recognise you, the both of us from a dream, in fact.'

The Russian Godfather smiles joyfully, his hands trembling. 'Seen us in dreams, I dare say you have.'

'Talk about fucking déjà vu, why is it I feel I know you?' Yanson asks.

The mafia Godfather doesn't answer but just smiles beatifically.

Yanson decides to get straight to the point regarding Princess. 'I have to take Penelope with me. You have my word, she'll not speak of this place to anyone.'

Mikhailov raises a palm in a gesture of submission. 'Two things Mr Bailey, firstly your word is valued above all, secondly she's not for sale.'

Yanson goes to stand up and object, but Mikailov bids him, 'Please be seated Mr Bailey and allow me to explain…'

Nevertheless, Yanson interrupts him. 'Sir, you don't understand my feelings in regards to this girl. Look, half a million Euros, an extra twenty kilos of cocaine delivered in Ibiza with your next delivery, I have to leave with my Princess…'

Mikhailov raises a hand. 'Please Mr Bailey, Mr Bailey… Koolah, allow me to speak. She's not mine to give you, and call me old fashioned, but I've just recently learned she was not here totally of her free will. You sir, take your Princess with my blessing.'

The Russian Godfather is cursing himself for having inadvertently called Yanson by the name Koolah, but Yanson himself is too astounded by the Godfather's response to have even noticed.

'Princess is neither mine neither anybody else's property to sell or give away,' Mikhailov continues. 'By the way, I rarely visit my Moscow palace and only God knows what my organisation, especially my sons, get up to here. I had no knowledge of her being in my home against her will. Now take her with our blessing.'

About twenty minutes later, a nervous Princess enters the dining room.

'You're coming with me, my Princess.' Yanson says with a reassuring smile. 'Get your things together. We've to wait a while for your passport. I'm on the flight to Madrid tonight and you'll be flying Paris France in the morning, connecting Ibiza.'

After the lovers have left the Russian Godfather alone in the room, he stands and his joyful soul momentarily moves his body as it did at the ceremonial parties in ancient Africa.

Ibiza, Balearic Islands, Spain

Two days later Princess wakes at Yanson's classy villa, trying to work out when her mind recently visualised her grandmother.

Was it a previous night in Russia, or waking just then? On her mind there's still a beautiful picture of her grandmother's face and the sound of her voice softly saying the words, 'Princess, please stop feeling bad about not being with me when I passed through. It was not your fault. I am – my soul is – with you in heaven. I will physically be with you soon. Princess, avenge your cousin for what he did.'

Happy at the fact her grandmother came to her in the dream reassuring her, Princess sits up in bed with a smile. No stranger to luxurious surroundings, she feels at home in Yanson's villa with him sleeping at her side; but there's something more, more than the fact that Yanson's Ibiza home is kitted out to the highest order, more than the pleasurable ache in her vagina that told of the sex they'd enjoyed – there's a feeling she has of knowing she's been there before.

Yanson wakes next to her and they share an uncontrollable smile – a smile that let's each other know how they feel without the need for words.

She gets up, puts his dressing gown on and goes to explore the home she's newly arrived in. In the downstairs living room, she hears a woman humming from an adjacent bathroom. She looks through the gap where the door is slightly ajar to see an attractive voluptuous local Mediterranean woman of around thirty years of age preening herself in the mirror: putting on make-up, undoing the top buttons of her blouse, puffing out her huge breasts and squeezing them out her bra, making sure her provocative suspender belt and garters are showing. Princess says nothing, and instead sits on the sofa, cross-legged, waiting.

Within a few moments, the woman emerges from the ground floor bathroom. The look on her face shows she's surprised to see Princess on the sofa wearing Yanson's bathrobe and a proud smile. The local woman is Yanson's cleaning woman, herself attractive but not in the same league as Princess. The cleaner busies herself with her work, feeling both annoyed and intrigued by Princess's presence. After a little while, the two exchange some words in Spanish.

Upstairs, Yanson hears their voices, and realising it was the day for his more-than-personal cleaner's visit, he sits up quickly, saying out loud, 'Fuck, it's Friday, Magdalena, fuck, fuck, fuck…'

He throws himself back, head hitting the pillow, as downstairs Princess points to the huge state-of-the-art TV and directs, 'Please don't forget to dust and polish the TV, noticed a lot of dust gathering on it when myself and my husband came home from the airport late last night.'

After an agonising wait, Yanson sees Princess coming back into the bedroom. It's obvious she knows he and his cleaner have a sexual relationship. 'I get it,' she says smiling, 'but Yanson…'

'Yeah, what is it baby?' he says sheepishly.

'I think it's time we changed our cleaner and found someone more suitable, Mr Bailey.'

He smiles a defeated smile. 'Anything you request, Mrs Bailey.'

'Mrs Princess Bailey, yes, certainly could get use to that,' she says and they begin to kiss again, as downstairs Magdalena sourly gets on with her job.

'Yanson,' Princess says when they have finished kissing. 'I dreamed about you many times in Russia. Strange fucking beautifully complicated dreams in ancient Africa and we were obviously a Black couple. One dream showed we were in Jamaica and had a black panther beast with us. We walked toward a crowd, like a party all eating food and looking at us. And this is the crazy part, when we got closer to the people, we saw you and I, like we were different people talking to us as we are now, talking to ourselves as other people.' She places her hand over her mouth. 'Please don't think I'm crazy.'

He shakes his head and the look in his eyes tells her he feels she's anything but crazy. Moments later they're again vocally making love. They'd both forgotten about Magdalena downstairs and at the sound of the cleaner slamming the door on her way out, they stop, laugh together and in a short while carry on where they left off.

Later that evening, Yanson sits on a poolside bed making a phone call, watching the sunset. Princess joins him on the luxury sunbed, smiling at him. The sight of her dainty but curvy body causes him to end the call abruptly. He knows he wants her to remain with him more than anything, but has to be sure of her feelings.

'Princess, you're now free,' he says. 'You don't have to stay here with me.'

A look of disappointment crosses her face, and she says sincerely, 'Yanson, you couldn't force me to leave your side. I'd rather take my own life. I'd never find another love out there to match the richness of our soul. How can I leave you, Koolah? We are joined at the soul; you can't run away from yourself. We're lovers in every life, couldn't leave you if I wanted.'

'Why do you call me Koolah and how did you know that we're lovers in each life? How do you know all that?'

Tears run down her face. 'I told you, I've called you it before we met in Russia in another place, another time. I've known you three days and on the flight here I thought deeply of our meeting in Russia and what we spoke about. Seeing your face in the arrivals last night, that feeling, the vibration told me we're soul mates, darling. I remembered something else on the flight over. Since I was a little girl, Nana always said my knight in shining armour would rescue me from the evil palace and we'd have everything, love in abundance...'

'I'd love to have met your nana,' Yanson says.

'Oh, you would have got on great.'

They kiss and can't help touching one another sexually, but they're interrupted by Yanson's phone ringing. He answers it and after listening to what's been said gives his orders, 'Yeah, pick up Mr Mosquera from the airport and bring him to the usual spot.'

His Colombian business partners were landing a major shipment of cocaine on the island and Yanson needed to be on hand to supervise receiving it and securing payment.

'Princess,' he says to her after finishing the call, 'I've arranged to meet some guys throughout today. Their employees have just docked with my product, important business. I'll be back this evening and we'll party.'

Princess tries her best to disguise her nervousness at having heard the name Mosquera. She knows who he is: a major cocaine trafficker she and her gang once ripped off in Madrid, a man who could identify her.

Nevertheless, she smiles and says, 'No it's cool, really, you do what you have to. I got to go meet my brother Django and old friends. They were all really eager to meet you.'

Yanson gently taps his own forehead. 'Oh I forgot, Julie's over today as well. Can you keep her company till later and we'll all get together?'

'Yes, no problem, it will be nice to meet some of your friends. Yanson, I want you to listen. I always speak the truth to those I love. You can keep Gemma and the others, but please, I wish to remain your gypsy Princess. I'm not a weak woman, but I understand you and agree with the laws of nature, you're a King and deserved to be treated so. Just the respect as your alpha lioness is all I'll ever ask.'

Her words bring a truly vibrant smile to his face.

Later that morning, Princess is lounging, sunbathing on the huge balcony sunbed, and there's a ring on the doorbell. As she's walking to the door, she feels pleasantly light-headed and before she opens it she starts to feel the Koolah tribe chemistry between herself and the two people on the other side of the door, Julie Marney and Stacey Holley.

'Hello, you must be Julie and Stacey; you're both beautiful, just like how Yanson described you. Come on in.'

'You're beautiful too,' Stacey says and Julie nods in agreement, both women feeling the Koolah tribe chemistry too and subconsciously aware that Princess embodies a soul their both familiar with.

'I'm afraid Yanson's not here,' Princess explains. 'He has some business with guys come from overseas, won't be in till later today. He's asked me to look after you. I know the island very well, lived out here a few years already.'

CHAPTER 66

Santa Eulalia, Ibiza

A moped rider and his passenger cruise the main strip, shops, bars and restaurants. The passenger's on the lookout for easy pickings and is eyeing up the gold diamond-encrusted Rolex he's spotted on a foreign lady's wrist. She's sitting with two other women, but as the moped team are ready to go into action, the three women are joined by four more people: another woman, an Italian man, an Eastern European man and a short stocky Black man wearing Gucci sunglasses.

The moped passenger is off the bike; helmet still on, tinted visor down, as he enters the restaurant and pretends to look at the menu board whilst getting ready to make his play for the Rolex.

But one of the newcomers, the Eastern European Django is on his feet, not only does he know what the moped passenger is wanting to do but he also recognises him. 'You got a problem with the ladies, Marku?' Django asks.

'Didn't recognise it was you sat there, Django,' Marku says sheepishly, at that moment recognising Django's sister, Princess, too, who previously had her back to him. 'You're back,' he says to her, 'but you look so different. Honestly you look beautiful.'

Princess, who had been on many a criminal enterprise with Marku in the past, smiles at him, saying, 'Marku, I thought they'd deported you back to Romania after your last arrest. How are you?'

'Deported yeah, but after twelve months I used my brother's passport to come back.'

'Can be beneficial having a twin, Marku,' Princess says.

'I think Marku was admiring your Rolex,' Django says to Julie

Marney, and she understands his meaning and also knows that Django's thwarted Marku's would-be robbery.

The would-be robber Marku himself is all too ready to make his excuses and leave, and in a moment he's back on the back of the moped speeding off.

'Thanks Django,' Julie says, beginning to feel smitten by Princess's handsome brother, who seems equally attracted to her.

He smiles, gently holding her wrist. 'No problem, Julie, but you have to remember my countrymen love the Rolex and like to take it rather than paying for it, ok.'

Julie turns to Princess and says, 'You know, only two things make a woman blossom as beautiful as you are, shopping's one...'

Princess purses her lips as though to indicate she's in deep thought, but actually thinking about the amazing vibration caused by the way she and Yanson are currently making love. 'Julie, let's just say I haven't been doing any shopping in a good while.'

The women laugh.

Yanson's Ibiza villa

Later that evening, Yanson and Princess lie in bed naked after making love. She's had her hair cut and styled in a shorter classy bob style and he can't stop smiling at it.

'Love your hair, babe. My God, Princess, you were designed for me. The female wanting to be the dominant partner, wanting to be the man, goes against the laws of nature and is unbalancing relationships. The lioness couldn't equally rule a pride breeding six males and they bear her cubs. Princess, I love nothing more than a strong beautiful woman. A King cannot rule his kingdom without the strength produced from the love of a natural, alpha Queen. A lion couldn't defend the pride without the love and spiritual strength of his alpha Queen lioness. You understand the laws of nature, Princess.'

The familiar Koolah city soul tribe vibration flows through them at that moment prompting another passionate kiss.

Princess pulls away from Yanson. 'That just then was a sort of déjà vu. We've only just met and yet I know you've explained creation's law of human nature to me before in another place, another time.

I fucking love you, you're my knight in shining armour… you make me feel like the children's storybook fairy-tale Princess you rescued from the evil palace tower, remember?'

Yanson smiles, delighted by her words. 'Darling,' he says in a sombre tone. 'I have to go to London in a day or so to take care of some business. I'll be back but, you can make yourself at home here. We'll live together here. This is our home now.'

'Our home,' she nods, but he detects a worried look on her face.

'Is everything alright?' he asks.

'I was just thinking of Nana, that's all.'

Princess could strangely see and hear in her mind her grandmother on her deathbed as the dying woman were speaking to her directly saying, 'I will soon physically be with you. Princess, avenge your cousin for what he did.'

She brings her mind back to the present and says, 'Our home… Oh Yanson, that's so sweet. It seems we share the love I feel for you. But, Yanson, listen, I have to fly to Romania to see mother with my brother Django tomorrow night. We are to bury Nana in a few days. I was actually going to ask you to come but it's not necessary.'

'Anything Princess, if you wish for me to come…'

'No, you have business to attend to. You've met Django; he's known of your strength on the island and Spain. I wish to tell Nana and Muma of our love and will be back home to you directly after the funeral. You obviously know life is cheap in countries like Russia. Django can't stop speaking about you, singing your praises of how you saved his sister. He's actually told friends he'd take a bullet for you, Yanson.'

Princess takes a plastic bag containing MDMA powder. 'This is the best on the island. Tonight we hit the town and party, my husband.'

Both dab some of the powder, and Yanson puts some house

493

music on, loud. 'Let me quickly get showered and dressed. I'll let Pacha know we're coming and reserve us a table.'

CHAPTER 67

Yanson comes from out of the shower to see a naked and smiling Princess blow-drying her hair. They're already both extremely high on the powerful MDMA.

'What you smiling at, Gabi?'

'Uh…' She doesn't hear the question, but turns off the hair dryer and raises her head questioningly.

'What you smiling at?'

She laughs a little. 'Oh, just happy to be here with you, but you just called me Gabi again then, didn't you? Second time you called me Gabi, need to make sense of it. There's something deeply connected between us and this name Gabi. My Nana was an old gypsy clairvoyant Voodoo witch. She practically raised me from birth and always called me Gabi. I told you earlier she explained I was an African Princess in another life and I feel somehow I'm becoming familiar with how come you know the name. Strange.'

'Your grandmother told you that, strange coincidence, my Princess. Don't know why I began calling you Gabi.'

A tear rolls down Princess's cheek.

'Don't cry, why are you crying?' Yanson asks, and, both naked, they hug one another.

'Yanson, I spoke to my brother on the telephone yesterday and he told me Nana... she'd passed away the night we met, darling. Since then she's come to me in a dream explaining she was in my heaven and something about coming back to me soon. She always spoke that way, of things I couldn't understand. But anyway,' she adds trying for the moment not to worry about what her grandmother meant, 'let's go dance. I've missed dancing at a party. Where did you say we're going?'

'My guys from Colombia, guys I met today, I've invited them to party with us at Pacha.'

495

Earlier this reply might have worried Princess, but she'd got her brother to ask around and it wasn't the same Mosquera cocaine trafficking organisation they'd ripped off in Madrid a year ago. The previous gang had been arrested and convicted in mainland Spain of cocaine importation charges.

Pacha Night Club, Ibiza

Yanson and Princess are in the club partying, totally loved up, on the centre of the dance floor, clenching one another in their subconscious soul memory of ancient Koolah ceremonial parties, dancing to the beat of quality house music. Earlier in the villa, the sight of Princess in her clubbing outfit had taken Yanson's breath away: she wore stiletto-heeled, thigh-high white boots and short Gucci mac that barely extended down far enough to cover her shapely bottom and the tops of her provocative thighs. Now, Princess decides to blow Yanson's, and every other man in the club's, mind by taking off and putting down her mac-type jacket, to reveal just a skimpy cream-coloured Gucci swimsuit, the revealing costume perfectly complementing her body.

Enhanced by the MDMA high, Yanson's mind focuses on her angelic dancing. Princess's soul moves her body in the same way Princess Gabi danced in the days of Koolah. She dances around, repeatedly twirling in front of Yanson, showing off her amazing protruding sexy rounded bottom and elegantly powerful feminine legs. She pulls him close and he thinks she wants to whisper something to him but instead she twirls her soaking wet tongue in his ear, again creating the Koolah ceremonial party familiarity, bringing back another blissful sensation.

She pulls him close again. 'Yanson, I know we've just met and everything but what I want most in this world is to give you a child.'

Dancing, she crosses her eyes and repeatedly rolls her shoulders to the rhythm, moving her torso back and forth, wobbling her head, twirling around wiggling her gorgeous bottom, her nose almost touching his nose. As she repeats her silly dance move, the soul of Koolah looks through her eyes, deep into her soul. As he comes from inside her, his mind can't yet fathom what's happened. He's no longer dancing with his Romanian girlfriend Princess; it's Gabi instead in the open air on the Koolah coast, and instead of Julie Marney and Stacey in their company, it's Gabi's sister Monifa and another Koolah soul tribe angel. The magical sensation lasts a few moments and then his mind's conscious back inside the Ibiza nightclub.

Claudette emerges from the crowd to stand close by Yanson and Princess. She places an arm around Yanson and Princess, and at first the Twin Flame lovers think it's just another loved-up raver wanting to be friendly — but there's more to it than that. Claudette knows this is the beginning of the soul tribe reunion and can feel the Twin Flame vibration from Yanson and Princess's souls having reunited, and all the Koolah souls present are feeling their unique, ancient, deeply divine, spiritual bond. Julie Marney and Princess don't know why they're unable to stop hugging one another. The MDMA is giving them the same trippy feeling their Koolah souls felt as biological sisters intoxicated on the ancient tribal love juice.

With the strobe light and other lighting effects in action, the nightclub smoke machine is turned on and suddenly fills the dance floor head high with smoke. Julie Marney closes her eyes and finds herself dancing as Monifa moving to the same house beat but on the ancient African beach not an Ibiza nightclub. Trancelike, intoxicated on the love juice and non-satanic Earth tropical atmosphere, Monifa's dancing close to Koolah, Gabi and others amid the head-height off-white mist of the magic circle, her mind in a state of pure ecstasy.

In ancient Africa, Monifa in turn becomes conscious of her future regression state: the vibration of the 20th century atmosphere; the interior of the futuristic Ibiza nightclub; the future incarnations of her ancient soul tribe, the White gypsy Princess, Black Londoner Yanson and others dancing and enjoying the music. With Princess, she experiences a remarkable soul familiarity.

In Ibiza, Julie Marney knows Princess is the girl she's grown up with in her childhood dreams, knows she's the future soul reincarnation of Princess Gabi – the distinctive colouring of her eyes, her body shape, but most of all the unique spiritual vibration she felt from Princess told her so.

Julie and Princess hug again, and Princess says in her ear, 'Yanson tells me when you were little at school you used to tell him you dreamed of having a Black sister with a blonde streak in her hair.' Princess holds up the dark strand that grows from her temple. 'Was it in the same place as this?'

Julie looks into Princess's eyes. 'Since I was a kid I've dreamed us being sisters. Gabi, you have the same eye, and what's really crazy is I know she is somehow you. From the moment we met I've felt the same beautiful feeling you gave me in my childhood dreams.'

'Oh fucking hell, you as well, Julie,' Princess says, feeling an amazing rush of euphoria. 'You called me Gabi.'

By now Yanson and Princess are extremely high on the powerful MDMA powder. The music the DJ plays carries a deeper, sweeter, more heavenly, rhythmic vibe that again catches Princess's soul, bringing her Princess Gabi incarnation to life – but now Princess not only feels Princess Gabi's spirit but actually sees a vision of her ancient African self. Princess Gabi, the equally beautiful ancient indigenous Princess of the Koolah tribe, is looking directly back at her. Gabi's dressed only in a tan suede G-string and slightly heeled clog-like shoes. She dances angelically, mouth pouted, feet shoulder length apart, gyrating her hips and seemingly looking up to the ceiling of the nightclub but in the magic circle tribal dimension looking up out to space and to the stars. The ancient African Princess shows her modern incarnation how to do the dance movement, shaking her head side to side, twirling her index finger head high.

Gabi physically places her palm on Princess's neck and gently caresses it as she speaks to her in ancient Koolah. 'Allow our soul to move your body to the rhythm; this is part of our way of praying before they forced their religions upon us. Yanson's soul will connect to the love vibration.'

Princess understands the instruction and begins mimicking the dance movement with ease, the characteristic of her inner soul. Gabi rewards Princess with a kiss, their identically shaped bodies coming together in an embrace before Gabi's form disappears. But as Princess dances with Yanson, again the dimension phases cross. For a moment, Yanson sees Princess as Princess Gabi and sees the black panther Jojo affectionately brushing his body against her thigh. Yanson is sure the black panther then looked lovingly towards him, asking him to stroke its head – but not yet fully understanding the crossing of physical dimension phases, the Black Londoner tells himself he must be hallucinating.

But the way Princess is dancing – mouth pouted, feet shoulder length apart, gyrating her hips, looking upward, shaking her head, twirling her index finger next to her head – continues to stir subconscious memories and feelings in Yanson's mind.

For Princess, at that moment, the crossing of dimension phases is again even stronger. She sees Yanson as Koolah and the vibration tells her that in another dimension she'd been totally in love with the African man with the dreadlocks, but furthermore she knows the soul of that man with the dreadlocks is Yanson.

Princess takes from her purse a little clear plastic bag, and, without realising she's speaking in the ancient Koolah language, says to Yanson, 'It's all making sense now. Nana always spoke specifically about you, oh my God...'

Somehow Yanson understands her words, and she continues, 'For as long as I can remember, since I was a little girl, at least once each year, my Nana Dinah told me what you were doing in your London life and I could feel the love she had for you. Nana loved the Black race, Yanson; some from our gypsy community couldn't understand why. We are the Twin Flame, one soul, a soul divided into two and our purpose in life is finding one another and the love we create making the planet more positive and loving. When she spoke of you, I felt the sad trauma you went through as a child. She would always say one day I'd get a chance to help make it better for you because the day we meet our soul would be whole again.'

He interrupts, 'We saved one another, Princess.'

She smiles and carries on speaking. 'I can hear her words as clear as when she spoke them all those years ago: "Princess, you and your Twin Flame will have a little girl together; you're to name her Dinah." She explained we, us and Nana, we'd be inseparable. I know about your childhood. Your brothers and sister are mixed race and you have a White stepfather, your auntie Elsie named you, right?'

Yanson nods in amazement as Princess continues, 'When I was growing up, she'd look into her crystal ball, turning tarot cards for you sending protection, love and light. She'd look into her crystal ball for hours every day. Told me I'd have Gabi's bum again, the Black girl's beautiful bum. She would never tell me too much about what you'd look like, said her soul tribe were asked not to spoil the surprise. Nana told me I was designed for you, you're a uniquely special soul I'd been in love with many times, and I'd know you when I met you. Didn't understand what she meant and lost faith until we met. In that Russian palace I gave up hope on her words, but then you came.'

She dabs some more MDMA, puts it in his mouth, and dabs some for herself. 'Told you earlier you're my knight in shining armour.'

'Wow, this magic is fucking good,' he says. 'What is it we drank in Russia the other day?'

She smiles. 'Oh that... a pot of Ayahuasca. Yanson, for the past I don't know how long, I've known I'm someone else in my body. Like our souls live somewhere else, but we've become conscious in the bodies we're in now.'

Yanson says nothing, and he and Princess finger-dab yet more of the powder. She goes to whisper in his ear but instead twirls her tongue inside it, again giving him that familiar ancient Koolah soul tribe tingling loving sensation.

They both laugh and she pulls him in, so he can hear her over the loudness of the music. 'Crazy high, this MDMA, Yanson. I saw this Black girl earlier. She was not showing me but reminding me how to move to the beat.'

'I saw her too,' Yanson replies.

She gazes at him excitedly. 'What... you saw her?'

Yanson proudly smiles. 'Yeah, Princess, I saw her as well. Listen, you've made me so fucking proud, I've truly found my fairy-tale Princess.'

A little later Yanson's stood at the bar, talking to friends – some of those he calls his Ibiza family, among them the Italian they called Rome and the Black Frenchman, Antoine – both prolific jewellery robbers.

The charismatic Rome, dressed in Italian designer fashions of the day complimenting his olive skin and silver-fox grey hair, suddenly finds himself locking eyes with Claudette.

'Hello again Raphael,' the pretty Haitian witch says.

'No sorry, my name's Riccardo; friends call me Rome,' he replies, his soul, however, feels an instant familiarity within the vibration, the French accent and the name she's called him.

'Rome now, ok,' Claudette replies still thinking of the love between her 18th century incarnation as Lana and this man's 18th century incarnation as Raphael.

'Yeah, Rome as a nickname because of where I'm from.'

Before he knows it, Yanson is looking across at Rome and Claudette dancing in a loving embrace, gazing deeply into one another's eyes.

As Yanson's getting in more drinks, two Russian millionaires, wannabe playboys, approach the captivating gypsy Princess. She politely explains she's with her boyfriend, but they ignorantly feel they have the right to encroach. Before long the Russian guys are surrounded by a part of Yanson's party, two notorious Russian gangsters included. One of them has a peaceful word and the two wannabe playboys are suddenly most apologetic, feeling it best to take the advice they've been given promptly.

A photographer takes a picture of Princess and Yanson dancing on that Ibiza nightclub dance floor, looking into each other's eyes, high on MDMA – their souls jointly feeling a love vibration that seemed not of this Earth, an emotion they'd shared countless times as eternal Twin Flames, in countless lives.

'Dance with me, baby,' Princess says, 'You know our soul loves to dance. The only thing we love more is making sweet love.'

In unison they say, 'I love you.'

Princess giggles, then adopting a straight face says, 'Koolah, I want to have your child. Never before have I ever felt this fucking way for anyone or anything.'

As they speak, an African youngster looking vaguely familiar to Yanson approaches the couple. He looks like a typical lucky street vendor.

'Yance, I had to come back, I had a dream and...' the African says, feeling humble in Yanson's presence.

Yanson interrupts him. 'Yeah, I remember you now. Now's not the time; come by and see me later in the week.'

The young man Yanson remembered had been sent on an errand delivering cash but he'd disappeared.

Yanson's Ibiza villa

By sunrise, having spent the night partying at the club, Yanson and Princess are back at Yanson's villa now alone. A shirtless Yanson sits up to drink coffee and something makes Princess ask for the first time about the tattoo Yanson has covering his back. She'd first noticed it only when he was asleep face down on the bed in the Russian palace suite, and at the time she'd thought it strange she hadn't seen it before. It made her feel she was tripping on the high – the detailed, lifelike artwork revealing the shape of the African continent, its coastline and lush vegetation, the actual city of Koolah with its palace, waterfalls, stone circle and the angels of the magic circle, and as the tattoo's main feature in its centre, the ancient Messiah Koolah's face with dreadlocks.

'Where did you get the tattoo on your back?' she asks. 'He's the fucking guy I told you about and often think of him and the beautiful coastal city. Somehow, I saw him last night when we were really buzzing. What made you have that exact tattoo? Where did you...'

He interrupts her mid-sentence. 'Thailand, was down there with Gemma, seriously fucked up, wasted in Bangkok.'

She points to the tattoo. 'Who's the guy?'

Yanson thinks for a while. 'I asked who it was in the picture and the Thai tattooist replied "Jesus". Something made me ask him, "Who are you?" and he replied, "One of the angels with you, always with you."'

Princess gulps. 'This is all so fucking trippy, my love.'

She drops to the ground the dressing gown she's wearing, revealing her remarkable naked body once again to Yanson. As she turns to look at the beautiful sunset, he admires her slender neck, feminine muscular back, shoulders, large backside and thighs.

'Babe,' he says, 'please go put the swimsuit and white boots back on.'

She gives him that raised eyebrow oh-ok-you-want-it-like-that smile.

A short while later, Princess has the crotch of her swimming costume pulled to one side as Yanson's tongue caresses her clitoris and his hand her breast. As she climaxes, she hears the sound of the Koolah Palace monkeys usually perched on the window ledges and becomes conscious as Gabi inside her palace quarters fondling her own breasts in her sleep, her body movements as though she's having sex and climaxing.

Later that day, Princess lies naked in bed, her body entangled with Yanson's as the couple wake from a much-needed rest. He wakes with a huge lingering MDMA-assisted erection. She smiles and reaches a hand towards his groin, masturbating his penis. Again, they begin to make tender love – a coming together of their Twin Flame union that awakes the vibration of all their deep subconscious past-life Twin Flame love memories, human and alien. After making love, they lie, head on the pillow, looking at one another.

'Yanson, my dreams were deeply spiritual before I met you, but now it's as though we're living a magical fantasy where our dreams are connected to the same ancient African reality. When we were making deep love and I climaxed, I was someone else, somewhere else, and woke from dreaming of what we were doing here.'

He looks at her with a smile. 'What just then?'

'No, that's the weird part, it was when we came back from Pacha and our friends had left, when we were intimate outside on the sunbed early this morning. When we were actually making love, I woke up somewhere else wondering who you was. It was like I was someone else waking from dreaming about making love to you. Fucking beautiful Yanson, so surreal. You tell me that isn't fucking weird.'

CHAPTER 68

Bucharest, Romania

Three days later, inside a city apartment, Princess's overweight dark-haired typically Romanian- looking cousin is sat alone eating biscuits and watching television. There's a ring on the doorbell and he sighs in his efforts to get up and answer the door. Opening the door, he's startled to see his cousins Princess and an aggressive-looking Django.

'I saw you two months ago,' Django spits out angrily, 'and you knew my sister was in Russia. We spoke about her.'

'Why… I trusted you?' Princess says tearfully.

Their cousin tries to close the door on them, but Django and Princess push their way in and slam the door closed behind them.

The now frightened overweight Romanian pleads, 'Princess, you agreed to do it. They insisted on the most beautiful women, and look at you, you are faultless. I owed them a lot of money, they were going to take out my family, threatened to sell my kids. I would have brought you back soon, Princess. We've been on more daring missions, come on…'

By now Django has heard enough of such lies and cuts his cousin's words short, saying, 'You were supposed to be watching out for my sister,' before bringing his hand out from the back of his waist brandishing a Rambo-style knife, which he uses to repeatedly stab at his cousin's throat.

Blood spurts across the apartment and gushes from the wounds. With their cousin now lying dead, Django and Princess share a smile of satisfaction, knowing they have carried out their nana's last wish and avenged the dead man's ill treatment of Princess as Nana Dinah wished.

'Nana, that was for you,' Django says, and Princess strokes her belly.

As they're using the dead man's kitchen to clean themselves up, Django comments, 'Yes, he shared our blood, but I never liked or trusted him.'

Later the same day Princess is alone in the caravan next to her grandmother's coffin with a large gathering of her family outside. She looks around at the family pictures, of her and her family posing outside gypsy caravans.

Django enters, and she smiles as she says to him, 'Nana said to not let the fat bastard get away with it and to avenge me. We thank you, Django.'

'How did you know she said that? You were in Russia.'

'We're ancient African soul mates. I saw it somewhere.'

A spine-tingling sensation rushes through the young man as his sister picks out some select old clothing she liked seeing Nana wear. She tries a few headscarves on, packs them in a suitcase and slams it shut.

Marigold Bay Hotel, St Lucia, the Caribbean

Meanwhile on a bright sunny day on the island of St Lucia, Diego Juan Carlo sits in the Marigold Bay Hotel's beach area, looking out at the sea in deep thought. The sudden ringing of his satellite mobile brings a smile of intrigue to his face and he begins listening to what his contact Fernando on the phone has to say:

'Bingo, Juan Carlo, got it, but you're not going to like it. Your cousins, fatty and skinny, were arrested Miami Florida four years back.'

Don Carlo frowns but remains silent as Fernando reels off information about the cartel's informant family members, tallying with what Hercule had mentioned about two males within the family informing:

'One hundred twenty kilo cocaine bust, deal went sour. Messy one, two guys and a broad sadistically tortured to death. Your cousins only ones didn't escape the cops. They ratted out other

506

outfits for their freedom and have been on the DEA books as top-level informers ever since. Look no further, my friend, there's the rat in our kitchen. Times like this I respect your intelligence. In this case, keeping my identity from the organisation.'

Diego Juan Carlo frowns and spits out the single word, 'Ratas.'

Yanson's Ibiza villa

Seven weeks later, Yanson is sitting by the pool on the sunbed that he and Princess shared in the short time they'd spent together at the villa.

Django joins him. 'Yanson, I can see your sadness about Princess in your eyes.'

'I still don't get it,' Yanson replies. 'She came back from Romania with you, and everything was fine. Then suddenly without a word she just disappears, and not a word for almost seven weeks. I dream about her day and night, every day — powerful dreams telling me we're still together.'

'The Peter', Cottle mansion, Essex, England

The Peter is a luxuriously fitted out large basement room situated beneath the Cottle mansion, rigged so that the authorities can't bug or listen in on any conversations there.

Daniel Cottle takes a sip of coffee from his mug and returns his attention to the Uzi 9mm sub-machine gun he's working on putting back together. He sprays WD-40 through its mechanism and checks the top safety lever.

He sits working on the gun at his antique desk. There's a video tape of silent CCTV footage playing on a TV screen and across the room Daniel's friend Terry Lewin lounges on the sofa. Terry's thirty-one years old and shares his pretty boy good looks with his uncle to whom he bears a distinct resemblance, Ricky Lewin.

'Fuck me, I done the ole woman this morning,' Terry says, breaking the silence.

Daniel chuckles. 'You had sex with your wife Mandy, makes a change, Terry. Tell me, what was the occasion?'

'You know the one, Jarrod, you know when for no reason you just wake up with that raving fucking hard-on with the urge to do the ole woman.'

Daniel doesn't respond, instead concentrating on his work, expertly servicing the illegal firearm.

Terry watches him work, impressed with his friend's expertise. 'Getting a bit warm at servicing the yogar nowadays, Dan,' he says.

Daniel smiles as he proudly wipes the miniature machine gun down with a black tea cloth. He studies Terry, looking up at him through the Uzi's silencer's perforated nozzle as he meticulously cleans it.

'Terry, you got a darker tan than usual, blood. Where d'ya go?'

'In between three months in Spain I stopped over with Yance for a few weekends in Ibiza,' Terry replies excitedly, 'flew home for the odd weekend. Hey listen, Yance was really down, mate; his new Romanian bird had disappeared on him.'

'I know, Julie said. Strange one, birds don't usually disappear on the Dread; that's not like Yance, usually has trouble getting rid of 'em.'

'Yeah, he's a proper good-looking cunt, like his ole man.' Daniel pauses to work something out in his head and adds, 'Fuck, it's been, must be about three months since I last see Dread. So, what happened in Spain? You weren't out there for an 'oliday.'

Terry smiles. 'Valencia, Spain to meet that little Newcastle Geordie lorry firm I was telling you about, putting some business together. We got some registered companies in Spain now, by the way. Fucking roasting hot weather the whole time we were there. Geordies reckon they can bring in a hundred kilos three times a week.'

'Three hundred a week, you say, Terry?' Daniel asks, his head down, concentrating on the gun he's servicing.

'Yeah, they got a fresh, unused set of wheels.'

Daniel looks up. 'Fresh lorry, good, nothing worse than when a driver brings in work for too many firms, one in ten has got to be old bill or a firm being watched bringing heat to the wheels.'

Terry shakes his head in protest. 'Na, these are fresh wheels, Jarrod... Oh and fuck me,' – he slaps his thigh mid-sentence – 'I took that little Asian babe off the manor, Sacha, with me, filthy, fucking bitch. While sorting the business, I swear twelve weeks a pure filth. Some nights both out our nuts, fucking the life out of each other.'

Daniel places the machine gun down and begins inserting bullets into its extended magazine gun clip, systematically cleaning each shell with the same black tea cloth.

'Twelve weeks in Spain, you'd only just come back from a month away in Thailand with the other bird. Don't you ever take Mandy and the kids away on holiday anymore?'

Terry shrugs his shoulders. 'You know the game, Jarrod. Mrs gets the family holidays, bits a fluff on side are for the business trips. Thailand was a business trip with Iftica's lot. Anyway look, even the straight goers do it that way, MPs, royalty, you fucking name it.'

Terry suddenly points at the TV screen. 'Jarrod, what's on the video?'

Both men watch the images on the screen that show the electric gates to Daniel's drive opening to let Terry's BMW saloon in.

As the gates on the screen close behind the car, Terry says, 'It's your fucking pad, isn't it? There's me driving in through ya gates earlier.'

'Yep Tel, you're driving past the ole bill observation team and they've made a note of your arrival. Nowadays they have to share and log everything with all observation teams, their bosses and an independent body because of how corrupt they are, doctoring observation notes months later and even during trial, lying to trick juries into convicting us. Make me laugh. They still sometimes doctor their notes later during trials to get illegal convictions. Their bosses and independent bodies are in on it. Cunts got the cheek to call us the fucking criminals.'

There's laughter between the two and Daniel presses a button on the TV's remote control. The image on the screen now shows what's supposed to be an inconspicuous dark-coloured works van opposite Daniel's mansion. There's no other parked vehicles around it.

'Right, there's filth watching me gaff,' Daniel says. 'Silly fuckers, it's been there a month and no work's been carried out but different men have been seen sat in it. Never were the cleverest old bill, I must say.'

'Yeah, fuck me,' Terry says peering at the van on the screen, 'that's the van I drove passed earlier coming in. So, you're watching them, watching you.'

'Something like that, Tel.'

'Anyway, about Yance, I meant to tell ya, he introduced me to people to put the shipping companies together for us. He's doing his usual, smuggling gear, but had the two women I met putting a company together for him, a legal business importing yams and bananas from Jamaica to here in the UK. He was telling me how he wants to promote Black business. Sick of how Asian people in general look down on and distance themselves from Black people, putting Blacks down for being lazy and sell Black products to the Black community.'

Daniel smiles. 'Yeah, that sounds like the Dread. Heard he's back in London now. Always on something, you know Yance, he don't fucking stop. Secretive brother, don't even let me know what he's doing half the time. Haven't seen him for months and last time I spoke to him was, fuck me, must have been two months ago; he was in Russia to meet with them Mafia lot he's serving in Spain. Fucking rather him than me, I've heard it's minus forty out them sides at times.'

'Tell you what, he really gets about, got some powerful, double sensible links, the Dread. He's got a lovely little operation set up in Ibiza. Did you ever see the little Romanian bird, Princess, who's disappeared?'

'No, but Yance tells me she pretty like money, didn't stop talking about the back off, my Lord God.'

'In Love, he's in love with her and don't even really know her. Not like the Dread to go falling in love quick like that.'

'Yeah, I could feel he checks for her,' Daniel agrees. 'We spoke the first night. Dread properly buss it down in Russia, said something about her being the one and one of us.'

'He's got it properly boxed off in Ibiza, though, Jarrod.'

Daniel nods in agreement. 'I know, Terry, it took him years putting his Ibiza click together. He began it when we was yuteman.'

Daniel thinks back to his and Yanson's last meeting. They were having a lunch at an East London Nando's restaurant, and Daniel remembers Yanson taking a phone call.

Nando's restaurant, East London

Yanson smiles looking at the caller ID. It's one of his cocaine runners, probably wanting to stock up on more cocaine to sell. But as Yanson answers the call, he instead hears the voice of David Hughes, a local bullyboy – a huge, blond-haired mountain of a man, now addicted to crack cocaine and willing to take advantage of anyone who'd suffer it in order to feed his habit. Yanson's employee had been approached by David Hughes and made to call Yanson.

'Yance, it's me Dave Hughes. Mate, we need to speak face to face,' the voice on the other end of the line says.

Yanson isn't too surprised to hear from Hughes, having expected him to try something sooner or later. 'Speak to me yeah, what about?' he says.

'That bit a thing you're putting out, it looks a lot like the same thing someone chored from us. Not being funny, but long story short, someone's gonna wind up getting one in the nut if this ain't sorted. I want me gear otherwise there's gonna be murders. I ain't saying you knew it was my gear when you bought it, but...'

Yanson interrupts him. 'No, not a problem, so sad to hear of your loss, and if such is the case, David, you'll be fully reimbursed and I'll take it up with my suppliers. I won't be happy to learn they stole it from you, not the way we do business. I can't meet you now; I'm flying abroad tonight, urgent business. Why don't you fly down to Ibiza over the next couple of weeks and we'll put this right? I'll cover the travel expenses, it won't be a problem, I assure you…'

'Yeah alright and it better not be a problem. Oh yeah, got me partner here, he wants a word and he's not too 'appy either,' David Hughes says, handing the phone over to Stephen Dack, a greasy dark- haired skinny heroin addict and slimy weasel of a man, who's been there at his side, nodding along in agreement to what Hughes has been saying.

A Manchester-accented voice comes on the line. 'Hello… me name's Stephen Dack, lad. Yanson, we don't know one another, so I'll keep it short, alright. Me and arr kid, Dave Hughes, want our gear back.'

David Hughes's voice comes back on the phone. 'You know how he don't take too kindly to your firm, as it is, so I think you had better sort it, alright.'

'Ok David, it will definitely get sorted, trust me on that. Can I reach you on this number?'

'Yeah, and don't keep us waiting,' Hughes replies, ending the call.

David Hughes's mother's home

David Hughes looks pleased with himself, and punches the air as his fellow gang members congratulate him.

'Told you Dave,' one of the men says. 'They're shit scared of us, should have put it on 'em ages ago.'

Hughes laughs. 'I bet the coon's shitting it hearing Manchester Steve's voice.' He then attempts mimicking Yanson's well-spoken voice, '"Can I get you on this number?" – he's flapping.'

Another of Hughes's gang members isn't as convinced. 'I'm not totally sure. Yance and his firm have been bang at it for donkey's. Yance can be one naughty cunt, and his close mate Danny Cottle's killed his parents and I remember he killed one of the Hudsons when he was just fourteen.'

Hughes snorts a line of cocaine, places down the straw and

calmly answers, 'Yeah but that was a long time ago, and now he's gonna hear the Manc's on the firm.'

Nando's restaurant, East London

Putting the phone down, Yanson smiles. He's pleased to have got a handle on the whereabouts of Stephen Dack. He knows Dack's responsible for the murder of a Black nightclub doorman, cowardly shot in the back of the head, in Manchester; and that the reason Dack's in London is that he's in fear of a reprisal from the Black Manchester gangs. The man he killed was related to the boss of one of Manchester's most feared gangs, and Yanson had been asked to let them know if Dack turned up on the Cottle gang's or any other's turf.

'Stephen Dack, yeah,' Yanson says out loud, sipping his Coke.

'Problem Yance?' Daniel asks.

'Problem, Jarrod? Na, is it fuck, fam. A problem's only a problem if you can't solve it, blood. Muscle-head, stead-head muppet Dave Hughes is trying it, feeling the waters. He's feeling the waters.'

'Dread, if such is the case, he'll soon find the water, way, way too hot. They must think this is all about the fistfight ting, whum to dem? 'Cos we're getting paper, people think we getting too soft and too much to lose.'

'Jarrod, this Dack geezer's on bail, had to surrender his passport, can't travel.'

'How do you know?'

'One of the man dem Alex is in talks with, one of the Manchester lot who are looking for him for shooting the bouncer.'

'It's a good thing, Dread; gives us an opportunity to let everyone know what time it is lately.'

'Let me handle it, Jarrod. Perfect timing.'

'The Peter', Cottle mansion, Essex, England

As Daniel Cottle is thinking back to his last London meeting with Yanson Bailey, Terry Lewin thinks back to a meeting with Yanson on the island of Ibiza.

Le Marquis, Ibiza

Yanson is chilling in the company of Terry Lewin, another close friend Liam Donahue, Princess and some of his new-found Romanian friends, including her brother Django, in the backroom of the local criminal hangout bar, Le Marquis. He's popular with the Romanians having, after all, rescued Princess. At a table nearby are some of his Columbian associates including Raul, who's retained the youthful looks of his childhood, earning himself the nickname Baby-face. He's also quite remarkable for his fair-haired, blue-eyed but Hispanic appearance.

The relaxed mood in the room is broken by the arrival of Dave Hughes and some of his newly formed gang, four White men, although Stephen Dack is not among them. All Dave Hughes can do at first is moan about the local food, foreigners in general, and the heat – his pale facial and body skin having instantly burnt bright red in the Ibiza sun.

'Please take a seat, gentlemen,' Yanson says to Dave Hughes and his men. 'I just need to finish off a meeting and I'll be with you shortly. Please order some refreshments.'

Although secretly nervous, Dave Hughes puts on a show of strength by replying in a surly tone, 'Yeah hurry up, ain't got all fucking day, mate.'

Yanson doesn't answer, but instead smiles and looks away. He approaches a mixed-race man who's sitting at a nearby table, and says aggressively to him, 'Right cut the bullshit, you need to tell us who's setting up my guys to be robbed over there in London, and quickly.'

The man's immediately filled with fear. 'Yance, I'll tell you, but you got to let me go, man,' he stammers, and then whispers a name to Yanson that none of the others can hear.

Yanson stands with a smile. 'You what, it was him all along. Why am I not fucking surprised? I've looked after you and your family since infant school and you were working with that no-good cunt stealing from me.'

As Yanson is giving the frightened man this dressing-down, Dave Hughes's gang look on nervously.

East London

Meanwhile, Stephen Dack in his secret hideaway hears the almighty crash as someone breaks down the glass and PVC front door of the flat he's renting. Before he can get to the living room door, he's bundled over and wrestled to the ground by one of four men, three of them Black and the other White.

A man wearing a balaclava, but who he could see was Black, brandishes a nine-millimetre pistol with its silencer attached and snaps at him in a Manchester accent, 'What think you kill my family and get away with it, unoo lickle smack rat racist pussy-hole?'

Knowing what's coming, Dack begins shaking nervously. He doesn't have long to do anything as those words quickly become the last ones Stephen Dack would ever hear in his life. The man in the balaclava shoots him four times in the head and face, making sure he's dead.

The White man present makes a call from his mobile phone.

Le Marquis, Ibiza

One of Yanson's employees in the Ibiza bar answers the call. He listens carefully to the short message, then nods his head at Yanson.

Yanson nods back at him in a prearranged signal and then turns to Django saying, 'You can go ahead now.'

The Romanian with a new-found taste for blood produces his own high-powered nine-millimetre pistol with which he shoots the frightened mixed-race man in the face. Not content with firing a single shot, he continues firing until he's emptied the gun into the now dead man's head and body.

515

Although none of the men in the room are strangers to gunfire, there's a lot of shocked reaction to what's just happened, during which Yanson's employee who took the phone call makes his way out the room. From outside he makes a call from his mobile to David Hughes.

Hughes picks up his ringing mobile and listens to a voice on the other end of the line saying, 'Dave, watch yourself. Manchester Steve's been shot dead at the slaughter. Probably someone you lot had robbed and it's come back on yous.'

Yanson smiles to himself as he watches Hughes's face as the big White man takes the call.

'Who is this?' Hughes manages to stammer, but the line's already dead by the time he gets the words out.

'What's wrong, mate? Who was that?' one of his gang asks.

'Someone who's said Stephen's been ironed out, he's gone mate.'

'Probably someone from up the road who wasn't happy with him,' the gang member responds.

In a matter of moments, the world of David Hughes and his gang had caved in, his red sunburnt complexion going as white as a sheet.

Yanson meanwhile is completely calm and unfazed. He uses his napkin to wipe spattered blood from his face and sits down to resume eating his meal, but, noticing something on the table missing, protests, 'Where's the fucking vinegar? How can you have a chip without fucking vinegar?'

Princess retrieves a bottle of vinegar from a nearby table and as she does so locks eyes with a flamboyant young Columbian who's sitting at Raul's table. She knows him and he knows her, and she's instantly filled with fear. This was a man who could identify her as one of the members of the Romanian gang that had swindled an outfit he's connected to. This combined with her missing her period sends a deep wave of nervousness through her in regard to her newfound love.

She places the bottle in front of Yanson as four local island men professionally wrap the dead man's corpse, getting it ready for disposal.

When Yanson has finished eating, he stands, points towards Raul and his gang's table and says, 'Ok Mr David Hughes, these chaps are my suppliers, and seems we have a major problem. This is the thing: you've accused them of stealing your cocaine and they swear you are making this up. They claim they have proof they've supplied me direct from Colombia and there's no way it could be the gear that you've lost. What have you to say?'

All eyes are on the big White man, David Hughes, who offers no resistance.

'Alright Yance, look if they say it's their gear, we ain't arguing, we must be mistaken… and you know what else, you are one proper geezer.'

Yance smiles. 'Ok that settles that little misunderstanding. All's well that ends well as they say. David, enjoy Ibiza. If you like, Django and some of the guys will take you for a night tour around the island. The night view of the coast from a mile out is spectacular. Django, Raul and some of the boys here will take you for a delightful boat ride.'

Hughes is trembling with fear as he replies, 'It's ok, thank you,' and he and his men make their way out the bar as quickly as they can.

Once they're outside, still visibly shaking, he says, 'Mate, that could be any of us with one in the nut. We better get off this island; that cunt and his mob are a fucking bunch a lunatics.'

'Right with ya there, mate,' one of his men agrees.

Back inside the premises, the flamboyant young Colombian at Raul's table who Princess recognised takes a call on his mobile and becomes angry. He ends the call, looks towards Yanson, and Yanson demands, 'What is it?'

The Colombian shakes his head as he explains. 'Pulpo, that's the second time this week, just robbed two hundred kilos, our English customer in Mallorca. He tried to kill them, but the English got away.'

Django chips in, 'Yance, you said to him, if it happens again, he's gone.'

The man they're referring to is really called Hector, but he had earned his nickname, Pulpo, the Spanish word for octopus, precisely because he always had too many hands to watch.

'Fucking little bastard Pulpo,' Yanson growls.

'Bastardo, Pulpo,'Raul adds angrily, 'won't have any customers left if he keeps robbing and killing everyone.'

CHAPTER 69

Terry Lewin brings his thoughts back to his conversation with Daniel Cottle and says, 'Yance does like his MDMA, though.'

Daniel laughs as he agrees. 'Yeah, always says it takes him back to the olden times, back to the beginning, ancient Africa… Fuck me, talk about ancient Africa, you've fucking reminded me, I didn't tell you what happened in the Dam when I was last there with Emy few months back. Mad ting…'

Terry's intrigued by Daniel's obvious excitement. 'Na, you didn't tell me, Jarrod. What happened?'

'In me Amsterdam hotel room, night before visiting Lickle, and fuck me, the dreams and a serious presence.'

'Presence Jarrod, what do you mean like a ghost, spirits and all that?'

'Yeah, not just that, Emy and me found we shared the same fucking dreams, Terry. Listen to this, that morning it wasn't like a dream, it was fucking real. The whole thing got me researching on the internet and the way it all happened is known as a kind of astral travel and astral projection. Like I left the physical body and travelled the dimensions of the universe, like travelled through time. I was with this beautiful little mix race French woman, Claudette. She took me on a spiritual journey. I was there, watching 18th century slavery, moving around a right naughty slave fort in West Africa known as the "Door of No Return". Still feel the pain and sorrow of the families, can hear the harrowing screams of the kidnapped men, women and children held there. She took me into a secret location with the leader of the slave rebellion on the island Haiti. I saw the leader of the slave uprising, a man called Toussaint Louverture. I knew nothing of all this before I experienced all this in Amsterdam, and when I researched it, it's all documented in history, mate. There was so much more to it, Emy's Dutch mates connecting to the dreams, deep, blood.'

'You're right,' Terry agrees, 'sounds fucking deep.'

Whilst Terry sits thinking on what Daniel has said, an amazingly beautiful Black African woman comes into his own mind, a woman he'd physically met briefly just once but who he can't help thinking about day and night as though he had some sort of spiritual connection with her.

He shakes his head and says, 'Ghosts, Jarrod, you've always seen them. Who was you dreaming about, that little Colombian bird you use' to go on about when we were kids, Sofia?'

'As it happens, I was taken to her New York apartment and shown her in bed asleep,' Daniel says, feeling a slight pang of jealousy as he thinks back to seeing her in bed with another man.

Terry smiles and changes the subject, again talking about their friend Yanson Bailey. 'Yance loves the Ibiza, mate. Put a right click together, local islanders, African, European, Colombian. The cunt's even started speaking bits of fucking Romanian now.'

Both men laugh and Daniel says, 'Typical Yance.'

'Dread's hanging with Romanian gypsies out there,' Terry continues. 'He's got a pucker villa in Santa Eulalia, Ibiza but always in the little ghetto part of the old town playing backgammon with the locals, African migrant and other foreigners.'

'He likes anyone clever at making dough,' Daniel comments. 'The gypsies and Africans across Europe seem to be good at it.'

'He's fucking proper at the game backgammon. Cunt beats everyone, never met anyone so fucking lucky with the dice. His Romanian ting who's gone missing's a sort. People were calling her the gypsy Princess on the island of Ibiza. She's a classy sort, fuck me for a slim upper body girl, size of the ass and legs on her, the pair of you like that big ass. From what I'm told she's born and raised on a Romany gypsy site but naturally classy and designed to the life.'

'Ooman botty fe swell an roun, Iyah,' Daniel laughs. '"The

woman's bottom has to be large and round," – for me, the foundation of a successful relationship. Yanson's new Romanian sort was like a sex slave in the Russian mafia's Moscow palace.'

Terry looks surprised to hear this, and Daniel adds seriously, 'That stays between the family, though, Tel.'

'Yeah fucking hell, course, Jarrod,' Terry replies, a little disappointed that Daniel even felt the need to say that.

Bucharest, Romania

As Daniel and Terry are having their discussion, Princess herself wakes from a confusing dream, lying on a plush bed in the five-star luxury City of Bucharest Hotel.

In her dream she was consciously awake in that ancient African magic circle dimension feeling terrible about running from Koolah. The dimensions seem to her to be all confused in her mind as she thinks herself as Gabi running from her Twin Flame Koolah because she as Princess is worried about Yanson learning about deceitful and embarrassing acts she's carried out in her paralleled modern- day Princess incarnation.

Yawning, she opens her eyes and is amazed to see before her Romanian aunt Rosella in her mid-twenties accompanied by another woman in her mid-twenties both in 1960s clothing and with 1960s hairstyles, together in conversation with her nana Dinah who herself looks younger than Princess can ever remember seeing her.

Even stranger the image of the woman she doesn't know keeps changing, flickering back and forth between the image of the 1960s White woman and an ancient African Black woman.

As she sits up on the huge king-size bed, Princess finds herself uttering one word in a language she doesn't understand. Then, she smiles at Rosella and says, 'Aunty, how did you know how to find me here? You are so fucking young and...'

Rosella answers with a smile, 'My mother, your grandmother Dinah showed us how to cross over.'

Princess can't help staring at the woman whose image seemed

to change, and gradually she begins to recognise this woman she thought she didn't know – recalling her from her amazing dream of the island of Jamaica, the 1994 reunion awakening, although at the reunion this woman appeared twice the age.

'Who are you?' Princess says to her, suddenly feeling a positive loving vibration.

'I've just shown you; I'm your mother, Queen Lulu,' Cindy Nevin replies, speaking in ancient Koolah. 'And, Gabi, I want you to listen; you've been very immature in regard to Koolah. You're to go back to Ibiza. Your mirror soul is powerless without you.'

Princess somehow understands every word, and is about to protest, but Dinah interrupts her saying,

'Release your fears; confide in Yanson. He's the other half of you; your actions are his actions and vice versa; therefore, he will understand all you've done no matter how embarrassed you feel about it. Princess, I'm with you all the time, part of you, present in your heaven as we speak.'

Later, the hotel phone rings and it's Princess's brother Django calling from Ibiza.

'Django,' she says breathlessly, 'Nana came to me in a dream with Aunt Rosella and someone else. I'm coming home to Yanson in Ibiza.'

After she's said goodbye to a relieved Django, Princess caresses her belly, and she hears a lion roar come from inside the hotel suite and a faint vision appears. She's somehow walking along the Koolah City beach crowded with local indigenous African families. She's walking side by side with the dreadlock-haired Messiah Koolah and a pride of lions, two males, four lionesses and eleven cubs. She knows the Messiah has the animals in a trance, telepathically communicating with them as he is able to communicate with all animals of the jungle. Still accompanied by the lions, they walk onto the magic circle to be greeted by the image she'd just seen, her mother, Queen Lulu, who looks directly into her eyes and says, 'Gabi,' then into the eyes of Koolah, and says, '...and your Twin Flame Yanson.'

CHAPTER 70

Later that day, Princess lies face down, jogging bottoms lowered to reveal her large, shapely, toned bottom, the waistline of her black G-string tight around her muscular feminine waist, as the expert tattoo artist puts the finishing touches to a love-heart-shaped tattoo covering one of her angelic protruding buttocks. It's early evening and the large tattoo shop that would normally accommodate four tattooists is empty apart from Princess and her tattoo artist, Ollie, a dark-haired handsome Australian beach-bum type with a tanned complexion and an athletic physique. House music beats in the background as Princess allows her mind to think deeply about the spiritual visit of her grandmother, aunt Rosella and Queen Lulu/Cindy Nevin, and specifically the advice she received concerning her Twin Flame, Yanson Bailey.

The tattoo is a composite image, a fine example of the tattooist's art. The love heart is made up of half Rasta flag and half Romany flag, against which the faces of Princess and Yanson are depicted kissing one another's lips, their portraits expertly rendered using an enlarged on screen photo taken of their faces dancing in a loving embrace at the Ibiza nightclub as reference. In the design, Princess wears a traditional Romany gypsy headscarf, her face in front of the flag of the Romany people, and Yanson, in front of the Rasta flag half of the love heart, has been given Bob Marley Rasta man–style dreadlocks, and his fingers hold a gigantic lit spliff, half of it sticking outside the love heart.

Ollie disturbs Princess to ask if she'd like to view the progress in the shop's wall mirror, handing her a smaller hand-held mirror too. She nods smiling in appreciation of the fine artistic detail. Ollie meanwhile finds he has to stop himself complementing the mirror reflection of her large flawlessly shaped backside. Instead, he finds himself wondering why his mind increasingly feels he's seen the unmistakable shape of her bottom and experienced the vibration of the sight before.

As he resumes his work, Ollie can't help but finally air his thoughts.

'I began doing tats as a kid in jail down under in Oz,' he says, 'and now thanks to the proceeds from my work I'm able to surf the waves, bum around scuba diving the best beaches and oceans of the world. I've tattooed people all over the world, in the most amazing countries, movie and pop stars even. Look, I don't want to sound like some weirdo creep, pervert or nothing and mean this in the most respectable way: I often get beautiful Sheilas often wanting tattooed backs, tits and arses but none ever with a natural backside to rival yours. You have the most incredibly perfect Sheila's arse I've ever seen. Tattooed chicks' arses all through the coasts back home, the States, Thailand, Caribbean, across Europe and can't remember one as horny as yours anywhere.'

Princess laughs and he suddenly feels relaxed in her company.

'I explained to my brother in Ibiza I wanted a quality, detailed tattoo done in Bucharest,' she says, 'and the Romanian community on the Balearic Islands all strongly recommended you.'

'Ever thought of modelling underwear?' Ollie asks seriously but Princess laughs.

'No, I'm not joking,' he continues. 'Seriously, I spent a long time in Jamaica, had some casual affairs with the local Black chicks and the first thing I thought when you walked in was you definitely have that native African Sheila's bum. Seriously, you've got an amazing arse. It's all natural, right?'

'Completely natural, unlike my breast implants, and thanks Ollie, you're not the first to say that. Buffness is what the other half of my soul Yanson calls my bottom.'

'Yeah, buff is a term Jamaican guys use describing an arse and legs like yours,' Ollie says.

'But when I was growing up here in Romania I got teased by some of the local guys and girls when I went to school, owing to the way my big arse really sticks out. It actually depressed me.

Nana always told me not to worry, that I have an amazing bum actually inherited from her mother, my great grandmother. She'd say when I get older the right guys will go crazy for it. Nana would always say European women pride their selves on having the so-called small sexy butt because the Western media has placed into the human psyche the idea the Black woman's larger rounded bum and larger lips represent ugly and unattractiveness.'

She pauses for a moment, then adds, 'My God, that's so fucking weird; I was lying here earlier thinking of my Nana who's passed on but after she died visited me, showing herself and actually speaking to me. Now it feels as though she hasn't left me; her powerful presence gets stronger by the minute.'

Ollie's immediately intrigued by her talk of the spiritual, but before he can think what to say Princess continues, 'Nana always told me when I get older it will all change: the brainwashed European and Asian male and female won't be able to help finding humanity's original look attractive because in the beginning the entire human race were Black. All other nations began as Black people from Mother Africa and later inhabited faraway lands of the world. Nana was clairvoyant with a very special gift, and I'm also the spiritual ancestry and blood of a long line of the ancient African and Romany Voodoo.'

'Your Nana was very knowledgeable. Sounds like what the Maroon and spiritual indigenous people back home speak of. We all, humanity, originated Black in Africa. Some left in man's first ships as Black people and evolved White, Asian and all other nations according to the climates of the destinations they reached. Fucking racist Whites in my country, White supremacists in the U.S., racist Asians and Europeans all over the world originated from the Black man. What happened along the way? How did every nation begin hating the image from which they began?'

'How do you know all this spirituality, Ollie?' Princess asks the tattooist as he pauses in his work. 'Yanson also explained Black Africa being the cradle of civilisation and the fact finally being recognised by Western scientists and the mainstream.'

'How do I know? Mate, just being around spiritual people like yourself, dreams and clairvoyants showing me stuff. Getting back to what I was saying, nowadays women pay heaps of money for all kinds of surgery to get an arse like yours. By the way,' he asks wiping the tattoo, 'what's the specific meaning of the two flags? I mean, I know what they are, but what do they mean to you?'

'The Romany flag represents who I am, where I'm from, my culture, and the Jamaican Rasta culture's deep within my future husband, my eternal Twin Flame.'

'Jamaica,' Ollie reflects, at the same time in the back of his mind wondering where he's heard the words Twin Flame before. 'A few years back I tattooed a rich Sheila, a divorcee. She'd moved across from Bellevue Hill, Sydney and relocated where we met, where I was hustling further along, Bondi Beach. We travelled the world and ended up on a crazy cocaine adventure on board a luxury liner passing through the Caribbean. Stopped in Jamaica, and fuck, there was an amazing pull on this soul, a familiarity, falling in love with the island's culture, history of the people, music, food – the vibe just fucking pulled me in. We decided to leave the cruise liner and instead backpacked the island, ending up in the Blue Mountain smoking the gunja chalice with the Rastafarian and Maroon community, constantly for days. That was when it began to get freaky because I'd never been to Jamaica but previous to setting up camp up on the mountain – I'm still not sure whether or not it was on board the cruise liner or back in Oz where I'd previously dreamed having visited the exact spot and meeting the people in the village. I felt at home with those guys, the Maroons and descendants of other runaway slave communities. You got everyone up there; I even got friendly with two White guys from Liverpool in the UK. They were evading the British authorities, wanted for landing a huge quarter ton shipment of cocaine at Liverpool docks. One of the local Jamaican guys, a tall Black Jamaican Rasta man called Leonard, an Obeah man, he explained I'd lived on the island before and had been brought back to be among my spiritual family, my soul tribe. At first, I was sceptical and insisted it was my first time on the island, I'd stopped off to surf, scuba dive, and mostly of all get high. I told him the Caribbean cruise was my Sheila's idea, and on the advice of a guy, a local beach hustler, we spontaneously decided to stay and backpack the Blue Mountain. But Leonard said no, no matter how I arrived, it was no coincidence I was there. Told me I'd lived there many lives and had been guided back by spirit to be among my soul tribe again. As Leonard enlightened me, my previous dreams of camping that spot of the mountain made pure sense. I hadn't thought much of the supernatural before then, but that déjà vu experience opened my mind to higher realms of spirituality. Then the second night up in the mountain and, strewth mate, that's when it all began. I woke from dreaming being in that very same spot, seeing that terrain view from the mountain but dreaming different olden-day people, Black, White, Mediterranean and a little pretty Chinese woman. The Obeah spirit is fucking powerful in those Jamaican mountains. I also felt the same Voodoo vibe on that cruise when we docked in Haiti before stopping in Jamaica.'

The mention of the pretty Chinese woman sets Princess's subconscious psyche experiencing vague thoughts of a past life where she's the Black girlfriend, and later wife, of the Haitian revolutionary called Destin, the sister-in-law of Toussaint Louverture. The pirate captain Morgan's female pirate Yu Yan was often a guest at the huge plantation house slave-uprising rebel base, Princess's home during that incarnation.

'One night,' Ollie continues, 'we were high on the sensimilla, and the Haitian witch Claudette came to us. She was completely naked, and she walked slowly through the campfire towards us, but the fire didn't burn her hair or her body, and the flames were nearly as tall as her. She spoke with a French accent, and everyone present, even the most deeply spiritual souls, Obeah men and women, had the utmost respect for her. She's highly regarded in the universal spirit world, an ascended master, able to physically travel the universe watching over us her soul tribe today in past dimensions and even into the future. Suddenly her image disappeared walking away back through the fire, but I'll never forget her face and occasionally her voice giving me advice.

Leonard explained that today she lives a physical life as a wealthy type of recluse on the powerful Voodoo island of Haiti, but astral travels through time watching over us and always spying on the enemy.'

As Princess listens on in silence, the familiarity to her of the character Ollie's describing sends a shockwave through her body and sets her heart racing.

Ollie puts down his tattoo machine, for a moment too absorbed in what he's saying to use it. 'Leonard helped me become conscious in two consecutive past lives. First there was an 18th century life where I was captured, abducted, enslaved and brought over to the Caribbean island Jamaica as an adult woman from Ghana, West Africa. The clear-as-life regression reading made me re-live that past life joining a courageous Jamaican woman freedom seeker known today as the legendary revolutionary leader, Nanny of The Maroons. She freed us from the clutches of the British slavers to fight alongside her, freeing other kidnapped and enslaved people, maintaining our freedom. The campsite we stayed when we docked here on the luxury cruise liner was the exact spot, one of the 18th century bases we used to hide from the British in between Nanny's scheduled attacks on them. The British fought hard for many years to re-enslave us, but when they realised they couldn't defeat us, they sued for peace and gave us land, signing a treaty. When you experience the Black magic African spirit in the mountain, you realise how we'd defeated the British. The media has always kept glorious Black rebellious slave uprising stories quiet and portrayed the Voodoo as evil but...'

Princess interrupts him, 'I love the sound of Nanny. My grandmother liked to be called Nana or Nanny pronounced in the English way. What's fascinating is now you've mentioned her, my Romanian Nana spoke of the Jamaican woman's stories a lot.'

She pauses for a moment, her psyche strongly picking up on the vibration of her grandmother, lifting her inner spirit. 'Wow, Nana has let me know you're speaking of her soul. She's the soul of the historic rebel against slavery, the freedom fighter you speak of, Nanny. God's spiritual universe is awesome. I now know I shared that incarnation with you and Nana, Ollie. All of the sudden, I know of her spiritual connection with Claudette and God's other angels during our war with the British on the island of Jamaica.'

As Princess again falls silent, wondering in amazement how her grandmother could still spiritually communicate with her, Ollie in his own excitement talks quickly, keen to tell Princess about the other past life regression reading the Juju man Leonard helped him into.

'My rich girlfriend, she wanted us to move on, but I told her I wouldn't be carrying on with her – felt terrible, broke her heart – instead I had to stop in Jamaica alone. Time flew and before I realised I'd been up there, high on the sensimilla, for months, living off the land and sea with them. After experiencing my Maroon past life regression incarnation fighting alongside Nanny, I self-hypnotised into the consecutive next past life incarnation, my life after that one. As clear as life, I was living the life of a West African Black boy. I re-lived the horrific life of a Black kid and my home was on the West Coast of Africa, known today as the Gold Coast...'

Ollie pauses, shaking his head and becoming choked up and tearful on reflection, again feeling the sadness of the revelation. He gathers and composes himself with a clearing of the throat.

'Strewth, I'd entered our family hut finding my grandmother and baby brother mutilated by British slave companies, and the rest of my family, parents, other siblings and cousins...'

Ollie's voice falters again and he sobs with uncontrollable chest movements. He wipes away the tears and tries his best to recover.

'...parents, aunts, uncles, siblings friends and other villagers within the community had been kidnapped by those British slavers, one of the world's nations who felt they were justified to enslave Black people...'

Princess interrupts, 'Yanson has explained slavery wasn't something the Asians and Europeans just decided to do; their countries' leaders were under the influence of Satan; they'd made a deal with the evil beast in return for showing them how to become dominant in this world. A massive part was to enslave and oppress the African and other indigenous nations, take away our spirituality and exchange it with man-invented religions.'

Ollie nods and continues with the story of his 18th century spiritual regression reading:

'Months after finding my family members killed or kidnapped, my little sister Anci and I were rescued from the West Coast of Africa and as promised by Koolah taken to the safety of our soul tribe. I remember being that rescued little boy arriving from Africa and docking in Jamaica, looking around at the same unmistakable terrain of St Ann's Bay. During the regression reading there's 18th century ships and boats and people in and around the bay, but it's the same shape bay and waterfall now as when I saw it then. I was taken on a long, long mule trek for days along a secret underground route – a string of mules tied together being led by a cowboy-hat-wearing Black horseman, guiding them through the trees, up a mountain. There was a dirt road to the safety of the secret pirate hideout within the same Maroon mountain village that we stayed two centuries later when we arrived off the cruise liner. Two hundred years ago we were taken there for an emotional reunion with our rescued African parents and other family members. Gave me a feeling of joy I've never before consciously felt in this life. I felt the powerful emotion; I was actually there reuniting with my kidnapped family again. Princess listen, the historic pirate Jim Morgan was present in the Maroon village. I actually saw and heard him speaking to his legendary nephew, the child swordsman, Jarrod. And the Chinese pirate who featured in all of the written novels and Hollywood movie, Yu Yan, I was present, saw and spoke with her on the island of Jamaica two centuries ago, and when I was in Jamaica just recently the regression reading allowed me to re-live it.'

'Yes,' Princess interrupts excitedly, 'I too was overcome with emotion watching the Hollywood movie, Ollie. It's actually my favourite. I could relate to the characters, especially Charlotte, the Duchess.'

'Before my return to Jamaica,' Ollie carries on, 'I was fascinated with the pirate captain Jim Morgan novel, and movie; read it in jail as a kid and many times afterwards. Unfortunately the writer Wilfred Turner hadn't fully captured the locations and political or spiritual Voodoo content...' – he slaps his own forehead signalling that he's just realised something – 'That's it, I began thinking about it on the Caribbean cruise liner and that's when I started waking from the dreams being in the olden-day Maroon village. Sad waking from dreams receiving the news Yu Yan and the rest of the crew – Lana, Morgan and others – were eventually hung at the London gallows. During that regression reading, the Haitian witch Lana helped Morgan and myself into a joint regression reading that showed our Maroon lives where I was the Black female and he a Black male when we were freedom fighters. Yeah, while conscious in a past life I became conscious in another previous past life; spiritual experiences don't go much deeper. The sensation revealed that in my female Maroon life the White pirate Morgan was my Black Maroon friend fighting as freedom seekers alongside Nanny. Morgan was never meant to stay in the King of England's Royal Navy in that life where he was born White. He was born into that life so that his military expertise could help our soul tribe rise up.'

In his mind Ollie recalls being conscious as the little African boy stood with his sister Anci looking up at the smiling suntanned dreadlock-haired historical pirate Captain Jim Morgan. Bongo drumbeat music's playing at the Blue Mountain hideout and people dance as Morgan congratulates his entire crew on another successful, fruitful voyage. Ollie knows it's the exact same campfire spot with the same mountain views that he knows in his modern-day incarnation.

'Funny how the indigenous people of their invaded lands are given the bad name,' he says. 'Other than this historic story Hollywood made me grow up feeling the Native Americans and the Black native Zulus were the bad guys in the movies, the savages attacking the righteous European settlers. In reality, the indigenous were just trying to resist the intruders taking their land, enslaving, killing and raping their families. We're taught the indigenous peoples of the world are savages, but one day I looked up the meaning of the word and read it means a person who is violent, cruel, fierce and uncontrolled. That's the question: the violence, mutilation, murder, mayhem the Europeans inflicted on the indigenous populations around the world, is it not the epitome of uncontrolled savagery? I mean what could they have done to make their actions more barbaric?

'I was born and raised under the notion the original people of Australia are a lower form of life to the Whites, and led to believe the religions of the world represent God, but later found the nations under the world's leading religions today are the true savages. The European governments under the umbrella of religion committed the most hideous crimes against humanity, enslaved hundreds of millions. One evil bastard, satanic devil European Catholic king tortured and mutilated, removing limbs from twenty million, and killing the same amount in just one section of the Motherland they named the Congo. Every other European government did the same in the parts of Africa they sectioned off for the purpose of dividing the people, stealing their wealth, creating a paradise in their homelands and also in Africa for themselves. Other European intruders killed and drove the indigenous natives from their homes in what's known today America and Australia. This so-called evil criminal pirate Morgan and leaders such as Toussaint Louverture helped free the oppressed slaves with the assistance of the so-called evil Voodoo spirit.

'I shared my regression vision with Leonard and he explained that myself, sister Anci and other members of our village escaped the massacre and slavery and were rescued in that life. I re-lived that incarnation where some of my family were killed, others shackled, and we children actually watched our family sail away on board the slave ship from the Devil's 18th century slave fort known as the "Door of No Return". During the regression reading, Anci explained we'd met the one known globally today as Jesus and he explained to us we would somehow in the future meet my baby brother and grandmother who were murdered by English slave companies. Leonard and myself did a joint regression practice because he actually lived the life as my brother who was with me when we met the one our ancient soul tribe knew as the Messiah, ten thousand years before they invented the Christian religion and this Jesus of Nazareth type character. We were rescued and reunited with our parents; they too had been rescued from the slave ship by Captain Morgan and led up the Blue Mountain hills to safety within the Maroon community.

'Don't you see, Princess? Leonard was right; I'd fucking been there before. Spirit brought me back to the very spot we lived in two other lives. After watching the slave ship sail away with our parents, family and others on board, myself, Anci and others walked, dying of thirst and starving, to the Devil- built West African coast slave forts. Jesus appeared and told us to come away from the area and go back to the village. During the walk back, he put a food and drink parcel on the road for us. But Jesus wasn't the guy my parents, school and church showed me. Instead, he was a handsome dreadlock-haired Black man with a beautiful Black woman on that day walking with their black panther companion. He explained we would be rescued and we were – saved and brought back there to Jamaica again. Our parents, relations and a ship full of kidnapped Africans were rescued by the legendary captain Morgan's mixed-nation crew.'

A tingling sensation sweeps over Princess's entire body. 'That's fucking crazy, Ollie,' she says. 'Yanson and I have spiritual connections with the panther and the dreadlock-haired guy called Koolah you mentioned, the one you call Jesus.'

Digesting the words she's just said, Ollie looks directly into Princess's eyes and subconsciously, maybe even consciously, he knows the uniquely coloured eyes of Princess are the eyes and same soul of the Black Princess Gabi, the woman accompanying the Messiah. He's about to try and put his thoughts into words when Princess beats him to it.

'We, myself and Yanson, are the same Twin Flame angel, the one-soul couple you speak of. I'm the reincarnated Black African

Princess Gabi who was revealed to you in your regression reading. Ollie, I actually specifically remember Koolah leaving the food and magical wristband for you and our other angel soul Anci. You're a cute African boy around ten.'

Ollie can picture in his mind the wristband Princess is talking about: a platted elephant-leather wristband. A feeling of joy washes over him, the equal of what he felt when reuniting with his rescued West African family. He knows he is not just in the presence of one of his soul tribe but Princess Gabi, the Messiah's Twin Flame, herself. For the moment, he finds it hard to speak.

'For a good while,' Princess says, 'I felt they were just unexplainable dreams, but meeting my Twin Flame and moments like this, meeting you and us sharing parts of the same dreams, and my meeting my auntie and ancient African mother earlier both from separate dimensions make me know it's all fucking real. Ollie, we have a spiritual connection; meeting you today was no coincidence. I came for a tattoo, but your famous art was the way spirit guided me here to you.'

Ollie nods. 'That's true, the Jamaican clairvoyant assured me I would meet Koolah's beautiful Black Princess Gabi again soon, but I thought he meant during another regression reading. I wasn't aware I'd physically meet this later incarnation of you.' He begins joyfully laughing. 'It's just come to mind, and has to be said, I remember from the regression reading the Sheila with Jesus had the same type remarkable backside, in fact exact same sexy physique, as you. Had smaller tits but...'

She giggles and says, 'Yes, so did I in this life, and that's why I went for breast implants.'

'Well,' Ollie continues, 'Leonard explained when we begin meeting one another again the awakening will be near. You're not the first I've met. The Haitian witch Claudette explained you and others would soon begin to show up and spoke of the reawakening, a coming together of our unique soul tribe on the island of Jamaica. Earth's authentic bible is buried on the island of Jamaica. We'll soon retrieve it and use its magical spells to lift the Devil's curse, reverse the work of Satan to remove physical and spiritual borders, reuniting the Motherland and her children.'

Ollie smiles brightly as he recalls the revelation Claudette had showed him during a future life progression reading. He remembers a future Africa thriving, one voice, one country, one people, one currency, and most of all he vividly remembers the face of the future Queen of Africa.

'The Haitian witch Claudette showed us what the African continent and Queen of Africa will look like in not too many generations from now,' he says. 'That transformation begins early next century, less than thirty years from now. Koolah will lift the curse and people will begin to tune into soul tribe angels, Dr Arikana Chihombori and others. During the future life progression reading I was conscious in the year 2019 where Dr Chihombori educated me on the Berlin Conference of 1884-1885 – where each European country sat and decided which part of Africa they'd forcibly take by inflicting bloodshed and misery in the process – and what it meant for Africa and her children. I specifically remember one French colony in Africa that Dr Chihombori spoke of in the future, one of many parts of the Motherland the French sectioned off as their own, the one they named Mali. I only remember parts of what she told us from the future life progression reading. The French are raping Mother Africa's natural resources, oil and other rich minerals. Every forty billion they are taking out of Africa, rich minerals and bank deposits from poor African people invested on the stock market, returns the French three hundred billion U.S. dollars each year to this day in line with inflation for the past hundred years, year in, year out...'

Princess interrupts him. 'Where's the shame? European countries have shown no remorse and continue to show no empathy in what they continue to put the indigenous of Africa through.'

'I know, Princess; the French are making trillions off of the back of sorrowful African human suffering every year with inflation since the Berlin conference. Then they have the cheek to leave the people of the land starving and tell the rest of the world that they are poor countries, the poor people of Africa. The Western media constantly show helpless Africans and their diseased children on television, claiming there's nothing in Africa for Africans around the world, just poverty and disease, as a diversion while they continue to take the wealth from them. The same Western European governments buy the oil from Arab countries that prosper. They will not allow the Black race to prosper at any cost.

'But not just Black but billionaires and millionaires, wealthy people with empathy from all nations around the globe will come together and back a soul tribe angel Dr Arikana Chihombori's international rescue mission demanding reparations, and the world will compensate for over a thousand years of criminal acts against Mother Africa and her children. We will step in where the United Nations have refused to do so.

'More rappers, sports personalities, entrepreneurs, Black and White, singers, film industry, Black billionaires such as Oprah Winfrey and even future lone wolves.' Ollie recalls the progression reading showed and spoke of reincarnated African descendants and future star celebrities such as a music artist Akon, tennis and soccer stars Roger Federer and Sadio Mané. 'I was shown future sports and music celebrities will come together to help create a one leader one country Africa. We will welcome outside business such as from the Chinese, Asians and Europeans but create systems similar to the one in place in the United States and Australia where migrant companies have to employ and train the locals as well as have enough money put into a banking system which benefits Africa. Claudette showed future reparations, compensation awarded to the African continent, and Africa becoming the leading nation in the future, back to be what it was designed to be. Princess, Claudette put the images of the Black psychic Queen of Africa into our minds when we were up in the mountain.'

Princess looks at herself in the mirror and her subconscious tells her Ollie's speaking of the soul of Cindy, the woman recently in her hotel. She looks back at Ollie and he's smiling brightly.

'Princess,' he says earnestly, 'I remembered none of this regression reading until you came to me today. Now I remember Claudette explaining that on meeting you I'd remember past lives and all what was revealed to me in Jamaica. During regression, the Haitian witch Lana also explained that I'd meet you, Princess Gabi, and you would trigger my memory of my past life regression and future life progression reading experiences. Now you've got me thinking of the spirituality of Jamaica and I can't wait to go back.'

Princess looks him directly in the eye. 'Since I was a little girl, Nana always told me I would meet members of my soul tribe, the likes of you and my Twin Flame.'

'Twin Flame?' Ollie asks. 'You've mention that before and Claudette and others speak of the awakening of the Earth-based alien twin souls. What exactly is your Twin Flame?'

'My Twin Flame,' Princess replies, 'my divine counterpart, the other half of my soul, literally the other half of me. Nana was a psychic medium, could see the future, always telling me the way I would meet you my soul tribe members and the exact way I'd meet my Twin Flame.'

'That's so strange your grandmother being clairvoyant. Nana of the Maroons was an Obeah clairvoyant too, and Leonard said I would be in her physical presence again. What's fucking crazy is earlier your words were that she spiritually let you know she's the soul of Nanny of the Maroons.'

Princess smiles. 'There's some words Nana said: "Keep reincarnating, perfecting yourself every life to finally be at one as the divine, the process that the newly man-invented Western religions call joining God in heaven." She used to tell me bedtime stories as a child, explaining the right man for me will be my knight in shining armour. He'd rescue me from the evil castle and be the one for life and it's happened.'

Ollie puts down his tattoo machine, the finishing touches having been put to her tattoo whilst they were talking.

'Tattoo complete,' he says, 'and you can tell Yanson from me, he's a lucky guy, must be someone special… Strewth, met a lot of spiritual people on my two visits to Jamaica; your guy's one blessed Jamaican dude, that's for sure.'

Princess's face displays a look of frustration. 'Ollie, it's as though you missed what I've said. My Twin Flame and I are the one soul of Jesus. Don't know how, just now realised we're Jesus.'

Ollie joyfully explains, 'Your subconscious is telling you, Princess, and I missed nothing. I'm just finding all this fucking hard to take in.' A thought suddenly comes to his mind and tears of joy begin to well up in his eyes. 'Oh my God... of course, the process of reincarnation. Up in the mountain we were shown by Claudette and others that the Greek philosopher Aristotle, Asians and rest of the European invaders had come back to Africa to be educated. They were visually shown that when the angels first arrived on Earth humanity was only Black and also shown proof that the Messiah was Black African. Part of the process of oppressing Africa was to trick us into hating ourselves and worshipping them and their version of God. In order to do this, they had to take away our spiritual knowing that humanity and the rest of the beings and animals of the universe are God. The knowing that some of God's authentic angels descended on the Earth and are occasionally still here, continuously reincarnating as humans.'

Princess and Ollie lock eyes as he goes further into his explanation.

'Yeah, fucking serious, Princess, I remember as a kid at school, religious studies and Sunday school, we were taught heaven is in the sky and God sits on the clouds with the angels choosing who comes through the pearly white gates into heaven or goes beneath the ground to hell. Claudette explained Earth-based Twin Flame authentic Angels – souls – left Africa and spread among indigenous tribes of the world. We are the true angels. The outsiders, intruders of Africa, invented religion and whited out the true Messiah, but even if the world went with the White Christian's Jesus of Nazareth story, the soul of Jesus would have to still be somewhere around the universe today.'

Ollie stands, raising his voice. 'Even if they wanted to see it in the Sunday service Christian religion version of Jesus, no one can argue with nature's cycle of life, spiritual reincarnation of the soul. When the body dies, nature planned that as a female anywhere in the universe alien or human conceives, we souls again return to heaven, going through the heaven process, part of which is the time spent in the female womb and we're repeatedly born from heaven – the womb – in a new body. Therefore, the spirit of Jesus has continuously reincarnated to different bodies and has to be reborn someone in the universe. I now know that someone is yourself and your Twin Flame, Princess.'

Princess smiles as she too gets to her feet and stands next to Ollie admiring her tattoo in the mirror. Then she looks up into Ollie's eyes in the reflection of the mirror, and Claudette's image joins them.

Princess looks at them both and, smiling a radiant smile, says, 'Yes, precisely my angels. Ollie, everything you say is true. My mirror soul and I are here today within human bodies, and, my God, if what I'm thinking is correct, I'm carrying Yanson's child, the reincarnated soul of Nana.'

Princess now realises how since the beginning of her and Yanson's Twin Flame separation period she had yearned for and visualised her and Yanson's – her and Koolah's – unique Twin Flame lovemaking all along.

She smiles nodding. 'Yanson's lucky, special and blessed, you say. My God, Ollie, you have no idea.'

The three of their images fade from the mirror to be replaced by short, intense bursts of light exactly like those from a powerful modern-day party strobe light. The flickering light is suddenly all around them, filling the room. And as it slows and comes to a stop, Princess and Ollie find themselves surrounded by a vivid real-life image of the ancient Koolah city magic circle. They're suddenly present with Claudette amid this virtual reality, accompanying the African King, Queen and their three adult children who are sat resting on the magic circle sacred stone. The ancient Koolah tribe angels are oblivious to their presence as Claudette narrates the scene, pointing to the Prince of Koolah.

'Ollie, you're an angel soul. In this dimension you live the life of Princess Gabi's elder brother, the man you see sat next to her there.'

Again they find themselves conscious in their bodies at the tattoo salon, and gobsmacked, the White Australian smiles, nodding. The image of Claudette remains in the mirror, jogging Princess's memory. She smiles back at the dainty Haitian witch and says, 'Claudette, I remember after our night out at Pacha, you and your sister coming back to our Ibiza villa for a while with Rome, David, my brother and the others. On my balcony you showed me pictures of your nephew, Hercule. His eyes told me he's our fellow alien from Delica and I knew instantly the purpose of your visit and showing him was to awaken me.'

Recalling Hercule's huge eyes and just now visiting the magic circle helps Princess again become aware of a deep subconscious Princess Gabi incarnation, in the actual dimension dancing near to the magic circle experiencing meeting with her own self Blee, her own futuristic Delican incarnation. Princess smiles continuously as she explains the sensation. 'I once crossed dimension as a futuristic alien, showing my Princess Gabi self my Delican incarnation.' Princess looks deeper into the eyes of the dainty Claudette. 'I felt it a coincidence meeting you and your sister in Ibiza...'

Claudette's face suddenly looks annoyed and she steps quickly out from the mirror to interrupt Princess. Physically gripping Princess's hand, speaking with her French accent, Claudette snaps in a tone of authority, 'Coincidence, Princess Gabi! I was there when your Twin Flame Koolah explained to you thousands of years ago that there's no such thing as a coincidental meeting or, for that matter, a coincidental anything else in God's entire universe.'

Princess nods as she recalls the bumblebee boy Imani, Claudette's ancient African incarnation, and the actual conversation with Koolah. Claudette releases her grip and realising she's there in the flesh, Princess says excitedly, 'You've physically crossed dimension, Claudette. I now actually remember you crossing to meet your Koolah era incarnation, Imani.'

Smiling vibrantly, Claudette responds, eyes open wide. 'Princess Gabi, I also remember someone leaving the magic circle with Koolah and Jojo. Sharing with the rest of us angels events of a modern day reawakening, a possible future dimension on the island of Jamaica that's scheduled to happen not too long from now, next year in fact.' Her smile grows brighter as she looks directly into the eyes of Ollie. 'Princess, you and your Twin Flame will leave the food parcel for Anci and other rescued child relatives on the West African coast.'

Princess looks to the Haitian witch with an inquisitive expression. 'Yes, I recall it from deep meaningful dreams, but, Claudette, you say the possible future reawakening; I don't understand...'

Claudette's energetic smile is quickly exchanged for an expression of concern, which stops Princess's words. 'Tap into your psyche and remember, Princess. Your dreams are possible outcomes of what's to come, possible future and previous dimensions that we could or could have explored. Although it's a possible outcome that could be available to us, our Jamaican reawakening reunion is far from a certainty. We've work to do in order to make it a happen. The age-old evil enemy is powerful and at work trying to change future dimension phases stopping us retrieving our bible, therefore preventing bringing love and equality to the earth and humanity....'

ACKNOWLEDGEMENTS

Thank you to all the following, who have, in one way or another, helped or inspired me to write this book.

Actress Jan Anderson, for your heartfelt, kind words of encouragement. The uplifting vibration of those few sweet words stay with me each day as a continuous divine inspiration. I thank you, Angel. All you need is the right material, the right platform, to show your true awesome potential. Trust me, I know.

Activist Dr Arikana Chihombori, for your tireless work in waking everybody up to the idea of bringing the land of Africa together as one. One country, one president, one currency for Mother Africa – it's the only way to bring harmony to the planet. If Momma not happy, no one happy. Thank you, our Queen, spirit has your back.

Actor Idris Elba, for your straight talking and no-nonsense advice. You've rejected and accepted some of the greatest Hollywood screenwriters' scripts, and after reading some of my early material and ideas for this story, you saying you feel I'm a great and talented writer gave me such a much-needed boost to get this book completed. Thank you, Sir.

Actor Winston Ellis, for having faith in me and telling me how epic this project is overall and the amount of lives it will positively affect. Your eagerness, after reading parts of the script, to want to play a part in the movie has been a source of great inspiration to me.

Film producer Nick Love, for your advice on screenplays and uplifting words. My friend, your in-depth advice during our initial three-hour meeting in the luxurious surroundings of Soho House, having faith in me and urging me to not give up really helped me after some early knock backs.

Actor Ray Winstone, for having faith in my work and your advice on the story and how to structure it for a feature film or TV series screenplay. Your words about the elder pirate captain Morgan role – "That sounds like a bit (of) me, can I read the script?" – have been another fantastic inspiration to me in my ambition to one day see this story put under the lights of a movie set.

Artist Tom Garfirth, for producing the jacket design and artwork.

Centreforce Radio 88.3 or DAB during the daytime and Ibiza Global Radio throughout the night, for inspirational music. The entire novel was written to the beat of quality music, the African drumbeat. The magic within the text of the story connects to the beat in all music. Listening to live soul and rare groove, funkadelic sound system and all the other '80s sound system raves from back in the day also helped the story along.

My dog Simba, for the love shown by your smiling eyes. The love and life in your eyes when I repeatedly throw your ball never fail to inspire me and have been the trigger for many of my bursts of creative ideas.

But, above all, this book is dedicated to my little baby brother Yanson Barnard who was tragically taken from us. Thank you God for returning this beautiful soul to me fifty years later as my grandson Yanson Barnard.

I would also like to pay a special tribute to my number one fan Teresa Lesley Owen who promised to read this but her body died. Ms Owen passed on before I finished writing this novel, but I know she (her soul) has reincarnated and is living somewhere in the universe – and who knows maybe she's been born into a future dimension and has already read the book before I completed it. Or at least I like to think she's been reincarnated to planet earth in this dimension phase and when she grows up she'll read this. That would be special.

Like people and animals, books are like our soul mates; they gravitate to one another. Wow, take a deep breath and think of what you've just read and how fascinating this dynamic universe really is.